⸙ LEGACIES ⸙

The First Book of the Corean Chronicles

L. E. Modesitt, Jr.

TOR®
fantasy

A TOM DOHERTY ASSOCIATES BOOK
NEW YORK

This is a work of fiction. All of the characters, organizations, and events portrayed in this novel are either products of the author's imagination or are used fictitiously.

LEGACIES

Edited by David G. Hartwell
Map by Ellisa Mitchell

A Tor Book
Published by Tom Doherty Associates
175 Fifth Avenue
New York, NY 10010

www.tor-forge.com

Tor® is a registered trademark of Macmillan Publishing Group, LLC.

ISBN 978-0-7653-9717-1

Our books may be purchased in bulk for promotional, educational, or business use. Please contact your local bookseller or the Macmillan Corporate and Premium Sales Department at 1-800-221-7945, extension 5442, or by e-mail at MacmillanSpecialMarkets@macmillan.com.

First Edition: October 2002
Second Mass Market Edition: July 2017

Printed in the United States of America

0 9 8 7 6 5 4 3 2 1

To Kristen:
For quiet competence and the ability to see the
best in every situation

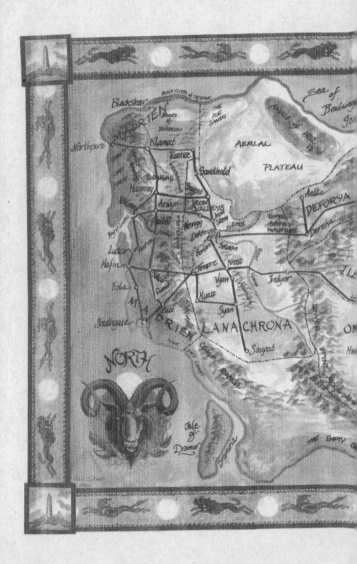

I.

❊ A LEGACY ❊ PROMISED

1

In the quiet of the early twilight of a late summer day, a woman sat in a rocking chair under the eaves of the porch, facing east, rocking gently. Except for the infant she nursed, she was alone, enjoying the clean evening air, air swept of sand grit and dust by the unseasonal afternoon rain. So clear was the silver-green sky that the still-sunlit Aerial Plateau stood out above the nearer treeless rise that was Westridge, stood out so forcefully that it appeared yards away rather than tens of vingts to the north and east.

She rocked slowly, looking down at her nursing son, a child already with dark hair, more like deep gray than black. Through the open windows set in the heavy stone walls, she could hear the occasional clatter of platters being replaced in the cupboards, and the squeak of the hand pump.

The glittering and scattered light reflected from the quartz outcroppings on the top edge of the distant and towering plateau died away as the sun dropped farther. Before long, pinlights that were stars appeared, as did the small greenish crescent that was the moon Asterta. The larger moon, Selena, had already set in the west.

She brought the infant to her shoulder and burped him. "There . . . there, that's a good boy, Alucius." Then she re-settled herself and offered the other breast.

As she began to rock once more, a point of light appeared off the north end of the porch, expanding into a winged feminine figure with iridescent green-tinged silver wings. The nursing mother blinked, then turned her head slowly. For several moments, she looked at the soarer, a graceful feminine figure somewhere in size between an eight-year-old girl and a small young woman—except for the spread wings of coruscating and shimmering light, which fanned yards out from the soarer's body until it bathed both mother and infant.

The woman chanted softly,

> "Soarer fair, soarer bright,
> only soarer in the night
> wish I may, wish I might
> have this wish I wish tonight . . ."

For a long moment after she had completed her wish, the woman watched. The soarer's wings sparkled, their movement seemingly effortless, as she hung in midair, in turn watching mother and child, less than twenty yards from the pair on the porch. As suddenly as she had appeared, the soarer was gone, as was the green radiance that had emanated from her.

Slowly, the woman murmured the old child's rhyme to herself.

> "Londi's child is fair of face.
> Duadi's child knows his place.
> Tridi's child is wise in years,
> but Quattri's must conquer fears.
> Quinti's daughter will prove strong,
> while Sexdi's knows right from wrong.
> Septi's child is free and giving,
> but Octdi's will work hard in living.
> Novdi's child must watch for woe,
> while Decdi's child has far to go.
>
> But the soarer's child praise the most,
> for he will rout the sanders' host,
> and raise the lost banners high
> under the green and silver sky."

She looked beyond the north end of the porch once more, but there was no sign that the soarer had ever been there.

Within moments, the door to the house opened, and a lean man stepped outside, moving near-silently toward the woman in the rocking chair. "I thought I saw a light-torch out here. Did someone ride up?"

"No . . ." She shifted the infant and added, "There was a soarer here, Ellus."

"A soarer?"

"She was out there, just beyond where you put the snow fence last winter. She hovered there and looked at us, and then she left."

"Are you sure, Lucenda?" Ellus's voice was gentle, but not quite believing.

"I'm quite sure. I don't imagine what's not there."

Ellus laughed, warmly. "I've learned that." After a moment, he added, "They're supposed to be good luck for an infant."

"I know. I made a wish."

"What did you wish for."

"I can't say. It won't come true, and I want it to come true for Alucius."

"That's just a superstition."

Lucenda smiled. "Probably it is, but let me have it."

He bent over and kissed her forehead. "For him, as well as for you."

Then he pulled over the bench and sat down beside her as the evening darkened into night.

2

In the warm sun of a clear harvest morning, five people stood beside the stable door, two men, two women, and a small boy. The child had short-cropped hair that was a dark gray, rather than true black, and he clutched the hand of the younger woman and looked up at the man who wore the black-and-green uniform of the Iron Valley Militia. Tied to the post outside the stable were a roan, saddled, and a gray mare. The gray tied beside the roan had no saddle, but a harness and two leather bags of provisions across its back.

"Father?" offered the boy.

The uniformed man bent down and scooped up the child, holding him against his shoulder so that their faces were but handspans apart. "You'll be a good boy for Mother, won't you, Alucius?"

"Yes, Father." His words were carefully articulated.

"He's always good," offered the older woman who stood back from the couple.

"You'd say that anyway, Veryl," countered the older man.

"I might," Veryl responded with a smile, "but Alucius is good. Lucenda knows that."

"You'll be careful, Ellus," said Lucenda. "You will, won't you?"

"He'll be fine," boomed the older man. "Best officer in all Iron Valley. Just going after brigands, that's all. Not like the border wars with the Lanachronans when I was his age. They had Talent-wielders. Not very good, but they did call out sanders—"

"That was then, Royalt," Veryl pointed out. "You and Ellus can compare stories when he comes back. Reillies, sanders, Talent-wielders . . . whatever you want."

The three other adults smiled at the dryness of her tone.

Ellus handed Alucius back to Lucenda, then bent forward and hugged her, kissing her on the cheek. "You two be good. I shouldn't be gone that long."

Alucius squirmed, and Lucenda set him down beside her, and threw her arms around her husband, holding him tightly.

Alucius looked up at the pair, embracing, then to the corral not two yards from where he stood. His eyes met the black-rimmed red orbs of the lead nightram, and he gently let go of his mother's trousers, taking one step, then another toward the black-wooled ram with the red eyes and sharp horns.

"Alucius!" Lucenda cried, lunging toward her son.

"Let him go," came Royalt's voice. "Best we see now. He's protected by the fence. Rams don't hurt children, unless the children hit them, and Alucius won't do that."

Lucenda glanced from Alucius to the fence, and to the

nightram on the far side of the four rails. Then she looked to Ellus. His lips were tight, his eyes fixed on their son.

In the silence that had settled across the stead, Alucius took three more steps, until his chest was against the second railing. The nightram stepped forward and lowered his head, until his eyes focused on the child. The curled and knife-pointed black horns glittered, reflecting the sun from their lethal smoothness, standing out from the light-absorbing all-black face, and from the black fleece that was so deep in color that the ram was darker than any night. Even the sharp-edged hoofs were night-black.

The boy smiled at the nightram, then reached out with his left hand and touched the beast's jaw, fingertips from the sharp teeth. "Good! Good ram."

For a long moment, the nightram's eyes took in Alucius. Then the ram slowly lowered himself to the ground, so that his eyes were level with those of the boy.

Alucius smiled. "He's a good ram."

"Yes, he is." Lucenda's voice was strained.

"He likes me."

"I'm sure he does."

Deliberately, slowly, Alucius lifted his hand away from the nightram. "You be good, ram." He stepped away from the railing. The ram slowly rose, lifting his head and sharp horns, but only watched as the boy stepped toward his mother.

"He was a good ram."

Lucenda swept Alucius up into her arms, hanging on tightly. "Yes, he was. But you must be careful with the night-sheep."

"I was careful."

The ram tilted his head, before turning and walking toward the far side of the corral.

"He'll be a herder, for sure, Ellus." The older and broad-shouldered Royalt laughed. "He's already got a way with them. He'll be ready to take the flock with us when you get back."

"That's good to know—and so young, yet." Ellus smiled

and straightened the green and black tunic. The smile faded as he looked at Lucenda and Alucius. He stepped over to them and hugged both of them for a moment. Then he looked at Alucius, his face serious. "You'll take care of your mother while I'm gone, won't you?"

Alucius nodded.

"Good." Ellus smiled once more. "I'll be back before long. Sure as there are five seasons, I'll be back."

"I'll be here," Lucenda replied.

Still holding the smile, Ellus untied the roan and mounted, leading the gray as he rode down the lane toward Iron Stem. He turned in the saddle and waved as he passed the end of the outermost section of the southernmost corral.

The older man and woman took several steps back toward the main house, before stopping and watching the rider. The younger woman stood by a fence post, ignoring the nightram on the other side, tears streaming down her face. The fingers holding her son's hand did not loosen as she sobbed.

Alucius looked at the departing rider. "Father . . ."

"He'll be back," Lucenda managed. "He will be."

Alucius watched until his father was out of sight. To the south, above the high road that lay beyond vision, an eagle circled upward into the open expanse of silver-green sky, a black dot that also vanished.

3

Outside, the evening was darkening, with neither moon to offer illumination. Inside the second lambing crib, with only a small, single-crystal light-torch to dispel the blackness, Alucius watched. His mother held a bottle filled with goat's milk, feeding the small nightlamb. The lamb sucked greedily for a short time, then stopped, lowering his head slowly.

"You have to drink more," Lucenda told the lamb gently.

"It doesn't taste right, but you have to drink it." She stroked the lamb.

"He doesn't like the sand. I wouldn't like sand in what I drank," Alucius said solemnly.

"It isn't sand. It's quartz. It's powdered as fine as we can make it with the crusher."

"But why?" Alucius gave a small frown.

"The ewes have it in their milk. They get it from the quarasote shoots. So we have to put it in the goat's milk so the lamb will grow strong."

Alucius could sense the doubt in his mother. "He's very sick, isn't he?"

"He isn't as strong as he should be. It's hard for lambs who lose their mothers. The other ewes don't have enough milk for two. Sometimes, they don't have enough for one." Lucenda tendered the bottle, and the lamb sucked for a time, but the amount of milk left in the bottle remained almost the same.

"He doesn't feel good," Alucius said. "He's tired."

"He has to eat, or he won't get well," Lucenda said evenly.

"Will he die?"

"He might."

Alucius sensed the concern in his mother's words, and the darkness behind them. He looked at the lamb, then sat down on the old horse blanket beside the animal. Slowly, he reached out and drew the small creature to him, his arms around the lamb's neck.

The lamb bleated, then seemed to relax, looking up at Lucenda. Alucius waited.

She offered the bottle once more.

Alucius held the lamb until the bottle was empty.

Lucenda looked to her son. "How is he?"

"He's tired. He'll be better."

"He made a mess of you," Lucenda said.

"I'll ask Grandma'am how to wash it off." Alucius yawned and lay down on the blanket next to the lamb. "I'm staying here. He needs me. He'll be better."

"For a while, dear."

"All night. He'll get well. You'll see. He will."

"If you say so, Alucius."

"I just know he'll get stronger." The child's treble voice held absolute conviction. He yawned again, and then again. Before long, his eyes closed. So did those of the lamb.

Lucenda looked at the sleeping child and the sleeping lamb. A faint smile crossed her lips.

4

The wind of late fall whistled around the dwelling, but the warmth from the big iron stove in the main room had infused the front parlor as well, as had the heat from the kitchen, with the associated smells of baking apples, biscuits, and mutton. Because it was Decdi, when Royalt did not graze the nightsheep, the older man sat behind the table desk, studying the black leatherbound ledger. He dipped the iron pen into the inkwell and added several figures to the column of figures. Then, with a satisfied half-smile, he swished the pen in the cleaning bowl, wiped it gently with a scrap of cloth and set it in its stand. After closing the ledger, he stood and put it on the top shelf of the bookcase. As he lowered his hand, his sleeve slipped back over his herder's wristguard, a seamless band of silver, with a strip of black crystal in the center.

Alucius watched from the leather hassock by the bookcase, his eyes on the herders' wristguard for a long moment. While chores still had to be done on Decdi, the day ending the week seemed special, perhaps because there was time for the adults to talk, and Alucius could listen, and no one urged him on to the next chore.

"Could I play a game of leschec with you, Grandfather?" asked Alucius. "A short one before supper, if you wouldn't mind?"

"You finished your lessons?"

"Yes, sir." Alucius pointed to the lesson book on the one shelf that was his, and that held his learning books as well. "Do you want to look at them?"

"You say they're done, they're done." Royalt leaned forward and offered a wide smile. "You've been watching us, haven't you?"

"Yes, sir." Alucius did not move from the hassock.

"Supper'll be ready before long." There was a twinkle in Royalt's eyes as he watched his grandson. "We're having an apple pie. You can smell it."

"I know. I helped mother pick the best baskets at market. This afternoon I cored the apples and sliced them."

The herder frowned slightly. "How did you pick the apples?"

"I was careful. I just said some baskets looked good." Alucius put both slippered feet on the polished wooden floor. "You said I had to be careful."

"I did. A good herder has some of the Talent, and most people are not comfortable with it. They especially don't like children with it."

"I was careful," Alucius said again.

"I'm sure you were, boy." Royalt grinned. "You think you can beat me?"

"Probably not yet," Alucius replied. "I can't see far enough ahead."

"None of us can, boy. We'd always like to see farther than we can. That's being human." Royalt took the board from the shelf and set it on the table, followed by the plain lorken box that held the pieces.

Alucius stood and pulled the hassock to the side of the table opposite his grandsire. Then he knelt on the hassock.

"You want black or green?" asked Royalt.

"Don't we choose?"

Royalt laughed. "You pick. I'll choose."

The boy took two of the footwarriors, one green and one black, and then lowered his hands below the table, switching the pieces between hands several times before lifting both hands, backs up, and presenting them to his grandfather.

Royalt touched Alucius's right hand. The boy turned his hand over, opening it and showing the black piece. Then he turned his left hand and displayed the green footwarrior.

"Black it is."

Alucius quickly set up the pieces, beginning with the foot warriors in the first row, and ending with the soarer queen and sander king.

"Do you have any questions before we start?" asked Royalt.

"No, sir . . . except why is the soarer a woman and the most powerful? Sanders are powerful, too, and they kill nightsheep. The soarers don't." He paused. "Do they?"

"No, the soarers don't." The older man laughed. "I can't tell you why the soarer is the most powerful piece. It's always been that way."

Alucius waited for his grandfather's move. Not surprisingly, it was the fourth footwarrior, two squares forward. Alucius matched the move, so that the two blocked each other. His grandfather moved the pteridon out, and Alucius countered by moving his fifth footwarrior a single square forward.

By several more moves, Royalt was smiling. "You have been watching. You're playing like your mother, but that last move was like Worlin's."

Royalt attacked, taking Alucius's lesser alector, but losing a pteridon, and a footwarrior, before capturing the boy's greater alector, at the cost of the other pteridon.

"Supper's ready!" called Lucenda from the main room.

"We can finish after supper," Royalt suggested.

Alucius studied the board before looking at his grandfather. "No, sir. You'll win."

"I might not."

"You should win," Alucius said. "But could we play another tomorrow?"

"I think I could manage that, if I'm not late bringing in the flock." Royalt stood. "Before long, you'll be besting me." Royalt laughed. "Time to wash up, boy."

Alucius followed Royalt to the washroom off the kitchen

where Royalt took the lever of the hand pump and put it through several cycles, until the chill water was flowing into the basin. Alucius waited and then took his turn, before returning to the kitchen.

Royalt sat at the head of the table, at the only chair with arms, facing into the kitchen, while Veryl sat at his left, closest to the serving table. Lucenda set a wide platter of mutton—from a town sheep bought the week before—on the table, and then seated herself at the end of the table, with Alucius on her left.

Veryl cleared her throat gently, and the other three bowed their heads.

"In the name of the One Who Is, may our food be blessed and our lives as well. And blessed be the lives of both the deserving and the undeserving that both may strive to do good in the world and beyond." Veryl smiled and looked up, glancing at Royalt.

The herder returned the smile, and then speared a slab of the mutton and set it on his wife's platter before serving himself and passing the platter to Veryl, who in turn passed it to Lucenda. Lucenda served Alucius and herself. The gladbeans, doused and lightly fried in sweet oil, followed. Alucius took one biscuit after his grandfather passed the basket to him.

"You can have two," offered Veryl. "You're a growing boy, and there's more than enough. We got some of the best honey from Dactar last week."

Alucius grinned. "Thank you, Grandma'am." He knew about the honey, having already snitched the smallest of samples several times during the week.

"Of course," his grandmother continued, "there isn't quite so much honey as there might have been."

Alucius flushed.

Lucenda shook her head, in what Alucius knew was mock-disapproval—or almost mock-disapproval.

"It was awfully good," Alucius admitted, "and I only had a little."

At the end of the table, Royalt coughed to smother a smile.

"You might have asked," suggested Lucenda.

"You would have said no."

"Sometimes that happens," his mother replied. "We can't always have what we want. You know that. Get too greedy, and you might get a Legacy of the Duarches."

"Yes, ma'am." Alucius wasn't too sure what that meant, but it didn't sound good.

After the momentary silence, Royalt spoke. "Been wondering if we'll be having a long and cold winter this year." He took another slab of mutton, and ladled gravy over it.

"You think so, dear?" asked Veryl.

"Haven't seen a sander in near-on a month. Not many sandwolves, either. Or even scrats. Saterl says the sandwolves have moved closer to the town, that folks there are losing dogs, and the wolves are going after food sheep. They all forget that the wolves don't leave a scent, and that food sheep don't sense them. Most times, sandwolves don't like town sheep, unless they're starving. Last time that happened this early in the fall was in the big winter, fifteen-sixteen years back." He took a swallow of the weak amber ale. "Wind's colder early, too."

"Do you think we should lay in another town sheep or two in the holding barn?"

"Three, maybe. And some of the big sacks of dried beans. We've got the coins."

Alucius hoped that his grandfather happened to be mistaken, because Alucius hated the beans. But he knew that Royalt had a feel for weather, and his own feelings had already told him it was going to be cold.

"And some of the dried maize," suggested Lucenda.

"You never did care much for the beans, did you, dear?" asked Veryl.

"You know that, Mother." Lucenda grinned. "Neither does Alucius. One of my faults that has been passed on to him."

"One of your few faults," suggested Royalt. "If you'd pass the biscuits, Alucius?"

Alucius looked around the table, at the three adults, and took another biscuit, smiling, before handing the basket back to his grandsire.

5

The Duarchy of Corus blessed all the lands with peace and prosperity, for generation upon generation, from the times of the Forerunners onward. Never was there so fair a realm, so just a world, and so blessed the peoples of a world.

The Myrmidons of Duality and their pteridons controlled the heavens, and they conveyed dispatches, orders, and messages from one end of Corus to the other, from the northern heights of Blackstear to the warm waters of Southgate, from Alustre in the east to mighty Elcien in the west, all so that the peoples of the Duarchy might prosper, and that their children and their children's children might do so as well.

Likewise, the Alectors of Justice and the Recorders of Deeds made sure that evil gained no foothold in any city, not even in the courts and chambers of the Duarches, nor in the meanest of city quarters, for without justice, nothing endures for long.

The Engineers of Faitel created the mighty eternastone highroads that crossed Corus from west to east, and south to north, excepting only the Aerial Plateau and the Anvils of Hel. Upon these highways moved all manner of goods and travelers, each secure in the knowledge that all were safe from any manner of harm.

Even the oceans fell under the sway of the Duarchy, with the fleets of the Duadmiralty built of dolphin ships so swift and fierce that no pirate and no brigand could contest or escape them, and the ways of the seas became as highways upon the waters, bringing goods and travelers to all manner of places.

The sun shined its favors out of a silver-green sky and blessed the Duarchy and all its peoples through all five seasons of each year, every year.

Then came the Cataclysm, and the old ways and webs weakened, and the world changed for all time . . .

> —*History of Corus* [fragment recovered from the Blue Tower at Hafin]

6

Mist sifted from the clouds overhead, and fog covered most of Westridge, bringing with it a faintly acrid scent of damp quarasote mixed with that of nightsheep dung. The supply wagon stood outside the stead stable. Wearing his oiled leathers and a battered brown felt hat, Royalt held the leads to the dray horses. He sat on the left side of the wagon. Beside him, slightly more to the middle of the wagon seat, was Alucius, who wore an oiled leather cloak over his nightsheep jacket.

"It's miserable weather to go to town." Lucenda stood bareheaded under the slight overhang of the stable eaves.

"Best weather to go," replied Royalt. "We don't miss grazing time. We need the salt, and the flour. Your mother's not up to taking the team . . ."

Alucius sensed that his grandma'am might never be up to taking the team. Something about her leg hadn't healed right. He felt that he should have been able to do something. Not that he hadn't tried . . . when no one was paying attention. Sometimes, she felt better, but it never lasted.

Lucenda looked at her son under the oiled leather cloak that was too big for him. Alucius returned the gaze with a calm smile.

"Alucius will be fine. He needs to get off the stead more, daughter."

"I suppose he should," Lucenda replied. "You be good for your grandfather, Alucius."

"Yes, Mother." Alucius smiled. "I'll be good."

Lucenda flushed. "I don't know why I say that. You're always good."

Royalt flicked the reins, and the pair of dun horses moved forward. "Should be back around supper time."

Neither the man nor the boy spoke until the wagon was on the narrow track that led southwest, through the treeless expanse of low and barely rolling rises, covered with scattered quarasote, toward the main road.

"You take it to heart, don't you, boy?"

"Take what?" Alucius wasn't sure he understood.

Royalt laughed. "I could be wrong. Let me ask you something. Do you remember what your father said before he left?"

"He said to be good and to take care of Mother."

"That is what I meant," Royalt said.

Alucius turned in the wagon seat and looked at his grandfather. "Did I do something wrong? You sound angry." Except that wasn't right. Alucius could feel it wasn't anger behind the words.

"I'm not angry." Royalt shook his head, and a strand of light gray hair flopped across his forehead. He brushed it back absently. "No, Alucius. You haven't done anything wrong. You never have. That was what I was talking about."

"I threw stones at the grayjays."

The grandfather laughed. "That wasn't wrong in the same way I was talking. You didn't mean to hurt them. You listen. Suppose that's what comes from growing up without any brothers or sisters and so far from other steads."

Alucius nodded. "I have you and Grandma'am and Mother. You play leschec with me."

"You're already better than I am, young fellow."

"That's because I can think about it more," the youngster said solemnly.

Royalt laughed.

The wagon bumped and jolted along the track from the stead for two vingts, and it seemed like it had taken glasses to cover the distance when Royalt finally spoke. "Here we are—the old road. Don't have to worry about sinkholes, washouts . . . and it's a smoother ride." Once he had the wagon headed south on the gray stone road, Royalt shifted his weight in the seat and smiled. "Good roads. Have to admit the ancients built good roads."

The ever-present red dust had drifted into piles beside the road, now dampened by the mist, and in places, encroached slightly on the gray stones that, even when scratched or cut— and that was hard to do—showed no trace of damage by the next day. The road ran straight as a rifle barrel from north to south between Soulend and Iron Stem. That much Alucius knew. He also knew that not many people lived in Soulend, and that it was much colder than in Iron Stem or in any of the more southern Iron Valleys.

The boy glanced back over his shoulder. The clouds had lifted some, and the mist-blurred Aerlal Plateau scarcely looked any smaller or any farther away, even after two vingts of travel. If the clouds did not descend again, the plateau would look almost the same from Iron Stem, he knew. His eyes went to the empty gray stone road ahead.

"This is a good road, isn't it, Grandfather?"

"That it is, lad."

"Not many people travel it."

"When it was built, back before the dark days, there were more people in the world, and it was a road many people traveled."

"The dark days were a long time ago," Alucius pointed out, hoping that his grandsire would offer more than his usually clipped explanation.

"That they were." Royalt paused, glancing sideways at the boy. "So long ago and so terrible that we can't count exactly the years." He paused again. "They were dark years, because everything changed. Some of the legends say they were dark because the sun did not shine for a year. Others said that was because the Duarchy ran dark with the blood of men and women who fought demons from beyond the skies. Still others claimed that those days were so terrible that no one will ever know what happened except those who died or lived through them." He cleared his throat once more before continuing. "Life changed. We know that. Iron Stem—do you know where the name came from?"

"From the iron mines and the mill, you said. That's all you said."

"Iron Stem had the mines and the big mill, and the mill used to make iron ingots as big as a man, and they put them on huge wagons and drove them down to Dekhron and put them on barges. The barges carried the iron to Faitel, and the artisans and engineers there formed the iron into tools and weapons and beams that held up buildings all over the Duarchy."

"An iron ingot as big as a man?"

Royalt nodded. "Some were bigger than that. I saw one, when I wasn't much older than you. They found a stack of them, buried under clay, coated in wax or something. Looked as if they'd been formed maybe a year before." He laughed. "Took a double team to move each one. Sold them to the Lanachronans. Town had golds for years."

"What happened? Why did the mill stop?"

"The weather changed. That's what they say. Some say the soarers did it. Whatever caused it . . . it takes lots of water to make iron, and it stopped raining. We used to have forests here, like the big trees on the river. You have to have rain for that. People needed the trees and cut them, but new trees didn't grow. It was too dry. The air got bad in the coal mines, and then there were creatures there, like black sanders . . ." Royal shrugged. "No coal, no water . . . and for a long time, no one needed much iron. So many people died everywhere that there were tools and weapons enough for anyone left."

"That's sad," Alucius said.

"Well . . . we wouldn't be herders if it hadn't changed," Royalt pointed out. "Nightsheep need the dry and the quarasote bushes. They say there weren't any quarasote bushes before the Cataclysm—and no nightsilk anywhere. There's little enough now. That's why the Lanachronans pay well for our nightsilk. They can't raise nightsheep there." He snorted. "That's also why we need a militia. Didn't have one, and they'd be here, taking everything we have."

"Did the dark days change anything else?" asked Alucius.

"They changed plenty." The older herder pointed. "There's the tower. Won't be that long now."

The first building that was considered part of Iron Stem was the ancient spire that loomed over the Pleasure Palace. Its brilliant green stone facing could be seen from several vingts to the north. Alucius flushed as he recalled the first time he had asked about the name.

After they had crossed several low rises, the long wooden sheds of the dustcat works appeared to the left of the road, a warren of enclosures, all sealed to the outside.

"Have you ever seen a wild dustcat?" Alucius knew the short answer, but hoped Royalt would say more.

"Not since I wasn't much older than you. You know that."

"They aren't many, you said."

"There are more than most folk think. The dustcats aren't stupid. They know people are trouble, and want to capture them, and they've moved into the rock jumbles just below the plateau or into the deeper swamps of the Sloughs. They still hunt people, but they only do it in packs, and they won't attack unless they can kill, and make sure that the hunters won't survive."

"Are they that smart?"

Royalt frowned, then replied. "Old man Jyrl used to say that the soarers warned the cats when hunters were around. Claimed he'd seen it happen. Said that was why he never hunted them again, that any man who had both dustcats and soarers against him was as good as dead."

"But people still hunt them, and they keep them in the sheds there."

"And the cats kill one or two scutters a year."

"I don't understand. Why do people work there if they are going to be killed."

Royalt sighed. "It's hard to see it when you're young. But the dust—it's dander really—that comes off the cats makes some people feel . . . well, the best they've ever felt, better than a good meal, better than . . . lots of things. That's why the scutters work for so little. They're around that dust all the time, and they never think about anything else except gathering the dust. Gorend and his son Gortal sell the dust to the Lanachronans—and anyone else who will pay good golds for it, and they'll pay ten or twenty golds to hunters for a cat that's healthy. Ten golds is more than most crafters make in a year, Alucius. It's a huge amount of coin."

"Do you make that much?"

Royalt laughed. "We don't bring in the kind of coins Gorend does, but we make enough."

"I don't think I'd like caging the dustcats like that."

"Good, because I don't think much of those that do. But keep that between us, boy."

"Yes, sir."

Before long, the wagon rolled over the low rise and past the empty green stone tower and the lower building next to the road. Despite its brilliant color-faced stones laid in an alternating pattern, the structure looked more like a night-sheep barn, garishly colored, and was only fifteen yards in length, with almost no windows. The five lower courses were of alternating blue and green stones, and the six above had blue alternating with a faded yellow.

The tower stood alone, fifty yards north of the smaller building, its gutted interior empty.

"Grandfather?" Alucius asked tentatively. "The people who built the building in front—" He didn't feel he should use the term "Pleasure Palace," especially since it was anything but a palace. "Why didn't they just alternate the yellow, blue, and green stones from the bottom?"

Royalt laughed. "Asked myself that very question for years. I can't tell you, boy, because the place was old when I was your age."

"Are the same . . . people there?"

"Sanders, no. The women there change, they say, sometimes as often as the wind shifts the sands around the plateau. Some stay. Most don't. I wouldn't know, for sure." Royalt cleared his throat and went on quickly, "Hope Hastaar has some of those sweet yams they bring up from Dekhron. Your grandma'am would really like them."

Alucius understood. "I hope he has some of the early cherries. They're good."

Royalt kept the wagon moving toward the center of Iron Stem, past the empty vingt or more separating the Pleasure Palace from the nearest cottage. Despite the chill and the mist and rain, the reddish brown shutters were half open, as were the shutters of the cottages closer to the square.

Alucius leaned to one side, watching intently as they neared the metal shop. He listened for the hammermill, but the mill was silent, although the odor of hot metal and a line of smoke rose from the forge chimney. The road flattened into an absolutely level stretch more than a hundred yards from the square. The buildings around the square were all of two and three stories, and although boardinghouses, all were well kept and swept, if not always painted so well as they should have been.

On one side of the square were the trade buildings—the cooper's, the chandlery, the silversmith's. On the corner adjoining was the inn, with its blue-painted sign, showing the outline of the old mining mill. Alucius had only seen the mill once, a cavernous and empty set of walls on the far west side of Iron Stem.

In the center of the paved eternastone square was a short line of carts and wagons, several with canvas awnings to protect either produce or goods from the threatening weather. Alucius wondered why. Even the worst storms produced little rain, just winds that were more likely to damage the awnings than the goods.

Royalt eased the wagon over to one of the stone posts on the west side of the square. After setting the wagon brakes, he climbed down and threaded the restraint ropes through the iron rings on the back of the harness of each dun dray horse, then tied both the ropes and the leathers to the big iron ring on the posts. Then he took out the two watering buckets and motioned to Alucius, who had just finished folding the cloak and slipping it under the wagon seat.

"You can water them, can't you? The public pump's right there."

"Yes, sir."

"I'll be over checking to see if Hastaar's got any of those yams. Likely be from last harvest, but he sometimes brings 'em."

After taking the buckets from his grandfather, Alucius pumped what he felt was enough water into one bucket and then the other, and carried them back to the horses. He set the buckets before them, and then stood back.

"Don't see how you herders do that," came a voice from beside him. "I'd risk having them kick it over."

"They won't do that." Alucius turned and looked up at the older man in a shapeless gray jacket, wearing a battered gray felt hat.

"You're Royalt's grandson, aren't you."

"Yes, sir."

"I'm no sir, young fellow. I just run regular sheep south of town, where it's wet enough we don't worry about sanders."

Alucius nodded politely.

The man returned the nod, before turning and walking toward the nearest produce wagon.

When the horses had had enough, Alucius reclaimed the buckets and took them back to the pump, where he rinsed them out before replacing them in the back of the wagon. Then he walked toward the endmost cart, where two boys stood, admiring the display of knives on the dark cotton.

One of the boys looked up. His eyes scanned Alucius, and he used his elbow to touch the other, before whispering something. Both nodded to the itinerant knife-smith and stepped away.

"Are you interested in something, young sir?" asked the gray-haired man.

"I don't have any coins, sir," Alucius said. "You don't mind if I look, do you?"

The man, younger than Royalt, smiled. "Look all you want. I come here every Septi during the spring, summer, and harvest seasons. I'll even make special knives when you're ready for one."

Alucius could sense the friendliness—and a hint of something else, sadness perhaps. "Thank you." He looked over the array of knives. Most were for use in a kitchen or stead, but a handful, on one side, were clearly weapons. Alucius thought that the two on the end were a matched pair of throwing knives, but there was no reason to ask.

After a time, he nodded to the knife-smith. "Thank you, sir."

"Thank you, young sir."

Alucius rejoined Royalt by a cart containing a few small baskets of breads and some half-bushels of early cherries from the south.

Royalt glanced down at the boy. "I was thinking . . ."

"She'd like the soft bread, with all the raisins and the browned sugar . . . and the cherries."

Royalt raised his eyebrows.

"I heard her talking to Mother. They won't ever ask for anything, Grandfather. And Grandma'am won't let Mother ask for her, either."

Royalt burst into a loud laugh. "You know more at ten than I did at twice your age." He turned to the redheaded woman at the end of the wagon. "How much for the cherries?"

"Had to bring them up from south of Borlan. I'd say three silvers, but I'd not want to carry them back."

Royalt nodded. "What about two silvers, and throw in two loaves of the soft current bread there?"

The woman pursed her lips, calculating, as her eyes ran over the nightsilk covered herder's jacket that Royalt wore.

Alucius waited for a moment, then added. "It's for my grandma'am. I have one copper."

The woman shook her head. "Done. Two silvers and a copper." She looked at Alucius and added, "Let your grandsire pay them."

Alucius noted that his grandfather actually handed over two silvers and a pair of coppers, not just one.

"You carry the bread, Alucius."

"Yes, sir."

The two walked back toward the wagon through a mist that was getting cooler and heavier, under clouds that had once more thickened and lowered.

"I'd stay longer," Royalt said, "but there's not as much here as I'd hoped. Happens when you come midweek. We need to go out to the mill for the flour and hope Amiss has some salt."

"Yes, sir." Alucius didn't know what else to say.

"The produce woman, she wasn't going to let those go for less than two silvers and five." Royalt stopped beside the wagon. "You knew that, didn't you, you imp?"

"Yes, sir."

Royalt covered the bushel with a cloth before easing it into the covered bin behind the wagon seat. He wrapped the two loaves of bread in another clean cloth before easing them onto a position on top of the coarse sacks of potatoes and yams he had apparently gotten while Alucius had been looking at the knives.

While Royalt untied the horses, Alucius climbed up into the wagon seat.

Then the herder swung up into the driver's seat. He released the wagon brakes, and gave a gentle flip to the reins. "Won't take long for us to get out to Amiss's place. Should make it easy for us to be back to the stead by late afternoon. That way, your mother and grandma'am won't be worrying. And if it starts to mist more, you need to put the cloak back on."

"Yes, sir."

As Royalt guided the wagon onto the westbound road out of the square, Alucius could see the two boys returning to the knife-smith's cart.

"Why do people think we're different?" Alucius asked.

"You saw that, didn't you?"

"Yes, sir."

Royalt sighed. "Herders are different. You know when the horses have had enough to drink, don't you? Or when a nightsheep is hurt? Sometimes, even when people are hurt inside?"

"Sometimes," Alucius admitted cautiously.

"Most people can't do that. To be a herder you have to have some Talent. Not much, but some—I've told you that—and most people don't have even that much Talent. People are afraid of the Talent. Some of them even think that Talent was what caused the dark days."

"It didn't, did it?" asked Alucius.

"It doesn't matter whether it did or didn't, boy. What matters is how people feel. If they think the Talent caused the Cataclysm, then they're going to be afraid of people with Talent, and nothing we say is going to change things. That's why some people don't care much for herders. Something you have to get used to, if you want to be a herder."

"Is that why herders wear the wristguard?"

Royalt laughed. "No, boy. We know we're different. You can tell a herder, young as you are. It's a symbol, in a way, something to remind us who we are."

Royalt eased the wagon to the right edge of the road as a rider neared, coming from the west. The man tipped his battered felt hat to Royalt. The herder returned the gesture.

Alucius nodded to the rider, as well, even as he still wondered why people would want to believe things that weren't true.

7

The full moon that was Selena cast a pale pearly glow across the stead, softening the hard edges of the fences, the main dwelling, the maintenance barn, and the sheds that held the nightsheep. Not even the cicadas or the distant howl of a sandwolf disturbed the silence.

The dark-haired woman sat on the porch, slightly crosswise on the wooden chair she had carried out from the kitchen. She cradled the four-string gitar and looked out into the patterns of moonlight and darkness. After a time, she began to sing, softly.

> "Don't be lookin' for soarers free,
>   dear, with anyone else but me . . ."

In the loft above, Alucius listened through his window, a window open to catch the light night breeze. He liked to hear his mother sing. She often sang that song, softly, late at night, when everyone else in the stead was sleeping. Or supposed to be sleeping.

> "Don't be seeking the distant sea
>   dear, with anyone else but me . . ."

His mother never sang when Asterta was in the night sky, and Alucius wondered if that were because the green-tinged Asterta had once been considered the horse goddess—the one who offered both death and glory to the horse warriors.

> "Don't be off'ring the homestead key
>   dear, to anyone else but me . . ."

At the gathers and the fests, there was always someone asking his mother to sing and play. Alucius was always amazed at how many songs she knew—from the upbeat and cheerful ones to some so mournful that even the eyes of the hard-edged Militia riders brightened.

> "Don't sit under the loving tree,
>   dear, with anyone else but me . . .
>   with anyone else but me . . ."

As the words from the porch below faded, Alucius lay back on his pallet bed, recalling that, of all the songs she knew, he had never heard her sing that song at the fests or when the growers got together after harvest. She only sang it at night and when she was alone.

8

A yellow-red arrow knifed through Alucius, searing through his stomach, and then running in a line both through his shoulders and arms, and down his back and his left leg. He woke abruptly and sat up in the darkness, panting, sweating, and recalling the intensity of the pain, a severity he recalled, but no longer felt. Except that it was still there . . . somewhere.

Voices drifted up the ladder.

". . . hurts so much, Royalt . . ."

"I know . . . I know."

Sensing the helplessness in his grandsire's voice, Alucius crept out of his bed and to the top of the ladder that led to the end of the hall below. Although his grandparents' room was a good five yards away from the base of the wooden ladder, the door was ajar. Like all herders, Alucius could hear from much farther away than could most people.

"I'll fix some root-tea and put some of the aspabark in it. That will help."

Alucius waited at the top of the loft ladder until his grandsire had walked toward the kitchen and until he heard the clank of the stove door and the clunk of the coal scuttle. Then, he slipped down the ladder. He glanced toward the kitchen, and then toward the closed door to his mother's room. He eased through the open door.

His grandmother lay propped up with pillows in the wide bed. Her eyes were closed, and she was breathing heavily. Even in the near-darkness—the only light being a glowstone on the bedside table—Alucius could see the tightness in her face and the pallor, an almost yellow-green tinge that came as much from within as from the greenish light of the stone.

"Royalt? . . ."

"It's me, Grandma'am . . . Alucius."

"You would know . . ." A faint smile appeared, one that vanished as her entire body stiffened.

Alucius could feel that same stabbing pain, not so severe as when it had wakened him, but the same. He didn't know what to say. Finally, he murmured, "It hurts a lot, doesn't it?"

"Yes . . . child . . . it does."

Alucius edged closer to the bed, standing next to the finial rising from the post on the right side of the footboard and resting his right hand on it. "It's been hurting for a long time."

Veryl did not reply, instead silently going into another spasm of pain.

Alucius reached out and touched her leg, and the intensity of the agony almost convulsed him, and tears began to seep from the corners of his eyes. No one should have to bear that pain. No one, and certainly not his grandma'am.

He swallowed, and then let his senses, his small Talent, become himself, as though he were lost in the Talent. He kept one thought, fixed it within himself—that the ugliness and the pain had to end, and that his grandmother *had* to get well.

Yellow-red shot through him, and he trembled, and grasped the finial ever more tightly.

Then a wave of whiteness washed over him, and then a wave of blackness.

Alucius woke to find himself on the long couch in the main room, his mother looking down at him, her face drawn.

"Alucius . . ." She bent forward and hugged him. "You're all right. You're all right. I was so worried."

"I'm . . . fine." He yawned. "Tired . . ." He frowned, realizing that he'd been in his grandparents' room. How had he gotten into the main room? What had happened?

He squinted. He remembered fighting with the yellow-red pain, and wanting her to get better. His eyes widened. "How is Grandma'am?"

"She's sleeping." Lucenda's hand went to her mouth. "Alucius . . ."

"She'll be better," Alucius said, yawning again, and turning on his side. "I know she'll be better." This time, now, he could sleep.

9

Hieron, Madrien

The long and narrow workroom was lit by three crystal light-torches, their radiance far brighter than those few antiques remaining and used throughout the rest of Corus. On the racks that flanked two sides of the chamber were objects of various sizes and shapes, and of varying degrees of complexity. All exuded antiquity. The workbench was newer, with its smooth-finished lorken surfaces and the polished tools set in brackets.

The only person in the chamber was a clean-shaven man who sat at the drafting table, dressed in brown, from his vest to his heavy boots, except for the silver torque around his neck. He studied the object in his hand, turning it, noting the way it flared in the light as the ancient purple crystal came into the direct beam of the light-torch.

After a time, he set it aside and began to draw upon the sheet before him. "Has to be a part of the energy release . . . somehow . . . but how?"

The door at the east end of the room opened, and a tall and broad-shouldered woman stepped inside. She did not close the door, and a line of afternoon sunlight falling through the opening space illuminated dust motes in a pyramidal pattern.

She did not speak until she was within a few yards of the man, and her voice was quiet, yet powerful, its effect reinforced by the intense violet eyes that fixed upon him. "Have you anything new, Engineer Hyalas?"

"Engineer? I am a mere artisan, honored Matrial," Hyalas replied in mock servility, "grubbing through the buried ruins of lost Faitel to reclaim a faint glimmer of what the ancients had created."

"I understand that," the woman replied. "I am paying you to provide devices of use to Madrien from that grubbing. You may recall that, from time to time. I am spending good golds to reclaim what you can of the Legacy of the Duarches." With her flawless white skin and dark hair, she might almost have been Talent-creature, or a sculpted image of beauty, had she remained silent, but her voice was full and musical.

"You may recall what the plaque said," Hyalas said, quoting,

> "That heritage, that legacy of old,
>   Duarchial bequest to ages new—"

A gesture by the woman cut off Hyalas's words, and the Matrial completed the stanza.

> "—unseen by fair Elcien's sages bold
>   will grant power even the wisest rue."

She raised her finely drawn eyebrows. "Power great enough that the wisest rue it? There is none such remaining now, but you will find it."

"Yes, Matrial." Hyalas inclined his head, before easing his squarish body from the armed stool where he had been sitting and walking toward the second rack toward the door.

He stopped and picked up an object. "This . . . it is a working model—"

"It appears to be a cannon. We have cannon, Hyalas. They are heavy, bulky, and even with the best of trunnions and scales, they are less than accurate, and anyone with Talent can touch off the powder before they can be loaded. They

are useful only against brigands, perhaps the herders in the
Iron Valleys, but not against the Lanachronans or others."

"Ah . . . but this is not the usual cannon, Matrial. I thought
as you did at first, but . . ." Hyalas paused, then smiled. "It
is a Talent-cannon. That is, it can only be used by someone
with the Talent, and it amplifies the power of the powder, so
that a heavy ball can be fired with perhaps one tenth the use
of powder, and . . . most important, it appears that it cannot
be touched off by another Talent."

"That is an improvement . . . but it takes someone with
Talent to operate it, and there are too few of those. Far too
few, though we cultivate the illusion, as you know, that our
officers all can wield Talent."

Hyalas moved to the next rack, containing all manner of
scattered parts. "This . . . I have just discovered it. If the
plates are correct, it takes no Talent to operate, and it creates
and throws crystal knives so long as there is sand nearby that
can be poured into its hopper."

"Can you rebuild it?"

"I would think so, but one never knows until one tries."

"I suggest you try. Or find us something else of even
greater use."

"Matrial, what do you think—"

The Matrial fingered the silvery loop on her belt.

Hyalas turned red, then blue, unable to speak.

The Matrial released the loop.

Hyalas took a long desperate breath.

"You know what you are to do. You are to find weapons,
usable by any, without a need for Talent, and effective
against small arms, armor, walls, or all three. That is what
we need. That is what you will provide." The Matrial smiled.
"You will find us the true legacy of the Duarches. Do you
understand?"

"Yes, Matrial." Hyalas inclined his head, more deeply.

"Good."

The artisan/engineer did not look up until the door closed.
His lips moved explosively, but the words were silent.

10

Alucius woke with a start in the dim light. His stomach ached, but the pain was hunger. He felt dizzy as he turned his head, and then caught himself, barely avoiding tumbling off the couch. Slowly, he sat up and eased his feet to the floor. He shivered, although the floor did not seem that cold. His mother was lying back in the armchair next to the couch, snoring softly.

Alucius stood, and she jerked awake. "Alucius?"

"My stomach hurts. I'm hungry."

"How badly does it hurt?" Lucenda asked, immediately standing.

"I'm hungry, Mother. That kind of hurt."

"Is he all right?" That was his grandfather's voice, sleep-roughened, and Royalt emerged from the hall.

"Should he eat?" asked Lucenda.

"He feels all right. But he's white. Let him eat." Royalt's voice was firm, but not harsh, and he smiled at Alucius, as if they shared a secret. "He can tell us later."

"Grandma'am?" Alucius asked.

"She's still sleeping, but she'll be fine. Better than she's been in years. I can tell that," Royalt offered. "Now, you need to eat, as much as you can."

"No prickle," Alucius said, shivering once more, and taking a step toward the kitchen.

"No prickle," his grandfather agreed. "But plenty of cheese and meat. You can even have the soft current bread. You just sit at the kitchen table and let us get you what you need."

Alucius trudged into the kitchen, aware that his legs were unsteady, and his vision blurring.

Almost immediately, Royalt thrust a chunk of soft bread and a tumbler of the costly berry juice he had been saving for Veryl before his grandson. "You need to eat. Start with this. Eat slowly while we get you something warmer." He pulled a blanket around Alucius's shoulders.

Alucius looked at the food blankly.

"You need to eat it, dear," Lucenda said.

Royalt left and then returned wearing trousers, boots, and a jacket thrown over his nightshirt. "I'll see about eggs, daughter, if you'll get the stove going."

Lucenda nodded, and immediately went to the coal scuttle. Alucius smelled the acrid scent of coal, both burning and unburned. He nibbled at the soft bread and took a sip of the juice, carefully. He didn't want to spill anything that cost more than a copper a tumbler. Before long, he looked down. Although he had eaten slowly, there weren't even crumbs before him. With the growing warmth of the stove, and what he had eaten, his shivering subsided.

"Your grandfather should be back with some eggs soon," Lucenda said. "I've got some ham from that shoulder Dercy brought, and I'll fry that up with some egg toast."

"I am hungry, still." Did using Talent take that much energy? He'd fallen asleep when he'd tried to save Lamb, and all he'd done then was persuade the little ram to take a bottle.

It didn't seem long before Royalt returned. "Not so many eggs as usual, but enough."

"The stove is heating up. The coals hadn't burned down, not really . . . You'd started it up for tea last night."

Alucius watched as his mother made the egg toast. He found his mouth watering, and he wasn't exactly surprised to find himself eating three pieces, and two large chunks of ham—and then another piece of egg toast. Both his mother and grandfather ate as well.

"Alucius . . ." Royalt said gently, after finishing his own breakfast. "Your grandma'am is much better. She might even be as strong as she once was. We won't know that for a time, though." He paused. "Last night . . . can you remember what you did?"

Alucius took another swallow of the berry juice, trying not to feel guilty about drinking two glasses of it. It did taste so good, and he'd been so hungry and thirsty. "I woke up, and

I thought I'd been stabbed. I hadn't been. Then I heard voices. Grandma'am was saying something hurt so much, and you said you'd be getting her tea and aspabark. You don't give that unless it really hurts. So I climbed down the ladder and sneaked into your room." Alucius moistened his lips. "I know I wasn't supposed to, but . . . she hurt so much . . . I just held her ankle, and I wanted the pain and everything that caused it to go away. Forever. Everything felt white, and then black." Alucius shrugged. "Then I woke up on the couch, and Mother was crying and hugging me."

"I was worried," Lucenda explained.

Royalt nodded, then tilted his head to the side, fingering his stubbly chin for a time before speaking. "You have more of the Talent than I do, or than your father did. If anyone knew how to train you, you might even have become a healer."

"A healer? There are healers?"

"No. Leastwise, we don't know of any." Royalt coughed. "That's not a blessing."

Alucius felt confused. Being able to heal someone wasn't a blessing?

Royalt looked directly at Alucius, his gray-green eyes intent. "You must remember one thing. Until you are a full herder, with a family of your own, you are not to tell anyone outside the family that you can do this. Not your friends, not any girl you love, not anyone."

Alucius swallowed at the total seriousness in his grandsire's voice, and the iron resolve behind the hard words. "Is what I did that bad?"

"It is not bad at all, Alucius. It is dangerous. You felt very weak. Your mother worried about you all night. What would happen if, say, the Council of the Iron Valleys knew? What if they threatened to kill your mother if you did not heal a wealthy trader? Or if the Lord-Protector of Lanachrona sent his men to kidnap you? What if he threatened to kill us if you did not heal his son? Or, even if he rewarded you, would you like to spend the rest of your life in a palace tower, guarded day and night because you were so valuable? Unable to walk anywhere without guards? Unable to see a sunset alone? Unable to walk the stead with Lamb?"

Alucius swallowed a second time. Those were things he'd never considered. All he'd wanted was to help his grandma'am.

"If . . . if you keep your secret to yourself," his grandfather continued, "you can do whatever you are meant to do. If you do not, then your life will be short, and someone else will tell you what to do every day that you live. Whenever you want to tell someone beside the three of us . . . think about that. Do you want to live your life, or have a life where every step is commanded by someone else? Where people surround you every moment, watching you?"

Alucius shivered.

"You're scaring him," Lucenda said.

"I have to. He looks more like a herder than any in generations. It's his life, and he *must* understand." Royalt went on. "Talent is not like a powerful explosion. It is not a force that can stop a falling boulder or bend metal. It grows like the quarasote, slowly. It underlies everything, and is everywhere, but few indeed can even sense it. Even when they do, fewer still can use it. Yet people would believe you could, and failing to do what people wish makes them angry."

"I understand," Alucius said slowly. "Even . . . even if herders kept it to themselves, someone would always want me to heal a lamb or someone in their family. And if I didn't . . . they might tell, or be angry, because they'd know?"

"That's one reason why herders *never* tell those outside their families about Talent and herding—even other herders," his grandfather said. "It will be hard enough, Alucius, even keeping it to yourself. If you can indeed heal others, you will always have to measure, to choose who you can heal, and how much. And never tell anyone. It must always seem like the person just got better. And that, too, will be difficult, because we all want others to know our value."

His mother's eyes were bright, and Alucius looked from one to the other.

Finally, he said, "We can tell Grandma'am, can't we?"

"She already knows," Royalt said gently.

"I have you three I can talk to."

"For now, Alucius, and for years to come," Lucenda promised.

But Alucius could sense the sadness that went with her joy and pride.

11

Hieron, Madrien

The Matrial sat on the south side of the circular ebony conference table, with the wide glass windows behind her. The deep violet of her tunic almost seemed to match her eyes, and the green emerald choker around her neck shimmered against her flawless alabaster skin as she listened to the officer who sat on the far side of the table.

"In the past year, we have only found two more with enough Talent to be trained," reported the gray-haired over-captain. "We are stretched thin in maintaining the discipline for the torques."

"Do we need more public demonstrations?"

"Not yet, honored Matrial, but we may need them in the future."

"What about lamaials?"

"Again, we have found no male children with Talent in the last year. That may be because their fathers have hidden them or spirited them away, but outside of the herders of the Iron Valleys, Talent is usually far rarer in males. And, as you know, Talent in males does not mean they will grow up to be lamaials. There have been no reports of one in nearly twenty years."

"That does not mean that there have not been such," the

Matrial pointed out. "That is their danger. They can appear to be men like other men."

"Matrial . . . even among the herders of the Iron Valleys, even among those with the black-gray hair, Talent is rare indeed. We have tested many as captive troopers over the years, and watched them for years, and . . ."

"You are doubtless correct, Overcaptain Haeragn, but we must be most careful, because, as the ancient lines declare,

> Then too, the lamaial will rise, but once,
> Where none yet will suspect, nor think to dare,
> and his hidden strokes may kill aborning,
> Duality of promise bright and fair . . ."

"We have been most careful," replied the overcaptain, her voice even but firm, "as you have instructed, but the herder captives also make the best squad leaders, and the ones most effective against the Lord-Protector's Southern Guard."

For a moment, the even smile vanished from the face of the Matrial. "It is sad to think that the traits we must control within Madrien are those which are also the most effective at retaining our prosperity and freedom, but ever has it been so." The smile returned, not quite hiding the darkness behind the violet eyes. "What about the women and girls who have fled from Southgate after the recent floggings? Are there more of them with Talent?"

"We have never seen any from Southgate with Talent, but that is because for generations, the Seltyrs drowned any woman-child who manifested Talent." An expression of revulsion briefly flashed across Overcaptain Haeragn's face.

"What about the Lanachronan captive troopers?"

"We have never found any with Talent, and we have far more of them than of those from the Iron Valleys. It is most surprising that the Lord-Protector even has a Recorder of Deeds."

"He does, unfortunately," the Matrial replied before rising

to signify the end of the meeting. "We will deal with that. You will let me know if you feel the need of public demonstrations?"

"Yes, Matrial." Overcaptain Haeragn rose and bowed.

12

Alucius woke slowly, the bright spring light stabbing through the cracks in the shutters at his eyes. He lay on the narrow pallet bed in the loft for several moments, listening to the sounds drifting up the ladder, half wondering why he had been dreaming about climbing the Aerlal Plateau. The clanking of the iron skillet on the stove stopped that speculation and told him that he had overslept—and that his mother was irritated.

He sat up, sliding the light-torch and the book into the bottom drawer of his chest. He groped for his work trousers. After pulling on his work shirt and trousers and his boots, he straightened the quilt on the pallet bed and then scurried down the ladder to the washroom. After quickly washing, he headed to the kitchen. "Can I help with something?"

"Just sit down and eat." Lucenda's voice was clipped.

Alucius repressed a sigh. He shouldn't have read so late, but there was so little time, and he wanted to read more than just the lessons sent from the school. He might not have read so much had his friend Vardial lived closer, but with more than fifteen vingts between steads, they seldom saw each other. "I'm sorry."

Lucenda dropped four overfried eggs on his platter, followed by dry toast, and a slab of hot and dry ham, and then two slices of honeyed prickle. "You're a growing boy, Alucius, and I'd not be wanting to treat you as a child." His mother paused. "The sun has been up for near-on a glass. Your grandfather left with the flock two glasses ago, and here you are, just out of bed. Your grandma'am needs help with the carding, and I need to get to cleaning the spinner-ets."

"I'm sorry, ma'am. I was tired." Alucius didn't meet her eyes.

"I can imagine so, staying up so late reading those old stories. You are becoming a young man, and must act as such."

Alucius flushed. People kept saying that, but long as it had been since he had first played leschec with his grandsire . . . time went by so slowly, and he wondered if he would ever grow up.

"There's nothing wrong with reading, son, but you can't let it get you so tired that others have to do your work."

"I'm sorry." He looked down at the platter heaped with eggs, and with the ham slice and toast to the side, and the honeyed prickle slices. Even overdone, most of the breakfast was good, but he hated eating the prickle slices.

"Don't leave the prickle. You want to grow stronger, you have to have vegetables and fruits, and this time of year prickle's all we've got. I mean it, Alucius." Lucenda turned back to the sink where she wiped out the cast iron frying pan and then dunked it into the soapy water.

"Yes, ma'am." Alucius understood, but didn't like it. Southern fruits cost golds and then some out of season. He took his belt knife and cut the largest prickle slice in half, slid it into his mouth, and swallowed convulsively. He took a gulp of the cold spring water, trying not to grimace. Then he had a bite of the eggs, and drizzled the honey syrup over the dry toast before taking a bite. He repeated the sequence three times more, until he had finished the prickle. He still had half the eggs and toast left that he could enjoy.

"The prickle's not that bad, Alucius."

"Yes, ma'am." He wasn't about to argue. To him, it tasted like soap mixed with sand and flavored with soured milk. "The eggs are good. So is the toast and the ham."

He ate quickly, then washed his own platter, and cleaned the sink, and scoured and oiled the frying pan. Then he went back to the washroom and washed his hands and face.

He went out onto the porch, stretching, and looking eastward, out toward the plateau that loomed over the valley, wondering how far out his grandfather had gone with the flock. A flicker of reddish brown at the base of one of the nearer quarasote plants told him that a scrat had made a nest there. Scrats could mean trouble, because the cute little rodents got into everything. And having cats was out of the question, because the nightsheep killed cats.

"Your grandma'am's waiting, Alucius," his mother called from the stable door.

"Yes, ma'am." Alucius squared his shoulders and walked quickly across the open ground, and past the stable to the processing barn, where he opened the door cautiously. The odor of the solvent from the tanks in the front room almost gagged him, and he hurried down the corridor. He paused and looked into the cutting room where the huge shears glittered in the indirect light. It always amazed him that something as thin as nightsilk could only be cut so slowly and by such massive shears, even though his grandsire had explained time and again why the treated threads became harder than iron against mild pressure and harder than that against sudden violent pressure. He caught himself and hurried to the third door.

"I wondered when you'd struggle up," his grandmother offered pleasantly, from where she sat at the first carding table.

"I'm sorry." All Alucius had done since he'd gotten up was to apologize. "I overslept."

Veryl laughed. "That's the way your mother does things. Me and Royalt, we'd just wake you and tell you to get to work. That's what we did with her. She didn't like it. So she lets you sleep, and then makes you feel guilty all day." The laugh and smile vanished. "Sit down. I had to go over what you did yesterday. I want you to look at the difference between the wools here . . ."

Alucius sat down and bent forward, dreading the next words.

"See the fine strands here . . . those are the undercoat, from a ewe's." She put another set of fibers beside the first. You see how those are thicker? It's undercoat, but it's from a ram. Now . . . here is the overcoat from a ram. What do you see?"

"It's much coarser and thicker," Alucius admitted.

"I don't know what you were thinking yesterday. You had all these in one batch, and you never separated them. You have to separate the undercoat from the overcoat, all of it, Alucius."

"Yes, ma'am." Alucius held the groan inside. Carding was *so* tedious.

"The solvent affects the wools differently. If you leave the undercoat threads in the tanks as long as the outer coat of the rams, then the undercoat is weaker than cotton thread. If you have overcoat threads in with the undercoats, then you get sharp fragments that can cut the cloth. So if the wool isn't carded and spun correctly, the thread is worthless. All the work that your grandsire and you do with the flock is wasted . . ."

Alucius had thought oversleeping had been bad, but it looked like it was going to be one of those days when he found out that nothing he'd done had been right, and it was only just past the second glass of the morning.

13

The wagon rolled northward on the eternastone road under an afternoon harvest sun. A light breeze carried the faintly astringent mintlike scent of quarasote. Alucius sat in the second seat, the one that he'd bolted in place in the morning. His mother sat beside him, while his grandparents sat in the front seat, where his grandsire guided the team.

"I'm glad you decided that you'd come to this with us," Lucenda said to her father.

"Not as though you left me much choice," grumbled Royalt. "Wouldn't get much besides a cold shoulder to eat, no help with anything."

"Dear, it's not as though Kustyl has a gather every week," Veryl pointed out.

"No . . . but now we'll have to give one sometime next year."

"That won't destroy us. Besides, Lucenda and Alucius need to see other folk more often."

Alucius squirmed in the seat, then looked at his mother. Lucenda grinned, then bent over and whispered in her son's ear, "He just likes to complain. He'll enjoy it as much as any of us."

"I don't complain, daughter. Much good it would do to sulk and waste good ale. Besides, you'd be put out if we didn't go, and when you get put off, you cut like quarasote."

Alucius didn't always understand the by-play. He knew his grandfather could hear a quarasote spine rustle a vingt away, and he knew his mother knew that. And he knew that his grandfather knew that his mother knew. So, instead of trying to puzzle it out, he looked to his right, at the great plateau, where, under a cloudless silver-green sky, some of the quartz outcroppings at the rim were sparkling, reflecting the sunlight with a green-tinged silver.

"It'll do you good to see other herders, Royalt," Veryl continued. "You can all complain together, and then you'll feel better. You always do."

Royalt laughed, and half turned in the seat to address Alucius. "Never argue with a woman, boy. If you're right, and you won't be often, they'll never forgive it, and if you're wrong, they'll never forget it."

"Royalt," snorted Veryl, "don't be giving the boy ideas."

"I don't have to give him ideas. He's got more than enough of his own. Needs to understand something about women, though."

Veryl turned in her seat to face her daughter and raised one eyebrow.

Lucenda grinned for a moment.

After more than a glass on the ancient eternastone highroad, Royalt turned off onto a lane heading west, a much rougher ride, one that took nearly a half-glass to travel a vingt, until they neared a stead, similar to the one where Alucius lived. Although there was no ridge like Westridge near the stead, the rolling quarasote plains were much the same, treeless and with the red sandy soil. The main house was longer, and lower, without an upper level or loft rooms, and the eaves were longer and hung out over a wide covered porch that ran around the entire dwelling. But the walls were of the same reddish stone and the roof the same split slate. The stone-walled outbuildings seemed lower than the ones at his own stead, but there were more of them.

As the wagon slowed, a grayjay squawked from one of the posts by a lambing pen, and then took flight. Alucius watched the blue and gray scavenger until it landed on the ridge of the stead house's slate roof, clearly waiting for any scraps that might come from the gather.

"Over here, Royalt!" called a thin and wiry man, one who definitely made Royalt seem stocky, even though the older herder was not.

Royalt slowed the wagon and eased it toward the open shed beside the stable, where the wiry man stood.

"Royalt . . . glad you all could come. Mairee was hoping you'd be here."

"Wouldn't have missed it for anything, Kustyl," replied Royalt as he set the wagon brake.

"You mean your lady wouldn't have." Kustyl grinned.

"That, too." Royalt vaulted down from one side of the wagon as Kustyl offered a hand to Veryl to help her down on the other side.

"You can put the team in the shed there. Got water and some grain."

As the two men talked, Alucius offered a hand to his mother, who took it with grace, although she did not need it to descend from the wagon.

Lucenda looked at her son. "You be careful with that clean shirt, Alucius."

"Not that careful," Royalt added with a laugh, interrupting his conversation with Kustyl. "Have a good time, boy."

Alucius looked toward the long porch, and then to the three boys on the far corner who were playing shoes.

"Go on," urged his grandfather. "The shirt be sanded."

Alucius grinned and began to run toward the three, although he only recognized Vardial. He heard—and ignored—the words behind him.

"Father . . ."

"He is a boy, daughter. Let him be one before he has to be a man."

Alucius slowed as he reached the end of the long porch.

"Here's Alucius," called Vardial, perhaps a span shorter than Alucius, but far broader. "That makes it even. Alucius and me against Jaff and Kyrtus."

"Fine," called the tallest youth, "Kyrtus and me, we'll make it quick."

Kyrtus's eyes lingered on Alucius, focused on the newcomer's dark gray hair, for just a moment. "That we will."

"No, you won't," Vardial predicted.

Alucius and Jaff took the pit closest to the porch, a sandy circle with an iron rod pounded deep into the ground and projecting about a third of a yard above the sand.

"Odd or even?" Putting one hand behind his back, Jaff looked at Alucius.

"Odd—on two. One . . . two." Alucius thrust forward two fingers.

"Even, it is." Jaff had offered two fingers. "You start."

Alucius picked up the pair of black-painted horseshoes, and shifted one to his left hand. Standing to the right side of the iron rod, he pitched it toward the opposite pit, where it landed two spans short of the rod and skidded perhaps a shoe's width past.

"Not bad for starters," Jaff said, taking his place on the left side, and tossing a green shoe toward the other pit. His shoe skidded past the rod, touching it enough for a brief *clang*.

"Jaff's within a shoe," Vardial called back to Alucius.

Alucius tossed his second shoe. While it struck a glancing blow to the green shoe, it didn't knock it away from the rod. Jaff's second shoe struck the ground just short of the pit and bounced sideways.

"Too short . . . wanted to slide it in," explained Jaff.

Kyrtus began from the other end, but his shoe skidded well past the rod, as did Vardial's first throw. On the second pitch, Kyrtus got his shoe close to the rod, but Vardial knocked both away.

Jaff started the second round, with a pitch that ringed the rod, and then spun off, landing nearly half a yard away. Alucius slid his first shoe almost to the rod, deep enough into the loose sand that Jaff's second shoe bounced off. Alucius tried to slide his second shoe to the rod on the second side—and did, but not quite close enough.

Over the next glass and a half, the four played five games, and, as Jaff had predicted, the two older boys won, but not easily, with all games being decided by less than four points, and with Alucius and Vardial winning two, if each of those by only two points.

"Wind it up, young fellows!" called Kustyl. "Ribs and chicken'll be ready in a bit. Wash up and get yourself some punch."

"Good game," offered Jaff.

"It was," Alucius replied. "You and Kyrtus are good. Thank you."

". . . he always that polite?" murmured Kyrtus to Vardial.

". . . his grandsire's strict . . ."

As Alucius walked up the steps to the porch, he glanced toward the other end where a girl in pale blue trousers and a white shirt and a brown leather vest was helping ladle out the punch. She wasn't as slender as Kyrtus's sister Elyra, and her hair was straight and brown. But there was something about her. Alucius looked away for a moment.

"That's Wendra," whispered Vardial. "She's Kyrtus's cousin. Her father Kyrial is the cooper in Iron Stem. He never had enough Talent to be a herder, like his brother Tylal. Father says he's the best cooper Iron Stem ever had, though."

Alucius glanced back at Wendra, watching as she smiled and then laughed. He looked away quickly when she lifted her eyes in his direction. Then he crossed into the house, following Jaff to the washroom. After washing, and patting his hair back into place as best he could, Alucius eased through the large kitchen, not that any stead had a small one.

Vardial slipped up beside him. "I saw that."

"Saw what?" Alucius kept his voice even, stopping himself from turning to go back and help his mother and another woman who were wrestling a kettle off the iron stove.

"You were looking at Wendra."

"I was also looking at where the punch was."

Vardial laughed, but softly. "Just be careful. Kyrtus is sweet on her."

"They're cousins," Alucius pointed out.

"That makes it worse."

Alucius could see that. "Thanks."

"She is nice. I like Elyra, though."

The two slipped onto the porch, and Alucius eased up to the punch table behind Jaff. When the taller youth had taken his punch and walked along the railing, Alucius stepped up and smiled pleasantly. He hoped his smile was merely pleasant.

"Do you want the lemon or the berry?" Wendra asked.

"The berry, please."

"You're Alucius, aren't you?" She handed him one of the tumblers, three-quarters filled.

"Yes, and you're Wendra?" Alucius looked directly at her.

"Yes." She smiled, not quite meeting the directness of his eyes.

"Vardial said you lived in town."

"We do, but Grandfather Kustyl always insists we come to the summer gather. He says that no one can make ale like Father, and he won't drink it unless Father's here."

Alucius made the slightest of gestures toward the one empty bench. "Everyone has punch."

"I shouldn't . . ."

"Go ahead, Wendra," interjected the older Elyra. "You've been serving everyone. I can get a glass for Vardial."

The slightest flush ran up Wendra's long neck.

"If we sit there," Alucius nodded to the bench, "you can see if you need to help Elyra."

"I suppose that would be all right." She slipped onto the bench gracefully.

Alucius sat down and turned to face her, careful to leave space between his leg and hers. "I've never seen you in town."

"During the week, I'm in school."

"I get lessons from there, but they come in a package, and it's usually for a month."

"Your mother goes over them with you?"

Alucius shook his head. "Mostly, my grandsire does."

"Vardial said he was strict."

Alucius shrugged. "He's fair, and he wants me to learn." He could see that Wendra's eyes were a greenish gold, or maybe a gold flecked with green. He wasn't quite sure, because they seemed to change. "How do you like school . . . I mean, learning with all the others?"

She grinned. "I like it, especially the mathematics. Madame Myrier is going to start teaching me bookkeeping next month. That way, I can help both Mother and Father."

"Your father's the best cooper . . ."

Wendra's laugh was musical. "You sound like Vardial. Everyone he likes is the best."

"He's my friend." Alucius flushed. He flushed even more when she touched his hand, even fleetingly.

"I know." Wendra grinned.

"What about your mother?" Alucius asked quickly.

"She's a seamstress. She has a special machine that makes flour bags, too, so that Amiss can sell flour in smaller lots than just the barrels . . ."

"The food's ready! Don't let it get cold!" called Kustyl, stepping onto the porch. "We've got tables on the side porch and in the big room and in the kitchen."

"Would you like to eat—" began Alucius.

"I promised Mother I'd help her." Wendra smiled once more. "I really did. After supper . . . ?"

"After supper," Alucius affirmed.

He didn't really remember much about dinner, except that he didn't see Wendra, but for when she served him, and that he thought the ribs were better than the chicken. And that Vardial kept looking at him and grinning.

Alucius finally managed to draw Wendra aside in the late twilight, and because the porch was crowded with the older folk, they walked out toward the low ridge to the east of the stead. The air was warm, and the scent was that of sand and quarasote and the lingering odors of chicken and ribs. Alucius had to blot his forehead with the back of his forearm. At least, he thought it was because the air was warm.

The last sparkles of light were fading from the quartz-studded western rim of the plateau, and the three-quarter orb of Selena hung in the greenish purple sky above the plateau—appearing as a massive stone rampart that marked the eastern borders of the Iron Valleys. They stopped at the top of the low rise, a good hundred yards from the main house, far enough not to be heard, and visible enough not to worry anyone, Alucius felt.

For a moment, neither spoke.

"Have you ever wanted to climb the plateau, just to see what's there?" Wendra asked.

"I've dreamed about it, and once I asked Grandfather about that." Alucius smiled wryly and briefly. "He said that there were more than enough mysteries in the Iron Valleys, and that anyone who wanted to climb more than six thousand yards straight up was a sanded fool, and anything but a hero."

Wendra laughed. "From what I've heard, that sounds like your grandsire."

"He's very practical. He's a good herder, and I've learned a lot from him."

"Are you going to be a herder?"

"What else would I be?" He frowned. "I wouldn't want to

be crowded in with other people. There's something about the valley, and even about the plateau."

"Nightsheep can be dangerous. That's what Grandfather and Uncle Tylal both say . . ."

"We understand each other. I mean, the nightsheep and I do."

"Is it true that you raised a ram from when you were only five? And that he'll do whatever you want? Vardial said . . ."

"That's Lamb. Not a very good name for a grown night-ram, but I was only five. He was an orphan, and I got him to nurse from a bottle for my mother. We've always been close."

"You understand him . . . with your father . . ." Wendra swallowed. "I'm sorry. I wasn't . . ."

Alucius touched her shoulder. "That's all right. It was a long time ago."

"How about the others . . . the other nightsheep? Do they obey you?"

"They seem to. I haven't ever taken out the full flock by myself, at least not out of sight of the stead. Grandfather says I should be ready to any time."

"So you are a herder." She smiled again, warmly.

"Well . . . I'm going to be."

"We'd better get back," she said abruptly. "I can see that Father's getting the team ready."

"I wish . . ." Alucius laughed, softly. "Yes, I suppose we'd better. Grandfather will be getting restless before long. Even with the moonlight, he doesn't like to drive that far at night."

"Neither does Father."

They turned and began to walk slowly back down the ridge to the west, and toward the stead. Alucius reached out and took Wendra's hand, gently.

Her fingers linked with his, and she did not release his hand until they neared the stable.

"There you two are!" called his grandfather. "Told Kyrial you'd be here before we had the teams hitched. I was almost right."

"Wendra?" called another voice, feminine.

"I'm right here. Alucius and I just walked a little ways."

"Your father has the team ready."

Alucius turned to her. "I don't get to town often."

"I don't get out to the valley at all, except for the gather. But, if you do get to town, I'm usually at the shop, in the back." Wendra smiled, then stepped back and hurried to the wagon with the sign on the side—KYRIAL, COOPER.

After watching the cooper drive away with his daughter, Alucius had to hurry and climb up into the rear seat of his family's wagon, settling beside his mother.

"She seems awfully nice, Alucius," Lucenda murmured.

"She does." He just hoped it would not be that long before he could see Wendra again.

"It was a lovely gather, Royalt," Veryl said. "Now, aren't you glad you came?"

"Suppose so. Worked out a trade with Jelyr, and a few other things . . ."

No one said another word about Wendra on the entire ride back to the stead.

14

Alucius and Royalt rode on opposite sides of the flock, behind the lead rams, as the sun rose over the rolling rises south of the plateau. The morning was clear and cloudless, like any other working morning, and chill, as was often the case in early spring. So chill that, until the sun was clear of the plateau and filled the valley with light and warmth, Alucius's breath steamed.

The youth kept his eyes moving, looking to the flock and beyond, and then back to his grandsire, trying to keep an even two hundred yards between them. The tenth of a vingt separation would widen to twice that, or more, once the nightsheep reached the area where Royalt decided they could begin grazing on the tender new stalks of the quarasote bushes, bushes that generally grew no closer than a yard to each other, and often much farther apart. After a year's growth, the lower shoots of the bushes toughened. After two years, not even a maul-axe with a knife-sharp blade on the axe side could cut through the bark, and the finger-long thorns that grew in the third year could slice through any boot leather. In its fourth year, each bush flowered, with tiny silver-green blossoms. The blossoms became seed pods that exploded across the sandy wastes in the chill of winter. Most of the seeds ended up as food for the ratlike scrats or for the grayjays, but enough survived to ensure new quarasote every year.

Within weeks of seeding, the old bush died and left behind stalks that contained too much silica to burn or to break or cut. Yet by spring, those stalks were gone, devoured by the shellbeetles that burrowed through the red sandy ground, and new bushes were sprouting.

The two rode slowly, without speaking, in a northeasterly direction down the long eastern side of Westridge. After almost a glass they reached the quarasote-covered flats stretching for more than ten vingts eastward to the rolling hills that formed the approach to the plateau. Overhead, the silver-green sky shimmered, and the early morning stillness had been replaced with a wind out of the northeast that carried the faint, but cold and iron-acrid smell of the plateau itself.

Alucius glanced up, catching sight of an eagle almost directly overhead, circling ever higher into the sky.

"Alucius!" Royalt called and then gestured.

The youth eased the gray mare toward the older man, around behind the flock, absently using his Talent to chivvy some of the laggards forward.

"Good. Saw you moving the stragglers up," Royalt noted as Alucius rode closer. "Best keep 'em moving early, when they're ready and restless, and then let 'em graze their way back in the direction of the stead." Royalt eased the bay alongside the smaller gray mare that Alucius rode. "See the marker wedge there?" He gestured to his left.

The youth squinted, slowly scanning the low rise beyond

his grandsire, well to the left of the black backs of the night-sheep. Finally, he caught sight of a crystal on top of a black pole striped with yellow. He pointed. "Is that it? A quarter off north-northeast?"

"Good! Another glass past that and we'll swing south for about two glasses, depending on how they're grazing and what the shoots look like. So far, they've not been growing back so quick as I'd like. Been drier this spring, though. Hope we're not coming up on another drought."

"How can you tell?"

"You can't. Not until it happens. Except less rain falls." Royalt glanced back.

Alucius followed his eyes. "Those three are dropping back again."

"Having you along makes it easier for an old man," Royalt said. "One herder to watch the flock and the other to keep in stragglers before they get too far out."

Alucius liked it when his grandsire called him a herder. "You're not old, sir."

"Old enough, son. Old enough. It was a long time since I was your age."

"Things were different then?"

"The things dealing with people were different. People change faster, and maybe it's just different people. The land is the same. The stead was pretty much like it is now, except the processing barn is new. Had three sheds then. This way is better." Royalt gestured toward the plateau. "That looked the same then as now. So did most of Iron Stem. Few more people then."

Alucius would have liked to have heard more, but he could see the three laggards were getting more and more separated from the rest of the flock. "I'd better get to them, sir."

Royalt nodded.

Alucius turned the gray and worked his way through and around the scattered quarasote bushes, making sure his mount avoided the larger and older bushes particularly. The animals needed to graze more to the east, nearer the plateau, for their wool to be the best, and dawdling near the stead would only cut back on nearby forage, which might be needed in times of bad weather and make the wool less valuable.

The nightram's black undercoat was softer than duck down. It was also cooler than linen in summer, and warmer than sheep's wool in winter, but stronger than wire after it was processed into nightsilk. The wool of the rams' outercoats was used for jackets stronger and more flexible—and far lighter—than plate mail. The fabric stiffened to a hardness beyond steel under pressure, although its comparative thinness meant bruises were not uncommon, something that Royalt had stressed to Alucius. The underwool from the yearlings or the ewes was equally soft, but not as strong under duress. The fabric loomed from it was used mostly for the garments of the lady-gentry of such cities as Borlan, Tempre, Krost, and Dereka.

"Come on, you laggards," he murmured as he chivvied the three, mainly with his Talent, watching as they ambled forward, slightly more quickly than the rest of the flock, to catch up.

Another glass passed as the flock moved through the scattered quarasote bushes, and past another crystal-tipped marker. Alucius could sense something, coming and going, as if in the distance, and not with his ears, but with his Talent. Yet he couldn't pinpoint it. Sometimes it wasn't there at all. He checked the rifle in the saddle holder, then glanced toward his grandsire.

At that moment, Royalt stiffened, turning in the saddle, looking toward the group of rams leading the flock.

Alucius watched. Two of the nightrams had lifted their heads, and tossed them, before lowering their horns. He could sense the smoldering feeling in each ram, even as his grandsire rode toward the pair, projecting disapproval. Both black-wooled rams looked up, either at the sound of the herder or his Talent-projection—or both.

Alucius smiled as the pair backed away from each other, and the calming voice of Royalt murmured across the flats. Belatedly, he cast out his own Talent senses again, but he

could sense nothing. Had what he felt been just the smoldering anger and jealousy of the rams? That was always a
problem, but gelding a ram reduced the strength of his
wool—and the value. So his grandfather only gelded those
males who were so intractable that they always wanted to
fight for dominance, and it was as though the others understood. Certainly, after a gelding, the other rams were far
more manageable, sometimes for months.

Another glass passed, and Royalt had turned the flock due
east, through an area that had seemingly received more rain,
and where the new quarasote shoots were more plentiful.

Once more, Alucius had begun to sense the uncertain
something, edged in redness. Another ram building up to a
challenge? What else could it be? Then, a feeling of red-
edged cold darkness rushed over him.

"Alucius! Get that rifle ready. Sandwolves somewhere
near here, maybe even sanders. Look sharp!"

Alucius had the rifle out and cocked. He glanced eastward,
but the ewes grazing there seemed unperturbed. To the north,
though, two of the rams had lifted their heads, and two of
the younger males—one of them was Lamb—had started to
move toward the flock leader.

Apprehension, if not fear, radiated from them.

Alucius rode northward, toward the violet-red feeling and
the rams, who had formed a semicircle facing to the northeast. He reined up to the east, just slightly forward of the
nightrams. The lead ram pawed the ground and snorted. Even
Lamb snorted, although he did not paw at the red ground
between the quarasote bushes.

Seventy yards or so to the north of the rams was a more
open space, a good thirty yards across with no vegetation at
all. There, the red-sandy soil shivered. One stonelike projection broke the surface, and then another. Then, there were
two blocky figures less than two thirds the size of a man.
The sanders were tan, and their skins sparkled in irregular
patches, as if crystals shone through in places. The eyes were
silvered green, also hard like crystal. Neither wore clothes,
but Alucius could see only the same rough skin all over,

without breasts or udders or any visible animal or human organs.

"Aim for the spot where the chest and neck join!" Royalt called.

Crack! A shot followed Royalt's call.

Belatedly, Alucius fired his rifle. His first shot missed. The sander shook itself and started toward the rams. Alucius recocked the rifle and fired again. The heavy bullet struck the upper arm of the creature, and it turned toward Alucius and the gray.

From well behind and to his left, Alucius heard a frantic bleating, but the sander he had hit and scarcely jolted was lumbering directly at him.

He cocked and fired. *Crack!* Sections of skin, like rock chunks, fragmented away, and the sander slowed. He fired again, and a larger expanse of crystallike skin broke off from the sander.

Abruptly, the creature shuddered, and halted. As Alucius recocked the rifle, it seemed to melt back into the sandy ground. He glanced toward his grandsire, but the first sander was lumbering northward, well out of range for a good shot.

Alucius turned the gray toward the sound of the bleating, a sound followed by snorting. He rode almost a hundred yards toward the rear of the flock, where as Alucius neared, a younger nightram hurled himself against a reddish tan sandwolf, nearly three yards long, with fangs more than a handspan in length, fangs that glittered crystal sharp in the sunlight.

Alucius raised his rifle, but the nightram blocked a good shot at the sandwolf.

The sandwolf snapped, its teeth seeming to close on the ram's snout, but at the last moment, the ram lowered his head and then twisted upward. The sandwolf lurched aside, trying to escape the knife-sharp horns, but a pair of long gashes scored the beast's heaving chest. The sandwolf growled, backing away.

The nightram snorted, a hoof pawing the ground.

Alucius saw another tannish red shape farther to the south.

"The sandwolf!" called Royalt.

Alucius caught himself and raised the rifle, firing his last shot.

The wounded sandwolf growled, turned, as if to retreat . . . and collapsed.

Several other shots echoed across the quarasote flats, but Royalt missed, for the other two sandwolves sprinted away through the quarasote.

For a moment, Alucius just looked at the sandwolf— taking in the reddish tan fur that shimmered in places where the sun struck it, the fangs that looked more like crystal knives, the broad paws and large chest, and the yellow-amber eyes.

A snort turned his eyes to the nightram, streaks of blood on the curled horns whose forward edges were every bit as sharp as the fangs of the sandwolf, and the red eyes set in the black face, eyes that seemed to carry both satisfaction and sorrow.

From the ewe came a soft bleat. She licked at the dead lamb sprawled in the open space between the quarasote bushes. For a moment, Alucius just looked. The sense of loss and sadness that emanated from the ewe was as palpable to him as the sunlight and the wind.

Then he jerked his head around, expecting another sander, but there were none . . . and the sense of violet-red that had nagged him all morning had vanished. But there was a sense of something shimmering and green. Alucius studied the flock, then glanced up, his eyes tracking to the northeast. There, a good hundred yards away, was a soarer, hovering just above a clump of quarasote bushes, her features and figure shrouded in the indistinct shimmer that had surrounded the handful of soarers Alucius had seen over the years.

Royalt reined up beside his grandson. His eyes took in the soarer. The older man had his rifle out and cocked, but he did not raise the weapon.

"Why . . . ?" murmured Alucius.

"Don't know. Sometimes you see them around sanders. Mostly not, though. Old tales say that soarers favor us by not meddling with people. Don't know for certain, but one thing's sure. You don't shoot at them. Bullets don't hurt 'em, and, besides, they don't do anything if you leave them alone."

"If you don't?" Alucius asked.

"Saw a fellow who tried to shoot one, years back. Bullet hit her and vanished. Three sanders rose right out of the ground around him and killed him. Not worth it."

As suddenly as the soarer had appeared, it vanished.

Royalt glanced down at the lamb and nodded sadly. "Diversion. When the sanders got us worried up with the rams, the sandwolves sneaked in back here."

"What . . . what do we do now?" asked Alucius.

"Leave the sandwolf. Not good for anything we need, and don't want to spend the effort on the pelt. Just pack the lamb up behind you. Nothing else we can do. Cold enough that we don't have to skin it here. Besides, we don't really have the knives. The sanders won't be back. Nor the sandwolves. Not today, and the rest need to graze. Have this feeling it'll be a hard year, Alucius. Sanders don't come after nightsheep this early."

"Why? They look like they're stone. How could eating . . . or killing . . ." Alucius wasn't quite sure what he meant, but the feeling was clear to him, that sanders were different, and that should have meant that they didn't need to kill sheep, not for food—although the nightsheep weren't good for human eating either, but when they died or were killed, the fleece and skin were always put to use. Did the sanders hunt to provide food for the sandwolves? Or did the sanders hunt for another reason and the sandwolves followed to get a meal?

"Don't know. Sanders sometimes carry off animals, and sometimes, they just kill them, leave them for the sandwolves. Never seen one eaten by a sander."

Alucius dismounted and handed the gray's reins to Royalt. For a moment, he looked down at the dead lamb before lifting it, heavier than it looked.

"Here . . . I've got the rope," Royalt said.

Alucius tied the lamb behind his saddle, on top of his

saddlebags that held food he wondered if he could eat later. Then he remounted.

He had sensed something, almost a violet-redness, in the part of his mind where he felt things with his Talent, but the feeling had come and gone since they had left the stead at dawn. He hadn't realized that the feeling represented lurking sanders, but now he knew. The soarer had felt the same, except for the differing "color" of the image his Talent sensed, more of a green. Most people he had met felt "black," although his grandsire and the other herders had flashes or flecks of silver and green running through the blackness. Scrats and grayjays were just thin flashes, brown for the scrats and bluish gray for the grayjays.

Even though he had not known, somehow, exactly what those violet-red feelings had meant, Alucius felt guilty about the death of the lamb, even though he had done all he could once he'd understood. Was life like that, seeing and often not understanding until it was too late? Or was that the curse of the Talent? Did others just not see?

15

Alucius was standing by the shed door, holding it open in the early summer twilight as Royalt herded the nightsheep flock back into their evening quarters. Once the last yearling was inside, the youth closed the door and slid the bolts in place.

"Thank you," said Royalt. "How did the spinnerets work today?"

Alucius walked alongside his grandfather and his mount. "I had trouble at first, but I got the hang of it after a while. Grandma'am came out and watched—"

"She was supposed to rest." Royalt snorted. "That was why you stayed here."

"She couldn't rest until she was sure I was doing it right."

Alucius laughed. "Then she went back to the house."

"When was that—midafternoon?" The older man reined up outside the stable.

"No. She did watch for a glass, though." Alucius grinned. "Mother came over from the processing vats, and they both decided I was doing it right, and the thread was fine. Mother checked again a couple of times, but I only ruined about two yards of the first bobbin, and she thought she could run it back through processing."

"You have to learn sometime." Royalt dismounted from the big bay.

"I've been watching, but it wasn't as easy as it looked, and . . . you know. The shears are less trouble. You just make sure everything is straight, and the slower you cut, the easier it is." The youth laughed. "About a half a glass after noon, just after I got back to work, someone came in a wagon, but I don't know who it is, because I had to clean out the spinnerets for the night. Mother checked a few times, and said we'd have company for dinner. An old friend and her daughter." Alucius rolled his eyes.

"It might not be so bad. Except you're still sweet on that other girl. Kyrial's oldest." Royalt laughed and clapped Alucius on the back. Then his expression turned serious. "Something was bothering Lamb today. He kept looking eastward at the plateau."

Alucius glanced back over Westridge toward the Aerial Plateau, rising like a fluted wall across the northeastern horizon. Light sparkled from the quartz outcroppings at the top of the plateau, more than six thousand yards straight up, outcroppings still highlighted by the rays of the sun that had already set in the valley. The scattered clouds were turning the sky into what his grandmother called sky-green-pink. "Sanders, you think?"

"I don't know. But he's one of the steadier rams—and good outercoat. Hope it was something. Thought you might check him out." Royalt smiled. "Seeing as you were the one who saved him, and he looks to you more than me as his herder."

Alucius returned the smile, knowing what his grandsire was thinking—that nightsheep shouldn't be named, and that Lamb was an absurd name for a nightram with horns as sharp as iron razors who could hold his own against one or two sandwolves. But Alucius had been young, and the ram didn't seem to mind, even after he'd grown up. "I'll see what I can do. Oh . . . Mother says grandma'am will be fine—just a touch of flux."

"Flux isn't good at any age." Royalt looked at his grandson. "You didn't . . . ?"

"No, sir. She feels a little weak. It's not the same, and I don't know that it would do much good. It doesn't have that same feeling, where everything is all in one spot."

"Good. That kind of Talent—it's something best saved . . ." He looked up, almost embarrassed. "If you'd see to Lamb?"

"I can do that." Alucius reopened the shed door and slipped inside, sliding the inner bolt in place—although the outside flange would allow his grandfather to follow, if he so desired.

Lamb was with the older rams, near one end of the group, and Alucius moved along the wall. Lamb eased away from the group, as if to acknowledge Alucius's presence. Alucius moved forward and ran his fingers through the thick wool of the ram, scratching his neck, oblivious to the pointed and sharp-edged horns.

"Was there something strange out there today?" While Lamb didn't understand words, the ram did understand the idea of inquiry, and Alucius projected that. The red-eyed ram looked up, then tilted his head ever so slightly. Alucius could only catch a sense of unease, a memory or feeling of possible danger, but the feeling wasn't specific.

"There was something, wasn't there?" He scratched Lamb's neck for a moment longer before easing away. Royalt had already stabled his mount and was waiting outside the shed. He looked to his grandson.

"There were sanders out there, I think," Alucius told his

grandfather. "I can't be sure, but Lamb had the feelings that they get when sanders are nearby."

"Afraid of that. Think maybe you'd better come with me tomorrow. Might bring an extra rifle, too." Royalt shook his head. "Need to go back and groom the bay. Tell your mother I'll be up for supper in a moment. She didn't say if her company happened to be staying?"

Alucius shrugged.

"I imagine so, but the women never tell us." Royalt laughed. "Women are like nightsilk, smooth and warm, and they turn to steel under pressure."

Was Wendra like that? Alucius wondered.

He checked the bolts on the shed door once more, then crossed the open ground toward the house. His mother was waiting on the porch. Beside her was a blonde girl, perhaps nine or ten.

"Alucius, this is Clyara." Lucenda nodded toward the girl. "Her mother and I need to go over some matters. I think she'd rather be out here."

Whether Clyara would or not, Alucius understood. "I'll be here. Grandfather said he'd be up for supper after he grooms the bay."

"It may be late." Lucenda smiled. "Would you tell him if you see him before I do."

"Yes, ma'am."

With a nod, Lucenda stepped back into the house, leaving Alucius with Clyara.

He gestured to the bench. "Do you want to sit down?"

"For a while." She sat on one end of the bench.

Alucius took the other. "Do you have sheep?"

"We have sheep," the girl said. "Not like yours. Ours are white. They get dirty."

"Ours get sandy . . . when the wind blows the sand. But nightsheep are different."

"A lot different? You couldn't put them together, could you?"

"They're different enough that it would be hard to put them together. They're good for different things. The white town sheep are good to eat. Nightsheep aren't, and eating them can make you very sick. The nightsheep have better fleece, but they're more willing to fight with other animals. A nightram can kill a sandwolf. That's why the sandwolves hunt in packs. Nightsheep have tougher wool, and they have much sharper and stronger horns. Their horns are sharper, especially the rams. We have to have more rams. That's because their wool is more valuable. You have to keep the rams from fighting. In other ways . . . they're alike. They like to be in a flock, and they have lambs in the spring."

"They say that your rams are dangerous. Only herders can touch them," the girl said. "Your mother said you could, that you raised a big ram. Are you a herder?"

"I'm still learning," Alucius answered. "Some days, I go out with my grandsire. I had to work here at the stead today. I'm supposed to learn everything before I become a herder."

Once she began to talk, Alucius discovered, Clyara had more than a few questions.

"Have you ever killed a sandwolf? . . ."

"Do you see soarers all the time? . . ."

"Are there any dustcats near here? . . ."

"Do you think there are Forerunner cities on the plateau? . . . Have you tried to climb it? . . ."

"Have you ever killed a brigand?"

At the last question, Alucius smiled. "I don't think I've ever seen a brigand. Sanders and sandwolves are the dangers." He paused. "At least, now they are."

The door to the porch opened, and Lucenda stepped out. "Alucius, would you show Clyara the washroom? You two can get washed up now." With a quick nod, Lucenda disappeared back into the house.

Alucius stood. "Washroom's off the kitchen. We can go in by the back side door." He turned and walked along the porch, past the kitchen window, casually glancing in, but only catching sight of his mother at the serving table. He held the door for Clyara, and then followed her inside. He cycled the hand pump several times, and then stepped out of the washroom.

After Clyara finished, he washed up himself and tidied the space, just in time for his grandsire.

Before long everyone was gathered around the kitchen table, set for six, instead of four. Lucenda nodded to Alucius. "If you would . . ."

He cleared his throat, conscious of both Clyara and her mother, and spoke. "In the name of the One Who Was, Is, and Will Be, may our food be blessed and our lives as well, and blessed be the lives of both the deserving and the undeserving that both may strive to do good in the world and beyond."

Lucenda began to hand platters from the serving table, speaking as she did. "Father, you remember Temra. She used to help me with the carding in the summer." Lucenda looked at her son. "That was years ago. Her Dysar is the second man in command of the Militia." She looked to the red-haired woman.

"They call him a majer," Temra explained. "Clyon is in charge, and he's a colonel."

Lucenda went on. "Temra was nice enough to bring out some of the hams that we'd bought from Junhal—we're having one, tonight—and she also brought some of the early greenberries from her sister's place near Dekhron. We were also talking about whether Clyara might come and spend a summer with us, in a few years, the way Temra did when she was Clyara's age."

Clyara glanced from her mother to Lucenda, and then to Veryl.

Alucius could sense that the conversation meant much more than the words conveyed, but what? He could also sense that his mother did not care much for Dysar.

Royalt cleared his throat, before offering the basket of fresh-baked bread to Temra. "Be good to have another young one around here. Specially in a year or so, even if it be just for the summer or harvest."

"Clyara could use some time seeing what happens on a stead," Temra replied. "It would be good for her before she gets too old to appreciate it."

Alucius wasn't sure that Clyara thought of that, but the petite blonde girl continued to eat her ham and biscuits. Like Alucius, she ate the prickle slices sparingly.

"Anyone who doesn't know should see and work at it," Veryl suggested serenely.

After a moment of silence, Lucenda spoke. "Temra was telling me that Dysar thinks the Reillies are beginning to raid some of the older steads to the west and north of Soulend."

Temra added, "He and Clyon think that's because the Matrites have taken over the Sloughs on the western side of the Westerhills and moved their horse soldiers in."

"So the iron women are moving out the Reillies?" Royalt passed the prickle platter to Clyara, who passed it to Alucius, who passed it quickly on, ignoring the frown from his mother.

"Dysar doesn't know," Temra replied, "but the Lanachronans have moved more Southern Guards from Krost and Vyan to patrol the river roads around Tempre. That's what he heard from the wine merchants."

"Bad business," Royalt grumbled. "Sounds like the Matrites are moving east. Means the Reillies won't raid west or south, and that doesn't leave anywhere but us."

"Why do they raid, sir?" asked Clyara. "Why don't they grow things like we do?"

"Because, young woman, the soil in the Westerhills is poor and because they have . . ." Royalt flushed, and then continued, "ah . . . too many mouths to feed."

Temra and Lucenda exchanged knowing glances.

"That's always been the case," Veryl said quietly, "and there's no reason to dwell more on that now." She smiled, a bright false smile. "Who's for a slice of honey cake?"

Even as he murmured, "Yes," Alucius could sense the undercurrents around the table.

"Lucenda," Veryl said, almost imperiously, "it seems everyone would like some."

"Yes, Mother."

Behind his mother's pleasant acquiescence, Alucius could sense a certain . . . something. Accomplishment? He wasn't sure, but it had to do with more than the honey cake.

Somehow, although Alucius should have enjoyed the cake, he didn't, and no one said much more. Then, it was time for Temra and her daughter to leave.

"Thank you for everything," Lucenda murmured as she hugged her friend. "Good luck."

"Good luck to you," replied Temra.

Clyara half-bowed to Lucenda, and then to Royalt and Veryl. "Thank you for supper, and for the honey cake."

"We'll get the wagon ready, Alucius," Royalt declared, starting for the door.

Alucius followed.

Once Royalt and Alucius had rehitched the two horses to Temra's wagon and seen the two off, Royalt turned to Alucius. "You need to get washed up and head for bed. No reading tonight. Be a long day tomorrow. Be waking you a half glass early."

"We're going farther with the flock?"

"No. Have some chores before we go. We'll talk about it in the morning."

"Yes, sir." With the sense of resignation that Royalt projected, Alucius didn't press his luck in questioning, but headed directly for the porch and the back door to the washroom.

He washed quickly and was getting to head into the main room to say goodnight when he heard voices in the kitchen. He paused just outside the washroom door, listening.

". . . very effective, daughter."

"You think I like it, Father? I've already lost one. In a way, I've even lost Temra. We were much closer until Dysar . . ."

The bitterness in Lucenda's voice shivered through Alucius, and he remained almost frozen in place.

A sigh from Royalt followed. "No . . . hoped it wouldn't come to this. Or that it wouldn't come till I was laid under the soil."

"Don't speak like that. You're still young and strong."

"Strong enough. Be better to be ailing and failing."

"I won't hear that."

"You'll be right, daughter. We'll start tomorrow. You think we'll have a full year—or two seasons?"

"Temra doesn't know."

"Let us pray we have a year or more."

Alucius frowned. After a moment, he opened and closed the washroom door. "I'm through in the washroom," he called loudly before walking toward the kitchen.

"I'll be there in a bit," his mother replied.

Alucius looked blandly at them. "Grandsire said I needed to get to bed early."

"That you do, young fellow. That you do." Royalt offered a forced smile.

"Well . . . good night," Alucius said, turning and heading down the corridor to the ladder up to his loft room. He hoped he could go to sleep early.

16

"Alucius?"

The young man jerked awake at the low sound of his grandsire's voice at the foot of the ladder. He hadn't thought he'd sleep, but he had, and it was now barely even gray in the east.

"Alucius?"

"I'm awake, Grandfather. I'll be down in a moment."

"Try to be a bit more quiet than usual," murmured the older man. "Your grandma'am is still asleep."

Keeping that admonition in mind, Alucius dressed as quietly and quickly as he could and made his way down the ladder and to the washroom. When he finished, his grandsire was standing outside in the corridor.

"Let's go."

"We're taking the flock out now? Before breakfast?"

"Soarers, no. We're going to the armory."

Armory? Alucius knew what an armory was, but did the stead have one? He'd never seen it, and he'd been through every building on the stead. Still wondering, Alucius followed his grandfather through the grayness of predawn from the house to the maintenance barn.

Royalt continued into the machining area where the foot lathes, the drills, and the grinders were set on their mounts and benches. He walked to the tool rack set flush into the middle of the north wall, reached high on one side, well above his head, and pushed up what had seemed to be a bracket bolted into both the rack and the wall. Then he pulled on the rack, which swung easily out into the workroom, revealing a lorken door—an old lorken door.

Royalt opened the door and picked a light-torch off the wall to the staircase that led downward.

"I never would have guessed," Alucius said slowly.

"That was the idea," Royalt pointed out, gesturing for Alucius to follow him. "There are bars behind the door, if we needed refuge from brigands. The door is two layers, with nightsilk between each layer of lorken and an iron plate on the back. That's so that it will hold for a long time. There's water and dried food down here as well. We rotate that every so often. Haven't had to use it since I was a boy, but you never know."

The room below was spacious, if without windows, measuring a good twenty yards in depth and fifteen in width. On the south wall were racked ten canvas cots on iron brackets. There was another door—barred and narrow.

"That's an escape tunnel. Runs a good eighty yards west, and comes out in the wash."

"I've been through the wash, and I haven't seen any caves or doors," Alucius said.

"You wouldn't. It's a concealed drop. Pull the levers at the end, and the dirt falls into a pit and breaks free of the door."

Royalt gestured to the racks on the eastern wall.

Alucius just looked, taking in the rifles and pistols racked there, the short-swords, and the daggers and knives. All of the weapons had a dullish sheen. The rifle cartridges were locked in a heavy iron box, except for those in the two ammunition belts, but the cartridges, thicker than a big man's thumb, were so heavy that the belts only carried fifteen. While their size was necessary to deal with sanders and sandwolves, it was also why a magazine carrying more than five shells was impractical.

"They're covered with an oil wax. I rotate the rifles we use, but they're all alike. Didn't think you'd notice."

Somehow, Alucius felt stupid for not noticing either the hidden doorway or the armory, and especially the switch in rifles, but then, he reminded himself, he hadn't expected concealment and deception from his own family.

Royalt cleared his throat and looked directly at Alucius. "What I'm going to teach you are things your father would have taught you."

The youth's eyes went from the knives on the table to the spear with the cross-bar below it, and then to what looked to be a small pistol.

"You already can handle a rifle, and you're adequate with a blade. Not great, but adequate. I can help you there."

"But . . . I'm a herder . . ."

"Are you ready to take on a pack of sandwolves by yourself—or a pair of sanders? Or will you take a few shots with your rifle and then let them make off with your best ewe? You've seen what they can do against both of us."

"Yes, sir. I mean, no, sir."

"There's another reason, lad . . ." Royalt sighed. "You heard what your mother's friend said last night. The Reillies and the other brigands are beginning to raid towns in the Westerhills."

"That's fifty vingts away."

"Fifty vingts isn't that far." Royalt paused. "With the brigands being pushed toward us by the Matrites, and more Lanachronan Southern Guards being moved north, it won't be long before they're talking about conscripting more young fellows for the militia. If the Council calls the need for conscription, each stead owes one man to the militia, if there's more than one man. Two, if there's more than five. You'll be eighteen in a little more than a year."

"Mother won't like that."

"She knows already. She doesn't like it. Neither does your grandma'am. Doesn't change things. You have a lot to learn in the next year."

"Yes, sir."

"Before we start, there's one other thing you need to remember . . ." Royalt said slowly. "I'll keep telling you, and I don't want you ever to say that you know it or that I've told you before." His voice hardened. "You understand?"

"Yes, sir."

"There are old troopers, and there are bold troopers. There aren't any old bold troopers. There also aren't many cowardly troopers left, either. That means you have to act, but only when you can stack things in your favor. When you don't know what's happening . . . watch, listen, and stay alive until you know what to do. Watched more men get killed 'cause they thought they had to do something, but they didn't know what. You get killed doing something stupid, and you can't live to do the right thing. If you think, you got a lot better chance of staying alive. Might die either way, but it's a sanded lot better to die doing the right thing that counts for something than just dying."

Alucius understood that well enough.

"Now . . . we'll start with the knives, and how to use them. Should be carrying three. Bootknife, one at your belt, and a small one *in* your belt . . ."

17

Hieron, Madrien

The Matrial walked around the dais holding the high bed whose curtains had been pulled back slightly when she had arisen earlier. Her steps were measured, but with a forced grace. She stopped before the full-length mirror on the inside north wall of her bedchamber. In the early morning light, she studied her face intently, noting the faint trace of wrinkles beginning to spread from the corners of her violet eyes, the hint of slackness along her chin.

"The Matrial, eternal and unaging . . ." she murmured in a voice so low that no one more than a yard away could have heard the words. "Unaging . . . if they but knew the cost . . ."

She turned from the mirror, and took a deep breath. Her eyes went to the circle of golden stone floor tiles, ringed with black, that lay two yards toward the door from the foot of the dais. The gold and black circle stood out starkly against the muted green tiles that comprised the rest of the bedchamber floor.

After a long moment, she took one step, and then another. Just short of the edge of the black-tiled circle, she slipped out of the violet nightrobe, revealing that she wore nothing beneath. She clamped her lips together and, with a convulsive movement, stepped into the circle, moving as though she were forcing her way through an invisible barrier.

Once within the circle, her entire body jerked, then shuddered. Welts, and then dark blotches, appeared across the once unmarked white skin, as if she were being struck by an unseen rod, until her entire body was a mass of bruises. And still she stood within the circle, her form seemingly being twitched and jerked as if she were a marionette whose strings were being plucked at random.

Her eyes closed, the Matrial clamped her mouth shut, so hard that her upper teeth sank into her lower lip and blood oozed down toward her chin. A low moan escaped her as one extraordinarily forceful yet unseen blow shook her entire frame. The Matrial pulled her head erect, but made no immediate move to escape the circle and the torment within.

In time, perhaps half a glass, she fought her way back through the unseen barrier, and stood, panting, outside the black tile line. Then, as she lurched away from the stone circle, the bruises that had covered her almost from crown to heel began to fade. She stopped short of the mirror and took in her reflection. Blood still flowed from her lower lip where she had bitten through it, but, even as she watched, the tissues scarred, and then healed. Within moments, there was no sign of the wound, nor of the bruises. Nor were there wrinkles, not even the hint of a trace of such lines, radiating from the deep violet eyes. Her chin line was once more firm and youthful, and her alabaster skin radiated perfection, without a sign of the bruises that seemingly should have taken weeks, if not months, to heal.

She stepped away from the mirror and walked, with the unforced grace of youth, toward the dressing chamber to ready herself for the day ahead.

18

"Alucius?" Royalt's whisper knifed up from the hallway beneath the ladder.

"Yes, sir." Alucius dragged himself out of his bed, into the cool air that held the faintest scent of quarasote. He pulled on his work clothes and boots.

He was long past dreading the morning sessions with his grandsire. They had become an accepted torture that he only wanted to complete as well as possible. If he didn't try, Royalt got angry and ended up bruising him so badly that Alucius could scarcely get through the day, especially if he had to ride with his grandsire to watch the flock.

If he tried, he got praised, but he was almost as sore, and then he was expected to remember what he had done well— and do better every morning thereafter.

Still, he hurried, as he did every morning, but Royalt was waiting in the armory for him, in the open area in the middle of the big room that had become a training arena. He tossed Alucius one of the blunt wooden knives. "Take the rifle. Check it to make sure it's unloaded."

Alucius caught the knife and put it through his belt, then checked the rifle. "Chamber's empty, magazine's empty." He cocked the weapon, then uncocked it, and checked again. He frowned. There was a cartridge in the chamber.

"Good. Sometimes, if a cartridge is just in the top of the magazine over the lip, you can't see it unless you look closely. Two things can happen. Either you shoot yourself or someone with you, or when you load the magazine and you cock it, you jam it."

Alucius nodded and removed the cartridge.

"Not the best design, and it usually doesn't happen. Took me a while to jigger that just right. But it's the things that don't happen often that can kill you."

From what Alucius was beginning to feel, everything could kill a man. Or at least, his grandfather felt that way.

"Now . . . you've fired your last bullet, and you've got a knife. So does the Reillie that's just overrun you." Royalt circled toward Alucius, holding the other blunt wooden knife. "Go on . . . what are you going to do?"

Alucius tried to circle away, but felt hampered with the heavy rifle, especially when Royalt jumped toward his right side. No matter what he did, he felt off-balance, and the useless rifle slowed him.

Finally, he set it down as he circled, and squared himself, finding his eyes tracking his grandsire's.

"Stupid move . . ." Royalt murmured, and feinted.

Alucius backed in a circle.

From nowhere, Royalt's booted foot slammed the knife

from Alucius's hand, and before Alucius could recover, he was on his back with the wooden knife at his throat. Royalt shook his head and released his grandson. "In a real fight, wouldn't put you down and put the knife to your throat. Put the knife right up under your gut. Won't kill you immediately, but the pain's so bad you won't be able to do anything, and you'll die anyway."

Alucius swallowed as he scrambled up.

"You were watching my eyes, not my body."

"It's hard. I've grown up watching the eyes."

Royalt snorted, tucked the wooden knife into his belt, and picked up the rifle, holding it in both hands. The black crystal band in the center of his herder's wristguard glinted, even though there was no direct light falling upon it. "Why didn't you use both hands?"

"Then I couldn't use the knife."

"All right . . . you attack me with your knife. That's what you wanted, wasn't it?"

Alucius reclaimed the knife off the stone floor, then circled in.

Royalt ducked, glanced to his right.

Alucius ignored the glance, but the rifle barrel snapped down on his weapon, and the knife went flying, and, again, Alucius looked up at his grandfather from the floor.

"How many times do I have to tell you? You don't watch a man's eyes. He can move his body one way while looking another. You watch the middle of his body. That's where his weight is, and that tells you where he's moving. He can't go anywhere without bringing it with him. Now, on your feet."

Alucius wanted to groan. His grandfather was ten quints plus, with the gray hair of age, and he was handling Alucius as if he were a toddler.

"You want to die out there?"

"No, sir."

"Then act like you want to live and start listening. How long is the rifle?"

"A yard or so."

"How long is a knife?"

Alucius nodded slowly, understanding the point. "But I didn't know how to handle the rifle that way."

"You're going to learn, just like you're going to learn every possible way to kill and to avoid being killed." Royalt smiled, not exactly warmly, but not coldly.

Alucius realized that the expression was one of concealed resignation.

"We'll work on the rifle for a while this morning, and then we need to get some breakfast and get the flock out as far as we can today."

Alucius wasn't nearly as eager to ride herd on the flock as he once had been—not with his grandfather. On the previous Tridi, his grandsire had made him trot alongside the gray and mount from a run—time after time. Alucius wasn't even sure what good that would do in the militia or in a fight. He could see the knife work and the unarmed fighting. But trying to mount a horse on the run? Or was it just to toughen him up and improve his legs?

He didn't know, and he wasn't sure he wanted to.

19

"Alucius?" Royalt's whisper wakened the younger man immediately.

"I'll be right there, sir."

"There's not as much hurry this morning. You need to wash up and wear your better outfit. You're going into Iron Stem with your mother today."

Alucius frowned as he climbed out of his bed and eased toward the ladder. For more than a season, his grandfather had not allowed him a single day of respite from the glass of grueling training that had begun every day. "Is there something wrong?" He leaned over the opening through which the ladder rose, looking down in the dimness of early harvest at his grandsire.

Royalt grinned. "You could use a day off, and so could I. Your mother would also like your company—and your strong back."

"Yes, sir." Alucius couldn't quite conceal the relief in his voice.

Below, he could hear his grandfather's snort, but the expression concealed amusement, rather than anger.

After laying out his better trousers and shirt and the vest he'd gotten a month earlier, Alucius started down the ladder. He had to wonder, and not just about the need for his strong back, but he wasn't about to complain. Perhaps he could even have a moment while they were in town to see Wendra.

He was still wondering when he sat down for breakfast and looked across the table at his mother. "What are we going to do in Iron Stem?"

"Now that the harvest produce is coming in, the prices in town are going down, and it's a good time to lay in goods and stock for the winter." Lucenda handed the basket of biscuits to him.

Alucius took one and passed the basket to his grandmother.

"Thank you, Alucius," Veryl said.

"Most people don't realize what's coming yet," Royalt added. "To them, those who know, it's a story. Been so long since we've had a real fight that most folk don't understand."

"Don't some people?" asked Alucius.

"There are some. Kustyl sees it, and so do his offspring, I'd wager, since he'd beat it into them. Gortal does. He's been charging the Lanachronans more for dreamdust . . ."

". . . price of cartridges has been going up. Good thing we've got plenty . . ."

". . . not the price of flour . . . not yet . . ."

As Alucius swallowed the last fragment of egg toast, his mother looked at him. "Will you get the wagon ready? Make sure that we have the oilcloth tarps in the back. It doesn't look like rain, but . . . if something blows up, we'd not want goods spoiled."

"Yes, ma'am." Alucius eased his chair back.

As he left the house, he did smile as he caught a few words.

". . . good boy . . ."

". . . getting to be a man . . ."

In walking to the stable, Alucius studied the sky. There were thin hazy clouds across the silver-green of the heavens, but nothing that augured rain. Still, the first thing he did was fold the oilcloth tarps and put them in the wagon bed. He was hitching the dun dray horses to the wagon when Royalt appeared with two leather cases in his arms. "Better take a brace of rifles."

"You think we might see brigands?"

"If I did, I'd be with you two, but it's more likely than it's been for years. Besides, now you know enough that the rifles are safe with you." Royalt laid the cased rifles in the wagon bed behind the seat. "The magazines are full, and there are spares in the cartridge packs. Need to talk to your mother. Bring the wagon up to the house."

"Yes, sir."

Royalt strode off back toward the house.

After Alucius hitched the team and set the rifles and their cases in the brackets mounted beside each seat, he drove the team up to the house. There Royalt was talking to Lucenda.

"I'd like ten half-barrels, and five full ones—if Kyrial can have them ready in the next two weeks. If he has any, take what you can get. Order the rest. You know what to get for stocks."

Lucenda nodded. "We'll do the best we can." She turned and climbed up into the right seat and turned to her son. "You can drive, if you'd like."

"You don't mind?"

"Drive," his mother said with a laugh.

Royalt laughed as well.

Neither spoke until they were a good quint down the lane from the stead.

"Your grandfather says that you're coming along well."

"It doesn't feel that way," Alucius admitted. "Every time

I learn something, he shows me another way to overcome what I just learned."

"How old are you, Alucius?"

"A little past seventeen. You know that."

"How old is your grandsire?"

"Ten quints or more."

"He was with the militia almost eight years in the Border Wars. Are you going to learn everything he knows in less than two seasons?"

Alucius looked down, then back at the road and the team. After a time, he spoke again. "Grandsire's worried, isn't he?" He knew that. He wanted to hear what his mother had to say.

"He is."

"But we've fought before, and won."

"When he was young, the militia fought off the Lanachronans. They really didn't want to take over the Iron Valleys. They just wanted the sources of the nightsilk and to get rid of the dreamdust. But if the Matrites are going to take over the Westerhills, then it won't be long before they'll take the Iron Valleys. Or the Lanachronans will ride north to keep out the Matrial."

"We could fight them off," Alucius suggested.

Lucenda laughed. The sound was harsh. "How many cities do we have, Alucius?"

"Dekhron's pretty big, and then there's Iron Stem and Soulend . . ."

"Dekhron would fit in less than the trade quarter of Hieron or Tempre. Madrien holds the entire coast up to Northport and all the Sloughs east to the Westerhills. The Matrites took over the Salceran lands more than thirty years ago. Only Southgate has held out so far—if they still have."

"You make it sound like we're a nightram caught between sanders and sandwolves, between the Matrites and the Lanachronans."

"That's a fair description of the situation," his mother replied dryly.

Alucius was silent for a time, as he considered her words.

"You make it sound hopeless," he finally said.

"We don't have enough militia to invade and defeat them. Thank the soarers, we don't have to. We only have to make it so difficult for either the Matrites or the southerners that it's easier to leave us alone. That's what happened with the Border Wars."

"Should we be fighting now?"

"The Council has discussed that, Temra told me, but we'd have to fight through the Reillies and the other hill clans— or trust them as allies." Lucenda's face turned bleak, and her lips twisted on the word "allies."

Alucius wasn't quite sure what else to say on that, and didn't.

Before too long the dustcat enclosures came into view on the left.

"Has a dustcat ever escaped?" asked Alucius, wanting to break the silence.

"Not that I know of. I wish they'd all escape. Filthy habit."

"I thought that all the dreamdust was sold to the Lanach-ronans."

"It is, but the scutters want it so much that they'll work for almost nothing."

"Aren't they . . . well . . . people who . . . maybe . . ."

"People who are mostly worthless? Is that what you're asking?"

Alucius flushed.

"They are when they've become scutters. They'll do any-thing. I knew some girls—they're women now. They'll do things that even the worst slut in the Pleasure Palace wouldn't, just to keep working where they can sniff the dreamdust. And the men are worse." Lucenda's voice carried a chill Alucius seldom had heard.

While there was a single mount tied up outside the Plea-sure Palace, Alucius saw no one outside as he drove the team past the barnlike building that was anything but a palace. His eyes had still lingered on the bright green spire that soared heavenward, far taller than anything else in Iron Stem, seem-ingly taller than anything except the plateau itself. He still wondered what the ancients had used the tower for, so magnificent was it, especially in comparison to anything else within hundreds of vingts.

Once they had passed the Pleasure Palace, Lucenda said, "I thought we might stop by the cooper's first. Your grandfather wanted me to order more barrels. He thinks we need to put aside more flour, and a barrel of rice."

"Rice? That's costly." Alucius wasn't about to say anything about seeing Wendra.

Lucenda nodded. "It is, but if you keep it dry, it will hold for years without spoiling. Then, after the cooper's, we'll see what we can find in the way of supplies, first in the square, and then out at Amiss's mill."

As was always the case during harvest season, there were more people in Iron Stem—or so it seemed to Alucius as he guided the team down the north road toward the square. The shutters of most cottages were open, and the hammermill was in full operation, with its muffled but thundering *clangs*, and the acrid odor of hot metal spilling out across the road.

He slowed the wagon when they entered the north side of the square, quickly counting the carts and wagons in the center paved area—almost twenty, and some were piled high with maize and apples and other produce.

"Looks like there's some good produce."

"I don't see any rice or beans, but some of them are still setting up. We'll have to come back and look closely. Put the wagon on the side street by the loading dock there."

Alucius nodded and guided the wagon into the indicated spot on the side of the deep building that held the cooperage. Then he set the wagon brakes, and secured the rifles in the locker under the seat. The lock was simple, but was sufficient for midday in Iron Stem. After that, he took the harness restraint ropes and tied the two dun geldings to the stone post.

Kyrial looked up from the work bench as the two entered the front of the shop. "Lucenda! We haven't seen you in almost a season."

"We've been working hard, and there aren't ever enough

hands to run a stead." Lucenda smiled politely. "We're also looking for some more barrels."

"Barrels I have." The cooper shook his head, then looked at Alucius, before lowering his voice as he continued. "With the trouble in the Westerhills . . . I ordered in more wood from Dekhron, and made barrels that I didn't have orders for. But so far, no one seems worried."

Lucenda laughed. "Father wants five full barrels and five half. Do you have that many?"

Kyrial smiled. "How about four full barrels and five half right now, and the other full one in a week?"

"How much?"

"The usual. A half-silver for the full, and four coppers for the half-barrels." The cooper grinned. "Not a good time for the millrights in Dekhron, and I got a good price on the wood." The grin vanished. "That'll change by fall, but I've got another order in with a fixed price."

"The terms are good," Lucenda agreed, "If you'll add two more half barrels, and hold all three of those you haven't finished until we get into town again."

"Done."

To their right, a squeaking of the opening door and then a thump indicated that someone else had entered the cooper's shop.

Kyrial glanced toward the door.

A faint smile crossed Lucenda's lips, and she said, "We've put off replacing the solvent barrels for too long, but you know Royalt—he hates to part with coin." She looked up abruptly at the newcomer, a man of medium height and build, wearing gray trousers, and a silver-gray vest over a while silk shirt. "Oh . . . Gortal . . . I didn't hear you come in." She inclined her head to Alucius. "Have you met my son Alucius?"

Alucius inclined his head, managing a pleasant smile, rather than the frown he felt. "Sir."

"Pleasure to meet you, young Alucius." Gortal's voice was calm, polite, and emotionless.

Kyrial nodded to Gortal. "Your lined and sealed lorken quarter barrels are ready."

"Good. I've got my wagon on the side." He nodded to Lucenda, "Just behind yours, I believe."

"Most probably."

Kyrial looked to Lucenda. "If you wouldn't mind . . . it will only be a few moments."

"Go ahead."

After the two men left, Alucius looked to his mother. "Neither you nor Kyrial like him."

"He's the owner of the dustcat farms. He has been since his father died two years ago."

"That shirt must have cost a gold itself," Alucius said.

"I wouldn't doubt it. The Lanachronans pay dearly for dreamdust." Lucenda glanced toward the rear of the shop. "Why don't you head into the back and say a word to Wendra? She's peeked in here several times. I'll call you when we're ready to load the barrels."

"Are you sure?"

"I'll call you. Don't fret about that." Lucenda cleared her throat. "Alucius . . ."

"Yes?"

"Her mother's name is Clerynda. You might have forgotten."

Alucius grinned. "Thank you." He inclined his head to his mother, and walked toward the door to the rear, noticing that it was ajar. He opened it gingerly, and stepped into the back room.

Wendra was standing at a table, holding a pair of shears.

"I hope I'm not interrupting," Alucius began, offering, first, a head bow to the squarish gray-haired woman who sat behind a treadle-operated machine, and, second, one to Wendra.

"We are working," Wendra said, but there was a hint of a smile in her eyes and words. She set down the shears, and half-turned. "Mother, this is Alucius. Alucius, this is my mother."

"Pleased to meet you, ma'am" he offered.

"I'm pleased to see you again, young man. Wendra has wondered when you might be in town—"

The green-eyed girl blushed. "Mother . . ."

"Hush. What is, is. No sense in making over it. You be here long, Alucius?"

"Not too long, ma'am."

"Why don't you two just go upstairs to the rear parlor? Leave the stair door open, and we can call you when we need you."

"Are you sure . . . ?" Alucius began.

"Sure enough. Don't waste the moments."

Alucius didn't need any urging, but he looked to Wendra. "If you wouldn't mind . . ."

"For that alone, were I thirty years younger, I'd have you," Clerynda commented.

"Mother . . ." Wendra was blushing even more furiously.

"Go and leave an old woman to get some work done." Clerynda smiled knowingly at her daughter.

Slowly, still blushing, Wendra turned. "We . . . *will* leave the doors open."

Concealing his own smile, Alucius followed the young woman to the door and up the narrow stairs, all too conscious of how close she was.

"Mother . . . sometimes . . . she's impossible." Wendra opened the door at the top of the stairs and left it open as she stepped into the room that held but a small loveseat, two chairs, two high tables flanking the window, and a low table around which the chairs and love-seat were arranged. The shutters were open, and a pair of clean but faded white curtains framed the window.

Alucius could sense frustration—and apprehension. "Aren't most mothers?"

"She's . . . more impossible," Wendra hissed.

Alucius made a vague gesture toward the table, not wanting to suggest where Wendra would sit. She sat on the love-seat, but as if it were expected. Alucius took the straight-backed ladder chair across from her, and could sense her relief.

"I'm sorry I couldn't come to see you sooner, but this is only the second time I've been away from the stead since spring—and you weren't here the last time I got to town. Except for herding, of course, but that doesn't get me anywhere close to Iron Stem." He smiled, trying to reassure her.

"Father did say something about that. He said it had been more than a month since he'd seen any of your family in town." Wendra shifted her weight on the love-seat, and for the first time, she actually looked directly at Alucius.

For a moment, he just met her eyes, the eyes that were somehow green and yellow and gold, and yet not exactly those colors or any combination of them.

"I'm glad you came," she finally murmured.

"So am I. I wasn't sure . . . if you really wanted to see me."

"I did. I do." She dropped her eyes for a moment. "You could have anyone, you know."

"Me?" Alucius had never even considered anything like that.

Wendra laughed, softly. "Vardial said you were nice. You are, you know?"

"I'd never thought about it." Alucius wished, in a way, that he'd seated himself beside her, but moving would have been awkward—or worse. "I just hoped that I could see you."

"So did I," she admitted, again looking away.

After a moment of silence that seemed far longer than a mere moment, he asked, "How are your bookkeeping lessons?"

"Madame Myrier says that I'll know all she can teach me in another season."

"That's good."

"What . . . I mean, how does a herder learn . . . ?"

Alucius laughed. "I have to learn by doing. My grandsire has been teaching me how to use weapons, all of them, it seems."

"Weapons? Like a sword or a rifle?"

He nodded, "I've already been out with him and the flock

when the nightsheep were attacked by sandwolves and sanders. You know that sandwolves don't leave a scent, not one that most animals can smell. The nightsheep can sense them, but regular sheep can't. That's why they're called townsheep. Anyway, a herder has to be good with weapons to protect the flock."

"And you have to know them in case you get called into the militia, won't you?"

"I guess so," Alucius temporized.

"Kyrtus said that all of you may have to fight." After a moment, Wendra added, "I hope you don't, but Father thinks it will happen."

"My grandsire worries, too," Alucius admitted.

"Grandpa Kustyl worries more than Father. He and your grandfather are friends, aren't they?"

"They are. Sometimes, Kustyl will come to see Grandfather, and sometimes, he'll ride over to see Kustyl." After another silence, Alucius asked, "What were you doing downstairs?"

"I was cutting out the patterns for the flour bags that Amiss the miller ordered." Wendra laughed. "They're hardly patterns—very simple—but someone has to do it, and that way Mother can sew more of them. It's more interesting to help Mother with things like the militia uniforms or the linens for the inn. The linens are easy, but the ones for the grand rooms, they want embroidered monograms, and I like to do those." She smiled. "I've already embroidered the ones for my own dowry chest." Abruptly, she flushed.

"I'm sure that they're very elegant," Alucius said quickly.

"They are. I followed one of the old patterns—"

"Wendra!" Clerynda's voice carried up the stairs. "If you would tell Alucius that he's needed to help load the barrels?"

"Yes, Mother!"

Wendra rose quickly—but gracefully—from the love-seat. "You have to go. We really didn't get much chance to talk."

"We did get some," he said with a smile. "Maybe it won't be so long before the next time."

"I hope not." With a smile, warm and slightly wistful, she turned toward the steps.

As he followed Wendra down to the shop, Alucius wondered. Had he missed some sort of opportunity? Failed to do something? Or if he'd tried to kiss Wendra, would that have spoiled everything? Even sensing some of what she felt, he was still at a loss, because he didn't know what the feelings meant.

Just before they reached the bottom of the steps, he reached out and squeezed her shoulder, gently. "I'm glad you were here."

"So am I."

They were both blushing when they stepped into the back workroom.

Alucius swallowed, and waited for some acerbic words from either his mother or Wendra's.

Instead, Lucenda merely smiled politely. "I wish we could have stayed longer, Alucius. I would have enjoyed talking to Clerynda longer, as well, but there's much we have to do, and I'd prefer to be back at the stead before dark."

Alucius nodded. "I'm ready to load the barrels." He turned to Wendra. "Thank you. I did enjoy talking to you . . . very much." He managed not to flush again, even as he thought how stilted his words were.

Wendra smiled and inclined her head. "Thank you."

"We do need to go, Alucius." Lucenda smiled at Clerynda. "It was a pleasure."

"For me as well, Lucenda."

Then Lucenda turned, and Alucius followed her, expecting some words about Wendra, at least after he finished loading the barrels or when they were on the way back to the square.

But his mother never mentioned Wendra.

20

In the darkness of a cloudy harvest night, Alucius turned over in his bed, wincing at the bruise on his hip, the result of a throw by his grandsire. He turned again, trying to get comfortable, then stiffened as he heard voices in the hallway below.

". . . has bruises everywhere." Lucenda's low voice carried enough for Alucius to hear.

He eased out of his bed toward the ladder, where he could hear more easily.

"Of course he does. How else is he going to learn, daughter? If it doesn't hurt sometimes, it's as though I don't know anything or it's so simple it's not worth learning."

"You were different, I suppose?" Lucenda's laugh was muted.

"No, I was worse. My father had to crack my ribs. Alucius is better than most his age . . ."

"I suppose you're right . . . how long . . ."

Alucius strained, but couldn't catch the rest of his mother's question.

"If he'll keep at it, I can train him better than anyone in the militia in the basic skills. They haven't got anyone who's been in a real fight. Haven't had for years."

"I wish . . ."

"I know, daughter, but it's hard for a man to be trained by his wife's father, and even harder to marry into a stead that way."

"But . . . if he had . . ."

"Might not have changed . . . When folks are shooting at each other, anything can happen."

Alucius could sense the untruth in his grandfather's words—the untruth and the sadness.

"You're kind . . . know better . . . just wish . . ."

"Wishing doesn't change what's been. We have to work to change what will be. Sometimes, we can. Most times, we can't."

There was a long pause, before Lucenda spoke again.

"You *will* hold a gather? A small one?"

"With Kyrial and his family invited?"

"Why else?"

"You think . . . ?"

"I don't know," Lucenda said quietly, but firmly enough that Alucius could sense the determination in her voice. "Either way, it will be good."

"Helps to have something to hold to," Royalt said.

Alucius frowned. Something to hold to?

"You think . . . ?"

"Who can say?" Royalt coughed. "Good night, daughter."

"Thank you, Father . . . good night."

After the two had closed their doors, Alucius slipped back to his own pallet bed, his face solemn, his brow furrowed in thought in the darkness.

21

The early afternoon sun was intense, as it often was in harvest season, and to Alucius's left, light sparkled off the crystal battlements of the distant Aerlal Plateau. Alucius rode alone, southward along the eastern side of the low rise, just above a streambed that held water only immediately after a heavy rain. There had been no rain for a month, and with each step that the gray gelding took, sandy dust rose. The new quarasote shoots were few and short, and the ground so dry that both scrats and grayjays were scarce.

Alucius needed to keep the nightsheep moving, or they'd eat all the new growth, leaving nothing at all for later.

He had the flock in the more southern reaches of the stead—almost as far from the plateau as possible. That had been his grandsire's orders, because sanders and sandwolves were usually less likely to roam in the southernmost areas—especially on bright and sunny days. Over the past year, Alucius had taken the flock out by himself perhaps a double handful of times, first close to the stead, and then farther and farther—although always in the southern ranges. He also took two rifles.

This particular Octdi, Royalt had gone to Iron Stem to work with Feratt at the ironworks on some replacement parts for the nightsilk spinnerets, leaving Alucius to take the flock, but not without the usual warnings and cautions.

"Keep your eyes and Talent on the lead rams and the old ewes . . . they'll sense something wrong first . . . You see a sandwolf, make sure there's not a sander too close . . ."

The lightest of warm breezes wafted out of the south, not even enough to ruffle Alucius's short and dark gray hair, but welcome nonetheless after days of still and blistering air.

Alucius frowned. Once again, he sensed the flash of red-violet that indicated sanders were somewhere around. He'd never felt them so far from the plateau, but his grandsire had often stressed that sanders could appear anywhere in the Iron Valleys—perhaps even in other dryland settings. They were just more likely to be nearer the plateau.

He watched the lead rams, and concentrated on Lamb, but the big ram seemed not to be upset. Neither were the other lead rams or the older ewes. Alucius checked his rifle once more, still surveying the clumps of scattered quarasote for the black shapes of the nightsheep.

As he studied the land and the flock, he could see that the nightsheep had nearly finished most of the newer quarasote shoots, because a number had lifted their heads and begun to move southward. Alucius checked the sun, and then, with a nod to himself, he decided that he could begin to work the nightsheep back westward. That might also move them away from the sanders, although the Talent indications were so faint that Alucius had no idea exactly where the creatures might be.

After remembering to study the sky—eagles often circled

sander kills, and sanders sometimes did kill sandwolves or other creatures—he circled behind the flock, chivvying the laggards into an ambling walk that was mostly westward, not relaxing his Talent-projection until the entire flock was a good half vingt farther west, and well clear of the dry stream bed.

The sense of the sanders—that vague red-violet feel—had vanished, at least for the moment. Mindful of his grandfather's warning about revealing the extent of his Talent, Alucius had never mentioned the details of his sense of sanders, although he had always told his grandsire when he thought sanders were nearby. But did he and Royalt sense the same thing?

Somehow, Alucius doubted it, and that was why he had never brought up the details of what he felt through his Talent, even to his grandsire. He'd certainly never mentioned any of it to Wendra, although he would, if matters worked out between them.

He caught his breath as a wave of red-violet washed over his Talent-senses, and immediately stood in the stirrups, scanning the flatter area where the flock grazed. Several nightsheep had lifted their head, and three of the rams—Lamb among them—had turned and were moving slowly back toward the ewes behind them.

Lamb snorted, the first sound Alucius heard, and pawed the ground.

Alucius urged the gray toward Lamb and the front of the flock.

Less than fifty yards ahead a swirl of sand and dust marked the emergence of a sander.

Alucius kept riding, then reined up a good ten yards short of the creature.

The sander, before even breaking clear of the red sandy soil, had clutched a young ewe in its oversized pawlike hands.

"You won't take my sheep . . ." Alucius threw out the single mental pulse. *No!* Without really thinking, he had the rifle out and cocked.

The sander halted and turned. It was wider and blockier than the handful Alucius had seen with his grandfather, but its skin was the same sandy tan, if with fewer of the crystallike patches that reflected sunlight. Deliberately and slowly, the sander tightened its grip on the young ewe until its heavy arm snapped the ewe's neck. Then . . . it just held the animal for a moment, long enough for Alucius to lift the rifle and fire.

Crack! The first shot struck exactly where Royalt had trained him to place it. *Crack!* So did the second. Chips and crystalline fragments flew from the impact of the bullets, but the massive sander shook itself once, twice.

Alucius cocked the rifle and fired again. *Crack!*

More chips flew, but the creature did not try to sink into the ground, the way most of the sanders did. Instead, it dropped the dead ewe and lumbered toward Alucius and the gray gelding.

Alucius recocked the rifle and fired. With the fourth impact, the sander slowed and shook itself more. A thin line of crystal seemed to ooze from the wound area.

Crack! The last cartridge rocked the sander back, but only for an instant. Oozing crystalline fragments, it leaned forward and then lumbered once more toward the young herder.

Realizing that he would not have enough time to reach the second rifle and cock it, Alucius dropped the first rifle and yanked out the sabre, bringing it down in a cross-slash aimed at the point where his bullets had weakened the sander. Hitting the sander was like hitting a lorken post, and the shock ran all the way up the herder's arm.

Surprisingly, the sander froze for a moment, and despite the numbness in his arm, Alucius managed another slash. His fingers were so numbed that he could barely hang on to the sabre long enough to transfer it to his right hand.

A green shock emanated from the sander, like a cry of despair, and ran through the herder. Then . . . the creature exploded into crystalline fragments that pelted Alucius and rained down upon the dry and sandy ground.

Panting, Alucius stared for a moment. As he stared, he

could see the fragments melting, disappearing into the soil. The quarasote plain was silent. Even the light breeze had died away. Alucius could sense nothing of sanders or sand-wolves—just an empty silence. Shaking himself, he checked his blade, but it was as clean as if he had never used it, and he sheathed it.

As he surveyed the area around him, he took the second rifle from its case by his knee. Nothing moved. He dis-mounted and quickly scooped up the first rifle, holstering it, but not daring to reload it until he cleaned it.

One of the lead rams had eased over to within several yards of the dead ewe. Alucius could sense the ram's unease . . . and something more. Loss? Alucius wasn't sure. He'd felt something like that before, when a ewe had lost a lamb, but he'd never sensed that feeling from a ram. They didn't slaughter the nightsheep. There was no point to it, since they weren't edible, but Alucius was still glad of it at that mo-ment.

Even before he finished packing the dead ewe behind his saddle, the last fragment of the sander had vanished. Except for the dead ewe, his sore arm, and the expended cartridges, it was almost as though nothing had happened.

Alucius remounted quickly, checking around him once more. He saw and Talent-sensed nothing but nightsheep. He pushed the flock farther westward.

After a time, he holstered the second rifle and took out the first to clean it. There was only a trace of sand in the barrel and almost no grit in the action and chamber. After cleaning it and checking it over again, he reloaded and replaced it in its case.

As he guided the nightsheep on their grazing path back toward the stead buildings, he still wondered about the sander—and about that green sense of despair. At the same time, he was angry, angry at himself for not being able to stop the sander from killing the ewe, for not somehow being able to foresee what would happen.

He had *known* there were sanders around—but he had sensed them many times before when none had appeared.

Would he ever be able to tell the difference, between when they would and would not appear?

Alucius frowned, but he kept watch, both with his eyes and Talent.

22

The harvest afternoon was cooler than usual, with a wind out of the northeast that mixed the scent of quarasote with the acrid and near-metallic odor that emanated from the Aerlal Plateau. The coolness suited Alucius, wearing a new nightsilk and sheepskin vest, as he stood behind the table that had been moved out to north end of the front porch and served the berry punch and the weak ale that his grandfather favored. He was still somewhat amazed that Royalt had decided to hold a harvest-gather. He also kept looking for the cooper's wagon and Wendra.

Vardial stepped to the table, holding up a tumbler. "I'd like the ale, but . . ."

"So would I . . . but I only get a small glass with supper." Alucius grinned.

"Do they decide this among themselves? A poor young herder has no choice at all . . ."

"You poor misbegotten fellow . . ." Elyra stepped up beside Vardial.

Alucius took her tumbler and refilled it with more of the berry punch, and then refilled Vardial's as well. "All of us who would be herders suffer great hardship. Surely, you know that, Elyra?" Alucius couldn't quite manage a straight face as he finished.

Elyra laughed. "You're too honest to lie well, Alucius—even in a good cause."

"You must admit it is a good cause," Vardial said.

"You will have to persuade me, I think." Elyra smiled at Vardial as the two moved away.

Kustyl walked toward the table, carrying two tumblers, both empty.

"Ale, sir?" asked Alucius. He could have told that Kustyl was a herder, like his grandsire, even without the silver and black crystal wristguard, because the older man had the flecks of green and silver that flashed through the basic blackness that all people seemed to have. Even Wendra had a few, but they were scattered, but that might have been because she had never had to do anything requiring Talent.

"I wouldn't be having anything else, would I, now?" answered the thin and wiry herder with a wide smile. "Especially not as Royalt's bought Typel's best." He held up both tumblers, and his sleeves dropped back, just enough to reveal the herder's wristguard on his left wrist.

Alucius hadn't realized that the guard could be worn on either wrist, but it had to be a choice by each herder because Kustyl was most definitely a herder, and wore his silver and black on his left, while Royalt wore his on his right. Alucius refilled both tumblers, and then pumped out more ale from the keg into the pitcher. He had finished refilling the pitcher when Elyra and Vardial reappeared together.

"Wendra's just arrived, and we thought we could serve the punch and ale. Your mother and your grandsire said that, if we wanted to relieve you, we could."

"Thank you." Alucius stepped toward Vardial and away from the table. Everyone knew everything—about some aspects of life, at least.

The stockier youth grinned at Alucius and mouthed, "Thank *you*."

Alucius returned the grin. Vardial would do anything to corner time with Elyra, and seemed oblivious to the fact that she could have easily avoided his obvious ploys.

After stepping off the porch, Alucius forced himself not to run toward the stable and the shed being used as a stable for some of the guests, but he did find himself walking quickly. As he neared the stable, he could see Kyrial, Clerynda, Wendra, and a boy standing beside the cooper's wagon. Wendra was wearing dark green trousers, with a matching vest, and a lighter green shirt. The greens set off her hair and eyes. Absently, Alucius also saw, in the back of the wagon, four full barrels and two half barrels.

"Greetings," Alucius bowed to the cooper, his wife, and then Wendra and her younger brother.

Before they could answer, Royalt stepped out of the shed where he had been stabling Kyrial's horses. "Thought you might be coming down."

"I just found out they were here. Would you like me to unload the barrels?" Alucius looked to Kyrial.

"If we each take two," Royalt said, "we can just set them inside the shed and out of the way, and then Alucius and I will take care of them tomorrow."

"Fine by me," answered Kyrial. "They were done, and I thought I'd spare you a trip." He smiled at Alucius. "Though I'd not be sure that the young man would have minded that."

Alucius managed not to flush as he lifted one of the larger barrels and carried it into the shed.

"This time of year, he'll be there sooner or later," Royalt predicted, taking a barrel as well. "There's always something needed."

"I'd be apologizing for being a trace late," offered Kyrial, "but I was delayed by Gortal. He wanted to order some special barrels."

"We've all got legacies to bear," Royalt replied. "Herders have to deal with the weather and sandwolves, coopers and merchants with difficult buyers."

"At least, Gortal's not a Legacy of the Duarches," suggested Clerynda. "Close . . . but not quite that bad."

"Might as well be," replied Royalt humorously.

Alucius nodded, knowing that "Legacy of the Duarches" meant different things to different people, although to herders it referred to something left that was not what it was supposed to be, usually less than good.

When they finished with the barrels, Royalt looked to his grandson. "Alucius . . . would you like to show the young woman and her brother to the refreshments? We older folk take longer."

"Yes, sir." Alucius offered his arm, and Wendra took it.

"I'll stay with you and mother," announced the boy. "They'll just say—"

"Korcler . . ." Clerynda's voice was low and stern.

"Yes, ma'am," Korcler said very contritely. "But might I?"

"Yes, you may."

Alucius kept his smile to himself as he and Wendra moved away from the larger group. "I'm glad you could come." He took a long look into her gold-green eyes.

"So am I." This time, she did not look away. "I like your vest."

"Thank you. It was a harvest gift from my grandparents. I like your vest, too."

"Thank you."

"Have you finished with Madame Myrier?"

"Weeks ago. Right after you came to the shop. I've started to keep the ledgers at the shop now. Father checks them, and so does Mother, but I haven't made any errors so far."

Alucius sensed the pride behind Wendra's words. "You *are* sitting with me at dinner."

"You might have asked me." There was a hint of mischief in Wendra's words.

"I didn't want to give you a choice." Alucius offered an embarrassed grin.

"What will your family say?" she asked, amusement still coloring her voice.

"I told them already. We can sit with your family or mine, but together."

"And which death do you prefer, young herder Alucius— death by sandwolves or sanders?"

"It won't be that bad," Alucius protested.

"If you have to sit beside Korcler, it will be."

"He seems nice enough."

" 'Seems' is a good word. He's been warned by Father. That will last but a short while. If . . . *if* I have a choice, I would like to sit with your family."

"If that is your choice, then that's what we'll do. Probably,

Mother won't sit down for long. She never does, but my grandparents will." The two went up the main steps onto the porch.

Vardial gave a broad smile as Alucius escorted Wendra toward the refreshment table.

Elyra elbowed Vardial and murmured, in a voice Alucius was not meant to hear, "Not a word, or I won't eat with you."

"That's not fair," Vardial mumbled back, even as he offered a tumbler of the berry punch to Wendra. "Would you like a glass, Alucius?"

"Yes, please. I could get it."

"Maybe . . . after you and Wendra have a few moments, you could . . ."

"We'd be happy to," Wendra replied.

"In a moment," Alucius added. "It's a long ride from town. Let Wendra have a moment to enjoy her punch."

That moment passed quickly, and before long both Alucius and Wendra had finished their tumblers and were standing behind the table.

One of the first to arrive was Kyrial. "I see you put her to work immediately, Alucius."

"She volunteered." Alucius paused. "Ale for you and Madame Clerynda?"

"Ale for her, punch for me."

Alucius filled one tumbler with ale, while Wendra filled the other with punch.

After Kyrial left the table and before anyone else came up, Alucius glanced at Wendra.

"Father says the ale doesn't serve him well," Wendra replied to the unspoken question. "He never drinks any. He said I'd have to be careful with it when I'm older to see whether I'm like him or like Mother."

"Wise man, your father," said Royalt, who had eased up to the table. "Takes after his father that way. Pleased to see you here, Wendra. You have your mother's good looks, and from what I hear, your sire's judgment. Don't hesitate to use both on this young fellow."

Alucius managed not to flush as he refilled Royalt's tumbler.

"You're much too kind, sir," Wendra replied.

Royalt laughed, genially. "Kindness isn't an offense I'm often accused of."

"That's probably because you take care not to show it in public, I'd think."

Royalt shook his head. "Alucius . . . you show this lady the greatest of kindness. Were I your age, you'd not see her again." He grinned at Wendra.

She returned the grin with a cheerful smile. After Royalt had left, she murmured, as Kustyl neared the table, "I think I'll like your grandsire."

Alucius hoped so.

"Are you treating this young fellow right, Wendra?" asked Kustyl.

"I'd hope I am," she replied with another smile.

"Good . . . he deserves it." Kustyl grinned at Alucius. "But then, so does she."

"I've always thought that," Alucius said.

As Kustyl walked away with the tumbler of ale that Alucius had refilled, Wendra and Alucius looked at each other. Then they both laughed.

"Supper's ready. Serving in the kitchen!" called Veryl from the front door.

"We'll wait and see if people want more to drink with their supper," Alucius said.

"I thought so. That's the way Grandfather always wanted it, too," Wendra replied.

"Your parents didn't mind coming?"

"Late on Novdi, business is slow anyway. No one had been in the shop for a glass or more, and we were already closing when Gortal showed up. Otherwise, we would have been here sooner. Mother was very pleased to be able to come. So was Father—once Gortal left."

Wendra stopped as Tynan—the son of Veryl's brother and a herder from farther north—neared the table.

"More ale?" asked Alucius.

"Please, young fellow. Can't enjoy supper to the fullest without a healthy tumbler of ale."

He winked at Alucius. "Course, a pretty girl helps, too."

Alucius couldn't help flushing.

After Tynan stepped away, Wendra murmured, "You're blushing."

"You are pretty, and I am enjoying being with you, but everyone is watching us."

Wendra laughed softly. "What do you expect? Why else would you have a new vest? Why else did Mother insist on new clothes for me? Everyone wants to know if we'll get along."

Alucius knew he was blushing even more furiously.

Wendra reached out and squeezed his hand. "It's all right. Don't you think that it's good they care? My cousin Syndra had to marry a butcher in Emal, and she didn't even know him."

Alucius winced at that.

"It's not for me, Alucius," Wendra added. "It's for you. All this will be yours one day, and everyone knows it's important that you have the right woman." She smiled. "I'm just lucky to be someone you're interested in."

"I'm the lucky one," he protested.

"I hope you always feel that way."

They both looked up as Korcler marched toward them.

"Mother said I could have another glass of punch." He looked up at Alucius. "If you please, Alucius?"

"I'm sure we can manage that, Korcler." Alucius took the proffered tumbler and refilled it.

"Thank you." Korcler bowed, turned, and headed for the kitchen.

"He was very polite," Alucius remarked.

"Father probably threatened him with having to smooth the inside of the barrels."

"That sounds as bad as sharpening blades on a grindstone."

"It's worse," Wendra said. "I've done both."

In time, Alucius and Wendra walked toward the round

table for five that had been put in the corner of the main room. Although he and Wendra had been among the very last to serve themselves, there had been more than enough food, and they had piled their plates with not only the spiced mutton rolls and the cheesed lace potatoes, but with the fresh buttered gladbeans and the maize-carrot salad, and the warm current biscuits.

As Alucius had predicted, even after everyone had been served, the place reserved for his mother was vacant.

"You both know Wendra," Alucius said to his grandparents as he seated the brunette.

"We've known about her for years. Kustyl never stopped talking about you, his little granddaughter." Veryl smiled at Wendra. "And now you're a grown woman."

Wendra returned the smile, shyly. "I'm not sure my brother would agree to that." She managed one bite of the mutton roll after speaking.

"Brothers never do," Veryl replied, dismissively. "Mine still call me their little sister . . . and I'm the oldest."

"Your father says you've a fine head for figures," Royalt suggested.

"I like working with numbers. Madame Myrier even gave me a book that has some ways to calculate how strong parts of buildings should be. I don't understand it all yet, but I will."

As he took a mouthful of the potatoes, Alucius nodded approvingly at the determination in Wendra's voice.

"Lucenda!" called Veryl. "You've done enough. Come here, and sit down and eat."

Alucius stood and pulled out the chair for his mother.

"Thank you." Lucenda settled at the table. "It is good to sit down." She turned to Wendra. "I'm glad to see you. Thank you for helping Alucius serve the punch and ale."

"I enjoyed it, and I'm very glad to be here. It's so beautiful, and everyone is so friendly."

"Beautiful it is, if in a stark and barren way," Royalt answered. "Not the best place for those who aren't comfortable with themselves."

"I can see that," Wendra replied. "Grandfather is like that."

"That's a lovely outfit," Lucenda said.

"Mother and I made it."

"Specially for the gathers?" asked Veryl, with a twinkle in her eyes and a lilt in her voice.

"No—just for this gather," Wendra answered. "The last time I saw Alucius, I was working on making flour bags, and what I wore wasn't that much better than the bags."

Alucius hid a grin at the directness of the pleasant response—and the iron beneath the gentle words.

Royalt didn't bother to hide his smile. "A young woman who knows her mind and who's pleasantly forthright!"

"And one who needs to eat," Lucenda said firmly. "Like all of us, she's had a long day, and I imagine she's more than a little hungry."

"I am," Wendra admitted.

"Nothing wrong with being hungry after hard work." Royalt nodded to Lucenda. "Good mutton rolls."

"The lace potatoes are good," Alucius added, wanting to keep the conversation on the food. "I always like them."

Before all that long, supper was over—even the apple pies and the pear-cream tarts—and people began to gather on the front porch in the twilight. Alucius and Wendra sat on a bench on the north end.

"I always like it when there's singing," Wendra said.

"I like to sing, if no one's listening. Sometimes, when I'm working alone, I'll sing, too."

"You have a good voice, I'd wager."

Alucius shrugged.

"Is everyone ready for some singing?" asked Royalt loudly, stepping into the middle of the porch, standing less than a yard from where Lucenda sat on the wooden chair, tuning her gitar.

"Of course we are," Kustyl called. "We're just sitting here quiet-like to give you a chance to yell at us."

More than a few laughed.

Royalt shook his head and nodded at Lucenda.

Holding the gitar easily, she played several chords, and then launched into a song.

> "Sing a song of silver,
> sing a song of gold,
> pocketful of coppers,
> makes a fellow bold . . ."

When the song ended, Wendra looked at Alucius. "She sings well."

"She always has. Her voice is truly fine."

"You like things to be the best, don't you?"

Alucius was saved from answering that as another round of song swept over the porch.

> "Gone, gone from Westridge,
> with little to say,
> the herders we knew
> have long gone away.
> Saddled, and booted,
> and bridled rode they . . ."

Alucius tried to suppress a wince at the song, wondering as he did why his mother had allowed that mournful ballad to be sung.

Wendra leaned closer and whispered directly in his ear, "That bothers you, doesn't it?"

He nodded.

She reached down and squeezed his hand.

The next song was far more cheerful.

> "I rode home one night, as drunk as I could be,
> and found a white sheep flock
> where my flock ought to be.
> I asked my wife, my dear wife,
> what's this flock a doing here,
> where my flock ought to be . . .

"... I've traveled these valleys
a thousand quints or more,
but nightsheep without their horns,
I ain't never seen before ..."

After several more songs, Alucius looked at Wendra, then glanced toward the rear door into the house.

She frowned.

He leaned forward and whispered over the singing. "I'd just like to take a walk, a few moments alone with you."

She nodded, then whispered back, "I'll leave first. I'll meet you on the north side of the house."

Alucius forced himself to sit and sing yet another song after Wendra left. Then, he eased himself off the bench and across the porch and into the house, as the group enthusiastically continued with another raucous favorite.

"There once was a herder so bold,
a herder from Soulend so cold ..."

Wendra was waiting in the shadows of the house. Alucius took her hands for a moment, then offered his arm, and they began to walk westward, away from the voices and their songs. The cool wind had died into a calm that made the evening seem warmer than it was, and the faint sweet scent of blooming quarasote filled the air.

"I am glad you came." He looked at her, taking in her face, before their eyes met, and they stopped walking.

"It's hard, isn't it?"

"Hard?"

"Trying to say what you feel, when ..."

Alucius nodded, sensing both her feeling of wanting to be close to him, and not wanting to be. At least, that was what he thought she felt, but it wasn't anything like with the nightsheep—or even his family. "Feelings aren't the same as words, and when you try to say what you feel, the words aren't right, or they sound too simple ... or too cold."

"You are sweet, Alucius. Promise me . . . promise me you won't lose that."

"How could I be anything but what I am?"

"I don't know, but people change." She looked at him for a long moment. "I like you the way you are. Please promise me."

"I promise."

She reached out and squeezed his hand. "Thank you."

They stood silently.

"Look, Alucius." Wendra pointed.

Alucius turned and followed her gesture. There, in the eastern purpled evening sky, Selena shone above the long rise that was Westridge. Beside the larger pearly-lighted moon was a single brilliant star.

"Isn't it just beautiful?"

"It is beautiful." Alucius thought Wendra was even more beautiful.

Behind them, Alucius could hear that the singing had stopped. Various voices echoed into the darkening night.

"I can hear Father rounding up Korcler. He'll be calling for me," Wendra said softly.

Alucius put his hands on her waist and looked into her eyes once more. "I'm so glad you came. It's been a wonderful day."

"The best day of harvest." She parted her lips slightly.

He drew her into an embrace, then kissed her, gently, barely touching her lips.

For just a moment, her arms tightened around him, and the kiss was no longer gentle. Then, she turned her head, so that they were cheek to cheek, and she whispered, "I wish we had more time."

"So do I."

They kissed once more, fumblingly and desperately, before Wendra eased away.

"We need to go back. I can hear Father calling."

So had Alucius, but he had not wanted to say anything. He caught his breath, and then offered his arm. They walked slowly southward, back toward the house, the gather crowd, and the uncertain future.

23

In some ways, Alucius had thought things would change after the gather. Yet nothing substantial did change. He still got up before dawn and did the exercises his grandfather prescribed, and went through all the drills, and practiced with the throwing knives, sparred against Royalt with the shortsword, and grappled with the older man as well. He no longer had nearly so many bruises, and Royalt often was breathing hard when they finished. But the sessions got longer, rather than shorter, and that meant that the days were also longer.

It was the end of another too-long day, one threatening rain, when he and his grandfather guided the flock back down the western side of Westridge and toward the stead. For all of the enjoyment he'd had at the gather, even after two weeks had passed, it seemed like it had been a season, if not longer.

A mist drifted from the low clouds that were darkening more than from the twilight. The drizzling mist foreshadowed the fall—just damp and cold enough to make riding and herding uncomfortable, but without enough real moisture to improve the forage or encourage more shoots on the quarasote bushes.

"This could last," Alucius said.

"It's the kind that does." Royalt glanced toward the stead and the lane beyond the buildings. "There's someone riding down the lane from the main road. Looks to be Kustyl. Wonder why he's here. Best go see." He looked to Alucius. "You can bring 'em in."

While Royalt rode toward the other herder, Alucius guided the flock toward the shed for the night. The two were still talking when Alucius finished closing up the shed, and continued even after Alucius had stabled and groomed the gray he had ridden. So he walked toward the house, knowing that Royalt preferred his talks with Kustyl not to be interrupted— or intruded upon.

"Where is your grandsire?" called Lucenda from the kitchen as Alucius headed for the washroom after hanging up his jacket on a peg in the back hall and using the boot brush.

"He's talking to Kustyl out by the sheds."

"Have to hold supper, then."

Alucius could hear both his mother and grandmother chuckling.

They were both seated at the kitchen table when Alucius joined them. The big iron stove exuded a welcome warmth, and the rich scent of a spiced beef stew and the smell of biscuits filled the room.

"Might as well sit down at the table, Alucius," suggested Lucenda. "I poured a glass of ale for you."

"Thank you." Alucius sat down on the side, opposite his mother, who had her chair turned so that she could get up easily. He took a slow and small swallow of the ale. "Tastes good."

"How did they handle the weather?" asked Veryl.

"Some of them—Lamb and some of the rams—prefer the cooler weather."

"Doesn't look like it's raining much," Lucenda observed.

"Just a mist. We could use more, especially out toward the plateau. Not much in the way of new growth out there. Could hurt their winter coats."

"And we'll be paying for that come spring," Veryl pointed out.

"We might get some rain," Alucius said. "Clouds were getting darker, even before dusk."

"Best we hope so."

The *thump* of a closing door announced Royalt's entering the house through the north porch door. Shortly, the three heard the sound of the hand pump in the washroom, and then Royalt walked into the kitchen.

"What did Kustyl want?" asked Lucenda.

"He was stopping by on his way back from town," Royalt said, settling into the chair at the head of the table. "Just stopped to talk for a moment."

"Kustyl *never* stops just to talk." Lucenda pointed out.

"You didn't invite him for supper?" Veryl rose from the table and turned to the stove.

"Asked him. He said Mairee would have his hide if she made supper and he didn't get there to eat it. Said he was already late and too old for two suppers." Royalt grinned. "What are we having?"

"Stew, from the beef shoulder we had last night." Lucenda eased the basket of biscuits onto the table.

"Better than mutton."

"Mutton's good," Alucius said. "If we don't have it too often."

"That's true of anything. Absence sharpens the appeal." Royalt grinned.

Lucenda shook her head.

Veryl turned. "Alucius . . . if you would . . . Then I'll just serve from the stove. Be hotter that way."

Alucius glanced at his grandsire, then began. "In the name of the One Who Is . . ."

After the supper prayer, and the serving of the stew into the big bowls, there was silence for a time, before Royalt cleared his throat and set down his big spoon. "The Reillies hit two steads south of Soulend. That's what Kustyl said."

"How bad was it?" asked Lucenda.

"Wiped out everyone at the first. Second was ready. Lost some of their stock, but no one was hurt."

"Do you think they'll be headed south?" Lucenda held her glass of ale without drinking.

"Kustyl doesn't think so. They wouldn't try that until they've taken the softer steads to the north, and that wouldn't be till midwinter at the earliest. They also might just move north."

"Hard life there," Veryl pointed out. "They'd not like that."

"No. But the Matrites are moving into their western

reaches, and we'll be raising more for the militia here. Better a hard life than none."

"Hope for their sake they see that way," replied Veryl.

"I'm not that charitable," Lucenda said. "The Reillies are reaping what they've sowed."

"That may be, daughter," Royalt replied, "but we could get caught in that terrible harvest."

Like his grandsire, Alucius wondered if they would. Or how long the Matrites would hold off. Another half year—or year?

II.

⸸ THE LEGACY ⸸
CONFLICTED

24

As the grays pulled the wagon southward toward Iron Stem in the early summer morning, under a clear silver-green sky, Alucius looked to the west, then to the east, sending out his Talent-senses as far as he could, but he couldn't discover anything except the distant red-violet of a sander and the muted gray-violet of a sandwolf—and, of course, the looming sense of the Aerial Plateau to the northeast, and its dead-metal feel. With not a single tree anywhere around, not until they reached Iron Stem, which had but a handful, the plateau always dominated the eastern horizon.

"Grandfather's worried," Alucius said, his eyes still on the road ahead. "More worried than he's been in years."

"Why do you think so?" asked his mother.

"The water barrels we're picking up. The only use for them is if we have to retreat to the armory or the hidden retreat off the cellar."

"He wants to be prepared. In another few weeks, you'll be eighteen. Some time after that, you'll be called into the militia. He's not going to want to leave the stead as much once you're gone. He's even talked about hiring Tynan's second-oldest grandson to help."

Alucius nodded. He understood. If his grandfather left the stead, with his grandmother's slow weakening—something Alucius could do nothing about—that left only his mother able to handle a rifle. "I worry about you and Grandfather and Grandma'am."

"We managed before, and we can do it now," his mother replied.

"I'm sure you can, Mother." He offered a smile.

The road was empty of other travelers until they had almost reached the green tower before the Pleasure Palace, when four riders in the black and green of the Iron Valleys Militia rode past.

The lead rider nodded to Lucenda. "Morning, Madame Lucenda."

"Good morning, Delar. Are you patrolling?"

"No, ma'am. We were running dispatches to the Council. We're heading back to the new outpost on the midroad west of Soulend."

"Have a good trip."

"Thank you, ma'am," returned Delar.

Alucius waited until the militia riders were well behind them before speaking. "New outpost on the midroad? Grandfather didn't mention that."

"He might not know," she pointed out. "We can tell him when we get back."

Even with as little experience as he had, Alucius understood what setting up new outposts meant, especially given the Council's tightness with coin. "I'm sure he'll want to know."

Lucenda nodded, but did not speak on it more as Alucius drove toward Iron Stem.

The town itself was quiet, as if it were winter rather than early summer, with the shutters on many dwellings closed, although the late morning was pleasant enough, with a light breeze out of the southeast.

Alucius studied the stone-paved expanse of the market square. There were but a handful of carts there, far fewer than normal, even for the time of year. "There ought to be more . . ."

"Everyone's hoarding," Lucenda said. "Maybe not everyone, but enough so that the growers don't have to travel north to Iron Stem."

"Because they're worried about the Reillies and the other brigands?"

"And because the Council in Dekhron is conscripting more young men, and people worry about planting and harvesting with fewer to help."

Alucius nodded, then turned the team to the right and

eased both team and wagon into place on the side lane beside the loading dock of Kyrial's shop. He set the wagon brakes, and then jumped down and knotted the restraint lines to the stone hitching post. He turned to offer a hand to his mother, but she had already jumped down from the wagon and was waiting for him.

They walked into the cooper's shop, with its scent of freshly planed and sawed wood.

"Lucenda, Alucius! It's good to see you." Kyrial set down a chisel and walked away from the larger workbench set against the inside wall and toward them.

Before her father could reach the two, Wendra slipped out of the back room. She gave a broad smile to Alucius, then rushed forward and hugged him. "Father said you'd be in this week. I've been watching."

"Watching more than working at times," commented Kyrial.

Their kiss was short—and proper. Wendra stepped back, but continued to hold Alucius's hand.

"I'd better load the barrels first," Alucius said.

"You load the barrels, and then I'll walk over to the square and see what there is in the way of early produce. You can spend some time with your intended. Soarers know, you've not had that much together." Lucenda smiled as she finished.

Kyrial laughed. "After that, we might get some work out of them."

"I remember a certain cooper's apprentice and the apple barrels . . ." Lucenda said, teasingly.

Kyrial shook his head. "None of you will ever let that lie."

"It's too good a tale, Kyrial, and you need to be reminded that you were young once, too."

Alucius caught the underlying sadness behind his mother's words, understanding that—unlike the cooper—she had had her youthful love cut far too short.

"Your barrels are the ones by the door there, the ones with the smooth finish," Kyrial said.

Alucius released Wendra's hand.

"I'll open the loading door for you," she said.

Somehow, it didn't take Alucius all that long to load all five barrels into the back of the wagon and strap them in place. By then, his mother was crossing the square, and Kyrial was back at work on the small lorken quarter-barrel that was probably for Gortal.

The back room was empty, and Alucius followed Wendra up the stairs to the rear parlor. He glanced around the room, but it was empty, and the door to the main living quarters was closed.

Wendra smiled. "Mother's at the miller's right now, and Korcler's at Aunt Emylin's." She slipped into his arms.

Their second embrace and kiss were considerably less than proper, for which Alucius was most grateful.

"I missed you," Wendra whispered.

"Missed you," he murmured back, still holding her tightly.

"Not as much as I missed you."

"I don't know about that."

"I can tell." There was the slightest of laughs.

They kissed again, then hung on to each other for a long time.

Abruptly, if gently, Wendra eased out of his arms, and eased toward the window, standing before the open shutters, the faded white curtains lifting almost to touch her face in the light and intermittent breeze.

"What is it?" he asked. "Did I do something . . . ?"

"No." Her voice was low. "It's not you."

"Are you sure?" Alucius didn't sense any anger, but worry . . . apprehension.

"It's just . . . it's only a few weeks before you turn eighteen, Alucius." Wendra remained by the window. "They say . . ."Wendra turned from the window to face him, but her eyes did not quite meet his. "They say that all of you who turned eighteen this summer will be conscripted and sent to training a week after the beginning of harvest season."

"Who said that?"

"Yuren's sister told me that yesterday. He's a dispatch rider for the militia now." She paused. "What will we do?"

"What we must," Alucius replied. "I serve my time in the

militia, and you work, and serve your time, and when I get out of the militia, we get married and run a stead."

"You . . . make it sound so . . . easy."

He shook his head. "I didn't mean it that way. It's just . . . what else can we do?"

"Don't you feel trapped? It doesn't matter what we feel. It doesn't matter what we want. You have to serve in the militia, and I'll have to work and wait . . . and hope."

Alucius swallowed. "I don't want to trap you. If . . . if you feel that way . . . I won't . . . I can't . . . make you wait."

Wendra's eyes brightened. "Are you . . . telling me . . . ?"

"No! I'm saying that I love you. I'm saying . . . that I don't have a choice, but I wouldn't want you to feel bound to me . . . not if you don't want to be." He stepped forward and put his arms around her.

"You do love me, don't you?"

"I told you that, my lady. I want you to be mine, now and . . . until the soarers no longer fly, until the trees return to the Iron Valleys . . . until . . ."

Wendra's lips found his for another long and lingering kiss.

"Just hold me," she finally said.

Alucius did.

25

East of Harmony, Madrien

Under the bright silver afternoon sky, a squad of heavy foot held formation around a shimmering hexagonal device set on the back of a wagon. The wagon had its wheels blocked in place on a knoll overlooking a meadow below. From the device projected a green-tinged crystalline barrel. The front third of the wagon held a hopper filled with sand.

Three other wagons, also filled with sand, were lined up to the west.

The Matrite Fifth Horse Company remained out of sight on the back of the hill to the south side of the midroad, while the Fourth and Fifth Foot remained hidden in the trees above the steeper incline on the north. In the valley below the knoll was a thin line of cavalry, troopers spread well apart and riding slowly eastward. Farther to the east, amid the scrub oak and scattered pines, were shadowy figures of mounted raiders.

Hyalas stood in the wagon next to the control panel of the device. Beside him waited another man, also in brown, and also wearing a silver torque and holding a shovel. Mounted on a black stallion beside the wagon was a tall and lanky woman, wearing the crimson and green of Madrien, as well as the crescent moon insignia of an arms commander.

Hyalas adjusted the mechanism.

"I would appreciate it, Engineer Hyalas," suggested the arms-commander, "if you would be ready to use your device before the barbarians decide to turn and run."

"It is almost ready, honored Vergya. I did suggest that it be improved before it was brought to the field."

From the saddle on the black stallion, the tall Vergya laughed. "Best you keep such sentiments between us, Engineer. The Matrial is not known for her humor." The arms-commander nodded to the bugler mounted beside her.

A series of notes rang out across the hill.

The troopers in the valley below turned their mounts, and an officer yelled, "Back! We're outnumbered. Back to the road."

Even before the Madrien troopers had completed their turn, mounted riders wearing a plaid of yellow and black burst out of the brush and pines, galloping toward the outnumbered Madrien troopers. The Madrien forces spurred their mounts into a full gallop westward.

On the knoll above, Hyalas sighted and then pulled the lever with the green knob slowly downward, listening as the humming of the device rose into a high-pitched whine, and then seemed to cease. For several moments, nothing happened.

Then . . . miniature crystalline spears seemed to form a yard beyond the crystal muzzle of the device, then blurred outward in a spraying pattern, moving so quickly that each looked more like a focused sunbeam rather than a crystal projectile.

The spray of crystal struck the left side of the oncoming barbarians, and the riders disintegrated into a pinkish spray. Hyalas began to spin the wheel on the side of the device so that the muzzle slowly moved to the right, and with it, the shimmering line of crystal destruction.

Behind him, his assistant continued to feed the sand into the hopper at the rear of the device, and the crystal storm of destruction scythed across the plain below, leveling mounts and men alike—even some of the laggards among the retreating Madrien troopers—until the few remaining barbarians rode or crawled beyond the range of the deadly device.

A handful of men in yellow-and-black worried their way eastward and back over the hill.

Hyalas eased the green lever back into the unpowered position.

"Most effective, Engineer," the arms-commander called. "I trust it will work as well against the forces of the Iron Valleys and the Southern Guards of Lanachrona."

"I do not know about those of the Iron Valleys. It will be less effective against the Southern Guards because their armor will shield them somewhat." Hyalas paused. "That is not quite right. It will be just as effective against those with armor, but it will take longer, because the armor will stop many of the crystal spears. There are so many spears that no armor will shield a man for more than a few moments, but I will have to track along the line of attack more slowly."

"It is too bad we do not have another," observed Vergya.

"The ancients built but one, and the records say that only one can operate at one time, anywhere in Corus."

"Still . . . if we did not fight our battles at the same time, it would be useful to have one in the south and one here."

"I can see that, honored Vergya. It would take much time and effort to construct another, and that is a decision not made by a lowly Engineer."

"I will speak to the Matrial. Then we will see." Vergya smiled. "Truly a lovely weapon. Yet we must be careful not to overuse it, or we will have fewer new recruits."

Hyalas nodded deferentially.

26

In the twilight of a late summer day, after he had said good night to everyone, Alucius sat on the end of his bed, thinking. He was already eighteen, and he had heard nothing about the militia. So far as he knew, neither had his grandsire or his mother, although he could sense the growing tension in both. Then, if Wendra were right, he might not hear anything until close to the beginning of harvest.

He froze, hearing a murmur from the kitchen, then strained to make out the words.

". . . should tell him . . . at least, let him have his guard . . ."

". . . too dangerous for him . . . especially . . . has the hair . . ."

Too dangerous? What was too dangerous? Alucius eased down the ladder, trying to be as quiet as possible, and along the side of the hall. His mother and grandfather were sitting at the kitchen table. His grandmother had already slipped off to bed.

Standing in the shadows on the other side of the archway, Alucius listened.

". . . Council's offer to let us buy out Alucius's conscription," said Royalt, his voice low. "We still have to decide . . . applies to all holders, but . . . costly."

"I've told you what I think. We could handle it." Lucenda's voice was hopeful.

"It's high—half the golds from each year's sale of night-silk for the three years . . ."

On the other side of the archway, Alucius winced. That much would destroy the holding.

"Three years?" questioned Lucenda. "You didn't tell me that. It used to be two."

"I did, daughter. You didn't want to hear it. The Council needs more bodies and more coins. The raids are increasing. I asked about that new outpost. It isn't that new, but the Council has tried not to say anything about it." Royalt offered a low snorting laugh. "Gortal bought out both his sons' terms. Then, he has the golds."

"We should agree to the terms," Lucenda said.

"No!" Alucius found himself saying, stepping out into the kitchen. "You can't give up the holding."

For a long moment, the two at the table looked at him.

"I overheard. It's my future as well," he pointed out.

"We could still manage. It would be hard, but we could." Lucenda's voice was matter-of-fact, almost as if she had known Alucius had been there all along. "And what is the point of having a holding with no one to continue it?"

"What is the point of being raised a herder with no holding? How will I be able to defend it or gain support in Iron Stem if all know that my family paid my way out of my conscription? What woman will wed a herder that none respects? And if she does, will she face scorn and sneers? Will I get the respect in dealings that my grandsire receives? Or that you, Mother, receive because of my father?"

"What good did respect do him?" Lucenda asked quietly. "What good was honor after they laid him in an unmarked grave?"

Alucius found himself momentarily speechless.

"Respect is a word everyone loves, but it does little good, son, if you're not alive for people to respect you." Lucenda rose. "You can talk it over with your grandfather. You know how I feel."

She walked by him and down the hall. Her door closed with a hard thump.

"Thought it might come to this," Royalt said slowly.

Alucius looked back over his shoulder toward the closed door.

"Go ahead and sit down."

After a moment, Alucius did.

"I didn't mean to upset her," he finally said. "I didn't."

"Your mother's not too impressed with anything having to do with fighting," Royalt said. "I thought you might have figured that out by now."

"Because of my father?"

Royalt nodded. "He said some of the same things you did. She wasn't impressed with them when he said them, either. He said he wouldn't purchase his life—even if it came to that—with the blood of his wife's family. Your mother . . . she couldn't answer that."

Alucius swallowed, and a long silence filled the kitchen.

"What really happened to my father?" Alucius looked to his grandsire.

"There are stories . . . but no one knows for sure."

Alucius could sense both the untruth and the sadness. "That's not true."

Royalt smiled bitterly. "You are a herder, and more. You can tell when someone isn't telling the truth, can't you? And you've been able to do that for years, haven't you?"

Alucius took a long breath. "Yes, sir."

"Part of what I said *is* true. No one knows absolutely what happened on the Lower Road, the one that runs from Iron Stem and all the way to the ruins of Elcien, or so they say." Royalt coughed, then cleared his throat. "The Reillies asked for a truce, under a green banner. Your father went to talk to their leaders. He was shot in the head by a sniper. Nightsilk doesn't protect what it doesn't cover. His company wiped out that part of the clan to the last woman and child."

"You don't think he should have accepted the truce?"

"Not with the Reillies. Maybe not with anyone these days." Royalt shook his head. "When I was your age, man's word was good. Man would rather die than dishonor his word. The world's changing, and it gets harder and harder to trust people's promises."

"Is there . . . how . . . ?" Alucius wanted to ask if his grandsire had any examples, any proof, but such a question sounded so cold, so . . . distrustful.

As if he understood, Royalt went on. "Last year, one of the big trading outfits in Borlan offered us a contract for nightsilk, at four golds a yard for ramsilk. When we came to deliver, they insisted they'd only offered three. I had the contract in writing, and threatened to sell the silk to one of the Madrien traders. The southerners paid four. They weren't happy, but they paid. Ten years ago, that wouldn't have happened. It didn't." He snorted. "It sounds like a little thing, but it's not. How can people deal with each other if no one can trust anyone else to do what they promised? Do we have to agree to become part of Lanachrona to get the protection of their laws? What would keep their Lord-Protector from changing the laws every time he felt like it?"

"You think they would?"

"I know they would. They're more like Gortal than Gortal is. Gortal at least can see what the dust does to his scutters. The Lanachronans don't look, and they don't see. Reillies never have, never will. That leaves us, and now the Council's trying to bleed us. That notice was aimed at the big herders and Gortal. Figure some of the herders, especially those with more than a few boys, will be able to pay, and the Council really wants the golds more than the young fellows. They need rifles for the foot; they need replacement mounts, powder, provender—most everything. That's because they lowered tariffs ten years back and never laid anything aside. Don't want to say that outright, and they won't."

"Grandfather . . . I've seen the ledgers. Even if I stayed here and worked. Even if Wendra came and helped, we couldn't pay that kind of tariff."

Royalt nodded. "I figure you're right about that. Your mother and I have been arguing about that for days. She's already lost your father; she doesn't want to lose you. She doesn't care about the cost."

"I won't be lost."

"You can hope that, Alucius. You can't be sure of it, though, and you sure aren't going to convince her."

Alucius could sense that. He paused, then shook his head. "It doesn't feel right. I don't want to fight. I'd rather herd. But . . . I can't . . . you'd lose everything, anyway, and what would there be for me? A job as an assistant cooper—if I'm lucky. Working as a scutter, if I'm not?"

"There are worse things . . ."

Alucius couldn't think of many, not after having ridden across Westridge in sun and in fog, and having looked to the plateau and seen the magic of nightwool being spun into nightsilk.

Royalt laughed, but there was bitterness in his amusement. "You're a herder just like the rest of us, Alucius . . . just like your father, like me, like my father, like my grand-mother . . ."

"What do I tell Mother?"

"You don't have to tell her anything," Royalt said sadly. "She knows. She always knew."

27

Alucius and Wendra stood in the upstairs rear parlor above Kyrial's shop, holding hands and facing each other. Despite the open windows, there wasn't a hint of a breeze, and the curtains hung limply. Alucius could feel the sweat oozing down the back of his neck.

"When do you leave?" Wendra asked.

"The day after tomorrow—like you said, the first Londi in harvest. We meet here in the square at the second glass. We have to supply our own mount. Grandfather's already bought another to replace the gray."

"They conscript you, and you have to pay for a mount?" Wendra's voice rose slightly.

"If you want to be cavalry," Alucius said. "According to my grandsire, the casualties are higher among the foot."

"I'm glad you'll be cavalry."

"I won't be much of anything if I don't get through training. I could still be foot if I don't do well."

"You will. You've ridden all your life."

"That should help."

After another silence, Wendra asked, gingerly, "Your mother . . . ?"

"She's upset. She understands, but she doesn't like it. She feels like she loses no matter what happens."

"Not if you take care of yourself. She'll still have the stead, and she wouldn't if they'd paid to get you out."

"I'm still not there, and that will make life harder for her and Grandfather. Grandmother is failing."

"The Council isn't fair," Wendra said. "I suppose they can't be."

"That's life. Someone always wants what someone else has. If you don't fight for it, you lose what you have. If you do, some people die and lose anyway."

"You're not going to be one of them." Her eyes were bright, but she had not shed any tears.

Alucius knew she wouldn't cry or weep, not while he was there. He'd never seen his mother cry either, but when she sang to herself late at night, he had often wished she had or would.

"No. I won't be." Alucius *knew* that. But he also knew that just surviving would be far from easy.

He stepped forward and held Wendra once more.

28

Standing outside the stable in the grayness before dawn on Londi, Alucius strapped the rifle in place. As a cavalry conscript, he was required to supply not only his own mount and gear, but his own rifle—one of a standard gauge and boring—and his own sabre.

In the already warm breeze that foreshadowed a hot beginning to harvest season, his grandparents and his mother waited beside the stable door.

"Take care, Alucius," Lucenda said quietly. "Don't seek friends just to have them, and don't put your trust where it does not belong."

"I won't," he promised, knowing that was as much as she could bear to say, knowing she knew he would understand. He stepped forward and hugged her warmly before releasing her.

"Take care, grandson," Veryl said slowly.

"I will." Alucius almost couldn't bear to look at her, so thin and frail had she become.

Royalt just nodded.

Alucius mounted the gray, turning his mount to look at the three who had raised him. "I'll write as I can."

"You won't have much time for a while," Royalt said, as much for Lucenda's benefit, Alucius knew, as to caution Alucius. "And remember, young man," Royalt said, "those undergarments will stop a blade, but they won't stop its force."

"Yes, sir." Alucius reflected on what was inside his saddlebags—the new vest that his grandsire and grandmother had made—of tanned nightram leather, and trimmed fleece, and covered in a double layer of nightsilk. There were also two sets of long-sleeved nightsilk undershirts and low-calf-length underdrawers. All were tailored to fit under the militia uniform. Without it ever having been spoken, Alucius also knew that the less said about his underclothing and vest, the better.

"I should be riding," he finally said. "Take care of Lamb and the others for me." He forced a grin.

"Likely he'll take care of me," returned Royalt.

With a last head bow, Alucius turned the gray, all too conscious of their eyes on his back as he rode down the lane toward the old road that would lead him into Iron Stem.

He sensed neither sanders nor sandwolves, and certainly not any soarers. He also saw no one on the ride into Iron Stem—not that he expected anyone. Vardial was not eighteen yet. Kyrtys and Jaff had been conscripted almost a year earlier, and he didn't know of any other herder youths within vingts who were close to his own age.

When he passed the dustcat enclosures, he thought of Gortal, and the man's ease in buying out his sons' conscriptions . . . and how that somehow felt wrong, although he knew his mother would have done that for him, had it been realistic. In a way, he was relieved—not glad—but relieved that it had not been possible.

"Then, you could just be a fool," he murmured to himself. Being a cavalry trooper was dangerous, that he knew, but he also knew it was something he had to do. He frowned, recalling once more the phrase he had overheard—"too dangerous." He'd asked his grandsire if a herder had anything dangerous or special to worry about, but Royalt had just assured Alucius that he had nothing to worry about on that count. It had been the truth, but not the whole truth.

Again, as he passed the bright green facing of the abandoned tower near the Pleasure Palace, he had to wonder at what the ancients had done. With the brilliant green surface on the exterior stones, a surface unscratched by weather or by time, the upper part of the tower looked as if it had been built within the past few years, yet his grandsire had insisted that it had been built closer to a millennium before, although no one in Iron Stem seemed to know exactly when that might have been.

Most of the shutters of the shops and buildings along the

road into town were open, although he saw few people on the road or on their porches. The iron works was already operating, the dull thudding hammering rumbling into the street with the acrid odor of hot metal.

As he rode into the square, he could see that the militia was ready for the summer season conscripts. A thin and trim man in the black-and-green of the Iron Valley Militia sat mounted before a half squad of rankers drawn up in formation. To the south of the rankers were two long wagons, each with four wide wooden bench seats behind the driver's seat.

Alucius could see another six youths who were mounted. As he neared the center of the square, another pair rode in from the west road—out from where Amiss had his mill. He reined up short of a group of four riders who seemed to know each other. No one made any effort to even look in his direction, even while they talked quietly among themselves. So, rather than interjecting himself, Alucius eased his gray more toward the militia cavalry.

Every so often, he glanced in the direction of the cooperage—but he couldn't see anyone on the porch. After a time, more than a quarter of a glass, possibly a half glass, the second bell rang. No sooner had the echoes died away than a voice filled the square.

"Cavalry conscripts! Cavalry conscripts! Form up by twos in front of the wagons!" The deep and powerful voice issued from the trim figure in front of the half squad.

Alucius shrugged to himself and eased the gray to a position that looked to be where he had been ordered. A lanky youth looking even younger than Alucius jockeyed a bay gelding beside Alucius. The two looked at each other.

Alucius didn't recognize the other. "I'm Alucius. From out on the north road."

"Kypler. From out west. Family runs the sawmill at Wesrigg."

"Pleased to meet you."

Kypler nodded in return.

"Cavalry conscripts! We haven't got all day. The rest of you form up behind those two!"

Alucius suppressed a wince. The last thing he wanted was to be an example.

"Not that they're any example!" added the militia cavalryman. "But they did follow orders. Foot conscripts! Take a place in the wagons. Two to a seat, and your gear goes with you."

Up close, Alucius recognized the insignia on the man's collar—that of a senior squad leader—and was thankful his grandfather had insisted on his learning the rank badges.

Before long, there were seven cavalry conscripts lined up behind Kypler and Alucius, and the squad leader who had called out the orders had ridden around and reined up facing them. His eyes raked over the group, and not with approval, although Alucius could sense that the man was not as angry as he looked.

"I'm squad leader Estepp. I'm the one who will make you into a semblance of a militia cavalryman. If I can, and if you don't kill yourself first. You call me 'sir' or 'squad leader' at all times. Is that clear?"

"Yes, sir," Alucius said quietly, but a number of the others did not answer or merely said, "yes."

"That's 'Yes, sir,' conscripts, and don't you forget it!"

The chorus of "yes, sir" was ragged but unanimous.

"A little better, that was. We've got a long ride ahead. A short one compared to what you'll be doing in a season, but a long one for most of you. You'd better be a summer conscript. We don't check that here, but they'll have your name at Sudon. Anyone not a summer conscript?"

"Sir?" came a voice from behind Alucius.

"Yes, conscript?" answered Estepp.

"I'm Velon, sir. I should have been a spring conscript, but the Council let me wait a season because my father's arm was crushed in the works. I have a paper here from the Council."

"That's fine, Velon. You're a summer conscript now." Estepp looked over the nine once more. "Anyone else." He waited. "We're headed to the training camp at Sudon. For those of you who don't know where it is . . . it's about twenty vingts south of here and then five west. When we get there, you'll be formed into training squads with the other cavalry conscripts, and issued a training tunic, and your weapons will be checked. If they're adequate, we'll lock them up, and you'll be given training sabres. They're rattan. That's a wood that hurts almost as much as a blade, but won't kill you unless you're a total fool. Why rattan? Because we don't want you killing each other. Then you'll be assigned to your barracks, and one of the squad leaders will brief you on what we'll do to try to make you into cavalry. That's all you need to know for now. No talking, except when I say you can. That will be at rest breaks and if I feel you merit that privilege. You'll ride two abreast, the way you're lined up now, and the man on the left keeps his mount exactly three yards behind the mount in front. The man on the right keeps his mount exactly even with the man on the left." Estepp looked at Alucius. "You're on the front left, and you take station on the guide. That will be a regular, who will set the pace. Is that clear?"

"Yes, sir."

"Good!" Estepp turned his mount. "Guide to the front!"

An older cavalryman, with a thin mustache and a scar across his left cheek, rode forward and eased his mount into position three yards or so in front of Alucius and the gray.

"Column forward! Take station on the guide!"

The guide urged his mount forward at what would be a quick walk.

As he followed the guide from the square, Alucius couldn't help but wonder if Wendra had watched. He hadn't seen her, but . . . that didn't mean she hadn't looked. He hoped so.

Two abreast, the conscripts rode southward, followed by the two wagons with the foot conscripts. Once they passed beyond the last dwellings of Iron Stem, Estepp rode along the left side of the road.

"You're going to learn a few songs. Here's the first one. Listen, and then you try it." Estepp stood in his stirrups and gestured.

Behind the conscripts came the words from the half squad of cavalry.

> "If the world you want to see
> try the militia cavalry
> as we ride through brush and sand
> till the brigands take their stand
> From throughout the Westerhills,
> from where the River Vedra fills,
> for it's hi, hi, he
> in the militia cavalry. . . ."

Alucius listened. It was always better to listen, and no one wanted to hear what he thought. That was already clear.

29

The first three weeks of training were comparatively easy for Alucius, and nothing compared to herding and what his grandsire had put him through. He did what he was told as well as he could. He listened and learned, both from what was said and what was not. His greatest problem was getting used to sleeping in a long room with fifty other men and always being surrounded by others. He did miss the solitude and the openness of the lands under the plateau.

The conscripts had been riding about three glasses a day, one in the morning and two in the afternoon, but most of the riding had been formation practice. They had also been practicing with the rattan sabres, but on foot. Since the exercises were elementary, and well beneath Alucius's level, and since he hadn't wanted to stand out, he'd decided that his best course was to go through all the exercises right-handed. Most people used their right hand anyway, and few would suspect he'd learned with his left. He'd gotten more than a few drubbings at first, but had caught up with most of those in the training company.

On the fourth Londi after he had arrived, he was grooming the gray and cleaning the stall before breakfast, looking forward to getting his rifle back, if only for target practice. As he closed the stall, he could hear Dolesy's loud whisper, clearly pitched to carry.

"Course he finishes with his mount first . . . herders sleep with 'em."

Alucius ignored Dolesy's comments and walked away from the stable and toward the farthest barracks, the one that held the conscript mess hall.

". . . doesn't like us talking about his being an animal lover, a *real* animal lover . . . wouldn't know what to do with a woman . . ."

Alucius tightened his lips, took a deep breath, and kept walking. He did wonder at times why Dolesy disliked herders so much, but the reasons didn't matter for some people.

Breakfast was the usual—lukewarm porridge, overdone mutton slices, greasy yellow cheese, bread not quite stale, dried apples with a slice of lemon—and cider. Alucius looked at the platter before him for a long moment, then used his belt knife to slice the cheese. It was greasy enough that he could only take it in small bites between the bread and the apples. Rather than squeeze the lemon over the apples, he just ate it, following it with a healthy swallow of cider.

Kypler joined him. "Dolesy sure doesn't like northerners." The lanky conscript looked at Alucius. "He doesn't like you at all. Did you do something?"

"Nothing. Never even saw him before we got here." Alucius gestured at the nearly empty table where they sat. "People sit with those they know. Not many know us, so . . ."

"It's not just that. He caught Velon in back, bruised his ribs . . . where it wouldn't show."

"He's that sort," Alucius said, taking a mouthful of the porridge.

"How can you eat that?"

"Because I feel worse if I don't."

Kypler laughed. So did Akkar, several places away on the other side of the long table.

After breakfast, as the sun was rising in the east, the cavalry conscripts lined up in formation outside the first training barracks—their barracks. The other three barracks were for the foot conscripts. Alucius found it strange not to see the plateau in the northeast, but considering that Sudon was well over a hundred vingts from the nearest part, he couldn't expect to see it.

Estepp marched down the line, studying each conscript silently, then returned to the front of the formation to address the forty-odd young men. "We're going to start rifle training today. You'll get your rifles for practice, and then you'll turn them back in. Some of you think you're good shots. Most of you aren't. If you are, just practice to keep your skill up. If you're not, listen and try to learn something. Remember that every bullet you put in a brigand means one more person who's not going to be able to put one in you."

The senior squad leader paused. "We don't like it when you waste cartridges. We can gather some of the casings. That's not the problem. Anyone want to guess what is?"

"The powder, sir?" ventured Velon from beside Alucius.

"Very good. Gunpowder. We've got charcoal, and we can find saltpeter, but the one thing we have to trade for is sulfur. That gets to be a little hard at times, seeing as everyone around us wants to make us part of their land.

"Now . . . fall out and get your rifles from the armory. Then mount up and re-form. We ride out to the range. You'll be issued cartridges there."

On the ride westward toward the range, Alucius and Kypler were side by side in the rear of second squad. If Alucius rode behind Dolesy, that seemed to cut down on the number of snide comments. Half a glass later, the five squads of the training company halted opposite a small structure and a very long railing.

"You must have used a rifle a lot," Kypler said as they dismounted and tied their mounts.

"Some," Alucius admitted. "You have to as a herder. What about you?"

"Some. My da took me hunting, but I'm not that good a shot."

"I imagine we'll get better."

"Form up by squads. Shoulder arms!" came the commands. "First squad forward . . ."

Alucius and Kypler stayed to the rear of second squad.

The range itself was simple—a line of wooden cutouts set fifty yards away in the shape of foot soldiers, covered in rough brown paper. Another fifty yards behind the cutouts was a berm. The range was clearly designed so that the targets could be moved back.

"You'll be issued ten cartridges, and you'll turn in ten empty casings," Estepp announced. "You'll load your magazines with five. After my command—and *only* after my command—you will fire. Take your time. Make each shot count. Is that understood?"

"Yes, sir."

"Then either Furwell, Jynes, or I will offer advice to those who need it. Most of you will. After that, you'll reload. You are not to reload until commanded."

Alucius fired his first five shots at what he thought was a deliberate pace.

Immediately after Alucius had finished, Estepp eased up behind him. "Conscript . . . I said to take your time."

"Yes, sir. I thought I did, sir."

Estepp smiled. "You only get to fire that fast if you hit the target. Did you?"

"Yes, sir."

"We'll see."

Once the last shots had died away, Estepp commanded, "Rifles at rest!" After a moment, he added, "Give me a check on target number seven, second squad!" Estepp called out.

"One moment, sir."

Alucius waited calmly. He *knew* where his shots had gone.

"All five in the center, sir," came back from the spotter.

Estepp looked at Alucius. "You're a herder, but not all herders shoot that well. Who's your father."

"His name was Ellus, sir."

Estepp frowned, then nodded. "Your grandsire is Royalt, Captain Royalt?"

"Yes, sir."

"He taught you?"

"Yes, sir."

Estepp nodded and walked on. "Dolesy, you're jerking the trigger. Squeeze it."

As the senior squad leader went on, giving advice to other conscripts, Alucius could hear Dolesy once more, whispering to Ramsat in the voice meant to carry. ". . . so he had a big name grandsire . . . someone who could murder lots of other scum . . . still northern sand scum . . ."

Alucius could sense the rage and antagonism from Dolesy, but hadn't the faintest idea why Dolesy was so angry with him or herders. He'd just have to watch the man, let him act, and catch him out—the same way he would have handled a sandwolf—except he had no intention of killing Dolesy.

30

Harvest had ended, and with fall had come colder weather. In the early morning, Alucius's breath steamed when he cleaned the gray's stall, and the warm cider for breakfast was actually welcome.

After two months, the conscripts had gone from sabre drills on foot to drills on horseback, but still with the rattan weapons. The drills ranged from full squad attacks or defenses to single combat. Alucius continued to drill mainly with his right hand, although when he worked with Kypler or Velon he sometimes used his left—if Estepp or Furwell were not following him closely.

Second squad was formed up in the gray light of a cloudy

morning in the maneuver field to the south of the camp complex.

"Five on five drills!" Estepp called out. "At my command!"

Alucius could see Dolesy had switched places with Adron. Dolesy grinned at Alucius, a grin without warmth.

"Attack!"

Alucius urged the gray forward, but not at the headlong pace of Dolesy's bay. He guided his mount head-to-head with the bay—until the last moment when he and the sure-footed gray cut left, leaving Dolesy unbalanced after the bigger man had made a giant lunge toward Alucius. Alucius swung the gray back toward Dolesy, still keeping his rattan sabre in his right hand.

Dolesy came in with his sabre high—on Alucius's right—then ducked and slammed the rattan weapon directly toward Alucius's knee. Alucius parried the slash, swung around, this time coming up on Dolesy's left.

Dolesy tried to bring his sabre across his body. But Alucius turned the gray slightly with his knees, switched his own rattan weapon to his left hand, and caught Dolesy with a sharp cut on the back of the wrist. The bigger man's weapon went flying.

Alucius ignored him and maneuvered the gray around him, attacking Ramsat from the other's left, disarming him, and saving Kypler from a blindside attack.

"Halt attack! Halt attack!"

Alucius rejoined the others in formation, slipping the gray in place between Velon and Kypler.

"Velon, forward!"

Alucius tried to hear what Dolesy might be saying, but the dark-haired man was massaging his injured wrist.

"Alucius, forward!"

Alucius eased the gray forward, reining up two yards short of the senior squad leader. "Sir."

Estepp looked at Alucius. "I saw something rather strange. You switched your sabre in the middle of an attack. That's dangerous. I've never seen you use the sabre in your left hand before today."

"Yes, sir."

Estepp looked faintly amused, as if he were going to say something, then just nodded. "Dismissed to formation. Kypler, forward!"

As Alucius returned to formation, he could hear Estepp's comments.

"If your flanker hadn't managed to break through, in a real battle you would have been dead. Even here you would have been hurt. Look *everywhere*. You don't and you'll be on your back with your eyes wide open forever."

To his right, Alucius could hear the faint murmur of Dolesy to Ramsat.

". . . used some sort of trick . . . get him yet . . ."

"How? Seems to know when you're layin' for him."

Alucius had been using his Talent for just that purpose, but he had the feeling he wouldn't be able to keep it up much longer.

31

Midmorning on the first Tridi of Decem, Alucius and the eight other remaining members of the second squad, still in well-worn black training tunics and trousers, were seated on backless wooden benches in the square room where squad leader Furwell discussed cavalry tactics—and anything else that came to mind.

". . . to repeat it all in simple terms," Furwell concluded, "always come from where you're not expected. Never charge a prepared position. It's a waste of men and mounts. They could have caltrops spread on the ground. They could have concealed pits with riflemen—or even pikemen waiting in ditches, and there's nothing that will stop you quicker than getting your mount spitted on a four-yard-long pike. If the fall doesn't kill you, one of the pikemen probably will. If you survive that, the best you can hope for is a very long run with soldiers shooting at you."

"What about warlocks or people with Talent?"

Alucius couldn't see who asked the question, and he didn't recognize the voice.

Furwell smiled. "Cold steel or a well-aimed rifle bullet will kill someone with Talent just as dead as anyone else."

"Sir . . . aren't folk with Talent more like sanders and soarers than real people? Can't they avoid a sabre?"

The squad leader snorted. "I can avoid your blade, Oliuf. That doesn't make me Talented. Having Talent is like having any other skill. It gives people abilities. For example, we use herders as scouts, and most herders have a touch of Talent. They make good scouts because they have a better sense of where sentries and ambushes are. They can also confuse tracking dogs. But they get killed and die like anyone else. People kill sanders all the time. It usually takes two or three men—but it would take two or three men to kill an experienced soldier—the kind we're trying to make you. Don't worry about Talent in battle. There probably aren't twenty people with a major Talent in all of Corus, and no one's going to waste them in a battle."

"Do you know if the Reillies, the brigands, have warlocks?"

"I doubt it. But it doesn't make much difference. You shoot him first, and he's dead. You don't, and he's got a chance to kill you, either with a crossbow or a rifle or a blade."

"Crossbow?" asked Ramsat.

"They're slow to reload, but you get hit with an iron quarrel and the whole time you're dying you'll wish that they'd shot you with a rifle. With crossbows, they don't have to worry about powder, and any backwoods smith can forge quarrels."

"What about the Matrites?"

Furwell laughed. "You just don't want to go out and go through drills, Velon. Right now, we're not fighting the Madrien forces. The hill folks to the west are. We might have to in time, but you'll have a chance to learn about that when you get to your permanent company." Furwell held up a hand. "They have cavalry, just like we do, and more foot. They've got rifles, and their officers carry pistols along with their sabres and rifles. They've taken over the entire coast from below Fola to well north of Northport. I'd say that they can fight." The squad leader grinned. "And don't ask me about the Lanachronans. You're dismissed. You've got half a glass to take care of whatever you need and to get saddled and mounted in formation."

The nine stood and stiffened at attention until Furwell had left the room.

". . . still say Talent can make difference . . ."

Anything that provided an advantage could make a difference. That was the whole point of what Furwell had said. And what an enemy—or an officer—didn't know was another type of advantage, Alucius reflected.

32

To the sound of a light rain pattering on the stable roof, Alucius finished brushing all the mud from the gray's coat, as well as checking his hoofs—and feed. After that, he left the stable for the barracks washroom to remove the mud from himself, his boots and his black training uniform. Once he'd cleaned up and stowed his gear, he hung up the damp riding jacket on the stand by his bunk and then headed for the barracks mess.

The evening meal—Alucius hated to call it supper—was mutton, with greasy fried potatoes and overcooked and soggy gladbeans. The bread was fresh, and the weak ale passable. Alucius sat down at the corner seat of an empty table. He had several bites of bread and mutton before Velon slipped onto the bench across the battered wooden table from him.

"Wet out there," Alucius offered.

Velon did not quite meet Alucius's eyes. "Watch out . . . Ramsat put Bowgard up to something, claimed something about his mount . . . got Furwell and Estepp out in the stables . . ." Velon's eyes flickered to his left.

Even before Velon had finished, Alucius could sense Dolesy's presence, and another figure behind the big conscript.

"You love sheep, don't you? You really love them, in just about every way possible, don't you?" Dolesy's voice filled the mess, as did the contempt in his words.

Alucius ignored the comment from the man, and concentrated on finishing the mouthful of bread and greasy potatoes.

"I was talking to you, sandscum."

Alucius took a quick and short swallow of cider, setting the mug down on the table without turning, although he could sense where the exchange would go, no matter what he said.

Dolesy put his beefy hand on Alucius's shoulder and yanked him around, intending to throw him to the floor.

Alucius kept turning as he came off the bench, bringing his knee into the other's groin, followed by a knuckle jab to the vee just below where the lowest ribs met. Dolesy lurched forward, gasping, and Alucius slammed his palm up under the other's jaw, then swept his legs out from under him. Dolesy went down like a sander-stunned sheep.

Ramsat charged forward. Alucius stepped inside the wide swing and slammed his elbow across the other's neck, then followed with a jab under the ribs, and another knee into Ramsat's groin.

Ramsat sank to the wooden floor retching.

"Halt!"

Estepp stood in the archway. His eyes went from Alucius to the two men on the mess floor planks. Then he laughed as he stepped forward.

Alucius remained at attention, waiting.

"You, Dolesy, haven't the brains of one of Alucius's sheep." His eyes raked over the second man. "You don't either, Ramsat." He waited. "It takes three of you with rifles to bring down a sander—if you're lucky. Alucius . . . how many sanders have you killed?"

"Just three, sir."

"By yourself?"

"Ah . . . the first one was with my grandfather, and the others by myself."

"Sandwolves?"

"Eight or ten."

Estepp laughed. "Sandwolves have a nasty habit, Dolesy. They can't be tracked by scent, and they can kill a dog or an unprepared man like that." He snapped his fingers. "Herders have to have senses that hear or feel one coming. Just like Alucius heard you coming. He'll always hear you coming."

Dolesy did not look at the senior squad leader.

"Now," continued Estepp, "I don't like trouble. Alucius can take care of himself. That's pretty clear. Only problem is that if he takes care of you two again, the militia's short two men. If you catch him off guard, I'm short a man who's worth both of you. The militia really doesn't like being short-handed. I *really* don't like it." He glared at the two on the ground.

"I won't do anything," Dolesy said.

Alucius looked at him. "You're lying."

Estepp grinned. "Another thing you don't know, Dolesy. Most nightsheep herders can tell when someone's lying. That's why no one ever cheats 'em. You want me to turn you over to Alucius right now?"

Dolesy paled. "No, sir."

"You're stupid, Dolesy. You got a man who could be your flank-rider who's twice as tough as any brigand. He could save your life, and you've spent two months trying to get him mad enough to kill you. He could have killed both of you. He didn't. Might have been easier for the rest of us if he had." Estepp looked to Alucius. "You weren't trying to kill them, were you?"

"No, sir."

"You two really are stupid. When you put Bowgard up to

that this evening, I thought you might have something in mind. Pack your gear. You, too, Ramsat. Furwell owes me, but, sander shit, I hate to call in a favor for this."

Dolesy looked blank.

"It's real simple, Dolesy. You don't learn. And you won't learn from me, because I've seen through you. Sooner or later, either Alucius will have to kill you, or you'll find a way to kill him, and then I'll either have to hang one of you or muster you out. Either that or spend all my time watching you. So, you're going to Furwell's squad to finish training. If you make trouble, if you even talk to Alucius or anyone in second squad until you finish training, I'll have you flogged and mustered out."

For the first time, Dolesy paled. Ramsat was wide-eyed.

"I hope you understand that." Estepp smiled. "I expect you and your gear to report to Furwell in a quarter glass." He looked at Ramsat. "You, too."

Once the two had gone, Estepp paused by Alucius's shoulder and said in a low voice. "You lasted a long time, Alucius. You'll have to do better in the future."

"Yes, sir."

"I just hope you're a tenth as good as your grandsire."

"Yes, sir."

"Alucius?"

"Yes, sir?"

"Some people don't need a reason to hate, and you have to learn to deal with it." With that, Estepp was gone.

Alucius stood alone beside the mess table, looking down at the remainder of his supper.

33

Standing before the thirty-one ranked men in new black-and-green militia uniforms, Senior Squad Leader Estepp surveyed them—those remaining from the more than forty that had entered Sudon two seasons earlier. A small table with a stack of flat papers stood by his left side. Standing behind him were Furwell and the other training instructors.

"Congratulations," began Estepp. "You're now militia cavalry. We don't have any more ceremony than this because you still have a lot to learn, but you've learned enough to be of use, and you've proved that you can learn. If you're smart, you'll make an effort to keep learning. Now . . . after I read out the full list of assignments, so that everyone knows where everyone else is going, I'll be handing out your orders, by squad, one by one."

Alucius stood third in line in the front rank of second squad, flanked by Retius and Kypler.

"You all have one week of furlough, starting in one glass," Estepp continued. "You report back here a week from Londi, no later than the fourth glass of the morning. That's when you'll pick up the rest of your gear. Now, your assignments . . ." He smiled briefly. "Most of you are going to Soulend. You'd better make sure you have warm undergarments. You can draw the winter gear before you leave, but if you don't bring them back, you'll lose three months pay.

"Caston, Deault, Kybar, and Thom—you four are being assigned to Third Company, first squad. Wualt is your squad leader."

Estepp paused before continuing. "Alucius, Akkar, Kypler, Oliuf, Retius, Velon. You six are being assigned to Third Company, second squad. Delar is your squad leader.

"Adron, Boral, Tyreas—you three are going to Third Company, third squad. Your squad leader will be Jult.

"Dolesy, Bowgard, Ramsat—you'll be in Third Company, fourth squad . . ."

Alucius could sense a sort of satisfaction in Estepp's assignment of Dolesy and Ramsat, and he wondered why the senior squad leader felt that way.

After completing his reading of the assignments to Third Company, Estepp added, "Squad Leader Gurnelt will be in charge of all of you on the trip north. He's taking over the fifth squad of Third Company. You'll also be escorting five wagons of foot replacements."

Twenty cavalry replacements for a company of one hundred? And more than fifty foot replacements? Were they for a year's losses? Or for just the two seasons they had been in training? Alucius kept his face impassive, wondering if the others had calculated what he just had.

"The rest of you are going to Fifth, Eighth, Tenth, and Twelfth Companies. Fifth Company is at Emal, Eighth is on the north side of the Vedra from Borlan at Nerle. Tenth Company is sixty vingts downriver from Borlan at Rivercliff. Eleventh Company will be moving to a new outpost west of Wesrigg on the old lower road through the Westerhills to the coast . . ."

An outpost in the lower Westerhills, not all that far from Iron Stem?

Alucius was definitely getting the message that all was not well with the Iron Valleys, and that the problems couldn't be just the Reillies or other brigands.

34

By the time they had gotten their orders, drawn their winter parkas and gloves, and reclaimed their sabres and rifles, almost two glasses had passed before Alucius and Kypler were actually mounted and on the road east from Sudon. Alucius was particularly glad for the inner warmth provided by his nightsilk undergarments, since the wind had come up and was more like a winter gale than the merely brisk gusts of late fall. But then, as Alucius well knew, in the Iron Valleys, late fall and early spring might as well be called winter. The two rode side by side, separated from the nearest other group of riders headed on furlough by a good hundred yards.

"It'll be good to get back home," Kypler offered. "Even for a week."

"Your sister will have all her friends waiting," predicted Alucius.

"That won't be so bad. I can't get married until I'm through with my first three years."

"You thinking of staying in?"

Kypler shook his head. "Don't know why I said that. Estepp has me thinking like the permanents. No, I'll do my time and go back to the mill. What about you?"

"I'm a herder. They need me on the stead. Grandfather can't keep doing it forever, and Mother can handle the equipment and the processing, but not the herding."

"Do herders have to be men?"

Alucius shook his head. "Grandsire said his mother was the herder. So was his grandmother. I think there are fewer women who have . . . who can herd." Alucius still had to remind himself to take care in the way he talked of herding and Talent. It was harder with friends, because that meant always being on guard.

Riding from the camp to the main road took more than a glass, and neither spoke much, not riding almost directly into the wind. Once they reached the eternastone pavement of the main north–south high road, they turned northward toward Iron Stem, unlike the majority of the new cavalrymen leaving the camp, who headed south toward Dekhron.

In time, the wind abated slightly, and shifted more to the east.

"Seems to me," Kypler finally offered, "that the cavalry needs a lot of replacements."

"I wondered about that," Alucius admitted. "Then, maybe they're pulling out some of the more experienced men as the backbone of those new companies they're forming."

"Hadn't thought about that. You think so?"

"I don't know, but it doesn't seem likely that they'd make them up from all new conscripts, does it?"

"Wager it's going to be colder than the Ice Sands in Soulend when we get there."

"Could be. We could also get a thaw. You never know."

"You think we'll have more trouble from Dolesy and Ramsat?" Kypler asked.

"They'll be careful when we first get to Soulend," Alucius predicted, "but I don't think they'll change."

"Makes you wonder . . ." mused Kypler. "Me . . . been Estepp . . . I'd have thrown them out."

"The militia's short-handed," Alucius replied. "Dolesy can be mean enough in a fight."

"He won't last his term," Kypler predicted.

Alucius shrugged. He had his doubts, but he also understood that actual combat could change anyone—for better or worse.

The glasses passed, and fine flakes of snow drifted around them as they neared the south end of Iron Stem. The shutters of the stone and brick houses were fastened tight against the wind, yet thin lines of gray smoke rose from but a handful of chimneys. The square was empty. Usually, there were at least a few peddlars or carts in the square, and in winter, there was always a coal wagon or two.

"Almost deserted," commented Kypler.

"It is." Alucius nodded. "I'm going to stop at the cooper's."

"I know what you have in mind." Kypler grinned. "I'll see you in a week."

"A week," affirmed Alucius.

As Kypler turned west, Alucius reined up outside Kyrial's shop, where he could see his mount from inside, since he didn't want to march in, rifle in hand. He tethered the gray carefully, and looked around the square and adjoining streets. He saw no one. Then he hurried up onto the narrow porch and into the shop.

"Welcome! You're now a full-fledged cavalryman." The cooper looked up from the staves he was smoothing with a plane—laboriously, because the stave was hard black lorken.

"More like barely fledged, sir." Alucius glanced toward the door to the back room. "Sir . . . I wondered . . ."

Kyrial shook his head. "Wendra took some work out of

town for the next few days, Alucius. She'll be back on Duadi. I'm sure she would have liked to see you, had she but known you'd be here. You're certainly welcome here anytime." He grinned ruefully. "Not that you'd want to be seeing Clerynda and me."

"Tell her that I'll be back to see her on Duadi."

"I'm most certain she'd like that very much. She talks of you often. She'd be most pleased to learn that you stopped here before heading home, and I'll make sure she knows that."

"Thank you, sir." Alucius glanced around the shop. There were few barrels in sight, and those few were all lorken quarter barrels in various stages of assembly.

"Aye," Kyrial said ruefully. "Business is slow this time of year—except for Gortal. The dustcats still shed their dreamdust, winter or summer, and the southerners still buy it."

"Perhaps things will pick up," Alucius temporized. "Please tell Wendra I was here."

"That I will. I surely will."

After he left the shop and as he remounted the gray, Alucius frowned. Kyrial had been hiding something, yet he hadn't seemed at all angry or displeased or sad. And the cooper had certainly felt welcoming. He'd been telling the truth about Wendra taking some work, but there had been more than that, and Alucius hadn't wanted to press for details.

He rode to the water pump in the square. He had to break a thin layer of ice to make sure the gray could drink, and he watched his mount carefully, with both eyes and senses to make sure the gelding had enough, but not too much.

As he rode headed northward away from the square, he shook his head. Having the Talent was useful, but at times he still felt it wasn't very helpful, perhaps because he still couldn't always figure out the meanings behind what he sensed.

Even the Pleasure Palace seemed nearly deserted with the few grimy windows shuttered and only one chimney showing a thin line of smoke. There were only two mounts tied outside, and the stable doors were closed. The tower to the north was as empty—and as unchanged—as ever. On the other hand, every chimney at Gortal's dustcat works showed a plume of smoke, and Alucius saw several scutters wheeling carts.

The road north was empty, and the thin dusting of snow on the unchanging gray stone pavement showed no tracks at all, either of mounts or wagons. The air held the faint and acrid scent of the Aerlal Plateau, although Alucius could not see it through the low-lying clouds and the ground haze to the northeast.

While the distance from Iron Stem to the stead was shorter than what he had already ridden, riding it alone made it seem longer, and he wished he'd been able to see Wendra for at least a few moments. He still wondered what she was doing, and why she'd had to take work elsewhere. Were times getting that tight, just in the two seasons since he'd left?

Finally, Alucius reached the lane to the stead and guided the gray along the rougher and narrower way. The wind picked up once more, and he had to squint to see more than a few hundred yards ahead through the blowing snow. When he could at last see the buildings, his eyebrows were coated with icy snow and his ears felt frozen despite the winter cavalry cap.

Even before he reached the stable, he could see three figures in winter coats walking from the main stead house to meet him. Had someone told them to expect him?

His grandfather was the first to greet him, even before he dismounted.

"Delar had a man stop by last week," Royalt said. "Told us you'd done fine and would be getting furlough today." He smiled, knowingly.

Alucius blinked as he took in his mother—and Wendra.

Wendra stepped forward, but not in front of or closer to Alucius than Lucenda, and smiled broadly, with a hint of mischief in those golden-green eyes.

"How . . . ?" Alucius stammered.

"I brought her back when I went to town early this morning," Lucenda explained. "We've been needing help, and there wasn't that much for her to do there in town. Clerynda was happy to have her help me with the looming. You can drive her back the day after tomorrow or on Tridi, whenever we're through this batch."

"Got a contract with a young trader out of Borlan," Royalt explained, "but he wants the nightsilk before winter."

Alucius nodded, then frowned slightly, sensing more behind the words. "Grandma'am?"

"She's up at the house. Getting to be a chore for her to move around much, but she's looking forward to seeing you."

"I'd like to see her." Alucius swung down out of the saddle.

Royalt stepped forward and, with a smile, took the reins, and murmured in a low voice. "You can greet 'em before you take care of your mount."

Alucius first gave his mother a gentle hug, but the embrace—and the kiss—he bestowed on Wendra lasted far longer.

"Can't tell he missed her or anything, can you?" Royalt laughed.

Both Wendra and Alucius flushed as they stepped apart.

Royalt handed the reins back to his grandson. "She can fill you in on what's happening while you take care of the stabling. We'll be waiting up at the house."

"We won't be long," Wendra promised.

"We won't," Alucius added.

After he put the gray in the waiting stall, cleaned out for him by Royalt, he suspected, Alucius did turn to the green-and-golden-eyed young woman for a longer and more personally embracing welcome. Only after that did he begin to unsaddle the gray.

"I would have been here earlier, but I stopped in town," he said, keeping a straight face. "I thought I might pay a visit to someone, but she wasn't there. Her father said she'd taken some work elsewhere. I worried about that."

"Oh, Alucius, I would have been there—except I could see you longer if I came with your mother."

"Things aren't going all that well for your father?" Alucius began to groom the gelding.

"No. I don't think he's sold a quint's worth of barrels in the last month—except to Gortal, and you know how he hates that."

"How was business during harvest and in the first part of fall?"

"Harvest was a little better than usual, and we even made and sold more of the flour bags for Amiss. By the end of harvest, no one was buying anything."

"I didn't even see a coal cart in the square," Alucius said, moving to the far side of the gray with the stiff-bristled brush.

"Coal has gotten very dear," Wendra said. "Father asked us to be most careful with it, and even your Mother said something about it when we were working the loom."

"It's probably a good thing she didn't have to do any processing," he replied. "The wool doesn't set into thread right through the spinnerets if it's too cold." Alucius didn't mention the obvious—that, if his comparatively more wealthy family happened to be worrying about the price of coal, the cost to those less fortunate could be unbearable.

"We still had to wear those fingerless gloves. It was so cold in the loom house."

"I imagine. I'd wager you did fine."

"Your mother seemed pleased," Wendra admitted. "She explained everything, even the other looms we weren't using. I never realized that there were so many . . . so much . . ."

"Didn't your grandfather show you around his stead?"

"I don't recall that. Then, we've never gone there except for gathers and birthdays, and once in a while for a special dinner."

"And your father wasn't the one to inherit."

"No, but he does like his work, if . . ." Wendra shook her head.

"If it were not so uncertain?"

She nodded. "He works so hard. So does Mother."

"Everyone in the Iron Valleys works hard. Some just get more for their work." Alucius set down the brushes. "I won't be too much longer."

"I like your family," Wendra said after a moment. "They've been so warm to me."

"Yours has been warm to me."

"That's different."

Alucius knew enough not to get into what was behind that. "No . . . it's not. Even Korcler has been friendly."

"He sort of looks up to you, Alucius, maybe because he doesn't have a brother."

"It could be." Alucius replaced the brushes in their leather case, then checked the manger and the grain and water. "I'm finished here for now."

He eased the saddlebags over his right shoulder, and carried the rifle in his right hand. Once he had closed the stable, his left hand took Wendra's, and they walked north to the main house through the scattered and tiny flakes of snow. A thick plume of dark gray smoke billowed from the main chimney of the house, and Alucius could smell the burning coal.

In one way, the house and the out-buildings all looked so familiar in the gray mist and early twilight—the oblong stones that formed the walls and pillars, the gray slate roofs. In another, everything looked unreal. There were no trees, no grasses, and even in the dimness before dark with the low clouds, the horizon seemed vingts and vingts away. The air held a bite even more severe than he had felt in the coldest weather at Sudon.

"I need to wash up and take care of a few things," he said as they stepped onto the porch.

"I'm sure you do. It was a long ride." Wendra smiled again and squeezed his hand before releasing it.

Once inside, Alucius brushed his boots and trousers, and then washed up, quickly.

Everyone was waiting for him in the great room, where his grandmother sat in the faded but comfortable brown armchair, pulled close to the big iron coal stove. She had her slippered feet on a low stool Alucius did not recall. Her hair was now entirely whitish gray and her face narrow and pinched, but not the broad smile she gave her grandson.

"Look at you! You look handsome in that uniform. Recalls your grandsire to me. You look so much like he did then."

Royalt shifted his weight from one foot to the other. "We are related, dear. Be a shame if we didn't look a bit alike."

Veryl laughed. "There you go again."

"Can I help with anything?" Alucius asked.

"Wendra can help me," Lucenda said firmly. "We'll need a glass to get supper ready. If you're really starving, there are some biscuits from breakfast that you could have."

"I think I'll be fine." Alucius understood the unspoken—that he needed to spend the time with his grandmother. Just a cursory sensing with his Talent told him that she might not last much beyond winter. He couldn't help but wonder if it were his fault—something he had done when he had tried to heal her so many years before.

Royalt, standing behind Veryl, caught Alucius's eye. Royalt shook his head to the younger man's unspoken question. At least, Alucius thought his grandfather was answering his question, but he'd have to see later when he could talk to Royalt alone.

Wendra glanced from Royalt to Alucius, a faintly puzzled expression appearing and then vanishing as she moved toward the kitchen.

"Come on, Wendra," Lucenda said. "He's probably starving, but he wouldn't admit it if he fell over in a dead faint."

Alucius offered a wry grin. He was hungry, and the food at the training camp had been filling, and little more. He took one of the straight-backed chairs from against the wall and set it down across from his grandmother, and then sat down. Royalt sat on the side of the couch nearest to his wife.

"We hoped the weather wouldn't keep you," Veryl began. "Soarers! It's so good to see you. Royalt, he said you'd be fine, but you never know . . . you just never know, not in these days."

"The days were long, and they kept us busy. I learned a few things, but it wasn't as hard physically as herding. We rode enough that I didn't get out of shape that way." Alucius grinned. "I am looking forward to a good meal. The food wasn't anything to talk about, except that there was enough." He paused. "I met a fellow named Kypler. His family has the sawmill in Wesrigg." Alucius looked at Royalt. "Do you know them?"

"His grandsire was Byaler. Spent some time in the militia with me. Good man, as I recall. They provided the beams for the new processing shed. Good timber, fair price."

Alucius wanted to smile. The "new" processing shed was older than he was.

"Delar suggested you might be going where he is," Royalt offered. "Said he wasn't sure, but might be likely."

Alucius laughed. "He'll be my squad leader . . ." As he glanced toward the kitchen and caught a smile from Wendra, he went on to explain, hoping it wouldn't be that long before dinner.

35

At supper, Alucius ate far too much of the mutton stew, but the meal was the best set in front of him since before he had been conscripted. Even the dried sweet melon slices tasted wonderful, and he had two large mugs of the good weak ale. Once they had moved into the great room, he felt comfortable and happy, sitting on the worn brown couch with Wendra beside him.

". . . think the southerners are worried about the raids, wanted more of the nightsilk for next year," Lucenda said. "Anyway, that's why we've been busy, and why Wendra is such a help." She looked up as Royalt re-entered the room. "How is Mother?"

"She's just tired." Royalt looked at his grandson. "I can tell you've missed good food."

"That's true," Alucius replied. He inclined his head toward the back hallway. "She gets tired easily, doesn't she? Grandma'am, I meant."

Lucenda nodded. "Her spirits are good, but the days are often long for her. I can remember when she could handle every spinneret in the processing shed, all at once."

"We all get old," Royalt said. "I couldn't keep up with what Alucius just went through."

Alucius laughed. "I got through it because of what you put me through, and that was harder than what the militia put me through. Don't talk to me about your growing weaker."

Royalt smiled back, not quite ruefully. "Let's say that I can do almost anything I once could, but it takes me three times as long to recover. And I need more sleep. A lot more." He offered a huge yawn. "Best I'd be getting to bed."

Alucius almost flushed. His grandsire wasn't that tired, although his grandmother had been ready to retire far earlier than she had.

"So should I," added Lucenda rising from her chair. "You two shouldn't stay up too late, because Wendra does need to help me tomorrow, and your grandsire could use a little help as well. After your own trip, a good night's sleep wouldn't hurt you, either."

"We won't stay up too long," Wendra promised.

Alucius wasn't about to promise an immediate retirement to the loft by himself, not with Wendra clearly headed for the guest bed at the other end of the house. So he just smiled.

"Listen to the young woman," Lucenda told her son.

"Yes, ma'am."

"He does listen," Wendra said. She turned to him and, after Lucenda had headed down the hallway, whispered in his ear. "You don't always obey."

Alucius slipped both arms around her. "I missed you."

"I can tell."

They shared a long kiss before Wendra eased away. "I'll

be here for a few days. It's not like we have but a few moments. Talk to me."

Alucius could feel . . . many things churning inside Wendra. Not fear, but apprehension mixed with both warmth and, he was happy to sense, strong attraction. "About what?"

"Anything . . . just talk to me." Her hand touched his cheek. "We have time."

Not so much as she thought, Alucius feared. "Was it all right with your family for you to come out here?"

"I think they worry a little. If your grandfather weren't such a close friend of the family, and especially of Grandfather Kustyl . . . it might be different." Wendra looked down.

"And coin is short?" Alucius said gently, easing back slightly so that he had just one arm around her shoulders.

"It's been a hard fall. Winter will be worse. Grandfather Kustyl can't help as much because the stead has to support him and Grandma'am Mairee and Uncle Tylal and his family."

"Kyrtus and Jaff are already in the militia."

"Jaff has two years before his term's up. He's down in Rivercliff now. Kyrtus is in Emal. Father said they try not to put brothers in the same place."

"Is Kyrtus still jealous?" Alucius laughed.

Wendra flushed. "He's a nice cousin. He just . . ." She shook her head. "He wanted to be more than a cousin and a friend, and that . . . it wouldn't work."

"Does *he* know that?" Alucius teased.

"Uncle Tylal made it clear, and Kyrtus apologized." Wendra grinned. "He did ask me to let him know if you didn't treat me right."

"Does everyone in the Iron Valleys know?" Alucius offered with mock-indignation.

Wendra cocked her head to the side, then offered in equal mockery, "I don't think the folk in Emal or Wesrigg know."

Alucius laughed once more, enjoying the moment.

Wendra bent forward and kissed him on the cheek. "Thank you."

He smiled. "You're welcome." After a moment, he asked, "How do you like the stead?"

"I love it. I love the space, and the open skies, and the air. And your family is so good to me. They make me feel like the intended of a Duarch." She blushed. "I suppose, in a way . . ."

"We're herders, nothing more, and it's hard work," Alucius pointed out. "You've seen that, not just here, but at your grandfather's."

A slightly pensive look crossed Wendra's face. "I worry . . . about you."

"I'll be fine."

"I'm young, Alucius. But I'm not stupid. People everywhere are worried. Father said that they're conscripting as many men as they can. Gortal is shipping wagons south to Dekhron, and that's just across the river from Lanachrona. The Council has ordered all sorts of supplies, and Father said they don't do that in the fall unless they don't think they can get them later."

"He's probably right about that," Alucius admitted.

"So . . . I can be worried about you."

"I'm glad that you are." He ran his fingertips along the line of her jaw, feeling the incredible smoothness of her skin. "And I'm glad that you're here."

"So am I."

The kiss was long and gentle, lingering, and Alucius held her tightly, wishing he could do more, and knowing, both within and from what he sensed, that to do more would destroy what he needed most from Wendra.

But he could savor the kisses and the embrace, and even the words they shared.

36

Alucius and Royalt rode about three yards apart as they urged the nightsheep east over the middle of Westridge in the silvered light that had followed a cloudy dawn and promised an iron-bitter morning. To the northeast, only the lower part of the Aerial Plateau was visible below the low and misty clouds. Alucius probably could have stayed at the stead, but his mother did need Wendra's help, without Alucius distracting them. Alucius also wanted a chance to talk to his grandsire without anyone else around.

Although the air was chill, it was still, and without any wind, the morning felt warmer than it was. The nightsheep were calm. Alucius couldn't sense either sanders or sandwolves, but hoped that wasn't because he had gotten out of touch with the land. Then, he could sense the faint bluish gray of the grayjays, and they were harder to Talent-sense than sanders.

Once they crossed the ridge and headed downhill, and Alucius was fairly certain no predators were near, he eased his mount closer to that of his grandsire.

"Sir?"

"Yes, Alucius. What did you want to talk about?"

"How . . . ?"

"Been obvious since you got home. Also, I was once young, and I recall feeling the same way when I first came home on furlough."

Alucius wondered how transparent he was. Like a window? Or was he translucent like quartz? Or was his grandsire just guessing based on Alucius's reactions and expressions? "You know what happened years ago . . . when Grandma'am was so sick?" He knew that Royalt had suggested an answer when Alucius had first arrived home, but Alucius wanted some reassurance.

"I recall." Royalt's voice was even.

"Did . . . I do something wrong then?"

The older man smiled sadly. "No. She would have died then. What you did—I think—partly borrowed from the rest of her body. You'll recall that she was never quite as strong as before. Healing, like everything, has a price. You might be able to have done more if you had been older, because an adult has more strength, but no one else could have done anything, and she would have died then. You gave us more than ten years together that we would not have had."

"I wish I could have done more."

"You did more than enough. You don't think I didn't feel helpless, that I don't now? She may not last the winter, certainly not more than two. You know that. She knows, too. You did what you could do. You have more of the Talent than I do. You also think through things more, at least when you want to. Haven't been able to beat you at leschec in close to ten years. The Talent's been obvious since you were a toddler. I still remember you taking on that ram—you couldn't have been more than four. Then Lamb . . . you were right about him. One of the best lead rams I've ever had. He listens to me, but he tells you things, doesn't he?"

"Sometimes," Alucius admitted. "I didn't try to save him for that. I didn't know. I just didn't want him to die."

Royalt shook his head. "Doesn't matter. You did what you felt was right. Listen to what you feel. What you *feel*, deep down inside, not what you *want*. Biggest challenge a man or woman with Talent has is to understand the difference between those two."

Thinking of the night before, with Wendra, Alucius managed not to blush. Still, he'd followed his feelings, not his desires.

They rode in silence for a time.

The younger herder studied the quarasote, taking in the graying of the fourth year plants that had seeded and would soon die, checking the land to the east, making sure that the outliers in the flock were not too far out. The lead rams remained quiet, always a good sign, but not necessarily always a complete measure of the flock's safety.

Royalt cleared his throat.

Alucius turned in the saddle. "Yes, sir?"

"You're militia cavalry now, Alucius. There are a few more things I want you to think about . . . in addition to the young woman—beautiful as she is." Royalt's tone was dry.

Alucius grinned. "Yes, sir."

"The first thing I told you a long time ago. You have Talent, more than might be healthy in some ways. Don't let *anyone* know. Herders never tell. That's how we've kept our way of life for so long. Second, the Iron Valleys can't afford to waste men, and it can't afford discord."

Alucius nodded. That had become so obvious that he wondered why his grandsire had even mentioned it. He looked eastward again, checking the flock.

"That means that your squad leaders and your captains will use you for what they think you're best at. That may not be good for you. Make yourself valuable at doing things that will help the militia without turning yourself into a target." Royalt smiled, tightly.

"How dangerous is scouting? They mentioned that herders were good at that."

"That depends on your squad leader and captain. They let you do it alone, and you're probably safer than in camp. They make you take others, and best you stay away from it. Some use scouts like a pole against a sandsnake—to stir up trouble before it can strike. Problem is that whoever's acting as the pole is going to take the first strike." Royalt paused. "You'll have to trust your feelings on that. Have heard tell that Delar's a good squad leader. Don't know about the Third Company captain, though.

"The other thing is to make your squad leader and captain look good. I'm not saying you should be polishing everyone's bars. Good officers hate toadies and flatterers. If an officer rewards those kind, find a way to get transferred if you can. If not, do your job and keep out of sight. Good officers want the job done, and they want it done with as few casualties as possible. Some of the glory hounds forget that. No real glory in fighting." Royalt snorted. "You do what needs to be done, and do it well."

"Sir? Are things getting worse? We haven't heard much, but you wouldn't be telling me this if they weren't."

"I'm afraid they are, Alucius. You know this as well as I do, or you wouldn't be asking."

"I don't *know*, sir. I feel that they are."

Royalt laughed. "When you're a herder, you learn to trust your feelings. You need to trust them in the militia as well . . . maybe more." He paused. "One other thing. Your mother, she measured you for a hat this morning?"

"Yes, sir."

"It's not for a hat. It's for a skull-mask—only leaves slits for eyes, nose, and mouth. They'll have you scout. Wear it when you're out there alone. Might save your life. Don't wear it around others, or some captain will try to take it, but it'll keep your ears from freezing in a gale and someone from putting a bolt in your neck. It'll protect your skull from shattering if you get hit with a bullet, but you'll still probably die because the shock will turn your brains to mush."

Alucius's mouth dropped open. "Ah . . . thank you."

"Not me. Your mother. She asked what else might save you." Royalt's voice was gruff, but Alucius could tell he wasn't angry.

"I'll come back, sir. You know I will."

Royalt nodded. "You will. Herders always come back. No matter where we go, we're tied here. You'll learn, as you get older and more able to use your Talent."

"Can't you tell me why, sir?"

Royalt shook his head. "That's something each herder must learn alone. It's a dark truth, but one that can sustain you. It can't be taught, only seen or felt and learned."

Alucius wanted to ask more, but knew all too well that Royalt would not offer more. After a time, he finally did ask, "Is there anything more, sir?"

"There's always something more, Alucius, especially from an old man. We've seen enough to have learned, and we're too old to act, and so we try to advise all you young folk, hoping that we can save you from the mistakes we made. Mostly, we don't. Sometimes, we do. Sometimes, that just means you make different ones, and some of them are worse than the ones we saved you from. That's life." Royalt looked eastward, then surveyed the flock. "Probably ought to start heading 'em southeast more."

"You feel anything?"

"No. Not yet, anyway, but the new growth isn't doing as well to the northeast. Drier there this summer. Don't know why."

Alucius suspected that also was life—observing and reacting, but not knowing why.

37

On Quattri morning, the sun struggled to burn through a high overcast as Alucius checked the harnesses of the dun dray horses a last time. He wore his militia uniform, and he had made sure he had a full magazine in his rifle before he had set it in the holder beside the driver's seat. He had put an old cartridge belt under the seat, and he'd managed to wrestle the covered coal bin into the wagon without smudging his militia winter parka. He hoped that there would be a coal wagon in Iron Stem. After a last check, he climbed up into the wagon seat, released the wagon brake, and drove the team and wagon from outside the stable to alongside the porch of the house.

Lucenda and Wendra stepped out of the house as he slowed the team to a halt next to the steps leading down from the porch.

"You take care." Lucenda embraced Wendra.

"You, too." Wendra stepped away, and climbed up into the passenger seat of the wagon.

"You'll get what you can at the square, now?" Lucenda

asked Alucius. "And another barrel of the hard wheat flour, if Amiss has it."

"And the coal," Alucius replied. "If there's anyone selling it."

"Be careful. Wendra can drive the wagon if someone looks to accost you."

"We'll be careful." Alucius intended that, and more.

As he guided the team down the lane that eventually led to the main road, he glanced at Wendra, bundled in her old sheepskin jacket, with heavy herders' gloves on her hands.

"Your mother insisted on the gloves. She said I could return them later, but that my hands would freeze on the ride back to town."

"I can't say I was unhappy that the looming took until yesterday to finish," Alucius said with a grin.

"I wasn't unhappy at all, but I hope Father and Mother aren't too worried."

"Mother did pay you?"

"She paid me too much, Alucius, but I couldn't say no. She insisted that she never would have finished it in time without me."

"Grandfather was worried. The traders are sending a wagon for the nightsilk tomorrow."

"It's so strange," Wendra said. "I know herders are better off than most, but you're not that much better off, and yet once nightsilk reaches the south, it is more valuable than gold."

Alucius wondered how much to say, before he finally replied. "We make more than most realize, but we also spend much more. The traders will be bringing barrels of processing solvents that are far from cheap, and you've seen all the machinery that we must have."

Wendra cocked her head to one side. "I had not thought of it that way."

"Most folk don't. It's costly to lose just one nightsheep, especially a ram. But if they don't graze the quarasote near the plateau, we don't get the best wool. Nearer the plateau is where there are more sanders and sandwolves. The losses can be high if you're not very careful."

"From the way your family talks, the losses can be high if anything goes wrong."

"That's true of your grandsire as well."

"He doesn't talk as much about it," Wendra said. "Not around us."

"Most herders don't."

"Why do . . ." Wendra frowned. "Because . . . of you and me?"

"They want you to know what it's really like," Alucius said. "Some people think it's exciting, and that we have piles of gold and hidden palaces, and that we don't work very hard." He paused. "My family likes you. If they didn't, they wouldn't talk so freely."

"They trust you . . . about me, don't they?" Wendra's voice was almost inaudible.

Alucius could sense a hint of fear. He laughed. "They trust that I not only want you, but that I like you. Very few herders have unhappy marriages."

"How much do you know about what I feel?"

"More than someone who's not a herder, but I certainly can't tell what you're thinking."

"Alucius . . ."

How much should he say? And how? After a moment, he replied. "If we're very close to each other, and if you feel something strongly—it could be anger or attraction—then I can sometimes sense it. People are much harder than night-sheep."

"Last night . . . I wanted you," Wendra choked out the words. "Did you . . . ?"

"I could feel that," he admitted. "I wanted you. But it wouldn't have been right. Your family would have thought I was taking advantage of you, and I would have been."

Abruptly, she eased across the bench seat until she was right beside him. Then she kissed him on the cheek. "I told you once you were sweet, and I love you for that."

Alucius flushed. He wasn't about to admit how close he had come to not being so sweet.

About the time that Alucius could see the gray line that was the main road, he also began to sense something. Not sander or sandwolf, but someone with a sense of urgency. He glanced back, but there was no one riding behind. His eyes took in the road, and then he could make out a trooper in a militia winter parka, wearing the green sash of a messenger, riding southward. Alucius studied the road to the north, but no one seemed to be pursuing the messenger. Yet the man rode quickly, not at a gallop, but at a fast walk, a pace for covering a long distance as quickly as possible with a single mount. The rider passed south of them on the road while they were still almost half a vingt from where the stead road joined the main road.

"What does the green sash mean?" Wendra asked.

"He's a messenger, probably reporting to militia headquarters in Dekhron."

"He's coming from the north, from Soulend, where you'll be," Wendra said. "I hope he's not bearing bad news."

"So do I." Alucius offered a laugh he did not feel.

The messenger slowly pulled away from the wagon until, by the time Alucius and Wendra were far enough south on the main road that they could see the ancient green-stone tower, the messenger was not in sight, even though the sun had finally broken through the clouds and brightened the day. Wendra's and Alucius's breath no longer steamed when they talked.

"I always wondered about the tower," Alucius said. "They took everything out of it, but they left the walls."

"Father said that the walls were put together the same way the roads were. After the Cataclysm, no one knew how to take it apart, or they would have used the stones." Wendra frowned. "But Iron Stem was so much bigger. Where did all the stones go?"

"I'd wager that there were more trees then—"

"And more of the buildings were of timber," Wendra finished. Her eyes flicked to the alternating stone patterns of the Pleasure Palace. "Bryanne—she was one of the girls Madame Myrier taught. She lives with her aunt in town . . . she said that was because she'd have trouble walking to school. But everyone knows her mother is at the Pleasure Palace. I feel sorry for her."

"Bryanne or her mother?" asked Alucius.

"Both of them. It's almost as bad as being a scutter for Gortal. I don't know. Maybe it's worse. They say the scutters have lost half their minds after a few years, and all they care about is being able to breath the dreamdust that the dustcats give off when they're combed and brushed. Just . . . doing that at the Pleasure Palace, and having to think about it . . ." Wendra shuddered.

"Maybe the mother does it so the daughter won't have to," Alucius suggested.

"That's sad, too."

Alucius agreed with that, but there was much in the world that was sad, and little enough that he could do about it.

All too many houses in Iron Stem still had shutters closed, and few chimneys showed more than the thinnest trace of smoke, even though there looked to be a coal wagon in the square. Alucius was glad he hadn't brought the coal bin in back of the wagon for nothing. He did worry about how much the coal might be going for, but he had a wallet of silvers and golds and instructions to fill the bin or get as much as he could for what he had.

Alucius slowed the wagon and then guided it down the narrow street beside Kyrial's shop, easing it to a halt short of the loading door. After setting the wagon brake, he turned in the seat and faced Wendra. "If I stop early on Londi . . . will you be here?"

"I'll be here." She smiled. "How early?"

"A glass before dawn."

"I'll be waiting."

Alucius squeezed her hand, then tied the team, before helping Wendra down. They walked through the front door of the shop together, and Alucius was careful to close the door behind them.

Kyrial looked up—his face bearing an expression of annoyance and relief. "I'm glad to see you, daughter. We had worried." For the first time, Kyrial looked sternly at Alucius.

"It wasn't Alucius, Father. He was herding all day every day. The looming took longer than Madame Lucenda thought." Wendra smiled. "But that meant she paid me more. Alucius was very proper."

Kyrial seemed to thaw, although Alucius couldn't tell whether that was from relief, or from the thought of more coin. "Your mother was worried, too, but she's at the miller's, delivering the few bags he wanted."

Wendra turned to Alucius. "Thank you."

"Thank you."

They did embrace a last time, but Alucius forewent the kiss, sensing Kyrial's concern.

"You didn't just drive Wendra in, did you?"

"No, sir. I have a number of things to pick up for the family. They're all working on finishing the goods Wendra was helping with. So it made more sense for me to bring her back and take care of getting what they need."

"Glad someone is selling something," murmured Kyrial.

"It's the first order from the south since summer, sir." Alucius did not explain that in normal times, there were no orders for nightsilk in the fall and winter.

"So times are hard for the herders, too."

"Yes, sir."

"Good luck, Alucius." Kyrial's words were as much dismissal as good wishes.

"Thank you, sir." Alucius offered Wendra a last smile before turning and leaving. He knew Wendra would face intense questioning. For her sake, he was glad he had been proper, although it had been a close thing the evening before.

He still had to get the coal that he could and another barrel of flour, as well as molasses—if he could. On the way out of the shop, conscious of both Kyrial's and Wendra's eyes on his back, he shut the door carefully.

He did hope Wendra's parents wouldn't question her too harshly.

38

Alucius sat at the kitchen table, wearing the almost-new militia uniform, as well as the nightsilk undergarments and the hidden undervest that made him look brawnier than he was. His rifle leaned against the wall less than a yard away. He watched as Royalt paced to the window, where the inside bars had been locked into place. They had set the bars in all the lower windows right after breakfast, and all the outbuildings had been secured as well. After a moment, the older man turned away. "Don't like doing it this way." His voice was barely above a murmur.

Alucius did not recall such elaborate procedures for selling nightsilk before. Usually, his grandsire and the other herders drove their wagons to the small counting house in Iron Stem operated by the Council in the spring and summer. He shook his head. Of course. The counting house was not manned in the late fall and winter, and there were no militia to provide security.

"You're worried about the year ahead, aren't you?" Alucius kept his voice low so that it wouldn't carry out to the main room where Veryl was dozing before the iron stove or to the front parlor where Lucenda was sitting, checking over the ledgers. She had a rifle with her as well.

"Yes." Royalt walked slowly back past the table. "The Lord-Protector of Lanachrona is ailing and expected to die. His eldest has made no secret of his scorn for his sire's caution. The Matrial is taking over the Westerhills and pushing the Reillies either into the Iron Valleys or northward. None of the Reillie raids make sense otherwise, but the Council isn't saying."

"Why wouldn't they?"

"They don't want to give the Lanachronans the idea that we might be vulnerable, especially with the possibility of a new Lord-Protector. In the past, the southerners haven't really wanted the northern part of the Iron Valleys. They just wanted Dekhron and the area around it and control of both banks of the Vedra. If old Lord-Protector dies and they know for certain that we are fighting the Matrite troops, the new Lord-Protector might decide to move on his own. That's why the Council is trying to build up the militia quickly and quietly—and hoping that the ailing Lord-Protector will last for a season or so yet." Royalt paced to the window for the third time in less than a glass, but this time he paused, then turned with a smile. "That'll be Kustyl and Tylal with their nightsilk."

Alucius followed Royalt out onto the porch, where a cold wind blew out of the northeast, carrying the acrid scent of the plateau. The two watched the wagon draw to a halt.

Alucius couldn't say that he was surprised to see Tylal wearing the uniform of a captain in the militia. Most herders served at one point or another, but the uniform fit Tylal well.

"Almost look like you've been called up," Royalt said.

"Almost as bad as if I had been," countered Tylal. He glanced at Alucius. "Two of us, it just might work."

"Oh, they wouldn't be able to take the nightsilk from four of us. Not from four herders," Kustyl said. "This way, though, they'll get the idea that there are militia in places they hadn't thought. Might help." He lowered the tailgate of the wagon.

"We can use anything that would," Royalt suggested. "Can't count on the Council to do the right thing, not for herders, anyway."

Tylal and Kustyl carried a plain wooden chest up onto the porch and set it beside the one that Alucius and Royalt had placed there earlier.

"You know what you're to do?" Royalt asked Alucius.

"You want me to stand guard over the nightsilk on the porch. But I'm really supposed to watch the traders and their guards. If they go for their weapons, I'm to kill as many as I can." Alucius paused. "Do you think they will?"

"No. You have to look as though you're ready to act, though."

"I understand, sir."

Royalt nodded, then turned to Kustyl. "You want to put the team in the shed?"

"Be warmer, and a mite safer."

Tylal and Alucius stood on the porch as the two older men took the wagon and team out to the one shed that had not been locked.

"You look just like a fresh-minted cavalry type," Tylal said with a chuckle. "Of course, that being the case, it's not surprising."

"Could they really call you up, sir?" asked Alucius.

"They could until I'm forty-five, but they'd have to release Jaff or Kyrtus, and I don't imagine they'd do that. They'd rather have younger men." Tylal paused. "Unless your grandsire is right, and things get much worse."

When the older men returned, all four slipped into the kitchen where they waited. Kustyl, Tylal, and Alucius sat around the table, while Royalt continued to pace, checking the window.

"Better doing this with both steads here, anyway," Kustyl offered. "Not sure I like partial shearing late in the year."

"We may not have any buyers in the spring or early summer," Royalt pointed out. "If we do, they won't pay as much."

"You could be right." To Alucius's Talent-senses, Kustyl didn't feel convinced.

"They're on the lane," Lucenda called from the loft, although Alucius had not seen his mother climb up there.

Alucius picked up the rifle and slipped out the back door to the north end of the porch where he took station as if he were guarding a post back at Sudon.

A single wagon rolled down the lane toward the stead. Four guards rode before the wagon, and two behind. With all the preparations required by his grandsire, Alucius had somehow expected a larger contingent of traders.

The wagon was narrower than many, and highsided and

enclosed, if not any taller than the head of a horseman riding beside, without shutters or windows, and with larger wheels than the stead wagon. The sides were painted a glossy maroon. The guards all wore maroon leather riding jackets, and bore blades in shoulder harnesses that were longer than sabres but shorter than the hand-and-a-half battle blades used by the Reillies. They also had rifles in saddle scabbards.

Alucius thought they looked more like cavalry than private guards.

The trader handling the wagon eased it up alongside the porch steps, where Royalt, Kustyl, and Tylal stood. Tylal stood back, more to the south end of the porch, so that he and Alucius had a clear field of fire at the traders and the wagon.

Royalt stepped forward. "Greetings, Salburan."

"Greetings, herder Royalt." The clean-shaven, dark-skinned trader glanced from Tylal to Alucius and back to Royalt before speaking. "Even upon a stead, your militia is present."

Alucius had to strain to understand the trader's words, delivered as they were in what seemed a thick accent, but both Lanachronans and people in the Iron Valleys spoke the same tongue, if with differing accents.

"Would you expect any less?" Royalt countered cheerfully.

"Ah . . . yes. Always the governments, they want their share."

"Is that not true in Borlan and Tempre as well?"

"Truly . . . truly . . ." After handing the leads to the other man in the wagon seat, who wore the maroon of a guard, Salburan swung down onto the hard ground. "Let us see the nightsilk. I would prefer a more, shall we say, relaxed transaction, but we have many vingts to return."

"We understand," Royalt replied.

Alucius continued to watch the guards, who had remained mounted and taken station several yards out from the wagon, so that they could survey the area around the stead. One had ridden all the way around the house before taking his position to the rear of the wagon.

Royalt opened the first chest, the one with the nightsilk from his own stead. The trader took out the bolt of the cloth, tilting it and looking at the weave and the texture from several angles. Then he took out a small frame from beneath his leather jacket and inclined his head to Royalt in inquiry.

"Go ahead." Royalt nodded to Kustyl, who placed two building stones on the stone floor of the porch.

Salburan unwound some of the black fabric and then fastened the two-sided frame over the shimmering nightsilk. He set the frame on the building stones, so that the framed nightsilk was two spans above the floor. Taking out a belt knife, he grasped it firmly and slashed down.

The nightsilk held, but the frame sprang open.

Salburan replaced the knife in its sheath and studied the fabric closely. Then he nodded.

Kustyl opened the second chest, and Salburan repeated his test—with the same results.

One of guards dismounted and stepped forward with a folding iron yard measure.

Alucius concentrated on watching the guards, as the lengths and widths of the nightsilk were measured and verified—and as Salburan tested the fabric at irregular intervals along its length.

Finally the trader spoke. "As always, it is the finest. Although times have been hard for us, as well as for you, we had agreed on ten golds a yard . . ."

Alucius managed not to frown. He knew that price was high, but he kept his eyes on the Lanachronan guards, rather than upon the golds coming from Salburan's strongbox.

Once the coins exchanged hands the trader took the nightsilk, wrapping each bolt in a dark fabric and carrying it to the wagon where someone inside took it. Then four large copper-bound barrels were lifted out by the trader and the man who had been riding beside him on the wagon seat. Kustyl and Royalt carried them to the porch one by one.

As they did, Alucius became very alert, his Talent-senses

seeking any hint of action, but everyone in the trader's party seemed almost relaxed, although the guards nearest to him were clearly taking in everything, much as Alucius was.

After the last barrel reached the porch, the door in the rear of the wagon closed, and Salburan turned. "Four barrels, as we agreed."

"As we agreed," Royalt confirmed, returning some of the golds to the trader.

"A pleasure doing business with you, herders," Salburan bowed a last time before climbing back into his wagon.

As the two Lanachronan guards who had remained mounted and closest to Alucius turned their horses to fall in before the wagon, one spoke, again with the thick accent, almost under his breath, to the one who had eased his mount nearer. "The dwelling, the out-buildings, they are almost like a fort. Stone walls a half yard thick. Stone roofs—double doors, iron bound. Three of their militia out here in the middle of nowhere."

"Much easier to let them take the risks, and purchase the nightsilk once it is ready . . ."

Alucius could not hear more as the guards rode to lead the carriage back toward the lane—and toward Iron Stem. Three militia? Then he realized that his mother had probably let her rifle be seen from the upper window.

Once the traders' wagon and the guards were well out of sight, Royalt turned to Alucius. "You did well."

"I didn't do anything," Alucius protested.

"Yes, you did," Tylal said with a laugh. "You looked like a very determined junior cavalryman who was looking for an excuse to shoot one of the Lanachronans. They could tell you were recently trained, and in service."

Alucius wasn't sure about that, but he smiled. "The last part is true enough." He paused. "I'm not very experienced, but I was watching their guards . . ."

Tylal laughed. "They were Southern Guards, dressed as a traders' guards. Your grandsire was right."

"They don't get much chance to scout out what we're

doing," Royalt said. "Wouldn't have been surprised if one or two weren't captains or undercaptains."

"Was that why . . . ?" Alucius didn't want to mention the price and realized he shouldn't have said anything.

"One reason," Royalt said quickly. "The other is that they won't go back through Dekhron. They'll go east of Emal and take a boat to the south side of the Vedra, then back roads to the old east road to Deforya."

"That way, they won't pay full tariffs to their own Lord-Protector," Kustyl pointed out. "They'll claim they sold less than they did. They'll have to pay extra to the Southern Guards, but the Guards won't say anything because they like the coin and because they want the information.

"And we don't have to pay any, because tariffs are only required when trades are taking place at the counting house," added Tylal.

"Of course," Royalt pointed out, "it's so dangerous to do this that we can't make a common practice out of it."

The three older men all nodded in relief.

Alucius didn't feel relieved at all.

39

Hieron, Madrien

The entire north wall of the study was composed of shelf upon shelf of ancient tomes, with the shelves running from the floor to the four-yard-high ceiling. A small walnut book ladder rested in the corner. The Matrial and a thin red-haired woman in a purple-and-green uniform tunic sat on opposite sides of the small circular table on the west side of the study. The Matrial frowned as she set down the written report and looked up. "This says nothing."

"Yes, Matrial. No one in Southgate will commit anything to writing."

"They do not seem able to commit to anything involving us."

"No, Matrial. They cannot afford to trade with us, nor to fight. So they say little."

"They fear the traders of Dramuria that much?"

"Most of their wealth comes from acting as the midpoint between Dramur and Lanachrona. We could, as I recommended, block the high road to Tempre to traders coming out of Southgate."

"Not now. The old Lord-Protector is failing, and his son might well use that as a way to consolidate his power. We cannot afford to fight in the north and the south at once. We must finish the conquest of the Iron Valleys first."

"As you wish, Matrial."

"Do any in Southgate say why they will not trade directly with us?"

"Ah . . . there are rumors . . ."

"Of what?"

"Seltyr Benjir says that his faith will not allow him commerce with a land that places collars upon its manhood."

The Matrial's lips tightened momentarily before she spoke. "So . . . he can chain and whip his women, and that is acceptable. We merely collar men so that they can no longer do violence, and that is not?"

"Matrial . . . I can only tell you what I have been able to discover. You had requested that we attempt to procure the alyantha more directly . . . or to discover why we could not."

"I did, and my anger is not at you, Sulythya. We create a land where men and women are at last equals, where unthinking muscle does not rule everything, and we can gain nothing through trade—only through force. Our golds are rejected, and where accepted, we must pay twice what the traders of any other land must . . ."

"Yes, Matrial."

The Matrial stood, leaving the report on the conference table. She forced a smile. "You may go. You have done what I requested, and done it as well as possible."

"Thank you, Matrial." The woman bowed, and then retreated, from the private study through the foyer, and out through the guarded doors.

Only when the outer doors had closed did the Matrial turn and depart the study, crossing the main sitting room and stepping through the arches and out into the enclosed garden. Her lips were tightly pressed together.

The garden-girl bowed, then slowly backed away, not taking her eyes away from the alabaster-skinned ruler.

Ignoring the girl, the Matrial glanced at the row of bright yellow and white daisies, nodding in the slight breeze that dropped from the open silver-green sky above. Her eyes lighted upon a squat cactus, set in the drier and sunnier northeast corner. She looked at the cactus, frowning, her violet eyes seeming to darken.

Behind her, the garden-girl slipped through the small doorway into her room, quietly closing the door.

The Matrial stared at the cactus for another long moment. Then the tip of the yard-high barrel browned, then blackened. Swiftly, blackness swept down the desert plant like a growing shadow. Behind the wave of blackness, the cactus shriveled. Putrid water oozed onto the sandy soil, then vanished into the sand.

For an instant, bluish flames played over the blackened remnant of the plant. Within moments, all that remained was a circle of black on the soil.

The Matrial nodded to herself, then took a long and deep breath, alone in the enclosed garden.

In time, she turned and walked slowly back to the study.

40

The week of furlough flew past, or so it seemed to Alucius. He spent most of the week herding, and helping his grandsire with various projects that required two bodies, such as reinforcing the doors on the main nightsheep shed, or a great deal of time and effort, such as carting barrels of flour and dried fruit and water down into the hidden fortified room beneath the house, a room even with an equally separate and concealed ventilation system.

He did spend Novdi—half of it—visiting Wendra, and helping her, as he could, and staying close, but out of the way, when he could not. Then came Decdi, with a few more chores, and a huge dinner, and a supper not much smaller— and a few tears from his grandmother, who tried to conceal her fears that it was the last time she would see him.

All Alucius could do was give her a careful and warm embrace and tell her how he'd think of her all the time he was at Soulend.

All too soon, it was a very dark and very early Londi, and Alucius was on his way south to Sudon. Although his night vision and Talent helped, he was still glad for the smoothness of the old road south to Iron Stem. He was also glad that the air was still. He could feel the folded square of nightsilk inside his tunic, the skull-mask his mother had pressed on him before he had left that morning, and he wondered if he would be able to use it, not sure whether he worried about wearing it or not wearing it more.

The town was dark and silent when Alucius rode up to the side door of the cooper's shop nearly two glasses before dawn. As he dismounted, he hoped that Wendra would be awake, for he was earlier than he had said he would be—on reflection and on Royalt's advice about cutting his travel time too close.

He did not reach the door before it opened. Wendra held a candle-lamp that, despite the glass mantle, flickered in the light and cold wind. She wore a heavy sheepskin jacket, and her hair was pulled back. Even in the dim light and from several yards away, he could see the warm smile, and feel the relief.

"I'm sorry. I'm early, and I was afraid . . ."

"Come into the shop. It's chill, but not so cold as out here." She stepped back, holding the door. "Father said you would be early. I didn't sleep. I kept waking up."

"I didn't get much sleep either," he confessed. "I can't stay long, but . . . I don't know when I'll get furlough, and I wanted to see you before I reported."

"I'm glad you did." Wendra eased the door shut, set the lamp on the barrel inside the door, and then lifted her lips to his, despite the chill of his face and lips.

The kiss and embrace did not last nearly long enough, not for Alucius, before he stepped back. "It's still a long ride."

"I know." She kissed him on the cheek, then stepped back and reclaimed the candle.

Alucius opened the shop's side door and stepped back into the cold. He untied the gray and mounted, his eyes still on Wendra, standing in the partly open side door. Finally, with a wave and a last smile, he turned the gray back toward the square and the road south.

He was nearing the outskirts of the southern side of Iron Stem when he saw a rider ahead, one wearing a cavalry winter parka.

The other rider glanced back. "Kypler?"

"No . . . Alucius."

The other rider slowed his mount, and as Alucius neared, he recognized Velon.

"I waited for Kypler in the square," Velon explained, "but I got worried. So I started out."

"I didn't see him either," Alucius confessed.

"When did you get up? Midnight?"

"A little after." He didn't mention his stop along the way. "The first couple of vingts are slow. That's before you reach the main road."

"Some of them, like Retius, were talking about reporting last night," Velon said.

"I'd thought about it—but not for very long."

"Did you stop at Kyrial's this morning?" asked Velon good-naturedly.

"Of course. But only for a few moments."

"She's beautiful. I saw her last Quattri when we were bringing in some late juice for the square market. I had to pick up some half-barrels, and she had come in from some-where."

Alucius couldn't help but feel slightly anxious, even though he could sense that Velon was being only friendly. "She's wonderful." He gave a rueful laugh. "It's going to be a long three years that way."

"I can see why, but I wouldn't worry."

Alucius hoped not.

They didn't see Kypler, or anyone else, on the main road as they continued south. Most of the snow of the previous week had vanished, and by the time they turned their mounts westward from the old stone highway, a cold white sun had lifted cleared of the horizon and shone out of a clear silver-green sky.

As they neared the gates to the camp, Velon cleared his throat. "Alucius . . . you know anything about second squad?"

"I've met Delar before, and my grandsire has heard he's a solid cavalry leader. That's about all."

"But six replacements out of a twenty man squad?"

"Could be that some were promoted to squad leader, or that they've been transferred to one of the new companies."

"Let's hope so," suggested Velon.

Within himself, Alucius agreed.

Estepp was waiting outside the barracks at Sudon, check-ing off names as the new militia cavalry returned. Alucius and Velon put their gear in the chests and spaces of their old bunks. Alucius lay down and promptly went to sleep, only to be awakened in what seemed moments, by the chiming of the bell.

He and Velon hurried back to the assembly space of the barracks, just in time to see Estepp appear. "Form up, close interval. By assigned company squad!"

Alucius found himself as the guide for the other five who would be joining him in Third Company's second squad.

"As some of you already know," Estepp said, "you won't be leaving until tomorrow at dawn. Today, after this briefing, put on work tunics and then form up in a quarter glass in the wagon yard. You'll be working with the new foot to load the supply wagons. After we load out, you'll form up here again for a briefing on what to expect at the various companies. Now fall out and get ready for work duty."

When he reported to the wagon yard, Alucius and his squad-mates found themselves detailed to roll flour barrels from the farthest warehouse to one of the wagons, and then lift and stack them. After the flour came ten barrels of salted pork, and then three of dried apples. In time, Alucius lost track of what they stacked and lashed in the wagons.

He was exhausted when they all reformed in the barracks, possibly because he'd only had the bread and cheese he'd carried for the ride from the stead.

Estepp waited until he was certain everyone was listening.

"For those of you being assigned to Third Company at Soulend—it's the coldest station in the Iron Valleys. I wasn't joking when I suggested warm undergarments. It's likely you'll see the most action this winter. The company has seen attacks on steads somewhere in the area once or twice a week. You'll have more scouting patrols than many companies, and you could run across brigands at any time. Most of them are Reillies, and for those of you who don't know, they usually wear a black-and-yellow plaid cloak of sorts. They're good shots. That's because many of them have older Lanachronan rifles that have to be reloaded after every shot. They have to make every shot count. They also carry hand-and-a-half blades, not sabres, and they use them very well. You either need to back off so that a flanker can shoot them or move in close where your sabre can actually do some damage.

"Those of you going to the Fifth Company at Emal will also find it cold, because you're close to both the plateau and just above the river . . .

"Those of you going to the Eighth Company . . .

"Tenth Company is in the middle of nowhere . . ."

Alucius stiffened as Estepp finished with his briefing on Tenth Company.

". . . and don't ever let yourself be captured by the Matrites if you ever want to see the Iron Valleys again. They put Talent-twisted collars on their captives, and turn them into troops fighting the Lanachronans . . ."

Alucius had heard something like that before, but never so clearly stated.

"Those of you going to Eleventh Company . . .

"You can fall out for supper. You're free to do what you want until the second glass of night. Then you'll turn in. Dismissed."

Retius, a stocky black-haired man from east of Dekhron, turned to Alucius. "You're from up north, Alucius. Is it as cold as he says?"

"Colder, at times, even where I live, and Soulend is another hundred and thirty vingts north of our stead."

Retius shivered.

Alucius was thinking more about eating, and then getting some sleep. The day had been all too long, and the next would be longer.

41

On Duadi, the bell rang at an hour before dawn, and Alucius had to struggle to get up and washed and to breakfast. Surprisingly, it was egg toast with mutton, and dried apples and hot cider—by far the best breakfast Alucius had seen in the cavalry.

While he had seen Dolesy and Ramsat from a distance, they had stayed away from Alucius, and that had been fine with him. Alucius had no illusions that Dolesy had either forgiven or forgotten, and he didn't like the idea of being even in the same company as the man. He couldn't help wondering why they hadn't been placed in different companies—especially based on what Estepp had said. But then, did Estepp control the assignments, or were they made by some officer? There was still so much Alucius didn't know.

Gurnelt had the replacement cavalry for Third Company mounted and in column before dawn. His eyes were as gray as the sky, and as cold. "We have a long ride ahead. I expect order and discipline. North of Iron Stem, we could run into raiders. If we do, you'll be expected to follow orders, either to pursue, or not to pursue—as I decide. On the open road, you can talk, quietly. No talking in ranks when we ride through any hamlet or town. Look sharp there, and no slouching in the saddles. Understand?"

The column began moving eastward out of Sudon just before dawn, and they rode eastward, into a hazy and cold day. The haze reduced the glare of riding into the rising sun, but it also meant the sun gave little warmth.

Even with the slower pace required by the heavy wagons, and a brief stop at the public pump on the south edge of Iron Stem for rations, they made the main square in Iron Stem by early afternoon. Alucius thought he saw Wendra standing on the porch of the cooper's shop, but Gurnelt took the column around the far side of the square, and Alucius couldn't be certain. He would have liked to have gotten a glimpse of her, but he hadn't counted on it. Already, he missed her green-golden eyes, her laugh—and, he had to admit, her kisses and the feel of her body as he held her.

As they rode northward out of Iron Stem, Akkar, riding beside Velon, just in front of Alucius and Kypler, pointed to the green-faced stone tower. "What's that?"

"That's the tower," Alucius said. "It's from the old days. The low building in front of it is the Pleasure Palace."

"Awful small for a palace," quipped Akkar. "Wouldn't think they'd have one of those in Iron Stem."

"Many wish that they didn't," Kypler said dryly. "It's been here since before the Cataclysm."

"And probably the women in it, too," came a voice from several ranks behind Alucius, a voice that he recognized as Dolesy's.

"That kind never learns," Kypler murmured to Alucius.

As they rode past the dustcat enclosures, Alucius wondered

if Dolesy or Ramsat would say anything about scutters—or
if the two even knew what they were passing.

From somewhere ahead, the singing began.

> "If the world you want to see
>   try the militia cavalry . . .
>   from throughout the Westerhills,
>   from where the River Vedra fills,
>   for it's hi, hi, he
>   in the militia cavalry. . . ."

Riding and singing helped in taking Alucius's thoughts
away from Dolesy—and Wendra.

42

Four days later, on Sexdi, there was much less
enthusiasm in the singing of the cavalry replacements. The
sky had turned leaden gray and cloudy. The wind blew un-
remittingly out of the northwest, as if it had come directly
from the Moors of Yesterday, damp and freezingly chill.

Intermittent snow flurries, with tiny flakes as sharp as miniature burrs, came and went. The wheels of the supply wagons creaked and shrilled in the cold of the afternoon.

Not for the first time, Alucius wondered how Wendra was
doing, and how long before he would see her again. He also
wondered about his grandmother, and her sense that she
would not see him again. With a headshake, he brought his
attention back to the road.

According to the last distance stone, they were less than
ten vingts south of Soulend, but the hamlet that had been a
town generations before was nowhere in sight. Alucius's face
was numb from the wind, and even under his winter cap, his
ears were chill.

The road continued to run due north, like a rifle barrel, as if it would stretch straight to the Ice Sands and the Black Cliffs beyond, and the slightly rolling plains on either side looked little different from those immediately north of Iron Stem, with small drifts of snow piled against the quarasote and frozen bare sandy red soil in most places. To the northeast, the Aerlal Plateau loomed larger than he'd ever seen it. That was as it should have been, because it was less than thirty vingts from Soulend and more than twice that from Iron Stem.

Alucius frowned. He could smell smoke, but it was more like wood burning than coal, and it carried an unfamiliar scent.

"All squads! Quick-step!"

At Gurnelt's order, Alucius looked up, even as he urged the gray forward. To the left of the road, a lane led to the northwest, and the column had turned down the lane.

"Raiders ahead. Pass the word. Raiders ahead . . ."

Raiders? South of Soulend, and so close to the town?

Above the riders in front of him, Alucius could see a thin column of smoke.

"First six riders! To the left, cut off their access to the back road there! Don't push your mounts until you're within a hundred yards!"

Abruptly, Alucius found himself in the front of the column as the six riders before him had veered to the left across flat and hard ground, empty even of quarasote.

Less than two hundred yards ahead, four men, outlined against the flames, struggled to remount horses. One of the horses pulled its reins from the rider's hands, leaving the man standing before the burning hut. Behind the hut was a low hill scarcely two or three times the height of the hut itself.

"Next four ranks—Alucius through Tyreas—charge straight ahead. Sabres at the ready. No quarter . . ."

"Fourth and fifth squads, follow me!"

Alucius urged his mount forward even as he unsheathed his sabre. From the corner of his eyes, and with his Talent, he could sense the half-squad-sized group that Gurnelt was leading quick-stepping slightly to the left.

He was perhaps fifty yards from the hut when there was

a single *crack*, followed by two others. But the three mounted raiders did not remain to face the charge. After firing once, they turned and rode eastward, leaving their unmounted comrade behind.

As he rode toward the hut and the one brigand, from somewhere, Alucius heard another command.

"Halt and fire! Halt and fire!"

The remaining brigand held a long blade, and stood defiantly, awaiting the shorter sabres of the militia cavalry, smiling, almost mockingly.

Not knowing quite why, Alucius pulled up his mount short, a good ten yards back from the man, left his blade across his thighs, hoping the gray would not rear, and yanked out his rifle, cocking and aiming it in one motion.

The first shot missed the Reillie. The second did not, and the man staggered. His knees buckled, and he fell backward.

"Company regroup! Regroup at the hut!"

For a moment, Alucius just sat on the gray, stunned at his aim, although he should not have been, not after the years of dealing with sanders and sandwolves. After a quick glance around that showed no brigands standing, he slipped the rifle back into its holster and resheathed his blade before it slipped to the ground. Then he eased the gray into formation.

Gurnelt rode toward the second group, the one that Alucius had led. He reined up opposite Alucius. "Alucius, why did you handle the brigand that way?"

"Sir. You gave a command to halt and fire. He had a longer blade. I wasn't sure if the command was to us, but it made sense. So I did."

"All right." Gurnelt nodded, then raised his voice. "Reform in column. Same order as before."

"Sir! Oliuf's hurt."

"It's not bad, sir," Oliuf protested.

"Let's see." Gurnelt turned his mount toward the injured cavalryman. "Retius, collect the blade and the rifle from the Reillie. When we get back to the wagons, hand it over to one of the drivers to take to the outpost."

"Yes, sir."

As Gurnelt rode toward Oliuf, Alucius looked eastward where two militia troopers had collected two of the raider mounts and were returning to the cavalry column with the captured horses. The third and fourth mounts had escaped. Alucius could see three figures in yellow-and-black, sprawled on the cold ground.

His eyes went back at the brigand he had shot, lying about ten yards in front of the hut. The man lay face up, darkening blood across his plaid and a sheepskin jacket so old that in places the leather had worn through to reveal the back side of the inner fleece. The gray-haired and gray-bearded man's face was thin—gaunt—and his body angular.

"Don't look so tough," Ramsat muttered.

"Some are, and some aren't," Gurnelt replied absently as he bound Oliuf's arm. "Best you treat them all as dangerous until you find out otherwise. Another handspan or so to the left here, and Oliuf would have been on the ground with them." He looked at the injured man. "You're luckier than you know. Doesn't look deep, but let me know if you feel weak. Don't wait."

"Yes, sir," replied Oliuf.

Alucius looked beyond the dead raider toward the small stone hut from which only thin trails of gray and black smoke drifted. What little wood there had been had already burned.

"They were surprised, and they only fired three shots," Gurnelt said. "One of them hit one of us. Think about what might have happened if there had been ten of them with time to fire."

There was silence, broken only by the faint hissing and crackling of the few last tongues of flame coming from the hut.

"Column forward! Back to the road and the wagons!"

Alucius did not look back. All he sensed beyond the riders who surrounded him was the absolute emptiness of death.

43

In the dimness of a winter twilight, the column of replacement troopers rode past two militia foot sentries occupying a small hutlike guard post. Behind the cavalry came the supply wagons, their wheels shrilling even more loudly than before. Alucius glanced back to the east. Although the hamlet of Soulend was less than two vingts away, there was not a lamp or a fire visible from the score or so of dwellings huddled among the heaps of stone that dominated what once had been a far larger town.

"Column halt!" Gurnelt ordered.

Once the tired riders stopped, the squad leader addressed them immediately. "Stable your mounts and groom them. The stone building with the green posts is the stable. You can take any stall that doesn't have gear or a name on it and seems empty. Just like at Sudon, you're responsible for keeping it clean. The company ostlers are supposed to take care of feed and water, but you make sure they do. After you get your mounts settled, form up in the open space just inside the barracks. That's the long building with the black posts. You'll report to your new squad leader by squads after that. Then you can eat. Some of you may have to help unload the supplies, but that will be decided by the captain and the company senior squad leader . . ."

As the blocky Gurnelt finished, Alucius studied the outpost, clearly a stead that had been abandoned, and then partially restored. The stone building serving as the stable had been a sheep shed, and the slate roof had been pieced and patched back together hastily with broken slates and bitumen. The barracks looked to have been a larger stock barn, and the replacement slates used were larger and matched the original roof more closely. The stead dwelling, in far better shape, was probably where the officers, and perhaps the squad leaders, were quartered.

". . . fall out by squads. First squad replacements!"

"It could be worse," murmured Kypler under his breath, breath that steamed in the chill air.

Alucius could see smoke from various chimneys and hoped for some warmth, although the ride from Sudon had not been any worse than a series of long days herding in the winter. The sleeping in a bedroll in waystations that barely blocked the wind had been worse, and he missed being able to wash up.

"Second squad . . ."

Alucius rode toward the stable, then dismounted. A white-haired and thin man in a worn brown leather jacket was standing just inside the stable.

Alucius offered a smile. "You might be the ostler."

"Brannal, trooper, and yes, I'm the head ostler."

Brannal didn't feel hostile, but almost indifferent. Alucius tried to project friendliness and deference. "Alucius, very new to the second squad. Have you any suggestions?"

A faint smile cracked the weathered face. "The far end on the right. Troopers avoid it because they have to walk the length of the stable, but it's drier and warmer."

Alucius inclined his head. "Thank you, Brannal. I appreciate it."

"No bother." But Brannal did hold the smile for a moment as Alucius led the gray past him.

While the stalls at the far end were a walk, almost fifty yards, Alucius could see why they were drier. The ground sloped upward, if barely, and there were fewer watermarks on the timbers underlying the slats holding the roof slates. Alucius took his time unloading the gray and grooming him, checking hoofs, and then his tack. As he was finishing, a younger ostler appeared carrying water buckets.

"Thank you." Alucius paused, then asked, "What do I do about feed?"

"We're a bit short on grain, trooper, until the wagons get

unloaded, but there's already some hay in the manger there, and we can spare some grain."

"Anything that you can, I'd appreciate it." Alucius smiled and offered friendliness. "I'm Alucius."

"Kesper, and I'm one of Brannal's assistants."

"He seems to be careful about watching everything."

"Good man, he is, and there's not much he doesn't know about horses." Kesper looked over the gray. "Yours for a while?"

"Five years," Alucius admitted.

"You're a herder, then?"

"From north of Iron Stem."

"You'll be knowing what to do then." Kesper nodded. "We'll see about that grain."

"I'd appreciate it, and so would he." Alucius inclined his head toward the gray.

As Kesper walked away, Kypler looked over the stall wall at Alucius. "How do you do it? They growled at the rest of us."

"I just try to be friendly," Alucius said. "Most of the time, it can't hurt."

Kypler laughed. "Unless you're dealing with brigands— or with Dolesy."

The two shouldered their gear, and carried their rifles, walking down the center of the stable and then out through the middle door—a door that had been created recently, Alucius could tell from the rough masonry that had yet to age or weather. Like the barracks in Sudon, the front of the Soulend barracks was an open assembly area. A trooper who appeared younger than Alucius stood just inside.

"What squad?"

"Second," Alucius answered.

"That's Delar's. He's the big blond squad leader over to the right."

Retius and Velon were already standing at rest before Delar, their gear at their feet.

The squad leader glanced across the two, then said, "You're Alucius, right?"

"Yes, sir."

"And you?"

"Kypler, sir."

"Good. Fall in. I hope we don't have to wait too long for the last two."

Before long, Oliuf and Akkar appeared.

"Now that you're all here," Delar began, "we can get through with matters, and then you can get something to eat. It's better than at Sudon, but not much, but there's usually plenty. Oh, and Oliuf . . . I want you to see the company surgeon right after dinner. The Company bunk spaces are laid out by squad. Take any one that's vacant. I'll be inspecting all your gear in the morning, and I mean all your gear. Rifles are to be stored in your footchest unloaded. Unloaded. I'll have your pay docked a copper if I find cartridges in the magazine or chamber. You load in the stable, after you're saddled. Is that clear?"

"Yes, sir."

"No fighting. Not in the squad. Not in the company. First offense is a month's pay. Second is a flogging. Self-defense is allowed . . . *but* . . . you'd better have a witness, and if I find anyone's lied about it, that's also a flogging. Understood?"

With barely a pause, Delar went on. "Gurnelt reported that you ran into some Reillies earlier today and took care of them. That's good. That's also the easiest fight you'll have in a long time. The better armed brigands, and they are mostly Reillies, have moved to the north of Soulend. This year most of them grew very little, and there are more of them in the steads they took over, so whatever the previous owners grew wasn't enough." Delar glanced across the faces of the new men. "Some of you are asking why we didn't protect those stead holders. It's simple. First, some of them were outside the boundaries of the Iron Valleys. Second, none of them ever paid tariffs for protection. Third, we don't have enough squads to patrol and hold every stead in more than a hundred vingts.

"We do regular patrols, by squad, and you're all lucky,

because second squad has tomorrow off. We will mount up and run through some commands and drills tomorrow, so that you're familiar with how I do things. I'm not supposed to say much, because Captain Heald will say more when we form up in the morning, but the Reillies don't look to be the big problem . . ."

Alucius refrained from nodding.

". . . we're beginning to get reports of Matrite patrols as close as twenty-five vingts to the west. Like I said, the captain will say more. Now . . . you're hungry, and you won't hear much more, So go pick out a bunk, and then I'll take you all over to the mess."

Alucius was more than ready for supper, no matter what it was.

44

Hieron, Madrien

The **Matrial stood before** the long windows, glancing at the two marshals still seated at the far side of the circular conference table.

"You are certain that the Iron Valley Militia has but one company of horse in Soulend?"

"Yes, Matrial," answered the blonde marshal. "They have one company of foot, and their Council has agreed to add one more company of horse by spring. If we attack, they may add one or two more companies, but with the new Lord-Protector reinforcing the Southern Guard along the Vedra, they will not be inclined to move many companies north."

"Even under attack?" The Matrial's eyebrows arched.

"They cannot provide what they do not have, and they do not have the golds to raise and supply additional militia forces. Certainly, neither you nor the Lord-Protector would lend them the golds."

"The Landarch of Deforya might, if only to keep the Lord-Protector occupied elsewhere."

"That is possible," agreed the graying and older marshal. After a long moment, she went on, "I beg your pardon, Matrial, but I must ask once more. Do we need to pursue this attack against the Iron Valleys? While they are not our friends, they will never present a threat to us, unlike the Lanachronans. Could we not lend them the coins and let them serve as a buffer between us and the Lord-Protector?"

"I understand your concerns," the Matrial replied, "but the Iron Valleys present a great threat. That threat is their very weakness. If we send them coins, we will not change the situation, and we will end up impoverishing ourselves. Their Council will take the coins and do little to strengthen their own forces. If they do spend more on their militia, they will place the new companies on our borders, not on the Lord-Protector's, because they worry more about raiders than about him." She turned from the window and walked back to the chair she had vacated where she seated herself gracefully. "As Marshal Aluyn said a few moments ago, the Council of the Iron Valleys cannot raise the coins to expand the militia. The Council is so short-sighted that its lack of preparation has made certain that the Iron Valleys will fall to someone. That would happen even if we sent coins. We all know that the Iron Valleys under the Council are not a threat. The Iron Valleys once taken by the Lord-Protector are a great threat. If we take the Iron Valleys, then Madrien will hold Dekhron and control the upper reaches of the River Vedra. That is a natural barrier that is far easier to defend—and far shorter than one running through the Westerhills. We will also be able to place forces across the river from Borlan or Tempre—or both. The seltyrs of Southgate will fall in the next few years. If we take Southgate, then we can control western Corus. If we do not, but if we hold the Iron Valleys, we are balanced. But if the Lord-Protector holds both . . ." The Matrial looked at the older marshal.

"We would be hard-pressed," the woman admitted.

"It will take the young Lord-Protector some time, perhaps

as long as a year, to consolidate his power in Tempre and throughout Lanachrona. He will not wish a war with Madrién during that time. Nor will he want to attack the Iron Valleys now. He would rather have them weakened, and he will wager that we cannot take them, since none have ever done so. But none have ever attacked in the way we have, and with the troopers and devices we have. The crystal spear-thrower is a fearsome weapon, already tested and proven against the barbarian Reillies. Also, we have three good high roads to use in attacking from the west and north. By the time he is ready to act, we will already have acted."

"You wish to take captives?" asked Aluyn.

"As we can. They will be useful against the Lanachronans." The Matrial smiled—coldly. "The Lord-Protector will attack in time. There is no doubt of that. A dustcat always uses its claws. That is why we are acting first, and while we can."

To that, both marshals nodded.

45

The entire Third Company lined up by squads— on foot—in the front inside area of the barracks, right after the second bell of the morning. Even inside the barracks the air was chill. The Third Company commander was Captain Heald, dark-haired, shorter than Alucius, and broader, with shoulders that would have better fitted a man two and a half yards in height. The senior squad leader was Ilten, a graying and rangy man with deepset eyes.

"Squad leaders, report!" Ilten ordered.

"First squad, all present."

"Second squad, all present," reported Delar.

When the reports were completed, Ilten turned to the captain, "All present or accounted for, sir. Third Company stands ready."

"Thank you, senior squad leader." Heald stepped forward. "Take ease, men."

The arrayed cavalry relaxed—slightly.

"We're finally at full strength for the first time since last spring, and we're supposed to get another company here by winter's end. That's why the masons are working on the other shed off to the back of the stable. They'll get to break in a new barracks, just like you veterans here did . . ."

Alucius could sense a certain humor in both the captain and the older men.

"That's the good news. The other news is that we're seeing more fires in the Westerhills. The Matrites are sending out their own raiding parties and burning every stead and hut they can find. So far, they're not moving in permanent camps for either foot or horse. With luck, they won't try that until spring. We can't count on luck, and once the replacements are settled in, we're supposed to intercept those raiding parties and destroy them. Depending on how everything goes, I'd judge we'll start in two weeks. We'll know more in a week.

"Fourth squad has the midroad patrol today, and first squad has the northside patrol. That's all. The rest of you have drills." Heald smiled. "You new men, take them seriously. They might save your life—or your flanker's." The captain paused, then snapped, "Dismissed to your squad leaders."

As simple as that, Alucius reflected. The Matrites were coming, first uprooting the Reillies and other brigands, and later to consolidate their hold on the Westerhills.

Delar cleared his throat. "Second squad. We'll be doing drills . . . one thing we'll be working on is the wheel from a column to a line abreast to bring the full firepower of the squad to bear on the enemy. That's real useful here, and we need to do it quick. All of you are dismissed to mount up— except Alucius and Geran. I need a few words with them, but they won't be long."

Both Velon and Kypler glanced at Alucius as they left to get their gear.

Geran was at least several years older than Alucius, a small bearded man with bright blue eyes and ginger hair.

Delar motioned for the two to step forward. "Geran, this is Alucius. Alucius, Geran. Geran's been our scout for the past year, but he'll be going to one of the new companies as a squad leader by spring." Delar looked at Alucius. "You mind being a scout?"

"No, sir. Not so long as I can do it myself, once I learn what's needed."

Geran grinned. "Another herder."

"How many sanders have you killed, Alucius?"

"Just three, sir."

"Sandwolves?"

"I'd guess a good ten-twelve."

"You killed one of the Reillies yesterday. Gurnelt said you kept your head and handled yourself well. I'd have expected that, but it's good to see in the field." Delar smiled. "You and Geran are going to do the scouting. That means you two lead the column, so that I can send you out when I need to, without wasting time because you have to move around or ahead through the column. It also means that I'm going to ride your ass, Alucius, on these drills, because you won't know enough. You understand it won't be personal."

"Yes, sir."

"Good." Delar nodded. "After the drills, and after we eat, we'll meet again. Then Geran will take you out and show you a few things. Now, you two mount up."

Alucius stiffened for a moment, then turned and hurried for his gear. Geran did the same, but without the impression of haste. Alucius noted the difference, hoping he could keep it in mind.

The mounted drills were just that—drills, set on the open ground to the east of the stead proper. Delar concentrated on basic formation moves, time after time, until the entire squad got them. First came the wheel to a firing line, then a wheel back to a double column, then an attack on the oblique. True to his word, Delar landed on Alucius.

"Alucius! You're on the outside. You have to move faster. You have more ground to cover."

"Alucius! You're slower than sander shit! Move that nag!"

"Alucius! The entire right flank lines on you! Set the interval right!"

"Alucius! . . ."

Despite the chill and the cold wind, by the time Delar called a halt to the drills, Alucius was sweating and soaked inside his undergarments and glad to get back to the stable.

Kypler looked over the stall wall. "Delar was hard on you."

"He was. I have a lot to learn."

"You were doing better than I could have."

"I feel like I'm back in camp at Sudon."

"Delar wants us all to feel that way."

Alucius laughed.

After their mounts were taken care of, the two walked from the stable to the mess. As Delar had said the night before, the midday dinner—a mutton and potato stew—was better than at Sudon, but not much. They had barely finished when Delar appeared with Geran.

Alucius carried his platter to the messman and tried to hurry back to Delar and Geran without giving the impression of haste.

Kypler smiled at Alucius as the three walked away from him and into the corridor outside the mess, where Delar stopped and addressed Alucius and Geran.

"I'm not a scout. I never will be. Good scouts save lives. Bad scouting costs lives. I have to leave *how* you scout to you two, but I hold you responsible for the results. The more you can tell me—or Ilten or the captain—about what's out there, the better we can do." The squad leader nodded. "Geran gets the job done. I've leaving it to him to make sure you can, too."

"Yes, sir."

With a nod, Delar was gone, leaving Alucius and Geran.

"Let's go back to the mess, and sit down," the older man suggested.

Alucius nodded. He was happy to do that. They took an empty table in the corner.

"You're a herder, and you've got that dark gray hair. That means you've got Talent," Geran said.

"Some," Alucius admitted cautiously.

"Enough that you can sense people?"

"If they're not too far away. A hundred yards, maybe farther. I've sensed sandwolves from farther, but I've never tried with people."

"That's good, and it's bad," the older scout said. "What I mean is that some herders just use their Talent. It's not enough. You have to look at the ground, the trees—when we're farther west and there are trees. Talent's best for sneaking around at night or in a storm when it's hard to see. A good scout without Talent will live longer than a Talented scout who doesn't learn."

That made perfect sense to Alucius. "I can see that. You'll show me what to look for?"

Geran grinned. "We'll do just fine if you keep thinking like that."

Alucius hoped so, but he was well aware that there was all too much he didn't know.

46

The winter morning on Londi was like so many in Soulend, gray and cold, with a thin wind whistling outside the mess, and chill air that had seeped through the old stone walls.

"You think we'll see any Reillies today?" asked Kypler.

Alucius looked across the table from his nearly finished egg toast, toast seemingly springier than coiled nightsheep wool, if more edible. "I don't know what we'll see."

"You've been the one scouting the roads and the steads with Geran," pointed out Kypler.

"That was teaching me what to look for. Tracking raiders and people is different from watching for sandwolves and sanders." Alucius took a last swallow of the hot cider, then stretched and rose from the table.

"How are you doing?" Kypler stood as well.

"Let's say that Geran thinks I might learn enough by the time he leaves for Seventeenth Company. There are too many little things I don't know."

Kypler laughed. "You don't like admitting you know anything."

"I have a lot to learn."

"Don't we all?"

At Kypler's dry tone, Alucius chuckled.

The two managed to get their mounts ready and to make it into formation outside the stable ahead of most of the new troopers, and about the same time as the fourteen veterans.

Once everyone was present, Delar rode up one side of the double column and down the other, offering a quick inspection, before ordering, "Squad forward!"

The wind more like a cold breeze than the harsh and bitter gales of previous days, and the smoke from the outpost chimneys rose directly up, rather than in the horizontal lines created by the fiercer winds. Still, Alucius was grateful for the warmth of the nightsilk against his skin.

"Less wind," offered Delar, riding for the moment at the head of the column, just in front of Geran and Alucius. "Might see some raiders today."

From the outpost, second squad turned right onto the eternastone midroad, called that because it was the middle road of the three high roads running east through the Iron Valleys. They rode due west across the open and gently rolling quarasote plains. Another seven or eight vingts ahead, was the last—and only—inhabited stead left near the midroad and on the eastern edge of the Westerhills. Just beyond the stead, in the first real hills, occasional junipers mingled with the quarasote that grew ever more scattered as the hills became higher and steeper.

"Scouts! If you'd ride van, about a vingt up front."

"Yes, sir."

"Squad! Guide on Vaskel!"

Alucius and Geran rode forward away from the main body of the squad.

For the next several vingts, as the road began to cut through the lower rises that were not quite hills, Alucius studied the ground and the road. Neither he nor Geran saw anything except the tracks of other militia patrols.

"Wager it'll be colder tomorrow," Geran ventured.

"Why do you think so?"

"When the wind's light, usually comes before a shift." Geran grinned. "In the winter, most shifts are colder."

Alucius could occasionally sense the red-violet of a sander, but the feeling was different, as if the sanders were deeper underground or somehow shielded. He could also feel but passing traces of the grayish violet of sandwolves. Even the scattered blue-gray flashes of grayjays were few.

Close to midday, on the midroad between the lower hills beyond the last true herder stead, where some of those slopes were treed thickly with pine and juniper, Alucius caught a whiff of acridness, not like the scent of the plateau with its metallic bitterness, but of fire. He glanced to Geran. "Something's burning . . . or burned."

"I smell it, too. Wood. You want to tell Delar that we're headed out to see if there's another burned hut? I'll wait."

"Will do." Alucius turned the gray back along the road toward second squad.

Delar rode forward to meet him. "What is it?"

"Something burned. Geran suggests that we should investigate and report to you."

"Where?"

"On the north side of the midroad, probably northwest. I'd guess within a vingt of the road, but we don't know."

"Go ahead. We'll close up after you."

Delar didn't have to add any cautions about being careful. Alucius could sense them as he replied, "Yes, sir."

When Alucius reached Geran, the older scout had reined up beside a track that led north, beginning between two junipers, positioned as if they were gateposts to the barely worn trail.

"Tracks here," Geran noted. "They're not ours. Not that new, either."

Alucius followed Geran's gesture. "They're headed north. The wind's from the north."

"We might as well check," Geran said, looking back over his shoulder. "Squad's less than half a vingt back. They can hear a rifle shot."

Alucius tried to sense if anyone was nearby, but neither eyes nor senses showed him anyone amid the scattered evergreens on the north side of the midroad. Both scouts had taken out their rifles as they rode along the gentle incline of the narrow trail as it wound between the trees. Even after several hundred yards, Alucius could still see sections of the gray stones of the midroad, and, occasionally, second squad as Delar neared the turnoff.

The smell of burning gradually grew stronger, but was far from overpowering.

As they rode around a thicker clump of bushy pines, a hut appeared. It had been little more than a two-room dwelling with a stable that had been more of a lean-to than a good shelter for a mount. The fires in both structures had long since burned out, except for a few lingering and smoldering embers, and the roof had collapsed inside the charred log walls of the hut.

Both men studied the hut, and the area around it, silent except for the faintest whisper of wind in the pines. The crude plank door lay where it had fallen on a rough stone stoop. The leather hinges had burned through, but there was no sign the door had been forced.

Geran eased his mount closer to the door, then shook his head. "Doesn't look or smell like anyone was killed here."

Alucius frowned. "Why would someone burn a hut if no one happened to be here? Matrites . . . just to force people out?"

"Could be. Most likely, but . . ." Geran paused. "More tracks. They head that way."

Alucius still could sense no one, but the two rode slowly, following the scattered hoofprints in the hard and near-frozen soil.

They rode less than half a vingt and found the bodies just past another denser clump of trees. They were sprawled in the open red-sandy soil between two junipers. There were a youth and a lean bearded man. Both were fully clothed, if in tattered rabbit-fur jackets and coarse brown trousers. Both men sprawled forward, as though they had been running and shot from behind.

"Notice anything?" Geran did not look at Alucius but continued to scan the area.

"Ah . . . there's nothing living within a vingt, Geran. Not besides rodents and snakes and birds."

"You can sense that?"

Alucius nodded. "Rather you didn't tell anyone but Delar." He already wished he hadn't revealed that, but seeing the bodies had momentarily left him off-guard.

"I won't. Now . . . what about the bodies?"

Alucius swallowed back the bile in his throat. "They're clothed . . . shot from behind."

"This was a Matrite raid," Geran said. "You see . . . no women. There were footprints of more than two. Matrites captured the women, sent them west, I'd guess." Geran gestured to the fallen figures. "They knew they'd be killed if they couldn't get away. Locals here wouldn't run unless there was a big Reillie raiding party, and you don't see many of those in the winter. Saw a bunch of clear hoofprints near the hut. All the shoes look the same. Military types, and that means either Lanachronan or Madrien."

Alucius nodded. A lot of the shoes of the militia troopers would still be different.

"Delar and the captain—they won't like this. Not twenty vingts from Soulend. Nothing else we can do here."

As Alucius turned his mount, he could feel the silver-green of a soarer. He glanced back over his shoulder. Geran's eyes followed those of Alucius. For a moment, they both looked at the hovering soarer, the green-tinged silver wings spread and moving so quickly that they blurred.

Alucius could feel something like sadness emanating from the soarer, but before he could feel more, the feminine-looking soarer vanished.

"What do you make of that?" Geran shook his head.

"I don't know," answered Alucius. Why would a soarer appear? And feel sadness? He'd never sensed that before, not that he'd seen more than a handful of soarers over his lifetime.

"Captain won't be happy with that, either. Don't need both soarers and Matrites showing up this close to Soulend."

"Soarers don't bother people. Not unless you bother them," Alucius said.

"That may be. Captain still won't be happy."

Alucius nodded. They still had to report to Delar, and the squad leader would want to see the bodies himself.

47

In the grayness before dawn, scarcely brightened by the oil lamps set at too-infrequent intervals in wall sconces in the mess, Alucius had no sooner seated himself next to Kypler and across from Akkar and Velon and set down his platter of breakfast than he heard his name.

He turned to see Delar crossing the mess. "Yes, sir?"

"Captain Heald wants to see all the scouts in his room right after breakfast, before morning muster. You've got time to eat. I'd advise seconds and whatever you can beg from the cooks."

With that, Delar was headed to the other side of the mess, calling out, "Geran!"

Alucius reseated himself.

"Glad I'm not a scout," Velon said. "Colder out there today."

"It's not that cold," Alucius said, cutting a strip of the tough egg toast with his belt knife.

"Not for you," said Kypler, "but for those of us who haven't spent every winter of their life fighting the icy winds on bitter rangeland, it's cold."

After Alucius had finished the egg toast, the overcooked pork strips, and the chewy dried apple slices, he went back for seconds. He even wheedled some biscuits from the cooks.

When all eight trooper scouts had gathered in the corridor outside the captain's spaces, a squad leader Alucius didn't know appeared and opened the door. "You scouts can all go in."

The captain's windowless room, lit by two oil lamps wedged in wall sconces, held an ancient rectangular table with stools set haphazardly around the sides and one end. At the other end was a chair as ancient as the table, and on the table before it, several stacks of papers. Heald stood behind the chair, his hands on the spooled back. "Take a stool."

Alucius hesitated slightly, then took a stool most of the way down the table.

The captain settled into his chair. "You all know the Matrite forces have raided within fifteen vingts of us. We need to know where they are—at least within four or five vingts."

He pointed to a map laid out on the table. "I'm assigning each of you a separate area. You're each to cover as much of that as you can each day for the next three. You'll report on what you find each night to Ilten. You are not to engage anyone in combat. You are to avoid fighting unless you clearly would be captured if you did not fight. Is that clear?"

"Yes, sir," came the murmured response.

"You will attempt to return each night before the second night bell. Be most careful. We will not send anyone to find you. If you get wounded, another scout may find your body by spring. Maybe."

All eight scouts nodded. Although Alucius was one of them, he wondered if they truly understood. Even on his own stead, Alucius had been very aware that if he vanished into a sandhole or a wash, even his own grandsire might not have been able to find him. Here, the land was wilder, the situation more dangerous, and no one would be looking.

"The cooks have a ration pack for each of you. You can pick those up on the way to the stable." The captain stood and pointed to the map. "You can see the sections here. Welkar, you have the northernmost area. Syurn, you have the area just south of Welkar's . . ."

After completing the assignments, Heald went on, "I have maps here for each of you. They're old, and they show some steads that are no longer there, but they're the best we can do."

Alucius had the southernmost section of those the captain had marked out.

"Do you have any questions?" After a moment, the captain nodded. "Dismissed."

The eight filed out, Alucius taking care neither to be first nor last.

After getting both gear and rations, and adding his hoarded biscuits to the rations, which seemed to be mainly hard cheese, travel bread, and dried beef of some sort, Alucius made his way to the stable, where he took special care in readying the gray and in checking his rifle. He'd planned to write Wendra, but, like many good intentions, that plan had been sidetracked. Perhaps when he returned.

Within half a glass, all eight scouts had formed up in a loose column outside the stable. The air was colder, and the clouds had lifted into a high silvery haze. The sun was without warmth, but the wind remained little more than a light breeze, but chill.

As the most senior, Geran led the way, with Alucius riding next to him. Geran didn't seem eager to talk, and Alucius wasn't about to break into the other's reticent silence.

Roughly three vingts west of the outpost, Alucius, Geran, and Henaar—the scout from squad five—turned off the gray eternastones of the ancient midroad, and south onto a narrow trail, leaving the five others to continue on their various ways. A good three vingts farther south, the three reached a stead of sorts—an oblong stone dwelling no more than ten yards long and five in depth, with two stone outbuildings, neither much larger than the dwelling. The stones were cut and dressed, but of all sizes and shapes, fitted together in jigsawlike walls. A line of gray smoke rose from the main chimney of the stead.

Geran took care to lead them well clear of the dwelling, and they were almost two hundred yards beyond the southernmost stone shed when they heard a voice.

"Troopers! Troopers!"

Geran turned his mount and brought out his rifle. Alucius did the same, as the three cavalrymen rode back toward the dwelling and the older man in a faded gray woolen jacket. They reined up a good twenty yards short of the holder. All had their rifles ready.

"Sirs . . ." The squat man bowed. "It's good to see you. I wish there were more of you, and you might be wishing that as well."

Alucius could sense the worry in the man, but inclined his head to Geran, as the most senior trooper. After a moment, so did Henaar.

"Why might that be?" asked Geran. "Have you seen brigands?"

The stead-holder laughed, gesturing toward the stone dwelling with the small windows. "Take more Reillies than live near here to sack my place." The laugh vanished. "Late the day before yesterday, that be Decdi, and it was near-on midafternoon, I was riding out west with my cart, gathering dead wood for my stove. At the top of one of the hills . . . there I saw riders, and there were more than a score, all in dark green, trimmed with red. Luck of a soarer, they didn't see me, and I hid behind a low pine till they had passed."

"Twenty of them?" asked Geran.

"Leastwise, sir."

"Have you seen any since then?"

"No, sir. But I'd be foolish to head that way, now, wouldn't I?"

Geran laughed. "That you would, good man. We will take

your words with great care, and we thank you for letting us know."

"Those wouldn't be the sander-souled troops of the Matrite bitches, would they?"

"Their colors are dark forest and crimson," Geran said evenly.

"The ancients save us," murmured the holder, although his tone conveyed resignation, rather than desperation. "That be them."

"Do you know if anyone else has seen them?"

The holder gestured around him, his arms taking in the low rolling hills. "There'd not be anyone I'd see to talk to, save Mereta, and she's been here with the fowl and the hogs."

"Thank you, holder," Geran said politely.

The man nodded, then backed away, and watched from his doorway as the three rode south.

"That's not good," Henaar said.

"We didn't expect anything else, did we?" replied Geran dryly.

Farther south of the holding, Henaar turned westward, leaving Geran and Alucius riding southward along the trail that was now scarcely more than a livestock path—if that.

After another half glass, Geran raised a hand. "Here's where I head west."

"Good luck," offered the younger scout.

"I don't rely on luck. You be careful, Alucius," Geran cautioned. "Dead scouts don't bring back useful information. They also don't return to their girls."

"I will." Absently, Alucius wondered how Geran knew, or was it that most young troopers had women they intended to wed? "You too. Dead scouts don't become squad leaders."

Geran laughed, then waved Alucius on his way.

Alucius rode southward alone, checking the small map against the terrain. A stead was shown on the map beyond a higher ridge that was supposed to have a creek on the far side. When Alucius reached the ridge, all he found remaining of the stead were piles of stone rubble, and the creek was dry and looked to have been for years. Not even quarasote grew out of the rubble.

Another vingt or so south, Alucius came to the remnants of what might once have been a narrow road. There were no tracks on the wind-and time-smoothed surface. He turned the gray westward. The morning had lightened, and he could feel a hint of warmth on his back, a sign that the sun was breaking through the hazy high clouds. The wind had earlier strengthened into a constant breeze, out of the north-northwest.

For the first few vingts, Alucius saw nothing large, although he sensed the deep and distant presence of sanders, and he could feel the gray-violet of sandwolves to the south, well to the south. There were the scrats that burrowed around the quarasote bushes, and the grayjays that scavenged almost anything, but nothing to command his attention. The hills became steeper with each vingt westward, and he passed two more long-abandoned steads. By late morning, he was seeing pines and junipers in scattered spots on the hills, as well as sections of ancient black lava beds. The road shown on the map did not exist, not in reality, save that where it had once run was a way that offered fewer bushes to avoid and no large gullies to work through or around.

He stopped in a sunny spot on the crest of one of the larger ridgelines sometime slightly after midday, a good glass after leaving the remnants of the road behind, and had some of the biscuits along with water from one of his two bottles. He'd already found a small pool where, after breaking the ice, he watered the gray.

The wind had picked up, and shifted even more to the north, and while he ate, Alucius studied the horizon to the northwest, where scattered clouds had appeared. By night, a storm might well be coming in.

With a deep breath he urged the gray on, westward, toward a thicker stand of trees that did not look natural. The stand of pines had indeed been planted, probably generations before, but there were only stone foundations left of what had once been an expansive dwelling, and several outbuildings.

After riding around the ruins, he also found tracks of a number of riders, and the shining brass of several recently discarded empty cartridge casings. The casings bothered him, because he could sense no large life nearby, and see no signs that anyone had lived there at any time recently. So at what had the Matrites been firing?

He circled the site, finally discovering the traces of an old road, heading west-southwest. Although the ground was hard enough that his own mount's tracks only occasionally showed, the traces of the Matrite riders were clear, if several days old.

Not without some trepidation he began to follow the old road, down along the hillside, and through a depression between hills, and then back along the ridgelines, heading more to the west, veering slowly northward.

It could not have been much past early midafternoon when Alucius sensed something . . . someone, at the edge of his Talent perceptions, a feeling of grayness, a sense-color he had not run across before. Most people came up as black, shot through with the brighter colors of emotion.

He eased the gray off the road and through the junipers on the eastern side of the ridge, and toward a farther crest, marked with an field of rugged black rocks. On the ridgetop, the wind was stronger—and far more chill, and the clouds on the western horizon had definitely thickened.

Less than three vingts away, in the flat between hills, on another road that apparently intersected the one he had been following, he could see, if intermittently, riders coming from the north. Despite the "grayness" of their Talent-feel, they wore riding jackets or coats that seemed black, although Alucius suspected, from what Geran had said, that the jackets were more likely a dark forest green. He watched for a time, until he had been able to count eight riders.

Carefully, he eased the gray along the back side of a rockier section of ridge, so that, if he were spotted, they would either have to climb over ancient broken rock or take a much longer circular route. He watched for nearly half a glass as the riders continued southward, and then turned west, presumably on the road he had been following. None of them so much as looked in his direction, and he could sense no other riders during the time he watched.

As they disappeared over another hill to the west, Alucius checked the sky. The clouds to the west were darker—and closer. The storm would be violent, and he needed to get back to the outpost, or as far as he could, before it struck.

Why would the Matrites send eight riders out? The number was too small to hold off a squad of militia cavalry and too large to scout effectively. Eight men sent separately could cover far more ground and report more. But . . . he'd report that as well.

48

The storm had come and gone in the night, leaving a handspan of snow dusted across the rolling plains and Westerhills. Quarasote, junipers, pines, and the occasional cedar, but slightly snow-dusted, stood out against the bright silver-green winter sky. Even without wind, the air was cold enough to freeze uncovered skin, as Alucius rode westward along the track he had taken earlier in the week.

In addition to Alucius, Geran and Henaar had reported seeing the Matrite patrol. Two other scouts had found burned-out cots. In one case, the inhabitants had either escaped or been captured. In the other, six had been slaughtered.

After hearing from all the scouts, Captain Heald had changed his orders. "Take rations for a week and head as far west as you need to—no more than three days. See what you can find . . ."

Now Alucius was already a good fifteen vingts west-southwest of Soulend, trusting to an out-of-date map and his own Talent-senses. This time, once he was well away from Geran, he had taken off his winter cap and eased on the black skull-mask, which had been quite an effort in itself, then replaced his cap. The skull-mask had two advantages, he discovered. His face was warmer, and the darkness around his eyes cut the glare of the light reflected from the snow.

In turn, the thin layer of snow also had advantages, in that Alucius could see the movements of small animals—and large ones—and would show more clearly recent travel, should he run across more Matrite patrols. It also left his movements far more open to be tracked, both by the Matrites and by sandwolves who liked to hunt, even in the Westerhills, after snowfalls.

By the time it was close to midday he was into the lower and easternmost sections of the Westerhills. He could sense, in the distance, the gray-violet of sandwolves, slightly to the south, but mostly west. He'd have to watch for them, for they were more likely to go after a single rider in the cold, especially if they were in a large pack.

Slightly after midday, Alucius found a thin trickle of clean water for his mount, and took the time to dismount, and stretch his own legs. He slowly chewed jerky that had been dried too long, then trail bread that made him sneeze because it was so hard and the crumbs from chewing were so fine that they ended up in the back of his nose. The cheese was cold and greasy, and he could only force down two small wedges before he packed up the rations.

After riding another glass or so, he studied the clear western sky and frowned, seeing the thinnest trail of smoke rising nearly straight up, so faint as to be almost undetectable. Even as he watched the smoke, it faded. He noted the direction on both the map and against the horizon.

He nodded as he sensed that the sandwolves seemed also to be located in that direction. Was the smoke the remnant of another holding burned out by the Matrites and where the sandwolves had found themselves a meal? Having nothing else to go on, and since the vanished line of smoke had been almost due west, Alucius continued riding in that direction, if with renewed caution. It didn't hurt that he was riding into the wind, although it was light, because that meant the sandwolves who lurked or roamed somewhere ahead wouldn't smell him.

He rode another glass, then two, up ridges and hills that all looked almost the same, with rocks poking up through thin white snow, then down into depressions where the snow had drifted boot deep. As he passed, scattered junipers and pines occasionally shed sprays of fine snow.

He stopped once more to water and rest his mount, and to have something to eat. All the while, he saw no traces of other riders. The few sounds were those of grayjays arguing over pine nuts and the scattered whisper of a winter hare slipping across the thin snow cover.

There was no further hint of smoke. Alucius wondered if he had imagined it, until he rode up the back side of a long slope and began to sense people—two sets of them, one the color-shot black that he expected from the hill-dwellers and the other the grayed feeling of the Matrite troopers. He immediately eased the gelding in behind a thicker clump of bushy pines until he could get a better feel for where each group might be.

The Matrites felt farther away, for they were almost at the edge of his Talent-perceptions, but their presence was growing stronger. The Reillies were nearby, very close, but obviously hidden, and silent. Alucius didn't care for that, and he urged the gelding forward, slowly, through the pines and farther upslope—only to discover that he was almost on the edge of an ancient wash. He reined up while still concealed by the pines and studied the miniature valley below.

After a time, tracks in the snow, mostly covered by the afternoon shadow, caught his attention, and he followed them northward with his eyes until he could see a hut, concealed with rock and brush, hidden on the western side of a small defile off the little valley. There was no movement around the hut, nor any sound. Recalling his grandsire's advice, he waited.

He waited half a glass, but still saw nothing except grayjays, two ravens, and a tree rat. While there was no movement from the hut, Alucius could sense the nearing presence of the Matrites, and the sandwolves that shadowed them. Absently, he wondered why he could feel the sandwolves from farther than he could the troopers. Did that have to do with the grayness that clouded them? And if whoever was in the hut knew about the Matrites, then why had he left such open tracks in the snow?

He stopped wondering as he heard the murmur of voices coming from the southern end of the small valleylike depression. He watched and waited. Before long, through his screen of pines, he could see the Matrite patrol below—eight strong, which Alucius was beginning to believe was the usual number for the Matrite scouting patrols.

The Matrites had their rifles out, as if they had been tracking something. Perhaps they had wounded the Reillie? Alucius didn't know. He was even more puzzled when the patrol halted, almost directly below him. Then he realized that the troopers must have worried about the narrowing of the wash. He looked down at the patrol less than a hundred yards from him—much more like fifty—then toward the cot. He didn't like the idea of watching while they slaughtered another family, but he liked even less the idea of taking on eight men.

He cocked his head. He could project ideas and senses to the nightsheep. Could he do the same to the sandwolf pack? Offer an image of fresh killed horses? He certainly wouldn't be attacking the patrol. The sandwolves weren't that far behind the Matrites.

He concentrated on sending the image, focusing on the image of the trailing rider's mount, suggesting it was lame, vulnerable, weak—and good prey. As he tried to send forth the image, he watched as the riders, rifles held at the ready, discussed something. Then two riders eased away from the other six, and circled back toward a gentler slope on the far side of the wash, where they began to climb up.

Abruptly, four wolves flashed from the pines beside the last rider of the six below, their glittering crystal fangs ripping at the mount. Within moments, two sanders had appeared out of the side of the wash—where there was sandier soil—almost upon the lead rider. The trooper's horse reared, and the Matrite trooper struggled to stay in the saddle.

The second and third riders had their rifles out and began to fire at the sanders. Chips of the sanders' hard skin splintered away, and crystalline liquid oozed from their wounds, but they turned toward their two attackers, closing the ground between them and the troopers with a speed every bit as swift as a galloping horse. Two more troopers began to fire at the sanders.

As the lead trooper managed to regain control of his mount, a single shot rang through the momentary quiet, a shot from above the cot farther up the narrow wash valley. The shooter caught the squad leader full in the chest, and Alucius could feel the cold black shock—and then the red emptiness—of sudden death.

With that, he had his own rifle out and cocked. His first shot missed, but no one heard in the commotion below. His second and third didn't. His fourth did, but no one was watching, because the second sander had grasped and killed one of the mounts—and its rider. Another trooper went down under the fire of the Reillie in the cot.

The trailing trooper had lost his mount, brought down by the sandwolves, and the trooper had jumped free. As the Matrite ran across an open space between two junipers, Alucius put a shot into his midsection, then quickly began to reload.

Quick as he was, by the time he had the rifle ready to fire again, none of the troopers directly below was standing, and the two who had been climbing out of the wash had urged their mounts into a gallop, back southwest.

A sense of shimmering silver-green flowed over Alucius, flooding through his Talent-senses. He could not help but look to the northeast, practically over his shoulder, at the soarer who had appeared from nowhere, its wings a twinkling silver-green. Then, as quickly as it had appeared, it vanished.

Why another soarer? Did they follow death? Or sanders? Alucius swallowed and gathered himself together. He could sense that five of the troopers were dead, and one was dying.

He forced himself to ease the gray downhill, out of any line of fire from the log hut, and then to the south where he could follow the fleeing men. He wagered that the two would be heading back to their encampment or outpost, and he didn't want to lose the opportunity to discover where it was.

The Reillie and his family could certainly take care of one mortally wounded Matrite. Still, Alucius wanted to be very careful in leaving the area, because he didn't want to be the next victim of the Reillie's all-too-accurate aim. He kept his senses spread, ignoring the gorging of the sandwolves on the two downed mounts, as he slipped south and then westward in the waning sun of late afternoon.

Only when he was well clear of the hut, did he take a deep breath. Then he concentrated on tracking the two men who seemed to be retracing their own tracks westward, along an old way that was more than a trail, less than a road.

The two Matrite troopers were still heading westward as the sun touched the western horizon, although they had stopped several times, as had Alucius. As day slipped into twilight, Alucius could smell smoke again, but it was the smoke of stoves or cookfires. He rode forward even more carefully, trying to be alert with all his senses, and his Talent, drawing in more of the gray-tinged Matrite troopers—and a handful of sandwolves to the north.

The Matrite encampment was on a rise in the middle of a long north-south valley, and the cookfires beamed out almost like beacons. The scent of roasting meat made Alucius's mouth water, but he swallowed as he tied his mount to a cedar branch—a sturdy one—and eased through the clump of trees to where he could look out toward the encampment to see what he could before the light faded.

Alucius located the position, as well as he could on his map. He also counted the numbers of mounts he could see on tie-lines, the number of cookfires, and the five wagons, including the three that seemed to be filled with something heavy, like stone, or iron. From what he could tell, there were close to five companies of cavalry and twice that of foot. Just in one force, the Matrites had mustered something like ten times what the militia had in Soulend and probably as big a force as the Iron Valleys could mount anywhere without stripping everything of protection.

As Alucius watched and took notes, and as the twilight faded, he could sense someone well to the north, also watching, perhaps one of the other scouts, but he didn't know.

He eased back to the gray, and then rode for almost a half a glass until he could find a spot where he could rest and water his mount, and where he could offer the small amount of grain to the gray. Before long, he would need to find a place to sleep, at least for a time, and one where he and his mount couldn't be easily surprised.

49

While the nightsilk undergarments and skull-mask kept Alucius warm, he had slept fitfully, although he could sense no sanders nearby, and the closer sandwolves seemed to be to the north of the Matrite encampment. The wind remained chill and biting, and his breath steamed. He noticed the chill mostly when breathing deeply, because his lungs protested and the inside of his nostrils felt frozen.

Since he scarcely had enough information to return and report, he was up well before dawn, and back checking the encampment. In the hazy, but stronger light of dawn, he could see that his initial judgment of the location of the camp had placed it too far south, for he could see the midroad less than half a vingt to the north of the low rise on which the Matrite force had camped. Alucius had clearly been more tired than he'd realized the night before.

He watched as the horns offered signals, and as the entire camp was packed up. A six-horse team was being readied to move the lead wagon, while those that followed had but four. He would have liked to see what was in the lead wagon. All his Talent-senses told him was that it was somehow both very new and very old, and that a sense of danger surrounded it. His best guess was that it was a weapon, and that the wagons that followed carried equipment it required. But those were only guesses, and he didn't like the idea of reporting something so uncertain.

The other scout was nowhere within his senses, and Alucius wondered if the man had headed farther westward or back toward Soulend.

Within a glass of dawn, scout patrols were assembling. Alucius remounted the gray and rode eastward, but onto a concealed position on a higher ridge, waiting and watching. The patrols headed eastward as well, and the entire Matrite force followed, with the four wagons in the middle of the column, rather than at the end.

Once Alucius was certain of that, he rode down the eastern side of the ridge, then angled northeast to pick up the midroad, and to make his way back to Soulend. There was little doubt in his mind—or in the actions of the Matrite troops—that they were headed through the remainder of the Westerhills toward Soulend—another Legacy of the Duarches that the Iron Valleys could ill afford.

50

Even with the greater speed afforded Alucius by taking the midroad, it was past midafternoon before he rode into the encampment. He had managed to wiggle out of his skull-mask before nearing Soulend, and the cold wind had made his face raw enough by the time he dismounted outside the stable that no one would have guessed he had such a mask. He hastily stabled and groomed the gray, and arranged for fodder and water with the company ostler before hurrying into the barracks to find Ilten.

He didn't see Ilten around and went to the captain's spaces

to inquire. A very young trooper, looking no older than Alucius, was standing guard.

"I'm looking for Senior Squad Leader Ilten," Alucius said. "I just got back from scouting, and there's something he should know."

"He's with the captain."

"They really should know," Alucius said politely, projecting a sense of urgency.

"He said they weren't to be disturbed."

Alucius swallowed silently, not quite understanding the rage he felt, then used his Talent to let it pour out toward the hapless trooper. The trooper almost cringed against the door.

"You'd best let them know . . . now," Alucius said mildly.

The man glanced at Alucius as if the scout were a sandwolf, then ducked inside the door.

Ilten appeared—without the trooper.

"Sir, reporting as ordered, sir," Alucius said.

"You're back early." Third Company's senior squad leader sounded less than pleased, and he radiated displeasure.

"That's because the Matrites are marching eastward along the midroad toward Soulend," Alucius replied. "They only have patrols out flanking the road. They have about five companies of horse and close to ten of heavy foot. They all packed up right after dawn and headed east on the midroad."

"Are you sure?" asked Ilten.

"Yes, sir."

Ilten sighed. "You'd better report this to the captain directly." He turned and opened the door, motioning for Alucius to enter before him.

The guard trooper eased out behind Ilten, not looking anywhere at the returned scout.

Captain Heald glanced from the departing trooper to Alucius. "Did you threaten Barka?"

"No, sir. I did tell him that Senior Squad Leader Ilten needed to hear my report now."

Heald frowned.

"You should hear what he has to say, sir," Ilten said mildly.

"What is so important, then, scout?"

"The Matrites left their camp and are marching the midroad toward Soulend. They should be clear of the Westerhills by twilight. They have about five companies of horse, and seven to ten of heavy foot."

"Show us where this camp was." Ilten pointed to the map on the long table.

Alucius studied the map, then checked his own, and finally pointed. "There. That's where they were set up, less than a half vingt south of the midroad on a rise."

"Have you talked to Waltar?" asked Ilten.

"Waltar?" Alucius didn't have to act surprised. "Sir . . . I don't know Waltar."

"You've met him. He's the seventh squad scout."

"I might recognize his face, sir, but I've never seen him close up outside of this room."

"Well . . . both you and Waltar gave the same location, but he came back in the middle of the night." Ilten nodded. "How did you find that encampment? And why did you stay? Oh . . . you can sit down."

Both Ilten and the captain reseated themselves.

"Thank you, sir." Alucius took the stool across the table from Ilten. "I was following orders, sir, trying to find the Matrites. It was maybe midafternoon yesterday, and I'd seen a thin trail of smoke. The Reillies had to know that the Matrites were around. So I thought there was a chance that it was another burned hut. With the snow, I figured I might be able to follow their traces—if they'd burned the hut, that is."

"Go on. I'd like to hear how the smoke led to the encampment," Ilten said dryly.

"I'm a herder, sir. I could sense that there were sandwolves around. I thought that meant bodies. I was very careful to keep downwind of the sandwolves when I was moving in to see what had happened. There was a hut, hidden up in the rocks, and there was a flat little valley below. The Matrites saw the smoke, too. I could feel horses, and that meant troopers. You told us not to get involved, but I couldn't move, not without being seen. So I waited. The sandwolves must have been hungry. They went after the mount of the last rider."

"They went after a Matrite trooper? I find that hard to believe," the captain snorted.

"You want me to take you out there and show you the bones and the hut, sir?"

"Go on," Ilten said quickly.

"The Reillie must have figured that was his chance. He put a bullet through the leader. Then things got really strange, because a sander appeared and took out a trooper and his mount. There had to be someone else firing, because two more of their troopers went down."

"And I suppose you sat there and did nothing?" asked Heald.

"No, sir," Alucius replied. "The trooper who lost his mount to the sandwolves got clear, but he started running right toward where I was hiding. I figured that with the Reillies all shooting, no one would hear me. I shot him. Then I waited a bit and circled south and followed the survivors straight back to their camp after that, but I got there so late that it was hard to see what they had. So I holed up out of sight and came back to their camp before dawn." Alucius cleared his throat. "There's one other thing, sir. They've got a big heavy wagon, and it takes a six-horse team, and there are three other wagons with it. They're not supply wagons, and they're all covered. They're in the middle of the column. I couldn't find any way to see what it is, but where they have it, and the way it's traveling, I think it's some sort of weapon."

Ilten and the captain exchanged glances.

"We'll keep that in mind," Heald finally said. "Is there anything else?"

Alucius considered. "Just one thing. The Matrites don't seem to send out single scouts. The few times I've seen them, they've had an eight man patrol."

"That might help us . . . a bit." Heald nodded to Ilten.

The senior squad leader stood.

So did Alucius.

Ilten walked out with Alucius. Once he closed the door to the captain's space, he motioned the young guard away, before turning back to the scout. "Alucius?"

"Yes, sir?"

"A couple of things. First, don't tell anyone the details of what you reported. That's the captain's job. He'll talk to Delar shortly, and he won't like it if your squad leader has already found out from you. Neither will I. You can say that you ran across the Matrites, and you gave the information. Let it go at that."

"Yes, sir."

"Now . . . just what did you tell Barka?"

"Just what I told you, sir."

Ilten laughed. "*How* did you tell him?"

"Well, sir . . . I *was* angry, but I didn't say a word, just what I said."

"I imagine you have a way of expressing anger within the rules, Alucius. Most herders do. Just don't do it often."

"Yes, sir."

"The captain and I know you left out a few details. Make sure that they stay left out."

Alucius could sense a wry amusement, not hostility or anger. "Yes, sir. I tried very hard to follow orders, sir."

"I'm sure you did, trooper. But you can't always rely on helpful sandwolves and sharpshooting Reillies to bail you out. You wouldn't know it, but two of you scouts aren't back yet. I hope they will make it back. Go get some sleep. You'll need it. We'll have to be ready for anything."

"Sir? What might happen?"

Ilten shrugged. "The captain's already requested reinforcements, after Waltar's report. We'd hoped the Matrites wouldn't move so fast. We'll do what we can. Now . . . you look like death. Get some food and rest. You can tell the cooks I said to find you something to eat."

"Yes, sir. Thank you, sir."

Ilten nodded, then turned and re-entered the captain's room.

As he headed for the mess, Alucius hoped that Geran wasn't among the missing.

51

The next morning—Alucius found it hard to believe it was Sexdi—found Third Company mustered in its entirety in the barracks. Alucius was relieved to see Geran, even if the older scout's eyes were rimmed with deep and black circles.

Outside, the wind had subsided into a moan, and the day was fair and cold. Inside, the captain's eyes surveyed the troopers. Finally, he spoke. "You all know we've been scouting the Matrite force. They're on the midroad moving toward Soulend. If they push, they could be here in two days, or sooner. I sent a second messenger to militia headquarters requesting reinforcements. We can't wait for them. So we're going to attack—like sandwolves, when and where they least expect it." Captain Heald stepped back.

Ilten stepped forward. "Pack your gear for a week's ride— light on comfort, except for warmth. You have one glass. Then you'll stand down. We could ride this afternoon or tomorrow. You'll get your rations and cartridges for your rifles from your squad leader after you've been inspected and passed, and before we ride out. Dismissed to your squad leaders."

Alucius kept his frown to himself. His grandsire had foreseen what was occurring more than a year before. Why hadn't the Council put more companies in the north? Was it that the north was expendable to the merchants of Dekhron?

"Second squad, stand easy," ordered Delar.

There was the slightest shuffling of feet.

"You heard the captain. When I dismiss you, get your gear

ready, and have it on your footchests. Then I want you to check your tack and your mounts. Then come back to the barracks bay." Delar paused. "Geran, Alucius, I need a moment from you two. The rest of you are dismissed to get ready."

The other eighteen troopers fell out, leaving the two scouts with the squad leader.

Delar looked at Geran, then at Alucius. "Anything I ought to know?"

"Sir, I don't know what Ilten and the captain told you," Alucius replied.

"He said that there were too many Matrites, but that we had to do something to slow them down, or they'd be marching into Dekhron by spring." Delar glanced from Alucius to Geran.

"I saw four companies of horse," Geran offered. "Could be more."

"Could be at least that many heavy foot," Alucius added.

Delar nodded. "Another frigging Legacy. Stinks worse than soarer shit. Anything else?"

"They don't like to send out small patrols. Eight or more," Alucius said.

"They've got smaller bore rifles. Probably have a larger magazine with more cartridges. Bullets go farther, maybe more accurate," suggested Geran.

Alucius's respect for Geran rose as he realized how close Geran must have gotten. Either that or Geran had ambushed enough of a patrol to collect arms.

"Good to know." Delar cleared his throat. "Anything else?"

"Not that I can think of," Alucius admitted.

"Dismissed."

As the two scouts walked toward second squad's barracks bay, Alucius said, "How did you get so close? If you don't mind . . ."

Geran grinned. "I didn't. I kept my eye out for spent casings. Found enough of them. They're all the same. You'd expect that from either the Matrites or the Lanachronans."

He fumbled in his tunic, then extracted a brass casing that he passed to Alucius.

Alucius examined it. "Only a little more than half the size of ours . . ." He realized, belatedly, that he could have discovered the same thing. He'd seen casings in the hills—another reminder that he hadn't thought things through.

"About two thirds. Shell is longer, too."

"They're not used to dealing with sandwolves. Some of them got surprised by them."

"They aren't fighting sandwolves. They're after us," Geran said.

Alucius could see Geran's point.

After packing his gear, Alucius left it on his footchest and headed out to the stable, where he checked the gray carefully. His Talent-senses confirmed that his mount was in decent shape."

Kesper appeared at the end of the stall. "Alucius . . ."

"Thank you. You gave him some extra grain, didn't you?"

Kesper nodded. "Try to do that with all the scouts' mounts. There's some extra in the corner there. Best you take it with you." He paused. "Word is that . . . things could get tight."

"They could. The Matrites are riding this way. The captain has some plan to slow them, but I don't know what it is."

"Nothing likely to stop the iron bitches."

"We'll see."

Kesper shook his head. "Wouldn't want to be any of you." He offered a forced smile to Alucius. "You take care." Then he was gone.

Alucius went over his riding gear. All the time, he just hoped that the captain had a *very* good plan. He had barely returned to the barracks when Delar and Geran appeared.

"The captain wants to see all scouts," Delar said. "In his study."

Alucius and Geran followed orders and made their way to the captain's study.

Ilten was waiting, as were several other scouts—Syurn, Henaar, and Waltar.

"The captain will be here in a moment," offered Ilten, who resumed smoothing out a long map on the table.

"This one's not going to be so easy," Geran predicted in a low voice. "The captain's going to want to know where everything is—sentries, picket lines—"

Ilten lifted his head and cleared his throat—loudly. "You might be right, Geran, but why don't you let the captain tell you?"

"Yes, sir." Geran did not sound abashed.

Two other scouts that Alucius did not know by name stepped into the room, so that seven scouts stood around the table.

Almost immediately, Captain Heald appeared. "I'm glad to see all of you. Before we can act, we need to know where the Matrites are set up—if they are, or if they're still on the march, and what their deployment or their camp layout is. Our patrols haven't seen them within six vingts of here on the midroad. There's only one decent stead out there—I sent a messenger, suggested to the herders that they leave, but we don't know if they did. Place would make a solid bivouac— with shelter for the troopers and most mounts. It's about eight vingts out, just at the base of the hills. I'd camp there, but that doesn't mean they will."

Heald paused and focused on the senior scout. "Geran, you'll be in charge of the scouts."

"Yes, sir."

"Once you have an idea of where the Matrites are, I want half of you to swing south of the road, and half north and each take a quarter. Geran will assign you as he thinks best. Try not to be seen. Don't do anything stupid. We'll need every one of you before this is all over." The captain looked from scout to scout, ending up with Geran. "I expect you all on the road in less than a quarter glass. Dismissed."

"Yes, sir," replied Geran.

Alucius waited for Geran to move, and then followed the older scout out and toward the barracks bay, where they collected their gear.

"Road patrols didn't tell him enough," Geran said to Alucius as the two walked toward the stable. "They never do."

"You think the Matrites are at that stead?"

"Where else?" Geran laughed. "In this weather, you go for shelter. They haven't tried to take Soulend. That doesn't leave much this far north."

After saddling their mounts and packing their gear, the two waited with their mounts inside the stable doors until they were joined by all of the other five scouts. Then, without ceremony, they led their mounts out into the chill, mounted, and rode away from the post and onto the midroad. Alucius rode alongside Geran, and Henaar and Waltar were immediately behind them.

Except for the road patrol, the midroad was empty, a gray line stretching westward all the way to the ruins of ancient Elcien, though that was more than six hundred vingts away. Alucius wondered if the road remained as untouched there as in the Iron Valleys.

By midmorning, a half-glass later and two vingts west of the militia outpost, there was still no wind to speak of. From the clouds to the west, Alucius knew another storm would be coming in. The snow had not melted in most places, but light as it was, the previous day's wind had swirled it into heaps around the quarasote bushes, so that the ground resembled a patchwork of snow, gray-green quarasote bushes, and red-sandy soil. Although he had a riding scarf wrapped across his face, it wasn't nearly so warm as the skull-mask. That was tucked inside his tunic.

Geran finally turned in the saddle and studied the six other scouts. "I'd like Narlet, Balant, and Syurn to take the north side of the midroad when the time comes. You probably won't have to circle out as far because the stead is on the south side, but there is one shed on the north, and they might have mounts or foot there . . . Waltar, on the south side, you'll have the quarter just south of the road, and I'll take the one after that. Henaar will take the south-southwest quarter, and Alucius will take the quarter south of the road on the west end of the stead. Remember, we need information. It doesn't do much good to leave your dead body there because we don't get any information at all that way, and killing one or two Matrites won't change much. . . ."

Alucius knew that part of the orders was for him, although Geran never looked in his direction.

"We won't try to meet. Once you've gotten as much information as you can, withdraw and take it back to Ilten and the captain at the outpost. Any questions?"

"Ah . . . does anyone know what happened to Welkar?" That came from Narlet, a stocky scout from the third squad, not much older looking than Alucius.

"No one's seen him," Geran said. "He still could be out there. Or . . ."

The others nodded.

After yet another half-glass of measured riding on the midroad, they all could see thin trails of smoke rising into a sky that was becoming less silver-green and grayer and grayer.

"Captain was right," murmured Henaar from where he rode behind Alucius. "Too many fires for a normal stead."

Even without the smoke, and from more than four vingts away, the concentration of Matrite troopers was obvious to Alucius's Talent-senses, the grayness so blatant that he half-wondered why he hadn't felt it when he'd neared the previous Matrite encampment while he had been tracking the two patrol survivors. Had he been too tired? Or did the "grayness" just blend into all the other sensations until he'd become aware of what it meant?

"Halt!"

Geran's order nearly took Alucius by surprise, so preoccupied with Talent-sensing he had been, but he managed to pull up the gray with the other scouts.

"We're nearing where they'll have road patrols, if they have any sense," Geran said. "Time to break off and circle around. Some of you may not be able to get close. If there's no cover, no washes, or gulches, or trees . . . don't force it. Just watch from a distance."

Henaar nodded. So did Waltar.

As Waltar angled away from the road and toward what looked like a low wash, Geran led Alucius and Henaar on a circuitous path behind another low rise that was barely perceptible. Once they were behind the rise, they couldn't see the lower sections of the smoke trails—or be seen by any road patrols that the Matrites might dispatch.

After they had traveled another two vingts and crossed a low depression to yet another long and low rise, Geran reined up. So did Henaar and Alucius.

"I'll be heading north-northwest from here. I'd judge you'll need to ride another vingt or so before you head in, Henaar. Alucius—I'd make sure you're almost in the hills before you head in, just south of the road."

As Henaar and Alucius continued riding, now moving almost due west, the wind picked up, even colder than the day before, and coming from a few points to the east of due north.

Henaar finally reined up, looking northward. "Looks like there's a series of little rises I can move north behind."

"Good luck," Alucius said. "I'll see you back with the company."

"Same to you."

Once he was well clear of Henaar, Alucius took off his winter cap and slipped the skull-mask out of his tunic. As before, it took a while to work it into place. Then he put his cap back on. Mindful of Geran's advice, he did not even begin to ease his way northward until the low rises began to resemble small hills, and showed scattered low pines and junipers. His Talent-senses told him that, except for small wildlife, there were no large living things within nearly a vingt, although he could sense the mass of gray that was the Matrite force to the northeast.

Another half glass later, he studied the land from the concealment of a juniper at the crest of a low hill, taking in the stead in the distance to the northeast. He began to move more to the east, through the junipers that offered concealment, but before long, he began to sense riders. From the grayness he felt, he judged they were Matrite riders.

Riding farther eastward and north, he found a low hill that offered more cover, and one where he could sense at least

one rider somewhere beyond the eastern side. Alucius tied
the gray on the back side of the rise, in the middle of a clump
of junipers halfway up. He took the rifle as he made his way
up the rest of the hill, then settled behind the base of an older
pine to survey the area. The trees thinned on the east side of
the rise below him, and continued to become more and more
spread toward the flat to the east, where there were few trees
and more than a few scattered quarasote bushes.

With the wind now blowing out of the northeast, he could
smell the cookfires—and an odor that was familiar—and yet
not. After a moment, he realized it was the smell of fresh-
cooked nightsheep. A cold smile crossed his face. If roasted
nightsheep were what the Matrites were eating, there would
be a number of very sick troopers for several days, unless
they were very different from other people, and he doubted
that. Only the sandwolves, the grayjays, the black vultures,
and a handful of other animals could tolerate nightsheep meat
without adverse effects.

He could sense someone nearing—not that close, but close
enough for him to be careful.

Below the rise, well back in the wide flat that was almost
a valley, a Matrite trooper rode north, toward the midroad.
Alucius watched as the man, his breath a white fog in the
early afternoon, let his mount carry him northward until he
reached the midroad. There, the mounted sentry surveyed the
road, before turning his mount and riding back past Alucius.

Alucius waited until the picket rider rode his post a second
time and passed southward once more. The rider took almost
a quarter glass each way on his post. Alucius's Talent-senses
showed him that there were others not too far away, and, of
course, a pack of sandwolves farther to the northwest. He
did not sense any sanders—or soarers.

Once the picket rider was out of sight, Alucius slipped
down the gentle slope, easing from tree to tree, still carrying
the heavy rifle. He vowed to concentrate on following
Geran's example, to pick up information in ways that would
be effective and less dangerous.

On the flat, the trees were spread farther apart, and Alucius moved deliberately from tree to tree, keeping low and moving slowly, trying to make sure he was concealed from the picket he had slipped past, as well as any sentries he might find ahead.

He found them, mainly through his Talent-sense—single foot patrols, each waiting behind the few remaining pines, each with a thin-looking rifle. The three posts he could find were each roughly a hundred yards from the next. Lying nearly flat, he checked his map against what he could see, and against where he knew the midroad to be.

Crack! The sound of the rifle was higher and thinner than those used by the militia, and Alucius froze, trying to determine if he had been seen. But he heard nothing, and he could sense no one moving toward him—or any of the sentries moving at all. The report had been close enough that it had to have been one of the foot sentries.

He forced himself to wait, to be patient, as his grandsire had told him, because he knew that he hadn't been seen. He would have sensed something—fear, excitement, apprehension. But why had a sentry fired? Or had the trooper fired at a grayjay or a scrat?

A good half glass passed, during which Alucius memorized as he could the positions of the sentries. There seemed to be little but open space—and scattered quarasote bushes—between the foot sentries and the stead and bivouac area. Certainly, neither his senses nor his eyes revealed any movement there, and it was open enough that the only way to cross it would be on his stomach—after taking out at least one sentry.

No other sentries fired weapons, and finally, Alucius squirmed his way back around the quarasote bushes and spines, back over one low rise, and then another, until he could sense the mounted picket. He waited some more, before he eventually slipped back to his mount.

He rode northward another half vingt to where he could clearly see the midroad from a taller hill. There was a hastily built revetment post of heaped earth with at least eight foot troopers guarding the road.

Then, in the light that was well past midafternoon, Alucius turned his mount back south and then eastward, feeling that he should have discovered more, but knowing that he didn't know enough to have done so, not without killing someone—and he'd been effectively ordered not to do anything of the sort.

As he rode eastward, well south of the midroad and the Matrite sentry lines, the wind blew into the side of his face, and he was glad for the skull-mask, and sorry that he did not dare to wear it except when alone, because the woolen scarf was barely adequate to protect his face against frostbite in the chill northern winds.

52

Although he was the last scout to return—well after twilight—and report his findings, Alucius managed to get dinner from the cooks before Geran found him in a corner of the mess.

"Thought you might be here. How did it go?"

"Long . . . cold," mumbled Alucius through a mouthful of overcooked stew. He took another bite of the bread, and a swallow of cider that was beginning to turn. "Picket sentries and foot inside them. Someone shot at a scrat or something. Thought they'd seen me." He took another mouthful of the barely warm stew.

"The captain and Ilten want all the scouts in a meeting."

"Now?" Alucius took another gulp of cider.

"Now."

Alucius groaned and gulped down another mouthful before rising and carrying the platter back to the mess boy. Then he followed Geran.

The captain's room was crowded, with Heald, Ilten, Troas—the undercaptain of the foot company—and his senior squad leader, and the five squad leaders of Third

Company seated around the long table, and the seven scouts standing behind them.

The captain looked around the room, then cleared his throat, before speaking. "I've heard from all the scouts. We're looking at a force of four to five companies of horse, possibly twice that many of heavy foot. They also have wagons not being used for food or transport, and that might mean some sort of weapons we haven't seen." Heald offered a grim smile. "We have a company of horse, and one of foot, and it will be at least a week before we get reinforcements."

Left unsaid was the possibility that they might get no reinforcements.

"We have to stop them, or at least slow them down. They've got more men and equipment. What we have to work with is the land and the winter. They've already lost a few men to sandwolves and Reillies, and Ilten and I have come up with a plan that should cost them even more, and shouldn't cost us much at all." The captain stood and pointed to the hand-drawn map on the table. "Once I've explained the plan, I'd like all of you, including the scouts, to take a good look at the map. That's so you'll see how your actions fit into the plan."

"First, we're going to set up before dawn. The plan is simple enough. They've got heavy patrols and revetments on the midroad. They've already figured that we're not likely to attack through the quarasote flats, not with what it can do to a mount at full speed or a footman under attack. They're wrong." Heald grinned.

Even Ilten smiled, if faintly.

"We've found a road—a lane, really, but it's clear of quarasote, that runs within a half vingt of the south side of the stead where they've camped. We'll attack before dawn tomorrow. But it'll be a different kind of attack. It'll be two-pronged. First, most of their mounts are in the old main nightsheep shed. Strong place. Stone walls, slate roof, hard-packed floor. The scouts are going to take out the sentries in the southeast quarter. Then fifth squad will ride in and storm the shed entrance, and throw in some special explosives and a few other items—and jam the doors shut. That will make a dent in their mounts and horse teams. Then, fifth squad will withdraw—and wait in plain sight. When they counterattack, we'll spring the second trap." Heald smiled, and nodded at Ilten.

"They've got sentries posted in two circles," the senior squad leader began, "one set of foot about a half vingt out, between fifty and a hundred yards apart. Another half vingt out, they have picket lines, roving patrols. It's a thin line of sentries, and we think they can be taken out. They'll hear some shots in the dim light, but they won't be sure where they're coming from."

"What about the quarasote?" asked the undercaptain. "That'll cut up men and mounts."

"There's a back lane on the south side that runs almost parallel to the midroad for about a vingt before it turns south," Heald replied. "The quarasote bushes are thick there. We've got five squads of foot. I want them set up just outside the Matrite perimeter. Then, when the scouts take out the sentries, they'll move forward through the quarasote here—" Heald pointed to a spot on the map to the south of the stead and the midroad.

"The Matrite horse will run them down," the undercaptain of foot protested. "You can't be sure of getting all their mounts."

"Not through quarasote that thick. They'll charge, and they'll lose a good third of their mounts. Your men will be in three lines. The first line will fire—one or two volleys—and then retreat to behind the third line. Once the first line is past, the second line will fire . . .

"They'll charge, you really think, and lose mounts?"

"If they don't," Heald pointed out, "they'll lose troopers, and we won't."

"What if they just stay put in the stead, sir?" asked Wualt, the first squad leader.

"Then, we'll start taking out their troopers all across the south side," Heald replied. "If they won't counterattack . . . we'll start making small raids on their sentry posts, day after day. The more Matrites we kill before we have to fight a pitched battle, the better."

Alucius didn't question the logic, but wondered how long those tactics would work if the Matrites just massed their forces and moved on Soulend. Unlike most of the troopers, who came from nearer the River Vedra, Alucius knew how difficult it was to live off the land in the north.

"I'd like to have you scouts take out the sentries about a glass before dawn," Heald continued.

Just like that, Alucius reflected, take out the sentries. Was war ever that simple? Was anything?

53

In the dim light of the stable two glasses after midnight, Delar arrived at the stall as Alucius was checking the fastenings on his saddle bags. "Can you carry an extra cartridge belt?" Delar handed it to Alucius before the scout could answer.

The younger man hefted the heavy leather belt. "Yes, sir."

"Good." Delar paused. "We'll be forming up in about a glass. Don't have to tell you, but wait in the stable till the last moment." The squad leader smiled, wryly. "Easier on you than most of us, I'd wager."

"Yes, sir, but it's still cold."

"That it is." With a rueful smile, the tall blond squad leader turned away.

Alucius rolled the second belt, with its heavy cartridges, into a tight circle and wedged it inside the left saddlebag. Then he walked the gray to the stable door, where he waited.

Ilten arrived within moments. He glanced at Alucius, then asked with a smile, "You think the sandwolves will give us a hand, trooper?"

"No, sir. Last time I could locate them, they were north of the Matrites."

"Could be better that way. Never know what the wild creatures might do." Ilten nodded and stepped back, waiting.

Waltar arrived next, followed by Narlet, and then Geran. Within moments, the other three scouts had joined the group. One of the mounts *whuff*ed, and the gray sidled toward Alucius.

"Easy . . ." Alucius patted his mount on the shoulder.

"Everyone's here," Ilten said. "You all know your orders, and you know where you're to meet up. If something goes wrong—it shouldn't, but if it does, fall back here." He nodded to Geran. "You have command here, senior scout."

"Yes, sir." Geran nodded. "Walk out your horses and mount."

Outside was almost pitch dark, the moonless night lit only faintly by starlight and by the single lamp on the outside stone wall of the stable.

Alucius had little trouble mounting or in taking station on Geran, but then, his Talent-senses gave him an advantage. Although he had the black woolen riding scarf across his face, Alucius wished for the skull-mask, but even beneath the scarf it would have been obvious.

Once the seven reached the midroad, the gray eternastone seemed to hold a faint glow in the darkness. That illumination was not the glow of light itself, Alucius realized, but something akin to what his Talent sensed—a residual energy put there generations upon generations into the past when the road had been laid down, seemingly for eternity. Did he sense it now because he'd been using his Talent more—and searching with it?

"Hardly see anything." Syurn's voice carried forward in the darkness, over the clopping of hoofs on the stone road.

"Neither can the Matrites. That's the point." Geran's voice held irritation and exasperation. "They won't expect an attack before dawn."

The Matrites must have expected something, Alucius reflected, or they would not have so many sentries out—unless the sentries were but a gesture to prudence.

After more than a glass and a half of riding, Geran slowed

his mount and began scanning the left side of the road. Perhaps a quarter glass passed before he nodded at a single post set on the south side of the midroad. "There. We'll follow that trail. It leads to the other road."

"How—"Syurn offered the unfinished question.

"Because I put the post there," answered the senior scout. "Took some doing with the soil frozen."

Progress along the trail was slower. Riding in single file after Geran, without the faint glow of the midroad to help him, Alucius had to watch the way more closely. The night seemed more still and colder with each yard that the scouts rode. Alucius flexed his fingers within the heavy herder's gloves, trying to keep them warm.

Another glass went by before Geran reined up. "To the northwest there, you can see a few lamps. That's the stead. We'll be riding behind a rise for another half vingt or so."

The distance before the senior scout halted the group again seemed far longer than a mere half vingt.

"Here's the rendezvous point." Geran kept his voice low. "You have to look closely for the marker on the north there." Geran pointed to another short pole rising less than a yard from the top of a quarasote bush a yard to the north side of the track the scouts had followed.

"Now . . . start moving off once I call your name. Wait at the edge of the road from where you're supposed to start north until I come by and check your spacing. Understood? Narlet?"

"Here . . ."

"Balant? . . . Syurn? . . . Waltar? . . . Alucius . . . Henaar . . ."

Alucius eased the gray along the road, first passing Narlet, then a hundred yards later, Balant, and then Syurn, and Waltar.

Again, the wait in the chill seemed interminable.

"Alucius?" called Geran as he rode up.

"Here."

"If you head straight in for half a vingt, you should be in the middle of the picket lines. About three hundred yards ahead is a shallow wash that angles northwest. You can ride along it for maybe fifty yards. Then you'll have to move in on foot."

"I understand."

Geran laughed softly. "See you later." The senior scout rode on westward.

Once he was on his own, Alucius wiggled on the skull-mask. Not only did it offer greater protection, but it also darkened his face. Moving slowly and carefully, he guided the gray northward through the quarasote, using his Talent-senses, hearing, and sight. He couldn't sense either sanders or sandwolves, but the Matrite sentries were definitely somewhere ahead.

It was more like four hundred yards before he reached the wash in the ground, a depression that was barely a yard and a half deep. After dismounting and leading the gray down a gentle slope, Alucius tied the gelding to the half-exposed roots of a quarasote bush on the south side of the depression that was barely a yard and a half deep. The horse would be all too visible in the day, or even by dawn, but if Alucius hadn't carried out his orders by then, that would be the least of his problems.

Then he eased his way to the northern side of the wash and tried to determine where the picket rider might be. He could sense the grayish points that had to be Matrite riders and sentries, but none were that close to him, but even farther north than the six hundred yards they were supposed to be. So he eased out of the wash, listening, sensing, and slipped from low quarasote bush to quarasote bush, but always heading north. Even with the skull-mask, some chill seeped in around the eyeholes and in through his nose, leaving his nostrils feeling frozen.

Scuttling over ice-hard ground and around the quarasote, he finally began to sense one Matrite mounted trooper coming closer, and he settled behind a larger quarasote bush, waiting.

A single rifle shot—heavy—came from the east, followed by a second shot, a lighter one, and then by a third shot from a militia rifle. There were no other shots. Alucius nodded to himself, thinking that Waltar had taken out someone.

As the picket rider neared, Alucius could sense not only the man's grayness, but his apprehension.

There was a faint clicking—a scrat—and, abruptly, the rider reined up and looked southeast, lifting and aiming his rifle—but nowhere close to Alucius. "Who goes there?"

That was a stupid question. In fact, saying anything in the darkness while riding a picket line wasn't very smart. Alucius just waited as the rider turned his mount. Between night-adjusted eyes and Talent-senses, Alucius could see his target almost as clearly as if it were day. He squeezed the trigger of the heavy rifle.

Crack!

The echo seemed deafening, but his aim had been accurate, and the sentry pitched sideways in the saddle—and that cold emptiness of red death washed across Alucius. He forced himself to push aside that void of finality.

The mount reared, then gave a sound that seemed like a cross between a whinny and a scream. Alucius winced. The horse had come down on a mature quarasote bush, but after a moment, limped away, favoring one leg, dragging the dead sentry, whose boot had caught in one stirrup. After the horse had gone less than ten yards, the body flopped onto the frozen ground.

Alucius recocked his rifle and turned westward. The sentry on the adjoining picket section should have investigated, but nothing happened. The moments passed, then perhaps a quarter glass, before his senses revealed another Matrite rider.

"Issop? Issop?"

The voice was low, and the accent strange, but it was clear to Alucius that the sentry was calling a name. Hadn't the Matrites ever fought anyone except in pitched battles? Or except against outnumbered enemies? With all the shots, they should have sent more than one rider.

Almost sadly, he aimed, waiting, before he fired once more. One shot was enough. This time, the mount backed away, riderless.

After adding two shells to the rifle's magazine, Alucius slipped through the darkness, past the first dead Matrite and toward the fixed line of sentries.

There were two—about seventy-five yards apart in the darkness—and each was behind a low mound of soil, soil that must have taken incredible effort by the Matrites to have broken free and heaped there. One man hissed something to the other, but Alucius couldn't understand a word. Nor did he understand the exact response of the other, except that he could tell by tone and his Talent-feel that it was negative. Both sentries were worried.

A muffled yell came from the east, then silence. Had Waltar used his sabre on one of the sentries? Alucius certainly didn't see how he'd get close enough to do something like that. He frowned. If . . . if Waltar had killed the sentry to the east, wouldn't it be possible for Alucius to slip through that way, and strike from behind? It would take time, and it meant a lot of scuttling and squirming, but both sentries were worried, alert, and keeping low behind their piles of rock-hard frozen dirt.

With a silent sigh, the young scout began to ease back and then eastward. A quarter of a glass later, or more, he finally slipped past the invisible perimeter line and began circling back in behind the sentries. Neither man looked behind himself often.

Slowly, silently, Alucius cocked the rifle, aimed and fired—and missed. The man had jerked his head sideways just as the scout had fired. The sentry lifted his rifle and turned.

Alucius waited until the man had almost completed the turn before he fired again, then scuttled sideways, knowing that, this time, the muzzle flash might well leave him a target for the westernmost sentry.

Crack! The single shot from the other Matrite was several yards off, but certainly the man had a good idea where Alucius might be.

Alucius moved westward, keeping low and behind quarasote, despite the heavy rifle.

Crack! Crack!

None of the shots were close, but with each shot, from both the muzzle flashes and through his Talent-sense, Alucius could see the other sentry, who was shooting from a kneeling position. The scout could also feel the near-panic in the sentry.

Still, Alucius forced himself to set up behind another quarasote bush and to aim carefully—and fire. The second sentry pitched forward, and his gun clunked dully on the hard ground.

Alucius swallowed the bile in his throat and eased his way back to where he had left the gray, keeping low, but not by crawling on his belly as he had to get close to the sentries. Before mounting, he reloaded, and then switched cartridge belts.

He was the second scout at the rendezvous point, even after reloading and worrying off the skull-mask. Waltar was waiting for him.

"Figured it'd be you," the older scout murmured.

Before either could say more, several shots rang out in the darkness, and half were from the sharper-sounding Matrite rifles. There were no more sounds of militia rifles, but Alucius could sense and hear riders.

"That sounded like number three area—Syurn's," murmured Waltar.

Four men rode toward them. Alucius could sense that they were militia.

"Scouts?" hissed a voice.

"We're here, Squad Leader," Waltar said. "Two of us."

"What was that?" Ilten reined up less than three yards from Alucius.

"Matrite sentry shooting at one of us, I figure," answered Waltar.

Alucius could feel an emptiness, distant but very real. He didn't know which scout had died, but one had, and Waltar was probably right.

"The column's about two vingts back. Slower on this side road," Ilten said. "How have you done?"

"Alucius and me—we cleared out the section just to the west of the middle."

"How soon will you know about the rest?" asked Ilten.

"There's one section not clear," Waltar pointed out.

Ilten was silent.

"Think we ought to go back in?" Waltar looked at Alucius. Reluctantly, Alucius nodded.

"Someone didn't clear his sentry?" asked Ilten.

"Doesn't appear so, sir. Alucius and me . . . we'll see."

"Two of you?"

"Might be best. They got one of us, and they're probably waiting," Waltar pointed out.

Alucius was content to let the older scout talk.

"You think you should wait for Geran?"

"Not if you want this to go right."

"Go ahead." Ilten's voice was reluctant—and doubtful.

"Yes, sir," Alucius said quickly.

As the two scouts rode back westward along the narrow road, Waltar snorted softly. Alucius said nothing. Syurn's section had no wash, but another of the gentle rises, and the two had to tie their mounts directly to quarasote bushes with rope leads.

"You go around this side, and I'll go around the other," Waltar suggested. "You can sense me enough not to shoot at me, right?"

"Right," Alucius agreed.

On the far side of the rise, a good sixty yards away from where Alucius had slithered through a low spot in the rise were three picket riders, on horseback, in a semicircle facing south. At each side was a trooper on foot. All had rifles near-ready.

Alucius took a deep breath. He was going to have to take longer shots than he would have liked. There was no help for it. He aimed at the center rider.

The bullet took the Matrite in the shoulder, spinning him half out of the saddle, but the man struggled to bring his rifle to bear. Alucius recocked the rifle and fired a second time, then a third.

A second heavy rifle joined in.

When he had emptied the magazine, a single Matrite foot trooper remained standing, almost frozen in place. Alucius fumbled out the cartridges from his belt, and reloaded, slowly, too slowly, it seemed to him, and raised the rifle again. A single shot was enough.

This time, it was harder to choke back the bile, but he did so as he quickly reloaded, smelling for the first time, it seemed, the acrid scent of gunpowder.

"Over here," hissed Waltar from behind a quarasote bush a good thirty yards to Alucius's left.

Although he could not sense anyone else besides Waltar, Alucius still kept low as he crossed the ground, but he did not do it on his belly.

"What about the ground sentries?" asked Waltar.

Alucius let his Talent-senses reach out. There was no one behind the bodies. "Think the two foot were the ground sentries. You wait here. Let me check a bit farther in," Alucius suggested.

"Fine by me."

Alucius slip-scuttled forward. By the time he had covered another hundred yards, it was clear that there were no sentries for at least a quarter vingt in each direction. He retraced his path carefully to where Waltar waited.

"That's it," Alucius said.

"Good. Let's get out of here. Done more'n enough."

Neither spoke until they were back untying their mounts.

"Too bad it won't be like that in a full battle," Waltar grunted as the two remounted. "Be ten of them to every one of us, and their rifles shoot farther."

"That's why the captain tried this, wasn't it?"

"Matrites aren't stupid. How many times you think they'll let us do this?" Waltar laughed. "They'll have more sentries, or pull them in closer. Also, you'll find it harder to use Talent to guide a bullet in a battle."

Using Talent to guide a bullet? "I don't do that."

"All you herders do, and you all say you don't. You make shots no one could make, otherwise."

Alucius didn't answer. Were his shots good because he could see better, or because of what Waltar had said? He certainly wasn't conscious of using his Talent to guide his bullets.

Another series of rifle shots punctuated the blackness of the glass before dawn.

Balant and Henaar were waiting with Ilten at the rendezvous.

"Geran went back out," Ilten said.

"Narlet," Henaar said.

"Captain and the column should be here before long," Ilten said.

The next rider was not the captain, but Geran. "Waltar? Alucius?"

"Here."

"You took out the sentries in Syurn's section, right? Did you see him?"

"No, sir," answered Waltar.

Alucius felt guilty. He hadn't sensed anyone alive, but he certainly hadn't thought about looking for Syurn's body.

"Didn't see Balant either." Geran turned in the saddle to face Ilten. "So far as we can tell, sir, we've taken out the sentries as required."

"Good."

In less than a quarter glass, Captain Heald appeared out of the darkness, riding a dark chestnut stallion. "We heard shots."

"We cleared out the sentries in this section," Ilten said.

"Fourth squad is right behind me, and the foot are only about a half vingt back. It's getting close to dawn. Wish it hadn't taken so long."

Looking eastward, Alucius could see the faintest light outlining the looming form of the Aerlal Plateau.

"We've had to change things—fourth squad will take the midroad out of the stead. If they move quickly enough, they'll hit the road guards from behind."

"But . . . then . . . how will the Matrites know we're here, and why would they attack here?" Geran asked bluntly.

"One squad of foot is going in farther, where they can fire directly at the buildings on the stead. That will work better. They won't open fire until it's clear that the attack on the shed holding the mounts has been successful. If it's not, they withdraw without firing—unless they're attacked. In that case, the plan will work anyway."

Except that the foot squad would take far higher casualties. Ilten added. "Return to your squads."

"Yes, sir." Alucius followed Geran.

"Glad to see you both made it," Delar said quietly as Geran and Alucius lined up at the head of the column.

"Thank you, sir," Alucius replied.

Fourth squad rode by in the darkness, in single file. Alucius didn't envy them.

After a good quarter glass of silence, a few scattered shots rang out, from the higher and thinner sounding Matrite rifles. There were a handful of shots from the heavier rifles, and then another, more scattered set of shots from the Matrites, and a few more shots from the militia.

Alucius looked toward Geran. Geran was looking toward the lamps of the Matrite outpost and the outline of distant structures barely visible in the faintest of gray predawn light. Alucius watched, catching sight of a light-colored mount now and again.

A few more shots echoed intermittently through the predawn dimness.

Then, after another period of silence, there were several muffled explosions, and flashes of fire. Thin trails of flame rose from a building on the former stead.

More rifle shots—heavy shots—came from the militia foot.

Figures small in the vingt-plus distance poured out of one of the stead sheds, heading southward. Alucius couldn't sense that many Matrite troopers—certainly no more than a company, and all were on foot. They didn't advance past their perimeter, but just dug in behind what cover there was and lay almost flat, firing occasionally. Was that by plan, or because so many of their troopers were sick from eating nightsheep?

More distant shots came from the midroad.

An order came from somewhere, shouted into a moment of stillness, "Militia foot! Withdraw! Withdraw by squads! Squad two!"

Then Ilten rode by, pausing before Delar. "Once the foot clear, by squads, to the rear."

"Yes, sir."

Alucius saw Delar's minute headshake once the senior squad leader had passed.

The second squad of militia foot trotted by, followed by the third, and then the fourth. Alucius didn't count, but there weren't a full twenty in any of the squads, and second squad didn't seem to have many more than ten.

"That's it," snapped Delar. "Squad, to the rear, ride!"

As they rode back to the midroad in the whitish orange light of dawn, Alucius wondered how many troopers fourth squad had lost—and how many foot had died.

54

Third Company and Fifth Foot returned to the Soulend outpost by midmorning. After stabling and taking care of their mounts, the entire company was dismissed for a late breakfast or an early dinner. Alucius dragged himself to the mess, where he took a platter without even looking at what was on it and slumped onto a bench at a corner table.

Kypler sat beside him. "We just waited. What did you do? Besides scout?"

"Killed people," Alucius said wearily, after chewing a mouthful of tasteless egg toast, and taking a swallow of warm cider. While the warmth helped, the cider seemed tasteless as well.

"Not enough," said Geran from the other end of the table.

"They'll just keep marching into the Iron Valleys until we kill them all. That's what they did when they took all the coast cities a generation back. That's what they've done to the Reillies in the Westerhills."

"They must have lost a lot of troops last night," Kypler suggested.

"Not that many. A little less than a company—mostly foot," Geran replied. "A squad or two of horse, and fifty mounts at most. Mounts might be their biggest loss."

"A company's not that many?" Kypler raised his eyebrows.

"You can do the figures, Kypler," Geran pointed out. "We've lost three scouts, out of eight. Fourth squad lost eight men last night, and the Fifth Foot lost almost two squads."

"That's almost a quarter of what we have here," Kypler said.

"And the Matrites lost twice what we did, and that was only a tenth part of what they have. We keep winning like that, and it'll be a real Legacy." Geran took a long swallow of cider. "Better eat what you can while you can."

"You're saying that we're going to get beat?" Kypler asked.

"I'm not saying that," Geran said. "But what happens if they march their fourteen-fifteen companies against Soulend?"

Kypler looked down at his platter.

Geran rose slowly and walked toward the messboy to hand in his empty platter and tumbler.

Velon cleared his throat. "Alucius . . . fourth squad. They took a lot of casualties."

"I know." Alucius had had his doubts about the captain's plan, but there was little he could have said. Not and have anyone listen.

Retius, sitting beside Velon, shook his head. "Did you hear about Dolesy and Ramsat?"

"Were they . . . ?"

Retius nodded. "Bowgard made it back. They didn't."

Alucius looked at Kypler. Had Estepp known that the two

would be more at risk in fourth squad? Was fourth squad the one used as bait and fodder? His lips tightened, understanding, again belatedly, some more of what his grandsire had tried to convey.

The smaller trooper shrugged. "Said they wouldn't last."

After a silence, Retius spoke again. "Overheard Brannal talking to Kesper. Most of the Reillies and the hill clans—those that were left—fled north of the midroad. Some say they're going to the winter tree forest south of Klamat."

"Cold land there," Alucius pointed out. "Winter's three seasons, and you have a half season of spring, a season of summer, and a half season for harvest."

"Too cold for me," grumped Velon.

"Better cold than dealing with the Matrites," Retius suggested. "We don't have a choice like the Reillies. We'll have to deal with the Matrites. If we don't want to end up wearing those silver collars."

"Well . . . you were the one who said you'd do anything to avoid the cold," Kypler parried, grinning at Retius.

"Almost anything," Retius replied. "The cold sounds better and better."

"Matrites or cold . . . some choice," mumbled Velon.

Wondering if anyone, anywhere, really had choices, Alucius kept eating, tasteless as everything seemed. After he finished, he decided that he'd head for his bunk and get some sleep. He had the feeling he'd need it in the days and weeks ahead.

55

Alucius did manage to catch up on sleep, even though the entire squad was mustered out after two glasses, only to be told to have their gear packed and to be ready to leave the Soulend Outpost in case of a full Matrite assault.

For all the warnings, the Matrites did not march or leave

their encampment on Octdi, as the captain had thought, nor on Novdi. They only sent out a handful of road patrols. Alucius thought he knew why—because the Matrites had eaten nightsheep. Since he hadn't mentioned it before, saying something so late would only create trouble for himself, and there was nothing he could do. On Decdi, everyone in Third Company was mustered out right after breakfast.

Captain Heald didn't offer any opening pleasantries. His jaw was almost clenched before he began to speak. "While some of you have been resting, the foot and our two engineers have been busy . . ."

Alucius didn't even know that Third Company had an engineer, let alone two.

"The Matrites are moving out toward Soulend." Heald offered a grim smile. "We have a few surprises. The Fifth Foot should be in place within the glass. Each squad here has a different assignment. Your squad leaders will fill you in. Dismissed to your squad leaders."

Alucius couldn't help but note that Heald's address was the shortest offered since Alucius had reported. His eyes went to Delar.

The second squad leader began, "Second squad will mount an attack out of the little wash four vingts to the west on the north side of the midroad . . ."

Alucius recalled the wash, and understood the idea. There was almost no quarasote there.

". . . can't see us until the last quarter vingt or so. We'll gallop up and wheel into a firing line, almost a broadside to the column . . . two or three volleys, and then wheel out and back up the wash. There are a few surprises for the Matrites, too . . ."

Surprises? The last set of "surprises" hadn't worked that well.

"You've got a quarter glass to get ready and pick up your cartridge belt. Dismissed."

Alucius walked quickly back to the barracks bay, avoiding other hurrying troopers.

Kypler scurried up, finally matching steps with the taller Alucius. "What do you think?"

"We'd better shoot and ride well." Alucius laughed—once.

Kypler looked as though he wanted to say something, but didn't.

Delar was mounted and waiting outside the stable by the time Alucius was mounted and formed up beside Geran. Alucius could sense Delar's anxiety. He glanced to Geran, then murmured, "Delar looks worried."

"Be stupid not to be," the older scout muttered back.

More second squad troopers rode up and into formation, and, without any warning, Delar ordered, "Squad forward!"

Second squad rode back into Soulend, rather than west on the midroad, and Alucius could catch both the murmurs from those who rode behind, and the senses of puzzlement.

The ruined square stone building that once might have been an inn was the first structure they passed. All that remained was a set of roofless walls. Past the empty gray walls were several small cottages, shutters fastened shut, and without a trace of smoke or life—the inhabitants gone.

As second squad rode into what passed for the town square, which had but an excuse for a chandlery and a wood shop that doubled as a cooperage and tinker's, Alucius could see two wagons on the south road, creaking on overladen wheels and axles. Seven people walked in front of or behind the heavy-burdened wagons. Not one looked back at the troopers.

"Not much faith in us or the One Who Is," murmured a voice.

". . . more faith in the Matrites . . ."

Delar led the squad through the square and onto the north road.

"We're not going to Sandhold?" Alucius murmured to Geran. "Just ruins there."

"We'll head off to the west just ahead. Old stead road reaches the wash. Matrites won't figure it because there's no connection between the midroad and the stead road."

"Your idea?"

"No." Geran's single word was terse, and Alucius could sense the disapproval.

While he didn't want to press the questions, Alucius felt that Geran understood more about tactics than either Delar or the captain, and that bothered him.

Delar led second squad nearly a vingt north on the old road, before turning the column westward on a narrow lane. Second squad then rode westward for a glass, until they reached a single rider, waiting at the edge of a trail to the south, through the quarasote.

"Column halt!" Delar rode to the other rider.

Alucius listened, trying to use his Talent to pick up what they were saying.

". . . about a glass away . . . traps in wash ahead . . . point them out . . ."

". . . how many . . . march order?"

". . . all of them . . . two horse . . . front . . ."

Delar turned his mount to face second squad. "Listen up! Follow me in single file. We'll form up in column after we're in position to begin the attack. We'll have to wait half a glass or so once we're ready, but they can't see us from where we'll be."

Both the other rider and Delar started down the narrow trail that wound between the quarasote. Geran followed, then Alucius, as second squad went from column to single file. After about half a vingt, the trail turned west and then wound down between two rises into a shallow wash that was almost invisible from more than a hundred yards away.

Second squad had traveled about half a vingt along the flat middle of the wash—hard-frozen soil on which a mount barely left a track—before the wash turned due west, and then, a hundred yards later, back to the southwest.

Then, just before the second twist in the wash, Delar called, "Column halt!" He waited and then continued. "I want you to notice the narrow trail to the left side of the wash. It's only wide enough for one mount. There are pits and traps in the middle of the wash. When we ride back, I'll order a line to the right, and you'll have to ride that narrow line at full gallop. Once you're past the little bluff there—" Delar pointed to the west, "you can spread back out into the middle of the wash."

Alucius was most careful to stay on the narrow trail. So were the troopers who followed.

Second squad drew up three hundred yards south of the trapped area, just behind another low bluff, less than three yards high, from where they could see nothing to the south.

"I'll be up on the edge of the wash," Delar announced, "watching for our signal to attack. The midroad is only a hundred and fifty yards south of here. No talking in ranks. Shouldn't be more than half a glass." Delar dismounted, handing the reins of his bay to Geran.

"Yes, sir," replied the senior scout.

The light wind had died to an even more intermittent breeze. Alucius tried to stretch his legs by barely lifting himself out of the saddle, as if shifting his weight. Time passed . . . slowly. Alucius wiggled his fingers inside his gloves, glanced around the wash, counted the scattered quarasote bushes on the western edge of the bluff—fifty-three fully in sight—and took several small swallows from his water bottle.

Suddenly, Delar scrambled down from the western edge of the wash, where he had been lying behind a quarasote bush, watching both the midroad and some trooper who was relaying hand signals from a hidden and prepared position on the north side of the midroad.

"On my command, quick-trot around the bend, and down to the wide section. Wheel to a fire line—on command! Now! Forward!"

Geran glanced at Alucius, raised his eyebrows and gave a near-imperceptible shrug, as the two followed Delar, the squad behind them, around the bend. Riding eastward on the road was a long column of riders in dark green riding jackets. Only a handful turned their heads for several moments as second squad moved down the wash toward the road. Then

. . . more heads turned, but no commands issued from the Matrite officers.

"Wheel to a line. Fire on my command!" Delar's command broke the comparative silence.

As they had drilled, the twenty riders wheeled into two staggered lines, leaving each man with a clear line of fire, less than fifty yards from the line of Matrite cavalry.

"Fire!" Delar's voice rang out.

The *crack!* of twenty rifles was nearly simultaneous.

"Fire!"

The second volley was almost as simultaneous.

"Fire!"

The third was ragged, and the higher pitched reports of the Matrite weapons were interspersed with shots from second squad.

"Wheel and withdraw!"

Alucius was more than happy to withdraw, especially as he could feel the massing cavalry, and the great number of Matrite weapons being brought to bear, and sense bullets closely around him. The frozen-hard soil of the wash was almost like riding on stone, and the sounds of hoofs echoed in nearly the same fashion as second squad galloped back up the wash.

"Line to the right! Now!" ordered Delar.

Second squad narrowed into a line and sped past the traps and the bluff.

"Center of the wash!" the squad leader snapped.

Alucius risked a glance over his shoulder. Possibly as many as twenty pursuers had been lured into the concealed pits in the center of the wash, and the pursuit had clearly broken off.

The sixteen remaining members of second squad reformed on the back road. Alucius could see Kypler and Velon, but Akkar was missing, as was Torbyl, one of the veterans. Alucius immediately extracted three shells from his cartridge belt and made sure he had a full magazine in his rifle.

"Better!" said Delar. "We took down at least a squad, maybe even a squad and a half. Now, we're headed back to

Soulend, and to whatever we need to do now. Column forward!"

Alucius glanced westward, at the heavy graying skies. The wind, light as it had been, had stopped, and a cold calm had fallen across the valley, the kind of calm that usually preceded a heavy storm.

Alucius occasionally glanced back, as did others, but the Matrite forces had not followed.

Second squad followed the trail out of the wash, and then the side lane back to Soulend. As they entered the hamlet, and reached the north side of the now-abandoned square, where the chandler's shop and the wood shop had shutters tightly closed, a militia rider with the green sash of a messenger rode toward them.

"Squad halt!"

Alucius strained to hear the conversation.

". . . Matrites lost almost a company of cavalry, sir, but they have a terrible weapon. It shoots crystal spears . . . right through the earthen revetment . . . cut it down. . . . killed most of the third and fourth squads of Fifth Foot. The Matrites lost half . . . more . . . First Foot Company, but we have less than three foot squads remaining . . . Captain requested that your squad not undertake the second attack. You are to return to the barracks, and pack out, with full ammunition. All squads are to meet him by the chandler's here in Soulend on the south side of the square. We're headed south."

Delar's face grew increasingly grim with each word. Finally, he turned his mount. "Back to the outpost. You'll have a quarter glass, no more, to grab your gear and get spare cartridges before we remount and withdraw."

Geran and Alucius exchanged glances. Geran nodded sadly.

Second squad rode in silence back to the outpost. There, all the wagons—except one—the one with the company's ammunition—had already left the outpost, and the only militia remaining were horse troopers gathering gear.

Alucius tied his mount in the stall, rather than outside. He found some little water for the gray, and then, hoping the gray would eat what was left in the manger while he was briefly gone, hurried to collect his gear from the barracks bay.

He didn't say anything, and neither did anyone else.

56

West of Soulend, Iron Valleys

The snow fell in fine white sheets, like an ice fog, around the covered crystal-thrower as Hyalas checked the lashings on the tarp that covered both device and the wagon that held it. He straightened, then looked around the converted stead that had been the enemy's outpost, a place truly too small for the forces of Madrien, but cramped shelter was far better than no shelter against the ice and snow and the winds that blew straight from the Ice Sands of the north.

"Engineer!"

Hyalas turned to find arms commander Vergya looking down at him from her mount. He bowed. "Yes, arms commander?"

"Why did your machine stop?"

"Because, honored arms commander, we ran out of sand with which to feed it. I had to use it as a spade to level that hill in order to flush out their riflemen." He bowed deeply. "You ordered me to do whatever I could."

"The wretches were slaughtering the Third Foot, and your machine does not leave survivors for us to turn into recruits."

Hyalas bowed again. "I know it has its faults, and I have suffered already for mentioning them to the Matrial. It was built to kill, and it does that well. It digs less well, and it captures men alive not at all well."

Vergya shook her head. "I do not fault your machine. How long before it will be ready for use?"

Hyalas bowed once more, then shrugged. "Honored arms

commander, if I had sand, it would be ready within the glass. But with the snow, and the cold, and no rivers—"

"Rivers?"

"All rivers have sand somewhere," Hyalas said. "Here, there must be sand, but in the cold, and with snow across everything, it might take days to find it and break it free."

"Days?"

"I cannot change what is, arms commander. I have men looking everywhere."

"Best you find that sand before days have elapsed, engineer." Vergya did not wait for a response, but turned her mount and headed toward the stable, inadequate though it was.

"Yes, arms commander." Hyalas did not blot away the dampness on his forehead, a dampness already freezing in place.

57

Alucius looked from Geran, riding beside him, up the high road in the direction of Soulend. The withdrawal to Pyret had been accomplished, through a blizzard, and now the remnants of Third Company, less than two thirds its original strength, waited there for reinforcements, while the two scouts patrolled to make sure the Matrites were not headed south.

For all that the wind had blown and the snow fallen on and off for more than two days after the retreat, only a thin layer of fine icy powder lay across the eternastone pavement, and some sections of the road were totally clear. Where there was snow, neither hoofprints nor wagon tracks marred the sheet of white. Part of that was because the old high road and its shoulders were often as much as a half a yard above the surrounding terrain.

While the late-morning sky was still gray, the clouds were

high and thin, and the wind had died away once more suggesting another change in the weather was coming. Alucius
felt that the next days would dawn bright and clear, and, for
the first time, he wasn't sure he wanted a bright and clear
day, not if that meant the Matrites could march south.

"They haven't even been sending road patrols," offered
Geran. "Not this far south."

"You think we'll have to go all the way to Soulend?"

"Wouldn't be surprised. Captain said he wanted to know
what the Matrites were doing. He wanted a lot of information. We just stop, and all we can say is that they're not
here."

Alucius could sense that more lay behind Geran's words.
"They'll probably be garrisoned at our outpost and all over
Soulend."

"We'll see."

Not until they reached a point on the road less than two
vingts south of Southend did they catch sight of hoofprints
in the snow on the road and the shoulder. The prints had
been made within the past few glasses because they were
crisp in most places, except at the edge of the road where
blowing snow had obscured some prints.

"Now what?" asked Alucius.

"We keep going," Geran said, "on the road. They're
headed away from us and back to their post. If we do run
into them, we can just turn around."

Less than a vingt later, Alucius began to sense the grayness of Matrite troopers, more than one, and probably one
of their eight-man patrols. "Matrites coming."

"We'll go east," said Geran. "Follow me."

"They'll see us." Alucius gestured to the almost flat expanse of quarasote plain to the east.

"They might. You think they're going to chase us through
it? And if they did, I'd say we have a good chance of either
losing them, or picking them off one by one."

"So we go east and then come in from the north or northeast? After dark, if we have to." Alucius added, "And I suppose we pick off a few sentries if we can?"

"Might make them think we've still got a presence around Soulend, but I wouldn't do it just to shoot or to let them know," Geran said. "Senseless killing's still senseless killing, even of a Matrite. Besides, our job is to get information, and it's easier if they don't know we're here. You got any better ideas?"

"Not at the moment."

"I didn't think so."

The two scouts were more than a vingt to the east in the flats when the Matrite patrol finally came far enough south on the main road for Alucius to see them when he looked back over his shoulder. Whether or not the Matrites saw Alucius and Geran, they made no effort to follow, but continued southward on the main road.

"You see? They don't care about two lonely troopers," said Geran.

The two circled to the northeast, slowly easing toward the dwellings and huts set amid the ancient piles of rubble, stopping once at a frozen stream where they managed to break the ice enough to water their mounts. They saw no other Matrite guards or patrols, even when they had come within a vingt of the inhabited section of Soulend.

The two reined up in the short and late afternoon behind a pile of earth and stone slabs—partly covered with red sandy soil and an occasional quarasote bush—that rose almost three yards against the hazy gray sky that was beginning to darken.

Geran looked at Alucius. "I'll skulk around Soulend. You see what you can find out about the outpost."

"Do you want to meet up somewhere?"

"That makes both of us more vulnerable," Geran pointed out. "Best place to meet up is back at Pyret."

The two separated, and, after leaving the rubble, Alucius continued to wend his way through the quarasote flats to the north and then west of town, finally ending up on the west-running road that second squad had taken on the ambush attack Delar had led. There were no traces of riders in the intermittent sections of thin snow drifted across the back road.

After a vingt or so of riding, he turned southward, picking his way through the spiny growth and eventually over a low rise. To his right, roughly southwest, was the former militia stead, barely visible in the twilight.

While listening and using his Talent-senses, he eased the gray down the rise far enough so that he would not be outlined against the sky. What he could hear, see, and sense told him that the sentries were posted only about a half vingt out from the stead. It took him a good half glass to find something to which he could tether the gray—an ancient stead marker pole back on the far side of the rise, out of sight of the stead. There he dismounted. In the cold, it seemed to take nearly as long to worry on the skull-mask as it had to find a place to tether his mount.

Carrying only his rifle—all too heavy, but he recalled his grandsire's lessons too much to rely on knives alone—he slipped through the deep twilight toward the former militia outpost, walking back toward the Matrite outpost, using what cover there was.

A good two hundred yards out, from behind a large quarasote bush and on his stomach, he watched as a mounted trooper rode along the north side of the camp—only one guard on the entire north side. There were no sentries walking the grounds out from the buildings. Instead, the Matrites had set up six boxlike little huts, each with several guards inside. Each hut was about a hundred yards out from the main compound.

For another half glass, Alucius watched, but he saw nothing except the outside of the guard huts and the mounted sentry—and three empty wagons. The larger wagon he had seen earlier was not in view. He eased forward through the scattered quarasote until he was less than fifty yards from the post being ridden by the Matrite trooper. That close, and Alucius could sense the man's discomfort, both with the cold and his duty.

Alucius wasn't exactly comfortable, either, and he didn't

really know much more than he had two glasses earlier. He definitely needed to get closer, but there was no way to get into the Matrite camp without somehow removing or getting by the sentries. He didn't like the idea of killing the sentries. It hadn't done much good before, and the way the guards were set up, killing any one of them would alert all the others.

Could he use his Talent to get them to overlook him—or keep them from looking at him? It was worth an attempt—after he decided what he wanted to see and where. Recalling how Geran had operated, he thought he might try the stable first. It was on the west end, and he could try his Talent idea while he was far enough away so that, if it didn't work, he could sprint back into the quarasote. In the darkness, he doubted that the Matrites would send anyone after him—not until they had a full force, and not after their experience the last time the militia had attacked their camp. By the time they had a large enough force, he'd be long gone.

He could slip by the mounted sentry easily enough, and if he moved another hundred yards westward, he could get within fifty or sixty yards of the stable before he'd really come into even a half-clear view from the northwest guard hut.

After timing the mounted patrol for several turns, Alucius counted, and then slipped downward and into the flat, directing his perceptions toward the guards in the huts, projecting the image of a stray dog slinking toward the stable, a mangy, scruffy stray, wary of humans. He kept his own doubts buried, even as he realized that he could not reach the stable without crossing a wide patch of snow, but he dared not hesitate, keeping the slinking gait he had imagined for the stray dog he had become to the sentries. Then he eased into the darker shadows between the manure pile and the stable. Once out of sight of the sentries he eased toward the second stable door, the seldom-used door to the ostler's work room.

As he stood in the darkness, panting slightly, all he could say was that no one called out, and no one shot at him. So his stratagem had worked. He was pleased when he slipped inside the empty ostlers' room, not much bigger than several of Kyrial's largest barrels, put end-to-end. He had to stifle a sneeze immediately. There were several troopers still in the stable, unsaddling and brushing down mounts, probably having just returned from road patrols.

Alucius waited until they left, then slipped into the dim stable, counting mounts. Most were double stalled, and there were no empty stalls. He did not find the missing wagon with the strange weapon. Nor did he find any weapons lying around loose. Or much fodder.

After more than a half glass in the stable, he went back into the ostlers' room, then used his Talent-sense to make sure no one was directly outside the stable before he slipped out into the night, and the cold that he had forgotten. At that moment, a purplish shock ran through him. He turned toward the spot from where he thought it emanated—and found himself looking toward the stead dwelling that had once housed the militia officers. There, he could sense something he had never felt before, a cold, almost crystalline, purple malevolence ... a feeling of evil that he could not explain, only sense. With it came the sensation of breathlessness. Then ... the breathless feeling was gone, and the purpleness subsided enough that it felt far more distant than merely coming from the stead house—except it was.

He frowned beneath the skull-mask. He'd never sensed anything like that before. Sanders were red-violet, sand-wolves grayish violet, and soarers silver-green, and the Matrite troopers grayish ... but an evil purple that varied so greatly from one moment to the next? With the strength and the projection, it had to be some form of Talent, but not one he had ever encountered.

Slowly, he edged his way around the west end of the stable and then back along the south side. He stayed in the darker shadows and against the dark gray stone walls as he moved toward the end of the stable across from the west end of the barracks. At the southeast corner of the stable he paused.

Someone was reprimanding someone else in a high voice, and far from gently.

Alucius froze, then peered around the corner. An officer was pointing to the ground, toward a patch of snow that Alucius had no doubt held his boot tracks. While Alucius couldn't understand all the words, he could pick up some, as if they were half familiar, and the gestures were clear enough. The officer was telling the guard something to the effect that a dog didn't leave boot marks in the thin snow, especially not tracks that seemed to have come from the north.

Another trooper emerged from the guard hut, and the two troopers and the officer followed the boot tracks toward the stable. When another trooper appeared with a lamp, Alucius decided to try and project being a cat as he made ready to sidle along the eastern side of the stable.

He was well away from the stable and close to the picket line when he heard a shout, and then a single shot that felt very close to his head.

He jumped sideways, then dropped lower and ran in an irregular zigzag path out to the north. He dodged through the quarasote, keeping as low as he could while scattered rifle shots peppered the air and quarasote all around him.

A high-pitched voice yelled, and the shots stopped—because the sentry turned his mount and began to pick his way through the quarasote. Another order followed, and the rider tried to urge the horse to move faster. The mount reared, probably because it had been run into a quarasote spine.

Alucius moved at almost a run, somehow hanging onto the rifle that felt like a leaden weight, the cold air rasping at his lungs. Once up over the rise, he darted down the back side, feeling his trousers rip as he lurched too close to a quarasote bush, and feeling thankful for the shielding effect of the nightsilk undergarments—better than armor for that sort of protection. Gasping for breath, he reached the marker post where his gray was tethered, waiting.

After untying the gelding, he mounted, forcing himself to be careful, walking his mount through and around the quarasote, fearing that, any moment, troopers or mounted troopers would burst over the low rise with their rifles firing. Nothing of the sort happened.

He had a long ride back—and not nearly so much information as either he or the captain would have preferred. All he really knew was that there were close to two hundred mounts in the stable, and that the mysterious weapon hadn't been there, and that the Matrités had changed their guard and patrol patterns—scarcely very much for the time, effort, and risk.

As for the purple malevolence . . . what could he say? He dared not say anything, and yet that might be the most important—because it meant some sort of Talent was being used.

58

On the morning after the reinforcements had arrived in Pyret, headed by Majer Dysar, and directly after what passed for breakfast, Alucius was in the front room of the small stead house which had become a headquarters of sorts. He stood there, along with the Third Company scouts, Ilten, Captain Heald, and a number of officers he didn't know.

"The only real problem we have," Majer Dysar announced, pacing slowly back and forth in front of the ancient iron stove, "is their spear-throwing device. According to scouts from Third Company, if we can rely on such, the spear-thrower is not in open view. If such is the case, that means that it cannot be used if we attack quickly, and depart quickly. We will do so in quick raids until it becomes obvious where the device is. Once we determine that, we can concentrate our attacks wherever device is not, as should have been obvious earlier . . ."

"Tomorrow evening, Sixth Company will undertake an attack on the horse outpost. The tactics will be simple. One squad will infiltrate the road south of Soulend, and allow the road patrol to pass southward. Once the patrol is well past, the rest of the company will attack from the south. The Matrite patrol will either perish immediately or retreat and be destroyed by the first squad. Then Sixth Company will move as quietly as possible to Soulend, where it will either take out the guards there, and proceed westward on the midroad, or dash past, if the guards are not in a position to challenge the company. Thirteenth Company will be standing by here, in the event that the Matrites think that they can outflank us and push southward. I doubt that they will . . ."

Alucius thought the plan was possible. What Majer Dysar did not seem to realize was that, effective as his plan might be, it was the sort of plan that Captain Heald had never had the resources to implement, not without risking his entire command and leaving the entire north open to a sweep southward by the Matrite forces.

"Third Company scouts will be required to familiarize scouts from Sixth and Thirteenth Company with the roads and terrain. Captain Heald will pick his four best scouts . . ."

Alucius concealed a wince. There were only five scouts left, and there was little point in excluding one just to have an even number. And if the majer wanted that number, he could have just drawn Captain Heald aside and asked him to assign four scouts.

Captain Heald smiled politely. "We only have five scouts, and they are all good."

"Sir," Ilten interjected politely, "Narlet's mount is somewhat lame, and that might slow him down. I would suggest the other four this time."

"That's fine," the majer replied. "You can work out your scouts, and Captain Tregar and Captain Vanas will provide two scouts each."

In less than a glass, Alucius found himself paired with Drengel, a wiry and black-bearded older trooper from Sixth Company. The two left Pyret, riding northward toward Soulend on the now clear eternastone high road. The sky remained clear, but the silver-green held the darker shade of winter, rather than the brighter hues of the warmer seasons.

"You're a herder, I take it?" asked Drengel, with the hint of a smile.

"How did you figure that?"

"You're young. You're good, and you've survived."

Alucius had used his Talent-sense on Drengel, but didn't feel anything like the faint tinge of silver-and-green flecks or streaks that herders showed. "And you're experienced and had to work a long time at reading the smallest of signs."

Drengel laughed, openly. "Just so as we understand."

Alucius understood. "How long have you been with Sixth Company?"

"Sixth Company's my second tour. Did four years with First Company when it was at Rivercliff. Sometimes, ran into Matrite patrols if we went too far west."

"Ever have to fight them?"

Drengel shook his head. "We had orders not to fire unless they fired first. They never did. Had big patrols, though. Either eight or sixteen."

"They do eight here."

"What do you think about the majer's plan?"

"The majer might be able to stop them—if he can keep away from the spear-thrower."

"Let's hope so. Tregar and Vanas are good captains."

Alucius wasn't exactly reassured by that answer, and Drengel's omission of the majer, but it squared with what he'd already observed. He glanced up the road. "We'll have to head out into the flats before long. Do you want to circle to the east and then north or west and north?"

"What do you think?" countered Drengel.

"East and north. There are some back roads that they don't use much . . . yet."

59

Alucius had not slept well on Quinti night, not after being grilled endlessly by Majer Dysar about his scouting, who questioned everything. Nor did he sleep well the following night, but few had. His dreams had been less than pleasant, with visions of the Matrites overrunning his stead and Iron Stem and slaughtering Wendra, even as he was unable to speak, unable to reach her.

With such thoughts and dreams, he wasn't surprised to find Third Company mustered out on foot on Septi morning. The majer was nowhere around.

Captain Heald was the one explaining matters to Third Company in the chill air. ". . . be taking some stead roads to the west, and then we'll attack from the west end of the outpost. The other companies will also be attacking. Thirteenth Company has a plan for dealing with their spear-throwing thing . . . Once we're on the road, Third Company scouts will be out front two vingts, with the vanguard a vingt before the main body . . ."

Alucius didn't mind being out in front with Geran and Waltar and Henaar, although he now clearly understood his grandsire's advice about the advantages of scouting alone.

"Draw your rations and cartridge belts, then meet out here with your mounts in half a glass. Dismissed to make ready."

Alucius nodded to Kypler, and to Velon, as the three readied their gear and then made their way to the stable, a scene of cramped chaos, with more horses than space or stalls. Like the others, Alucius was more than ready to face the cold after dealing with the makeshift stable.

Third Company was the first to leave Pyret, but stayed on the main road for less than two vingts before turning westward on another stead road. Then, Ilten dispatched the five scouts and the vanguard.

Geran glanced from scout to scout as they eased forward away from the vanguard and the main body of Third Company. "We'll alternate checking out the rises." Geran looked to Henaar. "You want to cover the north side of the road for now?"

"Fine by me."

"I'll take the south side," Narlet suggested.

While Narlet and Henaar headed out, Alucius, Geran, and Waltar rode abreast on the stead road, barely wide enough for the three.

"Do you know what everyone else is doing?" Alucius asked.

"I haven't heard, but it seems that the majer's idea . . ." Geran lowered his voice, even though no one else was within hundreds of yards, "is to attack from several directions around supper time. He figures their spear-thrower can't fire in all directions at the same time. He wants to take or destroy the weapon and their use of the outpost. Without the weapon, they lose their advantages, and we can attack them patrol by patrol until we destroy them or they retreat."

"Unless they send more companies," Waltar pointed out dryly. "Madrien is a bit larger than the Iron Valleys."

"I'd be more worried that they sent another spear-thrower," Geran said.

Alucius listened as they rode west-northwest on the stead road that seemed to angle, if gradually, toward the ancient midroad.

After about a glass, Geran dispatched Alucius to scout the parts of the land to the north of the midroad that were hidden by low rises, or washes, or the infrequent ruined hut or stead. The wind continued to blow out of the northeast. Even from his position well south of the midroad, Alucius could feel with his Talent that there were more sandwolves near the Matrite base. He could also feel the background red-violet of sanders, and that was something that was unusual in winter. Not unheard of, but unusual. He worried some about the pinkish purple Talent, but he didn't sense it—not yet.

Slightly after midday, Third Company halted for a ration

and water break, and Captain Heald gathered the scouts back to the main company. His face had gotten thinner and more drawn, and he had deep black circles under his eyes.

As soon as all five scouts had assembled around him at the head of the main column, the captain began, "The main body of the company will be taking station behind the second rise to the west of wash where we ambushed them before about half a vingt to the north of the midroad. We'll be standing down and resting there. First squad will be attacking the road posts and the road patrols, but the other squads need other ways to hit from the west. There have to be stock trails or something where there's less quarasote. I'm detaching you five to see what you can find. I want you back at the muster area at least a glass before sunset." Heald looked to Geran. "I leave it to you, Geran, to assign them as you think best. And to take whatever route you decide."

The captain eased his mount away from the scouts and back toward another group perhaps fifteen yards eastward— Ilten and the squad leaders.

"To get any information and get to the muster area," Geran pointed out, "we'll need to head northwest so that we get to the midroad almost at the wash."

"They have to have a sentry point somewhere. They had one at the base of the hills before," Alucius said. "Would it be faster to head west on this road for a time and then go north to try to catch the wash south of the midroad?"

"Might be," suggested Waltar. "A lot less quarasote and a lot more cover in the wash areas and those low bluffs."

Henaar nodded. Narlet just looked from face to face.

"That's what we'll do," Geran said. "Best we start now."

After barely a quarter glass, the narrow road ended abruptly at the ruins of an abandoned stead. Another road headed northward, slightly west as well, clearly straight to the midroad.

"From what I figure," Waltar said dryly, "that'd be the road that comes out at the old outpost. Be a quick way to get there."

"Be a quick way to get everyone chasing us." Geran laughed.

For the five scouts, the going through the quarasote to the west of the stead was slower, but not so difficult as it had been east of Soulend for Alucius because the quarasote near the Westerhills was farther apart and smaller. Alucius could see why the stead had been abandoned. The nightsheep that fed on the quarasote nearby would have had inferior coats, and the sparseness of the forage would have meant a smaller flock.

They continued riding westward until they reached a flat area where the outflow from the wash had spread across the land.

There, Geran reined up. "We'll follow this north to where the wash deepens. I'm going to take the area that runs off the quarter that's from northwest to west-northwest. Alucius will take the quarter from west-northwest to just above the midroad. Narlet, you see what you can see on the midroad and both sides—sentry posts, numbers, arms, guard huts. Henaar—west to west-southwest, and Waltar—west-southwest to southwest. We're looking for livestock trails, washes without much quarasote . . . ways to move quickly to the outpost without being seen." The senior scout glanced from one face to another. "Meet at the muster area at least a glass before sunset."

Waltar immediately headed northwest, and after a quarter glass so did Henaar. Narlet split off shortly afterward.

That left Geran and Alucius riding northward. They halted behind a low bluff, shielded by a turn in the wash to the west, just south of the midroad. The two peered around the bluff at the arched stone culvert that allowed the water to flow under the road—a culvert far too small and low for a mount. The road, a good two yards above the flat of the wash, looked to be clear of road patrols. Alucius did not sense any troopers nearby.

"I don't see anyone around." Geran looked to Alucius. "But we can't see eastward without climbing onto the road and exposing ourselves."

"The sentry posts on the road are to the east," Alucius replied. "It feels clear to cross."

Still, they rode out into the open section of the wash carefully, and then up the gradual slope on the west side. Once they reached the road, Alucius couldn't see any patrols on the midroad, and even the tracks on the light snow on each shoulder of the road and on the snow-dusted surface of the eternastone paving looked to be days old.

Before long, Alucius was on his own, riding carefully up to the back side of the next-to-last gentle rise before the outpost. The last rise might have patrols. He found a quarasote bush that looked stronger than most and used an extended tether rope to tie the gray gelding. Then, he eased up the rise to the top where he studied the next rise, a good three hundred yards away.

After a time, seeing no patrols, he slipped back down and reclaimed the gray. If he were discovered, he certainly didn't want to have to run through quarasote for up to half a vingt with mounted pursuers. On the back side of the more eastern rise, he once again tethered the gray, to quarasote, since there were no old marker posts, and eased up the back side of the slope. On the top, he flattened himself. He had recalled correctly. Half a vingt or so to the east were the stable and sheds of his own former outpost—and the current Matrite encampment.

Now, all he had to do was find a stock trail that led relatively directly back to the wash. For a time, he just studied the encampment, figuring how it might have been laid out as a stead. Then he studied the ground. After a good quarter glass, he found what he sought. He kept looking for a time, but there was only one possibility from where he was looking. There might have been one to the northwest, but to make sure of that, he would have to get within fifty yards of a guard post in full sun.

Instead, after slipping back behind the rise, he eased along the western side, heading southward. Less than a hundred yards to the south, he found a two yard wide patch of clear ground that ran uphill to a low spot in the rise. With a faint smile, he scuttled up along the ancient stock path to just below where he could be seen from the encampment, then wiggled to his left on his stomach, and then forward to make sure the old path did run toward the stable.

He wormed his way back to the western side of the rise, then followed the path downhill, keeping low. Once in the flat between the two rises, the stock trail turned southwest. Alucius reclaimed the gray and followed the trail, which did lead to the wash. He continued westward, and Henaar, Waltar, and Narlet were waiting as he rode into the muster area.

"Did you see Geran?" asked Waltar when Alucius reined up next to the other scouts, gathered to the north of where the main body of what remained of Third Company was standing down and sampling field rations.

"No." Alucius glanced at the bucket of water, only a third full, set beside a quarasote bush.

"That's for your mount. Delar left them for us."

Alucius dismounted, then looked at the gray as he picked up one of the two buckets, trying with his Talent to convey the need to lap up every drop. The gray gelding had just finished drinking when Geran appeared out of the wash to the east. Geran immediately watered his mount. As he was finishing, Ilten rode over from the main body.

The senior squad leader looked at Geran. "What have you discovered?"

In turn, Geran looked at the four other scouts. No one spoke.

After a moment, Alucius cleared his throat. "There's a narrow trail, probably worn by nightsheep, that runs almost due west until you get to the wash here. There's one part where it runs north-south, but that's out of sight of the encampment."

"How wide?" asked Geran.

Ilten frowned, but did not speak.

"Not much more than a yard and a half," Alucius admitted. "Two yards in places."

The older scout nodded. "We could run one squad there.

The one that runs from the bend in the old wash is about twice as wide, and it comes in on the northwest corner of the stead. It doesn't wind much, either."

Alucius silently admired Geran's ability to scout out that trail without being seen, since it had to have been the one he hadn't investigated.

Ilten looked to Henaar.

"Nothing that clear. There's a stock trail just south of the midroad, and it angles west-southwest, but it ends at the midroad, and it's exposed for the entire last three vingts."

"Waltar?" asked Ilten.

"There's one almost due south. Same problem as the one Henaar found."

Narlet shook his head. "Nothing next to the midroad. There's a road post about a vingt east of where the midroad crosses the wash. Two huts, and two mounted troopers, but they're messengers, I'd wager, to get help if they see any force coming."

"Geran . . . Alucius, you two come with me," Ilten ordered.

The two scouts repeated their information to the captain, pointed out the general locations of the trails on the rough map the captain had, and spent a quarter of a glass answering questions.

"Where is that . . . how long from there to the perimeter?"

"How many can ride abreast?"

"Where can we reform into a column or wheel into a firing line?"

When the questions finally stopped, the captain nodded, then looked at Geran. "You'll lead the main body on the northwest trail." His eyes went to Alucius. "You'll lead second squad along the trail you scouted. Ilten will tell the squad leaders."

After that, Alucius slipped back to second squad, where he munched a few of the tasteless travel biscuits and sipped from his water bottle. He could still feel the presence of sandwolves and sanders. Did they know there was a battle? Were the sandwolves hoping for carrion? Did the sanders feed on death of people the way they seemed to on the death of nightsheep?

"Are you all right?" asked Kypler. "You look worried."

"Shouldn't we all worry?" countered Alucius.

"Form up!" Delar called.

Alucius remounted and rode forward.

"You ready, Alucius?" asked Delar.

"Yes, sir."

"Then lead on."

As Alucius rode down into the dry wash, north for a hundred or so yards, and up the worn cut that nightsheep had not used in years, and then along the old stock trail toward the Matrite encampment, with Delar almost directly behind him, he didn't see any other militia companies. Nor did he sense them. He did sense sandwolves moving in from the north, still more than a vingt away, and the sense of sanders was somewhat stronger.

In the flat below the last rise separating them from the Matrite encampment, Delar raised his gloved hand, holding it aloft. Second squad came to a halt, unevenly, but silently. Alucius glanced over his shoulder. The white orb of the sun was seemingly much larger as it hung less than two fingers above the Westerhills.

The only sounds were a few shuffles of mounts, a scattered *whuff* or two, and the hiss of the wind as it swept through the winter-stiff quarasote spines.

"Torches." Delar's command was whispered, but it carried, and Velon and two others used their strikers to light the oil-soaked rags and wicker.

The sun touched the horizon—the lower hills that marked the eastern side of the Westerhills—and that was the moment for the attack. Delar dropped his arm, and Alucius urged the gray up the trail to the top of the rise. He wasn't supposed to move at more than a fast walk until halfway down the rise where the rest of the squad could follow at speed.

No one in second squad said anything, and Alucius was almost to the perimeter line, his body low against the gray, less than twenty yards from a guard hut before the first Matrite rifle went off. *Crackkk!*

"Wheel! Now!.... Fire!" Delar's orders were the first sound from second squad.

The heavy militia rifles sounded almost like thunder compared to those of the Matrites.

"Fire!"

The two volleys tore through the three guard huts on the west side, and Alucius could only see a pair of the Matrite foot scrambling clear.

"Charge! Torches forward!"

Crack! Crack! More rifle shots came from a handful of Matrite foot who had appeared outside one of the smaller sheds to the east.

Alucius heard more hoofbeats—from the north—but he concentrated on reining up and firing at the Matrite foot.

From somewhere else came a squad or more of Matrite horse, and Alucius barely had time to shove the rifle in its case and get his sabre up and out.

The first Matrite to charge him was so inept with a blade that Alucius was half-shocked when he swept inside the other's all-too-high strike and cut halfway through the trooper's throat. He almost lost the sabre, but managed to hang on, and turn the gray in time to block a slash from a trooper far better than his compatriot.

Alucius lost track of everything, except forest green jackets and black ones, as mounts and troopers from both sides mixed in a melee.

The oil-soaked torches had done their job—the stable was blazing, and there were horses screaming. A Matrite trooper, his uniform blazing, staggered from the shed, half-dragging, half-leading a horse that kept trying to rear.

Alucius parried a slash by the Matrite trooper, a parry he knew was weak, but managed to shift his body enough to avoid the next slash. A sharp blow to his right upper arm jolted him, and he automatically ducked and turned to see another Matrite, a surprised look on his face. Alucius didn't waste the surprise but kept low and urged the gray away from the two, ignoring the ache in his arm, an ache that could have been a deep slash without the nightsilk vest and undergarments.

Abruptly, a bugle sounded, and the Matrites pulled away, almost galloping to the south.

A humming filled the air—sharp-pitched, and cutting through the yells, curses, and the sound of both Matrite and militia rifles.

Alucius glanced toward where he knew the earthen ramp had to be, and felt a cold chill as he could see the shimmering metal of the spear-thrower—with its barrel swinging to the west.

In desperation, Alucius tried to create the feeling of a lamb—a lost and very alive lamb. He forced the projection to the north—to anywhere, knowing he should have done so earlier, far earlier. As he sent forth the projection, he urged the gray toward the corner of the stable, toward a spot where the crystal spears could not reach.

He had to rein up the gray short of the corner, for there was almost an entire squad of Matrite troopers re-forming. He considered a dash to the smaller stone shed.

The hum from the machine was rising in tone and pitch, and a line of crystal fire slashed through the twilight toward militia horse coming in from the north side of the encampment.

Alucius jabbed his heels into the gray's flanks, and the gelding dashed for the small stone shed. No sooner had Alucius pulled up behind the shielding of double stone walls than he sensed a strange surge of red-violet stronger than he had ever seen. To the north, the soil was boiling, and sanders surged out of the soil.

Overhead, the sky darkened, as clouds Alucius had not seen before thickened. Around him clashed the sounds of Matrite rifles, the thin shrieking hum of the spear-thrower, the screams of troopers and mounts.

Alucius turned the gray . . . when an enormous fist struck

him in the back of the shoulder. For an instant, he could feel himself toppling forward before silver-tinged blackness—and a green radiance—swept up over him and swallowed everything.

60

West of Soulend, Iron Valleys

Hyalas kept turning the aiming wheel, spinning it as fast as he could, so that the discharge formulator would swing around to the west to bear on the attacking horsemen in black. Already, a half company had fallen to the heavy rifles and the sabres of the attackers, and the stable where more than half the Matrite mounts had been was an inferno whose heat the engineer could feel from more than a hundred yards away on the mound where his device had been hurriedly pulled.

Hyalas gave several more twists to the aiming crank, then pulled down the lever with the green knob. A whine rose swiftly into a high-pitched shriek. As the shriek rose into inaudibility, a line of crystalline amber fire flashed from the crystal barrel toward the northwest corner of the encampment—slicing through mounts and men alike. Hyalas used the elevation crank to lift the line of fire slightly.

Screams and curses echoed across the twilight.

A different kind of chill swept over the encampment, and the engineer glanced around. He saw nothing. The crystal flame faltered.

"Keep shoveling the sand!" the engineer snapped to his assistant at the hopper from the sand-wagon. "Keep shoveling, or they'll overrun us!"

The man resumed shoveling with a redoubled intensity.

Hyalas turned the aiming crank, slowly sweeping across

the closest line of attackers, ignoring the pinkish mist that filled the twilight as the amber line of crystalline light struck the attackers.

The chill intensified.

Hyalas frowned, then swallowed. The frozen soil around the death sprayer was boiling. Boiling! From somewhere a green radiance seemed to sift across the land—and man-shaped figures were emerging out of the turbulent soil.

Two sanders rushed toward the sprayer. One stretched out a hand and touched the discharge formulator. Instantly, the crystal barrel sagged.

Then the device began to turn reddish. The heat from the turret was instantly hotter than the summer sun in Southgate, and rising with every moment. Almost without thinking, Hyalas threw himself out of the wagon and sprinted behind the sandwagon to the rear of the crystalline death sprayer.

Crump . . . Instants after the dull-sounding explosion, sand and tiny fragments of quartz rained down upon the engineer huddled behind the sandwagon.

Screams of dying horses, and the groaning of men beyond aid rose around where the death-sprayer had been—now a rough circle of molten quartzite glass and fragmented and bent metal on the hillside.

Hyalas shivered, then staggered erect, his fingers going to the torque at his neck.

Another company of Matrite troopers swept in from the south, from behind Hyalas, followed by yet another company.

Suddenly, the only riders in the encampment were those in forest green, and the attackers had vanished beyond the perimeter. The sounds of rifles diminished, then died away, and for a long moment, the only sounds were those of dying and wounded men and mounts—and the cracking of the burning stable.

"Engineer!"

Hyalas turned to see the arms-commander, looking down at him from her mount.

"What happened?" Vergya demanded.

"There were some figures—the things they call sanders—"

"Myths! Legends of a superstitious bunch of herders! Them and their sanders and soarers. They're even more ridiculous than the idea of the lamaial. And now you're saying that they are real?"

Hyalas could feel the torque at his neck tightening.

"They were there . . . something I'd never seen . . . Not as big as a man, and one was beside the discharge formulator—"

"The barrel?"

Hyalas did not correct the arms commander. "The formulator melted. I saw it and felt the heat, and I just threw myself behind the sandwagon."

The arms commander looked to the officer who had reined up.

"Arms commander, the attackers have all withdrawn."

"With heavy casualties, let us trust." Vergya looked to the overcaptain. "Did you see the . . . things . . . the engineer says destroyed his device."

"Yes, commander. They were manlike, but not so big. They killed several of my troopers. A rifle isn't much help. Not ours."

Vergya frowned, then nodded slowly. "That explains it."

Both the overcaptain and the engineer waited.

"Why their militia carries rifles with those huge cartridges and bullets. They're designed for those sander things. They can't afford to have two kinds of rifles, one for war and one for sanders."

The overcaptain nodded.

"Arms-commander?" asked Hyalas. "I fear I cannot rebuild the death-sprayer here."

Vergya shrugged. "No matter. It will take longer without the death-spray, but we will take the Iron Valleys, as we have taken everything else. We will send you back with the captives, if there are any."

Hyalas, still trying to catch his breath, merely nodded.

III.

⊁ LEGACY: ⊁
THE MATRIAL'S
ALTERNATIVE

61

There were low moans, coughs, and rasping breathing. The smell of fire was everywhere. Alucius lay still, his eyes closed, trying to listen. His head was splitting, and his right shoulder was one massive ache. The fingers on his right hand were half numb, half tingling. Words, half familiar, swirled around him, but they did not make any sense.

Finally, he opened his eyes. He had to squint because he saw two images of everything. He lay on the stones in the open area of what had once been the Third Company barracks. Several other militia troopers lay there. He started to turn his head, and even more pain radiated from his shoulder.

He swallowed, breathing heavily. Finally, he struggled into a sitting position. Only then did he realize that something had been fastened around his neck. He lifted his left hand to touch whatever it was. His fingers stopped short. He was wearing a Matrite collar. Below the collar, he could feel crusted blood. Gingerly, his fingers brushed the back of his head. He winced as an even more intense pain flashed through his skull. The huge lumps and matted blood made him wonder how he'd even survived. How long had he been unconscious? What had happened?

His sleeves had been rolled back, which seemed odd, but there were no cuts or scrapes there. And his parka had been opened, but not removed.

He glanced slowly to his left, but did not recognize the man lying there with a gash across his forehead, and his arm bound in a sling—except he knew he'd seen the veteran at some point. On his right was Haldor—a trooper he'd seen a few times.

Haldor had turned and propped his back against the wall. His leg was splinted with what looked to be broken rifle barrels. He smiled ruefully. "Wondered if you were ever going to wake up. Quite a lump on your head."

"I got hit from behind with something." Alucius gingerly felt the front of his skull. He had another lump, right above his forehead, in addition to those in the back. "What about you?"

"Right after their machine exploded . . . thought we'd do all right. Someone shot my mount from under me. Almost got clear. Then one of the Matrites rode over me, busted up my leg."

"Then what?"

"Rounded us up, asked our names, wrote them down, and left us here. Asked three of us your name. I guess to make sure we told the truth." Haldor stopped, then whispered, "Look out. Here they come."

The machine had exploded? How? And why were they asking names? Alucius turned his head. A tall blonde woman walked swiftly toward the small group of militia wounded. She was followed by a trooper, and without his riding jacket the dull silver torque around his neck was partly visible above his collar. The woman wore the forest green tunic of the Matrites, but with accented crimson piping on the sleeves, and a silver four-pointed star insignia on her collar. Even with his aching head, Alucius tried to sense what the woman was doing, although he needed no Talent to feel the arrogance she radiated as she stopped a yard away from him. He shivered as he realized that he could sense nothing with his Talent. Nothing at all.

Was his Talent gone? Or was it the collar around his neck, blocking his abilities?

The woman stepped up to Alucius. "Ask him how he is." Although she spoke in a tongue Alucius had never heard, he thought he understood her words. He looked blankly at her, wondering if she were the source—or one source—of the purplish sense that he had felt as evil, and could no longer feel. The loss of his Talent left him feeling more empty, made the splitting pain in his head seem as nothing, even though it was severe enough that almost any movement of his head made his eyes water and everything dance before him.

"How are you feeling?" The trooper spoke in the dialect of Lanachrona, similar to that of the Iron Valleys, thick, but understandable.

"My head is splitting, and my entire back is sore," Alucius admitted.

"His head hurts; his back is sore," the trooper said in the other tongue, which Alucius assumed was Madrien.

"Tell him he's lucky to be alive. Tell him about the collars."

"You're fortunate. You're alive. You have a collar around your neck. If you try to escape, it will kill you. If you try to remove it, it will kill you. If you disobey orders, you will be punished. If you fail in your duties you will be punished. Do you understand?"

What was there to understand? Alucius nodded.

"He shows no respect," the officer says. "Tell him he will be punished, and that is why."

The Matrite trooper looked to Alucius. "You must show respect. You must bow, and you must not look her in the eyes."

"I understand." Alucius looked squarely at the woman.

The officer fingered something at her belt, and Alucius could feel the torque around his neck tightening. He continued to look at the woman blankly until the blackness overwhelmed him and he pitched forward into it.

When he woke a second time, he was lying on something hard. A continued squealing and squeaking seemed to pierce his ears. For a time, he lay on the hard surface before opening his eyes. Above was a gray sky. A single thin blanket had been draped over him. He still had on his undervest and tunic, but his winter parka had been stripped from him. He looked around, then discovered it had been folded under his head—by someone. His belt knives and bootknife were gone, and, of course, his sabre. His nightsilk undergarments were still in place, but he guessed he'd only been searched for weapons.

"You all right, fellow?"

The words were in the hill dialect spoken by the Reillies and, supposedly, the Squawts, although the Squawts lived in the south hills east of Dekhron bounded mainly by the River Vedra, and Alucius had never seen or heard one. He'd heard only a handful of Reillies, women usually, at the market square in Iron Stem.

Alucius sat up slowly, steadying himself with his left hand on the sideboard of the wagon. His head still ached, slightly less than when he'd awakened the first time. He remained somewhat dizzy, but he only saw double images every so often. "I'm no worse."

"I'm Jinson. Used to live west a' Soulend."

"Alucius."

"They got some sort of thing, it's linked to the collars. You don't do what they want, they punish you. Send pain, or just choke you."

"How do you know what they want?"

"You learn real quick." The whispered words were sardonic. "You don't know, best you go right down on your knees and grovel. They like to see men grovel. They don't like you valley boys much. We don't either, but rather deal with your militia any day than this bunch. They got something bad against us—most of the time, they kill any one of us—especially men—just on sight. Only thought they killed me. Made me a captive after that."

"Where are we?"

"On the road back to Hieron. That's what one of the troopers said."

Alucius glanced around. From what he could tell, they were in a short column, guarded by no more than two squads of troopers. He saw no officers nearby.

"Don't try it," the Reillie said.

"Try what?"

"Escaping. See that silver box in the cage there?" The man pointed to an enclosure of steel bars, within which was a silver box roughly the size of a man's head, mounted on the front of the wagon between two posts.

Alucius followed the gesture.

"You go more than half a vingt from that, and you can't breathe. The officer in charge doesn't like you, and she'll tie you to a tree or a post and keep moving. When the box gets far enough away, you'll choke to death, slowly, as the wagons get farther away. Or maybe they'll leave you free, and not feed you when they're on the move . . . and you have to stay far enough away not to get shot and close enough not to stop breathing, and, sooner or later you die. Oh . . . and you even touch one of the officers—you stop breathing."

Alucius couldn't help frowning, even as he shivered in the cold. He unfolded the parka and struggled into it. His right arm would barely move, and any motion of the shoulder sent lines of pain through his entire body.

The Reillie—a burly man with his left arm heavily bandaged and bound—laughed softly. "Don't listen to me. One of your militia types—they already killed him. Actually got his hands on the captain—blonde and skinny, eyes like blue ice. He dropped over dead."

Alucius swallowed, then recalled his grandsire's advice about staying alive long enough to know what to do. He nodded. He had much to learn—and quickly.

62

Low thick gray clouds swirled barely above the midroad, touching the tops of the taller crests of the hills and cloaking them in gray. The snow on each side of the road was almost a third of a yard deep. There was less than half that on the eternastone paving itself, something that would have created more wonder in Alucius had he not been walking through the snow behind the wagon with the other captives, pushing it when necessary to keep the small convoy moving westward through the Westerhills. Fine icelike snow swirled down, needling the right side of his face. His head continued to pound, more so on the few times when he had tried to call forth his Talent—in vain.

His right wrist was chained to that of Jinson, and all the prisoners were chained in pairs. The chains were thin, thin enough that, with a solid rock and some time, or some tools, Alucius probably could have broken them—but he had neither rocks nor tools nor time. With the dull silver torque-collars, escape was out of the question, at least until Alucius could figure out how to disable the collar—if he could, with no Talent.

He still wondered who the militia trooper had been who had stood up to the Matrite officer and been killed. Had it been Haldor? He hadn't seen the man.

Except for his face, cold wasn't a problem—not yet, although some of the other captives were suffering. Alucius still had to wonder why he hadn't been stripped of his gloves and especially his undergarments while he was unconscious, but then, without special equipment, tailoring the nightsilk was virtually impossible. Or was it that once the Matrites had taken the weapons from the captives, they regarded them as beneath notice?

"Weren't for the chains . . . done harder work on my own place . . ." mumbled Jinson.

The Reillie had removed whatever binding there had been on his arm, and Alucius was surprised that the man seemed to have healed so well—or that he showed so little discomfort.

"I'm surprised that they let us have that much food and water," Alucius murmured. "And actual shelter at night."

"They're not being kind," retorted Jinson. "You feed and water your stock, don't you? Or are you a townie?"

"I'm not a townie, and I've fed a lot of stock."

"We're stock to them. Or rifle-fodder for their attacks on . . . whoever." Jinson's voice was barely above a murmur, but still conveyed bitterness.

"They're letting us ride in wagons some of the time," Alucius whispered back. "Why did they send wagons just for prisoners?"

"Didn't," Jinson said quietly. "These were some of the provisions wagons they sent. Got a regular line of them, least once a week. No sense in sending 'em back empty. Make better time if we ride some."

"No talking!" snapped the Matrite trooper—male, as all the rankers seemed to be—with the chevrons on his green riding jacket. He was riding to the left and back about three yards.

Alucius bowed his head, enough to acknowledge the command without obvious contempt. Ahead of them, the low rumble of the wagon slowed, as did the wagon, its wheels building up slush under the iron rims, and then beginning to slide sideways on a patch of ice.

"Move ahead! Give a push!" snapped the trooper. "Put some force behind it, now."

Alucius provided as little force as he could. His shoulder was still sore, and putting any pressure on his right hand and lower arm sent shooting pains from fingertip to shoulder, and even up his neck. The very worst of the aching in his skull was gone, but both lumps were still more than a little tender, even after three days' travel, and he'd definitely noticed it when he managed to use a little snow on the one on the back of his head. The cold had helped, but for the first few times, the snow had come away with the watered-down dark tinge of dried blood, more than a little dried blood.

"Show a little more effort there! Unless you want the captain to put the squeeze on your worthless necks!"

The six captives behind the wagon pushed it over the hump of slush ice, and, as the horses took up the full load again, resumed trudging through snow and slushy ice. Alucius had the feeling they were in for a long trip—and he had no idea where they were headed—except to Hieron—if the rumors were correct.

63

Alucius glanced up at the midafternoon sky.
High hazy clouds had begun to drift in from the south, lend-
ing even more of a silver cast to the heavens. After two days
of light snow, the sun had returned, and with it came a biting
wind out of the northeast. For the first time in his life, Alucius felt a northeast wind without the iron-acrid scent of the
Aerial Plateau. Also, for the first time in his life, on the
combined trek and ride, he had seen vingt upon vingt of
trees, mainly tall conifers, pole pines, some firs, and no junipers or cedars.

He'd also seen a convoy of more than twenty-five wagons
headed east, along with two more horse companies. In his
watching, he'd learned a bit more. Like the militia troopers,
the Matrites carried a rifle and a sabre, but their sabre held
a slightly greater curve in the blade.

Unlike the militia, the two levels of officers seemed to be
more distinct, both in conduct and uniform. The ones who
seemed to be squad leaders wore rank insignia on their shoulders and were always men. The higher-level officers had insignia on their collars, although there were but two officers
in the entire prison detachment guarding the prisoners, and
both were women. Neither wore the silver torque. The squad
leaders were distinguished by one, two, or three crimson
chevrons on the upper arms of their jackets, just below the
shoulder, and all of them wore the silver collars.

"For all your watching, friend," Jinson said in a murmur,
"you're not going anywhere, 'cept maybe to the One Who
Is."

"Not now," Alucius admitted. "But there's always a time."

Jinson snorted. "Where you going? Time you get free Matrites'll hold all your valleys."

Alucius inclined his head toward the officer who had ridden past. "She doesn't look like they're winning."

"Neither do you." Jinson held to the side of the wagon as it lurched to a halt.

"Everyone out!" a Matrite squad leader ordered.

As Alucius struggled out of the wagon, he could see that the column had halted for a watering break on the midroad—above a narrow stream. The rocks on the side of the stream were rimmed in partly melted ice.

Several of the prisoners were starting down to the stream with buckets. One slipped as he neared the water. Alucius felt relieved—and guilty—that he had not been one of them.

He took another bite of the hard travel bread that the troopers had passed out to the captives, still half amazed that the Matrites had kept them fed and as dry and sheltered as possible.

"You two!" The trooper with the chevrons that indicated he was a junior squad leader pointed to Alucius and Jinson. "Follow me."

Wondering what chore or task the trooper had in mind for them, Alucius followed the orders, as did Jinson, not that either had a choice, still chained together as they were. They walked forward along the left side of the midroad past another wagon of captives, and then past several troopers, who had dismounted, to another wagon, half covered with a silver tarp. Beside the tailgate that had been opened and hung down stood a man, not quite as tall as Alucius, who wore brown trousers and boots, and a brown jacket with silver piping.

"This is Engineer Hyalas," the trooper said. "You're to help the engineer as he orders."

"Sir." Even as he bowed his head, Alucius noted that the engineer, for all the deference accorded him by the squad leader, and his fine brown jacket, trousers, and boots, also wore a neck torque.

"Engineer will do," Hyalas replied in Lanachronan. "You two are to move the parts that I point out in this wagon to the wagon that is just in front of this one."

Alucius glanced at the wagon wheels and axles.

The engineer laughed. "For a trooper, you've got a quick

mind. That's right. The strain on this one is beginning to bow the axles. We need to hurry. The captain doesn't want to take too long. She's only allowing this because if the axle breaks it will delay us more."

Alucius looked at a stack of shimmering and irregular sheets of greenish metal, their color vaguely familiar.

"Not those. The section of crystal tube, there," said the engineer. "It will take both of you."

"That?" muttered Jinson, under his breath. "Not likely." He bent forward and tried to pull the section of greenish crystal—sheared irregularly at one end—that was less than a yard in length and but three fingers in width. His muscles stood out even under his old sheepskin jacket, but he could barely lever up one end. He winced as he released his hold on the tube, but the expression of pain vanished almost instantly.

"I *said* it would take two of you," the engineer said.

Alucius edged closer to the tailgate. Jinson started to climb up into the wagon bed.

"Don't step on anything. Be careful. The edges of some of the metal could slice right through you," cautioned Hyalas.

Jinson was noticeably more careful as he planted his feet in one of the few clear spaces in the rear of the wagon. "Slide this around. . . ." Using his legs, the Reillie captive edged the crystalline tube around the irregular shards of the shimmering metal.

Even in the chill winter air, Jinson's forehead was covered with sweat by the time he had the tube at the end of the wagon bed, just above the tailgate, which hung down, its lower edge almost touching the eternastone road.

"We need to go this way," Alucius said. That was so he could make sure that the crystal section would rest on his left shoulder.

Jinson just nodded.

It took all of Alucius's leg strength to straighten up after Jinson rolled the tube sideways and onto their shoulders. So short was the tube that there was almost no space between the two men. They took very short steps, and it seemed to

Alucius that they had walked far more than ten yards by the time they had the length of crystal in the first wagon, and were walking back to the second.

"Hope there's nothing heavier," Alucius murmured.

"Wouldn't wager . . ." muttered Jinson.

"Now you can take the side plate sheets." Hyalas pointed to the metal sheets Alucius had looked at first.

Alucius wondered why the engineer had wanted to move the heavy crystal first.

"Stack half of the sheets on each side of the crystal so that it won't move," explained the man in brown.

Alucius could see that no troopers were that close. "Engineer, sir—"

"Engineer will do." Hyalas's voice was gruff. "What?"

"Did you build this . . . before . . . ?"

"Before what?"

Alucius shrugged. "Engineer . . . I don't know what. I saw a machine that was killing troopers, and it was this color, but then I was wounded, and I never saw what happened, but I heard it exploded or something."

"That's enough." Hyalas glanced around. "No talk. We need to move enough of the parts so that the wagon will not fail."

Although his Talent-senses were not functioning, Alucius guessed that the engineer had built the machine, and was secretly pleased that someone had recognized what he had done. "Yes, sir, engineer." Alucius lifted the first of the silvered metal sheets to which Hyalas had pointed.

The sheets, like the crystal tube, were heavier than they looked, and one was all either captive could carry at a time. Alucius was sweating as much as Jinson after he had taken two to the first wagon. After the metal sheets, Hyalas had them move several silver boxes, also heavy, and then sections of what looked to be silver-plated copper cable.

When the original wagon looked to be about half empty, Hyalas spoke again. "That's enough." He raised a hand, and the junior squad leader rode forward.

"Engineer?"

"They've moved what had to be moved."

"Back to your wagon. Follow me," ordered the Matrite squad leader.

Alucius and Jinson did just that, not speaking until they were back in the wagon, and the convoy lurched forward, heading westward on the midroad once more.

"Why were you so interested in all that junk?" asked Jinson in a low voice.

"Because it was what was left of a machine that threw hundreds of crystal spears in a moment. I wanted to know if he had anything to do with it."

"Didn't tell you much, did he?"

"No, he didn't say much," Alucius replied.

The idea that the man who had created such a fearsome device wore a collar was as staggering to Alucius as the fact that someone—in the present time—had built or rebuilt something from the ancient times.

64

Another day passed. The Matrite convoy was still on the midroad, but moving through lower hills, with both firs and silver-trunked slough ash trees that would bear distinctive silver-veined leaves when spring arrived. Despite the splotchy patches of snow, Alucius could see hillside farms, with split-rail fences, and fields clearly well tended. By late afternoon, the terrain had turned more to rolling hills, with only the tops and the steeper slopes forested, and with vingt after vingt of well-tended farms.

As the column started down a low hill toward a stretch of flat road, Alucius, walking behind the wagon with Jinson and perhaps half the captives from the wagon, could catch glimpses of a town ahead.

"Move it to the right, closer to the shoulder!" ordered one of the squad leaders.

The wagon before Alucius moved to the right, hugging the shoulder of the road, and the captives followed. Alucius looked up to see two riders heading eastward on the left side of the midroad. One was an older woman, slightly graying, wearing a hooded riding jacket with the hood tossed back. The other was a red-haired girl—or young woman. Both appeared at ease and confident as they rode past the troopers and the captives.

The girl's eyes passed over Alucius and some of the others. The older woman did not even look in their direction.

The Matrite troopers did not look at any of the women, not even covertly, but kept their eyes on the road, the other troopers, or their mounts. Alucius wished he could sense what the troopers felt, but the loss of Talent left him without that ability, and feeling very empty. He looked at Jinson, and asked, "What do you think?"

"Wish I had that mount, riding that way," the Reillie replied, with a low snort.

After that, as the column neared the town, riders and farm wagons passed several times, almost always women, or even girls approaching womanhood. Alucius did not see a male rider unaccompanied by a woman.

"Pick it up! Captain wants to make the base before dusk!"

With the command from a squad leader, the wagon moved forward more quickly, and without the creaking that Alucius had come to associate with wagons from his time in the militia. The absence of creaking bothered him, because he knew it meant something, even if he could not have explained what.

By the time the column reached the first buildings, Alucius's feet were even more sore from walking the hard eternastone pavement. The captives had marched raggedly past several dwellings before Alucius looked up.

So many things struck him that he almost staggered. The town had not appeared that large, but the dwellings were close together, enough for the presence of hundreds. Although there were people beside the road, none of them paid the column much attention, save a child or two, and all of those in the streets and upon the neatly swept sidewalks, empty of snow, were well and warmly clad. The dwellings were all of well-dressed stone and of one story, and with brightly painted shutters. The odors of cooking, of bread, and of faint scents of flowers, filled the chill air.

The troopers, without orders, seemingly kept their eyes mainly on the road ahead.

The sun hung in the silvered dark-green sky, just above the western horizon, so low that Alucius could not easily squint through the glare, as the column continued through the town, perhaps a vingt in length along the midroad. At the western end, past the last dwellings, was a low redstone wall, no more than two and a half yards in height, and the first riders turned in through a gate, one seemingly unguarded. The wagons and the marching captives followed.

Once inside the walls, men and mounts and wagons halted on clean and swept stone pavement. Then the captives began to move, under the direction of one of the squad leaders with three chevrons. "Two by two through the open door."

Alucius and Jinson followed.

On the other side of the door was a man with a hammer and chisel, standing beside a small upright worktable slightly higher than waist level. He wore a plain gray tunic and trousers, and gray boots—and a gray collar. As each pair of captives came through, he placed the chain linking them on a thick wooden plank, and then used the hammer and chisel to break one of the links, so that each man, while wearing a wrist guard, was no longer linked to another.

"Through the archway," ordered another trooper.

On the other side of the archway was a third Matrite trooper, with an overcaptain standing behind him.

One of the taller militia troopers, his hands now free, charged the Matrite trooper, whose sole weapon was a sheathed sabre. Before the Iron Valley trooper took a third step, he pitched forward onto the stone floor.

Alucius winced within himself at the dull thunk of the trooper's body hitting the stone floor, but tried not to show any reaction, although, for some reason, his head ached again.

"You two behind him," the overcaptain ordered, "pick him up and carry him with you through the door."

Alucius didn't even look at Jinson. They just lifted the unconscious man and wrestled him up between them, walking toward the door.

Another trooper stood on the far side of the door. "All right. Prisoner barracks to the right. Overcaptain expects every man to wash thoroughly . . . not just hands and faces—your whole filthy body, and use the soap. Washrooms are at the end. That's before you lie down on your bunks. There are laundry tubs there, too, and tonight before you turn in, you're supposed to wash your undergarments. Anything else that would dry overnight would help. Only overnight. You'll be on the road again tomorrow."

Still supporting the unconscious trooper, Alucius and Jinson made their cumbersome way through the open, but iron-reinforced door into a long barracks wing. Before them were real bunks, with wooden frames, neatly lined up on swept stone floors, bunks with clean undersheets and a blanket folded at the base of each.

Alucius swallowed, getting a sinking feeling at the sight of the ordered quarters, even before he noted the heavy iron bars on the outside of the windows.

65

While Alucius had slept better in the ordered prison barracks, the captives were rousted out early on the next morning, and spent the next two nights in waystations. Three days later found the Matrite convoy entering the town of Harmony, again in the late afternoon. Alucius was sure of the town's name because they had passed several oblong stones set beside the road, with the name and the number of vingts from the stone to the town. The town proper lay on the south side of a narrow river in the middle of a flat land so far west of the Westerhills that the hills had vanished behind the eastern horizon two days earlier. Alucius knew that they had to come to the Coast Range sooner or later, but they had been on the road for more than a week, and after close to eleven days of riding in the wagon and walking behind for what seemed at least half the time, his feet were sore and hurt more than his shoulder, which did not hurt at all at times. His obvious head injuries seemed to have healed, although he still sensed nothing—neither sanders nor sand-wolves—and no soarers.

The waystations where they had stayed since the first un-named town had not had washing facilities, and the bunks had been pallets, but they had been under roof, if chilly roofs. The captives had not been rechained, but the wrist guards with links had not been stricken off, either.

"Think they'll have the fancy bunks here?" asked Lysal, a trooper not much older than Alucius, but one he had not met earlier.

"Course they will." Jinson gave a low laugh. "They want us to arrive in good shape."

Like the earlier towns and hamlets, the dwellings in Harmony were of well-dressed stone, with clean and shining glass windows, framed by brightly painted shutters. The mid-road was flanked by curbs and stone sidewalks, and the roads and sidewalks were well swept. The air was also fresh, if chill, and spiced with the scent of baking and cooking. Un-like the other towns, there were more men about in the streets, but Alucius noted that the men were either older, graying with age, or boys and youths younger than fourteen or fifteen.

They rode by a market square, and there Alucius noted that in several cases an older man seemed to be in charge of younger children, some barely knee-high. In the middle of Harmony, the midroad intersected another of the ancient eter-nastone roads, one heading north-south. The convoy turned south, and, once through the town, stopped at another outpost that could have been almost a duplicate of the one where their chains had been partly struck off—even to the yard and a half high redstone walls and unguarded gate.

Barely had the wagons come to a halt in the stone-paved courtyard and the captives scrambled out of the wagon bed when a Matrite squad leader rode up to the wagon.

"You two!" The squad leader pointed to Jinson and Alucius, and then to the two captive troopers behind them, "And you two. Follow me!" He turned his mount, expecting the four to follow.

Jinson looked at Alucius. Alucius returned the glance. The four captives followed the squad leader to the northeast corner of the courtyard, where three wagons stood—the two which contained the broken sections of the crystal spearthrower and an empty, and far larger, six wheeled wagon with heavier axles and larger wheels. The engineer stood waiting.

"The engineer needs you to move things. Do what he asks," the Matrite squad leader ordered.

"Everything needs to go in the larger wagon," the engineer explained. "Start by emptying the front wagon. Don't drop anything, and don't throw it. Set it down gently."

One by one, the four took their turns with carting items from the forward wagon to the larger wagon. Alucius said nothing, just followed directions, until they began emptying the rearmost of the two smaller wagons.

Alucius took care to make sure that he had the last piece of equipment, a small silver box, which he placed most carefully in the large six-wheeled wagon. Then, he studied the mass of broken equipment, and moved several pieces, so that they would not fall or be further broken if the wagon went over curbs or rough ground.

"As soon as you're through, form up!" ordered the Matrite squad leader.

Alucius moved another piece of equipment, then looked up to see the engineer watching. "I just wanted to make sure nothing broke anymore."

"I appreciate that," Hyalas said grudgingly.

Alucius did his best to project childlike, innocent curiosity. "Engineer, sir, how did it . . . all end up like this . . . with so many men with . . . these collars . . . here in Madrien?"

"Don't ask silly questions." Hyalas gestured to the torque around his own neck. "You know what would happen."

"Why do they . . . the women collar . . . even respected men like you?"

"Think that they should rule? Why not? They've taken the first words of the prophecy."

Alucius looked as blank as he felt. "Prophecy?"

"*The Legacy of the Duarchy*—the words go something like this . . .

> What lies ahead in dawns and dusks to come?
> Can we trust the rising sun, the stars of night,
> or will the ways of magic and of men
> betray our heritage, sacred birthright?
>
> That heritage, that legacy of old,
> Duarchial bequest to ages new,
> unseen by fair Elcien's sages bold
> will grant power even the wisest rue . . ."

"They believe that the ways of men betrayed them?" asked Alucius cautiously.

"The Matrial has said so. She is eternal and unaging. Would you question her?" A sardonic smile crossed the face of the engineer. "Now . . . you'd better get back to your group."

"Thank you, engineer." Alucius bowed his head in respect, then turned and hurried after the others, trying to ignore the squad leader who was riding toward him.

"Move it!" snapped the Matrite squad leader.

Alucius realized something else. The squad leader really didn't want to punish Alucius. He'd even waited and let the engineer talk to him.

66

Northeast of Iron Stem, Iron Valleys

In the early winter evening, just before supper, the silver-haired herder looked across the table at Lucenda. "I talked to Kustyl."

"Alucius . . . is he hurt?"

"He was wounded and captured . . . by the Matrites."

"But he is alive?" asked Lucenda.

"Before the Matrites took over the whole area around Soulend, some of the scouts claim they saw him in one of their wagons." Royalt took a slow and deep breath. "Good sign that he was alive when they carted him off to wherever they take them."

"Will they find out he . . . is a herder."

"Let us hope not. That's why I didn't want him to have a herder's wristguard . . . and he looks young. That might help."

"Can we ransom him back when this is over?"

Royalt did not meet her eyes. "Madrien doesn't ransom . . . the Matrites put funny collars on captives and train them as workers or cavalry," he finally said.

"What can we do?"

"We keep running the stead, and hope that Alucius can find a way home, in body, and not just in spirit," Royalt said. "And we don't tell Veryl. If she asks, we say that he was wounded, and he's recovering. That much is true."

Lucenda nodded. "She keeps hoping . . ."

"So do we all, daughter. So do we all."

67

Another four days of riding and marching southward on what the Matrite troopers called the east range road had brought Alucius and the other captives to the town of Arwyn, similar to Harmony, but slightly larger, with the same kind of captive barracks—and the same neat, well-dressed stone dwellings and buildings. From Arwyn they had continued southward through hills that had turned into low mountains in places, and then back to hills by early on the afternoon of the third day. Once south of the higher peaks, the air had warmed considerably, so much so that Alucius had unfastened his winter parka. The hills held leafless trees and silver-brown grass, but no snow and no evergreens.

"Oh . . ." someone murmured.

Seated facing the rear as he was, Alucius had to turn in the wagon to look southward. The convoy had emerged from between two hills and moved along a causeway that rose above the steep grassy slope toward an eternastone bridge that arched over the river ahead. The bridge was twice as wide as the highway, with a low stone curb in the middle of the roadway.

Beyond the river lay a city, a city larger than any Alucius had seen.

"That's Hieron," offered one of the squad leaders riding beside the wagon. "Where you'll find out what you'll be doing for a long time."

Alucius didn't like the idea of being in Madrien for a long time, not at all, but the squad leader moved ahead of the wagon.

Alucius looked back at the river, nearer than the city, and more than one hundred and fifty yards wide, a smooth expanse of shimmering gray-green water, framed in stone. Each bank was a stone levee that rose more than thirty yards above the water's surface. Upon the top of the levee was a broad highway, three times as wide as the old highways of the Iron Valleys, but made of the same imperishable eternastone. Gleaming silver-gray, the levee-highways stretched as far as Alucius could see, either upstream to the east-southeast or downstream to the west-northwest, and the one on the south side of the river formed the northern boundary of Hieron.

Alucius could tell that the Matrites had not built the bridge nor the levees; the sense of age and the resemblance to the ancient high roads were far too great. As the wagon rolled across the wide bridge, he looked downstream, taking in the straightness of the riverbank levees. He also noticed that there were no wagons and no riders heading downstream on those wide highways, although he could see riders and wagons heading upstream, as well as seven or eight wagons rolling northward across the bridge on the pavement on the other side of the stone center curb.

The high road which they had been traveling continued southward beyond the southern bank of the river, a raised causeway which effectively split Hieron in two. Alucius turned back around to look westward. On a hill to the west of the highway-causeway, just above and beyond the neat streets and stone-dressed dwellings, was a wide and low hill that appeared to be a spacious private retreat, a structure that hugged the line of the hill, no more than two or three stories in height, with low stone walls and trees and fountains.

Once on the south side of the river, which had to be the River Vedra, from what Alucius recalled of his geography, the riders and wagons turned eastward on the levee-highway. Alucius looked beyond the levee to his right, taking in what he could of the city of Hieron, stretching for at least a vingt east and west along the southern bank of the river. Beside the levee, the houses were smaller, but still well turned out, with the same painted shutters he had seen elsewhere in the towns of Madrien, and with people moving in all the streets, most on foot, but some mounted, and a few in small carriages drawn by a single horse.

On the wide river were barges using the current, and

guided by huge wooden sweeps, sailing craft, using the wind to move upstream, and a handful of boats powered by oars. Alucius was too far from the smaller craft to tell whether the rowers were men or women.

The river had cut a wide swath through the Coast Range, and the effect was that Hieron sat on the west side of the low mountains, the same range along whose east side the east range road had been built ages before. To the southeast of the city, the mountains climbed once more. In a way, it made sense to Alucius, because Hieron was a pivot point of both geography and trade.

Hieron had wide parkways, with silvered grass and green shrubbery in their centers, and open greens or squares in any direction where Alucius looked. He had to admit to himself that Iron Stem looked small and poor, and even mean, by comparison. He could sense that others shared at least some of his feelings, and those captives in the wagon were even more silent than usual, without even murmurs or whispers.

Even with the wide spaces, Alucius already felt closed in—confined—and he knew it would get worse. It had to. At that moment, he felt more like a herder than he had in weeks, and he missed the open spaces and endless silver-green skies.

The column traveled close to half a glass before turning southward on a slightly declining ramp from the levee-highway. Alucius could see that the ramp was not of eternastone and bore traces of wear.

Less than two vingts southward on the road paved with something like limestone, which was also showing traces of wheel grooves, the column turned into another compound— similar to those in Harmony and Arwyn, but larger, with walls almost half a vingt in each direction, and more impressive. The stone walls were three yards high, enough to deter an easy escape, but certainly not so formidable as the levee-walls bordering the river. Unlike the river levees, the walls around the fortress, if that were indeed what it happened to be, were of smoothed redstone.

"Out of the wagons and in through the square arch! In

through the square arch!" came the order, repeated by all the Matrite troopers.

Inside the arch was a large stone-walled room, larger than the inside mustering area had been in the barracks at Soulend, although there were only a few more than twenty captives. Once all the captives were in the room, a blonde woman Matrite officer with an insignia Alucius had not seen—a gold four pointed star with an arc over the top three points—stepped up onto a stone block that resembled a mounting block. She surveyed the captives slowly, before speaking in accented Lanachronan.

"You are captives of war. Unlike most lands, we provide you a second chance. For some of you that chance will be better than for others, depending on your skills. We welcome artisans and those skilled in engineering. We also seek skilled troopers. Those of you who lack those skills will become public laborers, building and rebuilding Hieron, or perhaps gardeners. Those of you who cannot accept such occupations will eventually die."

Alucius watched and listened intently. Although he wasn't certain, because Lanachronan was not her first language, and because he still had no Talent-senses, the officer seemed to be telling what she believed to be the truth, and that was as disconcerting to him as the size and scope of the city itself.

There was a long silence before she continued. "Someone, perhaps several people, will talk to you. You may be tested in various ways to determine your skills. You will be broken into groups of five. I wish you well." She paused again. "I remind you that disobedience is punished." Then she stepped down, and five junior squad leaders moved forward, breaking the captives into four groups of five and a group of three.

The group of five to which Alucius was assigned consisted all of younger men close to his own age, although Alucius was the youngest and the tallest, and the only one he knew on more than a name basis was Lysal. Because the room was far warmer than outside, Alucius had taken off his winter parka and cap, and folded the parka across his arm. So had all the others except Lysal.

"Follow me," ordered the stern-faced and clean-shaven Matrite squad leader.

Given the situation, Alucius followed. So did the others. The Matrite walked through an archway in the middle of the southern wall, and down a corridor a good five yards wide. Both the floor and the walls were of polished redstone. They walked a good thirty yards until the squad leader halted before a closed door.

"You will be interviewed. Do not attempt to lie. You will be found out." The Matrite pointed to Lysal. "Inside the door."

It was a simple five panel door, of dark oak, and oiled, with a brass door lever. Lysal opened it gingerly.

"Come in. Don't waste time," offered the firm, but not cutting, voice of a woman.

Alucius watched as the door shut.

"Wonder what—" began someone.

"No talking."

Alucius was third.

"Your name?" asked the gray-haired and square-jawed officer who sat behind a wooden table with a stack of papers on one side and a smaller stack on the other.

"Alucius."

"Sit down."

As he sat on the armless stool, the woman riffled through the papers, picked up one, and read it. She smiled, a friendly smile, but Alucius could see the calculation behind the expression. He also had the feeling that she was one of those officers with Talent . . . a feeling that was reinforced by the slightest sense of darkness around her. Was he beginning to regain his abilities, or learn to use them beyond the confines of the torque around his neck? Would he ever recover his previous Talent-abilities? Abruptly, he realized that the grayness he had sensed in the Matrite troopers—before he had been injured—had to have come from the collars, and perhaps the collar he wore also had affected his thinking abilities as well as his talent. It was something he had not considered, and he silently reproached himself for his slowness.

"You wear expensive undergarments, Alucius of Iron Valleys. The nightsilk is not usual for a common trooper. You are perhaps a herder?"

Alucius wondered how she knew about his undergarments. Had they taken notes on all the captives? Someone had rolled back his sleeves and opened his parka when he had still been unconscious after he had been captured. "No, honored one—" Alucius inclined his head and, following the example of the male Matrite troopers, did not look directly at her.

"Overcaptain," the woman corrected.

"No, overcaptain. My father died many years ago, and my grandsire is a herder. When I was conscripted, he gave me the undergarments in hopes that they might help protect me."

The overcaptain laughed. "Against blade, perhaps, but not against a collar—or against a rifle. If you are accepted to be trained as a horse trooper, you may keep them. It would be a waste to try to retailor them, and we would like you to be a long-lived trooper. So would you." She frowned. "Do you have skills as an artisan, an engineer?"

"I don't believe so." Alucius managed to keep his face regretful. If he admitted to skills with machines, it would come out that he was a herder in all but name, and he had a feeling that was not good. He tried to project both worry and truthfulness, but not strongly.

"You don't believe so?"

"Honored overcaptain, I don't know what skills you mean. I can do some leatherwork, and know how to tan. I've made leather vests, and belts, but they were not of good quality. I worked at carding wool before I became a trooper, but I never really learned spinning . . ." All that he said was certainly true.

"Then who would inherit your grandsire's stead?"

"My mother was of the opinion it should be sold to buy my way out of conscription, but that would have left my grandparents without a way to live."

"I don't believe you answered the question, Alucius."

"I don't have an answer, honored overcaptain. I was not

a herder. My mother and grandsire were looking for a suitable wife—"

"How would that help?"

At least Alucius had an answer for that. "Herders do not have to be men. The stead was held by my grandsire's mother, and her mother before her."

The overcaptain laughed. "Apparently, the Iron Valleys do have a few redeeming traits." She looked down at the sheet. "Does your head still hurt?"

"Only at times, overcaptain. Less so every day."

"Do you still have any bruises?"

"My shoulder was sore from where I fell—"

"A mounted trooper, and you fell?"

"I was struck in the back of the head, overcaptain. I could not see properly for days. I believe I fell. My shoulder was most sore when I finally woke."

"You speak well. How many years of schooling have you had?"

"I lived on the stead. I was sent lessons from the school in Iron Stem from the time I was seven or eight until I was sixteen."

The officer thrust a sheet of paper and a flat board at him. "I'll hand you a grease stick. I want you to write what I say."

Alucius took the paper, the board, and the grease stick.

"The best weapon is a prepared mind, and the greatest error is relying merely upon the strength of weapons and the thickness of fortifications . . ."

Alucius wrote as quickly as he could, and as well, but he was a good sentence behind when the woman stopped.

"Let me see."

He handed back the sheet, and the board and writing implement.

"Your penmanship is adequate, your spelling good, and your memory clear." She nodded. "You may go."

"Yes, overcaptain." Alucius inclined his head before standing, and bowing again.

Alucius waited outside with the others. Lysal glanced at him and raised his eyebrows. Alucius shrugged. He still wasn't certain about the interview, but he had the sense that the officer had at least a small amount of Talent, if not more, and had been using it. He could only hope he had deceived her.

The last man was a Reillie that Alucius had not met or talked to, and when he returned, he handed sheets of paper—five or six—to the squad leader.

"Let's go." The squad leader turned, and continued down the corridor until they reached the first intersecting hallway, where they turned and stopped at the third door.

The squad leader looked at the sheet, then spoke. "Ondomin, you go in here."

The Reillie swallowed.

"They want to test your woodworking skills. Good carpenters or cabinetmakers are hard to find. You could do well with that . . . if you're any good."

The squad leader returned within moments, alone.

Alucius did not even think of moving. Where would he have gone?

The remaining four were marched back the way they had come and then through the open courtyard to another building, and then into another stone-walled room where several troopers waited.

One of the troopers—a dark-haired and black-eyed man with olive skin of a shade Alucius had never seen—stepped forward and handed Alucius a wooden sabre, of the Matrite pattern with the slightly curved blade.

"You are to spar with him," said the escorting squad leader. "It does not matter how many times you strike him. The test is to see whether you can keep him from striking you without giving much ground."

Alucius set his parka on the floor stones, then hefted the weapon, not so heavy as a real sabre, but thicker so that it wasn't that much lighter.

The black-haired trooper bowed, then lifted his blade, also wooden.

Alucius was sweating when the squad leader called for a halt, but he had managed to avoid being struck by the other trooper, who actually had smiled once the two had lowered their weapons.

"He's good with a blade. Class one." The words were not Lanachronan, or the version spoken in the Iron Valleys, but Alucius understood their import.

Once all four had finished working with the wooden sabres, they were led through another warren of stone corridors until they walked through a set of double doors. There, Alucius looked out on an enclosed and roofed arena—one that was at least a hundred yards in length and seventy-five in width.

"This is the indoor maneuver area," said the squad leader who was leading the four. "You'll be asked to ride in patterns around those posts set on the sand."

The horse given to Alucius was a roan gelding of moderate height at the shoulder, perhaps a half hand taller than Alucius's gray. Absently, he wondered what had happened to the gray. Was he too a Matrite captive, carrying some Matrite trooper? Alucius hoped so, even if it might hurt some militia troopers. It wasn't the gray's fault that men fought.

He mounted and waited for his turn. He had to listen carefully to the instructions offered in heavily accented Lanachronan. The instructions seemed simple enough, and he followed them, he thought, accurately, returning to the point at the side of the area from where he had begun.

"He's got a good seat. Let's see how he does with Wildebeast."

The squad leader turned to Alucius. "We'd like you to ride another mount. Dismount."

"Yes, sir."

Alucius could tell that the second mount—who was led in almost immediately—was not only more spirited, but, for some reason, did not care to be ridden. Even as Alucius took the reins from the ostler, also collared, the beast *whuff*ed, almost angrily. Alucius took a slow deep breath and tried to project calm, then stepped up and patted the stallion's shoulder. He got another *whuff*. He mounted, still trying to project calm and control, not knowing whether he was successful, or whether the stallion settled down and accepted him because of his experience in the saddle. Either way, Wildebeast quieted, and Alucius rode him through a repeated series of the patterns in and out and around the posts and barriers. He was glad no one asked him to jump anything, but suspected that was for the mount's benefit, not his.

He reined up where he had started.

"How'd he do that?" murmured the squad leader.

The trooper acting as clerk looked at the sheet before him. "He comes from a herder family, but isn't one. Probably learned to deal with mounts as a child."

Alucius lost track of where they went, and all the small tasks they were assigned, from sharpening sabres to looking at an injured mount and being asked questions.

It was well past sunset when they found themselves in another room, this time with eleven others who had been captives, being addressed by the same blonde Matrite officer who had greeted them. Lysal, Alucius noted, was not among the eleven, having been led off somewhere along the way.

"You all are considered to have possibilities as horse troopers. You'll be escorted to the collar-forge and have the prisoners' collars replaced with troopers' collars. They're essentially the same, except that you can go anywhere without choking and you can touch them without pain. They'll still kill you if you try to remove them, and senior officers can administer punishment through them. So can the eternal Matrial and any of her assistants.

"You'll be fed after that, and you'll sleep here tonight, and tomorrow you'll be assigned mounts and be transferred to the training corps. Good luck."

With that, she turned and left.

"You're almost done," one of the more senior Matrite squad leaders said, "but you should be more comfortable—and safer—with new torques."

Safer? Again, that choice of words seemed odd to Alucius, but he took them in.

Another walk down another long corridor on tired legs ended with the eleven lined up before yet another door. Alucius was fifth. When he walked through the long archway beyond the door, he could smell the odor of hot metal, but the space did not seem excessively hot, not like the hammermill in Iron Stem.

A short, but muscular man stood between two benches. He motioned for Alucius to stand by the first one. An overcaptain stood on the far side of the bench, her eyes fixed on Alucius.

The smith looked at Alucius, then took a length of cord and measured the involuntary recruit's neck. "The overcaptain there has Talent. She doesn't need a collar to kill you. I'll remove the first collar, and she'll damp it so that you don't get hurt. I'll fit the torque and then I'll fasten it in place. After that, I'll slip the barrier under it and weld it. It's not a heavy weld, but it's enough to keep it from coming off unless someone cuts your neck in two, and then it wouldn't matter. You wouldn't want it separating on you. That's instant death, you know."

Alucius gave the faintest of nods. He was exhausted, and the headache had returned, so much so that he felt his head was splitting. Even so, he tried to concentrate on sensing what happened with the collar, but it was almost too quick for him to take in what happened. He thought that some sort of blackness wrapped around the back of the collar for several brief moments, and then the smith held the prisoner's collar, which he set on a lower shelf of his bench. When the smith fastened the troopers' torque on Alucius, the same thing happened, except there was a flare of that evil-feeling pink, if but for an instant, and for the first time he had sensed it since he had been injured. Alucius had the vague sense that the pinkness was a thread that led . . . somewhere . . . but he was so tired that he could hardly keep alert, let alone try to send his barely usable Talent-senses out, especially with a full-Talent watching him. Still . . . he could feel the relief that he would have some use of Talent, perhaps not so much as once, but any Talent was better than none.

Alucius waited . . . and followed . . . and perhaps another glass later found himself standing with the others in yet another spotless barracks, if again with barred windows.

A new junior squad leader looked over the group. "I've seen better, and I've seen worse. So will you. If you make it as a Matrite trooper, life's better than you'd imagine. It's better than in the Iron Valley Militia and a lot better than in the Southern Guard."

Alucius could well accept the second half of what the man said, and he wasn't so sure that the officers in the Matrite forces might not be an improvement over Majer Dysar. But Alucius wasn't free, and that would always bother him, because he was a herder in heart and spirit.

"There's even more freedom than you'd expect. That's if you make it." Another gesture was beyond the line of bunks. "The wash facilities are at the end. We'll feed you first, and then you can come back and wash, and turn in. We'll wake you at dawn to dress and eat, and we'll begin at a glass and a half past dawn. Eat well and have a good night's sleep. You'll work for every bite and moment of sleep from here on in until you complete training, or until you wash out and become a laborer."

Alucius didn't intend to end as a laborer. But then, he didn't intend to remain a Matrite trooper for life, either.

68

Alucius looked down at the breakfast platter he had been handed. Two large slices of something batter-fried rested beside some sort of eggs, with two golden-brown flat biscuits, partly covered with a whitish sauce or gravy. On the edge of the platter were fried sliced potatoes and a healthy pile of dried fruit, and half a lemon. He also had a mug of weak ale, and cutlery, which made a certain sense, because he'd long since been relieved of his belt knife.

Slowly, he carried his breakfast to one of the empty tables in the stone-walled and well-lighted mess, and seated himself on the bench. Shortly, he was joined by Sazium, a squarish militia trooper who he had seen but in passing at Pyret.

"Better food than I've seen in more than a year," offered Sazium.

"Since I left home," Alucius agreed.

"They must do a lot of fighting," the older trooper suggested. "Otherwise, why would they feed us like this?"

"Make us feel grateful over time, maybe." Alucius took several bites of ham and egg toast.

"Don't know as I ever will." Sazium paused to drink some of his ale. "Can't figure out how they took so much land. We fought better."

Alucius cocked his head. He'd thought about that. "A bunch of things. They have more people, and more golds, and more troopers. You saw what they sent past us. They also have machines like that spear-thrower thing. Their commanders have more experience."

"But we kept killing more of them," protested the other man.

"We were fighting on our land, and we used every trick we knew. Not one worked more than once. You really think Dysar is that good?"

Sazium laughed, if hollowly. "You're not going over . . . are you?"

Alucius shook his head. "I'll do what I have to, and I'll learn everything I can." He shrugged. "What else can we do?" He tried not to think about his mother, his grandparents—and Wendra. There was no way that he knew of to send them word, and he wished that he'd taken the time to dash off a letter or two. But he had always felt rushed and tired at Soulend. He wondered if he really had been.

"You all right?" asked Sazium.

"Just thinking. No way to let anyone know."

"You're right about that."

Alucius ate as much as he could, first, because it was good, even the fried fish, and, second, because he didn't know when they'd eat again. Then he stood and looked for somewhere to put the platter, cutlery, and tumbler.

"Over there, in the window," called the single Matrite trooper watching the mess area.

Alucius slipped both into the space that looked like a window without glass and watched as a white-haired man with one of the ubiquitous silver torques took both. Then he turned and walked back to the barracks where he washed up again and sat down on the end of the bunk to wait.

He waited less than half a glass before one of the junior squad leaders appeared, opening the locked door to the inner main corridor.

"Time to go. Form up. Five across."

When the eleven were lined up, the squad leader continued. "You'll be issued mounts here. This is actually two posts in one. You'll be assigned to the trooper section. That's Eltema Post. There, you'll have your hair—and beards, if you have them—cut to trooper standards, and you'll be issued a training kit. You'll spend the rest of the day getting you and your mount settled and your gear ready. Tomorrow your real work begins. We're headed to the stable."

As they followed the squad leader, Alucius pondered. The receiving area was huge. Did the Matrites use it for other functions? Or were they testing and processing that many captives every day? He wasn't about to ask—not until he knew more.

At the stable, Alucius almost grinned as the ostler, wearing the silver torque that all men seemed to wear in the lands of Madrien, brought forward his mount—Wildebeast.

The ostler did grin—broadly—and bowed. "Your mount, with squad leader Sywiki's compliments."

"Thank you."

The stallion seemed to recognize Alucius. At least, he calmed down and stopped edging sideways once Alucius had the reins, even before he led Wildebeast out into the stone paved courtyard.

When all eleven were mounted, the squad leader turned his mount to face them. "We're going to ride out about a vingt, and then come back and ride through the gates on the south side. Often, someone thinks that once we're on the highway, he can just ride away. It's true. You won't choke if you go too far." A cold smile appeared. "It's also true that one of the Talent-officers can kill you through the collar from dozens of vingts away, if not farther. I really wouldn't try it." He shrugged. "Every few months, someone doesn't believe me. Now . . . once you become troopers, you'll be riding a whole lot of places, and you'll have plenty of chances to ride off. If you want to try it, you'll have a chance. Don't try it now. Talk to the older troopers in your units first. Or let some other idiot try it so that you can see what happens."

Even with his faint Talent, Alucius could sense the absolute truth behind the man's words. He wasn't sure which was worse, that the Matrites could so convince a trained trooper— or that they in fact had that power.

After a moment, the squad leader said, "Form into a column, by twos. Most of you should know how. Help the others."

Only one of the eleven—Johens, a young, long-haired Squawt, Alucius thought—hadn't been a trooper, and in moments the column was formed. Alucius stayed back in the third rank, beside Sazium. The column rode out of the unguarded gates and continued southward on the redstone road. Wildebeast behaved well, and Alucius wondered if the stallion had been mistreated, or just needed a firm hand—or a herder.

Was the ride another test—with a Talent-officer somewhere watching and waiting to see if anyone tried to escape? With his bare shred of recently returned Talent-sense, he couldn't tell.

After about a vingt eastward, the small column turned south, along another redstone paved road, an older road with traces of wear on the smoothly dressed and mortared surfaces. Alucius knew that what he noted meant something beyond the obvious—that the ramps and redstone roads had been built later than the eternastone high roads and levees, yet . . . he could not quite grasp what that might be. He felt stupid that he could not, and frustrated by his inability to understand.

His head was beginning to ache again, and he concentrated on riding as the squad turned westward on another road, heading back to Eltema Post.

69

Spring came far earlier in Hieron than in Iron Stem. That was obvious, because the grass began to turn green and the trees to bud little more than two weeks after Alucius had arrived at Eltema Post. Even without the bitter cold of Soulend, the Matrite training—or retraining—was exhausting. The day began with a two-vingt run north on the road leading north on river causeway, in loose exercise clothes issued to them. After the run came a glass of individual arms training and practice. Sometimes they used the wooden sabres, sometimes longer blades, sometimes wooden knives, and sometimes no weapons at all. When they worked with instructors and no weapons, Alucius did better than most, although there were moves and techniques he had never seen.

Only then did they eat. After eating came showers and cleaning up, and wearing uniforms to actual classroom instruction for two full glasses every morning. Then they ran through mounted maneuvers, before a midday dinner, and after the midday meal, a glass of instruction in the Madrien tongue, and then back to mounted practice in small group tactics. This was different, because a Matrite company was made of ten eight-trooper squads, each led by a junior squad leader. After group riding tactics came practice at the rifle range, under *very* close supervision. The smaller Matrite rifle took some work for Alucius to adjust to, but he could see the advantage of the magazine that carried ten cartridges.

Then came another glass or so of hard exercise before supper. After supper, there was time to wash up and take care of cleaning uniforms and stable maintenance. Sometimes, there was time to read—the Matrites had a small library, and there was little else to do, except talk or game, and neither appealed to Alucius. The only problem was that the books were printed in Madrien. Alucius forced himself to start with the easy ones, telling himself that the more he knew the better his chances for eventually escaping.

Of all the work, he liked the class sessions the most. Alucius had never been in a classroom and usually enjoyed the learning, if not the circumstances. The instructors varied. Some were officers, always women. Some were senior squad leaders, and some were men or women whose backgrounds the trainees were never told. At times, the lectures were more than informative. They were disturbing, particularly one of the early lectures, with an older gray-haired woman.

"Our world has one large continent—that is Corus—and four small continents, as well as a number of groups of islands. The history of Corus is long, and much of it has been lost. Most of that you don't need to know. What you do need to know is what was lost, and what the Matrial has undertaken to reclaim and why."

Alucius had his doubts, but he had listened. He also noted the reference to "the" Matrial.

"There were four major cities of the Duarchy. Three of them lay in what are now the lands of Madrien. Those were Elcien, Ludar, and Faitel. Here, here, and here." The woman used the thin wooden pointer to show where on the large wall map each city had been. "Most of you should know that Ludar and Faitel were totally destroyed, so much so that little more than swamp and scattered stones remain. The isle on which Elcien was built sank so deeply into the Bay of Ludel that just the tips of a few towers are visible. Only in recent years have the Talent-forces subsided enough that the ruins could be investigated without risking instant death. The other great city was Alustre, far to the east, in the land now known as Lustrea, and Alustre was hardly damaged at all.

"In the time of the Duarchy, both men and women had great powers, and even the lowliest lived free from want and fear . . . the Alectors of Justice knew who those were who injured others, and justice was swift and fair. This is no longer true in much of Corus. Talent-power, save for the Talent-officers of Madrien, is rare and far less powerful . . .

"In Lustrea, women are blamed for the Cataclysm and may not own property, hold coins, supervise men, or become artisans or traders. In Lanachrona, only those who are born into the Ezerhazy may own land. In the Iron Valleys, vast tracts of land are held by herder families who live on luxurious estates, and the more lucrative businesses are held by merchants in Dekhron, while the majority of people have barely enough to live on. Even in Madrien, the torques are necessary to ensure that the violent are restrained . . ." The instructor smiled coldly. "What does all this have to do with troopers? A great deal."

She stepped sideways to the map. "You all can see the blue lines here. Those are the high roads of the Duarchy. Most of them still can be used. You can see how they create a web across all of Corus. In the ancient days, when there were the tireless sandoxes, food and goods and spices and people all traveled the roads swiftly. Grain grown in the fertile valleys that are now north Madrien was carried all across Corus. Fruits grown near Fola and Hafin traveled the world. The wines from the Vyanhills went everywhere. The golden rice and nuts of Lustrea came west. Great bison grazed the grasslands of Ongelya, and were transported everywhere for all to have fresh meat . . ." There was another pause. "Today, each land hoards what it produces. Madrien must either impoverish its people to buy goods—or have enough troopers to take the other lands for their goods because lands such as Southgate and now Lanachrona will not trade with Madrien."

The instructor pointed to Sazium. "Have you ever had a good glass of Lanachronan wine?"

"No, honored one."

"I'd imagine not. In Krost, you can get a glass of it for a copper. A small bottle, holding perhaps five glasses, costs two golds in Dekhron—two silvers for one small glass of wine. It certainly doesn't cost a silver and four coppers to cart that wine from Krost to Dekhron . . ."

Alucius understood the argument, but wondered what he was missing, although the woman felt she was conveying the truth.

". . . and that is why Madrien has troopers. As you ride through Hieron, and through any town in Madrien, look at what you see. You do not see masses of poor people. You do not see hovels and huts, but comfortable dwellings for all. Yes, you and many others wear torques, but those torques also free you from hunger, from want, and they allow you to walk anywhere at any glass in Madrien without fear and without danger. That is the greatest boon of the Matrial . . ."

Alucius knew what he had already seen, but it troubled him that everyone in Madrien seemed to accept the idea that men had to wear torques so the land could be free from poverty and danger. How could they believe so readily that men were so evil?

70

On the fourth Quattri that they had been in Hieron, Jesorak—the senior squad leader who directed their training—summoned all eleven to the stables at the time of their first morning classroom instruction. They wore no weapons, since those remained under lock except during weapons instruction.

"This morning, you're going to learn something in a different way. We're going to ride over to the southeast market." Jesorak gestured to a narrow tack table beside the stall door where he stood, on which were eleven forest green belt wallets. "Those are trooper wallets. Each has nine coppers in it, for each of you to spend as you wish—or not, as you choose. I'd suggest you not purchase more of the fruit than you can eat there. You have nowhere to keep it, and you're not used to too much fresh fruit at the moment. Also, I'd not buy anything terribly large, because you're troopers and all you possess has to fit in two saddlebags. Oh, and you get to keep the wallets, too, but you don't wear them except when you're traveling or going off post." Jesorak paused. "One other thing. Troopers don't steal. From anyone, and not from other troopers. If something's missing, I bring in an officer with Talent. She discovers who did it. You steal, and you're a public laborer for life, probably in the stone quarries. Life isn't very long there." He lifted one of the wallets and tossed it to Sazium, then the second to Murat. Alucius caught the fourth one and fastened it to his belt.

"Saddle up and meet in the courtyard."

Wildebeast seemed almost puzzled, Alucius sensed, to be saddled so early. Was the horse so spirited because he was more intelligent and sensitive than most mounts? Alucius was careful to project calm, and the two were ready outside the stable before the others.

Jesorak was already mounted. He had a sabre at his belt, but the rifle case at his knee was empty. The squad leader eased his mount over to Alucius. "Know animals, don't you, trooper?"

"Some, sir."

"Know weapons and fighting, too," Jesorak said, adding conversationally, "Good trooper can make squad leader quickly, less than a year, if there's heavy fighting. You serve fifteen years, get a good stipend, live well here, or anywhere you want in Madrien. Happened to my brother."

"Yes, sir." Alucius paused. "Where are you from, if I might ask, sir?"

"Me? Born a Madrien boy, down in Hafin." Jesorak laughed. "Don't you go thinking all the troopers are former captives. Less than a third. Most captives aren't good enough. Something like fifty of you came through that week. Three artisans, eleven of you, and the rest'll end up public laborers. Even a laborer in Madrien's better than being a scutter in the Iron Valleys or a field worker in Lanachrona, or seaman in Southgate—if you're not in the quarries."

"I've seen that, sir," Alucius replied politely.

"Just keep your eyes open, trooper," Jesorak said with a nod. "You'll see." He glanced toward Beral and Kymbes, who were mounting outside the stable. "Form up on Alucius here."

The other eight appeared within moments, and the small column rode out of Eltema Post gates. As they headed southward, Alucius noticed a full company of horse troopers moving through some sort of parade.

Jesorak turned in his saddle. "That's the Twentieth Company. They busted up an attack by the Lanachronan Southern Guards—trying to test us on the high road from Tempre to Salcer. Wiped out the entire company. Matrial's going to honor them at her residence tomorrow. They're practicing the parade." After a moment, the squad leader added. "Her residence is the big low dwelling on the hill park on the west side of Hieron."

Alucius recalled wondering what that structure had been. Now he knew.

Even before midmorning, the day was warm, under high and hazy clouds, with barely a hint of a breeze. The air held a warm dampness that would have suggested rain to Alucius in Iron Stem, but in Hieron dampness without rain was all too usual.

On the south side of the post, across another stone side street from the redstone walls, were at least five or six small shops. Like those he had viewed from the prisoners' wagon in Harmony and Arwyn, they looked spotless from the outside. Alucius could see several troopers in their uniforms on the streets, and going in and out of the shops. From the smell, somewhere there was an eating place, perhaps a bakery or a cafe. He'd never seen a cafe, because there were none in Iron Stem, but he'd read about them in one of his grandsire's books.

While not in groups of eight, most troopers seemed to be in pairs or groups of three. Alucius could hear them talking, and while their voices were not raucous, some of the conversations were animated, punctuated with expressive gestures. The more he saw of Hieron and Madrien, the less he understood.

Beyond the shops were more of the neat dwellings, again with painted shutters, but these shutters were painted in forest green with crimson edging. Housing for senior squad leaders or officers? They rode past the houses with the green shutters that covered three blocks, before passing houses that looked much as had those in other Madrien towns, but Alucius was able to see more now. The rear of every house contained a walled garden, and he did not see any gates in those walls, although he did see the tops of trees and a grape arbor in one place.

After riding perhaps another two vingts, the column reached a wider street, and to the right was a large walled structure with a stone-framed entrance a good twenty yards wide, without a gate. Jesorak rode through the entrance, and the other eleven followed into what looked at first to be a large courtyard in the middle of a square building. The courtyard was paved entirely in redstone. In the center were lines of posts, for tethering mounts, or teams—although Alucius could see but one of the small carriages, attended by a trim white-haired man with a high-necked tunic that concealed whether he wore a torque. There were so many people in the marketplace, and so many who projected the grayness brought by the collars that Alucius doubted he could tell who was wearing one and who was not—except by being so close that his eyes would tell him as well as his still-feeble Talent-senses. But then, he had not seen a man who did not wear a torque, not that he knew.

Unlike the market square in Iron Stem, there were no carts for vendors. Instead, the building held stone carrels of sorts, some large, some small, open to the inner square. Each contained goods and a seller, and there had to be over a hundred sellers there, if not more.

"Column halt!" called Jesorak. "The posts with the green bands are for troopers. You tie your mounts there. They'll be safe. You've got a glass and a half. When you see me mount, head back here." He grinned. "Enjoy yourself."

Alucius could tell that the grin was forced, that the squad leader was nervous. He also could feel a stronger sense of the pinkish power behind them, at the corner, and he had no doubts that one of the officers with the Talent had followed them—or had been waiting for them. In a way, that almost reassured him that there were some limits to the power of the torques. He just had to find out what they were. He was also feeling reassured by the fact that with each day, he could sense a bit more with his Talent. He just hoped that his abilities continued to improve.

Alucius dismounted and tied Wildebeast, spending a little extra time, soothing the stallion and projecting reassurance before he walked away from his mount, heading almost at random toward the north side of the marketplace.

His first stop was at the carrel of a silversmith, where he just looked, taking in the sleek lines of the work, mainly items such as ornate boxes lined with colored velvet, candelabra, and silver serving platters. The silversmith was a woman, without a torque, who studied him but for a moment before returning to discuss a silver platter with an older grayhaired woman and a younger woman in pale yellow.

Beside the silversmith's was a carpet seller. Alucius stopped and stared, not at the carpet displayed on the wooden rack, but at a smaller one, a yard and a half by two, which had a deep green midground with an eight-pointed pale blue star in the center. The border, a hand in width, was woven so intricately that the silver and crimson filigree pattern looked as though it were indeed enamel and metal. With a rueful smile, and a hidden laugh, he turned. Even as a herder, he doubted he could have afforded the carpets, not the ones he liked, and he certainly couldn't have justified spending the golds they must have cost, even if he had such.

Beyond the carpet seller's was a cabinet-maker's space. Alucius only gave the chests and cabinets a cursory glance. They were dark and heavy, cumbersome in appearance, if well made. He passed by a small space filled with bright scarves, scarves made of shimmersilk, not nightsilk. While he looked over the scarves for a moment, he knew they were far more expensive than his nine coppers, and, besides, how would he ever get one back to Wendra?

The western side of the marketplace held sellers of produce and foods. Alucius did buy a sticky honey roll, eating it carefully before moving on to the adjoining stone stall.

The fruit-seller was a woman with black hair shot with white. Unlike most of the women, she also wore a torque, with somewhat more filigree than a trooper's collar, but Alucius could sense that slight touch of the chill and evil-feeling pink. He studied the fruits—recognizing some, such as the lemons and the small bitter oranges, and the apples, although he wondered how they might taste, since they had to have been kept in a winter cellar somewhere. Others, such as the greenish oval that he thought might be a melon of sorts, were unfamiliar.

"What is best?" he asked in his still limited Madrien.

"The alewine." She pointed to the green melon, smiling faintly. "But it is a silver."

Alucius nodded. "Do you grow them . . . in . . ." He groped for a word.

"I have a glassed indoor garden. It isn't large, but I can sell melons a season before the ones in the fields come in. So I do."

Alucius was intrigued. "What else do you grow there?"

"The oranges, and the lemons. Some spices for cooking, but you would not need those now." The hint of a smile filled her voice. "You are young for a trooper."

"One of the younger ones," Alucius admitted.

She handed him an apple. "You may have this."

Alucius returned a copper.

"It was a gift." She smiled.

"Then the copper is also a gift." Alucius wasn't certain why he said that, but it felt right.

The fruit-seller laughed. "Then you must take two. They are two for a copper."

That felt right, and he accepted the second apple with a smile, and a slight bow.

"The best of fortune, young trooper," she murmured as he straightened.

"Thank you." He slipped the apples inside his tunic for later.

On the southern side were those who sold more practical goods. There, Alucius stopped by the cooper's stall, where there was an array of barrels, mainly finely finished half and fifth barrels, but no sign of tools. That indicated that the working shop was elsewhere. A young woman—a girl younger than Wendra, he decided—looked at him dubiously.

"I can't buy your barrels, but I know a cooper where I come from, and I just wanted to see yours and compare." He smiled gently as he bent to inspect a polished lorken fifth-barrel, bound not in iron, but bronze. The workmanship was good, but not any better than Kyrial's.

"How do you find them?" the black-haired girl finally asked.

"The workmanship is good, especially the bronzework."

"You speak Madrien almost without an accent," she observed. "Have you lived here long?"

Alucius smiled. The girl believed what she said. Perhaps his Talent had helped him in learning Madrien. Then, the language was not that different, and many words were almost the same. "I know less than you think. I've been here less than a year." That was true, but he decided against a more precise time.

"You must have a gift for tongues."

"Good teachers," replied Alucius with a slight laugh. "Thank you." He bowed and slipped away.

Long before the glass and a half was over, Alucius left the carrels and shops and walked back into the hazy warm sunlight, crossing the redstone pavement and carefully avoiding the other shoppers—again mostly women or older men wearing torques.

Once he was standing beside Wildebeast, he pulled out one of the two apples. Since he had no knife, he used a trick he had learned as a boy. Using his fingernail, he cut the skin of the apple all the way around, then put a hand on each

half, twisting abruptly and hard. The apple split into two
halves. Alucius offered a half to Wildebeast, then waited and
offered the second.

Only then did be begin to eat the second apple.

"A trooper at heart!" Jesorak laughed from behind Alucius. "The man gets two apples, and one is for his horse, and
the horse eats first. Your mount must have sensed that. Sywiki said he was smart." The squad leader shook his head.

Alucius couldn't help but like and respect Jesorak, enemy
though he might be.

71

More than a week later, again just before the
scheduled morning classroom instruction, squad leader Jesorak appeared with an order. "Mount and form up in the
courtyard."

Alucius could sense that the squad leader was less than
happy, but, as a trainee, he wasn't about to say anything. He
and the ten other troopers-in-training saddled their mounts
and led them out into the courtyard. There, under a clear and
hot sun that was more like summer than spring, a round-
faced, blonde woman wearing a captain's uniform and insignia was mounted beside the squad leader. Despite her
pleasant appearance, Alucius could sense the coldness behind
the facade.

As soon as the eleven were mounted and formed in a two-
abreast column, Jesorak announced, "You've seen the ben-
efits of what Madrien has to offer. Captain Tyeal is going to
take us to see what happens to law-breakers in Hieron."

Once the column was headed eastward, Alucius and Sazium exchanged glances, but not words. Sazium glanced forward and raised his eyebrows. Alucius shrugged in return.

As they rode away from Eltema Post and toward the center
of Hieron, Alucius could see that the streets, while not totally

empty, had far fewer souls on them than had been the case in the other few rides that they had taken since arriving in Hieron.

After about three vingts, they rode up another inclined stone ramp, and crossed the ancient road, descending on the far side into an area of the city where the dwellings were larger, and with walled courtyards in both the front and rear.

Their destination was a circular plaza two vingts to the west of the ancient north-south highway that divided Hieron into eastern and western sections. The plaza was unadorned, a paved expanse a good three hundred yards across set in the middle of a parklike expanse. Just to the west was the hill park with the Matrial's low and sprawling stone dwelling.

In the center of the plaza was a circular gray stone platform—actually a platform within a platform. The outer platform was roughly fifty yards across, and raised a yard above the redstone paving. The inner platform was twenty yards in diameter and raised two yards above the outer platform. Each platform had a set of stone steps on the south side. The lower paved section of the plaza was more than half filled, mainly with men and women on foot, although there were more than a score of small carriages lined up together on the southwest quarter.

The squad leader guided them to an open space less than twenty yards back from the edge of the lower stone platform, but on the southwestern side. "Double staggered line, six and five," Jesorak ordered. "Guide on me."

Once the trainees were aligned, Jesorak added, "Saddle ease . . . no talking."

Alucius shifted his weight in the saddle, then studied the platform.

Two people stood strapped in T-shaped braces on a temporary wooden stand on the south side of the inner stone platform. One was a powerfully built woman, her thick brown hair cut short. She glared at the assembled crowd, and a scabbed scar running from below her ear to the base of her nose stood out. Opposite her was a man, taller and even more powerfully built, if older, and partly gray-haired.

Both wore the silver torques, and plain gray trousers and shirts.

A squad of guards—all women—stood in the open space between the two prisoners. The guards wore forest green tunics, but the piping was not crimson, but a pale purple, and the cuffs of their tunics were also pale purple. Before the guards, stood another woman with a thatch of short gray hair and a firm, hard jaw. Her tunic and trousers were purple, and the piping green. She wore a black sash that ran from her left shoulder across her chest to her right hip.

As Alucius and the others waited, more people filtered into the plaza until, more than a half a glass later, it was more than two-thirds full. By then, Alucius was sweating in the heat. A trickle of moisture ran down the back of his neck, and he continually blotted his face and forehead.

From somewhere a bell rang, and all the murmurs and whispers died away.

The gray-haired official stepped forward. "We are here to do justice. You are here to see justice done. So be it." She turned toward the woman. "You, Luisine of Hieron, cheated the Matrial by failing to pay your tariffs, and lied about the revenues from your business. When you feared your husband would reveal your lawbreaking, you murdered him and falsely claimed you had acted in self-defense because he had abused you. He had done no such thing. When the auditors confirmed your dishonesty and your murder, you attacked and wounded them. For committing murder, for your treachery, and your dishonesty, you have been sentenced to die." A pause followed the words. "Have you any last words of repentance?"

"None! I have done no more than any of you. You cannot judge me fairly—"

"Justice will be done!"

Alucius expected the pinkish force to appear, but the manifestation of Talent that he felt was mainly purple, with but an overshade of pink, and felt even more evil. The silver torque did not tighten. That Alucius could sense, but the effect was the same, as the woman remained silently defiant, her face turning red, then blue. Abruptly, she slumped forward, but it was more than a few moments before Alucius sensed the void that signified death.

"Justice has been done. The Matrial—eternal and ageless—be praised." Almost without a pause, the woman in purple turned to the man at the west end of the platform. "Byreem of Hieron, formerly of Salcer, you have repeatedly abused your wife. Not only have you denied your actions, but you have continued that abuse. Do you confess your guilt? Do you have any last words of repentance?"

"I didn't do it!" The big man protested. "I didn't!"

Even from more than twenty yards away, Alucius could feel the truth of the man's protest.

"You lie. For your lies and your arrogance, and for forcing yourself upon a woman of Hieron, you will die. Justice will be done."

Alucius could sense the purplish force, rising, both around the assistant to the Matrial, and somewhere else in the city. Without moving his head, he tried to locate the source of that power. While he could not be certain, it felt to him that it came from the west, from the park that held the Matrial's dwelling or mansion, probably from the dwelling itself.

Again, the silver torque did not tighten, but the man's protests were cut off, and his face turned red, then blue, before he slumped and fell forward in the T-shaped brace.

"Justice has been done. The Matrial—eternal and ageless—be praised."

Justice? Power had been exerted. The woman had been guilty of all with which she had been charged, but the man had been innocent. Of that, Alucius was convinced. Yet he had died because a woman claimed she had been forced. Had the man used force, and had he not thought it was force? Alucius had known some like that. He had no doubts that Gortal would have felt that way, but the dead man had not seemed like a Gortal. Yet one never knew.

"Column reform!" ordered Jesorak.

While Alucius was far from absolutely certain, he was fairly sure that the power that had executed the two, and the power behind the collars, lay in the Matrial's compound. Not that he could do anything about it—but he clung to his grandsire's advice, and the hope that when he knew enough, he could act.

He also hoped he wasn't deceiving himself into accepting matters so much that he would never act.

72

Although spring had come before the calendar end of winter, the weather in Hieron did not remain cool and springlike, but continued to warm, so that by the time six more weeks had passed, spring was at least as warm in Hieron as full summer in Iron Stem. At the end of those six weeks, on Novdi, the ten experienced troopers were gathered before their morning "class" schedule in the teaching area. Two weeks earlier, the young Squawt Johens had been moved to another class of trainee troopers who had just begun.

There were no instructors, and Jesorak stood there. He was smiling. "Congratulations. Starting now, you're all troopers."

"Sir?" blurted Sazium.

"We don't make a big ceremony about it." He stepped forward and handed each man a silver collar pin—an "M" within a circle, covered with a sabre crossed with a rifle. When each had fastened the pin in place, he went on. "You're troopers. Your pay is standard, like every other base trooper, five coppers—a silver—a week. If you make junior squad leader, it will be doubled to two silvers. You also get two silvers for completing training." He lifted a leather pouch. "We'll take care of that, now. Everyone seems to think it's more real when it's backed with silver."

Alucius was the fourth to get the pair of silvers, which he slipped into his pocket, wishing he had the troopers' belt wallet on. He could not help but note that the Matrite pay was more than twice that of a militia trooper.

"You're going either to the Fortieth Company or to the Thirty-second," Jesorak said. "Both are stationed at Senob Post at Zalt. Alucius, Beral, Kymbes, Murat, and Sazium—you five have been assigned to the Fortieth. The rest of you are going to the Thirty-second.

"You'll be issued your full uniforms, and your sabres and standard belt knives, when we finish here. You'll get your rifles when you get to your company. I'll remind you one last time that sabres are worn only on duty, or when traveling, unless otherwise ordered, and never in a town or city, except when you're riding through or on duty.

"On your off-glasses you can leave the post, but it's strongly recommended that you at least go in pairs . . . especially until you're more accustomed to Madrien. After we finish, you'll have the rest of today and Decdi free, except for whatever preparations you need. I wouldn't try to travel too far from post. You'll be riding out right after breakfast on Londi, and for the first time in over a month, you won't have a weapons class." Jesorak grinned. "You'll be part of a resupply convoy—cartridges, travel rations, medicines—mainly that sort of thing. For the trip, you'll report to Squad Leader Gorak. Captain Sennel will be in command, with Undercaptain Porlel as number two.

"You should spend some time on your gear, but that's up to you. The shops south of the post are also open to you . . . In fact, any street where you can walk is open to you, but you're expected to stay close to Hieron."

Doing anything else would have been difficult, Alucius reflected, when they were effectively limited by how far they could walk.

"That's all . . . and congratulations!"

In a way, Alucius reflected as he returned to the barracks, it was a let-down, but it was probably more honest. He was one of the few who took his time checking his uniforms, as well as polishing his gear, and then going to the armory and waiting to be able to sharpen the sabre in the way he wanted it done.

Only then did he fasten on his belt wallet and decide to explore the shops south of the post.

Sazium appeared, clearly having waited for Alucius. "You don't mind?"

"Soarers, no." Alucius smiled. "This was so sudden, and I just had to think things over."

"I didn't expect . . ." Sazium shook his head.

"They have a way of keeping us off-balance." Alucius began to walk toward the doors, amazed in a sense that after months of effective captivity, he could just walk out, even if he were merely on a longer and unseen chain.

"I guess it's better than being in the stone quarries, and the Southern Guard isn't exactly a friend of the Iron Valleys, either." Sazium fell in beside Alucius.

The two walked out through the gate and turned south on the redstone sidewalk. The slight haze high overhead kept the day from being too hot, but Alucius could still feel a trace of sweat around his neck.

"You hungry?" asked Sazium.

"I could stand to eat—if it doesn't cost too much."

"What else are we going to spend it on?"

Sazium had a point, Alucius had to admit.

They crossed the narrow street just beyond the south wall of the post. The first shop was what Alucius would have called a miniature chandlery—one where numerous small items were on sale, including dried meats and triangular sections of cheeses in wax.

"Might not be a bad idea to pick up a few things," murmured Sazium.

"You'll be needing more than a few things, troopers!" The deep voice came from a surprisingly small white-haired man who was adding some waxed cheese sections to those on a small square table. "You can't always count on meals in the field. That's something I can tell you from experience."

Alucius noted the ubiquitous torque. "I'm certain you can. What would you suggest for those with very limited coins?"

"The dried beef keeps well—four strips for a copper. So does the dried fruit, and I make sure it's got dried lemon strips with it so that it helps keep your mouth from bleeding . . ."

"We'll be back," Alucius promised.

The second shop was a tailor's—of sorts. There were tunics that were not uniforms, and all were in subdued or solid shades—dark blue, deep maroon, a blackish gray that was close to the color of Alucius's hair. There was also a display of riding undergarments, as well as several vests similar to the one Alucius had been permitted to keep, if without the nightsilk. Besides the undergarments, everything else was far above what Alucius had in his wallet.

Outside, they passed Kymbes and Murat.

"You two looking for something to eat?" asked the taller Murat.

"We were thinking that way," replied Sazium.

"Down that passage just ahead. Little cafe inside the courtyard. Fair eats, fair price."

"Are you going back to the chandlery?" asked Alucius.

"Thought we might," Kymbes said. "Haven't seen anyplace else that has anything we'd need, not that we've got the coins for." He laughed.

"Always true if you're a trooper, no matter where," Murat added sardonically.

Sazium laughed. After a moment, so did Alucius, and he and Sazium passed the other two and turned down the passageway, little more than a yard and a half wide, between two stone walls.

The cafe was small—four tables in the open courtyard, and a stove and grill in a small wall alcove. At one table were two older troopers, finishing whatever they had ordered. A round-faced man with deep lines in his face, but with jet-black hair, presided over the establishment. The proprietor wore a brown apron, on which there were splatters of food. He stepped forward before Alucius and Sazium reached the nearest table.

"What would you boys like?"

"What are the choices?" replied Alucius good-naturedly.

"Fried oarfish roll, chicken roll, beef roll; weak ale, cider, redjuice; fried potatoes—that's pretty much it."

"How much for beef and ale?" questioned Alucius. He wasn't at all enthused about the fish roll, not after nearly two months of fried fish.

"Two coppers for the beef roll and one for the ale."

Alucius glanced at the chalkboard behind the man, checking the prices. Somehow, the written Madrien was even easier to figure out than the spoken. The prices seemed to agree with what the proprietor had said. "It says that the beef roll comes with fynel." He looked apologetic. "What is that?"

"This stuff." The proprietor held up a plant that looked to Alucius like green quarasote without the spikes. "Gives the meat a better taste."

"I'll try it—with the ale." Alucius laughed and handed over three coppers.

"Chicken roll—without the fynel," added Sazium.

"Coming up. Take a seat."

Alucius settled on the table on the south side, in the shade, and sat down on a sturdy wooden chair, varnished, rather than oiled, as was the square wooden table. Sazium seated himself across from him.

"Strange, isn't it?" mused Sazium. "One day, we're prisoners. A month later, we're trainees, and now we're troopers for the enemy."

"Not much choice," Alucius pointed out.

"Some folks would say we're traitors."

"They might," Alucius agreed. "They don't have collars around their necks, and we haven't been asked to fight against the Iron Valleys."

"Here you go, boys!" The round-faced proprietor set two platters on the table, then hurried back with two tall beakers of weak ale.

"Thank you."

"My pleasure. I can remember how good it was to get something besides from the mess."

"You were a trooper?" asked Sazium.

"Almost twenty years. Stayed the last five 'cause they double your stipend if you do. Saved a few silvers, then a few golds, and took this over ten years ago. Enjoy it." With a smile, the man turned and headed toward another pair of troopers who had entered the courtyard.

"First time in near-on a year . . . get to eat something I choose," mumbled Sazium through a mouthful of the grilled fowl roll.

Alucius nodded, then managed to hold back a frown as the two much older troopers, who had been eating when they entered the courtyard, stepped toward their small table.

The one who led was a junior squad leader, with a thin scar across his right temple, and another across his left cheek. He offered a friendly smile. "Jesorak said you fellows would be getting your pins today. How does it feel?"

"Better than not having it," Sazium replied.

Alucius took a small swallow of the ale and nodded.

"Fair enough," said the graying but junior squad leader. "Where are you being sent?"

Sazium glanced at Alucius before answering, "Senob Post, Zalt."

The junior squad leader looked to the other squad trooper. "Told you the Lanachronans would be moving there, making a play toward Southgate." He looked back at Sazium. "They always send the newest trainees to where they think the fighting will be—that's not against their own land, that is."

"Not at first," muttered a voice, the proprietor, Alucius thought.

"After a while, it doesn't matter," replied the junior squad leader. "You find out that who has the power doesn't matter. Only matters how they treat those who don't."

Those words chilled Alucius, but he managed to keep a pleasant expression on his face, even as he considered the implications.

"Have a good journey. Remember, the Southern Guards all try to kill you with the first two passes. Not much follow-through." With a nod, the aging junior squad leader turned.

"Good thought," Alucius murmured, almost to himself.

"What?" asked Sazium.

"Just thinking. It isn't how you start the battle. It's how you end up." Alucius needed to keep that in mind.

73

Londi dawned with low scudding clouds, but without rain, and Alucius and the other nine replacement troopers were ready immediately after breakfast. In the courtyard were five long wagons, and two of the eight-man Matrite squads. The experienced squads were forming up around the wagons, one before, and one after. Squad leader Gorak had already moved the replacement troopers in front of the first regular Matrite squad, in a column by twos. Alucius and Sazium were in the second rank, behind Kymbes and Murat.

Alucius patted Wildebeast on the shoulder, and projected calm as he listened to Gorak.

"You replacement troopers will act as one squad under my command. You'll all start up front with me. Once we're clear of Hieron, half of you will be in the van with Squad Leader Chanek," announced Gorak, a short and muscular man, clean-shaven with lank brown hair. He wore the two crimson chevrons of a full squad leader, but not the three of a senior squad leader. "There's one change from what Jesorak told you. You'll pick up your rifles at the armory in Salcer when we get there. You won't be needing them until then, but you might after that."

"Squad leader!"

Gorak turned his mount to face the trim older woman who had reined up just inside the gates. "Yes, captain?"

"Are your men ready?"

"We stand ready, captain, but the teamsters say that they need a quarter glass."

"So I heard." Captain Sennel's voice was hard, yet her tone conveyed a rueful acceptance, tinged with irony.

A second and younger female officer rode through the gate and halted her mount beside the captain. "Captain."

"Squad Leader Gorak, this is Undercaptain Porlel."

Undercaptain Porlel looked to be younger than Alucius. Her short hair was reddish blonde and tight-curled to her head, and she had a generous nose between deepset eyes. Her shoulders were broad, and despite her youthful and awkward appearance, she projected a confidence that suggested she was older than she appeared. From the few green flashes that his senses revealed as he studied her covertly, Alucius had the feeling she had at least some Talent. Alucius could not sense any Talent in the captain, but he was uncertain whether that was because she had none, or because she had enough ability to conceal what she had. There was still so much he did not know.

"We'll be picking up ten more wagons at the depot on the south side of Hieron. They're supposed to be ready." Sennel's voice conveyed some doubt.

"Yes, captain." Both the squad leader and the undercaptain spoke simultaneously.

A lanky woman wearing a plain forest green tunic and trousers walked toward the two officers and the squad leader. "Lead Teamster Sandjin, captain. We're loaded and ready."

"Thank you, Sandjin," replied Sennel. "As soon as you're on your wagon, we're moving."

The teamster turned, the iron taps of her boot heels clicking on the courtyard pavement.

Within moments, the captain commanded, "Column forward."

Alucius took his station on Kymbes, and watched Gorak as the squad leader rode, alone, behind the two officers.

Once outside the redstone walls of the post, the column turned west until it reached the ramp up to the ancient high road, and then turned south on the eternastone paving. Alucius studied the park of the Matrial. Once they were on the raised high road, Alucius realized that the thin pink Talent-threads from the torques led to the long stone dwelling, not in a way that he could have proved, even though he felt it. He also had a greater sense of an unseen evil around the dwelling. Were the torques the sole key to the power of the

Matrial—or just part of a larger set of Talent-powers she wielded?

A wry smile crossed his face and vanished, as he considered that he was acting as if there were something he could do when he was yet a captive of one of those torques, and when he had still to regain full control over his Talent.

Second, as he looked from the elevated road to the park and then southward, he understood what he had felt and had not been able to articulate when he had first come to Hieron—the city had been built entirely after the Cataclysm, and it had been built around a place where all the old roads had intersected. That was why there were ramps everywhere to access the roads. That also pointed out how close Hieron was to the ancient vanished cities of Elcien and Faitel—because such a crossroads would certainly have been a place for a city, unless there had been much better sites not that far from where Hieron now stood.

The column traveled a good three vingts southward on the high road until the dwellings abruptly ended. There was a space of close to half a vingt of meadow between the last dwellings and the depot. The depot was surrounded by three-yard-high stone walls that formed a square five hundred yards on a side. Within the walls, as they approached on the ancient high road from the north, Alucius could see more than forty warehouses, each close to a hundred yards long and twenty in width.

"More stores there than in all the traders' warehouses in Dekhron," Sazium murmured.

Alucius wouldn't have doubted it, but he had no way of knowing, except that most of Iron Stem would have fit within the walls of the depot.

Contrary to the captain's doubts, all ten wagons were loaded and lined up just inside the fifty-yard-wide opening in the walls—an opening that was too large to qualify as a gate and that was without fortifications, except for a small guardhouse set just inside the walls. Two guards in green, not troopers, but gray-haired women, stood beside the slate-roofed stone-walled guardhouse, watching.

Alucius could sense Talent there, and quickly decided against probing with his own Talent senses. Instead, he watched as the captain talked with two other teamsters.

Then the captain turned her mount and rode back toward the troopers.

"They're ready to roll, squad leader."

"Yes, captain." Gorak turned his mount. "First two ranks and the next man, replacement troopers, forward! Squad Leader Chanek, forward!"

Since Alucius was in the second rank, he and Sazium rode forward to meet with Gorak and Chanek. Chanek was a tall and thin junior squad leader with jet black hair and a short-square-trimmed black beard.

"Here are your five troopers for the van," Gorak announced.

Chanek glanced over the group, then nodded. "Yes, sir." After a moment, he addressed the six. "We'll be riding just thirty yards before the main column until we're a vingt south of here. Then we'll be moving to a half vingt. Follow me, in column."

Less than two vingts south of the depot, the land—good rich bottomland well to the south of the river and to the east of the low peaks of the Coast Range—was filled with small holdings, all intensely cultivated, all with neat dwellings that bespoke prosperity, rather than the huts and hovels that existed outside the steads in the Iron Valleys. But then, the land itself in the Iron Valleys was far, far poorer.

That self-explanation did not fully satisfy Alucius. He leaned forward, thinking, and patted Wildebeast on the shoulder.

74

Hieron, Madrien

There were but two figures in the stone-walled workroom on the lower southwest levels of the Matrial's residence, one a tall and broad-shouldered woman in purple trimmed in forest green, the other in the working brown of an engineer.

"For years we have been at the mercy of a device that the Lord-Protector of Lanachrona has, the . . . Table that allows him to see anywhere in Corus." The Matrial's purple eyes fixed on Hyalas, their intensity emphasized by the flawless pale skin of her face. "I asked you before to look into this. Is there a reason why we should not develop such a device?"

Hyalas bowed deeply. "Begging your pardon, most honored Matrial. The device is called a Table of the Recorder. As you well know, they were once used by the Alectors of the Duarchy to view crimes that had recently occurred, and I suppose, for other matters as well. There have been rumors for years that such a Table remained in Tempre."

"After my request . . . why have you not pursued creating such a device for us?"

"Honored Matrial, there were no plans and no descriptions. There were but a double handful of such, and all were constructed secretly through the use of Talent. So far as I know, there is only the one remaining."

"And the Lord-Protector could see where our troops are deployed?"

"That is true, Matrial, but each Table was fixed to a point on the earth, and the points could not be changed. Failure to link a table to the nodal points resulted in an explosion. That is what the records say. That is why several no longer exist. After the Cataclysm, they were removed from where they were, and someone attempted to use them. There is an ancient scroll that states that when the Landarch of Deforya invaded Illegea and tried to move the one in Lyterna it exploded and killed him and all those around him."

"He must have thought it possible," the Matrial suggested.

"Many rulers have thought the impossible could be done. At times, it can be. At other times, the cost is most high."

"Engineer . . . you come perilously close to insult."

Hyalas bowed his head, deeply, before speaking. "Yes, honored Matrial, but it is not out of desire to offend, but to speak the truth as I know it, always in your interest."

"Only because it is in yours." The Matrial laughed. "Tell me more."

"It is true that a Table would grant the Lord-Protector some information, but there are two limitations. First, there is only one Table, and it takes, if the accounts are correct, much effort by a Talent for each use. Second, its linkage to its location creates limits on its use in warfare."

"I do not see the bearing—" The Matrial nodded. "The Table is in Tempre, and so the information must go out from Tempre. So if we send troops well in advance, then move them suddenly . . . or deceive them . . . Or if we have a field commander who can act swiftly, the best information will avail them little." She looked at Hyalas. "Is that what you meant, engineer?"

"Yes, Matrial."

"Now . . . can you rebuild the weapon?"

"It took over two years the last time. This time, I would judge it might take a little less . . . but not much less."

"Then I suggest you begin immediately. Good day, engineer."

Hyalas bowed and watched with a lowered head from his position of obeisance as she departed.

75

Traveling the ancient high road south took nearly two weeks, almost eight days from Hieron to Salcer and the massive armory there, and another six to the smaller river town of Dimor. South of Dimor, the road left the bluff on the eastern side of the south branch of the River Lud and headed absolutely straight southeast. For most of the two days it took to ride the last leg of the journey, from Dimor to Zalt, Alucius could see, to his left, the hills slowly subside into rolling rises, and the orchards give way to a patchwork of grasslands, fields, and woodlots. The holdings remained far smaller than the steads of Iron Stem, but the stone houses were all neat and in good repair.

"There's Zalt," called out Chanek, as the vanguard rode out of a road cut through a rise slightly higher than most. "You can see the Senob Post on the east side, just north of the southwest high road. Where the roads meet—that's where the high road we're on ends."

Alucius, in the second rank, had to half-stand in the stirrups and look around Murat. What he could see was that the post had redstone walls, high enough to be visible from three vingts away, and was separated from the town proper. The high road arrowed both to the northeast and southwest all the way to the horizon. There was not a single rider or wagon on it. The north-south high road just ended, less than a hundred yards south of where the two roads intersected, almost as if the ancient builders had meant to go farther south, but had been stopped and never resumed. Had they been working on the road when the Cataclysm struck?

The vanguard rode another quarter glass southward before Chanek ordered, "Vanguard, halt! We'll hold up for a bit, until we're only a hundred yards out from the rest of the column."

While the vanguard waited for the rest of the supply convoy to move toward them, Alucius studied Zalt, as best he could. Unlike the other towns in Madrien through which Alucius had passed, where the town had been built on both sides of the high road, the town of Zalt lay entirely to the northwest of where the two high roads crossed.

On the northeast side of the crossroads was Senob Post, with a fair separation between its walls and the north-south high road, but the post appeared to be set only a hundred yards or so north of the southwest high road.

"Column's closed up enough. Vanguard forward!" Chanek ordered.

Alucius took in the town to his right as they rode past, but outside of the placement, nothing seemed unusual. There were the same neat stone-walled houses, the same brightly painted shutters, the same wide streets, and open areas of green. The two differences were that there were few trees in the open green areas—only within the rear courtyards of the dwellings—and that the roofs were a whitish stone of some sort.

"At the crossroads, vanguard left!" Chanek ordered.

With the others, Alucius guided Wildebeast into a left turn, and the column headed northeast toward the post.

Set almost a vingt to the east of the crossroads, Senob Post was a large structure, with walls half a vingt on a side, and close to four yards in height. The gates were indeed gates, heavy timbered gates bound with dark iron, each only about three yards wide. While they stood open, the cleanliness of the stones and the huge iron hinges showed that they could be quickly closed. Behind the outer gates—on the inside of the walls—was a second set of gates, but these were designed to be closed by sliding forward along channels in the stone paving.

Chanek led them straight through those gates and down what amounted to a wide stone-paved courtyard or avenue until they neared a series of long stone buildings.

"Vanguard, halt!"

Moments later came the command from behind Alucius, "Column, halt!"

Then Gorak rode forward and reined up. "Replacement troopers to the fore! Guide on Sazium. Column of two."

Alucius was already in place. He waited.

"For the moment, you'll stall your mounts in the visitors' section of the stable. Once you're done, take all your gear, except for your tack, and form up out here. Then I'll take you to the mess. That's where you'll meet the senior squad leader for your company. Replacement troopers, dismissed to duties!"

Alucius followed the others to the visitors' section of the stable, taking in as much as he could. Neither the captain nor the undercaptain had that much to do with the troopers, and hadn't, not for the entire journey.

After Alucius and the other replacement troopers had stabled, unsaddled, and groomed their mounts, Gorak led them to the mess hall—a stone-walled building that stood to the north of the barracks. In the late afternoon, the mess was empty, except for Gorak and the ten troopers. The stone floors glistened, as if just polished, and the smell of bread baking filled the air.

"Those of you for the Thirty-second . . . you wait there in the southwest corner. Those of you for the Fortieth. . . . the southeast corner. I'd guess it'll be a half a glass or so, but neither company is on patrol today. Best of luck."

"Thank you, sir."

Gorak turned and walked away, unhurriedly.

Alucius, Beral, Kymbes, Murat, and Sazium—the five replacement troopers assigned to Fortieth Company—found themselves standing in the southeast corner of the mess, gear at their feet, waiting for their new senior squad leader.

"Wouldn't have minded having him as a squad leader," Kymbes offered.

"Just have to see what we get," Murat said quietly.

"Here he comes . . ." hissed Sazium.

The man who walked toward them was of medium height with a few white hairs in his short-cut brown thatch and his short-trimmed beard. Behind him were four junior squad leaders. "You're all for the Fortieth?"

"Yes, sir," was the unanimous response as they straightened to attention.

"You can stand at ease, troopers. I'm Tymal, senior squad leader for Fortieth Company. I'm sorry if you had to wait, but I wanted to read over the reports that Jesorak sent before I decided on which squads you'd go to." Tymal paused. "Do any of you know what we do here?"

"No, sir," Alucius answered a moment ahead of the others.

"All of the companies here at Senob Post—regulars and auxiliaries—have the same task. We keep the Lanachronans from Southgate. We patrol the southwest highway and several of the smaller passes. We also pretend we're not at war and allow the traders to use the road. We're the force that makes sure they pay their tariffs. If any bandits or raiders show up, they're our task, too, but there haven't been many of those for years. Captain Hyrlui is in charge of Fortieth Company. She's the senior company captain . . . easy to recognize—she's very muscular and her hair is half white. The two undercaptains are Taniti and Kryll. Undercaptain Taniti is black-haired and big. Undercaptain Kryll . . . well . . . you can hear her voice from three vingts."

After a pause, Tymal gestured to the four junior squad leaders. "These are your squad leaders. Alucius?"

"Yes, sir?"

"You're now in the seventh squad." Tymal inclined his head to the tallest of the junior squad leaders. "Alben is your squad leader."

"Beral? You're in second squad with Sedyr . . ."

"Kymbes? Third squad with Yular."

"Murat and Sazium . . . eighth squad with Rask." Tymal looked over the five. "Now . . . I'll spend a few moments with each of you and your squad leader. We don't rate spaces. So we'll use the mess here. Alucius, come with me."

"Yes, sir." Alucius followed Tymal and Alben to the northeasternmost table.

The two squad leaders sat on the bench on one side, and

Alucius waited for Tymal to indicate that he should sit before he did.

"According to your training records, you're class one in all weapons, and unarmed combat, and you can ride anything." Tymal frowned. "If you're that good, how did you get captured?"

"I got hit in the back of the head and shoulder with something during a raid on a Matrite camp. It might have been debris from where the spear-thrower exploded or when it hit one of the buildings. I don't know." Alucius shrugged. "When I woke up I had a collar on."

"Spear-thrower?"

"There was this weapon. It created and threw hundreds of crystal spears, about this long." Alucius held his hands about a half yard apart. "It exploded." He caught the brief look and feel of surprise in Alben's eyes.

Tymal merely nodded. "How did you know that, if it knocked you out?"

"The engineer who built it carried the pieces back to Hieron in the wagons that went with those of us who were captured. The pieces were so heavy that the axle on one of the wagons started to bow, and they had some of us move the pieces from one wagon to another."

"How long were you in the Iron Valley Militia?"

"About a half year, sir."

Tymal shook his head, then smiled. "Welcome to the Fortieth." He nodded to Alben. "Alben will show you to the squad spaces and introduce you to your squad-mates."

The junior squad leader stood, and Alucius followed his example, but then bent to recover his gear, including the Matrite rifle that still felt far too light to be effective. Alben did not speak until they had left the mess and the corridor beyond and were walking southward across the paved courtyard toward the barracks.

"Are you a killer?" Alben asked conversationally.

"I've killed men, sir. Most troopers who've survived have."

Alben stopped in the courtyard and looked hard at Alucius.

"You're in my squad. I have to know who and what you are. You speak Madrien with almost no accent, but that hair screams Iron Valley. You're younger than almost all troopers, but your weapons skills are better than all but the very best. The officer who examined you in the field said you had no Talent. So did the overcaptain at Hieron. The only kind that are so good young and without Talent are born killers. At least, the only kind I've known. They'll master anything to be able to kill better."

Alucius met the glare from the other man without flinching. "I'm sorry, sir, but I'm not a born killer. I'll do what's necessary, and I'll do it as well as I can, but that's because it's the only way I know to stay alive."

Alben sighed, loudly. "Maybe you don't know. You ever shoot anyone who you could have captured?"

"No, sir."

"Then . . . how do you know so much so young?" Alben watched the younger man intently.

Alucius wondered how he could answer that, even as he began to answer. "My father died when I was barely able to walk. My grandfather—my mother's father—had been an officer in the Iron Valleys Militia in charge of some sort of training. He felt that my father died because he hadn't been trained well enough. He spent years training me before I was conscripted."

Alben laughed. "You expect me to believe that?"

"You can believe it or not, sir, but it's the truth."

"With all that . . . why didn't they make you a squad leader?"

"Because I was too young, and because they really didn't want me as one." Alucius paused. "I don't know that it's true, but I always had the feeling that those of us who lived north of Dekhron were looked down upon, and it had been many years since my grandsire had served, and none of the senior officers knew him."

"How far north of Dekhron?"

"Iron Stem." Alucius hoped there weren't too many more questions.

Instead, Alben nodded. "That makes more sense. I'm from Klamat." He paused again. "How many water bottles do you have?"

"Two, sir. Gorak saw that I needed another."

"After you meet the rest of the squad, I'll get you a third. In the summer here, you'll need it." Alben resumed his swift walk across the courtyard.

Alucius could only surmise that Alben had been just trying to draw him out, to get a better sense of who he was. At least, that was what he hoped.

76

On Quattri morning, Alben gathered up seventh squad after breakfast in the corner of the mess. Alucius hung back ever so slightly, standing beside Oryn because, as the newest and youngest member of the squad, he did not wish to appear too enthusiastic.

The junior squad leader looked briefly at each of the eight members of the squad. Alucius still found the Madrien organization strange, with ten eight-trooper squads, as opposed to five twenty-man squads used by the Iron Valleys, but he could see that each organization had its strengths.

"We weren't due to go on patrol until Septi, but Captain Hyrlui's sending us out today. We're only covering the north side of the high road, but we're going farther north. We had reports from local loggers. We'll be running patrol for the next week and three days—three days out, three days north, four days angling back to the high road, and three days back." Alben surveyed the squad again. "Eighth squad will be doing the same thing on the south side. From now on, we're only getting three days off between patrols, and we'll be running four patrols at once, instead of two." The junior squad leader paused, then added, "Once I've checked your gear, pick up your rations from the mess. You'll be getting two cartridge packs in addition to your cartridge belt and more rations. So don't pack anything extra." Alben looked almost directly at Alucius.

Alucius nodded.

."We leave in a glass. I'll inspect gear in half a glass. Fall out and get ready."

Alucius let the older troopers lead the way back to the barracks wing. Oryn walked beside Alucius. Like Alben, Alucius had learned, Oryn was from the north, but from Northport, rather than Klamat, and he was wiry and blond, and a good six years older than Alucius.

Oryn looked at Alucius. "He fired that last one at you."

"He doesn't know me yet," Alucius pointed out.

"You always so . . . reasonable?" asked the smaller man.

"No," admitted Alucius, with a laugh. "I can be very stubborn. This isn't the time." Or the place, he reflected, not a thousand vingts from home with a collar around his throat and his Talent still weaker than he would have liked.

77

Seventh squad rode northward through a clammy mist and along a rutted clay road less than four yards wide. Alucius shifted his weight in the saddle. He was stiff. For the last few months, he'd actually been sleeping on a real bunk. Now, for each of the past three nights, seventh squad had stopped at one of the stone-walled way stations beside the high road—essentially two rooms—one with twelve wooden frames on which to lay a bedroll and one with twelve crude stalls.

He glanced up, but the sky directly overhead remained gray, as it had been for the nearly two glasses since the squad had left the way station—and the high road. On each side of the road loomed tall spruces and firs, their tops lost in the misty fog. Infrequent bird calls, unfamiliar to Alucius—

issued from the woods flanking both sides of the hilly road.

Kuryt and Venn were scouting—in a way—riding five hundred yards ahead.

A call came from ahead.

"Timber wagon coming," called Alben. "Single file on the right. Single file on the right!"

Alucius was in the second rank, and he let Denal, the trooper he'd been riding beside, slip in front of him. The first wagon was a three-axled monster—pulled by eight enormous dray horses. On the wagon were timbers six yards long, rough cut to a size of two spans by two, and securely roped in place. Behind the timber wagon were four riders, followed by two other wagons. Even through the fog, Alucius could make out the loggers in the wagons.

"Squad halt!" ordered Alben.

A small gray-haired woman in a faded brown jacket who carried a brace of rifles had reined up opposite Alben.

Alucius used both his Talent and his ears, since sound carried even more in the fog.

". . . attacked yesterday afternoon . . . drove 'em off, but lost three loggers . . . couple more wounded . . . low on ammunition . . . couldn't see the point in staying . . . pulling out for now . . ."

". . . know how many . . . ?" asked Alben.

". . . couldn't tell for sure . . . might have been one of their squads—twenty . . ."

". . . be following tracks . . . you'll report this . . ."

". . . we'll report it, squad leader . . . need more than a few squads here . . . a whole company."

". . . we're scouts . . ."

". . . should have been here *before* the dirty southerners . . . could have used some warning . . ."

Alucius could easily sense the head logger's rage, and Alben's discomfort and deference, as well as the squad leader's own checked anger.

". . . giving poor Alben what-for . . ." murmured Oryn.

". . . he doesn't decide who to send . . ."

". . . she doesn't care . . ."

Once the loggers had left, Alben addressed the squad. "Looks like we've got a squad of Southern Guards running loose. They took a shot at the logging camp, then moved north. We'll follow, but we're in no hurry. From here on in, rifles ready to fire on command. You can leave them in the holder if you think you're fast enough—except for the scouts . . ."

Over the next glass, the fog burned off until there were only wisps in some of the darker parts of the forest and a faint haze overhead. With the sun came warmth and, for Alucius, a soaking sweat compounded from heat and damp air. Almost with every step Wildebeast took, Alucius found himself wiping perspiration out of his eyes or off his forehead—when he wasn't either brushing away the gnats or trying to ignore them.

"Rifles ready!"

At Alben's order, Alucius pulled the Matrite weapon from its holder.

"Squad left! Down the lane."

The lane, wider than the road they had followed, ran for less than a hundred yards before it opened onto a cleared area bright with midday sunlight.

The logging camp was more like a lumber hamlet, with nine neat bungalows, shuttered and locked, two drying barns, a sawmill, and a stable. Like every other hamlet, the houses had stone walls, but the roofs were shingled, rather than slate. Out in the hazy sunlight, the gnats vanished, but were replaced by large and hungry horseflies.

Alucius could sense that no one was nearby, not anything human. He could sense something—but his Talent showed it as brownish green, and he'd never sensed anything like that. Whatever the creature was, it was at least a vingt away, and showed no sign of approaching. Still, Alucius held his rifle as if someone might attack at any moment. He didn't want Alben getting ideas of any sort besides the one that Alucius was young.

"Venn—to the northwest corner of the cleared space. Get close to the trees and use one for cover. Kuryt! Northeast

corner . . . Daafl . . . southwest . . . Denal . . . southeast. The
rest of you . . . check the buildings. See if there's any sign
of anyone breaking in. All of you! I order a fall-back, and
you move! Full speed to the lane and south."

Alucius found himself riding around the two westernmost
bungalows. No one had tampered with the locks or the shutters. There were no recent tracks in the damp clay, not besides those of the loggers and their wagons and mounts, and
Alucius sensed no one. Although there was wildlife in the
woods beyond the camp, most of the creatures felt small,
except for whatever registered with his Talent as brownish
green. That was more distant, and it felt more like a soarer
or a sander than a sandwolf or a dustcat.

One by one, except for the perimeter guards, the rest of
the squad returned to Alben.

So did Alucius. "Checked the last three bungalows and the
ground nearby, sir. No sign of anything but the loggers, sir."

Alben nodded, and Alucius slipped Wildebeast into the
column beside Oryn.

"See anything?" asked Oryn.

"Not a thing."

"Good. Their squads are more than twice our size. Don't
know why the overcaptain didn't send two squads."

"We're only scouting," Alucius pointed out, even as he
wondered. Certainly, the Matrites hadn't had any problems
in sending more and more companies against the Iron Valleys. Lanachrona was more of a threat—and closer.

"Guards in!" Alben ordered. "Keep your rifles handy.
We'll keep heading north."

Alucius found himself riding in the first rank, beside Oryn,
continuing away from the high road and along a logging road
that, while it had not narrowed, had gotten progressively
more weatherworn, with higher underbrush on both sides.
Brekka and Fustyl rode a good two hundred yards ahead.

By midafternoon, seventh squad had ridden a good ten
vingts from the logging camp, but still had not seen any
tracks in the road. Then, Alucius wouldn't have left any
there, either, not if he'd wanted to set an ambush.

"How do you think the southerners got here?" Alucius asked his riding mate.

"Probably came down the old river road and then hit the logging road," Oryn offered. "They can cut off the southwest high road on their side of the border and make us travel farther."

Alucius nodded, his attention abruptly moving to his Talent-senses. There was something up ahead—several troopers, black as shown by his Talent, on the right side of the road, uphill and somewhere sheltered by the large tree trunks.

What could he do without revealing his Talent? And without having troopers slaughtered in an ambush, himself included.

He cocked his head to one side, as if listening, although he heard little except insects, and few of those. Then he eased the rifle up, so that he could fire quickly.

Oryn glanced at him. "You hear something?"

"I don't hear anything. That's the problem." Alucius could sense the anticipation of the four Lanachronans. What he couldn't understand was where the rest of the Lanachronan troopers were. He edged Wildebeast slightly more to the right side of the road, so that he could have a better line of fire—if he had any shot at all through the thick trunks of the trees. Finally, he could wait no longer.

"Sir! Blue! To the right!" As he spoke, Alucius fired.

Crack! Crack!

A deeper sounding *crack* replied.

"Fire from the right!" Alben snapped. Take cover and return fire."

Crack! Crack! . . . More shots filled the forest air, shots from both sides.

Alucius cocked, reaimed and fired again, even as he quickly guided his mount practically against one of the larger trunks. He could feel the sudden death void, and while the trooper could have died from any of the shots, Alucius *knew* he had killed the man.

Pushing that thought away, he concentrated on the other

three, but still worried about where the rest of the Lanachronans might be.

Sporadic shots continued.

Alucius waited, until he sensed one of the Lanachronan troopers easing from behind a trunk to fire, when he quickly brought his own rifle to bear and squeezed off a quick shot. This time, there was a reddish flash of pain—agony—before the death void.

Just as suddenly, the two remaining Lanachronans turned and began to retreat.

"They're backing off, sir!" Alucius called.

Oryn snapped off another shot, but there were none in return.

There was a cracking and swishing of brush, and Alucius could sense the two mounting and taking two riderless mounts with them.

A quarter glass passed, but there were no other sounds and no shots.

"Alucius . . . can you see where they were?"

"Yes, sir."

"Ease in there . . . see if they left any traces."

"I'll need to go on foot, sir."

"Oryn, hold his mount."

Alucius dismounted, handing the leathers to Oryn, while using his Talent to press a calming feeling on Wildebeast. Then, rifle in hand, he slipped from tree trunk to tree trunk, knowing no one was there, but also not wanting to show that he knew that.

As he had already known, there were two bodies, both in the dark blue of the Southern Guards. One, a clean-shaven young trooper, didn't look that much older than Alucius, and, despite the blood across one side of his head, reminded Alucius somewhat of his friend Vardial—who might well be in the militia now. The other was an older man, thin and tired looking.

"Sir!" Alucius called. "Two dead southerners. Southern Guard uniforms."

The two still carried their sabres, but their compatriots had taken their rifles.

Alben appeared within moments. He studied the bodies for a moment, then bent and checked them. "Nothing here. Their friends took their wallets and their rifles." He straightened and looked at Alucius.

Alucius returned the glance, not defiantly, but merely as if accepting Alben's scrutiny. After a moment, the junior squad leader looked away. "Let's go."

Alucius eased his way through the trees and back to the road and Wildebeast.

"Re-form on me!" snapped Alben.

The squad reformed, with Brekka and Fustyl riding back cautiously. Alben rode to meet them, his eyes taking in both sides of the road. The three stopped a good fifty yards north of where the rest of the squad waited.

Alucius listened.

". . . you didn't see anything?"

". . . no, sir . . . must have been lying low till we passed . . ."

". . . trying to get shots at all the squad . . ."

After a time, Alben nodded, and the two formed up.

"We'll keep moving north . . . except the two scouts will stay about fifty yards out," Alben announced. "Do I have to tell you to keep your rifles ready?"

"No, sir."

Seventh squad continued along the old logging road.

Another glass passed. The forest got warmer, and Alucius stickier, and the gnats more numerous. But there were no signs of the Lanachronans, and Alucius could not sense anything human in the forest on either side.

The squad leader eased up beside Alucius.

"Sir?"

"How did you know they were there?" Alben's eyes focused hard on Alucius.

"I saw a flash of color, sir. Never saw an animal in blue with white piping, sir. So I yelled, and I fired. I didn't know if I should have waited, but I wanted to upset them enough so they didn't get a clear shot."

Alben nodded. It wasn't a gesture of agreement. "How could you see through all that brush?"

"I come from a herder family. I wasn't the herder, but you learn to watch for the little things, the things that should be—or the things that should be and aren't. Didn't hear as many insects and no bird calls. So when I saw blue . . ." Alucius shrugged. He could tell that Alben was not totally convinced. "I yelled and fired as quick as I could."

Alben smiled. "Think you had a little luck there, Alucius, but we'll take luck."

"Yes, sir." Alucius wasn't going to argue.

"Keep looking."

"Yes, sir."

As Alben rode forward toward the scouts, Oryn looked to Alucius. "More 'n luck."

"Thank you. I was watching and listening, but I probably was a bit lucky."

Oryn grinned. "Don't care what it was. If it's luck, keep doing it."

Alucius nodded. He still wondered—about the Lanachronans, and, in a way, about what he and seventh squad were doing—and why they were undermanned compared to the Lanachronan forces.

78

Northeast of Iron Stem, Iron Valleys

As the late spring snow swirled around the stead house, the three sat around the kitchen table, taking in the warmth from the iron stove that had been used to prepare the supper they had just finished eating.

"Have you heard anything from Alucius?" asked Veryl,

her voice so thin that her husband and her daughter had to lean forward at the table to hear.

Royalt shook his head. "The militia has pressed every possible company of horse into the battle. They're not getting much time off."

"Have you heard how it's going?" asked Lucenda.

"I had so hoped we would get a message this month," Veryl said, almost querulously. "He's always been such a good boy. Has young Wendra heard from him?"

"If Alucius hasn't been able to send us a message, I doubt that she's received one," Lucenda said dryly. She did not look directly at her mother, but at her father. "I saw another company of horse riding north this afternoon on my way back from town."

"Kustyl says that we've pushed the Matrites back out of Soulend. They still hold the old outpost. He's worried that they're going to bring in even more troopers. They had some Talent-weapon, but it exploded. Without it, they're not as good as we are. The winter's helped too. They're not used to the cold."

"What will happen when it warms up?" asked Lucenda.

"Not much besides what's already happening—unless we get heavy rain. That could hurt, because we couldn't use all the back stead roads."

"I just don't understand why he hasn't written," fretted Veryl. "It's not like him. It just isn't. You're sure he's all right?"

"He should have recovered from that wound," Royalt replied. "If he hadn't, we would have heard." He turned to his daughter. "It's a good thing Clyon took over the defense of Soulend personally," Royalt said with a snort. "He sent that idiot Dysar back to Dekhron."

"Why don't they get rid of Dysar?"

"Because he's not too bad at handling administrative things, because he's related to half the Council, because the Council wants their fingers on the militia, and because they still think the Matrites are traders and that if we hold them off long enough, they'll go away, like the Lanachronans did."

"Will they?"

"Our only real hope is that we can bleed them dry enough that the Lord-Protector will make a grab for Southgate or the southern fruitlands of Madrien."

"That's a slim hope," Lucenda noted.

"Not so slim as it once was—"

"It's not like him not to write," Veryl repeated. "I just don't understand it, such a thoughtful boy, not writing his mother."

"He's trying very hard to do his job and stay alive, dear," Royalt said gently. "There are at least twice as many Matrite troopers as we have. Between cleaning his gear and getting sleep and fighting, I'm sure he has little time. He also may not have anything to write on or with."

"That's certain enough," Lucenda added.

Royalt nodded, both at her words and the second meaning behind them.

"You both say that. I still think he could write."

"I'm most certain that if Alucius could write, dear," Royalt said patiently, "he surely would."

Lucenda nodded, then looked down at the table, before turning and rising abruptly. "There are dishes to be done."

"He should write," Veryl murmured. "He should."

Lucenda and Royalt exchanged sad glances, before Lucenda went to check the kettle that held the hot wash water for the dishes.

79

After nearly a week of patrols, and no success in finding the Lanachronan raiders, seventh squad returned to Senob Post on Septi. The squad had Novdi off—after a very long Ocdi that had begun with cleaning of tack and riding gear and ended just before supper with an inspection where

Alben went over everything from uniforms to gear to bunks and spaces.

Midmorning had just passed when Alucius and Oryn straightened their undress green uniforms—their pass uniforms—and started to leave the barracks. Most of the older troopers in seventh squad had either gone back to their bunks, except for Brekka and Daafl, who were playing leschec with the pieces borrowed from the library and set up on Daafl's footchest. Alucius paused to study the positions on the board.

"You play?" asked Daafl.

"I used to," Alucius admitted. "It's been a while."

"Good to know," said Daafl. "Always good to have a third. You two going out?"

"We thought we would," said Oryn. "Alucius hasn't seen the town."

"Be careful of your many coins." Brekka laughed, good-naturedly.

"We'll try," Alucius promised, with a smile.

Oryn and Alucius left the barracks, worked their way through the linked and stone-paved courtyards of the post, and made their way to the south gates. From there, they began to walk westward along the high road toward Zalt.

"You're good at leschec, aren't you?" asked Oryn.

"I was all right. I learned from watching my grandsire."

"He was a herder, wasn't he?"

Alucius nodded.

"Figured as much, with the nightsilk undergarments." Oryn shook his head. "Lucky for you that no one else can wear them. Say they'll stop most sabre cuts."

"They'll stop an angled slash," Alucius admitted, "but they don't do anything for your hands, or head." *Except if you wear a skullmask.* Alucius was still amazed that he had his, flattened inside the left thigh of his underdrawers. "Bullets or hard blows with big blades, and you'll get a lot of broken bones, if not worse."

"Still . . . that's something. True that once they're made you can't retailor them?"

"Not without very special equipment, and you still could ruin the nightsilk and get nothing."

"Someone else wear them?"

"If they're smaller . . . but then they wouldn't do near as much good, because the silk would be loose and a hard cut would just transmit the thrust like an extension of the blade. Be worse with a bullet."

In turn, Oryn nodded. "Figured something like that. Might get hurt even worse that way."

Alucius shrugged. "Might help some, or it could be worse. Matter of luck."

"How come you didn't get to be a herder?"

"It didn't work out. I got conscripted." That was true enough.

"You might be able to go back by the time your service is up."

"In twenty years?" Alucius laughed, ruefully. "When Madrien holds the Iron Valleys?"

"Talbyr said that they're sending more companies to the north. Thinks we were pushed back some." Oryn shook his head. "Might take longer, but it won't change anything."

Alucius managed to nod. He had to hope otherwise. Whatever the reason, the spear-thrower had exploded. With it gone, he just hoped that the militia could throw back the Matrites.

"Now here, we got problems on both sides. Southgate—the traders own everything. Mean bastards, I hear tell, and they hire mercs from Dramur. The Lanachronans . . . you know what they're like. They don't take captives. Wouldn't do any good for troopers, and they hate Madrien women. Be better if we could clean 'em both out."

"We don't have enough troopers here to do that, do we?"

"A course not." Oryn frowned. "Not that I'm putting your place down, you understand, but takin' Southgate would do Madrien lot more good than the Iron Valleys would. Don't see why the Matrial did that. Not as though the Valleys were a threat the way the Lanachronans are."

From what he'd seen so far, Alucius would have had to

agree. Yet Madrien had been successful and seemed most prosperous, and little he had seen had been done without reason. He did not respond as they walked across the north-south high road, and he followed Oryn toward a wide street that angled northwest from the crossroads.

Abruptly, Alucius looked up. On the maneuver grounds to the south, there looked to be two full companies practicing. "Did we get more troopers? I didn't hear tell of that."

Oryn followed Alucius's glance, then shook his head. "No. Those are the auxiliaries. You'll see them practicing. That's one reason why we can get by with two companies here. If she needs to, the captain can call them up. There are either two or three companies here."

"Who are—"

"Mostly women, those who didn't want to try for officer training, and some of the troopers with stipends. They get another gold a month if they serve with the auxiliaries. They can do that for five years after they're stipended. Easy way to make a little more."

"Oh." Alucius wondered. Tymal had mentioned auxiliaries, but not any details.

"You'll learn to recognize them," Oryn added. "They say some of them are pretty good."

After another long look southward, Alucius glanced at the town ahead, even while his thoughts lingered on the auxiliaries. On the surface, Zalt looked like every other Madrien town Alucius had passed through, with the neatly dressed stone walls, the walled courtyards, the paved streets and sidewalks. The only obvious difference was that the roofs were of white tile, rather than of the dark slate of the more northern towns. There were but a handful of folk out, mostly older men and women, and not a one paid any attention to the two troopers, other than a casual look, or in the case of one gray-haired and bent man, a nod.

After three blocks, Oryn turned right. A hundred yards later, they stood in a plaza of sorts, and in the center was a marketplace—a smaller version of the one in Hieron.

"Ah . . . I need to see someone," Oryn said.

Alucius could sense both the truth and the unease behind the statement. He smiled. "Have a good time."

"How did you know?" Oryn looked slightly askance.

"I'm the most junior, and don't really know my way around. You thought no one would think much if you were showing me Zalt. And you wouldn't be going this early if it weren't for someone." Alucius was partly guessing. "I'll just look around."

Oryn looked sheepish. "You don't mind?"

"Sanders, no."

Oryn frowned at the word "sanders," but it had slipped into the Madrien Alucius had been speaking, really without thought. "You're sure?"

"I'll be fine," Alucius said.

With a smile of obvious relief, Oryn stepped away, heading toward the stalls and carrels on the west side of the structure, walking around the building, rather than into the central courtyard.

Alucius walked straight into the courtyard, studying the stalls. He finally made his way along the north side, eventually pausing by the carrel that held the cooper's wares. All the barrels were of a plain white oak—good and serviceable, but not nearly so good as Kyrial's work. A sense of emptiness filled him, for a long moment, as the barrels reminded him of Wendra. Would he ever see her again?

"You once a cooper's apprentice?" asked the woman tending the stall. Like Alucius, and unlike most of the women, she wore a torque. Her skin was dusky, and lined, with webs radiating from her eyes, eyes that were dark and intent. She wore a plain brown shawl over a long-sleeved tunic, also brown.

"No, but I knew one well, and spent time in his shop."

"You're a northerner. From Harmony or Klamat?"

"Nearer to Harmony," Alucius replied.

"Does it get as cold as they say there?"

"It gets cold, much colder than here." Alucius paused but briefly, before asking, "You must be from somewhere warmer than here."

"Southgate. When my mistress died, I fled here. That was ten years ago."

"You were a cooper's apprentice?"

"Me? No, young man, I was a lady's maid, and her master's whore. But then, all women are in Southgate."

Alucius tried not to wince at the bluntness, and the bitterness that he could feel—even with his weakened Talent—wash over him like an acid torrent.

"My man, he was a trooper like you, but he learned coopering when his leg was hurt, and the troopers kept him to work in the supply depot in Salcer, and then at Zalt. He got his stipend three years ago, and now we have a shop here."

"I wish you well, lady," Alucius said, "although it would appear that you need little in the manner of wishes." He gestured at the range of barrels.

"Thank you. You are kind. Business could be better, but it is not bad." With a smile, she turned from Alucius to a heavyset woman who walked toward the carrel. "Honored Yelen . . ."

Alucius slipped away, moving to the next stall, one where all manner of woven baskets were displayed, some woven so deftly that scenes were depicted in darker straw. The gray-haired and collared man who sat on the battered stool beside the wall watched Alucius, but said nothing.

After a time, Alucius moved on, checking the platters and kettles of a coppersmith, and then the blankets of a weaver, thick and soft, but not so fine as nightsilk. From somewhere he caught the odor of fried fish. While he had no trouble eating fish, it was far from what he preferred, but it was much, much better than honeyed prickle—even the pickled sea-lettuce often served in the mess was better than prickle slices.

Leaving the weaver's stall, he sensed a swirl of Talent. His eyes turned toward the central open space. A slender older woman wearing a purple tunic, and trousers—and a thin black sash—stepped into the courtyard. Without seeming to, people eased away from the woman, leaving her in a space of her own as she made her way toward the stalls in the eastern section.

There was something . . . Alucius almost nodded. She wore the same clothing as the executioner had in Hieron. He studied her with his Talent, not searching, but trying to receive. He almost staggered at the pinkish purple forces that swirled around her, and the sense of wrongness, even evil within them. The forces swirled into nothingness in one way, yet there was an unseen line of Talent-power that pointed northward. The lines of power beckoned to him, almost as if he could reach out and touch them. But . . . then what would he do—especially if she sensed what he was doing?

"Good thought, trooper," came the voice of the middle-aged woman weaver behind him. "Best you be careful with the Matrial's representative."

"Thank you," Alucius said, turning. "Is she the only one here in Zalt?"

The weaver, who also wore a torque, if of the more ornate style worn by those few women Alucius had observed, shook her head. "They always come in pairs. Zalt has four. Salcer eight, I've heard tell."

Alucius blotted his forehead.

"Northerner, aren't you?"

Alucius laughed softly. "Everyone seems to take one look at me and know."

"For Zalt, it's a pleasant day. You're already warm."

"You're from around here?"

"Fled from Southgate years back."

Alucius wondered how many women had done that. Finding two in less than a glass was probably more than coincidence. "You ever hear from anyone there?"

"How?" The woman laughed, ruefully. "Not that there's probably anyone left, but traders from Southgate are forbidden to take messages or goods or coins to or from Madrien. The Lanachronan traders—they would, if one had the golds, but not to or from Southgate." She shrugged. "No one else travels the high road beyond Madrien."

"You seem to know much about that."

"There's always a young trooper—like you—who wants to get a message home. It's easy if home's in Madrien. It's possible, and expensive, to get a message to Lanachrona, but not back from there . . . not to anyplace else . . . it's so seldom any other traders come here."

Alucius had hoped, but he would keep his eyes and ears open.

Oryn appeared from nowhere. "There you are."

Alucius bowed to the weaver. "Thank you."

He got a faint smile in return.

"I saw the Matrial's representative," Oryn said, drawing Alucius back into the shadows between stalls. "You want to stay away from them."

"That's what the weaver told me." Alucius paused. "They don't like troopers spending time with local girls?"

"There's nothing forbidding it," Oryn said.

"But you don't want to cause her trouble."

Oryn nodded.

In a sense, Madrien remained a puzzle. Alucius turned. "I think I've seen enough for now."

"You don't want to go and have a bite at the cafe?"

"My silvers are few," Alucius said with a laugh. "Remember, I'm new."

"What else are they good for but spending?"

"Next time," Alucius promised.

Oryn was probably right, but Alucius didn't feel like spending. After growing up and seeing his grandsire watch every silver, he'd never enjoyed spending coins for pleasure, or gaming. He wasn't that hungry, and he had yet to find any way to send a message home. So all he really wanted to do was go back to the barracks and hole up in the library and read more about Madrien. If he learned more, then . . . perhaps . . . what he saw would fit together in his mind. At the least, he'd feel better about trying to understand the culture into which he had been forced, and which he was defending, whether he wished to or not. And . . . perhaps he might find an opportunity . . .

"Are you sure?" Oryn had a worried expression on his face.

"I'm fine." Alucius offered a smile. "I just need time to feel more at home." Not that he ever would, he feared.

"You might pick up a honey roll before you go back. You can get two for a copper, and they are good," Oryn suggested.

"Thank you. I just might."

As he walked toward the stall where the baker offered her wares, Alucius could feel Oryn's eyes—and concerns. For that reason alone, he bought two of the honey rolls, wrapped in a broad leaf. They did smell good.

Then he turned and began to retrace his steps to the post. He had more than a little thinking and reading to do.

80

The back road that seventh squad traveled ran through a stretch of high meadow south of the southwest high road. The sun had already turned the meadow grasses half gold, with most of summer yet to come. Riding in the last rank, Alucius leaned forward in the saddle, patted Wildebeast on the shoulder and then lifted his second water bottle from its holder. Even before midmorning, the back of his tunic was damp, despite the breeze out of the southeast. As full summer drew closer, each day in the saddle was hotter than the one before, and Alucius went through bottle after bottle of water.

"Glad I'm not a northerner," said Daafl, from the left of the younger trooper.

"Does Dimor get this hot?" Alucius took a long swallow and then replaced the bottle in its holder.

"Almost . . . and it's damper, being on the river."

"I guess this is better." Alucius pushed back his felt summer troopers' hat and blotted his forehead, then eased the hat forward so that the shadow from the brim shielded his eyes. The road climbed slowly at the end of the meadow, turning downhill and through another stand of evergreens. With each step of the troopers' mounts, dust billowed upward from the dry road.

"A lot better," Daafl confirmed.

"Fire! Smoke and fire!" came the call from Brekka, riding a good five hundred yards ahead with Venn as one of the squad scouts.

Over the trees ahead, a column of white and gray smoke rose straight into the silver-green sky, a sky with more of a silver shimmer in southern Madrien than anywhere else Alucius had seen. Mixed in with the white and gray smoke were swirls of black.

Alucius reached out with his Talent-sense. In the distance, he could feel riders, moving away. There was nothing large living near the fire—except, strangely, the creature that he had never seen that his Talent showed as brownish green. Farther away he could sense animals, similar to nightsheep, but not the same. Probably they were white sheep raised for food and wool.

"Rifles ready!" ordered Alben. "Close up on the scouts."

Alucius slipped his rifle from its holder and checked the magazine and chamber.

As seventh squad followed the road where it entered the trees, Alben glanced from one side to the other, but there was little undergrowth, and the wide spacing between the evergreens allowed little concealment. Alucius concentrated on following the brownish green feel, which seemed to be centered in the stand on the right and below the road, but he could see nothing, although he could sense that the creature seemed to be one with a large bristlecone pine that stood almost alone in a clearing. Was there something like a soarer or a sander, except linked to trees, rather than the sands or the skies? He'd never heard a mention of that, but the Matrites had never heard of sanders, either, except as distant legends.

He shifted his eyes forward, watching as the next meadow

came into view, and with it, the long and low structure from which flame poured skyward. Even from more than a hundred yards away, Alucius could feel the heat.

Beside the access road to the summer sheep station lay the body of a gray-haired woman in brown trousers and tunic, sprawled on her back. One side of her temple was gone and beneath the streaks of blood, what remained of her face showed an expression of shock.

"Squad halt! Rifles ready!"

No riders, no other people remained alive around the burning building.

Looking down, Alucius could see dark splotches in the dirt, well away from the building, indicating possibly that some of the attackers had been wounded or killed. But there were no bodies other than those of the Matrites.

"Last four—Denal, Daafl, Alucius, and Fustyl—circle around to the back!"

Alucius followed the other three, keeping his rifle ready, even though he knew there were neither shepherds nor raiders alive behind the building.

Three other bodies lay in the dirt behind the main building of the station, one older man and two women, all shot as they tried to escape the conflagration, Alucius gathered. The stable doors were wide, and the stalls empty.

"Shot anyone who tried to escape and took all the mounts," Denal noted.

Daafl swung down out of the saddle and studied some hoofprints in the dust. He looked up. "Southern Guard shoes . . . got that star."

"There was blood on the road," Alucius pointed out, "but no bodies."

"Didn't want to leave proof it was them," replied Denal. "Check the stable. Alucius?"

"I'll do it." Alucius eased Wildebeast up to the low stable with the lean-to-type roof, then dismounted and tied his mount to a post. Carrying his rifle at the ready, he stepped through the open doors.

All the stalls were empty. On a low pile of hay was the

body of a young woman, scarcely more than a girl. Her body below the waist was unclothed. Her throat had been slashed. Her hair was the same color as Wendra's. Alucius swallowed, and turned, studying the rest of the stable, but there were neither any mounts, nor any more bodies. He finally stepped out.

Alben waited with the others. "What did you find?"

"No mounts. There's a woman in there. They used her and cut her throat."

Alben's face froze for a moment. "Bastards! Always do that. Captain will have to know that." He dismounted and walked past Alucius and into the stable, returning within moments. "Nothing we can do. Mount up! We'll see if we can track them."

Alucius untied Wildebeast and mounted.

Alben led the way back to the road, as seventh squad followed the trail of the marauding Southern Guards. Alucius knew that the Lanachronans had far too much of a lead to be caught, and he had no doubts that Alben knew that also. But they had to make an effort. That was also clear.

Daafl looked at Alucius. "Matrial won't like this."

"More patrols, you think?"

"Wager we have both companies up here within the month, with orders to wipe out any Lanachronan we find."

Alucius nodded. He wouldn't have taken that wager, not after what he had already seen in Madrien.

81

Seventh squad was formed up on a section of the southwest high road, just below a crest of the road a mere ten vingts from the border with Lanachrona. All of Fortieth Company had been called out, and they had ridden northeast for four days, following Thirty-second Company, which had ridden out a day earlier.

The early summer sun beat down on Alucius, its heat going through his felt trooper's hat, enfolding his face, almost as if his face had no protection at all. He leaned forward in the saddle. After a moment, he glanced ahead at the browning grasses flanking the high road, and at the wavering heat lines that rose from the highway and from the dry and rocky hills to the northeast, the lower slopes of the coast range. The slopes on both sides of the high road were mostly rock, sand, and red dirt, with occasional patches of summer-dried grasses, scattered clumps of low pines and junipers, and occasional cacti that bore a slight resemblance to quarasote, except that their spines were shorter, and less deadly, and their color more of a bluish green.

". . . what we waiting for?"

The murmur came from behind Alucius, who was in the second rank in the left hand file, directly in back of Kuryt.

". . . what we always wait for . . . someone to make up their mind . . ."

The murmurs died away as Alben rode back from the front of the company and reined up before his troopers. "Seventh squad! Listen up!"

The squad leader waited for a moment. "There's a company of Southern Guards on the back side of these hills. We're going to turn back and ride just out of sight, and behind the next lower line. Thirty-second Company is already in position to keep them from riding south along the sheep road. They'll move north along the road and flush them out toward us. The first five squads of Fortieth Company will keep moving eastward on the high road until they pass the next cut in the hills. Then they'll turn and reform. That will keep the Lanachronans from retreating. Our job is to wait until the Lanachronans start westward. We'll be on the south side of the road, along with sixth squad . . ."

"We'll need to be ready when Thirty-second Company starts to flush them out toward us. The foot squads are already in the hidden trenches along the sheep road they'll have to take to reach the high road. We'll let them get to the high road, those that can, we'll be waiting behind these hills." A hard look crossed Alben's face. "It's time to teach them not to raid Madrien."

The squad leader stood in his stirrups, turning and looking back eastward. After several moments, he ordered, "Seventh squad, to the rear, ride!"

Alucius brought Wildebeast around with the other mounts, keeping station in the squad formation. As his eyes crossed Denal's, the other trooper raised his eyebrows, as if to suggest that the tactics were less than ideal. Rather than express agreement, even silently, Alucius just shrugged. Denal shook his head, minutely, before looking ahead and keeping formation.

The hill behind which sixth and seventh squads finally repaired was only seven or eight hundred yards farther west. Where they waited was bowllike, with the open side on the north adjoining the road. Just to the east, around a jutting low bluff, was a second and far shallower bowl, with a clump of juniper trees perhaps two thirds of the way around the back curve on the west side.

Alucius slowly studied the rises surrounding them. Although they were concealed, they were also open to attack on three sides from above. The steepness of the slope would keep anyone from riding up or down, but there was nothing to keep a force from climbing up on foot and then firing down. He just hoped that someone was watching the back sides of the rises. He hadn't seen anyone doing that. The half bowl just to the east would have been better, because parts of the rises surrounding the flat were gentle enough for a mount to ride up. Where seventh squad was, the only way out was by the high road.

After perhaps half a glass, he reached out with his Talent. He could sense troopers, Lanachronan troopers, because the Talent showed them as black, rather than the collar-changed gray of the Matrite troopers, and those Lanachronans had been moving closer. He frowned. He couldn't tell exactly how far to the south and east they were, not with so many troopers from both forces within a vingt or so, but the Lanachronans were so close that someone should have been giving an order for sixth and seventh companies to ride.

No order came. Alucius forced himself to take a long swallow from his water bottle, then slowly surveyed the rises. No one looked to be up there, and he could sense that the Lanachronans weren't *that* close. But they were close.

An officer—Undercaptain Taniti—galloped up the road from the west. "Thirty-second Company's pinned down. Ride east and then go south on the sheep road!"

"You heard the undercaptain!" snapped Alben. "Forward! Rifles ready."

Alucius liked it not at all. As he followed behind Kuryt, he sent out his Talent-senses again. They only confirmed that the Lanachronans were nearby, very near. Once seventh squad cleared the bowl and the low bluff separating it from the smaller bowl to the east, one with its back ridges less than fifty yards from the road, Alucius could barely keep from screaming as he sensed the Lanachronans there. Both sixth and seventh squad would be fully exposed.

As soon as the first Lanachronan lifted his rifle, Alucius snapped, "Fire on the left!"

The first shot punctuated his words.

"Wheel and fire! Wheel and fire!" ordered Alben.

Alucius winced, but obeyed, even as a volley of shots rang out from the south side of the high road.

Alben toppled out of his saddle. Beside Alucius, so did Kuryt. Alucius could sense that there were close to twenty Lanachronans there, if not more. If one of the two squads didn't do something, the losses would be enormous.

"Reverse wheel and follow!" he snapped. "Reverse wheel and follow!" As he wheeled Wildebeast, he only hoped that the rest of the squad would obey him—and the seldom-used command.

Without looking back, he led the charge up the western and lower side of the slope. Wildebeast's hoofs scrabbled on the loose soil, but the stallion lurched forward, caught his footing and carried Alucius toward the junipers.

Alucius could feel the bullets flying by him, so close were they, but he pushed away the thought and concentrated on swinging uphill behind the clump of junipers. The firing moved away from him as Wildebeast scrambled across the sandy dirt to the junipers.

"Charge and fire!" Alucius ordered, bringing his own rifle to bear as he rode from behind the cover of the clump of scraggly trees.

He fired once, kept riding, and cocked and fired again.

"Fire! Fire at will!" Alucius snapped, knowing he was repeating commands, but he seemed to be the only one shooting at the Lanachronans.

The Lanachronans, who had been concealed behind a low berm they had dug, were without mounts, and seemed to turn so slowly. So slowly that Alucius had fired three times, before the first raised his rifle. Alucius cut him down with his fourth shot.

Alucius reined up, one-handed, and resumed firing, quickly but deliberately.

Abruptly, there was silence on the back of the berm.

Close to twenty Southern Guards lay sprawled in the dirt. Alucius glanced around him, his eyes running over seventh squad. Kuryt and Alben had fallen on the road. Oryn was holding gloves, or something, against his arm, and Fustyl had been cut down on the charge.

"We'd better get back to the road," Alucius said, as he quickly reloaded. He couldn't sense any more Lanachronans nearby, but he had no doubts that there would be more attacks. He let Wildebeast pick his own way down, using his Talent-senses to try to find other Lanachronans. So far as he could tell, all left alive were farther to the east.

As the squad reached the road, Undercaptain Taniti rode up. "Good work!" Her eyes traversed the troopers. "Who was the squad leader here?"

"Alben, honored undercaptain," Alucius answered.

"Didn't he fall in the first volley? I saw him go down."

"Yes, sir . . . undercaptain."

"Who led that charge and took out the Lanachronan snipers?"

Alucius didn't dare look around. "I did, undercaptain."

"Are you the most senior, trooper?"

"No, undercaptain. I was the first to see them, and when no one ordered anything, I did. I just hoped someone would follow. The whole squad did, and we killed them all."

Taniti nodded. "You'll need a new squad leader. Until then . . . who's senior?"

No one answered.

"I believe Trooper Brekka is, undercaptain," Alucius finally said.

"You knew that, and took charge?"

"He was in the last rank, honored undercaptain. I don't know that he saw what had happened, and he wouldn't have had time to ride forward."

The undercaptain looked away from Alucius. "Brekka!"

"Undercaptain, sir." Brekka rode forward.

"You're acting squad leader. The company's re-forming at the crest up there. We'll still have to take out the main body of the Lanachronans."

"Yes, sir. Seventh squad! Forward."

Once the undercaptain turned her mount and headed eastward along the high road, Brekka turned in the saddle and glanced at Alucius. "More guts than brains, Alucius."

"What else could I have done, sir?" asked Alucius. "They would have killed most of us if we hadn't charged them."

"That was right," Brekka replied with a faint laugh. "I meant answering the undercaptain."

Alucius had been afraid that was what the older trooper had meant. All he could do was shrug. "I'm inexperienced. Perhaps you could tell her that."

"*If* she asks . . . or Tymal does," Brekka agreed. He turned toward the five remaining troopers in seventh squad. "Close up. Forward to the company!"

As seventh squad rode eastward, Alucius glanced over what remained of Fortieth Company. From what he could see, almost a third of the company was gone. There were even more Lanachronan bodies, but that didn't offer him much consolation, not if seventh squad had to keep fighting the way they had.

IV.

⊀ THE MATRIAL'S ⊁ LEGACY

82

The sun had not yet cleared the timber-covered ridge to the east of the former logging camp where half of Fortieth Company was now stationed in the first week of its three-week rotation, a series of rotations begun in midsummer of the previous year when one more company had been shifted to Zalt. Alucius walked quickly toward the stable.

He found it hard to believe that he had been at Senob Post for over a year, that he had been on more than fifty patrols, and that he'd lost count of the number of raiders and Lanachronan troopers he'd shot and killed, and that seventh squad was now on its third squad leader—Solat. Solat seemed to have more tactical sense than Alben had. So had Relt, but Relt had just been unlucky on the patrol before the last one.

Alucius took a deep breath as he stepped into the stable, then nodded as he passed Oryn, who was already checking his mount.

"You think we'll find anyone today?" asked Oryn.

"Some tracks, not much more. They've been avoiding us lately."

"Could be they're getting ready for a big attack, try and push through to Southgate?"

"Who knows? Everyone says they want Southgate. Lot of folks in Zalt ran from Southgate when they could. From what the women in the market tell me, the seltyrs use the Dramuran mercs to keep everyone a serf, except a handful of traders."

"Matrial should have taken it years ago."

"Why didn't she?" asked Alucius.

"Got me. Relt told me that both Dramur and Lanachrona said they'd attack Madrien if the Matrial tried."

"The Lord-Protector's attacking anyway," Alucius pointed

out. "And neither one offers much trade." Or any way to send messages, he'd discovered.

Oryn laughed. "They call them raids. That way . . ."

Alucius shook his head and headed for the stall holding Wildebeast. Even before he stepped up beside his mount, he could sense the residual soreness in Wildebeast's left front pastern. He had no idea what had caused it, unless it had been a stone thrown by another mount, because they'd only been riding the logging roads and not going cross-country after the Lanachronans.

He bent down and spread his fingers across the bone, letting his Talent enfold the skin, sinew, and bone under his fingers. "Easy, fellow . . . easy. This should help."

Alucius had done the same the night before, and his healing had clearly removed most of the damage. Healing his mount wasn't something that would be obvious, and Wildebeast wasn't about to tell anyone.

Wildebeast remained calm, almost as if the stallion understood that Alucius was trying to help him. Finally, Alucius stood, smiling faintly to himself, then patted his mount on the shoulder. In the two glasses before they would begin patrol, there would be more healing, enough so that Wildebeast shouldn't have any trouble.

83

"Halt!" ordered squad leader Solat.

In the early afternoon, under a hazy silver-clouded spring sky, seventh squad reined up at the junction of the two rutted logging roads. As he waited in the second rank, Alucius patted Wildebeast. His mount had recovered fully from whatever had caused the soreness in his pastern.

Solat studied the dusty road, then looked up. "No signs of tracks here. Alucius . . . you take Venn, Oryn, and Astyl, and follow the tracks on east fork. We'll take the west road.

Whoever gets first to where they rejoin waits for the other group."

"Yes, sir." Alucius eased Wildebeast forward, waiting for the other three to fall in beside and behind him. One reason Solat picked him to take half the squad was that Alucius wouldn't say anything about it. There wasn't anything in the regulations about patrols smaller than a squad. It just wasn't done—except two patrols could cover more ground than one. Since they knew the area around the old logging camp well, it was certainly faster with two patrols.

Venn slipped his roan up beside Alucius.

Neither said anything until they were a good three hundred yards away from the fork. Then, Alucius turned in the saddle. "Let it open up until we're about ten yards apart."

"Got it," replied Oryn.

Astyl, who had only been with seventh squad two months, glanced from Alucius to Oryn. Alucius let Oryn explain.

"In a small patrol, we don't want to be too close together."

Alucius kept scanning the woods on each side, not only with his eyes, but with his Talent-sense. The only scents were those of dust and men and mounts, so dry had the weather been in recent weeks. By the time they had covered almost a vingt, he could sense that there was something—or someone—out there, even if there weren't any hoof-prints in the road dust. He paused, then raised his hand. "Halt!"

Venn just waited as Alucius dismounted and studied the road.

Alucius nodded to himself, then mounted again. "Keep your eyes open."

"What did you see?" Venn asked. "There weren't any tracks."

"There weren't any tracks at all. None, not game, not birds, and there were some faint lines."

"That's what—oh. You think they're close?"

"No. Not yet. The dust has settled. You can still hear birds and insects farther back in the trees. Also, there's no undergrowth here, and no low trees. It's too exposed." Alucius pointed more than a vingt ahead to where the old road swung more directly eastward and around a rocky ridge. "When we get near there . . . then we'll see."

After another four hundred yards or so, Alucius could feel the blackness of troopers, Lanachronan troopers, farther ahead, waiting in ambush. There weren't that many . . . and if his little squad took them by surprise . . .

"Halt!" He reined up, then gestured to a boulder almost the height of a mount at the shoulder on the right side of the road. "We'll go over there."

Oryn and Venn nodded. Astyl just looked puzzled as the four eased their mounts to the flat area between a fallen fir and the boulder.

"I can't be sure," Alucius said, "but I think the Lanachronans have set up an ambush up there, right below that ridge. It looks right down on the road. So we're going to see if we can do the same to them."

"Shouldn't we . . ." Astyl closed his mouth abruptly as Oryn glared at him.

"If we try to get help, they'll move," Alucius pointed out. "If we ride past, we get shot. If we go back and around, the other half of the squad might decide to come after us, and they could get ambushed from that side."

"Oh . . ."

"Astyl?" Alucius asked.

"Sir?"

"We're going into the woods and climb up behind them. I want you to wait here, right behind this boulder. Once we're out of sight, I want you to count to four hundred, and then fire one shot into the trees on the east side of the road— just across from you. Then I want you to count to two hundred and fire once more. Do that once more, and then reload and wait. If any Lanachronan troopers ride down the road, shoot them. Just make sure they're Lanachronan."

"Ah . . . yes, sir."

"We'll ride to the base of those rocks, and then we'll climb the back side. I'd wager that the Lanachronans are on the flat rock below. It's slanted, and they can't be seen from the road."

"How do you know that?" asked Venn.

"Maps," Alucius answered, less than completely truthfully. "There are lots of them in the library at Zalt. That's the only spot for an ambush, and they swept the road so that they could set it up."

Astyl looked puzzled.

"Dragged a pine branch behind their mounts or something like that." Alucius turned to Oryn and Venn. "Let's go." He looked back at Astyl. "Don't start counting until we're well out of sight. And count *slowly*."

Alucius eased Wildebeast back around the uprooted trunk of the fallen fir, and followed a narrow game trail under the pines and firs, a trail that angled downhill, and then back up to the southeast and the rocky outcropping that overlooked the logging road. Once he had to dismount and lead his mount around a bushy growth of pines that were but shoulder high where the trail was blocked by a pine half fallen and wedged against a larger fir.

"Glad he knows where he's going . . ."

". . . safer around him . . ."

Alucius ignored Venn's murmur, as well as Oryn's reply. He definitely disagreed with the idea that being around him was safer.

A single shot echoed from the north. Alucius smiled. "Not that much farther." He remounted, then froze in the saddle for a moment, as, again, he could sense the brownish green of the unseen creature. The feeling passed as quickly as it had appeared, and Alucius urged Wildebeast toward the western side of the base of the rocky ridge, now visible through the trees ahead. His Talent confirmed that there were no Lanachronans on the west side, although there was a single trooper with the mounts on the south side, almost a vingt away.

Just before Alucius reached the spot where the ridge began to rise too steeply for the mounts, Astyl's second shot echoed through the trees.

"We'll tie the mounts up there," Alucius said quietly. "We

have to climb up there to get above them. Then we'll shoot down at them."

After another fifty yards, he reined up and dismounted, studying the rocks with eyes and Talent, and waiting for Venn and Oryn to join him. He dropped two more cartridge packs inside his tunic before turning toward the jumble of rocks that rose like irregular steps punctuated with scattered cedars and barely leafing mountain birches. "Let's go. Try to be quiet."

Oryn nodded. So did Venn, but the older trooper's nod was more resignation than acceptance.

Behind them a third shot echoed over the trees.

Alucius began the climb by squeezing between the irregular gap formed when one huge bolder had been split by water and time, then easing up an angled ledge. When they had climbed another fifty yards uphill, perhaps ten short of the crest, he motioned for the other two troopers to move closer. "They'll be in some sort of line. Unless I tell you otherwise, Venn, you take the three on the right end, and, Oryn, you take the three on the left. Understand?"

"What if there are more than that?" whispered Oryn.

"Then move toward the center—after you take down the ones on the end."

Both troopers nodded.

Alucius eased across the sandy exposed rock that formed the top of the ridge, moving slowly, and keeping low, finally stopping several yards short of the edge, and dropping onto his stomach before edging forward, his rifle in his left hand.

When Oryn and Venn slipped into place beside him, Alucius pointed over the lip of the redstone boulder. Less than fifteen yards below were nine Lanachronans stretched out prone, their rifles aimed at the empty road.

He cocked his rifle, waited for them to do the same, and then whispered. "Fire!"

His first shot took the middle trooper in the back of the skull.

Alucius got off three shots before the troopers below even began to realize from where the Matrite troopers were firing.

Alucius pushed aside the empty voids of death washing over him, and kept shooting. The other two were slower, but less accurate, and Alucius had finished reloading before they had emptied their magazines.

By then, the ambush of the would-be ambush was over, and there were six bodies on the rock below. A single Lanachronan trooper—the one guarding the mounts—had galloped off, with two mounts. That Alucius had determined with his Talent . . . and said nothing about it.

"Now what?" asked Venn.

"Are you three ready to surrender?" Alucius called down to the three wounded men, who had tried to huddle behind low outcroppings of rock.

"You'll just shoot us."

"We could already have," Alucius called back. "Throw out your rifles, or I will."

"Frig you!"

Alucius sighted on the man who had replied, then squeezed the trigger.

The Lanachronan's rifle clattered onto the stone.

". . . how'd he do that?" Venn murmured.

". . . don't ask . . ." muttered Oryn.

"We'll surrender," called back another voice. Two rifles skidded across the stone.

"Sit up with your hands on your head!"

When he was certain that the two remaining Lanachronans were unable to fire at them, Alucius motioned for Oryn and Venn to follow him, taking turns moving so that a rifle was always trained on the two survivors.

In the end, Alucius and the half squad resumed their ride toward the rest of seventh squad. Astyl was leading six Lanachronan mounts, loaded with the captured rifles and other gear, and the two wounded Lanachronans. Oryn rode behind, his rifle at the ready.

It took more than a glass to reach where the roads joined.

Solat rode out to meet them. His eyes widened as he saw what followed Alucius.

"The rest of you form up with the squad. We'll be heading

back. The undercaptain will want a report, and she'll want to talk to the prisoners." He looked at Alucius. "You ride with me and tell me what happened." He raised his voice. "Daafl and Neyl—you ride as scouts."

Denal looked toward Alucius and grinned.

Alucius shrugged, helplessly.

"Let's go!" snapped Solat.

Alucius guided Wildebeast up beside the squad leader and his mount.

The squad rode almost half a vingt before Solat turned in the saddle. "Tymal told me things happened around you." The squad leader paused, then asked, "What happened? How many were there?"

"Half of one of their patrols, I'd say. We counted seven bodies, and only one got away. Thought the undercaptain might like to talk to the ones that we captured. They'd set up an ambush, but they were too clever."

"Too clever?"

"They used a pine branch or something, dragged it behind a mount, to sweep away the traces of their tracks. There weren't any tracks at all on the road dust, and we haven't had rain or snow in weeks. I kept looking, and there was only one place for an ambush. We ambushed them."

Solat shook his head. "How did you manage that without losing anyone?" He paused. "Don't answer that. I don't need to know."

"Sir . . . I just do the best I can." That was certainly true enough, and it was the only way Alucius could hope to live long enough to figure out how to escape and return home.

"I've already recommended you for promotion to junior squad leader."

"Thank you, sir."

"You get the job done . . ."

Alucius could almost read Solat's unspoken words . . . *and I don't know how . . .*

84

In the darkness, Alucius stretched out on his bunk in the logging cottage that held seventh squad, about to fall asleep after a long and three-day ride through the hills from the southwest high road, at the beginning of yet another three weeks plus patrol. A wave of brown-green washed over him, and all thought of sleep was gone as he sat up abruptly.

He could sense one of the unseen creatures—the one with the brownish green feel—and not all that far from the patrol station. Quickly, he slipped to the pegs on the wall that held his uniform and pulled on trousers and tunic, boots and jacket. As an afterthought he added his sabre.

Only then did he step out onto the stoop of the cottage.

"Alucius?" asked Daafl, who was sitting on the stool used by those on guard duty.

"I need some air."

"You're not . . ."

"I know. If someone complains, I'll say I went out the window. You didn't see me."

Daafl shook his head. "Long as you get back soon. Not like there's anywhere to go. Or anyone to go to." He chuckled softly.

"Thank you." Alucius nodded. The isolation and restriction were more obvious in the mountains, but they existed everywhere in Madrien, and it sometimes amazed Alucius that so many of the other troopers did not seem to notice. A few did, like Daafl or Oryn, but most did not. Everyone was polite in Zalt, but, except for the handful of former troopers in the market and the refugees from Southgate, said little beyond pleasantries.

Without a look back, Alucius slipped into the night, moving alongside the cottage in the deeper shadows cast by the full orb of Selena—the spring planting moon. The air was chill, with a hint of mold, but dusty as well, but still, without even a hint of a breeze. From the lamps in the main building, he could see that Undercaptain Kryll was still up and awake. The problem with having half a company with a semipermanent patrol station was that an officer was always around.

At the end of the cottage holding seventh squad, Alucius eased to his left so that he would be on the back side of the next cottage, well out of the undercaptain's sight, should she even look out. From the back side of the last cottage, he walked eastward, downslope, away from the buildings until he was out between the tall firs. He moved easily, his boots almost silent on the carpet of needles, still damp enough from the snowdrifts left from the winter storms that had not finished melting until a few weeks earlier.

He walked silently away from the camp and into the deeper woods, into a stand of trees that had never been cut. He paused, abruptly, wondering how he had known that, and let his senses run across the towering trees and the ground. He did not know how . . . but he *knew*, in the same way he had known the land of his own stead.

He could still sense the brownish green, even stronger than before, as strong as a sander or a soarer, and not all that far away. After stopping beside the trunk of a tall fir, he gazed out from the shadows across the open space which held little but a scattering of seedling trees and a few thin stalks of last year's grass. He could smell a faint scent of the caroli, just about the only early spring flowers, and the only ones with a night perfume.

Whatever had created the brownish green was not far away, yet even with the night vision of a herder, at first he could see nothing. As he stood by the tall fir, he kept scanning the forest, both with his eyes and his Talent. Slowly, he took in what lay before him, sensing a faint green that permeated the ancient bristlecone pine on the far side of the open space, a tree gnarled and seemingly dwarfed by the taller firs and pines of the forest, yet with a depth and presence that made the other ancient evergreen monarchs less than shadows.

A girlish figure, seemingly clothed only in a subdued shimmer of light, stepped away from the ancient tree. The moonlight seemed to focus on her, deepening the shadows around the edge of the clearing, and she seemed made of green-and-silver light, never quite the same combination of colors as she moved.

Alucius waited, uncertain whether to slip away or to watch, yet knowing he would not leave, and not knowing why.

She continued to walk toward Alucius, her hands at her sides, her feet not touching the ground. Then she stopped, looking from the circle of moonlight that bathed her into the shadows where he stood.

You will have to leave the shadows before long. The unspoken words chimed softly, bell-like, in his head.

He would, Alucius knew, because sooner or later the sun would rise. Somehow, he understood words were unnecessary.

Not those shadows . . . the ones cast over your soul. She beckoned again. *Come . . . if you would . . . herder from the high lands . . . even with the evil collar you wear, we offer no harm.*

Alucius stepped forward, but he stopped short of the focused circle of moonlight that surrounded the girlish figure. *You're like the soarers . . .*

You could call us cousins. We are the few souls of the woods, while they need the open skies where none watch. The wood-spirit looked straight at Alucius. *You are part of the soul of the land.*

How could that be?

What is . . . is. The dark ties are too strong to be questioned.

For the first time, he could sense the age of the youthful-looking figure . . . and the sadness.

Why do you allow them to hold you with the collar?

Alucius did not answer. The question implied that he had the choice, not the Matrites. *Because I fear I do not know how to remove it.*

It is less than a spider's web.

They are spiders.

There is but one spider . . . and all the unnatural webs spin from there. They are nothing to the strength of the ties that are. You could break that web whenever you wish. Do not wait until it is too late.

Alucius watched as her hand extended to his neck, to the silver-gray torque. He could sense how she untwisted the purple and the pink. The collar fell away, and for a long moment, she held it in silver-white slim hands. Then she replaced it, and retwisted the spider threads of purple and pink. *You must do what you must do. We cannot.*

Alucius understood that. *Thank you.* He bowed his head.

There was a sense of laughter, not unkind, but not without an underlying tone of irony. *In time, we hope to owe you thanks.*

Being thanked by the wood-spirits he'd never imagined even existed?

We hope. We have hoped for generations. We hope you will understand and act before it is too late. She stepped back, bowed gravely, and then turned and walked back to the bristlecone. As she reached it, her hand touched the nearest feathery branch, and she vanished. So did the circle of moonlight.

Alucius glanced up, but Selena still shone brightly. He looked back at the ancient tree. The greenish glow was gone from the bristlecone, yet he could sense that somehow it remained, though he could not see it. He watched for a time, but the brownish green was gone, as if it had never been.

Finally, he turned and began to walk uphill and back to the cottage.

Just short of the cleared area that held the camp he stopped. He let his senses drop over the torque he wore. Then he swallowed. Should he? If he didn't, would he remember what she had shown him. His fingers were almost trembling as he lifted his hands. Then he concentrated on following the pattern of unweaving the purple and pink—and letting a flash of light break the weld.

He was breathing heavily by the time he held the collar in his hands. He cocked his head. Then he slipped it back in place, using his Talent to lightly seal the weld, but when he rewove the purple and pink, he did not tie the threads of power to himself, but to the torque, so that he would still seem "gray" to any Talent-wielder who looked at him. While he doubted that he could pass a thorough scrutiny by a Talent officer, in more than a year, he'd never even been close to one. He wore a torque, but not one that could kill him while he slept. A quick smile passed across his lips.

Alucius made sure Daafl was alone before he slipped up to the small overhanging porch and the stoop of the cottage.

"Daafl . . . I'm back."

"What . . ." The older trooper shook his head.

"You all right?"

"Nothing. Was probably dozing. That's all. You feel better?"

"The walk helped," Alucius admitted.

"Understand. Sometimes . . . you just need some space to yourself."

"Thank you."

Daafl nodded.

Alucius eased back into the cramped confines of the cottage, slipping toward his pallet bunk through the darkness that seemed more than bright enough for him not to need a lamp.

He glanced at Oryn, snoring lightly on the adjoining bunk. He could see, more clearly than ever before, the thin line of purplish pink—evil purplish pink—that twisted from the torque at his throat around Oryn's head and then stretched up and northward. Northward to Hieron and the Matrial.

Alucius shivered.

85

Alucius stood at the doorway of the mess, looking out at the rain falling across the courtyard of Senob Post,
the first rain in months, a late spring rain that flowed down
from thick gray clouds, cleaning the dust out of the air, the
dust of a long and dry winter, one that the southerners had
thought cold, and one filled with skirmishes, endless patrols,
and two inconclusive battles—followed by the eerie absence
of Lanachronans during the past weeks.

He moved from the doorway, heading back to the library
in the center of the barracks wing, glancing at Culyn, walking out of the mess, a youngster out of trooper school at
Salcer less than two months, and the latest addition to seventh squad, greener even than Alucius himself had been a
year earlier, probably even less experienced than some of the
auxiliaries who drilled infrequently, although Alucius had
never seen their maneuvers up close.

"Alucius!"

Alucius turned to see Brekka walking toward him. "Sir?"

Brekka laughed. "You're so formal. Always following the
rules to the letter."

"Yes, sir." Alucius grinned. "Safer that way." Especially
for a herder out of the Iron Valleys. "How do you like ninth
squad? And being a squad leader?"

"It's a good group. Not quite as good as seventh, not yet,
anyway. Being a squad leader beats being a trooper, but it's
more work. You'll find that out." Brekka paused. "Solat was
asking about you. Wanted to know why you weren't a junior
squad leader."

"No one asked me," Alucius pointed out amiably.

"He's recommended you for the next vacancy in the company. The captain will promote you before long, now that
you've a year in service." Brekka shook his head. "Specially

the way we're losing squad leaders. Almost as if the Lanachronans are targeting us."

"They probably were, except that they've vanished."

"Not for long. They want Southgate. They always have." Brekka frowned. "Why do *you* think they're after squad leaders? You didn't say, except you thought they were."

"Because the effectiveness of a squad depends on the squad leaders." Alucius didn't point out that, effectively, the officers were primarily strategists, logisticians, and large-scale tacticians, but usually not combat leaders. That had become all too clear over the year. "The Lanachronans know that." He shrugged.

"That makes me feel even better," Brekka replied. "Talking to you could depress a fellow, you know?"

"Yes, sir."

Brekka laughed. "I'll enjoy the respect from you for now. You'll be getting your own squad by summer's end, if not before."

"I appreciate the thought, sir. If it happens, I'll do the best I can."

"Oh, it will, and you'll have to." Brekka turned, heading toward the courtyard, despite the heavy rain.

Alucius fingered his clean-shaven chin, then walked toward the library. The room in the center of the barracks was termed the library, for it held several hundred volumes, but only a handful of troopers ever entered it, and usually only squad leaders. Most of the books were on matters of arms and geography, but there were a few books on history. There was also an entire rack of maps, mostly on Madrien and the adjoining lands. But he had found nothing on wood-spirits, legends or otherwise. Since no one had ever mentioned them, Alucius wasn't about to ask.

Alucius had begun to draw his own maps, earlier, but now he would need to concentrate more. Before he began on the maps, though, he took down one of the histories that went all the way back to the Cataclysm, just to see if he could find anything which mentioned wood-spirits. He seated himself at a stool behind one of the two narrow tables and began to leaf through the history. The early pages mentioned pteridons and sandoxes, and there were even references to sanders near the Aerial Plateau—but the historian dismissed them as "herders' mirages." Alucius snorted to himself. Mirages indeed! There was no mention of any other creatures.

He frowned momentarily as he turned the page and found a folded and yellowed slip of paper tucked there, pressed into the inside of the binding where the pages joined. After easing it out, he unfolded it and read the two lines—just two lines—written there.

> The collar, weaker than velvet or rope,
> strangles souls by suffocating men's hope.

"Weaker than velvet or rope?" he murmured the words to himself. Why the word velvet? He refolded the paper and slipped it back into the book. He could recall the words if he wished, and there was little point in carrying the paper with him. In a way, the words reinforced what the wood-spirit had said, but she could not have known about the ancient slip of paper.

He glanced up as he heard voices in the corridor outside, even through the door.

". . . better get over there before someone does . . ."

". . . early yet . . ."

Alucius frowned. The two troopers had not even passed the library door. While he had always had especially keen hearing, he had the feeling that his ability to overhear others had improved even more. Because of the wood-spirit? Or the looser tie of the torque. Or because the wood-spirit's appearance had pushed him into becoming more alert. *Do not wait until it is too late* . . . Those words had echoed in his thoughts. Had he become too complacent, telling himself that he needed to learn more and more, rather than acting?

Part of the problem was that the library was one of the few places where he learned anything beyond skills at arms. Most troopers knew less than he did, and anyone he could meet, usually in the marketplace, was cautious in going beyond pleasantries, or the evils of adjoining lands. While he knew that he needed to act, he had no idea what act to take. With his herder's skills and his Talent, he could probably make his way back to the Iron Valleys. Probably, but that was far from certain, and would take months on horseback, and far longer on foot. And then what?

Would anyone believe him, without his demonstrating his Talent? Even if they did, that would either leave him back in the militia, being asked to do more dangerous missions, or worse. He wanted to get back to his family—and to Wendra—but not in a way that destroyed all hope for the future.

And then . . . there was the implication of the wood-spirit's words . . . that there was something else to do. She had showed him how to escape the torque. Did he owe her? What?

Still pondering that and the words of the couplet, Alucius skimmed through the next fifty pages of the history. Of course, there was no mention of anything like wood-spirits.

Undercaptain Kryll stepped into the library. Alucius immediately stood. "Sir?"

"I was told I'd find you here, trooper. Please sit down." Kryll held several sheets of paper and an officer's grease markstick. She gestured to the table behind which Alucius stood.

Alucius eased back onto the stool.

The undercaptain pulled up another stool and sat on the far side of the table, then looked straight at Alucius. "I'd like you to write down what I say, trooper. You can do that, can't you?"

"Yes, sir." Alucius wondered why, but questioning officers was never a good idea.

The undercaptain handed the paper and markstick to Alucius.

He checked the markstick, then eased out his belt knife, sharpened the point, and waited.

Kryll cleared her throat, then spoke slowly. "Squads two, four, and five will patrol south of the high road. They will use the sheep station on Bare Ridge as their base and quarters. One squad will remain on guard status at all times. Troopers will carry double cartridge belts . . .

Alucius wrote what the undercaptain dictated, hoping his Madrien spelling was adequate.

Kryll stopped talking and waited until Alucius finished. "Let's see what you wrote."

"Yes, sir." Alucius handed the sheet to the undercaptain.

Her eyes slipped over his words. Alucius could sense she was pleased, in a way, yet vaguely disturbed. Should he have deliberately made mistakes?

Abruptly, the undercaptain stood.

So did Alucius, stiffening into attention.

"That's all."

"Yes, sir."

Alucius did not sit back down until the library door closed, and he was alone once more.

After considering what the undercaptain had wanted, he stood once more and walked to the shelf where he replaced the history. Then he went to the map rack.

One way or another, he needed to know more about the roads and towns of Madrien.

86

The late spring sun had dried up the morning rain and shone brightly on the rain-washed streets of Zalt, and a light wind out of the south carried a fresh scent of damp fields. Alucius walked briskly through the early afternoon toward the market. He still wondered about his encounter with Undercaptain Kryll. Clearly, it had been an examination, but for what? To make sure he could write? Was Brekka right about Alucius's being considered for promotion? Alucius wasn't so sure he wanted anyone to examine him too closely, especially not a Talent-officer.

He stepped to one side, out into the street, bowing his head slightly, to avoid a woman and her daughter, careful not to look directly at either. Neither looked at him.

His eyes ran across the blue-painted shutters of the house he passed, shutters that matched the door, and the window hangings, and even the woven mat on the front stoop. The neat stone-walled houses past which he walked were as closed to him as if they had iron gates, as were the walled courtyards behind them.

A few yards farther north, as he neared an older woman with a cane, he smiled and nodded. "Good day."

"Good day, trooper." The woman returned the smile and continued onward.

That was how it always was. He smiled, more faintly, as he neared the marketplace, thinking about how, even after a year, the only people he really knew in Zalt were troopers and a handful of vendors and shopkeepers. And in the only tavern, it was clear troopers weren't welcome. Alucius had never gone back.

His first stop was at the cooper's, but Elhya, the wife of the owner and perhaps the first person who was not a trooper that he had spoken to in Zalt, was not there, and the stall was being tended by an apprentice. So Alucius merely made a cursory inspection of the smaller barrels and then slipped away toward the weaver's.

A white-haired woman was haggling with Hassai over the price of a thick blue blanket, and Alucius stepped away and looked over the wares of the coppersmith, well made, but not exactly of much use to a Matrite trooper.

Alucius waited until the white-haired woman had left the weaver's stall and until it appeared that no one else was nearby, before slipping in and looking at the scarves—some of which he liked and could have afforded. Then he looked up. "Hello, Hassai."

"Alucius, my curious trooper friend, how are you this fine day?" The darker-skinned weaver smiled, showing even white teeth.

"I'm doing well."

"You always look, and you never buy."

"You have fine scarves, and some I could afford." Alucius shrugged. "But how would I ever be able to send one to my family?"

"You still pine for someone in the Iron Valleys?"

"You know that." Alucius bantered easily.

"You will never return there."

"You always tell me that. Tell me something new—of a trader who will carry a message there, or of a courier between large traders who could be persuaded—"

The weaver raised her hand. "My trooper friend . . ."

Alucius laughed. "I know. It is not possible."

"It has never been possible. You wish to send a message hundreds of vingts. In fifteen years, I have yet to find one wool merchant, one of the many traders who come here to sell their wares, who would carry a message less than two hundred vingts to my sister in Southgate. Sooner or later, you will understand." Hassai smiled. "I know a girl here who watches you. She finds you most handsome and kind."

"Not yet, Hassai," Alucius said, looking down at the green scarf, a color that would certainly bring out Wendra's eyes. "How much is this one?"

"Surely you do not intend to buy . . . not after teasing me for so long?"

"I might." Alucius grinned.

"For you, a mere two silvers."

Alucius slipped the coins from his wallet. "Two, it is." He handed the Madrien silvers to the weaver.

"You are too easy. You do not bargain." Hassai took the coins, shaking her head.

"I've bargained with you for a year, but never bought. How could I bargain about such a little thing?" Alucius grinned.

"You are kind." The weaver woman shook her head once more. "Once you have a stipend, women will come from all over Zalt."

"That's a long time," Alucius observed, carefully folding the scarf and slipping it inside his tunic. "A very long time."

"Time passes, more quickly than you know." Hassai looked to Alucius's right.

Alucius nodded and slipped away to leave the weaver with the pregnant woman who stood before the smaller blankets on one side of the stall.

Hassai flashed a smile at the trooper before stepping toward the woman.

After deciding against spending any more time in the marketplace, Alucius walked out into the spring sunshine, sunshine that somehow did not feel quite so warm and welcoming as it had earlier.

Had he bought the scarf to remind himself that he needed to find a way to escape and return to Iron Stem? And to Wendra?

Except, he knew all too well, escape was not enough. That thought bothered him. For while his grandsire had warned him to trust his feelings, *why* did he feel that escape was less than enough?

He shook his head as he walked back toward Zenob Post. To the west, another line of clouds was gathering, promising evening rain.

87

After sitting down at the mess table, across from Oryn, Alucius looked at the golden brown fried fish on his platter. Well cooked as it was, after more than a year of batter-fried breakfast cod, he wasn't certain that he wouldn't have preferred even honeyed prickle slices.

"Gets to you after a while, doesn't it?" Oryn asked dryly.

"The cod?" Alucius nodded.

"Got to me a long time ago. Hard to raise anything in Northport, except winter deer, and the does only come in season every other year. We ate a lot of fish. Didn't mind the clams, but when all we could catch was herring . . ." Oryn shook his head.

Alucius had never eaten herring, but he could sense that Oryn felt about herring the way Alucius did about prickle.

The two shared a laugh. Then Alucius took a bite of the slightly elastic eggs. The ale helped, and he slowly finished off the breakfast, saving the dried apple slices, also elastic, but tasty, for last. Then he carried the platter to the messboy, and turned toward the archway from the mess, followed by Oryn.

"What are you going to do today?" asked the other trooper. "Last day before we go back on duty."

"Might go to the market later, if it clears." The rain of the previous night had stopped, although the sky remained gray, and seventh squad was due to ride out on the following morning, back to the logging camp post to watch for and prevent more Lanachronan raids.

"You won't spend much. You've got more saved than some ten-year troopers, I'd wager."

"Probably not," Alucius replied, not quite truthfully, since he knew more than a few troopers who spent every coin they received. He also had to wonder about his uncharacteristic impulsiveness in buying the green scarf. But it did remind him of Wendra.

The older trooper laughed.

Alucius shrugged helplessly.

"When you come to the market," Oryn said, "you can find me at Cherafina's."

"The perfumer's?"

Oryn nodded.

Since he wouldn't go to the market until later, Alucius turned and headed toward the library. Once there, he took out the rack of maps that held those for the midsection of Madrien—where the midroad ran from Arwyn eastward and toward Iron Stem. He was more interested in what the maps showed in the way of back roads and towns. He had the feeling he'd need to know them far better than he did, which was not at all.

"Trooper Alucius!"

"Yes, sir." Alucius snapped to his feet as Tymal entered the library.

The senior squad leader shook his head. "One of my deadliest troopers . . . and he spends his free time reading and studying."

"I can only spend so much time in the market, sir, and I have much to learn about Madrien."

"You've learned a great deal, and you're on your way to learning more." Tymal smiled. "The captain wants to see you."

"Me?" Alucius wished he hadn't blurted that out.

"It's nothing to worry about." Tymal turned.

Hoping Tymal was right, Alucius hurried after the senior squad leader.

The captain's room wasn't as large as Alucius would have expected, a space five yards by four, but it had two large windows looking out on the courtyard. Captain Hyrlui stood behind a table desk, with Undercaptain Kryll to her left.

"Trooper Alucius, sir. As you requested," Tymal said.

"Thank you, Tymal. If you would stand by."

"Yes, sir." Tymal offered a nod of respect, then stepped back out of the room and closed the door.

"Alucius," began the captain, remaining on her feet. "You've been here something like a year and two months."

"Yes, sir."

"Last year, when your squad leader was killed in an ambush, you led the squad to a successful counterattack before turning the squad over to the next senior trooper. Is that correct?"

"Yes, sir. I didn't know if Brekka could see what had happened, and we were under heavy fire, sir." Alucius could sense a slight wave of Talent from both the captain and the undercaptain, but so little that either would not even have made a marginal herder.

"You have also operated independently and successfully routed small Lanachronan raider forces with few or no casualties to the men you led. Is that not true?"

"Yes, sir."

"You understand that forces smaller than a squad are frowned upon?"

"I understood that we were not supposed to range far from the rest of the squad, and in those cases we were not that far away. It was hard covering that territory with only a squad, sir, and I'd thought that was why more squads were sent on patrol."

Hyrlui smiled wryly. "I'd appreciate it, trooper, if you did not guess at the reasons for actions."

"Yes, sir." Alucius waited.

"Undercaptain Kryll has verified that you write acceptably." The captain paused and looked at Alucius again. "In fact, you write and speak better than most, and yet Madrien is not your native tongue."

"My mother said I had a gift for words, sir. Also, I haven't been around that many who spoke my tongue for almost a year and a half."

"You've spent many glasses in the market and the library."

"Yes, sir."

"Why?"

"I'm here, sir. I have to do the best I can. In the market, I talk to those who will tell me things. The library is to help me learn more. I figured that if I read more and learned more, it couldn't hurt, and it might help."

Hyrlui glanced toward the undercaptain, who nodded.

"You were a captive, and yet you work harder than most born here. Why?"

"I didn't see that I have any choice, sir. My best shot is to be good enough to get promoted. I figured that meant being as good as I could be. In everything." All of what Alucius said was true.

"What do you plan to do next?"

"Keep learning, sir. Do the best I can."

"Have you thought about the future beyond that?"

"No, sir. I mean, not in terms of making plans or anything. I thought I'd be a trooper for some years to come." Alucius was shading things slightly, but not much.

The two officers exchanged glances.

Then the captain spoke. "If you'd stand by outside, trooper."

"Yes, sir." Alucius nodded, then stepped back. The two had begun to talk even before he finished closing the door, slowly and deliberately.

". . . darker gray, like his hair . . . but still gray . . ."

". . . you think . . ."

". . . better by far than anyone else . . . and with the new assault . . . then we'll see . . ."

Alucius stepped away, toward Tymal, not really wanting to be too familiar, but also not wanting to give the impression of avoiding the senior squad leader.

"You'll do fine," Tymal said. "They go through this with every new junior squad leader."

Alucius blotted his forehead with the back of his hand.

"It can be a little rough," Tymal added. "They ask you a lot?"

"They asked me about the time I took over the squad when Alben was killed."

"I told them you handled that better than most junior squad leaders."

"Thank you."

Tymal offered a rueful smile. "I need men who can think when they're moving and under attack. It's going to get worse."

"The Lanachronans, sir?"

"I'd wager on it, but we'll have to see."

The wait seemed interminable, but far less than a quarter of a glass had passed before Undercaptain Kryll opened the door. "If you would both come in."

"You first," Tymal said.

Alucius stepped inside, followed by Tymal, and set himself opposite the captain.

Captain Hyrlui studied Alucius slowly. She did not look at Tymal at all. "You've been highly recommended by two of your squad leaders and by the company squad leader."

"Yes, sir, captain."

"You're going to be the new squad leader of second squad. Sedyr is being promoted to full squad leader and being sent to Thirty-third Company in Dimor."

"Yes, sir." Alucius wasn't sure whether he should offer thanks, but decided against it. "I'll do my very best."

"According to everyone, you always do, and that is what the Matrial expects."

"Yes, sir." Alucius paused, then asked, "Would it be possible for me to talk to Squad Leader Sedyr before he leaves . . . that is, if he has not already?"

The captain nodded. "Absolutely." She glanced to Tymal.

"I'll take care of it, sir, and his chevrons."

The captain smiled. "Congratulations, Squad Leader Alucius."

"Thank you, sir." Alucius bowed his head momentarily.

"You both may go."

Once the two squad leaders were out in the corridor, the door to the captain's spaces closed behind them, Tymal glanced at Alucius and said cheerfully, "I told you."

"You were right, sir." Alucius had the feeling that much more had hung in the balance than Tymal knew or would ever know.

"Sedyr's leaving tomorrow morning. Let's see if he's still here." Tymal turned down the corridor.

They found Sedyr in the squad leaders' wing, talking to Solat.

"Congratulations!" Solat looked pleased as he saw Alucius. "I take it you're Sedyr's replacement."

"That's what the captain said," Alucius replied.

Tymal cleared his throat. "I'll be back with those chevrons in a moment. You can have the tailor start putting them on your tunics right away. You're lucky in one way. Second squad just got back last night."

Solat grinned at Alucius. "I know why you're here." He nodded to Sedyr. "I'll be back in a while."

"You want to know about the squad, right?" asked Sedyr.

"Anything would help," Alucius pointed out.

Sedyr frowned. "It's a good group. There are some things.

Beral's solid in anything, settles anyone down. Rhen doesn't think much. You tell him to cut his own arm off, and he would. Druw looks like he doesn't hear. He does. Just hopes you'll ask someone else . . ."

Alucius listened intently, hoping that he could remember it all.

88

Hieron, Madrien

The triple-crystal light-torches focused on the workbench and the silver brackets and crystalline components laid out upon its immaculate and smooth-finished lorken surface. The brown-clad engineer concentrated on fusing two silver clips that would eventually join two angular crystals.

Outside light filled the room as the door at the east end of the workroom opened.

The Matrial followed the light into the workroom, leaving the door open, and walked toward the engineer and the workbench.

Hyalas turned and waited, his face composed.

"I trust you are working on rebuilding the weapon, engineer."

"That comes first, Matrial, as I promised. There are times when I can do little, while the crystals are growing, and then I continue to search for other possible weapons."

The Matrial's dark eyes fixed on the engineer. "You said it would take less time, engineer."

"I did, honored Matrial. I said it would take less than two years. It has been a year. Growing the crystals cannot be hurried. Nor can refining—"

"How long?"

"The crystals will not be ready until early harvest, late summer at best."

"That is too long. Have you no other devices that will help in warfare?"

"Talent-wizardry is not like smithing, honored Matrial, where a blade or a spear can be hammered out in days. It can do more, but the preparation and the materials take far longer. Nothing you or I can do will change that." Hyalas paused, then added quickly, before the Matrial could speak. "That was one of the reasons why the ancients never recovered from the Cataclysm."

"Oh?" A note of curiosity entered the woman's hard voice.

"The power of the Duarchy rested on devices and creatures built or controlled by Talent. For a time, Talent did not work, or perhaps the Talent they used changed to what we now know. Exactly what happened is unclear. What is not unclear is that much of what they had devised no longer worked as it had, nor as powerfully, and they could not adapt and change quickly."

"I doubt that the destruction of the two capitals rested on Talent, Hyalas."

"There was a great concentration of Talent in Ludar and Elcien, honored Matrial. How that Talent was used or contained changed in some fashion. That we do know, because for generations nothing grew near those sites, and any who ventured too close or remained too long wasted away."

"That is interesting . . . but it does not address our current needs."

"That I know, Matrial, and I am looking for other devices that may prove useful."

"Please do."

Hyalas could not resist stiffening at the chill in the Matrial's voice. "I have done so, and I will continue, as always, Matrial."

The Matrial did not reply, but turned and left the workroom.

Only after one of the Matrial's personal guards, in the purple and forest green uniforms of those pledged directly to her, closed the workroom door did Hyalas take a deep breath.

He glanced down at the components on the bench. "Fools . . . all of them . . ."

After a moment, he spoke the ancient words . . . some of them.

> " . . . The brave, the craven, those who do not care,
>   will all look back, in awe, and fail to see,
>   whether rich, or poor, or young or old and frail,
>   what was, what is, and what is yet to be . . ."

He offered a lopsided smile to the emptiness as he re-phrased the last line he had quoted. ". . . and *who* will decide what is yet to be?"

There was no answer to the words, but the engineer needed none.

89

In the dim light just after dawn, Tymal glanced at the assembled squad leaders of the first five squads of Fortieth Company as they gathered in the open space of the squad leaders' barracks wing. Alucius was the youngest squad leader, even of the junior squad leaders, with all of three days in his new position, and he listened intently, not only to what Tymal said, but how he said it.

"Second and third squads—you'll be escorting Undercaptain Gerayn out to meet the traders from Southgate. They'll be at the trade waystation. We didn't get advance word about them. They're probably trying to get back or make a last run before we get into full-scale fighting. The undercaptain asked for your squads to be ready at the third glass of the morning. Yular . . . your squad will mount guard duty on the tariff chest. Alucius, second squad will provide the personal guard for the undercaptain. You'll have to act almost as her head bodyguard. Pick two of your biggest and meanest-looking troopers to stand with you and behind her as she's inspecting the goods and collecting the tariffs."

Yular nodded. Following his example, so did Alucius.

"We'll all be moving out a week from Decdi. The captain has been ordered to overlap patrols even more. First and fourth squads . . . after morning muster, your men can have the day off. Remind them to be back well before sunset. Fifth squad—Gholar—have your troopers form up after second and third squads leave this morning. I'd like to see them in maneuver practice."

"Yes, sir," Gholar replied.

Alucius wanted to nod sympathetically. He'd spent most of the previous day working with Tymal and second squad. For Alucius, being squad leader had been more draining than being a trooper.

"Any questions?" Tymal added quickly, "Except about the Lanachronans. I don't know anything new. I don't know why we're stepping up patrols, and the captain hasn't said anything, and there's no word from Hieron."

"Sounds like there'll be more attacks," suggested Lokyl, the first squad leader.

"That may be, but just tell your men the facts, not what you think." Tymal glanced around. "That's all."

Before Alucius could leave, Tymal drew him aside. "Undercaptain Gerayn is a tariff officer. She's not trained as a troop commander. You don't have to take her orders, if there's trouble."

"But . . . if I don't, I'd better have a very good reason?"

Tymal smiled. "You understand. I doubt anything will happen, but you should know."

Alucius had to hurry to get through breakfast and to the muster area in the courtyard before his new squad. Even so, Beral was waiting as Alucius strode up.

Alucius stood back and waited until the others arrived. Then he stepped forward. "Second squad. Two things. First, the patrol schedules have been moved up, and we'll be riding out a week from Decdi. Second, we'll be doing guard and escort duty for a tariff collection today. You've got half a glass to be mounted and ready in the courtyard. That's all. Dismissed to get ready to ride."

Alucius headed back to the squad leaders' wing to get his own gear.

A half glass before the third glass, Undercaptain Gerayn appeared in the courtyard, riding a gray mare. She was a short and round-faced woman with wispy brown hair that her officers' hat barely kept in place. The sole difference in her uniform from that of other officers was the single silver stripe just above the each cuff of her tunic sleeves.

With his Talent, Alucius could easily sense streaks of both green and a tinge of purple shooting through the blackness of her being. He resolved to be very careful, since the undercaptain showed far greater Talent than anyone he had seen in Madrien since leaving Hieron.

Alucius rode forward and reined up. "Undercaptain, second squad stands ready."

"Thank you, squad leader."

Yular rode up within moments and reported as well.

"Since we're ready," the undercaptain said, "we might as well head out. We'll be riding southwest to the trade waystation on the west side of Zalt. You're new, Alucius. You'll ride with me, and I'll tell you what you need to know."

"Yes, sir." Alucius hadn't heard of the waystation before that morning, but he was certain there was much he would learn in the days and weeks ahead. "Second squad, forward!"

"Third squad, forward!"

Gerayn did not speak until the column was on the high road, headed southwest. "All you really have to do, squad leader, is look ready to kill the head trader if he does anything wrong . . . and be in a position to do it."

"Rifle or blade, sir?"

"You have to use a blade. The two guards with you should bear rifles. Tymal said you're a class-one blade and rifleman. Is that correct?" asked the undercaptain.

"Yes, sir."

"You're a fairly big man, but I've seen larger. Are you especially quick?"

"Sir . . . someone else would know that better than I. I just do the tasks as well as possible."

"You're quick enough." Gerayn laughed.

Second squad rode southwest, and Alucius studied the road. It was empty of travelers and wagons, not that there were ever more than a handful. As they passed the south edge of Zalt, Alucius thought the town was quieter than usual, although it was always quiet in the morning.

The trade waystation was separated from the town by a good vingt of open fields, fields now showing perhaps a span of green growth. The trader was clearly ready for the tariff officer, because he stood by a small table under the slanted front overhang of the square stone building that was the trade waystation. Beside him were two bearded men in sea-green tunics, with blades in curved and gilded scabbards.

"Do you want a show of force, sir?" asked Alucius.

"That might be fun . . . but we'll dispense with it. That's Burlyt, and he'd protest for almost a glass about how I should trust him after all these years. I don't trust him, and he knows it, and there's little sense in giving him an opportunity to protest. He is close to both the Dramuran traders and Seltyr Benjir."

"Yes, sir." Alucius had no clear idea of what the two references meant, except that the undercaptain thought they were important, and he concentrated on remembering them before he turned in the saddle. "Second squad, rifles ready in holders! Keval and Armon—you two will act as the undercaptain's guards. You'll dismount with me. Bring your rifles. The rest of you . . . draw up on the south side, three abreast, two deep."

Only when the troopers were in position did Gerayn dismount and approach the older and bearded trader, Alucius beside her, and Armon and Keval directly behind her, both with rifles at the ready.

The swarthy trader wore a white shirt with a sea-green vest, trimmed in gold, and flowing white trousers above dusty white boots. Alucius managed not to change the intent expression on his face, as almost in passing, his Talent revealed that the bodyguard on the left was a Lanachronan trooper or officer. Did the trader know? Would Gerayn find out?

"Again we meet, Trader Burlyt," Gerayn offered.

"The most lovely and wise tariff officer . . . you are even more beautiful than ever, like the sunset on a calm sea, and cool water in the heat of summer . . ."

"And you are an even more gracious liar than ever," returned the undercaptain with a warm smile. "Shall we inspect your goods?"

"They are assembled in the courtyard within."

Alucius gestured for Armon to go through the archway first, although he sensed no one beyond in the narrow shadows, nor any excessive tenseness in the trader and his two bodyguards. The trader and his guards followed, then Keval and the undercaptain. Alucius came last.

An array of goods was laid out, each set on the stone pavement before the wagon from which it had come. There were bolts of southern cotton, dyed in swirls of color, and southern silk, as soft as nightsilk, and far brighter, but not so strong. There were jugs of perfumed oils, and smaller jars of bright pigments, and larger jars of cardamom and saffron, and the heavy cloves that came only from Dramur. There were ingots of tin, and two jars of a finely ground powder that Alucius had never seen, at which Gerayn nodded knowingly. And rows of amphorae, all filled with various liquids. At the end, guarded by two other men, was a strongbox.

Burlyt produced a shining brass key and unlocked the iron-bound chest. On an inset shelf, covered by a dark blue velvet pad that Burlyt lifted, were golden rings, amulets, and unset gem stones. Gerayn surveyed the items, then nodded. Burlyt replaced the pad and lifted the shelf. In the bottom of the chest lay long golden chains, seemingly dozens of them.

Alucius could sense the disgust that radiated from the tariff officer as she studied the chains.

"You may lock the chest."

"You see," said the trader, "just trade goods, and only trade goods."

"For men," Gerayn said mildly. "Few women would buy such."

"Ah . . . that is not so. The women of Tempre, they buy much."

"Do they buy much for themselves, or to please the men who own them?" Gerayn's tone was bantering.

Alucius listened. So did the Lanachronan disguised as a guard.

"We all seek to please someone, do we not, even since the days of the Duarchy? Always that has been the way of the world."

Gerayn nodded, producing several sheets of paper with printing upon them. "That is so, and the Duarchy fell, did it not?"

"The stars and the moons are in the sky, are they not, honored tariff officer?"

"They do not fall, but the Duarchy did."

A puzzled expression crossed the trader's face. "That is true."

"Why did the Duarchy fall? Might it be because it was controlled and ruled by men? Women were treated like brood mares—just as they are today in Lanachrona and Lustrea—or Dramur. If a woman there has children, she'd better have sons or risk being discarded . . ."

"I would not discard any of my wives, gracious undercaptain," suggested Burlyt, humor tingeing his voice as he clearly baited the tariff officer.

Alucius refrained from showing emotion, especially since he did not understand what was being played out. Gerayn was bluntly suggesting the need for better treatment of women, but why to a trader? And if the Matrites were so opposed to Lanachrona and Lustrea, why had they attacked the Iron Valleys, where women were treated so much better? Or were they? Certainly, his great-grandmother and great-great-grandmother had been herders. Why didn't his mother have the Talent? Alucius had to admit that he didn't know.

And Wendra . . . she had pointed out to him how everything was being arranged for Alucius, not for her, and that a cousin had been married off to a butcher she didn't even know.

"No . . ." laughed Gerayn, "for they might have you murdered, you charming scoundrel."

"Gracious tariff officer . . ." the trader protested.

"And what have men done since the Cataclysm?" asked Gerayn. "What was the Legacy the Duarchy left them? Generation after generation, they've fought over scraps of the Duarchy. When the Matrial first appeared, and that was less than four generations ago, Hieron was a backwater river town subsisting on the crumbs left by Lanachronan traders . . ."

Less than four generations? What sort of power had the Matrial—or Matrials, for Alucius still had strong doubts about an unaging Matrial—discovered that had forged such a strong land in so short a time?

"Today, Madrien is the strongest land east of the Spine of Corus. The Matrial has done more in three generations than have the men of Corus in more than a thousand years . . . Come . . . tell me how men are superior, Trader Burlyt."

"I am but a trader, arms commander . . . but if you have no children, you will have no future." Burlyt laughed genially, if uneasily.

"We have children. I have three. We have them when we wish them, and not at the pleasure of any man. That is why all women are trained in arms."

"Then it is at your pleasure, and for that I must salute you."

"I take your salute, trader, and my pleasure." Gerayn grinned openly.

Burlyt shook his head. "There are no women such as you in Southgate."

"You and Seltyr Benjir would hope not." Gerayn took the markstick and ran down the list, jotting figures, and then adding them.

Burlyt waited. Alucius studied the trader, his guards, and,

with his Talent-sense, the others who waited beyond the second archway.

Gerayn looked up. "For what you are transporting, eighty-one golds."

"Eighty-one? I will not get two hundred for all that I have," protested the trader. "Not one hundred and fifty on a bad week."

"Oh? You plan on getting almost fifteen hundred."

Burlyt shrugged helplessly. "Alas . . . you know me too well." He rang a small bell that appeared in his hand.

Alucius realized that Burlyt had staged the show of protest, as, in a different way, had Gerayn. Why?

Was each trying to let the Lanachronan know something? Or was there more there?

A thin youth appeared with a large leather pouch, which he tendered to Burlyt. The trader untied the thongs and emptied the golds onto the flat top of the strong box, where he counted out eighty one, which he then openly replaced in the pouch and handed to the tariff officer.

Gerayn laid two lists on the top of the strong box where the coins had been. She signed both with her markstick, and then handed it to Burlyt, who also signed both below her signature. Then she reclaimed one of the lists, rolled it, and slipped it into the pouch. She inclined her head but slightly to the trader. "Thank you, trader."

"My thanks to you, tariff officer. You are most prompt and quick." Burlyt offered a deeper bow, then reclaimed the other signed list.

Gerayn gestured, and Alucius nodded to Armon, who led the way through the archway and out under the overhang and to where the squads and mounts waited. Burlyt did not follow them.

Alucius was the last to mount. "Second squad, forward!"

They had ridden almost half a vingt before Alucius turned in the saddle. "Begging your pardon, undercaptain?"

"Yes, squad leader?" Gerayn's voice was even.

"I'm new at this, but the trader knew you. He knew that you'd know the value of his goods, but he protested, and then paid, as if he'd known it wouldn't do any good."

"You saw that, didn't you? Why do you think he protested?"

"Someone in his group is a spy for whoever runs Southgate?" Alucius suggested.

"A spy, but from Lanachrona. It was a setup. If I don't call his bluff, then we look unreasonable or stupid. If I do, then it shows we have power. Burlyt wanted the spy to know we see more than we reveal. He hopes that will discourage the Lanachronans from trying to attack Zalt or even Southgate."

"Thank you, sir." Alucius nodded. He had his answers, and he hoped that he had covered any interest he might have betrayed.

"And Burlyt is the cousin of one of the high seltyrs of Southgate," Gerayn added. "He should know better."

Know what better? Alucius wasn't about to ask, and the undercaptain didn't volunteer an explanation.

90

Hieron, Madrien

The Matrial turned in the wooden armchair, looking up at the rows of ancient tomes in her private library. "So much knowledge, Aluyn, sits upon those shelves, and so much of it is useless."

"Matrial?" inquired the blonde marshal from the other side of the ancient wooden desk.

"For knowledge to be used requires power. In the contests between cultures and lands, neither the greatest knowledge, or even sometimes the greatest power, triumphs. Look at where we stand. An accident, a simple accident, led to our present situation. Or perhaps it was lack of power." After seeing the puzzled expression on the marshal's face, the Matrial continued. "We sent the crystal spear-thrower to Sou-lend. While it functioned, we had almost routed the Iron Valleys Militia. It failed, and we did not have another. That was lack of resources, or golds, or power, or forethought, call it what you will.

"So I ordered you to send more troopers, and we pulled most of the garrisons and horse from Salcer, Fola, and Hafin to be able to reinforce our troops in Soulend. After all, who would attack our heartland? But the reinforcements were not enough against the Iron Valleys and the coldest winter in a generation. Still, once the winter ended, our forces there made some inroads, and had moved halfway to Iron Stem and almost to Wesrigg. Who would have expected that this past winter was even colder, and that we lost ground once more? Now, we have all our forces ready to act, with their Militia crumbling, and what has happened?"

"The Lord-Protector has attacked Salcer," replied the mar-shal. "But we repulsed them, and destroyed most of their force."

"They almost reached the walls. Could we defeat them once more? Do we have the forces in the south to stop them if they send fifteen or twenty companies toward Zalt and Southgate?"

"No, Matrial," the marshal admitted.

"So . . . we must pull back to the Westerhills borders, and send the forces in the north southward, as quickly as possi-ble." The Matrial smiled, sadly. "We have been beaten in trying to take the Iron Valleys—for now, and not by the power of men, but by the power of nature." She sipped the amber liquid from the fluted crystal before she continued. "By our efforts, we have stripped the entire midsection of Madrien. While Zalt is stronger than last year, there were less than two full companies of horse in Salcer now, and only one in Dimor. Without the auxiliaries, we would have lost Salcer, and they were so decimated that another five companies could take the city, the depot, and the armory. Eight companies lost to nearly the last woman and veteran? Is that not so?"

"That is what I reported."

"The Lord-Protector will attack in the south. He will attempt to take Southgate. He has always sought it, one way or another. So has Dramur. The attempted assassination of Seltyr Benjir and the rather unusual deaths of Seltyr Yasyr and his eldest son . . ."

"You believe that the traders . . ." ventured the marshal.

"They have close ties to the Dramurans. Dramur would dearly love to have a captive port on the west coast of Corus. We know this, and so does the Lord-Protector. The Iron Valleys must wait. If nothing else, we have weakened them so that when we do attack they will not be able to raise more militia." A wry smile crossed her lips. "They already do not have the coins. They borrowed six thousand golds from the Landarch of Deforya—at interest. They have raised enough forces that the Lord-Protector will not attack there. Not now, and not if he is trying to seize Zalt and Southgate, and that he will do."

"It will take time to move so many of our companies south."

"It will, but move what you can quickly, and have the others follow. The rebuilt crystal spear-thrower will be complete by late summer or early harvest, and that should aid greatly." The Matrial looked to the tomes filling the shelves on the wall. "So much knowledge, and so limited by the power we do not yet have."

91

A hot wind blew off the sandy and scrub-covered ground to the right of Alucius, whipping sandy grit across his face. His eyes watered, and he blotted them, then readjusted his trooper's felt hat to keep it from blowing away.

Behind him rode second squad, along the south boundary road that divided the easternmost cultivated lands of Zalt from the scrub rangeland where the handful of local herders grazed their white sheep. The wind was coming from the east, off the Coast Range, as it had for days, drying out everything.

In some ways, everything had changed over the past three weeks. First, half of Fortieth Company had gone east to the logging camp used as a staging base. No sooner had they gotten there than it had rained for three days straight, turning the roads into swamps. Then, a messenger had struggled through to recall them to Zalt, because the Lanachronans had attacked Salcer with more than ten companies, but the Fortieth Company squads had to wait until the roads were passable. Since then, the sun had been unrelenting, the skies clear, and there was dust everywhere.

A week had passed since second squad's first road patrol after returning to Senob Post—ten days of drills and road patrols, with no sign of the Lanachronans. Only the day before had the captain received a message from Salcer, and all she had conveyed to the Eighteenth, Thirty-Second, and Fortieth Companies was that the invaders had been repulsed, with heavy losses on both sides.

Very, very heavy losses, Alucius suspected.

When the last gust of wind subsided, he looked eastward once more, sending out his Talent senses. He neither saw nor felt anything except wildlife and a distant flock of the Madrien sheep . . . and a range fox, the kind that preyed on the weak or upon newborn lambs.

Neither he nor any of the patrols had seen or reported any Lanachronan activity, and no sign at all of troops or scouts. Had almost all of their forces been directed at Salcer?

To Alucius that made little sense, because the maps and everything he had heard indicated that the Lord-Protector was far more interested in taking Southgate than in undertaking a full war against Madrien. His lack of understanding told him, once more, that there was far more that he needed to know, and yet . . . the wood-spirit had been clear that he could not wait too long.

He blotted the grit off his cheeks with his tunic sleeve,

readjusted his hat, and looked eastward once more. Nothing, except wind and empty land.

"... keeps looking out there ..."

"... nothing ..."

"... anyone see anything ... be him ..."

"... someone ... said he'd been a militia scout ... one of the youngest ever ..."

"... must have missed scouting something ... wouldn't be here otherwise ..."

Alucius laughed to himself. He'd missed more than a little, and he still was.

92

For all of the captain's concerns, two more days passed without event. Messengers arrived, but the captain said nothing, nor did Tymal. The near road patrols reported nothing. The more distant patrols had returned late on Tridi, and, not surprisingly to Alucius, on Quattri, all the squad leaders at Senob Post were summoned to a meeting immediately after breakfast. The only ones missing were the two who had already left on local road patrol duties.

Alucius accompanied Pahl and Yular into the long room, nearly a third the size of the mess, a place in which he had never been. The walls were of pale green plaster over stone, the floors polished redstone rectangles, and the windows had narrow casements without shutters or hangings. At the south end of the meeting hall, a low dais ran from one side of the ten-yard wide room to the other. There were neither benches nor chairs.

The dais was empty until all the squad leaders had assembled. Tymal stood beside the eight remaining squad leaders of Fortieth Company, as Konen stood beside those of Thirty-second Company, and Kastyn did beside those of Eighteenth Company. After several moments, the officers marched in.

Captain Hyrlui, Captain Dynae, and Captain Marta took positions at the front of the dais, with the six undercaptains behind them, and Tariff Officer Gerayn slightly to one side.

Captain Hyrlui looked across the squad leaders, then spoke. "As you all should know, the Lanachronans attacked Salcer several weeks ago. Their losses were high, but so were ours. Now, the longer road patrols I had dispatched several days ago have reported that the Lanachronans have ten companies of Southern Guards on the southwestern high road, riding toward us. If they succeed in taking Zalt and breaking through to Southgate, they will send more companies. It is clear that their goal is to control the southwest high road and to take Southgate. We cannot allow this . . ."

Even had he not worn the collar, Alucius would not have wanted the Lanachronans to gain control of Southgate. But then, he really didn't want the Matrial in control, either.

"The most aid we can expect immediately is three companies of horse, and two of foot. They had been dispatched immediately after the battle for Salcer, and messengers have confirmed that they should reach us shortly, but possibly not before the Lanachronans do . . ." Hyrlui paused, glancing toward Captain Dynae, before continuing. "In addition, Zalt can raise three companies of horse auxiliaries. That will provide us with forces close to equal of those of the Lord-Protector. We will not ask for the auxiliaries unless it is clear we will need them. We expect to see the Lanachronans soon, either tomorrow or the next day."

Captain Dynae cleared her throat, and Hyrlui nodded to the younger woman.

"We've been assured that additional companies are also on the road south," Dynae added. "That's why it's important to stop the Lanachronans now."

Hyrlui waited for a moment, then went on. "After this, we'll be meeting with senior squad leaders. You squad leaders should brief your troopers, and make sure that they're ready for battle. It could be tomorrow, or as late as Septi." The captain paused once more, and looked toward the red-haired Captain Marta, who gave the slightest of headshakes.

Hyrlui then concluded, "That is all."

The officers left, with Captain Hyrlui the last to depart.

Then, Alucius led the squad leaders from the meeting hall. Once out in the corridor, he turned to find Tymal, but Gholar was already talking to the senior squad leader. Alucius listened.

". . . know whether they've got cannon?"

". . . have wagons, more than a score, ten trailing the main body . . ."

Tymal had known before the meeting. How much more did the senior squad leader know? Alucius kept listening, standing well back, but waiting for his turn to talk to Tymal.

". . . might have some field pieces . . . wouldn't have many . . . couldn't risk it . . . not with Talent-officers . . ."

". . . didn't know we had any here, sir . . ."

". . . only need one, Gholar . . ."

"Yes, sir." Gholar nodded and stepped away.

Alucius moved forward. "Sir?

"Yes, Alucius? Can you make it quick?"

"The auxiliaries? How good are they?"

"They are not quite so good as you, except for the elite companies, but they all have had much training, and, you have seen that they conduct maneuvers regularly. All able-bodied women are required to take arms training. They spend a season, sometimes two, in separate companies after their twentieth birthday, and some take it most seriously. They lost almost seven companies in saving Salcer."

Alucius wanted to look down. "Thank you, sir."

"You wouldn't know. You should." Tymal smiled almost kindly before turning away.

As he walked back toward the barracks wing that held second squad, Alucius wondered. How many women in the Iron Valleys would train so . . . and risk their lives? His mother would have. He had no doubts of that. Wendra? He hoped so, but honestly didn't know.

93

Midafternoon on Quinti found Lokyl, Alucius, and Yular sitting on one side of the end table in the northeast corner of the troopers' mess. Across from them sat Tymal and Vylor, and between them was a map.

"Some of the auxiliaries sent out scouts earlier today, disguised as herders and growers," Tymal began. "They just got back. The Lanachronans have six or seven field pieces—with a range of a good two vingts. They're placing them in the Barrow Mounds—those old low hills to the northeast. They'll be able to shell the post from there. Or even the town." The senior squad leader paused. "In addition to the gunners, they've only got a half company of foot there right now. They've set up their main camp on the other side of the southwest high road, along the southern boundary road, right where the lower reach of Spring Creek crosses the road."

"That's almost four vingts out," Lokyl said. "That puts a good two vingts between their main camp and the artillery. I wouldn't do that."

"You'd want all that powder near your camp?" asked Tymal.

"Don't know why they'd even risk bringing it." Yular scratched his ear.

"Because true Talents who can cast power over a distance are very rare," Tymal pointed out. "They're not going to let one walk up, and we're not about to risk one, even guarded with a company, trying to get her close enough to set off the powder." The senior squad leader shrugged. "So you three get chosen to try and do some damage to the guns. Vylor is going to take out first, second, and third squads in a glass—sooner, if possible. Your job is to locate exactly the cannon emplacements and send back a good map with a messenger.

Then, if possible, you're to attack the emplacements and destroy or capture the field pieces. The captain would prefer destruction, but even if you can't take the position, the attack should force them to move more troopers to defend there. We need to keep them off balance for another day, until the other companies reach us."

"You said they only had half a company of foot troopers?" asked Yular.

"That's now. Once the guns are dug in . . . they'll move in more. That's why you'll be heading out now, before they move in more foot troopers." Tymal gestured to the map. "You'll take the north-south high road back north. It's less than three vingts before you reach the place where you head east, along the field roads. The fields run almost to the base of the hills, but if you go another couple of hundred yards north, here, there's a windbreak of brush olives that you can follow to within two hundred yards of the northeastern end of the Barrow Mounds . . ."

"Are the Mounds talent-trapped?" asked Lokyl.

"No one has found anything there," Tymal said dryly. "The Mounds were built generations before the Duarchy was established. There won't be anything of power left. If there is . . . well . . . the Lanachronans are there now. I doubt if any traps will wait for you."

Yular laughed. Lokyl flushed.

After the short briefing, Alucius hurried to the second squad barracks wing.

Beral was on his feet. "Squad leader's here."

"Gather round!" Alucius ordered.

He waited until all eight troopers were there. "We're heading out now. Half glass at the latest, formed up in the courtyard. Three squads. Lanachronans are trying to establish a post in the Barrow Mounds."

". . . frig . . ."

Alucius didn't see who muttered the comment. "It'll be worse than that if we let them dig in. They're bringing in cannon."

"Only a third of a company?"

"We can't risk more than that," Alucius pointed out. "Not until tomorrow, or maybe Septi. We can't wait that long."

"Would happen to us," Keval muttered.

"Someone has to go, unless we want to sit here and get bombarded—or retreat and fight on worse ground." Alucius pointed out. "Get going. Draw double cartridge loads. I'll see you in the courtyard."

"Yes, sir."

Alucius turned away.

". . . doesn't coddle you . . ."

". . . doesn't coddle himself . . ."

Alucius hoped not, although he could recall sleeping in while others worked, and that hadn't been all that many years before. He picked up his own gear, and a triple load of cartridges from the small post armory, before heading to the stable.

He was the first saddled and ready in the courtyard, as it should have been, he felt, noting that Yular was close behind him.

The older squad leader eased his mount toward Alucius. "What did you tell your men?"

"That we had to take out the cannon before they got them in position to take us out." Alucius shrugged. "What else could I say?" He paused, then asked, "What did you say?"

"Same thing." Yular grinned. "I also told them you were part of the attack."

"That . . . and a bullet . . . will get them the same grave," Alucius replied.

"You and I know that, but you've got a reputation. I'll use it."

Alucius shook his head. "So it'll be my fault if things go wrong?"

"No. I'll just tell 'em that if you couldn't do it, no one could, and that they did their best."

"You're most helpful, Yular," Alucius replied with exaggerated courtesy.

"I know." Yular laughed, then turned his mount back to where third squad was forming up.

The half glass had not passed when second squad was formed up, and only a bit more time passed before Vylor appeared.

"Squad leaders, report!"

"First squad present and ready."

"Second squad present and ready, sir," Alucius replied.

"Third squad, present and ready, sir."

"Column, forward!" Vylor ordered.

After riding out through the post gates, and directly into the late afternoon sun for the several hundred yards westward along the southwest high road back toward Zalt, the small force turned northward on the north-south road, passing the town on the left. For the first time, Alucius was conscious that people in the town actually stopped to watch the troopers ride past. Absently, he wondered where the auxiliaries might be.

Once the three squads crossed the culvert bridge where the lower reach of Spring Creek ran beneath the north-south high road, Alucius began to look northeast, out across the fields toward the low mounds, almost lost against the fields from which they rose and the mountains farther to the east and behind them.

Before long, they neared a lane on the right side, one that was just on the north side of a long line of bushy trees with pale gray-green leaves—the brush olive windbreak. To the north of the lane, the fields showed shoots of green, mostly two spans high.

"To the right, single file!" Vylor ordered.

Alucius repeated the command, and the troopers formed a longer line along the narrow lane to the north of the brush olives, whose feathery-looking and heavily thorned branches overhung and thrust out onto the lane. Brush olives, Alucius decided after riding less than two hundred yards, were worse in a way than quarasote, because nightsheep could eat quarasote, while only the redbreasts and a few other birds tolerated the tiny bitter fruit that scarcely resembled olives.

Feeling more than a little uneasy, Alucius began searching with his Talent when the column was still a good half vingt

from the end of the brush olive windbreak. Not a single shot
had come in their direction. With the thickness of the windbreak, he couldn't see the Barrow Mounds, and certainly, no
one could fire at them—until they charged from behind the
olives.

Alucius could clearly sense the black auras of the Lanachronans—more than a full company, probably foot, since he
did not pick up many horses—and all dug in behind berms,
waiting for the late afternoon attack—or even for a night-
time attack—or so it seemed.

Less than fifty yards ahead, Alucius could see where the
olives thinned and then ended.

"Column halt!"

"Squad halt," Alucius repeated.

"Re-form in double files!" came the command.

"Double files."

Before long, Vylor would give the signal, and they'd
charge out—and, sooner or later, receive heavy fire from a
prepared position.

Vylor rode down the column, first stopping and saying
something to Lokyl, and then riding toward Alucius. "Second
squad will take the north side of the Mounds."

"Yes, sir."

Waiting, as Vylor continued past to give his orders to Yular, Alucius tried to make sense of what his Talent was showing him. Cannon—widely spaced, each within an earthen
berm, and each with a berm behind it. Almost belatedly, he
recalled the conversation between Gholar and Tymal—and
the mention of a Talent-officer.

Could he use his Talent to set off a cannon's powder? He
had to try.

Alucius reached out, trying to create a sense of fire somewhere . . . amid the powder bags.

Sweat poured off his forehead, and his eyes seemed to
blur. Just the smallest spark, the tiniest point of fire. He felt
like his entire face would burst into flame, and he channeled
that feeling into it.

Nothing happened.

He sat on his mount, shaking, and Vylor rode back toward the head of the column. There had to be a way. There had to be. Before Vylor ordered them into certain slaughter.

If the Matrial could use power for hundreds of vingts and use it to kill those who wore collars . . .

He straightened in the saddle. Perhaps that was it. He let his Talent range over Beral, the closest of his troopers, picking out the thin line of purple-pink that linked with other lines and then vanished into the distance.

The second time, Alucius visualized a thin line of purple, running from him eastward over the brush olives and toward the Barrow Mounds, a line of purple carrying the heat of not just a flame, but of red-hot metal, the heat of the hammermill in Iron Stem.

To his senses, the line of thin purple seemed almost like a flame flashing across the sky, yet no one else saw it.

Crump! The first explosion seemed distant, although he knew the cannons were little more than two hundred yards away. Even so, Alucius almost started out of his saddle, and Wildebeast *whuff*ed and pawed the hard dirt of the lane. The second Talent-spark seemed easier, as did the others, as he reached cannon after cannon. Still, by the time, he finished the last, he was trembling in the saddle, and could hardly see.

Crump! . . . crump . . . Explosion after explosion filled the late afternoon.

"Charge!" Vylor commanded in a lull in the detonations.

First squad cantered forward, around the end of the wind-break.

Second squad followed. Alucius's mouth dropped open as he looked toward the Mounds. There, lines of fire flared into the sky, and clouds of white and black smoke swirled up. His amazement was not because of the explosions themselves—gunpowder was supposed to explode—but because he had actually used Talent to set off those explosions.

Still, it wouldn't take long for the Lanachronan troopers to settle back in.

With the Lanachronans spread in an arc, if second squad

circled more to the north, the troopers would have to fire over each other. At least, Alucius hoped so. He turned in the saddle. "Follow me! We're going to flank them!"

Second squad reached the bottom of the northwestern corner of the Mounds before the bullets began to fly past. Almost absently, Alucius concentrated on leading the squad around, brushing away all distractions.

"Rifles ready! Hold your fire until we make the top! Rifles ready!"

"Stay close to the squad leader!" someone called out.

The sound of rifles firing became louder, more obvious, as the explosions of powder died away, although a crackling sound began to rise in the background as Alucius and Wildebeast came over the crest of the mound, right at the north end of the Lanachronan line. Less than a handful of Lanachronans had their rifles aimed northward.

Alucius aimed and fired, then recocked and fired, still keeping Wildebeast moving, if more deliberately. "Second squad! Fire at will!"

The command was unneeded, Alucius realized after he'd yelled it out, but it probably didn't matter. He got off two . . . three more shots. Then he saw a Lanachronan aiming toward a horseman who had appeared in the center of the defending foot.

Alucius shot the Lanachronan in the back, and then took down those beside him. Hurriedly, he kept Wildebeast moving while he fumbled more cartridges into his magazine.

Then he wheeled Wildebeast back north, once more firing until his magazine was empty, before unsheathing his sabre. He used it but once, before seeing, a good half a vingt to the east, a cloud of dust, dust of a company or more of Lanachronan horse. As his glance shifted to the thin line of second squad, he saw Rhen pitch forward from the saddle. There were only a handful of Lanachronan troopers nearby, and most of them were keeping their heads down. For the moment.

"Second squad! Withdraw! Withdraw! Follow me!" He waited but briefly, until he saw his troopers turning their mounts, before urging Wildebeast to begin to ride down, even more northward than before, hoping that the angle of the slope would shield them.

"Third squad! Withdraw!"

Alucius heard no commands from first squad. He turned in the saddle and yelled out, "First squad! Regroup on second squad. Withdraw!"

There were almost no bullets chasing them as they pounded back down the hill. Alucius thought he saw several riders that weren't his troopers trailing behind Armon and Hansyl as his squad swept behind the windbreak.

He glanced back over his shoulder and counted, trying to take in faces and names. There were nine immediately behind him, and then another group twenty yards or so back.

"Slow to a fast trot!" Alucius called, once he was sure all the riders had reached the protection of the windbreak. He wasn't about to stay around with at least a full company of horse coming as reinforcements, not when they'd accomplished their mission, but exhausting their mounts wouldn't help, either.

"Guess that's a good idea," came a dry voice from behind as Yular and five of his troopers rode up behind second squad. Yular eased his mount through the field beside the lane and then up alongside Alucius.

Alucius shook his head. "You're in command, now, acting senior squad leader Yular. Second squad stands ready."

"You only lost one trooper. They got Vylor. Only three men from Lokyl's squad left, they're back here with your men. Lokyl wasn't one of them." Yular glanced back at second squad. "You didn't suffer too bad."

"We went up the side. Caught them between us and the explosions," Alucius explained.

Yular laughed. "Did something like that, took that little ridge, just enough cover. Figured it didn't matter how we went, just so we did. How many do you think they have left?"

"Saw more than a company of foot . . . we got maybe

thirty . . . forty. But they had another company of horse coming in."

"Don't think we got more than twenty, thirty at the outside. They were waiting for us."

Alucius nodded. "We were lucky."

"You mean . . . with their powder blowing up? Wondered how that happened?"

"I don't care," Alucius said. "I'm just glad it happened. We'd have been chewed up."

Yular glanced back. "More than we were, you mean?"

Alucius suppressed a wince. "Much more."

"You're probably right."

The surviving troopers had almost reached the western end of the windbreak, just short of the north-south high road, less than a hundred yards ahead. Alucius did not sense any Lanachronans nearby, or following. That was fine with him. He turned in the saddle. "First squad! Second squad! When we reach the road, let third squad take the lead!" He looked back at Yular. "You're in charge, sir."

Yular shook his head, a tight and rueful smile on his face.

Alucius looked westward, half surprised to see that the sun was just dropping behind the trees in the distance beyond the fields on the west side of the north-south high road. Had the fight taken that long? Nearly two glasses? It hadn't seemed that long.

He also realized something else. Every muscle in his body seemed to feel weak and trembling.

As second squad—and the remnants of first squad—followed him back toward Senob Post, the smoky orange light of burning power and equipment already fading, the acrid scent of smoke and death trailing them, Alucius could pick up the murmurs.

". . . *knows* where things are . . ."

". . . been picked off like targets if we'd gone straight up . . ."

". . . did the mission, didn't we? . . . most of us came back . . . better than first squad . . ."

". . . not complaining . . . rather be in his squad . . ."

". . . don't say anything then . . . ."

Alucius had to use every bit of concentration to stay in the saddle, every last bit. He hoped he wouldn't disgrace himself by collapsing. But he couldn't do that. He couldn't.

94

The next morning, before breakfast, Alucius was still shaky, but determined not to let anyone know that as the squad leaders met with Tymal. Even the air in the open space felt warm and confining.

Tymal glanced over the nine squad leaders. "For the moment, the three troopers in first squad will be attached to third squad. I've already let them know. That will bring you up to full strength, Yular."

"Yes, sir."

"The scouts have reported that the Lanachronans have set up defense berms around their main camp, and they've pulled back from the Barrow Mounds. There's still smoke rising there." Tymal shook his head. "The first three squads . . . however it happened, the captain is grateful." The senior squad leader paused. "She wants a personal briefing from you two, Alucius and Yular, right after morning muster.

"Have your squads stand by, ready to mount and ride out in less than a half glass."

"Yes, sir."

"Now . . . go get something to eat. You might get a midday meal, and you might not eat for days. Make sure your men know that as well."

"Yes, sir."

"I'll see Alucius and Yular right after muster, and we'll go see the captain."

"Yes, sir."

"What do you think the captain wants?" asked Alucius as he and Yular walked toward the mess.

Yular shook his head. "Be happier not meeting with her."

"So would I," Alucius admitted.

"Probably be all right, now," Yular said. "They need every one of us." He snorted. "More than every one of us."

For that, Alucius suspected he could be grateful. He did take Tymal's advice and ate everything that he could stuff in himself. The food helped his shakiness as well. Before he knew it, he was mustering second squad in the courtyard, under a sky that was silvered light green, and promising yet another too-hot late spring day.

"Second squad. Fall in."

With all his remaining troopers in place, Alucius turned and waited.

"Squad leaders, report!" Tymal ordered.

There was a momentary silence, until Alucius realized there was no first squad. "Second squad, all present and ready, sir."

"Third and first squad, present and ready, sir," Yular announced.

"Fourth squad . . ."

"Fifth squad . . ."

After the reports, Tymal was brief. "You're all on standby. Have your mounts saddled and your gear ready. We could be going out to fight in a quarter glass—or not for days. The captain would rather not fight until our reinforcements arrive. We don't know what the Lanachronans will do. They took some losses yesterday. Without their cannon, they may need some time to regroup. We can't count on that. So be ready." After a pause, he added, "Dismissed to standby. Saddle your mounts."

"Second squad, dismissed to saddle up and stand-by." Alucius turned and headed to join Tymal.

Yular was right behind him.

The door to the captain's spaces was open.

"Come on in, squad leaders. Close the door behind you." Captain Hyrlui did not rise from the chair behind her table desk. Even more of her hair was white, Alucius thought.

Once Tymal and the other two were inside, she began.

"Yesterday's raid was more successful than we could have hoped. Yet . . . I'm a bit surprised. According to the acting full squad leader's report, the Lanachronan powder supplies exploded just *before* you began the attack. Is that correct?"

"Yes, sir," Alucius answered.

"Yes, sir," Yular concurred.

The captain looked at the two squad leaders, and then at Tymal.

"Do any of you know how the powder supplies of the Lanachronans exploded?"

"No, sir," offered Tymal. "Vylor might, or Lokyl . . . but they didn't make it back."

"No, sir," added Alucius, shading the truth, because he didn't know *exactly* how.

"No, sir," said Yular, "except it happened just before squad leader Vylor gave the command. It was almost like he was waiting. He kept looking at the squad leaders, and then at the Barrow Mounds . . ."

"I see." The captain's left hand dropped to her wide belt, and Alucius could feel the slightest pressure on his torque. Not on his neck, but on the torque. Yet he could tell that the captain had very little Talent. Still, she had enough to use the nooses on the belt.

Alucius felt very chill, and even shakier, inside. Vylor had probably suspected Alucius of something—or Yular thought Vylor had. Either possibility was bad enough, and the pressure from the captain reinforced Alucius's concerns. But why was there pressure on his torque? Or wasn't the captain that discriminating in her Talent use?

"You're not saying that Squad Leader Vylor had anything to do with this?" asked Hyrlui, looking at Yular.

"No, sir. I'm just telling you what I saw. Could be that I saw more, because I was the squad leader farthest back and where I could see everything."

Hyrlui nodded slowly. "However it happened, we're fortunate. The Twentieth, Twenty-Fourth, and Thirtieth horse companies are less than ten vingts to the north, and the Fifteenth Foot is less than a day behind. Still . . . the casualties were . . ." She tilted her head slightly and leaned forward over her table desk. "Vylor led squad one, is that correct?" The captain looked directly at Yular.

"Yes, sir. He took the center. That was where the most fire was."

Hyrlui looked at Alucius. "You had the north side, squad leader?"

"Yes, sir. The way the side of the hill sloped, we could ride almost halfway up before anyone could get a clear shot at us."

"So you had more troopers when you reached the top?"

"Yes, sir. We had a better field of fire, too. We took out close to forty of their foot."

"How many did you lose?"

"One, sir."

Hyrlui frowned, then turned to Yular. "You fared almost as well. Why?"

"There was a bit of a ridge near the top of the south side, sir. Anyone around it couldn't fire directly at us. So we got most of the way up before more than a handful of their rifles could get a clear shot."

"What about the middle section? The one where squad one attacked?"

"They had a clear field of fire, sir," Yular said. "I wouldn't have wanted to ride that slope."

"I see." Hyrlui studied the three.

Alucius could not feel the captain using Talent, but outside of the screening officer at Hieron, when he had still been injured, and not thinking so well as he should have been, and the tariff officer, Undercaptain Gerayn, he had not been that close to anyone else who had any great Talent.

The captain looked at Yular. "Would you have said it was unwise to attack the center?"

"I didn't have any reports, sir. I didn't know. Once we got to the top, it was pretty clear, but you can't act on what you don't know until after the fight, sir."

Hyrlui focused on Alucius. "You have a reputation . . . squad leader. What do you think?"

"I was told to take the north side, sir. I looked for the quickest and safest way. When we got to the top, it was clear that first squad had taken heavy fire, sir. From below, we couldn't see where they had their foot positioned."

The captain stood. "Thank you, squad leaders. I hope you will be as effective in the days ahead."

The three filed out silently.

They were a good fifty yards down the corridor before Tymal spoke. "You both handled that very well." He stopped. "See that what you said stays exactly the same."

"Yes, sir."

"Better check your men. I'll be by shortly to keep you posted."

Alucius and Yular kept moving toward the squad leaders' wing to pick up their gear.

"You know that a frontal assault was a hog-stupid thing." Yular said quietly. "The captain knew it, too."

"I thought she felt that way," Alucius offered, "but I'm still new at this."

Yular laughed. "You won't be able to plead inexperience too much longer, Alucius."

"Probably not." Alucius grinned. "But let me do it so long as I can."

They both laughed.

95

Octdi morning, right after muster, with all the companies still on stand-by, Alucius and the squad leaders were summoned to another briefing in the large meeting hall. Alucius noted almost twenty squad leaders of various ranks that he did not know—clearly those from the three horse companies that had arrived the afternoon before. There were also more officers on the dais, including a gray-haired overcaptain who stood immediately beside Captain Hyrlui on the dais.

Captain Hyrlui stepped forward and began immediately. "First, I'd like to welcome the officers and squad leaders of the Twentieth, Twenty-Fourth, and Thirtieth Companies. We're very glad to see you. Second, I'd like to introduce Overcaptain Catryn. She has assumed overall command of operations here in Zalt, and reports directly to the Matrial. Overcaptain Catryn." Hyrlui inclined her head to the older woman.

The overcaptain stepped forward, offered a warm smile, and nodded her head to Hyrlui, and then to Dynae and Marta. "Thank you, captain. Those of you here in Zalt have borne a heavy burden. I wish I could say that it will get lighter soon. It will not. The Lanachronans have completed rough fortifications around their camp, and they have dammed and diverted Spring Creek, in order to cut off water to Zalt. However, the reservoirs here are full, and water is not likely to be a problem any time soon.

"From what we can tell, the easterners lost slightly more than a company of foot along with their cannons. The raid cost us a little more than a squad and two squad leaders . . ."

Alucius was surprised to hear the Lanachronans referred to as easterners. He'd always thought of them as southerners, but Lanachrona was definitely east of Madrien.

" . . . We do not know with absolutely surety, but we expect that they will be sending even more forces from Tempre as quickly as they can. Whoever controls Zalt controls the access to Southgate, and if either Dramur or Lanachrona gains control of Southgate, it will cost us dearly. That's not just in golds. We'll be pushed into a defensive position."

Alucius frowned. For perhaps the hundredth time, he wondered why, if Madrien was so worried about Lanachrona, the Matrial had attacked the Iron Valleys?

"The Matrial had hoped that it would take some time for the young Lord-Protector to consolidate his power in Tempre . . ."

With that one piece of information, it all made sense to

Alucius. The Matrial had felt that the Iron Valleys would fall to someone. She had hoped for an easier and quicker victory there before the Lord-Protector could act. That would have secured a more defensible border all along the River Vedra and allowed Madrien to concentrate on the south where it faced challenges from both Dramur and Lanachrona. The Lord-Protector's actions also made a sort of sense. He didn't want to see Lanachrona denied access to the sea, and strangled on three sides by Madrien.

Unhappily, there was little Alucius, particularly as a junior squad leader, could do about anything, even if it all did make more sense.

". . . Captain Hyrlui will be meeting with the undercaptains and squad leaders of Fortieth Company immediately after you're all dismissed . . ."

Overcaptain Catryn concluded, "I am pleased to be here, and look forward to working with you to assure the future of Madrien."

Once more, Alucius led the way out of the meeting room, fairly certain that there were few if any squad leaders with less time in rank.

Captain Hyrlui's spaces were crowded, with nine squad leaders, two undercaptains, and Tymal standing before her table desk.

"We're still outnumbered," Captain Hyrlui said. "A direct attack on the Lanachronan position would bring heavy losses. But we cannot allow them to remain or to develop their position there. The overcaptain brought some engineers. We have reservoirs. They do not. Farther to the east, there are several places where Spring Creek can be diverted. We will do that. Without water, they will either have to move to water, or attack away from their prepared positions. If they move, we can raid or attack, depending on how they move. If they attack us, we have the prepared positions." Hyrlui smiled grimly. "Our task is to escort and protect the engineers and their equipment, while they change the flow of Spring Creek."

"How soon?" asked Tymal.

"As soon as we can. A glass or less. Assign the squads as you see fit, and let me know."

"Yes, sir."

"Dismissed."

After that very short meeting, Tymal gathered the squad leaders in the northeast corner of the mess, wasting neither time nor words. "Here are the basic assignments. Alucius, second squad is going to be the scout patrol. Your mission is to scout, not to kill easterners. Do you understand?"

"Yes, sir."

"Yular, you're going to be the actual van squad. Pahl and Gholar—fourth and fifth squads will cover the engineers . . ."

As Tymal went through the assignments, Alucius fretted. It was more than clear that Tymal had a good idea that Alucius had some abilities in looking out for danger. Was the senior squad leader making his assignments on the basis of the past—or did he have a better idea of what Alucius could do?

Then, in the current situation, what else could Alucius do? Desertion more than a thousand vingts from home didn't look appealing, especially not in the middle of a war. Neither did fighting battles against the Lanachronans.

96

Two days later, under the midmorning sun of early summer, a sun that, with a cloudless sky, promised almost blistering heat by later in the day, Alucius and second squad rode along the narrow canyon road. The old road wound back toward the southwest high road, following the path of Spring Creek. Alucius pushed back his felt hat and blotted his forehead with the sleeve of his tunic, then eased the hat back forward to shade his eyes from the intense sunlight.

Second squad was headed southward toward the southwest

high road. Alucius judged that they were less than two vingts away. Second squad's patrol duty was simple—to warn the rest of Fortieth Company if any Lanachronans appeared, particularly any forces of a size to present a danger to Fortieth Company and the engineers. The engineers—working to shift the course of Spring Creek—were two vingts behind second squad to the north and a good seven or eight vingts eastward of where the southern boundary road crossed the high road. Occasionally, Alucius could hear muffled explosions as the engineers moved soil and rock.

He glanced to his left. The ground, half rock and half sandy soil covered with brown pine needles, rose steeply enough that twenty yards into the pines, the roots of the trees were yards above Alucius's head. Then, the pines became fewer—because the uneven slope gave way to a series of sandstone escarpments, out of which grew but scattered and twisted pines. On the right, the ground—also heavily wooded—dropped sharply to the narrow creek. Beyond the creek farther to the west, the broken and sheer sandstone rose even more steeply than on the east side of the road. Alucius disliked the narrowness of the canyon, but it would be another vingt or so before it widened into something more like a wooded valley closer to the high road.

So far his Talent had shown him little besides deer, a mountain cat, handfuls of rodents and birds. He'd felt no other people—troopers or others—and there were no signs of the brownish green wood-spirits. Still, he kept scanning the trees on both sides of the road, and the narrow creek running to the right of the road, a good five yards below the road level. In the next day, the engineers had said, they hoped to turn the existing creek into a dry streambed that would deny the Lanachronan camp its water supply.

Alucius blotted his forehead again, and then reached forward for his water bottle—the first one, although, with the creek near, he didn't have to be quite so careful, at least until the engineers completed their work. He took a long swallow and replaced the bottle in its holder.

Behind him, he could hear some of the murmurs of the squad.

"... pick us?"

"... better than sitting around back there, waiting for someone ..."

"... was a scout ... want someone who knows what to look for ..."

Another quarter glass passed, and the creek kept flowing, but Alucius had heard no more explosions behind them. Were they far enough south that the detonations didn't carry? Or were the engineers doing something else?

Then, faintly, Alucius could sense riders ... a good distance away, too far for his Talent to feel anything but their presence. He eased out the water bottle and took another swallow.

Before long, he could tell that the riders were headed up the canyon toward them. He held up his hand. "Squad halt. Quiet."

From what he could tell, the oncoming riders—he felt there were two, Lanachronans with black auras—were less than two vingts away, and heading northward toward second squad. He shook his head. "Nothing. Squad forward."

He leaned forward in the saddle and patted Wildebeast on the shoulder, then settled back and tried to sort out what he could do if the Lanachronans kept closing on second squad. He had less than a quarter glass to decide.

He glanced ahead, looking for a spot where cover would be possible. Taking second squad into the trees on the east side would keep the on-coming riders from immediately spotting the Matrite troopers, but the pines were set far enough apart that, once the riders were within a hundred yards, the easterners could easily make out the troopers of second squad. About a hundred yards ahead of second squad, farther south, the road and the canyon curved slightly eastward, just enough that a rider coming north would not be able to see into the trees until he passed the gentle curve.

"Squad halt." Alucius turned in the saddle. "There's someone riding this way. If you look closely, you can see a little haze or dust over the road. There's no real cover from a distance. Armon, you and I are going to slip forward, riding along at the fringe of the trees here. The rest of second squad—you're to pull back at least ten yards into the trees here, and wait. Hansyl . . . you're in charge."

"Yes, sir."

"If there are a lot of riders, we'll be back in a hurry." Alucius grinned. "And then we'll all be in a hurry. If there are only a handful, and we can, we'll let them ride past us, and try to capture them. Armon and I will close from the south." Alucius looked at Hansyl. "If anything happens to us, you're acting squad leader."

"Yes, sir."

"Now . . . into the trees." Alucius looked to Armon. "Ready?"

"Yes, sir."

Alucius guided Wildebeast toward the left shoulder of the road, until his shoulders were almost brushing the pine branches. The two rode another fifty yards before Alucius eased his mount around a pine trunk and slowly worked his way southward, until they were just short of the point where the southernmost part of the curve in the road ended.

Alucius studied the pines and then edged Wildebeast farther east, but to where he had a clear line of sight at the road—from behind a thick pine trunk that afforded some cover. "We'll wait here. It won't be that long."

"Yes, sir." Armon had also eased his mount behind a pine trunk.

"If they ride past us without seeing us, we'll follow. If they shoot, we shoot back."

"Yes, sir."

Alucius blotted his forehead once more, before taking out the water bottle for another hurried swallow. Then he waited, knowing the two Lanachronans were still approaching and almost within sight.

Another quarter glass passed before two dim figures appeared on the road, their mounts raising but small clouds of dust. Alucius swallowed. "Rifles ready. Just in case."

"Yes, sir."

The two Lanachronans, standing out in the bright midday sun in their blue uniforms, continued to ride toward the two Matrite troopers half hidden in the pines.

For a time, Alucius thought the two scouts might ride past without noticing them. But the eyes of the lead rider, less than fifty yards south of Alucius, swept across the pines. Then his head turned back, all too casually, even as he grabbed for his rifle and hissed something to the second trooper. He raised his rifle and ducked, even while aiming toward Alucius. The second fumbled for his rifle.

As the first Lanachronan fired, Alucius raised his own weapon and squeezed off a shot, *willing* it to hit. The Lanachronan pitched back in his saddle, his rifle flying free, and the void of sudden death flashed past Alucius. The second trooper wheeled his mount, clearly trying to flee.

Alucius took two more shots before the man flailed out of the saddle, also dead.

Alucius lowered the rifle slowly, then turned to Armon. "There aren't any more. We need to drag the bodies into the trees. See if they had any dispatches, orders, anything like that." Without saying more, he turned in the saddle and began to ride toward the two dead Lanachronans.

After a moment, Armon followed.

The two rode side by side for almost fifty yards.

"Sir . . . ?"

"Why did I shoot the second trooper?" asked Alucius. "What was I going to do? Have him ride back and report that we're up here along the creek? Have them send a company or more?"

"If the engineers do their thing . . . they'll find out."

"But they won't know for certain, and we won't be here when it happens, outnumbered, with our forces split."

Armon was silent.

Alucius reined up by the first body, then dismounted and handed Wildebeast's reins to Armon. He picked up the dead man's rifle and extended it to Armon. Then, he turned over the trooper, a dark-haired and bearded man a good ten years older than Alucius, probably an experienced scout. He carried nothing in the way of orders or dispatches, and Alucius dragged the body into the trees, a good ten yards back and uphill. He was sweating profusely and breathing heavily when he finally walked back to the narrow road and remounted Wildebeast.

The second rider was far younger, and more muscular. Alucius swallowed. For a moment, the dead trooper had reminded him of Vardial. Was Vardial still alive? Serving in the militia? Alucius swallowed again before quickly searching the body, and then dragging it into the trees. His eyes burned for a moment as he laid the figure beside a tree. Then, he blinked and took a deep breath before walking quickly back to Armon. It took him longer to find the second rifle, beside a pine tree root on the western side of the road.

Both Lanachronan mounts had stopped two hundred yards south of the second trooper. Alucius managed to project enough reassurance to keep them from spooking again, and, without being asked, Armon took charge of the riderless horses.

Then Alucius and Armon rode slowly and silently back northward, around the gentle curve in the road. Absently, Alucius noted that Spring Creek still flowed unabated.

"Hansyl!" Alucius called as they neared where he had stationed the squad. "Second squad! Form up."

As the troopers eased their mounts from the pines and onto the road, Alucius could hear some of the comments.

". . . two mounts . . . four shots . . . just shot 'em . . ."

". . . think this is leschec . . . a game?"

"Form up!" Alucius repeated. "We're headed back to the engineers."

The afternoon, as he had feared, continued to get hotter, and he drank more water, sweated more, and collected more road dust.

Alucius kept his eyes and ears—and Talent-senses—out searching, but for the entire ride back upstream, for more than two glasses, he could find no sign of anything except wildlife, his own troopers, and, as they neared the work site, the engineers and Fortieth Company.

Tymal had clearly posted lookouts, because he rode out alone in the late afternoon to meet second squad. His eyes widened at the sight of the captured mounts trailing the squad, and he reined up, waiting until the squad neared before speaking. "Squad Leader Alucius. I'll need a word with you."

"Yes, sir." Alucius turned in the saddle. "Second squad, hold here." He shifted his weight in the saddle and urged Wildebeast forward on the narrow road. Behind him, he heard some of the murmurs.

". . . in for it . . . wager Tymal told him not to shoot anyone."

". . . what was he going to do . . . let 'em ride back and tell where we are . . ."

". . . had to do it . . ."

". . . doesn't miss much . . ."

"What happened?" Tymal's voice bore equal traces of resignation and curiosity, but his eyes were intent and focused on Alucius.

"We ran into two Lanachronan scouts. We'd hoped to surround and capture them . . . but they saw us and fired, then tried to escape." Alucius shrugged.

"You shot them both?" asked Tymal.

"There wasn't any way to catch them," Alucius replied. "There weren't any others with them. No tracks of other mounts nearby. They were under orders to get information and report back. I couldn't let them get back with it."

Tymal shook his head. "I suppose you couldn't."

"No, sir. Not if we want what the engineers are doing to work."

"I'll have to tell the captain."

"Yes, sir."

Far too much was getting reported to the captain. Yet . . . if Fortieth Company did not survive, the odds were poor that one junior squad leader would.

97

Decdi came and went, and so did Londi. Alucius and Fortieth Company had returned to Zalt. They waited . . . and waited. Spring Creek had dried up, but the Lanachronans remained behind their earthen berms beyond the southern boundary road. On Londi, second squad had ridden a patrol, but the Lanachronans had been silent, and even with his Talent, Alucius had detected no movement, no preparations.

Long after the sun set on Londi, Alucius had finally drifted into sleep, a sleep filled with dreams of shadowy figures with unseen weapons, and words that he could never quite hear.

"Sirs! Senior Squad Leader Tymal needs to see you! Northeast corner of the mess."

A light-torch flashed across Alucius's face, and he struggled into a sitting position.

"What glass is it . . . ?" he mumbled.

"A good glass before dawn," Pahl snapped from his bunk farther down the bay. "It figures. Keep us waiting, and then attack before dawn."

Alucius lurched out of his bunk and struggled into his uniform, making sure the nightsilk undergarments were smooth against his skin, not that such was the problem, since he hadn't gained much weight since they'd been tailored for him. Then he hurried down the dim corridors of the barracks toward the mess, following Yular, and with Pahl and Rask behind him.

The mess was brightly lit, and ration packs had been laid out on all of the tables.

Tymal stood at the end of a mess table in the northeast corner, shifting his weight from one boot to the other. His eyes had dark circles under them, and he snapped, "Over here!"

Within moments, all nine Fortieth Company squad leaders were gathered, their eyes on the senior squad leader.

"We've had scouts watching their camp," Tymal said. "They let the cookfires burn out last night, and they didn't relight them this morning. They're forming up and will be ready to ride in less than a glass. Have your squads mounted and ready with double cartridge loads in less than a half glass. You'll have to take the ration packs to your squads yourselves." Tymal glanced around. "The three full reinforcement companies will be in the center, as will Eighteenth Company. Fortieth Company will be to the left of center, Thirty-second to the right, and the auxiliaries in the rear, to be dispatched where they are most needed. The Fifteenth Foot will hold Senob Post. Is that clear?"

"Yes, sir."

"Take your squad rations and move!"

Like the other squad leaders, after gathering up seven ration packs, Alucius practically sprinted to the barracks wing holding the troopers. "Second squad. On your feet! You've got a quarter glass to get to the stables. I've got your ration packs here."

". . . frig . . ."

". . . dog-chewing bastards going to attack . . ."

"Get suited up!" Alucius ordered. "Get your gear; and pick up your ration packs here. Draw double cartridge loads. Double cartridge loads. I'll see you in the stable."

After that, moving as quickly as he could, Alucius reclaimed his own gear, and cartridges, before heading out of the barracks to saddle Wildebeast.

The courtyard of Senob Post was crowded, and names and orders flew above the stones, in the dim light that was barely brighter than night—without either moon high in the sky. Selena had long since set, and Asterta was but a thin green crescent in the west.

For all the commands, and with six different horse companies forming up, second squad was still ready in ranks within the half a glass set by Tymal—if barely, as Druw eased his mount into the last rank just as Tymal rode toward the front of Fortieth Company. The hubbub in the courtyard had already begun to die away. Only moments behind Tymal were Captain Hyrlui, Undercaptain Kryll, and Undercaptain Taniti.

"Fortieth Company will be sixth in the line of march," Tymal announced, "right after Twentieth Company. Squad leaders, hold your position until commanded."

Time seemed to pass ever so slowly, but Alucius doubted that even a quarter of a glass had passed before the first commands to move out were called forth.

By the time second squad followed Tymal and the officers of Fortieth Company out through the gates of Senob Post, the sky was pale gray, rather than dark gray, and a hint of orange played across the peaks of the Coast Range to the east. Behind them, the gates closed, the first time Alucius had ever seen the gates closed. The three companies of auxiliaries were drawn up on the high road, waiting for Fortieth Company, before following.

There was a light and warm wind out of the east, blowing gently into Alucius's face, and carrying the grit and road dust kicked up by the hundreds of riders already on the road in front of Fortieth Company and second squad. Alucius definitely preferred being in the front of the column. Still, the Matrite forces did not travel that far—less than three vingts east of Senob Post—before the column came to a halt. With the wind so light, what dust there was settled almost immediately.

As he waited, wondering why the force had halted, Alucius cast out his Talent-perceptions, trying to see where the Lanachronans were. From what he could tell, they were riding eastward on the high road—on and beside it. The Lanachronan strategy seemed clear enough to Alucius—just punch through any resistance and take Zalt.

Likewise, the Matrite strategy was equally clear—stop the attack.

It would have been difficult for the Lanachronans to take Senob Post, Alucius knew, even with cannon, but Zalt itself was not fortified, and the Lanachronans could easily lay

waste to the town without taking the post. So the Fifteenth
Foot was holding the post—for now.

Was that to keep the Lanachronans from moving on or
consolidating a position in the event the Matrite forces were
overcome? To fight a holding action until more Matrite companies arrived?

As more dust rose, Alucius could see that the Matrite
companies were beginning to re-form, the Thirty-second
Company riding southward in a line perpendicular to the
southwest high road. Then another company followed, and
Fortieth Company moved forward on the high road, then
came to another halt.

In time, after receiving some order from Captain Hyrlui,
Tymal turned his mount. "Fortieth Company to the left, keep
pace with me. Follow the lane."

"Second squad! Column turn left onto the lane. Column
turn left!" Alucius ordered, keeping station on Tymal as second squad rode down a narrow lane between fields.

After little more than two hundred fifty yards, the senior
squad leader halted. "Fortieth company, right wheel, halt in
place."

"Second squad, right wheel, halt in place!" Alucius ordered.

"Double ranks, double interval," Tymal commanded.
"Second squad first, third squad directly behind second.
Fourth squad to the left and abreast of second . . ."

Alucius was definitely not pleased with the "honor" of
being in the front rank, although he had thought that second
squad would have been positioned directly next to Twentieth
Company. Instead, second squad and third squad were the
ones holding the left flank of the entire formation.

With slightly fewer Matrite troopers, it appeared to Alucius that Overcaptain Catryn was simply trying to keep her
forces in position to avoid being easily flanked, but not so
thinly spread that a heavy attack could punch through the
center of the formation.

Alucius looked eastward. In front of him was a field filled
with low green sprouts, with no fences, not that there were

many fences anywhere in Madrien. The field stretched eastward, and farther east was another field, with shoots of a darker green.

Alucius shifted his weight on Wildebeast and waited . . . and waited. He took a long swallow from his water bottle and kept waiting. To the east, he could see the dark mass that was the Lanachronan force, but the enemy horse had reined up, a good half vingt away, out of easy rifle range, and also waited. The sun slowly crept up, until orange flooded the ground, glaring almost directly into the eyes of the defenders.

A single trumpet blast came from the east, its echoes wavering and dying away. The signal was repeated twice more.

Alucius had to squint against the brilliance of the rising sun to make out the dark mass of the Lanachronan troopers, not hurrying at first, but moving forward at a measured pace.

"Fortieth Company! Rifles ready!"

"Second squad, rifles ready. Prepare to fire!" Alucius checked his own rifle once more, then watched and waited.

At a range of around a hundred and fifty yards, the Lanachronan horse broke into a canter, sweeping forward. Alucius still waited, knowing that his troopers were most accurate with their rifles at less than a hundred yards.

"Prepare to fire at will!" he ordered, again, studying the attackers, calculating before he finally ordered. "Fire!" He raised his own rifle, and fired, then cocked it and fired again . . . and again. He got in almost seven shots before the Lanachronans were within thirty yards.

"Rifles away! Sabres at the ready!" He waited just a moment. "Charge!"

While the Matrite fire had reduced the number of attackers somewhat, Alucius felt more than a little outnumbered as second squad rode forward.

When the first trooper in blue slashed at him, Alucius parried and back-slashed, then ducked and took on the rider following the first, and then another, before turning Wildebeast and bringing down yet another Lanachronan from behind.

Horses wheeled, and some screamed. The reports of rifles died away, and blades flashed, seeming to flicker in the dusty air. Men grunted, and swore. Dust was everywhere, fine and pervasive enough to blur the outlines of anything beyond the circle of struggle that surrounded Alucius.

A lull of sorts filled the area, and Alucius could see no Lanachronans—or rather, they had seemingly been carried toward the center of the fray.

He marked the lane, a good fifty yards behind him, and called out. "Second squad! Second squad! Re-form on me!"

Figures emerged out of the dust, which had begun to settle. Alucius counted six. Keval was missing.

"Back to the lane and re-form!" Alucius cleaned his blade and sheathed it.

Somewhere to his left, he heard a similar command from Yular.

No sooner had second and third squads re-formed into a more solid formation, again defining the left flank of a battle that had looked disorganized and chaotic, than Tymal galloped up.

The senior squad leader reined in his mount and shouted, "Second squad, wheel to a line oblique! Staggered spacing. Fire a full magazine. Leapfrog back and reload." Then the senior stood in the stirrups and repeated the orders to Yular and third squad, telling them to take station on second squad.

More dust appeared to the east, and now that the sun was far higher, Alucius found it easier to make out the blue tunics of the Lanachronans galloping toward Fortieth Company. An even greater mass of troopers had hurled itself toward the center of the Matrite line.

"Wheel to a line oblique!" he snapped. "Staggered double file so all troopers can fire. Rifles ready."

As second squad wheeled, Alucius glanced to his right. There, the leftmost squads of Twentieth Company had already formed into an oblique firing line.

Crack! Crack! . . . A line of fire from Twentieth Company raked the oncoming easterners. Troopers in blue pitched forward, but the charge continued. A second volley, and then a third, followed.

"Second squad," Alucius called. "At my command . . . fire!"

Crack! The reports from his squad were almost simultaneous.

"Fire!"

By the end of the commands, the Lanachronans—those still mounted—had broken.

Alucius looked around. All six remaining troopers of second squad were still mounted. Alucius saw no reason to withdraw immediately. "Reload and stand ready!"

To his right and to his rear, he heard a similar command from Yular.

Alucius stood in his own stirrups, trying to see what was happening toward the center of the line. He could sense that something was not as it should be. Twentieth Company seemed to be pulling back—away from the center where the Lanachronan attack had been concentrated.

Alucius wanted to do *something*, but leapfrogging back seemed useless, since no one was attacking, and there was even less chance to support the center from farther back. Circling forward around Twentieth Company would leave a gap in the line, and his small squad was unlikely to make that much of a difference—and he didn't want to collapse the line more so that they could be flanked.

So . . . he waited. "Stand ready!" Ready for what, he had no idea.

Out of the turmoil in the center of the line, slowly, slowly, the Lanachronans were pushed back. Then the trumpet sounded, three short blasts, and then another three.

Alucius watched, through the dust, as the blue clad Lanachronans swung their mounts and pulled back.

Alucius became aware of a slight ache in his right forearm. He glanced down, taking in the slash in his tunic. The nightsilk had stopped the blade, turning what could have been a nasty slash into a bruise—probably a nasty one, but a bruise rather than a sabre wound.

He shifted his weight in the saddle and fumbled out the water bottle, taking a quick swallow, even as he surveyed the area around him. There were horses down in places, but more bodies in green and blue than mounts, many more. Alucius didn't count them.

The Matrite horse companies were already re-forming. Alucius smiled to himself, glad that second squad was already in order, although that had as much to do with the battle moving away from the left flank as anything he'd done.

Tymal rode down to the end of the line, less than five yards from Alucius. "Reload now, if you haven't already. Make sure your men drink!" Then he was moving back toward the center of Fortieth Company.

"Second squad, reload!" Alucius called out. "Make sure your magazines are full. Then take a drink. We may not have much of a break."

"Break, sir, what's that?" asked Beral, grinning.

"It's what we're not getting much of," Alucius replied.

Less than a glass passed, perhaps even as little as a half a glass, before the Lanachronan trumpet sounded once more, and once more the drumming of hoofs on hard ground and stone filled the late morning. Once more, the mass of the Lanachronan attack seemed directed at the center of the Matrite line.

Alucius blinked. A column of riders had broken off from the main attack and was riding northwest, aiming toward the Barrow Mounds.

"Fortieth Company! To the left, oblique! Charge!" This time, Captain Hyrlui's voice was the one that rose over the low thunder of hoofs. Had something happened to Tymal?

"Second squad, column oblique! Follow me!" Alucius urged Wildebeast forward. "Rifles out. Prepare to fire!"

Shooting while riding wasn't terribly effective for most troopers, but anything that would slow the attackers would be helpful. Alucius lifted his own rifle and concentrated on the one of the leading Lanachronan mounts. It took him three shots, but the mount went down, as well as two following.

He managed to bring down one more mount—slowing the attackers fractionally—before second squad neared the Lanachronan column. "Sabres at the ready!"

Alucius aimed Wildebeast at the standard bearer beside the lead rider.

The leading rider swerved toward Alucius, and Alucius switched the sabre to his right hand, ducking and coming in under the other's guard. The cut wasn't what he would have liked, but the result was acceptable—the Lanachronan was lifted out of his saddle.

The standard bearer never even truly saw Alucius before the sabre took his arm and the blue-and-cream banner dropped into the dust.

From there, the battle turned into a man-against-man struggle, with more horses turning, riders swearing and grunting—and more troopers dying.

Another retreat sounded from the east, and Alucius turned Wildebeast, trying to make sure neither he nor any of his men were cut down by retreating troopers. Once he was sure the Lanachronans had withdrawn, he called for the squad to re-form on him.

"Fortieth Company! Return to position!" called out the captain.

"Second squad forward. We're heading back to position!"

"Third squad, take station on second squad."

Alucius took a deep breath, and then began to cough on the dust he'd inhaled. He groped for the water bottle. After several more coughs, and then some water, and he could breathe. He glanced eastward. From what he could see, the Lanachronans had withdrawn so far that he couldn't see their forces. Could that really be? Had they thrown them back from Zalt?

At what cost? Alucius wondered. For how long? And whose reinforcements would arrive first?

He looked down at the bloody sabre in his hand, then slowly began to wipe it clean.

98

Alucius had not been certain that he would sleep the night after the battle, but he had, although he had awakened early and dressed and then checked Wildebeast before making his way back to meet with the other squad leaders before breakfast.

Gholar—the acting senior squad leader after Tymal's death—glanced at Alucius as he walked back into the open space at the end of the squad leaders' barracks wing. "I'll tell you before the others get here. The captain wants to see you now."

"Yes, sir. Now?"

"As soon as you can get there. I'll catch you at breakfast and fill you in—if she doesn't." Gholar cleared his throat. "The captain watches you like an eagle watches a stray mongrel. You want to tell me why?"

Alucius shrugged. "I was almost a herder. I was a scout. I learned some things, and it seems like every time I use them, someone thinks it's unusual. I wasn't close to the best scout in the militia, but I'm probably one of the best in the Matrite forces." He shook his head. "I can't not use what I know. Troopers will get killed; I might get killed. If I do use what I've learned . . . then I get questioned."

"You'd be better off as an officer." Gholar laughed. "Too bad you can't be one."

Alucius laughed as well, if falsely. He just wanted to get back to Iron Stem and be a herder, but that hardly looked likely. Surviving was hard enough, and getting harder.

"You'd better get moving."

"Yes, sir." Alucius half-bowed and turned.

Although he didn't wish to face Captain Hyrlui, being late would only compound the problem. So he walked rapidly through the dim corridors.

The door to the captain's spaces was open.

"Squad leader . . . come in and close the door." The captain did not stand, but motioned for Alucius to take one of the stools set against the wall.

Alucius pulled one out opposite the captain and settled himself there, waiting.

"What did you think of yesterday?"

"Everyone fought hard, sir." What else could he say?

"Yesterday was indeed hard fought, squad leader. Hard enough that the Lanachronans withdrew into the hills. They're waiting for reinforcements."

"Yes, sir."

The captain fixed her deep-set eyes on Alucius. "Second squad was most effective yesterday in leading the charge to turn the Lanachronans' attempt to flank us." She paused. "How many troopers did you lose, squad leader?"

"One, sir. We lost one in the earlier skirmishes with the Lanachronans."

"One . . . and yet your squad was in the first rank and met all attacks." Hyrlui nodded.

Alucius wasn't sure that he liked what the nod implied, an inner acknowledgement by the captain of a judgment, a recognition, almost self-satisfaction, rather than fear or anger. "Yes, sir, but we were also on the right flank, sir. We could see what was happening, and we didn't face quite so many easterners as the squads did more toward the center."

"You led the attack on the flanking attempt, and all of your men rode into the attack," the captain pointed out.

"I'd say we were fortunate, sir. This time."

"That may be." The captain's tone was polite, but Alucius could sense the doubt, even as she smiled. "That may be, and let us hope that we continue to possess such fortune, especially in the weeks ahead."

"Yes, sir."

"It's as I thought, but I wanted to hear it from you." The captain stood. "Thank you."

Alucius stood and bowed. He could tell that the captain wasn't lying, and that bothered him far more than if she had been, because it meant that she had a good idea he wasn't exactly what he seemed to be.

She wouldn't do anything . . . yet. But if the Matrites succeeded in throwing back the Lanachronans, he'd have to watch out. If not, he had another set of problems, beginning with surviving.

99

Another summer Duadi dawned bright, promising hot and dry weather, as Alucius formed up second squad in the courtyard of Senob Post. He turned Wildebeast so that he could study second squad. Every one of his men except Druw was already in formation.

Three more Matrite horse companies had arrived from the north two days earlier, along with two more foot companies, turning Senob Post into a crowded warren with pallet beds everywhere. Even the squad leaders' spaces had been halved, so that their bunks were almost frame to frame.

That crowding might not last long, reflected Alucius as he continued to check the courtyard filled with men and mounts, not when at least five horse companies had also come from Tempre, swelling the Lanachronan forces, from what the scouting patrols and the scouts from the auxiliaries had reported. The easterners had set up their camp in the low hills on the north side of the southwest high road, several vingts east of the eastern boundary road. Their locale in the hills had made it more difficult to determine exactly the size and composition of their forces. What was certain was that, at the moment, a large force was riding westward on the southwest high road, and was nearing the eastern boundary road.

According to Gholar, now confirmed as senior squad leader for Fortieth Company, with the arrival of two additional foot companies, Overcaptain Catryn had decided to let the easterners ride much closer to Zalt this time. Gholar had not explained why.

"Sir . . . sorry, sir." Druw eased his mount into place.

"You made it." Alucius paused, then added with a smile, "If not by much."

"Yes, sir."

"Fortieth Company, report!" Gholar called out.

"Second squad, present and ready, sir!" Alucius reported.

"Third squad, present and ready, sir," Yular stated.

When the nine squads had reported, Gholar in turn reported to Captain Hyrlui, "Fortieth Company all present and ready, sir."

"Stand easy," the captain called out.

Another quarter glass passed before the commands came, beginning with those for Thirteenth Company.

Shortly, Gholar called out, "Fortieth Company! Forward!"

"Second squad, forward!" Alucius ordered.

As the Matrite forces rode eastward, Alucius considered what little Gholar had said that morning. Once more, the Matrite troopers were outnumbered. Not badly in total numbers, but the Matrite force included five companies of auxiliaries, and the auxiliaries were nowhere to be seen. Had they been sent elsewhere? Alucius didn't know. All he knew was that, once more, Fortieth Company was bringing up the rear, at least for the moment.

Less than two vingts to the east of Senob Post, long before the eastern boundary road, the column halted, momentarily, before forming into a thick line across and perpendicular to the southwest high road.

"Fortieth Company, to the left!"

When second squad finally came to a halt, and the dust settled enough for Alucius to see more than a hundred yards, he could tell that Fortieth Company held the left flank of the entire force, and that second squad again held the northern flank of Fortieth Company. For all the haste, there was no immediate sign of the Lanachronans.

"Company! Stand easy!" Gholar called out.

"Second squad, stand easy," Alucius repeated. "Take a

break for water, but make it quick." He followed his own advice.

After that, he tried to sense what might be coming, but all that he could feel with his Talent was the mass of darkness somewhere to the east and north. With so many auras so close together and so far away, all he could determine was that the Lanachronans had brought a massive force into Madrien—far, far more troopers than on their last attack.

Alucius could easily understand why the Lanachronans would wish a pitched battle. If they won and destroyed the Matrite forces, they could easily take Zalt and rebuild it into a fortified outpost controlling the southwest high road—and the access to Southgate. Before long, Southgate and southern Madrien would be part of Lanachrona. But . . . without cannon, the easterners would have found it difficult, if not impossible, to take Senob Post.

So why was the overcaptain—or the Matrial—willing to risk such a battle?

Alucius swallowed a rueful laugh. Did it make any difference as to why? He was as low as one could get in the command structure, and his influence was nonexistent. His knowledge was but slightly more than that of most troopers, and what he said or thought made little difference to those above him.

For almost a glass, second squad waited before the dust rising on each side of the southwest high road neared enough that Alucius could make out the host of the approaching Lanachronan horse troopers—perhaps two vingts away.

Gholar rode along the front of Fortieth Company, stopping his mount and exchanging a few words with each of the squad leaders. Finally, he reined up opposite Alucius.

"Sir?"

"They're going to try to wear us down. They've split into two forces, and they're holding back the second group. That means the first attack won't have the force of the one they tried the last time. Don't fire until they get to within fifty yards. Then have your men fire as fast as possible."

"Yes, sir."

Gholar turned and rode back to the center where he reported to Captain Hyrlui. Neither undercaptain was in sight, but that was usual. Some of the officers were directly behind the company, and some in front. Usually, it was the undercaptains out front, but Captain Hyrlui preferred it the other way.

"Second squad! Rifles ready. Hold your fire until my command, then fire as quickly as you can . . . *accurately*." Alucius looked at each squad member, one after the other, then eased Wildebeast around so that he faced eastward. Once more, he checked his rifle, then lowered it, resting it across his thigh as he watched the deliberate pace of the approaching troopers.

As before, the Lanachronans walked their mounts until they reached a point just beyond accurate range for most rifles. There they dressed their lines—and waited. The two forces were less than a vingt apart, and neither line moved.

Another quarter glass passed.

Then came the trumpet blasts from the east, and the Lanachronan horse surged forward.

The Matrite troopers continued to wait as the easterners pounded toward them, with the drumming of hoofs and, except for those few riders who held the high road, the rising swirls and clouds of dust from fields where knee-high crops were being trampled into the dry soil. No yells or battle cries filled the air, nor did the *crack* of rifles. Just the sound of mounts rumbling toward the Matrite line.

Alucius watched as the gap between the two forces narrowed to two hundred yards, then a hundred. When the gap reached what he thought was sixty yards, he shouted out the order. "Second company! Prepare to fire! On my command! Fire! Fire at will!"

With that, he lifted and aimed his own weapon, centering his concentration on the nearest standard-bearer. *Crack!*

The blue-and-cream banner fluttered down, lost in the press of the Lanachronan troopers.

Alucius continued to fire, going through his entire magazine before the easterners were within fifteen yards, then shoving his rifle into its holder and drawing his sabre.

"Second squad! Sabres at the ready! Sabres at the ready!" He only waited a few moments before snapping out a second order. "Second squad! Form on me! Charge!"

Gholar's orders or not, Alucius wasn't about to have his squad cut down motionless, and he urged Wildebeast forward. Second squad formed behind him as a wedge, as if the other six troopers sensed that following him was their best chance.

Alucius kept low in the saddle as he guided his mount toward a slight gap in the oncoming line, aiming at the left side of an eastern trooper. There were definite advantages to being left-handed—provided he took the initiative. His blade slashed across the first trooper's shoulder as he rode past, but he had to lean and twist to parry a thrust from his right.

After that, second squad's charge slowed, then deteriorated into a horse-to-horse melee, where the seven troopers ended up in a rough circle facing out. The fine dust was foglike, and clinging, and occasional coughs mixed with grunts and the sound of metal on metal, and the occasional scream of a wounded horse.

Alucius cut down an already injured Lanachronan trooper, making a gap that offered some light to the west. "Second squad—on me! Charge!"

He urged Wildebeast onward, and the stallion responded.

Second squad burst into a clear space off the northern flank of the blurred line of the Matrite forces, and Alucius wheeled his mount back into position.

"Glad to see you back!" called Yular from twenty yards to the south.

"We do what we can!" Alucius ducked and parried a slash from a trooper in blue who had appeared, seemingly from nowhere, then offered a counterthrust that he twisted into a slash across the man's face and throat.

A triplet sounded on the Lanachronan trumpet, then was repeated, and the easterners disengaged.

"Second squad! Re-form on me!" Alucius wiped his sabre clean, then sheathed it. He surveyed the field as the dust began to settle, casting out his Talent-senses. From what he could tell, the Lanachronans who had attacked were moving back as another wave of their own forces moved to the fore. "Reload and check your rifles!"

Gholar rode to the front of Fortieth Company. "Re-form in squad order! Dress the line!"

"Hansyl!" Alucius called out. "Take station on fourth squad!"

"Taking station, sir."

This time Gholar started his rounds with Alucius. "Almost like last time. Don't fire until they get to within fifty yards. Then have your men fire as fast as possible."

"Yes, sir."

"Once they get close, you can charge, but try to keep your squad close to the line."

Alucius nodded, but Gholar was already moving to Yular, repeating the same orders. So Alucius addressed his squad. "We'll fire when they get within fifty yards, and then we'll switch to sabres and charge at my command."

"Yes, sir," someone said.

Alucius checked his rifle once more and watched as the blue-clad troopers thundered toward the Matrite lines. Then the attackers were within a hundred yards, dust swirling up from the dry beaten ground, blades flashing through the dust-fog.

"Second squad! Prepare to fire! Fire at will! Fire at will!"

The Lanachronans seemed even more tightly bunched than before. Alucius concentrated on shooting, taking just enough time to make sure each of his shots counted. He *thought* he had hit most of those he had aimed at, but with the mass of oncoming riders, how could he tell? His rifle empty, he holstered it and drew the sabre once more.

"Second squad! Sabres at the ready! Sabres at the ready! Form on me! Charge!" Alucius signaled Wildebeast forward, both with his heels and the slightest bit of Talent encouragement, and the big stallion charged forward toward the massed line.

Alucius concentrated on becoming a weapon of death—a

focus of destruction—and, almost as if the Lanachronans saw that focus, several riders tried to avoid him. Alucius didn't let them, his sabre becoming a flashing blade of annihilation—at least in his own mind—as he ripped through the first ranks of the Lanachronans.

Once more, second squad found itself in a circle, but a circle into which the Lanachronans seemed reluctant to enter.

Alucius saw another opening, deciding not to tempt fate too much by remaining where they were. "Second squad! On me!"

By the time second squad was free and back somewhere close to the Matrite line, the Lanachronan trumpet had sounded, and the easterners had pulled back. Alucius absently cleaned the sabre and sheathed it, taking stock of his squad. Karyl was missing, and that meant that second squad was at half strength.

". . . see that?" Hansyl asked someone behind Alucius. "Looked like he was a company by himself . . ."

Alucius frowned, then glanced eastward, where the Lanachronans who had withdrawn had turned and were re-forming yet again.

In the momentary break, Alucius tried another search with his Talent, beyond the immediate battlefield itself, where everything was far too confused for his perceptions to make much sense, even though the Lanachronans appeared to be re-forming in preparation for a third attack. To his left, to the northwest, there were more Lanachronans.

Were they coming down the north-south high road? He frowned as he tried to determine how and where.

"Dress the line! They're beginning another attack!" Gholar called out from the center of Fortieth Company.

Alucius looked east. The easterners' line began to gallop back toward the Matrite force, and it appeared as though both previous waves of attackers had been combined into a single force, determined to smash through the thinning lines of green-clad Matrite troopers and to sweep across Zalt.

Gholar rode down the line, calling out. "Fire when they're within a hundred yards! Within a hundred yards—" With the last words, the senior squad leader pitched out of his saddle, almost in front of Alucius.

Alucius rode forward fifty yards up onto the slightly higher ground. There he looked at the eastern assault to the east and then back to the northwest. His eyes widened as he saw the massed force of blue tunics less than half a vingt away.

What could he do? There wasn't time to pass the word. He didn't see either the captain or any of the undercaptains— and Gholar was down, perhaps dead.

"Fortieth Company! Fortieth Company! Oblique! To the left! To the left, oblique! We need to stop a flank attack!" Alucius hoped the explanation would help with the irregular orders. He was far from certain that a charge on the oblique was the best maneuver, or that his orders were technically correct, but unless he did something, the entire Matrite force would be smashed from the left rear, and that would be worse than obeying orders. Far worse!

"Follow second squad!" snapped Yular.

"Follow third squad!"

Someone was listening to his orders, Alucius realized, and even if only three squads did, it might help. He glanced over his shoulder. From what he could tell, all of the reduced Fortieth Company had responded. He glanced forward again.

The massed front of the Lanachronans looked like a wall of blue, nearing all too soon.

Alucius swung Wildebeast more to the west. "Column line! Column line!"

Again, the squads followed.

The Lanachronan force was at least as large as the one attacking from the east, and Alucius felt that Fortieth Company was riding against a stone wall, even if that wall happened to be riding toward them.

As the distance narrowed, Alucius calculated, waited, then called out the order. "Fortieth Company! Wheel to a line! Wheel to a line, and fire!"

The wheel was broken and irregular, and Fortieth Company stretched across something like two hundred yards and was little more than a hundred yards from the advancing easterners. But it stood between the easterners and the un-protected Matrite flank.

"Fire at will!"

Crack! Crack!

So solidly were the Lanachronans massed that every Fortieth Company shot seemed to take one of the easterners down. So many easterners were there that it seemed to make little difference, except perhaps by creating a slight delay—and buying some time for the overcaptain to reorganize the Matrite troopers.

Still, Alucius saw no point in sacrificing men needlessly.

What would save Fortieth Company from total annihilation, if Alucius happened to be right, would be that the Lanachronans were riding, and it was far harder to aim a rifle accurately while riding, and that they were massed while Fortieth Company was spread into a line with open space between riders and mounts.

Alucius counted, carefully, watched as the Lanachronans neared, and then shouted out another order. "Fortieth Company! To a column! To the right! Charge! Sabres at the ready!"

Alucius would have liked to have brought Fortieth Company to the western side of the attackers, but that would have left them too exposed to all of the front rank of the easterners for too long. The eastern side it would have to be.

Alucius pushed Wildebeast back eastward and to the fore of the column, where tenth squad was, and found himself at the tip of the all-too-small wedge that was Fortieth Company, aimed at the front of the right flank of the easterners. If . . . *if* he had judged correctly, they could sweep behind the Barrow Mounds, and then strike the right flank of the other eastern force on their way back to rejoin the main body of the Matrite forces. *If . . .*

Forcing that thought from his mind, Alucius concentrated on the point of attack—a squad's length from the flank of the Lanachronans. For the briefest of moments, he glanced to his left, where the west side of the Lanachronan force had slowed. Why had they slowed? That thought, too, he pushed away, focusing solely on the Lanachronans before them, again trying to force himself into the image of death and destruction, sabre gleaming.

Abruptly, as he was within less than ten yards of the Lanachronans, several troopers broke. Not many, but enough that Alucius drove Wildebeast through that narrow opening, his blade flashing. Behind him, Fortieth Company followed, seemingly like a red-hot blade through rotten spring ice.

Then, the company was clear and to the east of the Lanachronans.

Pushing aside thoughts of how many troopers had fallen, Alucius swung due east, and, once they were separated by a good three hundred yards, dropped Wildebeast into a fast walk. While he worried about the time it might take, he knew he could not push his mount, or any of the others, without a bit of a breather.

Alucius glanced to his right, up at the Barrow Mounds, where he could still see traces of blackened ground. Even at a quick walk, it seemed as though less than a quarter glass had passed before Fortieth Company broke from behind the southeastern corner of the Barrow Mounds. Ahead was a swirl of mounts and men.

Alucius turned in the saddle. "We'll strike their right flank as close to our forces as we can! Pass it back!"

All too soon, Fortieth Company was almost upon the Lanachronans. Although he felt sore all over, Alucius once more lifted the sabre as Fortieth Company struck the right flank.

"From the rear! They're everywhere!" The accented Lanachronan was loud enough that Alucius could understand it clearly.

From everywhere? That made no sense, but Alucius had no time to worry about that as he slashed through the awkward defense of Lanachronan trooper trying to turn his mount and twist in the saddle simultaneously.

Fortieth Company made it almost within three hundred yards of the original line of battle before it was slowed into another man-on-man melee. But this one was different, because the Lanachronans were fighting merely to escape, caught between Alucius's unplanned flank attack, and Twentieth Company and another company.

Alucius kept moving, trying to avoid being caught from behind or from his right side, striking where he could, parrying where he had to, and trying to keep the company together as he could. Then, as battles always seemed to end, he found that there was no one left to strike, no one remaining whose blows he needed to parry.

He looked around, surprised that the sun was well into midafternoon. Bodies lay everywhere on the trampled and churned fields that had once held promising green sprouts. From what Alucius could see, there were at least two fallen figures in blue for every one in green, perhaps even more.

To the east, the straggling remnants of the attackers rode slowly back along the southwest high road. Wildebeast stood stock-still, panting, as did most of the mounts of Fortieth Company. Alucius was breathing almost as hard as Wildebeast. At least, that was the way he felt.

From somewhere out of the confused mass of Matrite troopers, a single officer emerged and rode toward Alucius—Undercaptain Taniti.

"Fortieth Company! Re-form!" Alucius called out.

Slowly, the remnants of the company coalesced into squads, and then the squads formed into the company. Alucius took a quick glance, guessing that no more than half of the company's original strength remained.

The undercaptain rode deliberately, allowing the company to re-form. She reined up several yards from Alucius, studying him.

"Fortieth Company, sir." Alucius wasn't about to claim the company was ready for anything.

"Well . . . squad leader. You managed to disarray two separate Lanachronan forces in the same battle." Taniti studied the company. "Costly disarray."

"Yes, sir." Alucius saw no point in arguing. They had made it through, and he had his doubts that anyone could have survived if Fortieth Company had merely stood and waited to be caught between the two Lanachronan forces.

"I don't believe you're the next most senior squad leader, Alucius."

"No, sir, but we lost Gholar just as they attacked, and I couldn't find the captain."

"We lost her, too," Taniti said quietly. "And Undercaptain Kryll."

"I'm sorry, sir."

"Don't be. You did what you thought best, and it actually helped the overcaptain's strategy. Less than a handful or two of the attackers from the north survived."

"Yes, sir. Thank you, sir." Alucius was sure he looked as blank as he felt. He had no idea what Taniti was talking about. All he knew was that his shoulder ached, as did his right thigh, and most of his body. His tunic was splattered and stained, with assorted rents and cuts.

He'd survived another battle, and, hopefully, the last one for a time, since the undercaptain had implied that there were comparatively few Lanachronan survivors. And, once more, there was so much he hadn't known.

100

By Sexdi morning, clouds and a light rain had swept over Zalt. Undercaptain Taniti was commanding Fortieth Company, and Pahl was acting senior squad leader. Jumal and Hastyr—the two survivors of Rask's eighth squad—had been transferred to second squad under Alucius, and the eight remaining squads of Fortieth Company were mustered in the courtyard. All of the companies had taken heavy losses. Twentieth Company had been reconfigured into five squads, and some were not even fully manned.

Alucius stood on the barely damp stones of the courtyard before his six-trooper squad and reported, "Second squad, present and ready, sir."

"Third squad, present and ready . . ."

After receiving the muster, Pahl addressed Fortieth Company. "The road patrols and scouts report that the easterners have withdrawn well behind the border and may be returning to Tempre. The overcaptain feels that there will be other attacks later this summer, but it is likely to be some time. The rotation pattern for free days will continue. Third squad is on road patrol today, fourth tomorrow. Second squad is assigned to stable duty today, third squad tomorrow... That's all. Dismissed to your assignments."

"Second squad. Dismissed to stable duty." Alucius turned to see Pahl at his shoulder.

"Overcaptain Catryn and Undercaptain Taniti would like to see you in the overcaptain's spaces, Alucius. It's nothing to worry about."

"Yes, sir." Alucius had his doubts about that. Seeing senior Matrite officers always had risks for him. "Now?"

"Right after muster, they said."

"I'm on my way, sir."

Alucius re-entered the main barracks building and walked toward the officers' wing. What did they want from him?

Inside the overcaptain's spaces, the two officers sat on one side of a wide table desk, talking to each other, the overcaptain in a straight-backed wooden arm chair, Undercaptain Taniti in a straight-backed armless chair. They both looked up.

"Come in, squad leader, and close the door, please," said Overcaptain Catryn.

Alucius complied.

The gray-haired overcaptain looked tired, with dark circles under her slightly bloodshot eyes, and even a faint gray tinge to her face. She nodded toward the stools opposite her on the other side of the table desk. "Please sit down." Her eyes dropped to several sheets on the desk before her.

"Yes, sir." Alucius sat.

The overcaptain studied him for a long moment, and Alucius could sense the faint wash of Talent, not so powerful as that of a herder, but definitely Talent. Finally, she spoke. "You're a very able squad leader. Very few squad leaders have shown the presence of mind that you have consistently demonstrated."

Alucius waited. The overcaptain had not asked a question, and the less he volunteered, the better.

"You are also by far the youngest of the squad leaders in any of the companies here in Zalt. How did that happen?"

"I don't know, sir. I was raised where I had to be alone a lot and where I handled animals a lot. They can't talk to you, and you have to watch out for little things. I've just tried to watch for little things here. It seems to work."

"What sort of little things?"

"Questions, I guess, mostly, sir. You'd told us that the Lanachronans had more troopers than we did, a lot more. I didn't see them. So I kept looking for signs of where they might be." Alucius shrugged. "That sort of thing."

The overcaptain laughed. "So simple . . . and yet so profound."

For a moment, Alucius thought she might add something, but she did not. Undercaptain Taniti watched Alucius like a eagle might search for prey. Alucius smiled good-naturedly, waiting.

"Twice, according to Undercaptain Taniti, you've taken charge when there was someone senior to you who could have. Why did you do that?"

"Begging your pardon, sir, I didn't want to in either case. But no one else did take charge, and we would have lost more troopers standing and waiting for someone to act. As soon as I could, I let the next senior trooper take command."

Taniti nodded at Alucius's last statement.

"With all this, you've never been wounded," the overcaptain said mildly.

"Sir, I've had cuts and bruises, as many as the next trooper. And," he added slowly, "I was wounded back when I was captured."

The overcaptain paused and lifted one of the sheets, reading the one behind it. "That does answer a few questions."

For some reason, Alucius could tell that she was pleased. Pleased that he could be or had been wounded?

"I'd like to be the first to inform you that, based on your performance, you have been selected to be promoted to full squad leader." The overcaptain smiled.

The undercaptain extended several sets of the crimson double chevrons.

Stunned, Alucius took them. "Thank . . . you, sir."

"There is one minor difficulty, squad leader."

Alucius had a feeling about that. In any arms force, there were difficulties.

"You're more than capable, but you're also very young for the rank. For that reason, it's best that you be transferred to another company and another post. You're immediately detached from Fortieth Company to prepare for that transfer. There will be a convoy returning to Hieron the day after tomorrow with some of the recovering wounded who are injured enough to be mustered out and some of the empty supply wagons. You'll be one of the road squad leaders. The officer in charge of the convoy will be Captain Gerayn. Once you get to Hieron, you'll be interviewed there, and then assigned to a new company."

"Yes, sir." Alucius could sense, both in words and feelings, that more had been left unsaid.

"You may go, squad leader, and congratulations."

"Thank you, sir."

"Please close the door on your way out."

Once he had left the room, closing the door as requested, Alucius paused outside the door, bending down as if to adjust his boot, his hearing boosted by his Talent.

"There's something about him," said the overcaptain. "It's as though he's too gray, like his hair is a gray that's almost black. He sees too much for a trooper that young."

"Everything he said was true," pointed out Undercaptain Taniti.

"That's bothersome, too. He needs to be screened by someone in Hieron." There was a pause. "Either way, we've done our best. If he passes the Matrial's screen, he'll be assigned to another company as an assistant senior squad leader or to some detached duty, like a messenger or scout patrol. And we'll have a good squad leader when we don't have enough. If he doesn't . . . we'll have stopped trouble."

The words faded away, and Alucius slipped to his feet and walked briskly down the corridor. He would have liked to hear more, but he had certainly heard enough.

In some ways, it was better than it could have been. If he could engineer a good escape. If he could learn more about his Talent . . . and use it . . . So many ifs . . .

In the meantime, he was going to check with Pahl, to make sure someone was watching over second squad. Screening or not, he still didn't like leaving things unfinished, even as a captive trooper and squad leader.

101

After seeing to Wildebeast, Alucius spent almost a glass in the northwest corner of the empty mess hall briefing Daafl, who'd been promoted to junior squad leader and moved from seventh squad to take over second squad. That taken care of, Alucius headed for the squad leaders' wing of the barracks, and then to the bay housing the squad leaders of the Fortieth Company and, more recently, those of the Twelfth Company. He needed to pick up his gear and move it to the visiting squad leaders' bay so that Daafl would have a bunk with the other Fortieth Company squad leaders.

As Alucius entered the bay, he saw Pahl and Brekka sitting on stools on each side of a footchest that held Pahl's leschec board.

They both looked up.

"Leaving tomorrow?" asked Pahl.

"Right after breakfast. Escorting the wounded stipended-outs and empty wagons back to Hieron. We're also taking some broken rifles and salvaged Lanachronan gear to the armory at Salcer."

"They tell you more about where you'll be posted?"

Brekka grinned as if he already knew the answer.

"Do they tell anyone anything until it happens?" Alucius countered ruefully.

"Well . . . if you're going to act like a senior squad leader, maybe they figured they'd better make you one," Brekka suggested.

"I'm only a full squad leader. That means either an assistant senior squad leader in a company or something like being in charge of a messenger post or detail. Or something else I've never heard of. Just as it finally gets quiet here."

"That won't last," Pahl predicted. "A month, two at the most, and the easterners will be back. They don't know when to quit." He smiled. "You may be back by then, too, with another company. They need fighting leaders."

Alucius shrugged. "Anything's possible." That he'd already learned. "I need to move my gear, and then find Captain Gerayn."

"What squads are going with you?"

"They've two put together with about a third of what was left of Twenty-fourth Company. The overcaptain shifted the others into Twentieth Company."

"They took a real beating," Pahl pointed out.

"Almost as bad as Fortieth Company," suggested Brekka.

Pahl ignored the comment and looked at the leschec board. "Do you really want to move your lesser alector there?"

"You're bluffing," Brekka said with a laugh.

Alucius moved away, heading toward his bunk and footchest to pack his gear in his saddle duffel.

Behind him, he could pick up the murmurs the two leschec players thought were low enough that he would not hear.

"There's . . . something about him . . . Get the feeling that, cold as he is, if he's leading you, he'd take a blade or bullet for you."

". . . thought he did . . . once or twice . . ."

Cold? Alucius had never thought of himself as cold. He tried to be thoughtful, but cold?

". . . seen it happen . . . saw some easterner slash at his arm, so hard. Blade shattered . . ."

". . . nightsilk . . . you think?"

". . . doesn't matter . . . sorry to see him go. Get a squad leader like that, and they send him somewhere else . . . talk about Zalt being important . . . only an overcaptain and they send away the good ones? Doesn't make sense."

Alucius had the same feeling, except that he learned that some things that seemed to make little sense were senseless only from his point of view, not necessarily from someone else's perspective.

102

After three days, the convoy had passed Dimor and left the south branch of the River Lud, which wound more to the northwest before returning to a course largely parallel to the north-south high road. By midafternoon, the day had become hot enough that Alucius was sweating and had gone through two water bottles, despite the high hazy clouds that had turned the silver-green summer sky more silvery than green.

Captain Gerayn was the only officer with the convoy, and she and Alucius ended up riding beside each other more often than not.

"You were a junior squad leader for less than half a year, were you not? Before being promoted, I meant," asked the round-faced tariff officer, brushing back one of the wisps of brown hair from her face.

"Yes, sir."

"Overcaptain Catryn said that you have an excellent sense of the field, even in the fog of battle." Gerayn looked ahead at the road, as if she were just making conversation.

"I just tried to keep track of who was attacking where and how many troopers I had and where." Alucius tried to sound modest. He remained wary of the tariff officer, because she had traces of Talent, and he had to wonder if part of her job was to provide information for whatever screening he might be subjected to when he reached Hieron.

"I'm told that can be difficult in a battle."

"It is," Alucius replied, "but if you don't know where your troopers are, how can you lead them?"

"Undercaptain Taniti said that you could use a sabre with either hand."

"I'm far better with my left," Alucius demurred.

Gerayn laughed. "Do you always qualify everything good that someone says about you?"

"Probably, sir. There are always those who are better. At least, that's what I've found." And no matter how good he might be, Alucius had already learned that sometimes it didn't matter. That had been how he'd been captured, and his handling of the Fortieth Company had been unnecessarily foolhardy because he hadn't realized that Overcaptain Catryn had been a better tactician than Alucius had ever thought.

"Most people as young as you are haven't learned that," Gerayn observed.

"They probably would have if they'd been where I've been," Alucius suggested. "Having other troopers trying to kill you does sharpen your reflexes and wits."

"I wonder." Gerayn fingered her chin. "You speak Madrien now as if you were born to it. How did you manage that?"

"I listened, sir." All the time and very carefully, he reflected, knowing that, even so, listening wasn't really the total answer. Before she could ask another question, he spoke. "You're a tariff officer, sir, and that one time when I was in charge of a squad that escorted you, you spoke of the seltyrs of Southgate. Could you tell me more?"

"We certainly have time," she replied with a smile. "Where should I begin? Perhaps with what has happened most recently." The captain cleared her throat. "Seltyr Benjir is the most powerful of the seltyrs who rule Southgate. The seltyrs are the heads of the ten or so most powerful families. Most of their power lies in their trading networks, and their ships. They also all have their own fighting companies, loyal to the individual seltyr, and not to Southgate. Seltyr Benjir is a very shrewd man. He understands that if Southgate falls to the Lord-Protector, most of the seltyr families will have to flee, probably to Dramur, where they will be heavily tariffed until they lose much of their remaining power. If they do not flee, they could lose both lives and property. On the other hand, if Madrien takes Southgate, only a handful will lose their lives, but all will lose their power and property, especially their power over women. And if Dramur should invade and capture the city, then over time, quietly but surely, they will lose lives, property, and power. So the seltyr has been playing Dramur against Lanachrona for years."

"And not Madrien?" Alucius let skepticism creep into his voice.

Gerayn laughed. "Once or twice, he has suggested to the Matrial that it would be more in her interest to have Southgate independent than controlled by either Dramur or the Lord-Protector."

"Which would be worse? For Madrien?"

Gerayn shrugged. "Dramur would harm Madrien less, but the women in Southgate would suffer even more than they do now."

Alucius recalled Hassai, and the cooper's wife who had fled Southgate, as well as some of the other merchants in the marketplace at Zalt. And Dramur would be worse?

"Is Seltyr Benjir old?"

"He is not a young man, but he has a good ten or fifteen years of vigorous life ahead of him, or so I have been told. As seltyrs go, he is more fair than most, and that angers many. There have been several attempts on his life."

"Because he is fair?"

"No one really wants fairness, squad leader. Those who have little want more, and they claim that it is right and fair that they should. Those who have much claim that their prosperity and power come from their abilities, and that also is fair. Those who would be even-handed anger both those who have little and those who have much."

Alucius decided against asking whether Gerayn thought

the Matrial was fair. "I suppose it's always been that way. Does that mean that some of the seltyrs would support Dramur or Lanachrona?"

"There is one who comes from a Dramuran family, and who might prosper under Dramuran rule, but the rest would fall quickly. None would do well under the Lord-Protector, but they all fear each other, almost as much as outsiders."

Southgate sounded worse than Madrien or Lanachrona, but then, what he heard came from a Matrite woman officer. Still . . . women fled Southgate, and they did not flee Madrien, from what Alucius knew. He almost snorted, considering that men could not flee Madrien, not without almost certain death.

"You look amused, squad leader." Gerayn leaned back in the saddle for a moment.

"Surprised, and not surprised. You make it sound as though the seltyrs all know that they are doomed, and yet they will do nothing to change."

"No one who has power will give it up easily," Gerayn pointed out. "Even you would rather be a squad leader than a trooper, would you not?"

Alucius laughed, although he would far rather have been a herder than either, and he wanted the herding way of life to last, although he worried that it might not, caught as the Iron Valleys seemed to be between Lanachrona and Madrien.

"So are the seltyrs any different?" asked the tariff officer.

Alucius didn't answer the question. It needed no answer. But Gerayn had given him another answer as well.

103

Northeast of Iron Stem, Iron Valleys

In cool night air, three figures looked eastward, watching as Selena rose over the rim of the Aerlal Plateau. Once the full orb of the moon cleared the plateau, Royalt turned to face the wooden platform, set on a low rise west of the stone dwelling of the stead. The two women followed his example.

The herder said nothing. He squared his shoulders and faced the platform and the body that lay upon it.

Abruptly, a spike of light flared from the platform, a beam that fluoresced both black and green, yet not mixed, nor of either color alone.

Royalt's eyes followed the light. Then the light spear vanished—as had the figure and the platform upon which she had been placed.

For a long moment, Royalt remained looking, before he lowered his head. His rugged frame shook for a moment before he finally straightened.

The open lands remained silent, as if even the endless wind had ceased in recognition of what had occurred.

After a time, the younger woman looked to Lucenda. "She hung on for so much longer than . . ." Wendra's voice broke.

"I'm glad you've been here," Lucenda said. "You'll be able to tell Alucius. When he returns. One way or another, he'll return to you."

"You keep saying that he's alive. How do you . . . how can . . . ?" Wendra shook her head.

"Herders can tell." Royalt's eyes dropped to the silver wristguard with the seamless line of shimmering black crystal that circled it.

"The wristguard?" Wendra asked.

"That and Talent."

"Why doesn't Alucius have a wristguard?"

"He does," Royalt replied. "It's in the house, along with the ring."

Lucenda raised her eyebrows.

"She should know," Royalt said, before turning back to the younger woman. "A herder and his wife are linked in more ways than one, and the longer they're together, the stronger that bond is, and it extends in a lesser way to children and grandchildren. That's why Veryl hung on for so very long, until she knew Alucius would be coming home soon."

"He is?" Wendra asked. "He is? How . . . ?"

"It won't be that soon, but he will, one way or another."

This time, Wendra shivered, understanding all that the words meant.

Royalt smiled faintly. "I'll see you two in the house. I need to check the lambing shed."

With those words he was gone, leaving Lucenda and Wendra standing on the empty rise.

Wendra swallowed, realizing all of the implications of the older man's words, and she turned to Lucenda. "How long . . . ?"

"He's strong, Wendra. It could be two years, three, perhaps longer, but in the end the dark ties will not be denied."

"But you?"

"Ellus was not a herder born, and neither was I, for all that I am the children of herders, and we did not have that long together. Yet we had long enough that I would have no other. It happens that way, sometimes." Lucenda turned away from the younger woman. "We should head back to the kitchen. Father would like some hot cider. He won't ask, but he'd like it."

Slowly, Wendra followed Lucenda, back toward the lights of the stead house.

104

Salcer was less than a half day away at the pace the convoy was making, but Alucius felt impatient, as if he were being pushed, or told to keep moving. Yet no one had said anything, and it was just past midmorning, which meant that they would make Salcer well ahead of schedule.

Was it that he knew he had to find a way to escape? He almost shook his head. He could have escaped weeks before—except that merely deserting and trying to find his way back to the Iron Valleys was no answer, not when both lands well might regard him as a deserter. And he certainly didn't want to become a mercenary for the Lanachronans, which was the only task besides herding in which he had skills others would pay for. He had to find a better way—and he didn't have that much time left, he feared. Every time he looked at the green scarf, now in his saddlebags, he was reminded.

As he pondered, Alucius leaned forward in the saddle and studied the eternastone high road ahead. In the distance to the north, he could barely make out the shape of a south-bound resupply convoy, with several companies of troopers, headed toward them. The road patrol he had sent out had not reported back to confirm that the convoy was Matrite, but the grayness Alucius sensed with his Talent told him that the troopers had to be Matrite, not that he expected anything else so close to Salcer.

"Those must be the reinforcements for Zalt," suggested Captain Gerayn, riding to the left of Alucius.

"They may well be, sir. I can see wagons as well, and one looks overlarge."

"If they have supplies, so much the better. They'll need more after harvest, with all the damage to the fields."

Before a quarter glass had passed, one of the road patrol troopers rode back southward. In time, he reached Alucius and the captain, and swung his mount alongside Alucius.

"Captain, squad leader, sirs, the captain of the convoy requests the right of way. She has an overlarge and heavy wagon." The trooper inclined his head to Gerayn, then to Alucius.

"She shall have it," Gerayn affirmed.

Alucius studied the road and the shoulder ahead. From what he could see, the shoulder was broader and more firm close to a vingt ahead where the roadbed was level with the crest of a gentle rise. "I'd suggest that we pull over on the shoulder by that rise ahead, sir."

"That would be good, squad leader. Order it." Gerayn turned to the patrol trooper. "Tell the convoy captain that we will be pulling over ahead there on the rise."

"Yes, sir."

Once the trooper had turned and was riding back northward, Alucius swung Wildebeast back south. First, he told the squad immediately following, "We'll be pulling over and taking a break on the shoulder on the right side where the road and rise meet, about a vingt ahead."

"Yes, sir," replied the junior squad leader.

Alucius continued riding southward, informing the wagon drivers, and then the squad following the wagons, before turning and returning on the left side of the road to rejoin Gerayn.

When they reached the rise, Alucius turned Wildebeast to face those following him. "Onto the shoulder, and stand down. Forward squad, you may dismount and stretch your legs." Later, he'd have them remount, and let the rear squad dismount.

Once the entire short convoy was on the shoulder, he dismounted, then took a long swallow of water, and watched. The captain dismounted, but did not bother with drinking any water, but then, Alucius reflected, she was a southerner.

When the southbound convoy was a half vingt to the north, Alucius remounted, as did Gerayn.

"Forward squad, remount!" After that order, he rode past the three wagons and gave the command for the rear squad to stand down.

Then he rode forward and waited with the captain. A full company of horse led the column heading southward, with a vanguard of one squad, followed by an undercaptain and a senior squad leader, then by the remaining nine squads.

The undercaptain inclined her head to Gerayn as she rode past. "Captain."

"Undercaptain."

Behind the squads rolled a six-wheeled wagon with the oversized axles, rumbling over the eternastones toward them. Although a worn black tarpaulin covered what was in the bed of the wagon, the brown uniform of the man sitting beside the driver and the shape of the load told Alucius what the cargo might be.

He turned to Gerayn. "If you would excuse me for a moment to greet an old acquaintance?"

An expression between amusement and curiosity crossed the captain's face, but she nodded.

Alucius eased Wildebeast forward toward the oversized wagon, then swung his mount to ride beside the engineer, who looked up, startled.

"Engineer Hyalas?" Alucius was surprised that he had remembered the man's name. He was also surprised at the apparent vividness and strength of the purple-tinged pink Talent thread that seemed to flow northward from the engineer's torque.

"Yes?" Hyalas's voice was wary.

"Squad Leader Alucius, sir." Alucius gestured toward the huge six-wheeled wagon. "Is that the rebuilt crystal-spear thrower?"

"What do you know about that?" Hyalas's eyebrows lifted, and he seemed more curious than offended.

"Once I helped you transfer the parts after the time when it exploded in the north."

"Oh . . ." Hyalas nodded. "This is a better version. The Southern Guards will find that out."

"That's good." Alucius had thought about asking why the device wasn't headed northward and decided against it. "The companies in Zalt could use some help, sir."

"You came from there, I take it?"

"Yes, sir." Alucius turned and nodded to the captain who rode up. "Captain, sir."

"Why are you here, squad leader?"

"I'd helped the engineer before, captain, and I'd just wanted to tell him how welcome his work would be."

"You've told him, I take it?"

"Yes, sir." Alucius nodded, and eased his mount onto the shoulder.

He watched as the unknown captain rode over to Gerayn, spoke briefly, and then rejoined the resupply convoy.

After five standard-sized supply wagons passed, and then

the last of the additional two horse companies, Alucius rode
back to join Gerayn.

"You knew the engineer?" asked Captain Gerayn. "I hope
you did, because I told Captain Ulayn that."

"I'd done work for him, sir," Alucius admitted.

The captain laughed. "As a captive, I'd wager."

"Yes, sir." Alucius let himself grin.

She shook her head. "You're a dangerous man, squad
leader."

Not so dangerous as he needed to become. That was clear.
Alucius feared that he was far from dangerous enough, but
so long as he was not thought that dangerous, unlike the
unfortunate engineer, that might be an advantage.

He hoped so. He also hoped he could discover why he
suddenly felt that his time was so short—and that he could
do something about it.

105

Once Alucius had made sure that the wagons
had been properly blocked and secured for the night in the
wagon yard adjacent to the armory at Salcer, he arranged for
billeting both the wounded returnees and the escort squads,
and then unsaddled, groomed, and otherwise took care of
Wildebeast. Only after all that did he slip away, dropping
his gear on a bunk in the barracks bay for visiting squad
leaders, and then making his way down one empty corridor
and then another, looking for the equivalent of the library at
Zalt.

The search, although it took less than a quarter of a glass,
seemed endless, but his reward was that the small musty
room was clean—and vacant, the all-too-neatly shelved
books looked as if they had not been read in years. The late
afternoon light coming through the single narrow window

was barely enough to give the room the illumination of twilight—or so it seemed.

Alucius sat on a stool behind the reading desk and took a deep breath, trying to clear away all the thoughts and feelings that had besieged him in the last day. Why now? Because he knew that he had to do something to avoid being discovered in Hieron? Because he felt guilty for not acting sooner, for merely settling for survival?

For scarcely the first time, Alucius felt that he needed to act. The wood-spirit had told him not to wait, but he had not acted, not to escape, or even to learn as much as he could have, or should have. The power of the purpled pink thread that bound the engineer had been a fearful reminder—and from somewhere else came a dark and nagging sense of urgency. But why now?

It made sense to go with the convoy to Hieron—that would bring him two hundred vingts closer to the Iron Valleys without pursuit and faster than he could travel on his own without being discovered and chased. But what could he do to prepare himself to act when the time came? It was clear that it would—and soon, even if he could not say why.

He had once slipped through a Madrien camp unseen—or seen as a mangy dog. Did he still have that ability? Could he improve it? How could he not try?

The first test should be in a place where he had every right to be, but where someone would have to recognize him, and that someone should be a trooper, not an officer. He stood and slipped from the musty library, closing the door quietly, and turning back down the corridor that would lead him back toward the stable.

Halfway down the corridor, he met an undercaptain, a tall woman with red hair. He nodded in respect. "Sir."

"Carry on, squad leader."

Alucius hadn't dared to try the invisibility for the first time with an officer, but a corridor would be the perfect place, because he could look distracted, and if seen, apologize profusely.

After leaving the barracks wing, he crossed the stone-paved courtyard, which was moderately busy, with troopers bringing in mounts from patrols or maneuvers. After accepting several acknowledgments with a polite "Carry on," he entered the stable. Once inside, he eased himself to the outside stone wall, to the left of the open doors, and concentrated on projecting the feeling that nothing was there, nothing except a faint breeze drifting through the stable.

Trying to hold that feeling, he walked toward a trooper who had apparently just stabled a mount. The man walked by Alucius without even pausing.

In his effort to hold the illusion, paradoxically, it seemed to Alucius, he was more aware of the purple-tinged pinkish thread that ran from the trooper's torque, vanishing, even to Alucius's Talent-sense, somewhere to the unseen north.

Had it been just that trooper? Alucius waited, and shortly another trooper left a stall. Once more, he walked toward the man, this time almost directly. The second trooper ignored him, and, again, Alucius could see the pinkish collar thread.

He slipped back to an inside wall, thinking. There, standing in the shadows of the stable, Alucius wondered how many threads filled the world. He'd certainly seen the pink lines of power, and those tinged with purple, and how they turned a man's—or a woman's—black aura to an oppressive gray.

And he'd seen the brownish green ties of the wood-spirits to trees.

He closed his eyes and concentrated, trying to take in all the threads . . .

He gulped. Behind—or beyond—or beside—the pinkish thread that ran from his own torque to the indistinct north, there was another thread, less visible, yet different—an entwined thread of black and green. It seemed to be gathered in tiny filaments from him before joining in a larger thread that ran to the northeast, as if in the direction of the Iron Valleys.

Alucius swallowed. Black and green? Did everyone have such a thread? What had the wood-spirit said? Unnatural webs? Did that mean all people had natural webs?

He remained in the shadows, this time waiting for one of the stableboys.

As the boy passed him, seemingly oblivious to a full squad leader within yards, Alucius tried to concentrate. He wasn't certain, but beyond the youth's faint pinkish collar thread, he thought he'd sensed an even fainter brown thread. Brown only.

With his Talent-sense, Alucius "reached" for that thread, touching it.

The youth jumped, but only for a moment before his knees buckled. Alucius withdrew the touch and his screen and hurried over to the boy. He bent down. The youth was breathing. After several moments, his eyes fluttered open.

"Sir . . . I . . . I don't know what happened."

"You fainted. Have you been getting enough to eat?" asked Alucius.

"Yes, sir. I thought so, sir."

Alucius put on a concerned frown. "Were you out in the heat a long time this afternoon?"

"Ah . . . yes, sir. We had to clean all the wagons."

"Sometimes, that can do it. Still, you'd better be careful."

"Yes, sir."

After helping the youth to his feet, Alucius turned away, thoughts swirling through his head. He didn't know what had prompted him. Curiosity? He certainly hadn't meant to hurt the young fellow. He hadn't even known that the personal threads or webs existed.

Those could wait, and he could observe, as he could. He still needed to test his not-being-there screen on an officer. Where?

If he picked the rear corridor leading from the mess to the squad leaders' bay . . . Supper wasn't for another glass, and the corridor would be lightly traveled now, if not deserted. He certainly didn't want many people around, in case his effort failed.

He left the stable, without the holding the screen, and crossed the courtyard once more, passing several troopers, but no officers. Once inside the forward barracks wing, he found himself alone, not only on the main corridor, but on the next two.

Had the losses at Salcer been so great that the barracks were that empty? Or were the barracks so empty because of transfers to fight against the militia of the Iron Valleys?

Then, at the end of the corridor, an officer appeared. Alucius tried to project the feeling of the corridor being empty, even while he put a worried look on his face and continued to walk toward the officer, his eyes not exactly moving in her direction.

As she walked toward Alucius, at about five yards, the undercaptain cocked her head, then frowned.

Alucius swallowed. He could tell from the swirls of green through the black of her aura that she had Talent. One try, and he'd picked one of the few Talented officers. He hadn't even thought about that.

Suddenly, her eyes opened wide, and she looked at Alucius. "You!"

Her hands dropped to her wide belt, and Alucius could sense the pressure on his torque, but only on the torque, not on him. As he stood there, as if time had almost stopped, he saw her mouth begin to open, and he lashed out, not with his hands or body, but with his mind and Talent, seeking her thread—brown—and striking with all the force he had.

She pitched forward.

Alucius glanced around. There was no one in the corridor. He bent down and turned her. She was breathing, but he could feel no sign of the brown thread that had connected her to . . . whatever it was that the thread connected people to. What should he do?

Her eyes opened. They were blank, expressionless . . . empty.

Alucius stood and walked away. He knew she wouldn't remember. He feared she might not live that long, but he could only hope that no one would connect it with a trooper. If he had used a weapon, he had no doubt that every trooper would have been questioned. They still might be. It was a

risk to stay, but he felt it was less of a risk than fleeing
blindly. If he had to, he could still do that.

He did not look back as he continued on his way to the
barracks bay for visiting squad leaders. He had to struggle
to keep himself from shaking. What had he discovered? Why
had he had the bad luck—or bad judgment—to try out his
screening in front of one of the few officers with Talent.

He turned the corner at the end of the corridor and kept
walking.

There were no outcries behind him, no other steps. Even
when he was back in the bay for visiting squad leaders, Alucius found he was breathing hard, that he was sweating, and
that the palms of his hands were damp. He sat down on the
end of the bunk, head lowered.

He knew one thing. Once he reached Hieron, he had to
act—and quickly. And, even before that, he had to be ready
to run or ride away at any moment—without a question,
without hesitation.

106

       On the high road north of Salcer, the air wasn't
as hot as in Zalt, but the sky was overcast, and the midmorning air was damp and carried a scent of faintly rotting
vegetation, perhaps from the lowland swamp to the left of
the high road. Alucius was soaked, and perspiration ran down
the back of his neck. The perspiration and the heat were
giving him a rash on the neck where the torque touched his
skin. He'd never had that problem before, or he'd never noticed it.

Was that because he was worried about the captain he'd
disabled—or worse—in Salcer? He didn't worry so much
about what had happened to her. She'd tried to kill him
through the torque. But he couldn't help but feel that, sooner
or later, something might come up that would link her to

him. Gerayn had said nothing, not even indirectly, and Alucius had long since learned that there were times to probe and times to say nothing. The stunned undercaptain in Salcer was an event about which Alucius would never speak. That he knew.

Alucius shifted his weight in the saddle. They were two days out of Salcer, with at least another six to go before they reached Hieron. In the past week, they'd passed more than three companies of horse headed south toward Zalt. Was another Lanachronan attack imminent? Or was the Matrial trying to forestall such an attack? Gerayn hadn't speculated, and Alucius hadn't asked.

With each day of travel, the eternastone high road seemed even more endless. Then again, the high roads were endless. That had been the entire point of the Duarchy's constructing them.

After a glass of riding in comparative silence, Captain Gerayn spoke. "Undercaptain Taniti said that you'd killed more easterners by yourself than any two squads."

Alucius laughed. That idea was ridiculous.

"Don't laugh. She watched you shoot. She saw you hit at least seven men for every ten shots. She didn't want to lose you." Gerayn's gray eyes bored into Alucius. "Especially after she was given command. It's funny how that makes a difference, don't you think?"

"I wouldn't know," Alucius pointed out.

Gerayn smiled. "I do. I may not be a field officer, but I've seen enough. Those who succeed are those who are good at using people, and who worry less about some sort of purity than about results. You're a throwback, a man who would have led armies of conquest in the time of the Duarchy. You make us nervous, because you're so good at destruction, but without troopers like you, we'd have the Lanachronans in Hieron before long. It makes for an interesting situation."

"I'd rather not be interesting, sir. I'd rather just do what needs to be done."

This time, the captain was the one who laughed. "That's

why you're interesting. You do what has to be done, and you do it well, and you do it without hesitating."

Within himself, Alucius disagreed. He'd already hesitated far too long, and now he was having trouble disguising the sudden impatience whose cause he could not even identify. He'd survived nearly two years in two different armies . . . and now he was impatient?

Impatient or not, he needed to be more careful—far more careful.

He smiled at the captain. "Tell me more about Southgate, if you would, sir."

107

The small convoy rolled into Eltema Post in Hieron in midafternoon. Even just in the courtyard, Alucius could sense that the post didn't seem to hold as many troopers—or captives—as when he had last been there. He said nothing about that, just followed Captain Gerayn's orders.

Getting the wagons unloaded and in place in the repair yard took almost a glass in itself, and then Alucius and the two squads of troopers from Twenty-fourth Company had to wait almost another glass while the captain found out where the two squads would be billeted and where the disabled wounded would be quartered while they recovered enough to be stipended out of the Matrite forces.

In the end, Alucius found a stall for Wildebeast and left his gear there. Then he followed Gerayn back into the large training building, and through the warren of corridors to one of the unmarked doors.

A voice called out from the adjoining and open door. "The overcaptain's not there."

Captain Gerayn entered the room from which the voice had come. Alucius stood behind her in the doorway. He glanced down at the door, and the lock, actually a latch that only locked from within. Then his lips quirked as he realized that security probably wasn't that much of a problem when a Talent-officer could tell innocence or guilt and when a space like the undercaptain's had little in it of value. The captive trainees were securely locked away, and probably coins, with weapons in the armory, but when any officer could stun any trooper, locks weren't necessary everywhere.

"Squad leader Alucius is supposed to report to Overcaptain Haeragn for assignment," Gerayn offered, holding a folder containing several sheets of paper.

"She's been sent to Faitel for a week. It could be longer," replied the undercaptain. "There was some difficulty with the engineers there. I can offer the squad leader a temporary assignment, but she'll have to review that when she gets back." There was a pause. "We're short of squad leaders in the training group." She motioned for Gerayn to hand over the folder.

Gerayn did, seemingly reluctantly.

After scanning the sheets for several moments, the undercaptain nodded and looked past Gerayn to Alucius. "You're a class-one blade and a class-one marksman. You can help with that until the overcaptain returns. I'll have Fynal take you over to see Jesorak and then show you to the barracks bay for the squad leaders who are instructors." The undercaptain looked at Captain Gerayn. "Sir, we can take it from here."

Gerayn turned to Alucius. "Take care of yourself, squad leader."

"Thank you, sir. You, too."

"I will. They'll just have me audit reports until it's time for another supply convoy south." She nodded, then turned.

Alucius waited, but only for a few moments. A graying older man, a junior squad leader who came to Alucius's shoulder, stepped into the room and reported. "Undercaptain Sulkyn, sir?"

"If you'll escort the squad leader . . ." The undercaptain stopped and looked at Alucius. "You have gear, don't you?"

"I left it in the stable, sir."

"You can pick it up after Jesorak decides where to use you."

Fynal cleared his throat. "This way, sir. The instructors share a space on the next corridor."

"Thank you, sir." Alucius bowed.

The undercaptain didn't even look up from the papers on her table desk as Alucius and Fynal left.

Alucius took a moment to study the threads around Fynal. The obvious pink link ran almost due west, confirming Alucius's belief that the torque threads centered somewhere close to the Matrial's dwelling. Beneath the obvious was a yellowish brown thread, so thin and frail that Alucius made an effort not even to investigate with his Talent, and that thread ran to the southeast.

Unaware of Alucius's Talent investigation, Fynal led Alucius to the end of the corridor, past closed door after closed door, around the corner, and then another twenty yards to an open door, the first open door since they had left the undercaptain.

Inside, a full squad leader that Alucius had never met looked up from the long and narrow table where he was reassembling a rifle.

"I'm Alucius. I was looking for Jesorak. They've assigned me here."

"Heltyn." The squad leader looked to Fynal. "You can go. I'll make sure that he stays here until Jesorak returns."

Fynal frowned.

"I really will, old man. You can tell the undercaptain it's all my fault."

"Yes, sir."

Alucius took a quick Talent look at Heltyn, beyond the pink torque web. Heltyn's lifeweb thread, for that was what Alucius felt the deeper threads were, was a brownish amber and vanished into the northwest.

Heltyn said nothing until Fynal's bootsteps had died away. "Nice fellow. Got badly hurt, head wound, in a skirmish with the easterners a year ago. Needs another year for a full stipend, so he runs messages inside the post." He turned on the stool, ignoring the rifle before him. "I'm the head marksman instructor. You a marksman?"

"Ah . . . class one in blade and rifle."

"Jesorak and I will probably fight over you." Heltyn shook his head, ruefully. "They've stripped us clean."

Alucius smiled. "I don't know for how long. I was sent for reassignment—"

Heltyn laughed, long and hard. "Without the overcaptain around, Undercaptain Sulkyn can't offer directions to cross the courtyard."

Alucius took one of the empty stools and sat down.

"Where did you come from?"

"Zalt."

"They're sending a class-one marksman and squad leader back?"

"Only for reassignment," Alucius said.

"Because you're good and too young, and can't stay in the same company and post?"

"You don't seem surprised."

"No. It happens. Too often." Heltyn shook his head. "They want father figures as much as leaders. Too many young squad leaders, and the youngest get transferred to an outfit where there are older ones. You'll stay here for a season, or until they've got an opening where you can be the number-two squad leader, and you'll be the one who leads from the front."

Alucius nodded, although he doubted he'd have anywhere near that much time.

"The Lanachronan assault couldn't have come at a worse time. That's why it did. We've had to pull company after company out of the north. Had to pull back out of the Iron Valleys, establish a perimeter barely into the Westerhills. Soon as a returned company gets furloughs and replacements, they're pushed south. The new Forty-second left a week or so ago, along with the Thirty-seventh and the Eighth." Heltyn leaned back on the stool. "If you're lucky, and we're lucky, you'll be here two months." He grinned. "Least you won't be in the south for the hottest weather."

"I can't say I'll miss it."

"What sort of heroics got you promoted?"

"Being foolhardy. I took over my squad when the squad leader got potted in an ambush. Ordered a charge that should have gotten us all killed, but didn't. We killed almost two squads." Alucius shrugged. "Made me junior squad leader for that."

"And full squad leader?"

"Last battle with the Lanachronans, we lost the captain, one undercaptain, and the senior squad leader. Already had lost the assistant senior squad leader. Easterners tried a concealed flank attack. We were on the flank. I ordered the entire company to follow me. Slowed the attack enough to allow the auxiliaries to wipe out the force on the flank. We were down to half strength after that. Guess they didn't want any more successes like that."

"Why didn't they—" Heltyn shook his head. "Why do I ask. Let me guess. You weren't the most senior of the junior squad leaders?"

"Ah . . . actually, I was the most junior," Alucius admitted.

Heltyn laughed, harder than before. "If . . . if . . . it weren't so stupid . . . it'd be even funnier."

"What would be?" asked another voice.

Alucius stood as Jesorak stepped into the long room. "Squad leader Alucius, sir. I've been assigned here temporarily."

"Alucius . . . Alucius . . . didn't I train you?"

"Yes, sir."

Jesorak looked at the pair of crimson chevrons on Alucius's sleeve. "And they had the nerve to send you back to me?" His eyes twinkled, even though his voice was stern.

"Actually, sir . . . I was sent to Overcaptain Haeragn for reassignment . . . but . . ."

"She's in Faitel, and Undercaptain Sulkyn knew I'd been complaining, and she handed you to me until the overcaptain returns."

"Yes, sir."

"You were good with both blade and rifle, as I recall. Very good."

Alucius was more than a little surprised that Jesorak remembered.

"That means he was one of the best," Heltyn added. "You wouldn't recall otherwise."

"He's good," Jesorak admitted. "Doesn't mean he'll be a good instructor."

"I can see you haven't changed, sir."

"Not a bit." Jesorak smiled. "You have, though. Let's get your gear and get you settled. We can talk over what you'll do at supper." He glanced at Heltyn. "We'll come back for you."

"I won't wait for them to rebuild Elcien," Heltyn replied.

Jesorak snorted "You wouldn't wait for a pretty girl with a gold purse and a calligraphed invitation."

"You're right. I'd be long gone."

Nodding to Alucius, Jesorak said, "We'd better get moving. You can tell me about what's happening in the south."

"It's been a long year, sir . . ."

"None of that "sir" business except when others are near. Now . . . go on."

"First there were raids and ambushes . . ." As he talked, Alucius walked alongside Jesorak. He'd liked Jesorak when he'd been a captive, and was glad to find that he still did.

108

After supper with both Heltyn and Jesorak, and a long discussion that ended up with a joint decision by the two to try Alucius as an assistant to both squad leaders—at different times of the training day—Alucius walked out into the courtyard.

He stopped to let a messenger ride out from the stables. The man was a full squad leader uniformed like Alucius, but with the addition of a purple sash. The leather dispatch case was slung under his left arm, held in place by a wide leather strap that went from each end of the case and over his right shoulder.

Alucius watched as the rider went out through the gates alone. As the echo of hoofbeats on stone died away, Alucius crossed the courtyard and made his way up along the narrow and unrailed stone steps onto the top of the western wall of Eltema Post. Like all the walls of the post, it was unguarded, an undefended rampart that—unlike the gates and the southern wall—felt ancient. He wondered if the old wall had been part of a Duarchial outpost that had been later restored and rebuilt when the Matrite post had been constructed.

He stood there in the silence, first looking back down at the courtyard and the orderly buildings within the wall, each structure in its place, from the massive domed indoor riding arena to the overlarge training building.

Then he turned to watch the sun, just setting, moving until he stood against the smooth redstone parapet. From there he looked out across Hieron, first to the north, then the west, and finally to the south. In the fading orange light, under a darkening silver-green sky, the stones of the buildings glowed as if by an internal amber illumination of their own, but that illumination faded as did the sun, if more slowly, as though the stone had caught and delayed the departure of the sunlight.

Once the sun had dropped completely below the western horizon, and as the twilight darkened, Alucius looked westward, not just with his eyes, but with his Talent, trying to sense all that he could.

The weave of color assaulted him, and he staggered, putting out a hand and steadying himself on the wall. Fine pink threads from everywhere converged on the Matrial's residence, so much so that the grounds seemed lit with a purplish pink light. The pinkish cast was unseen and unfelt, he knew, except to those who could see it with Talent, but that was the first impression that swept over Alucius. The second impression was one of a subtle weave that filled the entire darkening skies, the warp and weft of life webs that seemed to intertwine, and yet never touch. Against the soft and warm and subtle and living web, the purplish pink was shudderingly wrong, an oppressive web spinning out of the Matrial's residence, rather than the tapestry of life formed by the softer life webs.

Could he do anything about that pink web? Was that what the wood-spirit had alluded to? And why him? Surely, others had seen what he was seeing. He couldn't have been the first herder, the first Talented man seeing what he saw. Or could he?

He repressed a shiver.

Then he straightened and studied the pinkish threads of that web again. Perhaps . . . perhaps if he could do something about it, difficult as it seemed, it might make his escape far easier.

He paused. Was that the problem? All he had been thinking was about escape, and, just as the pinkish web felt wrong, so did the idea of mere escape. Yet . . . what could he do?

Enter the Matrial's grounds? He'd been discovered by the first Talent-officer he'd run across, and surely there would be more experienced guards or officers with Talent surrounding the Matrial. Then, would anyone expect anything from a lowly squad leader in uniform?

He could escape . . . without doing anything. He could remove his own torque and ride to the northeast, and with what he knew, it would be hard for anyone to find him or catch him. But . . . he would know. And if he ever did return to the stead, on all the rides below the plateau, he would indeed recall that he had seen true evil and turned away.

He looked back at the Matrial's grounds—and the shocking *wrongness* of the purplish pink spider web that so few could see. He studied the interweaving and converging threads for a long time . . . until true deep evening fell across the city. Then, he took a long and slow deep breath, before turning and taking the narrow stone steps back down to the courtyard.

109

The rifle training came late in the afternoon, which made a sort of sense to Alucius, because most of the time, troopers weren't fresh when they had to use their weapons—at least that had been his experience, both in the militia and with the Matrite horse.

In his second day as an instructor, Alucius watched as the trainees filed into their positions on the range. A Matrite rifle was laid out at each firing position, already loaded. That was one of the setup chores that went with being an instructor. In addition to Alucius and Heltyn, there was an undercaptain—Jynagn—who sat in a raised booth above and behind the trainees, and who had enough Talent to stun or kill any trainee who turned a rifle in any direction besides the targets. Alucius made very certain he used no overt Talent around Jynagn, although he could still passively sense strong feelings and the world around him. Also, he suspected he was far more adept than she was, but there was little point in trying to determine that. But she was one of the very few officers he had seen who had more than just a trace of Talent. His experience had made it clear to him that there were not that many women with Talent, and all of those he had seen served the Matrial in one capacity or another—although he had heard or read nothing that would support that conclusion.

In addition to the undercaptain, there were also ten regular troopers and two spotters, also troopers, who watched the targets, replaced them, and moved them once each rotation was completed. The nonspotting troopers were each assigned to watch a trainee and count the shots. The trainees fired from a prone position, for a number of reasons, one being that it made it much harder to turn the rifle on the instructors.

During the initial rotation, Alucius noted an older trainee who consistently missed the targets, even at the closer range.

Once all trainees had fired their first ten rounds, he eased up behind the man. "You've been using a militia rifle, haven't you?"

"Yes, sir." The trainee looked down at the ground, not meeting Alucius's eyes.

Alucius could sense the man had trouble with understanding Madrien, and switched to his own native language for the next question. "What's your name?"

"Zerdial, sir."

"Zerdial . . . the Matrite rifle is lighter. You can see and feel that. The cartridges are smaller, and the weapon doesn't kick as much. You're reacting as if this were a heavier weapon even before you squeeze the trigger. Hold it firmly, but don't wrestle it, and squeeze the trigger slowly, especially until you get the feel of it. You want the trigger pressure to be firm but so even that you don't know the exact moment when the firing pin hits the cartridge. That way, you won't jerk the weapon."

"Yes, sir."

Personally, Alucius suspected the man had had the same trouble with the militia rifles, but the explanation might get him to relax enough to concentrate on the target and not on the rifle.

". . . speaks both tongues . . ."muttered one of the trainees under his breath.

"A number of squad leaders do," Alucius said loudly. "They also hear well. You're supposed to be concentrating on marksmanship, not on the language abilities of your instructors."

Someone gulped.

Heltyn looked up from the end of the line of trainees and grinned.

Alucius smiled back at the other squad leader, even as he made a mental note of the Iron Valley captive trainee's name—Zerdial—before he moved to the next trainee.

After Alucius and Heltyn had offered comments to those they thought needed them, one of the nonspotting troopers walked down the firing line, handing each trainee ten cartridges.

"Reload now!" commanded Heltyn from the far end of the firing line.

Every trainee was watched to see that every cartridge went into the rifle magazine.

Alucius caught a feeling of apprehension from the fourth trainee, the one after Zerdial.

"If I were you . . ." Alucius fumbled mentally for a moment for a name, "Kasta, I'd finish reloading that magazine. The undercaptain might get very upset if you only fired nine shots. So would I." Even if it weren't for exactly the same reason, Alucius noted to himself.

"Yes, sir. I was just slow, sir."

"You're lying," snapped the undercaptain from above.

Kasta twitched and stiffened. Alucius could sense the pinkish power in the torque, but the undercaptain released her hold before the trainee lost consciousness.

Kasta coughed, as if he were choking.

"Get that cartridge in the magazine, Kasta," Heltyn ordered.

Kasta started to swing the rifle toward the older squad leader. Then his whole body twitched, and went limp.

"Trainees! Leave your weapons on the pad. On your feet. Any man who touches a weapon is dead!"

Nine men stood up empty-handed. From the void that swept over Alucius, he knew that Kasta wouldn't ever stand up again.

Alucius could sense Heltyn's anger—and frustration.

The older squad leader waited a long moment before speaking. "You men are being given a chance. It's a chance at a far better life than most of you ever had. For those for whom it's not, it's another chance at a productive life. Kasta was stupid enough to think that he was smarter than squad leaders who've seen more than most of you ever will and officers who can kill you with a single gesture." He paused. "You've got a good half glass before practice is over. You're not going to practice. You're going to stand there and think about just how stupid a trick like Kasta's was. Then you're going to carry him back to the barracks. Now! Not a word!"

Alucius could also sense the satisfaction from the undercaptain above. Not glee, but satisfaction that a wrongdoer had been punished. Alucius knew Kasta hadn't been a wrongdoer, just a stupid young man who'd been arrogant enough not to realize his own limits.

Both he and Heltyn watched the trainees like eagles until they were marched out, carrying a dead body.

Only then did Heltyn walk from the other end of the firing line.

"How did you know?"

Alucius shrugged. "There was just something . . . it wasn't right, and after a while you have to trust those feelings."

Heltyn nodded. "That's what separates the squad leaders who live from those who don't. Anyone can act right when they know. It's what you do when you don't know that counts." He gestured toward the weapons. "We'd better check the rest of them."

As he unloaded and checked each magazine, counting the cartridges, Alucius reflected on Heltyn's brief statement. Perhaps that had been his own problem—not wanting to act until he *knew*.

But now, he did know one thing. It would not be long before Overcaptain Haeragn returned, and he would have to act before then.

110

At supper, after the incident with Kasta, Jesorak looked across the table in the squad leaders' mess at Alucius. Eltema was the only post Alucius had been where the squad leaders ate separately from the troopers, but that might have been because the troopers and trainees shared the same mess.

"Kasta was too stupid to be a trooper," the senior squad

leader said. "We should have caught that. Then, he was from Klamat, and a lot of the north forest boys are Reillies who think with their muscles." He took a slow sip of the weak ale, not looking down at his unfinished oarfish. "Still bothers you, though. Every time it happens—it doesn't that much, thank the Matrial—I think about asking the overcaptain to send me back to the field." He set down the mug. "I did ask the second time it happened. She wouldn't. Told me that part of my job was to weed out the stupid, that it made Madrien a better place."

A better place? Or a less rebellious one? Alucius sipped his own ale. He hadn't finished his own meal. "I didn't want him to get killed. Neither did the undercaptain. She stunned him the first time, and then he tried to use the rifle . . ."

"That's stupidity," Heltyn added. "How smart is it to try to shoot someone after you've been discovered and stunned once?"

"Some people can't stand to be confined," Alucius pointed out. "I've seen that."

"That's a problem," Jesorak admitted. "But before the Matrial and the torques, the whole west coast of Corus was a slaughterhouse. Every city was fighting every other city, and the towns and hamlets between were raided and terrorized."

Were the only choices for people between two evils? Alucius pushed that thought away and replied, "It's not that way now. It might not even be that way if the torques vanished, now that people have seen the good."

Jesorak laughed, ruefully, looking down but ignoring the near-empty mug of ale. "After what you saw today? There's always some lump of muscle who wants things his way, no matter how many people get hurt or killed. Without the torques, the only way to stop them is with more muscle, and that ends up with people getting killed."

Alucius nodded, not because he agreed, but because he could see no point in arguing. Instead, he cleared his throat and said, "The other night I saw a messenger. He was a full squad leader. When I left Senob Post, the overcaptain there told me that might be where I was reassigned." Alucius took another swallow of the weak ale. "What can you tell me about what they do here?"

"It's hard work. I did it once, right here. Glad I only I had to do it for a season." Jesorak looked up, his eyes somewhere else.

Alucius waited.

"I think they like every squad leader to do it for a while. You get to know more about how things fit together." Jesorak inclined his head toward Heltyn. "Except Heltyn here never did. I told him he'll never make senior squad leader until he does."

"I'm not much for bowing and scraping, Jesorak," Heltyn replied. "And waiting. Messengers do as much of that as riding. More, I'd wager. Take a message to the Matrial's residence for this or that overcaptain or assistant. Then stand or sit in some corridor until they tell you to go back, or wait some more for them to give you an answer to take back. I can do without that. Half the time, all you know is the name you're supposed to take the message to."

"I'd wager none of the names are ever familiar, either," suggested Alucius.

"Oh, Rydorak . . . he said he recognized some, like Nyasal, one of the overcaptains, who's now an assistant to some other assistant, and, of course, everyone knows Pelysr because she's the Matrial's chief justicer. But most of the names aren't people squad leaders come across."

"Do the messengers have a special bay in the barracks, near the stables or something?" asked Alucius.

"Why do you want to know?" asked Heltyn.

Alucius managed a grin. "If I'm going to be reassigned, I thought I might talk to some of them. If it sounds as bad as Heltyn says, maybe I'll grovel at the overcaptain's boots and plead to stay in training."

Jesorak snorted. "They're just like all the rest of the squad leaders. Their bay is on the same corridor as ours. They do get the spaces closest to the courtyard. Bartwyn is the senior squad leader. He'll tell you how wonderful it is. Don't believe everything." The senior squad leader leaned back, then stood. "I still have to write an endorsement on your report about Kasta."

"You have to write that up?" asked Alucius disingenuously.

"Anything where a trainee is seriously hurt or dies. It's even worse in the regular trooper school. Overcaptain Haeragn writes something on that as well, and then it goes to . . . who is it . . . oh, sub arms commander what's-her-name . . . Benyal. I suppose she reports that to someone else." Jesorak lifted his platter and mug. "Rather talk with you two, but that won't get it written."

As Jesorak walked away, Heltyn looked at Alucius. "You going to talk to Bartwin or the others now?"

"Why not? The overcaptain could be back any day. Maybe I won't have any choice at all, but I'd like to know something before it happens." Alucius stood and picked up the remnants of the supper, then his mug.

"Still say you'd be better off in training."

"Probably," Alucius agreed. "But, if I get asked, and I probably won't, what do I say when she asks me what I know about the messenger service?"

"You always look at things that way?"

"No." Alucius laughed. "That was how I got captured."

After handing his platter and mug to the messboy, Alucius walked briskly to the bay where Jesorak had said the messengers were quartered.

Except for two full squad leaders, both looking several years older than Alucius, both in full uniform, the bay was empty. The two had pulled stools up to a footchest and were playing a game with stiff placards about the size of a large man's hand. Both looked up as Alucius appeared.

"Evening," Alucius offered. "I'm Alucius, from the training section. For now. But I was told I might be reassigned to messenger duty when Overcaptain Haeragn returns." He offered a shrug. "I don't know anything about it. So I thought I'd ask."

"Lysan," offered the slightly built blond man.

"Gero." The swarthy dark-haired squad leader, gestured

toward a stool against the wall. "Sit down, and tell us about yourself." He set the placards on the chest face down, as did Lysan.

Alucius retrieved the stool. "I was with Fortieth Company in Zalt . . ." He went on to give a brief summary of his tour. ". . . and then Overcaptain Catryn sent me here for reassignment."

The two looked at each other, smiling.

"Well," Gero said, "I have this feeling we'll be seeing a lot of you, Alucius. I think Lysan will be seeing even more of you. I'm supposed to be rotated north to one of the Westerhills perimeter companies before long, and you just might be the one they've been waiting for. Seems like every trooper who makes full squad leader young gets a tour as a messenger."

"Could you tell me a little about what you do?"

Lysan grimaced. "Besides ride and wait?"

"I've seen the sashes and the dispatch cases . . ." Alucius glanced to the wall where two sashes and cases hung. "You're on duty now, waiting?"

"We wouldn't be here, if we weren't," Gero pointed out.

"It's simple enough," Lysan said, pointing to the bell on the wall. "That rings and whoever's up first puts on his sash, and case, and then goes to the main duty office. The duty squad leader either has the message or tells you where to go to get it. If he does, he tells you where you're riding and who to give it to . . ."

When Lysan had finished outlining the procedure, Alucius asked, "Isn't it a little . . . strange . . . if you have to take a message to the Matrial's residence . . . or spaces . . . whatever?"

"Just call it the residence. Like a palace, but it's the residence. That's simpler. You just ride up to the western portico, that's the small one on the far side, and tell the duty guards—they're women in green, but with purple sleeves, sort of . . . tell them who the message is for. Generally, if it's for the arms commander and her staff—that's most of what we carry—one of them will escort you there. If it's for the

Matrial or her personal staff, they take you to the second
level, and you just hand it over to the personal aide on duty.
They know what they're doing, not like when you have to
run a message to some captain who's assigned to the rifle-
works." Gero shook his head. "Most of the messages are
from Arms Commander Uslyn or her aides over to the marshal and her staff. Sometimes from Overcaptain Haeragn or
her deputy . . . what's her name?"

"Sulkyn?" suggested Alucius.

"Right."

"What else do you do?"

"Believe me, that's enough. Sometimes, you'll make five-
six runs a day."

"Is there another messenger service for messages from Hieron to places like Zalt or Dimor?"

"Those are the distance runs. You really don't want them.
They operate out of the Southside Depot . . ."

Alucius listened and asked more questions, listened some
more before saying. "I don't want to bother you more, but I
appreciate your explaining. I've never done much besides
fight."

Both Lysan and Gero laughed.

"Well . . . maybe we'll see you besides in the mess."

Alucius shrugged. "That's up to Overcaptain Haeragn,
whenever she gets back."

"Well . . ." Gero glanced at Lysan, "she's still in Faitel.
Will be for two-three more days.

"Then I should know before long," Alucius suggested.

"Don't count on that. Jesorak'll keep you as long as he
can."

After leaving the two messengers, Alucius headed back to
the Eltema Post library. The single room was larger than the
one at Zalt, but not that much better equipped, except with
local maps, which showed signs of having been perused, possibly by the messengers.

In the dimming light, even with the aid of the wall lamp,
it took more than a glass before he found what he needed, a
hand-drawn map of the lanes and roads leading into the Ma-

trial's Park and residence. He already had located a map of Hieron and traced out a fair copy of the roads leading from Eltema to the Matrial's residence, and he noted where the west portico was, and how to approach it.

With Haeragn returning before long, he had little time.

As full night fell, and the lamps were dimmed, Alucius left the library and slipped through the shadowed courtyard to the main training building. While he wished he had more time, it was all too clear he did not, and he had one more task to undertake.

There was only one problem. Not only were the doors locked, but, from his vantage point in the shadows, he could see the guards.

He headed back to his own bunk. He'd have to handle the last chore during the day.

111

After his last stint of the morning in sabre instruction—mounted—Alucius stabled and groomed Wildebeast before making his way to the quarters bay, where he washed up, then headed to the training squad leaders' staff room. By then, it was close to midday, and his stomach was growling, slightly, but definitely.

Heltyn was sitting on the left side of the long narrow table, near the door, pouring over a short stack of papers. "How did it go?"

"Some of them still don't know that a sabre has only one side that cuts. Most of those that do are pretty good, except for the two that think it's an axe."

"We're having to try to train more captives without arms experience," Heltyn pointed out. "They've got it even worse at the trooper school in Salcer."

Absently, Alucius wondered how his grandsire had stood it—either when he'd been a militia training officer or when he'd undertaken to train Alucius. "You be a while?"

"Not that long."

"I'll be back in a bit." Alucius walked out of the squad leader's staff room and headed back in the direction of Undercaptain Sulkyn's room—and Overcaptain Haeragn's, as well.

As he turned the corner, he looked down the corridor. The only people were thirty yards away, and heading in the same direction he was. He used his Talent to create the same kind of screen he had at Salcer, one that created the impression of an empty corridor space around him.

Taking care to move silently—boots clicking on the stone in a seemingly empty section of hallway wouldn't be at all helpful—Alucius slipped toward the undercaptain's room. He hoped she was at the officers' mess. The open door disabused him of that possibility.

He stopped well short of Sulkyn's door. Now what?

He could see a squad leader walking briskly along the corridor. He waited until the man passed, then had to wait for a captain to pass as well. Neither even looked in his direction.

Finally, he eased past Sulkyn's open door, still holding the screen, his heart beating faster. The undercaptain never even looked up from the papers on her table desk.

Alucius's Talent told him that no one was inside the room used by Overcaptain Haeragn. Hoping he remained unseen by the undercaptain, Alucius eased the inward-opening door back and stepped inside, careful to close the door behind him slowly and silently.

He surveyed the space, without touching anything.

There was a stack of papers in the center of the table, with a smaller piece of paper on top, held down by a polished wooden weight into which had been inserted an insignia of sorts. He looked at it, realizing that it resembled the ancient seal of the Alectors, a circle containing an enamel portrayal of a balance scale suspended from a red sabre. There were several words inscribed in the ancient silver that bordered the enamel. Alucius couldn't read them.

He could read the words on the paper, little more than a notation that the papers represented personnel decisions deferred until Haeragn's return. He decided against trying to read any of them. His time was short, and Sulkyn's note to her superior confirmed the fact that Haeragn was expected back at Eltema Post *very* soon.

Instead, he slipped to the cabinet in the corner, perusing one drawer as quickly and quietly as he could, then a second. In the third drawer, he found what he needed—a recent message from one sub-arms commander Benyal urging Haeragn to find ways to increase the number of captive trooper trainees, given the heavy losses sustained by the Madrien forces. Alucius slipped it inside his tunic, along with the copy of Haeragn's reply on a sheet of message paper, with "Eltema Post Training Center" across the top, the first time Alucius had seen that. It took him several moments more to find blank sheets of the same message paper, which also went inside his tunic.

After that he stood inside the closed door, using his Talent-senses to make sure the corridor was clear. He didn't need someone seeing a door open itself, or call the attention of an officer who might have Talent to such an occurrence.

He felt as though he had waited a quarter of a glass before the corridor was clear enough for him to leave the over-captain's room and close the door behind him. There was the slightest *click*. Alucius froze.

The undercaptain looked up, and then back at her papers.

Once Alucius was certain she was concentrating on them, he slipped past her door. Twenty yards farther on, when no one could see, he released the screen, with a silent sign of partial relief, and made his way around the corner and to the squad leaders' staff room.

Heltyn looked up as he entered. "Where did you go? Ready to get something to eat?"

"Had to relieve myself," Alucius explained. "I'm ready. It's going to be a long afternoon, after yesterday." And he had much to do after his formal duties were over.

"It probably will be. Jesorak didn't say anything, but word

does get around. Sometimes, it's more effective if we don't say anything at all."

Alucius could see that. He was learning, later than he should have, why his grandsire often had said little—to great effect. But then, he felt, he was learning much, also later than he should have.

112

After supper Alucius made his way back to the library. There, with a large and ancient history book propped open beside him for cover, he inspected the two messages he had taken from the overcaptain's file.

They were both fairly lengthy—one reason why he had chosen them—and had a text that would allow a follow-on from the overcaptain.

For all his hopes, it took him more than two glasses to write out the very short message, supposedly from Overcaptain Haeragn. The message itself wasn't all that difficult, but copying the hand that had written it was. It didn't have to be perfect, but it had to pass a cursory inspection.

Finally, he studied the third copy he had made, skipping past the formalities of the headings and salutations to the short text.

. . . in further reference to your earlier message, I have given this much thought while in Faitel, despite the difficulties. We have been trying to train captives whom we would have turned to the public labor pool in earlier years, but the training staff has also been reduced, and the casualties in training are now higher. If the Westerhills perimeter remains quiet, and the Lanachronans do not mount another heavy assault upon Zalt, it may be

possible to supply replacements for depleted companies.
It is unlikely that we can train enough captives to do
more than that . . .

Once he was certain that his forged message was totally
dry, he slipped all three messages inside his tunic and
made his way through the dim halls of the barracks in the
direction of the courtyard—and the bay that held the messengers.

As he neared the archway into the bay, he moved more
slowly, and quietly, and raised a screen that suggested only
empty shadows. After easing around the edge of the archway,
he could see that he almost didn't need the screen.

A single squad leader—not someone Alucius had met—
was on duty—if on duty meant asleep in a wooden chair
under the call bell. His breathing was not quite a snore, but
almost.

Rather than take the sash and dispatch case of the slum-
bering messenger, which would be most likely to be missed
sooner than others, Alucius moved toward the row of bunks
and footchests. Most of the bunks were occupied with sleeping men, and most had stowed their gear neatly with cases
and sashes out of sight. On the fourth footchest were both a
sash and case along with a hastily discarded set of uniform
trousers.

Ever so carefully, Alucius removed both sash and case,
and gingerly made his way out of the bay and back toward
his own spaces, still holding the screen until he neared the
archway to his own bay. Then he released the full screen and
concentrated on making sure his hands looked empty as he
walked into the bay and toward his bunk. He slipped case
and sash into his footchest and under a tunic, then straightened.

"It's late." Heltyn looked up sleepily from his bunk as
Alucius sat down and pulled off his boots.

"I know. I was reading in the library. There's so much I
still don't know."

"You won't know your sabre hand from your elbow if you don't get some sleep."

Alucius offered a low laugh. "You're right. Turn over. I'll probably be asleep before you are." He was lying about that. His heart was still beating too swiftly.

113

Alucius finished saddling Wildebeast. His skull-mask—unused for more than a year—was inside his shirt, above his nightsilk undergarments. The dispatch case and sash lay under some loose straw in the back of the manger. The green scarf was in his saddlebags, along with a spare uniform. In just a few moments, he was supposed to report to the staff room to meet Jesorak. He could still do that. He could, and no one would be the wiser. No one would ever need to know what he had done so far.

Alucius swallowed, not easily, because his mouth was dry. Did he really want to try this? He thought of the wrongness of the pink threads, the massive web converging on the Matrial's residence, of the innocent man he had seen killed in the square when he had been a captive, and of all the militia troopers slaughtered by the crystal spear-thrower. He also thought about his grandsire—and his father, who had died doing what he had felt was right.

How could Alucius ever return to the Iron Valleys if he had not at least tried to remedy what he knew was wrong? He'd felt the wrongness from the beginning, even before he had learned how to see the threads and webs, but he'd been more worried about his own personal problems. Did he want to spend the rest of a life wondering if he could have done something? Yet . . . could he? Was he deluding himself to think that he could?

With a deep breath, he slipped the sash out of the manger and brushed away the loose straw, then eased it over his uniform tunic. Next came the dispatch case into which he had already placed the forged message. He walked to the back of the stall and checked the stable.

There was no one close.

He led Wildebeast out of the stall, then cast a loose screen. The idea was to create a general idea of "messenger" without revealing a face.

Outside the stable, he mounted. No one seemed even to look his way as he rode out of the courtyard and through the open gates. Once beyond the walls, he turned Wildebeast westward, and as he passed the corner shops, and the small chandlery, an older woman waved. Alucius waved back, wondering whose face she had seen. He continued to ride west along the paved redstone road that led to the intersection with the north-south high road.

After he was a good vingt west of Eltema Post, he released the bit of Talent-power that blurred his face. While it was highly likely that someone would eventually figure out what he had done, he thought he had a good chance of getting away with the first part of his plan, only because no one would expect a squad leader to ride toward the Matrial and into a place where he could be so easily destroyed.

Once he was inside the residence . . . he pushed aside those thoughts and shifted his weight in the saddle. Wildebeast *whuff*ed, as if he sensed his rider's unease.

Wildebeast carried Alucius westward with an easy stride, and Alucius realized that this was the first time in years that he had ridden anywhere alone. He held to the center of the road, as he'd seen other messengers do, and kept his eyes forward. Even so, he could see the neat dwellings and the sheltered courtyards, and feel a certain order. Yet he could also feel a tension beneath that order—or was that his tension?

Before all that long, he arrived at the redstone ramp that rose to meet the roadbed of the north-south eternastone high road that divided the city into its eastern and western halves. He crossed the high road just after two traders' wagons that were heading southward, seemingly empty. He headed down the ramp on the far side, and then, later, past the circular paved square where he had seen the public execution where a guilty woman and an innocent man had been killed. The area was empty, and he took the road that curved to the right and around the northern side of the Park of the Matrial. The park was enclosed by a low redstone wall, only about a yard and a half high. The residence was roughly in the center of the park, set upon a low hill that, to Alucius's eyes, looked as though it had been built just for the residence.

While there were trees amid the grass, most were low evergreens and junipers. The white stone pathways were bordered by knee-high boxwood hedges, and beyond each hedge was a narrow flowerbed, although none of the green plants there showed blooms. The grassy expanse of the park was vacant except for a small flock of white sheep and a herder.

Alucius tried to use his Talent to see exactly where the purple-pink torque threads converged, but from the north all he could tell was that they seemed to reach below ground somewhere on the south side of the residence.

He was grateful he had not seen any other messengers, nor heard any coming after him.

The road continued to curve around the park until it was headed south. Then he neared the pair of gate posts on his left. He turned Wildebeast toward them, and the narrower way beyond that led to the Matrial's residence. The single sentry—in green and purple—watched as he rode toward her. Almost without looking, she waved Alucius through.

Once he was inside the gates and riding through the grounds, a faint scent of some flower wafted past Alucius, although he had seen no blooms. So quiet were the stone lane and the park that Wildebeast's hoofs on the stone sounded preternaturally loud.

On the lane, he could sense more clearly that the torque threads wove together into a treelike trunk that ended somewhere in the hill on which the residence was built. He frowned as his Talent revealed that the residence was more like four levels, with only two above the hill.

He rode up to the west portico, and glanced around, then

saw what he was looking for—a pair of bronze hitching posts near the base of the stone steps, each circled with a pink enamel band.

Two guards—women in green with purple cuffs on their tunic sleeves—stood above it. They watched as Alucius dismounted and tied Wildebeast to the left post. They wore sabres and holstered heavy pistols, the first Alucius had seen in Madrien. With only his sabre, Alucius definitely felt at a disadvantage in weapons. So far as he could tell, neither guard had any Talent.

Then, one stepped forward. "You're new."

"Very new. Alucius, reassigned from Fortieth Company in Zalt."

The hard-faced guard nodded. "Soon as we get to know you messengers, they send you someplace else. Who's it for?"

"Sub-arms commander Benyal. That's what the duty officer said."

"That figures." The guard turned. "Follow me. She's on the lower level."

"How many levels are there?" Alucius asked naively.

"Just two." Her words and feelings had the ring of truth, and that meant the existence of even lower levels was kept from most people, because guards usually found out almost everything.

The guard walked briskly, but not at a headlong pace, and Alucius followed, trying to use his Talent to sense any officer who might be looking for him.

Inside the archway was a stone-walled foyer ten yards square, and at the front sat an undercaptain behind a small table from where she could watch everyone who entered. She studied him for a moment, but said nothing as he walked past following the guard who headed for the corridor leading from the back wall on the southern end of the east wall of the foyer. The residence had a feeling of age, almost as if the very stones felt older than they were, and there was a faint odor, somewhere between flowers and incense, that reminded Alucius, in an odd way, of his grandmother. He frowned, because he did not recall her wearing any scent.

The two entered a rear corridor about four yards wide, and within ten yards, they passed a window on the right, revealing an inner courtyard on the same level, but open to the sky. Ten yards past the window, they walked by another, slightly smaller corridor. "Where are we going?" Alucius asked politely.

"You'll learn, probably by the end of the day. We're on the lower level. This is for all the officers who handle logistics, training, and oversee the field commands. Off the north corridor are those who handle the domestic functions, roads, engineers, tariff officers. . . ."

"I thought this was the residence of the Matrial . . ." Alucius ventured.

"Her quarters and offices are in the southern half. If you were delivering a message there, we'd go up the stairs here, and then turn right, and you'd hand it over to the duty assistant at the end of the corridor."

Alucius glanced at the circular stone stairs as they passed. "Thank you. I suppose I'll learn my way around."

"Oh . . . you will. You'll spend more time waiting here than you ever thought."

Alucius nodded and kept pace with her. The main corridor ended at another corridor that ran both left and right. The guard turned right.

The guard stopped at a closed door, on the left side of the corridor. Alucius stepped forward and knocked on the golden wood of the five-panel door.

"Yes?"

"Messenger from Eltema Post."

"Just a moment."

Alucius waited.

The door opened. A square-faced captain stood there, the first person Alucius had seen who was not in the green and purple.

Alucius opened the case and handed over the rolled message. The woman scanned it, albeit briefly, frowning slightly, and then nodded. "There won't be an immediate answer, squad leader. You may go."

"Yes, sir."

Even before he finished responding, she had closed the door. Alucius turned, looking at the guard.

"This way."

Following the guard, Alucius waited for a few steps, then reached out with his Talent, ever so gently, touching the guard's life web, and simultaneous suggesting that the messenger had been requested to wait for a response.

Then he held his breath. The guard shook her head, and squinted.

Alucius raised the screen that conveyed the impression that no one was there.

The guard paused, stopped, and turned, looking down the corridor that Alucius hoped was empty to her. She squinted again, then frowned before murmuring, "Better check later, just to make sure." Then she walked away, back toward the west portico.

Alucius was alone in a building whose structure he knew but roughly and with perhaps a glass, two at the most, before someone—or many people—became exceedingly suspicious.

He turned, letting his Talent seek the source—or the destination—of the torque threads.

From where he stood, he judged that convergence point to be a good sixty yards to the south, and two levels down. The problem was that he'd seen no sign of stairs or shafts that led down, and there was a solid wall twenty yards to the south.

He shrugged to himself. That meant he had to go up a level, somehow cross to the southern half of the residence— the Matrial's half—and descend four levels, all in less than a glass and without being discovered.

He might as well start.

Still holding his screen, he moved deliberately back along the corridor. He kept about a yard from the wall and walked as quietly as possible. A young woman in the green and purple that almost everyone in the residence seemed to wear stepped out of a doorway to his left, crossing so closely in front of him that he lurched to a stop. The room from which she had come adjoined a larger one, but neither had another exit.

Letting her precede him, he moved toward the staircase, but she passed the staircase and headed down the side corridor to the left. Alucius started up the smooth and polished stone steps. At the top of the circular stairs, he paused, looking to the right. There was a wide hallway that ran southward, brightly lit from the high windows in the raised roof. At the end of the hallway was a silver gate. Before the gate were two guards in purple and green. There were two more guards standing on the other side of the closed gate.

Alucius thought. A gate with that many guards indicated that it was used. He eased along the left side of the hallway, avoiding the morning sunlight angling onto the shimmering oblong green stones of the floor. He doubted that his Talent-screen would help if he cast a shadow.

He stopped a good five yards short of the gate, easing to the side of a tall ebony cabinet with a glass front. He did not look to see what was in the cabinet. From where he stood, the guards could not have seen him even without his Talent-screen.

As he waited, he used his Talent to study the gate. The faintest hint of Talent played around it, and especially around the iron lock inset above the silver lever handles. Even if he could have used his Talent to work the lock, the disruption of the Talent flow would tell someone that the gate had been opened.

He took a slow and deep breath and continued to wait.

Behind him, after a good half glass, he heard the rapid click of boots on the stone tiles of the hallway. He turned and watched. Two women in Matrite uniforms, but with collar insignia he did not recognize, walked toward the gate. One looked to be ten years older than Alucius, the other more like his mother's age. The older woman showed definite signs of Talent, though it was well contained within her. As they neared him Alucius stiffened, but both passed without so much as looking in his direction.

He slipped away from the wall and the cabinet and followed them, perhaps a yard back, listening.

"She's summoned us . . . don't know why this time . . . unless it's the Dramurans . . ."

They stopped opposite the silver gate.

After several moments, a woman clad almost entirely in purple, except for the forest green cuffs on her tunic sleeves and uniform collar, appeared on the far side of the gate. She inserted a key and opened the gate.

Alucius edged forward, slowly, hoping he remained unnoticed, his heart still beating fast, because he felt someone should have noticed him, even as he scarcely wanted that to happen.

The aide swung open the silver gate, which, surprisingly to Alucius, squeaked slightly.

The two officers stepped through, Alucius practically on their heels.

"Marshal, the Matrial is expecting you in the situation room." The aide turned, and the other two women followed. Returning quickly to the left-hand side of the corridor, Alucius let some distance grow between him and the women, since he had absolutely no intention of ending up in the same room as the Matrial. Every feeling he had screamed against that.

The walls were smoothly plastered, the finish slightly off-white with a green tint. The floor remained the same polished oblong green stone tiles, with light pouring in from the high clerestory windows above the corridor.

The three women headed for a set of double doors directly ahead, where another pair of armed women guards waited. Rather than follow, Alucius slipped into the first side corridor, hoping that the rooms there might give him a clue. There were three doors on the short corridor. The first was without a lock and was little more than a storage room containing brushes and what he thought was cleaning gear. The second was empty, he could tell, but held a table desk and cabinets.

The third was locked, but empty inside. He took another long and slow deep breath before reinforcing his screen and stepping into the main hallway.

Although the guards at the double doors looked in his direction, and he was certain they could not have missed seeing him, neither moved. Ten yards short of the dead-end main corridor that stopped at the double doors was another wide corridor to his left. With nowhere else to go, Alucius took it.

He passed another short corridor to his right, leading to another set of double doors, unguarded. He could not have said why, but that set of doors did not lead anywhere he wanted or needed to go. The next side corridor was to the right, and he slipped into it. There was only one door, a double door to his right. Since he could sense no one inside, he eased it open, glancing inside to view the vacant sitting room of what was clearly an opulent guest suite, and one that felt as though it had not been occupied in years, immaculate though it appeared, with the upholstered green leather settee, the golden oak writing table, and thick green-and-tan carpet over the polished parquet floor.

He eased the door closed without entering the chambers, and moved back to the main east-west corridor he had just left, following it until it ended where it joined another north-south corridor. Alucius turned south.

Ahead was a brightly lit rotunda.

Alucius stopped just short of the columned arch—half buried in the sides of the corridor—that marked the entrance to the rotunda—roughly fifteen yards across.

A quarter of the way around the rotunda on the east side was another set of double doors, these set in what appeared to be false columns, but were not. There were two guards outside the double doors, doors Alucius felt led to the Matrial's private chambers.

He paused, thinking.

There was no help for it. He eased into the rotunda and moved along the curved wall until he was within less than two yards of the guard on the north side. From there, with his Talent, Alucius reached out and touched their life webs, as he had with the guard on the floor below. One hand rested on his sabre. Nothing happened.

Then he implanted the suggestion that someone had rapped on the other side of the door.

The two guards exchanged glances, before the one on the left opened the door.

He slipped between the guards, just before the one on the right closed the door, and into the chamber beyond, a small and spare foyer with neither furnishings nor wall hangings. He was getting a strong impression that the Matrial liked matters simple and spare—at least for a ruler.

By now, his head was beginning to ache, and he hadn't even begun to discover how to get down four levels, although he knew he was close to the point where the purplish pink torque threads converged. Leaning against the wall on the north side of the foyer, he massaged his forehead and temples.

On the east side of the foyer was a square arch. Alucius moved toward it, sensing that there was someone somewhere before him. Beyond the arch was a sitting room of sorts, less than five yards deep, but more than twice that in width. The north end of the room ended in an archway into what looked to be a library. The south end also provided an archway, fitted with doors currently open, into a courtyard garden. On the east wall was a single door.

As Alucius surveyed the room before him, he almost jumped at the sight of a young woman sitting on a chair, but she had been so quiet and drawn into herself that he had not even observed her. She wore a torque and did not even look in his direction.

He waited for several moments, wondering whether she would move, or whether he would need to stun her or try to persuade her to move. As he watched, she gave a deep sigh, then stood and picked up a small basket, which she carried with her as she moved toward the courtyard garden.

Alucius eased his way across the sitting room, around two settees and a low table, and past a simple bronze holder that contained another of the ancient light-torches. The handle to the door was a simple silver lever. He could sense neither Talent nor other energies in the door, although there was a sense of great power—and purple-pinkness—beyond the door.

After a brief hesitation, he pushed the lever down and opened the door, slipping past in and closing it, even as he scanned the chamber. He staggered as he stood inside the closed door of what had to be the Matrial's bedchamber. Staggered because, less than three yards before him was a cascade of that horribly wrong and shocking purple-pink, looking to his Talent-senses both like a silent waterfall and the twisted pink trunk of an ancient and somehow evil tree.

The rush of power was centered and seemingly contained within a circle of golden stone floor tiles, ringed with black. Ignoring his distaste, he studied the wrongness and power that flowed from above down through the circle. The focus was so narrow that he had not even sensed the vastness of that power until he had stepped inside the bed chamber and within a few yards of the circle. Whatever focused those threads lay directly below.

He stepped around the circle, his trousers brushing the edge of the dais on which the high and curtained bed was set, moving toward the dressing chambers on the south side of the room.

In the back of the small closet off the dressing room, a closet empty of anything, Alucius could sense a staircase. He studied the wall—totally devoid of anything except an ancient light-torch in a bracket. He tried to concentrate on the torch, and then the bracket. There was something about the bracket.

He tugged on it. Nothing. Then he twisted. When he twisted to the left, there was a solid *click*, and a crack appeared in the corner where the walls met at a right angle. The left side swung back, revealing a narrow circular staircase, also lit with ancient light-torches.

Alucius examined the back side of the concealed door. After making sure that there was a lever on the inside, he stepped inside, and then eased the panel shut. The light-torches were dim but adequate as he descended the narrow stone steps, moving downward, all too conscious of the power so few yards away.

He could feel the silver torque around his own neck getting warmer and warmer with each step that he took down the staircase. Perspiration began to well up on his forehead, although there was a breeze of sorts flowing up from the depths below. His fingers brushed the metal of the collar. The heat radiating from it told him that it was getting hot enough to brand him.

He could feel he had no choice. He reached up and, using his Talent to contain the force in the lock, broke the torque apart. Immediately, he felt as though a weight had been lifted from him, as though his vision were clearer, sharper. He thrust the broken torque inside his tunic. He paused, then drew out the nightsilk skull mask and wiggled it over his head and into place. He also dropped his concealment shield. If he were caught now, anyone who could reach him could certainly sense his Talent use, and being seen would be the least of his problems.

With a grim smile behind the nightsilk, he resumed his descent.

The staircase, if narrow and ancient, was clean and without dust, although the centers of the stone steps were slightly hollowed out. When he reached the bottom, there was a landing less than a yard deep and not much wider, and a silver door, with a crystalline door lever, which shone with an inner purple glow. Talent-links surrounded the latch on the door, as well as the handle itself.

For a time, Alucius puzzled about them, but no matter how he traced them with his Talent, he could see no way to unravel them, and they were so pervasive that he could not use his senses to look beyond the door.

Finally, he unsheathed his sabre, and shrouding it in his own Talent, pressed the silver door lever down, letting the door swing inward. Then, using the sabre he *cut* through the Talent barrier and stepped through the doorway.

A line of purplish light flared around him, then subsided. He stood in a small antechamber, empty, unfurnished, with smooth white alabaster walls, dimly lit by two light-torches set in brackets on each side of a solid oak door, a door without locks or iron binding, and only a simple latch. Alucius did not hesitate, but took three steps and lifted the latch, then pulled the door toward himself.

He was enfolded by blinding purplish pink light, light that was visible not just to his Talent-senses, but to his eyes as well. Slowly, he stepped into the room, finding that the very air itself seemed to thicken, to resist his advance. He took two more steps until he could make out the source of the light.

For a moment, he just looked.

Hanging in midair, suspended in the circular underground room by no visible means of support, was a massive, multi-faceted crystal. Talentlike roots, of a purple energy so dark it was almost black, vanished into the rock below the crystal, but the roots were invisible to the eye. Above the crystal, the compressed trunk of purplish pink torque threads seemed to writhe, with energy of some sort flowing to and from the crystal, although Alucius had the sense that most flowed into the crystal, rather than out and back upward.

His eyes registered another oak door, a quarter of the way around the circular wall to his left. He looked back over his shoulder. The door through which he had entered had vanished! Then, he realized that it lay behind some sort of Talent-illusion.

His eyes went back to the floating crystal.

What had he expected? He wasn't certain, only that it was wrong, and that he had to do *something*. He looked at the massive crystal, seemingly hanging in midair.

How was he supposed to destroy *that*?

Alucius could feel the heat building inside his nightsilk undergarments, and somewhere outside the crystal chamber in the room behind him or on the staircase—or behind the door to his left, he could hear voices, and steps.

He looked at the crystal, then at the sabre in his hand, then back at the crystal.

He willed dark-Talent to enfold the blade of the sabre. After a moment, with all his effort, mental and physical, he swung the shimmering edge of the blade toward the massive crystal.

114

Hieron, Madrien

As always, the Matrial sat on the south side of the conference table, her presence somehow standing out even against the light of the wide windows behind her. "What does Overcaptain Haeragn have to say about it?"

"We received a message this morning," replied the marshal. "She has grave concerns about our ability to significantly expand the number of troopers under arms. She had already pointed out that even a total conquest and impression of all possible men in the Iron Valleys would not be likely to raise adequate numbers and now . . ." The marshal let her words fade.

"With the Lord-Protector's attack and the failures in the Iron Valleys, you think the situation in the south will soon become impossible? Is that what you are suggesting?" The Matrial's beautiful smile was as cold as the winter ice on the Black Cliffs of Despair. "Marshal Aluyn sent a dispatch last night. She should be returning—" The Matrial broke off in midsentence, her violet eyes glazing over.

Without speaking, she stood and walked to the bell pull on the wall. "You must excuse me. If you would wait . . ."

The marshal and her assistant stood and bowed, but the Matrial did not acknowledge the obeisance as she strode from the conference room. Outside the double doors were the two guards, armed with sabres, and with large-bore heavy holstered pistols. Two others immediately appeared, followed by a tall woman wearing a guard's uniform, but the collar insignia of a submarshal.

"Yes, Matrial. Is there difficulty in there?" asked the submarshal.

"No!" snapped the dark-haired woman with the flawless skin and violet-purple eyes. "There is a lamaial in the residence."

"A lamaial?" stammered the submarshal. "How?"

"They can cast an illusion that there is no one where they stand. They can convince a careless guard that no one is there, even as they pass. It has been many years, but I knew there would be another. I can sense the focus of the life webs. He is nearing the crystal chamber."

The submarshal's eyes flickered but once. "We should go, then."

The five walked but ten yards to a seemingly blank wall, where the submarshal touched and then twisted the bracket holding a light-torch. The wall opened to reveal a staircase broad enough for two abreast, a staircase that led straight down to a landing, where it turned back upon itself.

A set of guards started down immediately, followed by the submarshal, the Matrial, and then the last two guards. Behind them, the wall panel slid shut, and a series of light-torches flicked on, illuminating the stone stairwell. At the base of the stairwell, three flights down, was a silver door with a crystal handle. The submarshal stepped in front of the guards, concentrated, and then touched the crystal with a short rod of deep purple, before she turned the lever.

A straight corridor three yards wide and thirty long stretched beyond the silver door, ending in a solid oak door, held closed by a simple iron latch.

"He's in the crystal room," the Matrial announced.

"Has anyone . . . ?"

"No. The defenses have destroyed all those before."

"Sidearms ready!" snapped the submarshal. "Fire as you enter. Avoid shooting at the crystal. If you hit it, the bullet will rebound and strike you." She reached down and lifted the latch, then pulled the door toward her.

The four guards surged through the doorway into the crystal chamber, followed by the submarshal and then the Matrial.

115

The sabre stopped . . . less than a span from the edge of the crystal, then rebounded. It took all of Alucius's strength to keep the weapon from slamming back against his body and then flying out of his hand.

Holding the sabre, Alucius extended the faintest touch of Talent to the crystal, trying to concentrate, even as he could sense both a concentration of Talent and guards moving toward the chamber—and him.

He concentrated . . . thinking about the way in which the wood-spirit had released the torque the first time . . . the way blackness had enfolded the pinkness of the torque thread. Slowly, deliberatively, he visualized a sphere of blackness around the purple crystal. As he extended that blackness, he could feel a pressure, a resistance, but he continued to press, to visualize, to extend a blackness suffused with green. Slowly, slowly, a thin and unseen layer of darkness slipped around the crystal, and the room dimmed, with the faintest of green overtones to the fading light.

Caught in the thinnest of coverings of darkness, the crystal pulsed, shuddering, and then contracted ever so slightly. Alucius concentrated yet harder—

The door to his left, the one that had remained visible, burst open, and four of the purple-clad guards burst into the circular chamber. They paused for an instant.

Alucius slipped to his left, putting the crystal between him and the guards, and forced his concentration back to thickening the darkness around the dimming crystal, and to suffusing that darkness with the sense of greenness that seemed to help.

"Shoot him!" commanded someone.

"Where is he?"

The crystal vibrated, shuddered, and gave a high whining sound that began to rise in pitch.

Alucius pressed more darkness around the crystal.

The four guards split into groups of two, one set moving to the right of the door through which they had entered, the other moving to the left.

"There he is!"

"Shoot him!"

With the command came a bolt of purplish black power that shook and pummeled Alucius like a ripe wheat stalk in a harvest hailstorm, but he continued to build the darkness around the crystal, hoping, somehow, that he could finish before it was too late.

A second vibration shook the entire chamber, so violent that Alucius went to his knees, as did three of the four Matrial's guards.

A dull splintering sound echoed through the space, and cracks appeared in the stone walls of the chamber, widening almost instantaneously from spidersilk thinness to rents in the solid stone wide enough for a trooper's arm to pass through.

On his knees, Alucius pressed more darkness around the crystal, darkness that seemed to flow from somewhere, almost effortlessly now. Then, he was thrown to the floor by another bolt of Talent-force.

For a moment, the dark cocoon wavered, but he shored it up, held it tight.

Abruptly, a brilliant greenish light poured through the now-huge cracks in the chamber wall, and the remaining faint purplish light swirled as if it were smoke, smoke pressed back by the greenness.

Alucius struggled to his knees, pouring more blackness around the shrinking purple crystal. The whining from the crystal rose in pitch into a piercing shriek, and then into a

frequency so high that while Alucius could not hear it, he
felt as though his very bones were being sawed apart from
within, that his entire being was being sliced into slivers by
invisible knives.

He forced more blackness, backed with green, looking up
as a single point of fire brighter than the sun replaced the
dark-enshrouded purpleness, throwing his darkness back at
him.

At the same moment, in that moment of clarity, three
guards fired.

One shot hammered the back of his shoulder, another his
lower back, another the back of his thigh. He tried to turn,
to throw himself flat on the stone splintering beneath him.

Silver-green surged across the chamber . . . a blinding
wave of color and power . . .

. . . then darkness claimed him.

116

Someone was groaning.

After a moment, Alucius realized he was the one groaning.
His head throbbed, and his eyesight was blurred. He was
lying on something hard, very hard. Stone.

The chamber was dark. Black, with but a faint glow from
a single dying light-torch, its crystal cracked and its energies
dissipating.

The guards! He tried to move his head, and sharp pains
jabbed through his skull. Gingerly, he turned his head, and
looked across the chamber. There was no sign of the purple
crystal. There was no flow of pink or purple thread power.
There were figures on the stone floor. There were still large
fissures in the walls of the chamber, but no light—sunlight
or green light—came through those cracks.

Alucius slowly pulled himself into a sitting position. Outside of his head, which ached, his body did not feel as sore

as it should have. He looked down at himself. There was a hole in his trousers on the side of his thigh, but his thigh was not sore. Carefully, he stood, looking around the chamber, and particularly at the floor around himself. There were stone shards around him, except they lay in a semicircle almost a yard from where he stood.

The feeling of silver-green? The only creature he knew that felt silver-green was a soarer. But what had a soarer been doing in the chamber? Or had he imagined it? And what would a soarer have been doing underground?

He frowned, then moved a step around to his left. Even though the space in the center of the chamber was empty, as if the crystal had never been, he had no intention of walking through where it had floated. Before him, there were five bodies, and all lay in pools of blood. He looked at the body of the nearest guard, and then looked away from the splinters of stone that had riddled her. He had to swallow to keep from retching.

He stepped carefully around the other four. The last one had been an officer of some sort, but Alucius did not recognize the insignia. Slightly behind the five figures was a line of clothing—a deep violet tunic, matching trousers, black boots, and an emerald necklace of some sort—all stretched out as if someone had been wearing it and then vanished. But there was not even dust within the clothing.

He reached for the necklace, then drew back his hand. There was something about it—very old and very evil, as if it had been imbued with the pinkness, even though the purple and pink had vanished from the chamber. He looked at the clothing once more, and then at the ancient emeralds. Although he could scarcely prove it, he *knew* who had worn those clothes. He swallowed and straightened, and then glanced around.

After a moment, he eased toward the open oak door and peered into the corridor beyond. It too was empty. He walked steadily to the end of the long corridor, and stopped at the silver door. There were no Talent energies playing around the door, and the crystal handle looked like dull glass. There was no one on the other side of the door either. The handle was cool to his touch as he pressed it down. He opened the door and stepped through. On the other side was a staircase wide enough for two that led straight upward to a landing.

He walked up the three flights of stairs, slowly, listening, but he could hear nothing. When he reached the top, he faced a blank wall—except for a small handle.

He cloaked himself in his screen, ignoring the headache that intensified, and then pulled the handle. The wall slid apart, and Alucius stepped out in one of the side corridors he had thought led nowhere when he had been looking earlier in the day. The corridor remained empty.

It took him several moments to figure out that the light-torch bracket served the same function it had in the Matrial's closet, but the wall closed, and Alucius moved back toward the center of the building, staying next to the shady side of the corridor. From the position of the sun, it was early afternoon.

He could not believe that no one had seen or heard what had happened. But then, it had all occurred three levels down, behind stone walls, and past three doors. Also, he suspected that no one had dared question the Matrial too closely about what she did behind such closed doors.

Alucius smiled.

Several of the women in purple and green moved along the corridor, radiating concern, but they were preoccupied and did not near Alucius.

Again . . . it took patience, but only about a quarter of a glass before one of the Matrial's aides appeared and opened the silver gate to allow someone in uniform to depart. Alucius followed. This time, even before Alucius could let the officer move away from him, the overcaptain looked over her shoulder—twice, frowning—then shook her head and continued. He swallowed, silently.

On the north side of the residence, it appeared as though nothing had happened, and Alucius made his way past the guards. Neither even looked in his direction.

Once outside the west portico, he made his way down to

where Wildebeast remained tethered. There he mounted, and then expanded the cloak to cover the horse.

He couldn't quite believe that he was riding away, but no one stopped him.

117

Alucius decided to wait until well after dark before he returned to Eltema Post. He felt guilty for using his screen to cover the theft of a meat pie from a vendor on the fringes of the market, but that theft was minor compared to the problems he had already created in Hieron—or those to come that he had planned while he had waited. He found a sheltered and concealed spot below the river high road, where he tethered Wildebeast, and managed to doze in the shade, a fitful rest interrupted by nightmares, but a rest of sorts.

Once full darkness fell, he rode Wildebeast back though the gates of Senob Post, wearing the messenger sash and using his screen to blur his face. He left the horse saddled, and stalled the stallion in one of the stalls used for visiting officers, rather than his own. He also left the sash and empty dispatch case in the manger under the straw.

As he left the stall, in the dimness, he could sense someone—with Talent—walking toward him, an officer clearly not deceived by his screen and coming to investigate, and more. The gray-haired officer carried only a sabre, sheathed, and Alucius recognized her as the one who had initially interviewed him. He suspected that she was Overcaptain Haeragn, although he had never been introduced to her as such.

He stopped. "Sir?"

The Talent officer looked at Alucius. "Who are you, squad leader? What sort of mask is that? Remove it!"

Beneath the skull-mask Alucius smiled. "No."

"I command you." Her fingers touched one of the loops

on her belt, and then he could sense a gathering of Talent, blackness gathering to smite him.

"It won't work." Alucius was only mildly surprised that she had not noticed he was not wearing a torque. People tended to see what they thought they saw.

The puzzlement turned to alarm when Alucius touched her life thread, in the instant before she pitched forward. The Talent-force she had been about to cast at him dissipated. Alucius had intentionally severed her thread—with enough force that he had killed her. The fewer Talent-officers left in the Matrite forces, the less the Iron Valleys would have to worry, since it had become all too clear that there were far fewer officers with Talent than he or any of the troopers had been led to believe. He also wasn't surprised by her apparent slowness. It had been generations since a squad leader had not worn a torque and had not been able to be disarmed or killed instantly by a Talent-officer.

He dragged her body into an empty stall, under the manger, and covered it with loose straw before closing the stall door and heading to the stable doors.

Once out of the stable, he kept moving, crossing the courtyard briskly, as though he had every right to be there. He made his way into the barracks building, then walked toward the bays for the squad leaders.

Jesorak rated a bunk in an alcove in the bay, apart from the others. Alucius raised his screen as he neared the senior squad leader, who was sitting there alone, reading a stack of papers under the light of a single oil lamp.

Alucius tried to be quiet, but the older squad leader dropped the papers and looked around. "Who's there?"

Alucius dropped the screen.

Jesorak came with a belt knife from somewhere. "Hold it. That's you, Alucius, isn't it, behind that mask? What have you been doing?"

"You could say . . . I got into a fight," Alucius said slowly. He didn't want to hurt Jesorak, who had been more than fair.

Jesorak looked at the hole in the thigh of Alucius's uniform trousers, barely visible on the forest green in the dim light. "Do I want to know?"

"Probably not." Alucius straightened. "I'd like a favor. I'd prefer it as a favor."

"You want me to turn the captives over to you, don't you?"

"Yes. How did you know?"

"I can tell. There was trouble with the torques this afternoon with one of the new captives. They don't work. The Talent-officers are trying to keep it quiet." Jesorak smiled, sadly. "The hair. I don't know how you got through, but only herders have that hair."

"I had a severe head injury when I was screened."

"And you were young and very good, and we were terribly short of troopers."

"Well?" Alucius asked.

"Would you kill me if I said no?"

"I'd rather not."

Jesorak moved . . . but not quickly enough.

Alucius reached out with his Talent, and touched, lightly, he hoped, the senior squad leader's amber-brown life thread.

Jesorak folded.

Muttering at himself for being a fool, Alucius took a moment to tie Jesorak's wrists behind his back. He dragged the limp figure under the bunk and out of sight before taking the keys from the senior squad leader's footchest.

Next he headed for the wing that held the captive trainees. He didn't know of a way to release all the captives who had been impressed and scattered throughout the Matrite forces, but he could do something about those in the training center.

He stunned the single guard outside the locked door to the captive barracks wing, and then propped him up in the chair, as if he were sleeping on duty. Then, he used Jesorak's keys to unlock the door. After a moment, he wiggled off the skull-mask and tucked it into his tunic. Then, he opened the door and stepped inside.

While some of the captive trainees were sleeping, a number looked up.

"Zerdial!" He made his voice hard.

"Yes, sir." Zerdial scrambled forward.

"Who's the other Iron Valley trainee—the one you trust?" Alucius kept his voice hard.

Zerdial looked blank.

"I could question everyone."

"Anslym, sir."

"Anslym! You and Zerdial suit up. We have a chore for you two. It won't take long."

"Yes, sir."

Although both men looked puzzled, neither questioned, and in but a few moments, they reappeared. Alucius opened the door and motioned them out. Once outside, he relocked the door.

Then he smiled and asked in the speech of the Iron Valleys. "Do you two want to go home? Back to the Iron Valleys."

"Who are you?"

"Squad Leader Alucius. I used to be a herder before they captured me. Now . . . do you want to go home?"

"Yes, sir. But how?"

"We're going to form a few squads, and ride out of here."

"They'll kill us," Zerdial protested.

"No, they won't. Close your eyes." Alucius projected command.

Almost involuntarily, both men closed their eyes. Alucius reached forward and snapped the weld at the back of Zerdial's torque, then, as he opened his eyes, handed him both pieces.

Anslym's eyes widened, but he did not move as Alucius removed his collar as well.

"Sir . . ." Zerdial offered tentatively, "what about the others?"

"We won't leave them, but I need help getting rifles from the armory, and I don't want trainees running around making noise until we're armed and ready to move. That's what you two are going to help me with."

"What?"

"We're going to raid the armory, and then we're going to gather the others and ride out of here. Once we're north of Hieron, we've got a fair chance that we won't see too much opposition." Alucius turned.

After a moment, the two others followed.

They crossed the courtyard and reached the armory without incident. Alucius walked up to the trooper on guard, who looked both interested and confused as Alucius stepped forward.

"Special detail from Senior Squad Leader Jesorak."

"No orders in the book."

"Last moment," Alucius said, stepping closer, using his body as a shield so that neither trainee could see what he did, before touching the man's life web. He lowered the figure to the courtyard stones, and took out the keys. The third one fit.

"What did you do?" asked Anslym.

"What was necessary." Alucius had already decided to conceal his use of Talent. "Drag him inside here and tie his hands and feet with his belt or anything else." Alucius opened the iron-banded oak door and stepped inside. He could tell there were no sentries within.

Anslym slowly dragged the sentry through the door

"Take the rifles from the second rack, Zerdial. Anslym, you load them. We'll take as many as we can, and, if we can on the way out, we'll bring a mount by and get more, and more ammunition."

In less than a quarter glass they were headed back across the courtyard, with Alucius in the lead. They were five yards from the outer doorway to the barracks wing holding the trainees when a squad leader stepped out of the shadows and moved toward the three. "What are you three doing?"

Alucius again stepped forward and touched the trooper's life thread, swinging the rifles he carried toward the man. The blocky trooper collapsed. Alucius swayed on his feet for a moment. There was clearly a limit to how much of that he could do. He set down the rifles and dragged the man back into the shadows around the corner, then scrambled back and picked up the rifles he'd been lugging.

"What did you do?" whispered Zerdial.

"Hit him with a rifle," Alucius lied. "He wasn't expecting it. Come on. We need to get these back to the trainees. You two will need to follow me in and stand ready with your rifles. I'm hoping they'll be reasonable, but . . . some might not."

When Alucius walked back into the barracks section holding the trainee captives, Zerdial and Anslym followed with the loaded rifles. They set them on the stones, except their own weapons.

"Form up! Listen up!"

Alucius could hear the mutterings.

". . . some sort of night drill?"

". . . sounds like the new squad leader . . . tough . . ."

"Just form up!" Alucius snapped, knowing he was tired and losing patience. And he had a great deal more yet to do.

The trainees milled into formation. There was an aura of sullenness, not that Alucius had expected much else. He looked over the captive trainees—roughly forty. "No one's told you. The torque collars don't work anymore. I'm leading anyone who wants out of the Matrite forces and who wants to go to the Iron Valleys. I've got rifles here. The rules are simple. You obey me as senior squad leader until we're back in the Iron Valleys. There's no way you'll make it, unless we do it as if we were a horse company."

For a long moment, there was silence.

"Why should we follow you?" came a voice.

Alucius smiled. He could tell it wasn't a friendly smile. "Because I'm not in the mood to let anyone out who doesn't. Because I'm tougher, and I know more than any of you, and because anyone with any brains would know this is your only chance. You want to go—you get suited up and line up one at a time. You come to the door, and you get your rifle. We form up without a word in the corridor, and march quietly to the stables. We saddle up, and we ride out."

"What if someone tries to stop us?"

"In the corridor, I'll take care of it. Once we're mounted, we may have to fire. You only fire those rifles if and when I command. I'm going back to the Iron Valleys. Anyone who wants to come . . . suit up. We may have to fight our way out of Madrien, but we'll never have a better chance."

"What about the collars?"

"Oh, those. I told you already. They don't work any longer. Alucius smiled beneath the skull-mask, then fished his own from his tunic and held up the broken sections. "Anyone else want theirs removed?"

Finally, a thin man stepped forward, from one the third rank back. "I'll see. Living death here anyway."

Alucius snapped the heavy clasp and handed the torque back to the man. "Make sure you have your bedrolls and riding gear."

Even before he finished speaking, men scrambled into their training uniforms and lined up to receive their weapons. And to have their torques removed. Not one chose to remain.

Less than a fifth of a glass later, Alucius looked over the ranks of trainees, hoping he could keep them under control. "Remember. No shooting unless I tell you."

". . . deserve it," muttered someone.

"They may deserve it, but they're a lot less likely to send several companies after us if they wake up and find us gone, and no one's dead, than if we leave bodies all over the place. And we have a long way to ride."

Even before he finished speaking, he could sense the general agreement. Now, all he had to do was get them out into the stables, saddled, and on their way.

"For now, Zerdial and Anslym are going to be acting squad leaders. The first half of the group—back to there"— Alucius pointed—"will answer to Zerdial, the last half to Anslym. The first half will set up a perimeter line on foot just inside the front of the stables, while the second half will saddle up. Then, you'll switch. Once everyone's saddled, we'll take some extra mounts, and load ammunition from the armory, and ration packs from stores. Then we'll leave. Let's go. Quietly."

The column walked down the corridor.

No one approached until they had just entered the court-yard when a duty sentry walked around the corner of the barracks. His eyes widened, and then his mouth opened. Al-ucius struck with his Talent, moving like a streak toward the trooper, fast enough to catch him and lower him to the ground back against the wall and out of obvious sight.

"Keep moving to the stables," he hissed.

". . . no one moves that fast . . . "

"Quietly," he whispered, taking the sentry's rifle, and hur-rying back to the head of the column.

Alucius was only three steps into the stable when the duty stable boy scurried forward. "Sir?"

"Night maneuvers and training," Alucius explained. "We'll also need four packhorses. What do you have?"

"There are six, but Captain Julyn—"

"We only need four, and I'm sure the captain can find others. We're needed down south immediately." Alucius pro-jected authority.

"Ah . . . yes, sir. I'll get them ready."

Alucius took a quick look at the trainees inside the door of the stable, then walked to a point a third of the way down the line. He pointed to his right, at the larger group. "We don't need all of you. Those over here, go get your mounts saddled."

"Anslym, you get saddled, too. I've got a task for you when you're ready."

"Yes, sir."

That left six men. Alucius stood with then, scanning the quiet courtyard with both eyes and Talent, but nothing moved.

Before long, the green troopers of Zerdial's group—a militia-sized squad, overlarge for a Matrite squad—were leading their mounts forward.

"Zerdial, take over guarding here."

Alucius reclaimed Wildebeast, then returned to the front of the stable where the stable boy had brought forth the pack-horses. He pointed to two of the troopers who stood by their mounts and who felt solid. "You two, each of you take a packhorse and follow me. Mount up outside."

He turned, relieved to see Anslym returning with his mount. "Anslym?"

"Yes, sir?"

"I'm going to ask you to take two men and the other two packhorses back to the armory. Get a few more rifles, but mostly ammunition, and load them. Don't skimp, but don't overload them, either. I left the armory unlocked. Can you do that?"

Anslym nodded.

Alucius looked at him coldly.

"Yes, sir," the trainee said quickly.

"Good. Load them and bring them back here. We're going for stores."

The small stores room was off the side of the armory, and one of Jesorak's keys worked there, as well. If it hadn't, the lock was so flimsy Alucius probably could have pried it loose, but the key was quieter.

The ration packs in stores held food far less appealing than the normal Matrite fare, if still good and edible—dried meat, rubbery dried fruit, white cheese that could have substituted for building stones. But they were accessible without going back into the training center—and they were packed to travel.

Alucius made it back to the stables before Anslym did with the spare ammunition and rifles, and he waited, mounted, nervously scanning the courtyard, wondering why he had seen no more troopers or sentries.

Something moved to the south, and he had the rifle aimed before he realized that it was Anslym.

"Any problems?" Alucius asked.

"No, sir."

Alucius eased Wildebeast to the outside front of the stables. "Get out here and mount up. Quiet as you can."

The sounds of hoofs on the stones, and occasional grunts and whispers sounded like thunder to Alucius, and he kept scanning the courtyard, still quiet, even after both his make-shift squads were mounted.

Once everyone seemed there and mounted, he eased Wildebeast out to the head of the rough column, then turned to look back as he ordered, "Column forward." A wave of dizziness swept over him, and he had to struggle to remain erect in the saddle. He was exhausted, but there was no time for resting.

The last man had actually ridden out of the gates and the entire column was moving northward toward the river road that would lead to the north-south high road, before Alucius could sense movement in the courtyard.

Why had it taken so long? He'd fully expected to have had to fire at least some shots—or had some fired at them.

Suddenly, he smiled. First, along the way, he'd taken out most of the sentries, one by one. And second, most troopers had learned not to question too much so long as things looked normal. No one had been running around or yelling or shooting. Perhaps the trainees had looked awkward, but they'd done what troopers did, and that seemed to have been enough.

Still . . . they had a long, long way to ride, with minimal supplies and no grain for their mounts, and no coin. Through the intermittent waves of dizziness that washed over him, Alucius studied the road ahead, the eternastone glow even more pronounced to him than ever before, despite the faint stars that flashed across his vision, stars that reminded him of how little rest he had had, and of how much he had asked of his body.

Was the greater glow of the ancient stones because he was more accomplished with his Talent, or because of what he had done in the underground chamber?

He kept turning his head and checking, but no one followed, not that he could see or sense, but he did not relax, even after the two close-to-militia-sized squads turned westward on the river levee high road, and then northward on the north-south high road. In the darkness, not surprisingly, they saw no one.

Once they were almost at the north end of the bridge crossing the River Vedra, a swath of darkness beneath the white eternastone of the high road, Alucius turned in the saddle and looked back at Hieron.

Even with his Talent-sense, there was no sign of the pink threads, the web that had centered on the Matrial's residence, and the deeper life web that filled the sky seemed a little brighter, a little more colorful. Was it? Or was he hoping it was? Or was it because it wasn't washed out by the garish purple-pink. He didn't know. He also hoped that the disappearance of the Matrial would add to the consternation and confusion more than proof of her death would have.

He turned and looked at the enternastone road ahead. They had a long journey ahead, and he was making it with largely untested troopers. He stifled a yawn. He had to stay awake for a time longer. He just had to. He steadied himself by putting one hand on the front rim of the saddle.

118

Northeast of Iron Stem, Iron Valleys

In the late evening, Royalt looked at the stove, cold and unneeded in summer, then at the two women on the couch to his right. Abruptly, he stood and, without a word, walked toward the front door.

Behind him, the two women exchanged glances.

"He's been like that every since he brought the flock in," Lucenda murmured.

Royalt ignored the statement and stepped out onto the wide porch that faced east.

For a long time, he stood at the railing and looked into the night at the dark mass to the east that was the Aerlal Plateau. Then he went down the stone steps and walked south until he was clear of the house. There, he turned west and studied the stars, still without speaking.

In time, he returned to the porch.

Wendra and Lucenda stood there waiting. Neither spoke.

"Something's happened," he said slowly. "I felt it at midday, and it's still there."

"Are you all right, Father?" asked Lucenda.

Royalt laughed softly. "It's not me, daughter. The world's changed, and I don't know how, or what that change is, only that it's happened. There was a flash in my wristguard, pinkishlike, so bright it shone through my tunic. Then it was gone. I'd like to think it's something to do with Alucius, something good. I don't know. I thought, if I came outside, in the quiet, I'd learn or feel something." He shook his head slowly. "It's the same as earlier. It's different, and I don't know how."

"What about Alucius?" asked Wendra.

"How is it different? Can you even say how it feels?" pressed Lucenda, her words tumbling over those of Wendra.

Royalt turned to Wendra. "He's still alive and well. Beyond that . . . I cannot say." Then he looked at his daughter. "It's as if an unseen darkness had been lifted, a darkness none of us knew was there."

"An unseen darkness? It's a Talent thing?"

"More than that, I feel." He fingered his chin. "Tomorrow, I may ride over to see Kustyl and see if he felt what I did."

"Are you sure . . . I mean . . ."

"You're worried about the dark ties. No . . . this is different." Royalt smiled, an expression that was simultaneously hopeful, wistful, and worried. "This is different. The dark ties are stronger, and yet not so heavy, either, but that is not it. Not at all."

Lucenda and Wendra exchanged glances.

Royalt looked back at the darkness of the plateau, again, without speaking.

119

In the gray light just before dawn, Alucius studied the all-too-casual bivouac.

He'd had the men ride only three glasses the night before, a time sufficient to take them across the River Vedra and far enough north that they could find a place to make camp in the wooded hills leading to the pass through the Coast Range without getting too far off the high road. And, he had to admit, that had been as far as he could have gone without falling out of the saddle. At the end, he'd been holding on to the saddle rim with one hand all the time. After a short night's sleep, he didn't feel that much better.

"All right! Form up on foot!" He projected both voice and Talent-backed authority. "With your sabres!"

He stood quietly until he had the two squads in formation—a decent formation, if not outstanding. Then he spoke. "We're going to have to fight. We can't spend as much time training as I'd like. But we will go through sabre blade exercises every morning, and we will practice wheeling to a firing line a few times every morning. That practice just might save your life.

"We have to travel four hundred odd vingts to reach the border, and that's by the high road. Do you want to get slaughtered on the way? Or to be, if you're lucky, one of a handful to slink home? Or do you want to be able to get there with the fewest casualties and with your heads held high?" His eyes raked across the trooper trainees. "If there's any one of you who thinks he can do a better job . . . just step forward."

No one did.

He paused. "All right. You've got a quarter glass to eat—if you want to. That ration pack has to last you all day. Then we'll start the sabre exercises on foot. After that, we'll mount and do a series of wheeling maneuvers, and then we'll get on the road. Dismissed."

". . . still a friggin' squad leader . . ."

". . . quit flapping your jaw . . ."

". . . want to go home?"

Alucius repressed a sigh.

He hoped that they could make good time on the road, but he knew that, before long, he'd have to find either better forage, or grain, or both for their mounts. All the time now, they'd have to watch for messengers and trained Matrite companies out to stop them.

He did sigh, then.

120

In the late afternoon of the second full day of their ride north from Hieron, Alucius could tell that both mounts and men were tiring. They had passed only two traders' wagons, both headed southward, and neither trader— one a woman and the other a man, seemingly a Deforyan, with his red jacket—had done more than nod at the troopers. Was Deforya the only outside land that traded in Madrien? Alucius still didn't understand all the trading rules, but he knew that the reasons existed—somewhere. Just as he still didn't understand why the sprite and the soarers had helped him, but knew they had their reasons. Was it just because he had been the only one to destroy the pink-purple crystal? Would he ever see another soarer, except from a distance?

Because he needed to concentrate on the tasks at hand, he pushed the thoughts away and looked at Zerdial, riding beside him. "We should be looking for some place near the road to stop. There should be a way station somewhere ahead, and, with luck, there won't be any troopers on the road right now."

"Why do you want to stay on the high road, sir?" asked Zerdial. "Some of the men had wondered."

"And they asked you to find out if their squad leader had a reason, or if I happened to be less than thinking?"

Zerdial looked down.

"Because it's the fastest way to get where we're going. Also, it's the fastest way for the Matrites to send a message or troopers. That's why we've been camping beside the road and setting guards. If they do send a messenger, we can stop him from getting word to any companies to the north. And we can travel faster, for a while anyway, than can any companies coming after us."

Zerdial looked unconvinced.

Alucius smiled. "Zerdial . . . what do you think is happening in Hieron and elsewhere in Madrien?"

"Happening?"

"For more than a hundred years, men in Madrien have worn those torques. They've had to do what the women with the control belts wanted. Do you think that an arms commander is going to risk sending a company of troopers out of Hieron after us right now?"

"Then why do we have to worry at all?"

"There's something called the auxiliaries. They're mostly women, and they're all trained, and some of them are very, very good. I saw them wipe out five companies of Southern Guards. They won't know that we're coming—unless a messenger gets in front of us. While the Matrite officers probably won't risk sending a regular company out of Hieron after us, it won't be long before they will risk sending a messenger. And that message will tell the auxiliaries and companies stationed on the northeastern borders that we're deserters. We don't need to face that, or any forces that we can avoid. When we get to Arwyn, we're going to have to go through there late at night, and quickly. Then, we'll only have to worry about whatever forces they have set up as perimeter guards. Near the Westerhills."

"Perimeter guards? I thought the Matrites were in the Iron Valleys, weren't they?"

"There were so many attacks in the south that they had to pull back," Alucius said. "They pulled out of the Iron Valleys, for now, anyway. Since the torques don't work, it will be a while before they attack again, but I wouldn't count on it being more than a few years."

"But you said . . ." Zerdial's voice contained more than a little confusion.

"Right now, there will be a lot of confusion, and some men will probably try to even things with women who have been overzealous. But the fact is that life isn't bad for most people in Madrien, and when everything settles down, I don't know that much will change. I could be wrong, but I think that in time the Iron Valleys will have exactly the same problems we had two years ago—enemies to the west and enemies to the south. The ones to the south may be more dangerous, but you can never tell."

Alucius smiled. "Whatever may happen, right now, we need to find a place to stop. Send out a couple of your best scouts to replace the ones there now."

"Yes, sir."

Alucius nodded in response. The first two days had not been bad, but the next ones were likely to be more difficult.

121

A **woman with flawless** white skin and violet eyes walked toward Alucius, smiling, beckoning, suggesting that all manner of delights were within his reach. Yet Alucius hesitated, stepping back, feeling a deep chill from somewhere.

The woman beckoned again, and Alucius deferred. A bolt of purple flame flashed from her fingers, and he threw up a sabre that had appeared in his hand. Flame sprayed past him, burning his arms, searing his face—

"Sir! Wake up!

"What?" Alucius shook his head, trying to emerge from the dream, and the all-too-real feel of fire singeing his arms and his face. His fingers brushed his forehead, hot and damp.

"Rider's coming hard."

Alucius bolted upright, grasping for his boots, and his tunic and jacket. Then he grabbed his rifle, following the sentry whose name he did not recall, hurrying down the gentle slope of the redstone lane from the way station to the high road.

Overhead in the night sky, Selena was but a crescent, hardly enough to add to the summer starlight, and Asterta had long since set.

"Can hear a long ways at night, sir," the sentry said as he caught up with Alucius. "From the south, I thought, sir."

Alucius stopped, listened. Through the darkness, Alucius could hear the sets of hoofs. Sets of hoofs? He cast out his Talent-senses. The rider had a spare mount with him, and he was pushing both mounts.

The sound of hoofs grew louder, and before long Alucius could make out the shadowy figures of two horses and a single rider above the Talent-based glow of the eternastones of the high road.

"Halt!" Alucius called, hoping that the trooper would stop, knowing he would not. As he spoke, he raised his rifle.

The messenger flattened himself against his mount, and aimed the mount directly toward Alucius as if to make himself a smaller target in the darkness.

Using both Talent and skill, Alucius sighted and fired through the darkness, a darkness that was at most twilight to him. *Crack!*

The sickening void that swept over and by Alucius told him that he'd been accurate.

"Get his mounts!" snapped Alucius.

"His mounts?"

"He's dead. He had a spare horse."

The horses slowed, almost immediately, because the gelding was dragging the rider by one stirrup. Both Alucius and the sentry ran forward, the sentry grasping the rider's mount by the side of the bridle.

Alucius worked the dead trooper's booted foot from the stirrup and dragged his body—one-handed—to the side of the road. There, he took the dispatch case, hoping that it held a message worth the life of the messenger.

"Bring the mounts to the way station, and then have someone come down here and bring the body back up and out of sight of the road," Alucius called to the sentry.

"Yes, sir."

Carrying the dispatch case, Alucius walked back toward the way station, one of those stations unmanned with but a spring and long covered sheds with pallets for men and a rude barn for mounts.

As he entered the waystation and headed for the hearth, he could hear the sentry whispering.

"Need some help . . . one shot . . . in pitch darkness . . ."

". . . herder . . . see why you don't mess with herders?"

"How'd they capture him?"

"Wall fell on him, someone said . . ."

Alucius brought the case to the red coals in the hearth. There, he added a few pieces of thin wood, and waited for them to catch. After a time, red flames began to flicker up, and he opened the case, extracted the message, and began to read. The message was to a Captain Grenyl, in Arwyn. He skipped over the salutations.

> . . . a group of captives has escaped from the training center. They are led by a renegade squad leader with combat experience. He is said to be fearless and an excellent tactician . . . cannot emphasize how dangerous he is. You may have to call up the auxiliaries to ensure he is stopped, if he is indeed headed in your direction . . . should be halted at all costs . . .
>
> In the Name of the Matrial Eternal

Alucius did not recognize the name of the arms commander who had signed it, but his knowledge of officers' names had never extended above the rank of overcaptain.

The order in the "Name of the Matrial Eternal" nagged at him, as if there were something that the words signified beyond the rote.

The thought behind the message also bothered him, and he wondered if he'd been too charitable in his assessment of the women of Madrien. A group of forcibly detained captives who wanted to return home were so dangerous that they had to be eliminated "at all costs."

He could use the message—and he would. In the morning, he'd have all the men, those that could, read the message and tell the others.

In the meantime, there was little else he could do. He replaced the message in its case and headed back to his bedroll, hoping he could get some rest, wondering if he'd ever get a good night's sleep again. And hoping he did not dream once more the way he had, of the beautiful and deadly Matrial—for who else could have haunted his dreams? Absently, he wondered if she had indeed looked the way he had dreamed her—and if so, how he could have known.

122

In the hazy sunshine of the late afternoon in summer, Alucius shifted his weight in the saddle, before scanning the high road ahead, then the rolling hills to the east, hills that held woods and occasional holdings, and then to the west, where the land looked much the same as that to the east. High puffy clouds rose over the Coast Range that was more than thirty vingts to the west. He and his two squads were a little more than five vingts from Arwyn, and he had hoped that the scouts he had sent out near midday had been able to find what he had asked them to look for.

Less than a half vingt ahead, he saw a sole rider in Matrite colors, clearly one of the scouts. Sending them out alone was a risk, if they were seen, because that was almost never done by Matrite forces, but four men sent separately could scout far more than a road patrol of four could.

Before long, Zerdial and the older trooper, probably a former militia scout, from his appearance, rode toward Alucius.

"Ralzyr has a place, sir," Zerdial called.

Alucius motioned for the two to ride alongside him. He blotted his forehead with the back of his sleeve. "Tell me about it."

"It's a little farther from the high road than you wanted, sir, almost half a vingt to the west and not quite two vingts ahead. There's only one lane in . . ." As Ralzyr explained, Alucius listened and tried to visualize the terrain. When the scout had finished, Alucius nodded and said, "That sounds as good as anything." He looked at Zerdial. "Would you have someone ask Anslym to join us?"

"Yes, sir."

While he and Zerdial waited for Anslym to ride up from the rear, Alucius cast out his Talent-senses once more, but the road ahead was clear. Over the more than six days they had been riding, they had seen but a scattering of people on the roads, and all had been traders. As he considered the high roads in the Iron Valleys, he realized that the same had been true of those as well. Yet the high roads went everywhere.

Had there been that many more people in Corus when they had been built? There had to have been, but he guessed that in the more fertile areas, such as Madrien, the signs of abandoned hamlets and steads had vanished. He had thought that the depopulation he had seen in the Iron Valleys had occurred just there, because the weather had changed so much, but his involuntary travels were showing him that the same thing had happened everywhere as a result of the Cataclysm.

"Sir?" Anslym had eased his mount in beside Alucius on the left. Zerdial rode on his right.

"Thank you. I wanted you both to understand what we have to do. We need fodder and grain for the mounts and more provender for the troopers, or we won't make it back home. But how we get it is important. Zerdial's scout has located a holding that looks prosperous and is not close to others. There are two things we need to accomplish in taking this holding. We don't want anyone to escape, and, if at all possible, we don't want anyone killed—either in our squads or on the holding."

Both squad leaders looked mildly skeptical.

"If anyone escapes, we'll have to fight the auxiliaries from Arwyn, or end up spending weeks tracking through back roads to get home. The more time we spend in Madrien, the more of our troopers that are likely to get killed. If we kill their people, especially people who aren't troopers, there's going to be an outcry and more troopers—regular and auxiliaries—chasing us."

This time, Zerdial and Anslym nodded.

"So we'll have to sweep in with force, but leave one squad back to cover the lanes and exits . . ." Alucius went on to explain what he wanted from each squad.

He found himself more and more nervous as they neared the holding, something he hadn't anticipated. Was that because he was in charge, and there was no one else responsible?

The two squads stopped, at his command, just short of a woodlot that provided cover. There, Alucius turned to Anslym. "You know what to do."

"Yes, sir."

Alucius nodded to Zerdial, then moved to the edge of the lane. "First squad, forward!"

His Talent-senses out, Alucius kept close behind the first riders who swept down the lane and into the holding. Even before the troopers reached the yard area, someone left by the rear door and began to run for the woodlot—as Alucius had half-suspected would happen. Within moments, he had Wildebeast around the dwelling and in position to cut her off, his rifle out. He raised the rifle. "Move and you're dead!"

The woman didn't reply, but turned and sprinted toward the stone wall less than five yards away.

He hated to do what he had to, but he'd hate it even more if the woman escaped or if someone found out what he was truly able to do. As he swung toward the woman, he reached out with his Talent, and just barely touched her life web thread. He swung his rifle as if he had clubbed her, and she went down like an unbalanced and unsupported sack of flour, and he was practically on top of her unconscious form before two of Zerdial's troopers were close enough to see anything. "Watch the rear door!" He snapped.

He could tell there was no one in the stable or the trimly kept and brown-painted wooden barn, but he could sense someone in the holding fumbling with something.

"Shoot and she's as good as dead!" he called, turning Wildebeast, and riding straight toward the rear door.

In a sense it was foolish, but he barely reined up before he flung himself from the saddle and through the door, lashing out with his Talent at the gray-haired man who was raising the rifle. He did strike the Talent-felled man with his own rifle butt, but not terribly hard.

Two girls—red-headed and blond—stood frozen in one corner of the kitchen, where a white-haired woman stood before them, trying to shield them.

"We're not going to hurt anyone," Alucius snapped, "not so long as no one tries to attack us. We need forage and provender."

"You'll have to kill me first," said the white-haired woman.

"Why?" asked Alucius. "We're not going to hurt anyone."

"You already killed them!"

"No, I didn't. They'll both wake up with headaches."

"Sir!" called the two troopers who burst into the house.

"In the kitchen."

Alucius waited, then gestured. "Tie them all up, but try not to hurt them. Tie up the man who's in the hall, too."

He went back outside, where he hitched Wildebeast to a post by the back door, and then walked to the fallen woman—the holder. He was scarcely surprised to find the pistol inside the gray-haired woman's vest.

There were only five people in the holding. Two girls— one about ten and one about twelve, an aging white-haired woman, the gray-haired holder, and the gray-haired man who wore a torque. Alucius judged him as a former Matrite trooper.

He had the girls tied, hand and foot, and placed on their beds, with a trooper to watch them, and the same for the older woman. The holder and the man, her husband, Alucius gathered, were tied to wooden straight-backed chairs in the kitchen.

After giving instructions to Zerdial and sending for Anslym's squad, Alucius returned to the kitchen where the woman had begun to rouse herself. She said nothing for a time, just glared at him.

"So . . . are you going to be brutes, now that you're free of the torques?" The woman wriggled in her bonds.

Alucius judged her for a former Matrite officer, or possibly one still in the auxiliaries. She clearly understood that the torques no longer functioned.

"I have no intention of being a brute. Nor do I have any intention of letting my troopers be brutes."

"If you kill us, every woman and every auxiliary in every hamlet and town on the high road will come after you," she promised.

"I am not so sure of that. The torques no longer work. You know that."

"That's nonsense," claimed the gray-haired man bound in the chair beside her. Alucius hadn't realized that he also had recovered.

Alucius gestured to the trooper. "Blindfold him."

"More brutality."

After walking behind the man's chair, Alucius extended a thin tendril of that Talent-darkness, although he doubted he needed it, before reaching down.

"No!" screamed the woman, involuntarily. Clearly, she didn't want to risk her husband's life.

Alucius smiled, ruefully, at the illustration of how old habits and reactions died hard. He snapped the weld on the torque and lifted the entire collar away from the bound man's neck, then slipped the blindfold off, holding the broken torque before the older man. "I'll leave it for you to examine, once we've left."

The man and woman both looked as ashen as the dull silver gray of the broken torque.

"You may believe me or not, but I would have preferred not to forage off your land and holding, or anyone else's, but we lack enough provender to reach the Westerhills, and we are being far more gentle than were your troopers in my land."

"*What* are you?" Her voice was low, just above a whisper.

"Just a man, a squad leader who happened to be fortunate."

The two captives exchanged glances, a shared expression that expressed great disbelief with Alucius's words.

Alucius turned as Anslym entered the dwelling's kitchen.

"They have one wagon, sir, and two horses," Anslym reported.

"Is there enough grain? Enough other supplies?"

"Be tight, sir, but I think so."

"Load all that you can without overburdening the horses."

"They'll stop you in Arwyn," the woman holder promised, "and they'll hound you to the ends of Corus."

"That is possible," Alucius said. "It is also possible that they may find other matters taking their attention." He gestured toward the broken torque he had laid upon the table.

Then he left the two under guard and walked back outside to check the loading and take a survey of the holding, to make sure that his men—or he—had not overlooked anything. So far as he could tell, there was no sign that anyone else had been at the holding.

By the time everything was loaded, and the squads had rotated and eaten, twilight was beginning to fall across the holding.

"Have them mustered up in order, with the wagon ready to go." Alucius said to the two squad leaders.

"Yes, sir."

He turned and re-entered the dwelling, walking to the kitchen. "Troopers! Outside! Form up! We're heading out!"

Then he waited until only he and the two bound captives were left in the kitchen. He took out his belt knife.

"You going to kill us, now?" asked the woman.

"What gave you that idea?"

"The knife."

"We've taken your weapons, and your mounts, and the supplies we needed. Your girls are fine, and so is your mother. You'll have to untie them. Even so, it's far better treatment than your troopers gave the folk in the Westerhills or in Soulend." Alucius smiled, ruefully.

Then he touched her life thread, just gently.

She swayed in the chair.

"No! I'll kill you . . ." The man's voice was low, but intense.

"Be quiet!" Alucius snapped. "She's just asleep. She'll wake up in a glass or so." He bent down and made a cut in the rope binding the unconscious woman, then worked the bounds off her hands. "When she wakes up, she can untie her feet and untie you. By then, we'll be far enough away that whatever will be . . . will be."

"Who are you?"

"I told you." Alucius straightened and replaced his belt knife in its sheath. "I'm sorry we had to impose at all, but the Matrial brought this on you. If she hadn't attacked the Iron Valleys, none of this would have happened." He nodded. "Good night." The two might tell tales of what he had done with his Talent, but, if his plans went well, it would be a long time before those tales reached anywhere, and there was no real proof. If all did not go well . . . then, it mattered little.

He walked out of the house and mounted Wildebeast. "Column forward!"

Once more, in the fading light, Alucius scanned the lane ahead, and beyond it, the way back to the high road, but there were no signs of traffic on either, and the troopers stationed to watch the high road had reported neither troopers nor messengers.

"With the wagon, we almost look like a real Matrite company," Zerdial said.

"A resupply convoy, a very small one," Alucius suggested. He just hoped they didn't have to meet up with a real convoy, not with his men understrength and undertrained. He looked ahead toward Arwyn, straining to make out the lights of the town through the deepening twilight.

Almost a glass had passed, and Alucius's contingent was traveling in full darkness when they passed the roadstone that indicated two vingts to Arwyn. Even stretching his Talent, Alucius could sense no troopers out along the high road, but the sound of hoofs on stone, and the occasional creaking of the wagon seemed to blare the falsity of the impression he was trying to create.

Even so, his troopers reached the intersection with the lower high road to Iron Stem without running into travelers or opposition.

"Column! To the right!" Alucius ordered.

The trainee troopers swung right, and the wagon followed.

As he rode eastward, on the high road that split the town of Arwyn, Alucius glanced at the slivers of light that indicated lamps behind shuttered windows throughout the town. The scent of flowers drifted past him on the light breeze, and he could hear occasional murmurs or laughs.

The seeming juxtaposition of those sounds with the now-useless torques of the Matrial and the fact that life was apparently so peaceful that many folk had yet to discover that the torques were useless brought home to Alucius how much of life rested on belief and illusion.

Ahead, to his right, and less than ten yards south of the east-running high road, Alucius could sense a pair of women in the shadows on the south side of the high road. With ears and Talent, he strained to catch their words.

"Troopers . . . looks like a resupply convoy . . ."

"Late for them . . . and only one wagon . . . wonder why they didn't stop at the compound?"

". . . tell the auxiliary commander in the morning . . . no one could do anything now, anyway . . ."

While Alucius didn't like their words, anything he did would make things worse, and doubtless by morning the family that they had raided would have gotten word to Arwyn in any case. He and his troopers would have to travel until close to midnight and do with a short night's sleep, in order to keep ahead of any possible pursuit.

They were also traveling a high road Alucius knew little about, except its destination—Iron Stem—and they'd have to ride with a parley banner of some sort once they reached the border—if they made the border without incident. Or he'd have to come up with a better plan.

The last thing he wanted was to have escaped Madrien and then get shot by his own folk.

123

By midmorning on Quattri, two and a half days after slipping through Arwyn, Alucius was certain that at least two Matrite companies were following them, although the Matrites were at least two or three vingts behind Alucius's small force. The sun was beating down, and Alucius was blotting his forehead all too often as he turned in the saddle, trying to check the terrain, and then looking forward to see what lay ahead as they neared the Westerhills. The well-kept Madrien hamlets were farther apart, and the few inhabitants scarcely even looked at the troopers as they headed eastward—presumably toward the outposts near the border—or because they had been warned, although Alucius thought that unlikely, since he sensed neither fear nor worry.

His Talent had given him a vague sense of forces ahead, but so far, his scouts had not reported anything. Alucius had no doubts that they were there—somewhere beyond the clear reach of his Talent. What he had to balance was the speed his force could make on the high road against the maneuverability—but slowness and danger of being trapped—afforded by leaving the high road.

More than once, he wished they were on the midroad that ran from Harmony to Soulend, where he had a far better understanding of the ground, but his force would have run even more risks and dangers by trying to move that far north because they would have had to ride more than another two hundred vingts to reach Iron Valley territory.

After blotting his forehead yet again, Alucius glanced back in the direction of Arwyn. The Matrites weren't any closer—yet. Then he looked forward, where he could see a scout moving quickly toward them. That could only mean that there were Matrite forces ahead, and probably that they'd used a fast messenger to take the back roads that Alucius did not know.

He turned in the saddle. "Zerdial! Anslym!"

As he waited for the two squad leaders to join him, he studied the hills to the east, hills that were slowly becoming more rugged—and more heavily forested—as they neared the true Westerhills and the traditional border between Madrien and the Iron Valleys. He concentrated harder. His Talent-senses revealed that the Matrite forces held the road and a line running from the road northward, and that there was a larger concentration of troopers even farther to the north.

The scout and the two squad leaders arrived at almost the same time.

"Sir!" the scout began. "They've got two full companies on the road, and on the hills to the north. There's a swamp on the south side."

"How far ahead?"

"Two vingts, a little more maybe."

Alucius could sense the companies from Arwyn moving up their pace, as if they knew that they had the inexperienced troopers—and their very inexperienced commander—in a tight position. He studied the ground to the north. It was totally exposed, except for a slight ridge that ran mostly north, but slightly northeast. The ground looked firm. The high road dropped ahead, not much, but a good three yards over perhaps a hundred, then ran level for a half vingt through a stream valley, crossing the stream about six hundred yards ahead. The stream was probably what drained the swamp that lay ahead on the right side of the road.

He concentrated on trying to find a gap in the Matrite lines. From what he could tell there wasn't such a way. Was there another way, a way around, or a means to exploit the Matrite formation?

"Could they see us from where they are when we reach that bridge there?"

"No, sir."

Alucius could have created an illusion that his squad was moving north along the ridge, but then everyone would know that he had Talent—a lot of Talent, and what sort of life would that lead to when—and if—he returned to the Iron Valleys?

"What about the trees—the forest—on the hills to the north, short of where they are?"

"They're scattered, like in the Westerhills. Easy to ride through, not much undergrowth. Hard to shoot through, though."

"How much of their force is on the north side of the road?"

"Maybe like half, spread out in a line."

Alucius thought.

"What do you want us to do, sir?" asked Zerdial.

"For now . . . we keep moving, on the high road. There might just be a way to do this, if they handle their troopers the way they usually do."

As they began to ride up the gentle and long incline, behind which the Matrite troops waited, Alucius turned to the squad leaders. "I want your squads in as close as possible. You see that bush up ahead, about a hundred yards below the crest there?"

"Yes, sir."

"They're bunched to protect the road, but they're over the crest where they can't see us. They'll probably have a scout watching, but it will take a few moments for him to report.

When we reach that clump of bushes up there on the right, we'll make a column turn and move at a fast trot to the north. They'll leave some of their force to hold the road. You can be sure of that."

Zerdial and Anslym looked puzzled.

"We're going to look like we're making for that hill, to run around them . . . but once they're moving, we'll cut back between their forces. That's why I want the troopers close together in each of your squads."

"What if they don't follow?" asked Zerdial.

"What about the wagon?" That was Anslym.

"If they don't follow, then we ride north until we're clear and then head west." Alucius doubted that would happen, but it could. "Have the wagon come with us, but have the drivers ready to switch to their mounts, if they have to." They were close enough to the Westerhills that Alucius wasn't about to deny the drivers the same chance at escape as the others. "This will work," Alucius promised. "We'll get shot at, and we'll have to shoot at them while we're moving, but . . . it's far better than trying a stand-up battle." And what his men would not see would be the illusion that would make the difference—he hoped.

Anslym and Zerdial exchanged brief looks, expressions conveying extreme doubt.

"Could either of you gotten us this far?" asked Alucius quietly.

"Ah . . . no, sir."

"Have I gotten anyone killed yet?"

"No, sir."

"Then, let's get on with it. Go and form your squads into tight formations. Once we make the turn, I'll call for a fast trot. I'd guess we'll travel almost a vingt, and then we'll make a sudden right turn, and drive through the weakest spot in their lines. We'll keep moving until we're well clear and back on the high road. They may pursue for a time, but they won't go too far. There are bound to be militia troopers along the high road somewhere in the Westerhills—or farther east."

Alucius added a touch of command assurance, boosted ever so slightly with a touch of Talent.

"Yes, sir."

The two turned their mounts to head back to their squads.

Alucius sent forth a Talent-probe. As before, and as he had suspected, the Matrite forces were concentrated across the road, with a thinner line running northward to another concentration at the base of the hill a vingt to the north of the high road. He intended to give the impression of trying to ride around the Matrite line to the north.

He reached up and massaged his forehead, then blotted the sweat off his brow to keep it from oozing into the corners of his eyes. He glanced at the road head. Less than two hundred yards to go to the turning point—the decision point.

Looking back over his shoulder, he could see, that whatever their doubts, his squad leaders had tightened up the formation of each of their squads. Ahead, the Matrite forces remained out of sight over the gentle rise. Slowly, he eased Wildebeast forward so that he was riding with the first rank of the van, studying the road ahead, and, occasionally, the troopers behind.

Finally, after much less time than seemed to have passed, Wildebeast carried Alucius abreast of the clump of bushes. He moistened his lips, then half-turned and ordered, "Column left!"

Then he turned Wildebeast into the hock-high grass beside the road, heading parallel to the rise, slightly eastward, but mostly north. As he did, he did his best to create his first Talent-illusion—that of a full squad forming into battle order and remaining on the high road, while the other two squads moved northward and away from the high road.

The two squads rode a hundred yards northward, and nothing happened. Two hundred yards, and still there was no movement from the Matrite troopers.

Juggling the illusions and trying to sense where the Matrites and their auxiliaries were intensifying a growing headache for Alucius. He just hoped he could hold all the illusions together long enough.

His two actual squads were almost halfway to the hill when Alucius could sense movement among the Matrites—but only in the company holding the hill.

"Sir?" asked Zerdial.

"Not yet." Alucius barely managed not to snap. Riding, keeping track of where forces were with his Talent, and holding the illusion—all at once—were taking their toll on him. He was already tired. And now he needed yet another illusion.

He concentrated, trying to create the images of another few squads moving out of the trees to the north, flanking the Matrite company holding the base of the hill—but squads in the black of the Iron Valleys Militia.

Abruptly, the Matrites on the hill wheeled to the north, and about half of the Matrite troopers in the line between the high road and the hill—those closer to the hill—began to move northward.

Alucius—his concentration split in three directions—waited, only for a bit, until he could sense the break in the Matrite line.

"Column right. Rifles ready! Prepare to fire! Follow me! Charge!"

Alucius brought Wildebeast around to the right and then a shade farther to the southeast. At the same time, he tried to throw another illusion—this one just one of empty grasslands, in place of his outnumbered two squads.

His head was splitting, and with each stride Wildebeast took, it pounded more, almost in rhythm to his mount's hoofs hitting the dry ground.

The two squads reached the top of the gentle incline, thundering toward a thin line of Matrite troopers, who looked westward, squinting, as if they could see something, and then could not. Alucius could sense his control of the illusions slipping, and he dropped the concealment illusion.

He was less than a hundred yards from the startled Matrites.

"Hold your fire! Fire at my command!"

At fifty yards, he ordered, "Fire at will!"

The sound of rifles—from both ranks—merged with the muted thunder of hoofs. Alucius aimed and fired as quickly as possible, using his knees and his thoughts to guide Wildebeast. He tried to focus on the point where his squad would strike the thin Matrite line. He could sense the voids of death, but had no idea how many came from his shots at the Matrites and how many from those of his own trainee troopers—knowing only that some of his shots had been accurate.

At less than thirty yards, Alucius holstered his own rifle and called out, "Sabres out! Stay in formation!" He could see the nearest Matrite squad leader trying to move to intercept them.

As Alucius brought his sabre up, he tried to project an image of death and destruction sweeping along with him. At least one Matrite trooper winced, and that was enough for Alucius to get in a cut that disabled the man—at the very least.

Almost as soon as they had begun, the charge and skirmish were over.

Alucius looked back. It looked as though almost all of the trainees had made it through, including, incredibly, the wagon. He realized also that, somewhere along the way, he had lost or released his Talent-illusions, yet no one was chasing them.

Ignoring the pain that stabbed through his skull, and the waves of intermittent dizziness, he pressed out his senses ahead, but he could feel no troopers—Matrite or militia—ahead to the east. He slowed Wildebeast to a walk, and gestured for the others to do the same. After another half vingt they rejoined the high road—empty as far to the east as Alucius could see.

Before long, he knew, they would have to stop to rest the mounts, but he waited until they had covered another half vingt. Then he signaled for a halt. "Stand down for a quarter glass!" He dismounted.

Zerdial and Anslym rode up and joined him.

"How many did we lose?" Alucius asked.

"First squad lost three, sir," Zerdial answered.

"Four, sir," Anslym replied.

Alucius nodded. "I'm sorry for them, but that was about the best we could do."

"How many of theirs, do you think?" Zerdial glanced back westward.

"I'd guess close to twice our losses, but I don't know." Alucius did know that he personally had killed at least five men, and probably a few more.

"How did you know that they'd set their squads like that?" asked Anslym.

"I didn't. If they'd set them differently, we would have had to use another tactic. You just have to do what they don't expect."

Zerdial and Anslym nodded, but Alucius wasn't certain that they really understood.

After the stand-down, which Alucius extended to a half glass because he didn't sense anyone coming from the west, he had the column resume its progress eastward at a slow walk. He didn't want to pressure the mounts too much, but he also didn't want to remain too close to any Matrite force.

It was late afternoon, a glass after the squads had stopped by a stream for water for men and mounts, when Alucius began to sense a rider behind them, a rider with a spare mount. Before long, Anslym rode forward from the rear.

"Sir, there is a rider behind us. He has a spare mount, and he's riding with a white banner."

Tiredly, Alucius cast back his Talent-perceptions, well beyond the rider. There were more riders, indeed, a squad or more.

"Column halt!" Alucius turned to Anslym. "Have your squad wheel and stand ready with rifles."

"Yes, sir."

Alucius could sense his puzzlement.

"There's a good chance that they're also former militia who've realized that the torques don't work and who've deserted and want to go home. But there's no point in taking chances."

"Why are you—"

"I'm going to talk to them because the more troopers we have the better chance we have of getting good terms from the militia command." Alucius turned Wildebeast back to the rear of the column.

There he waited.

The lone rider neared the column slowly, his hands in the open and empty, except for the one hand around the long branch that held a crude banner—a white undergarment.

"I'd like to talk!" called the rider.

Alucius noted the single chevron on the man's sleeve. "You can ride up. We won't shoot."

Warily, the other squad leader approached.

Alucius rode out and stopped five yards short of the older man.

The other noted the double chevrons on Alucius's sleeve, and nodded, almost to himself, before speaking. "Sir? Is it true that you're an Iron Valley officer who's escaped from the Matrites and heading home?"

"Yes." Alucius wasn't about to get into technicalities about what kind of officer he was.

"We'd like to join you. We also got another bunch, two squads, really, that's farther back. They've got a wagon with some provisions and other stuff."

What could he do? After a moment, Alucius said, "You can join us if you want. The rules are simple. I'm in charge. No arguments. No discussion. We act like a regular company until we get to the Iron Valleys, and we stay together until we get good terms from the militia."

"Good terms?"

"Squad leader . . ." Alucius sighed. "What would you do if a company of horse showed up in Matrite uniforms. We don't stick together, and some idiot is going to get the wrong idea." Like claiming that the former militia troopers were deserters, or worse. "At the very least, we can probably get accepted into militia service as a company, and that's with pay, and without torques, and there isn't likely to be that much fighting for the next year or so."

The other considered what Alucius had said. Finally, he

spoke. "That makes sense to me. I think it will to the others."
He grinned ruefully. "Wish we'd have known before you
made that charge."

Alucius waited.

"Your men took out more than two squads, and the captain."

Alucius hadn't even recalled the officer. Then it struck
him, and he grinned back at the other man. "That's the way
it will be."

"Appreciate that. If you'll stay here, we'll rejoin you.
We'll ride in one at a time, arms empty."

"That's a good idea," Alucius agreed.

"We won't be that long. Appreciate the consideration. My
name's Longyl."

"Alucius."

"We'll be back, captain."

Zerdial glanced from the departing squad leader to Alucius. "Is that wise, sir?"

"Not totally. We'll be on guard, but I'll know, long before
they can do anything, if they're up to something. We'll either
have reinforcements—or more dead Matrites." His voice was
tired, almost cold. He could sense the chill it cast over the
two squad leaders.

Now . . . all he had to do was reach the Iron Valleys without getting attacked, negotiate an agreement, and make sure
that the Iron Valley Militia kept it.

All? He laughed, softly, almost bitterly.

124

The ragtag company that Alucius found himself
commanding had finally camped at an abandoned Reillie
stead, less than half a vingt off the high road. The spring
was still good, and between the two wagons, there were
enough provisions for the troopers and grain for the mounts.

In the early evening, after sentries had been set, and one group of scouts had returned, Alucius and his four squad leaders met in the main room of the three-room Reillie hut.

"There's one other thing we need to do," Alucius said to the squad leaders who had joined his force. "I want to remove every torque from your men. We'll keep them to show to the militia."

Longyl nodded. "Proof."

"People like proof," Alucius said. "Also the torques are mostly silver."

That got a nod from Longyl, a short barrel-chested man, who, Alucius suspected, was or would have been a militia squad leader. The other junior squad leader was Egyl, taller than Longyl, but also stocky. Next to them, Zerdial and Anslym—and Alucius himself—probably looked green.

"You're herder born, aren't you?" asked Egyl.

"Yes."

"One reason why you look so young. All herders do."

"That's true," Alucius admitted. It was true, but it also gave Egyl and Longyl a way to explain Alucius's apparent youth to the troopers. "I also entered the militia young."

Both older men nodded.

Alucius got a sense that Longyl was solid to the core—the kind of squad leader that men would follow and who would do his best, and also the kind who wasn't afraid to question a bad order, but tactfully.

"You saw a lot of combat, didn't you?" asked Egyl.

Zerdial looked at the square-jawed Egyl, clearly puzzled by the question.

"Pretty obvious," Egyl explained. "He knows combat tactics. He kept you moving when someone who hadn't seen a lot would have dithered. He saw the weakest spot in our line, and he kept you tight. Most times, that's dangerous, but not with what he had in mind." Egyl looked at Alucius. "Sorry, sir."

Alucius smiled. "It might be for the best that you explained. The two squads I brought were all captive trainees I broke out of Eltema Post. I was there, for reassignment, when the torques failed." Alucius shrugged. "I saw a chance and took it."

Egyl and Longyl actually looked impressed.

"You got two squads of trainees from Hieron to the border, and through four companies?" asked Egyl.

Alucius nodded, although it would have been more accurate to say that he had avoided two companies and broken through two with deception.

"What did you do before you were sent back to Hieron?"

"I started out as a trooper with Fortieth Company. That was after I got captured. Part of something fell on me at Soulend. I was a scout for Third Company in the militia . . ." Alucius gave a summary of his Matrite career, such as it was.

"Shame the militia didn't make you an officer," Longyl said. "You're still our captain."

"Right," added Egyl. "Won't hurt to have a herder speaking for us, either."

After a moment of silence, Alucius asked, "What did the scouts find out?"

"Just like you thought. No sign of a militia encampment near here. Probably at the eastern side of the Westerhills . . ."

"Tomorrow, we'll keep moving, but we'll send scouts out a good two vingts ahead. We'll need that much warning if we see any militia patrols."

"What will you do if we see any?"

"We'll use a white banner," Alucius replied, "but we'll see if we can make first contact from a higher point, hilltop, bluff, cliff, that sort of thing. I don't trust anyone, not the way this war has gone. I don't imagine anyone in the militia would either. But they have to be hurting for troopers—and for information. We've got both." He knew it wouldn't be that simple.

There was little else to be said, and they all knew it. So he nodded and added, "We'll talk in the morning."

Then he watched as the four left the hut, studied them closely from the shadows.

Zerdial glanced back, then shrugged.

"Zerdial?" Egyl gestured to the fresh-faced squad leader.
"Sir?"

Alucius used his Talent to listen.

"You want to stay a squad leader . . . don't look so stupid.
The captain, and you'd better think of him that way, he's
been through more in the last year than most officers see in
a career. You owe your friggin' life to him . . ."

"You don't," Zerdial said.

"You don't get it, do you? Before long, the Matrites would
be killing or putting chains on any man, trooper or not, who
isn't from Madrien. This way, we all got a chance to go
home, and the rest of us want to. Sometimes, I wonder if
you care. You do what the captain says because he scares
you."

"Ah . . ."

"Captain's right. We'll probably have to stay troopers for
a while, but when it's over, we're home, and we're not serving where someone can decide that they don't like what you
did or said and choke you to death before you know what
struck you. Even the Reillies we got, most of them'd stay
with a good captain. The captain rode point on your attack.
Two things. First, he didn't get shot, and second, he killed
a lot of people who could have killed you. You find another
officer who can do that for a year, and I'll eat your sabre."

Zerdial was silent.

"Might be a good thing to tell your friend Anslym that.
Or do you want me to?"

"I'll tell him." After a moment, Zerdial asked, "Is he . . .
the captain . . . that good?"

Egyl laughed. "I spent four years in the militia and three
with the Matrites. Made junior squad leader. He made full
squad leader in two, and he had enough guts to take on the
Matrites in their capital, and enough smarts to take a bunch
of green-assed trooper trainees four hundred vingts through
an enemy land, and he only lost something like seven. He
looked at Longyl and me, and he *knew* who we were and
what we could do. Just like we knew he'd bust his ass for
his men, and break anyone who didn't. You don't shape up,

and he'll break yours. You could be a good squad leader, you know, if you tried harder, and we need good squad leaders."

Zerdial looked down.

In the shadows, Alucius swallowed. Not only was life not simple, but he was making it even harder for himself.

125

Not surprisingly, to Alucius, it was two days later, midmorning on Septi, when the scouts reported finding a militia encampment, right where Egyl had predicted, on the eastern edge of the Westerhills. Egyl, Longyl, and Alucius sat astride their mounts in the warm morning, in the middle of the high road that led to Iron Stem, with Anslym and Zerdial on their mounts, but slightly farther away from the other three.

"They've got an encampment on the stream just east of where the trees end," Egyl was pointing out. "There's a hill-side above that, and it looks like they water the mounts be-low that."

"So we could get their attention there?" asked Alucius. "They aren't running any patrols?"

"None that the scouts could see, and not many tracks in the dust of the high road," Longyl pointed out. "Trees are pines and junipers . . . scattered, but enough cover if we're careful."

"It's like they've left the Westerhills as an unprotected buffer between the Iron Valleys and Madrien," Alucius mused. "That's not good. What I'd expect from Dysar, but . . ."

"Patrols cost coins," Longyl said slowly.

"And the merchants in Dekhron aren't interested in paying to protect what they don't see will hurt their profits," Alucius concluded. "So we'll be there in force, but we'll need to be prepared to move back." He looked toward Zerdial. "You don't get good terms if you shoot people—not unless you can shoot them all, and we can't do that."

"We could probably wipe out the company there," Egyl said. "Not a good idea, though."

Alucius took a deep breath. "We might as well push on. But make sure the scouts and patrols let us know about anything."

"Yes, sir."

Less than a glass before noon, Egyl rode back down the road. Alucius could see a broad smile on the squad leader's face.

"The boys cornered one of their road scouts," Egyl reported. "Thought it might make working out terms a little quicker."

"How far ahead?"

"Just a vingt."

"Good. We'll see what we can do."

As they rode on, Egyl looked to Alucius. "This isn't going to be easy."

"No. It won't. But I have some ideas. The way they're set up shows that they really don't want to fight. Not two months since the Matrial pulled out of the Iron Valleys and the Westerhills, and they've already reduced the militia forces. I'd bet that there's only one company at the encampment."

"Town sheep," Egyl said.

Alucius didn't argue with that. He just nodded.

A little more than a quarter glass later, Alucius reined up about five yards short of the militia road scout, a young man not that much older than Alucius had been when he had been with Third Company, a time in his life that seemed far more than two years before.

"Greetings," he offered. "What company are you with?"

The scout, clearly uncomfortable with the Matrite uniforms and rifles trained on him, finally spoke. "Cylpher, Eleventh Company . . . that's all—"

"I'm not asking for any more," Alucius said. "All we want is for you to take a message back to your captain."

"That's all?"

"Despite the uniforms, we're mostly all from the Iron Valleys. A lot of us were captured in the Soulend campaign and later, some earlier. The Matrial slapped Talent-collars on us and impressed us into her forces. The Matrial is dead, and the collars no longer work, and we escaped. It's very simple. We'd like to come home, and we want to make sure we get treated fairly. So I want to talk to your captain. I'll meet him—or another officer—by the place on the stream where you water your mounts—one glass after you return to the encampment. He can stay on the east side of the stream. I'll be on the west."

"Ah . . . sir . . . what if . . . ah . . ."

"Trooper," Alucius said firmly, "we are coming home. Now . . . if the good captain doesn't want to talk to me, we'll just avoid the encampment and ride on to somewhere closer to Iron Stem, and we'll find a sympathetic herder, and then we'll work out details from there, and the captain will look foolish. I'd rather not make him look foolish, and I don't think he wants to look foolish. As for an ambush . . . if we'd wanted to do that, all we had to do was take you, and slip into the encampment. I imagine we could have wiped out about half the company before anyone knew what happened. We didn't."

The scout's eyes widened. "Who do I tell the captain is in charge of . . . your company?"

"Alucius. Scout and trooper with Third Company in Soulend. Grandson of Royalt, captain and herder out of Iron Stem. I was hit on the head and captured at the raid on the Soulend encampment, after the Matrites took it. That was the battle where they used the crystal spear-thrower until it exploded." Alucius paused. "That should be enough."

"And you'll let me go, if I tell him that?"

"Once we're closer to your encampment," Alucius promised. "We're going to ride back with you until we're just a vingt or two away. That way, your captain doesn't get any strange ideas, and you'll have time to think about how you're going to convince him." He gestured at the column that had followed him. "You can see that we do have a few troopers here."

"Ah . . . yes, sir."

Alucius turned to Longyl. "We'll send him back with a broken torque and an empty Matrite rifle. The captain will find it harder to ignore that way." Alucius turned back to face the scout, projecting an air of command, "and I'm sure that our friend here will understand that he should tell all his compatriots about our meeting *before* he meets with his captain, perhaps even show them the broken torque collar and the rifle. Not that I wouldn't trust the captain, but trusting him would be a lot easier if the captain knew that most of the company knew." Alucius smiled. Even before he finished speaking, he could sense the approval of Egyl and Longyl, and, belatedly, that of Zerdial.

"Column forward!"

For another glass the company and the captured scout rode eastward, until they reached a gentle incline that led down to a higher valley that held the militia encampment.

Once they had sent the scout on his way, with the rifle and the broken torque, Alucius and his company left the high road and crossed the vingt of hilly land, partly forested with junipers and low pines, to the hillside overlooking the bend in the stream that served as a watering hole. They had to leave the wagons within a few hundred yards of the high road, with their drivers and half a squad, but Alucius doubted that the militia would come storming out after wagons.

Alucius had the remainder of his entire company set up in concealment, ready to rake the land below. He watched the militia encampment, both with his eyes and his Talent, to make certain that the militia did not send out messengers or squads. Then they waited for almost a glass before Alucius had one of the troopers from Zerdial's squad begin to wave the makeshift white banner.

Shortly, the militia captain rode out to the stream, accompanied by a squad, all with rifles at the ready.

Alucius rode Wildebeast just enough into the open that he was visible, but with a clear path behind a clump of junipers—just in case. He recalled the story of his father's death all too well, and he wasn't about to be trusting.

"You . . . you say you have a whole company," called the captain. "Where are they?"

Alucius ordered, "Company, ready rifles! Into the air! Into the air, fire!"

The hillside seemed to explode.

As the sound died away, Alucius replied, "As you can see, they're up here."

"You disarm, and we'll talk about your request," the captain said.

Alucius laughed. "I don't think so. Majer Dysar and Colonel Clyon don't have enough troopers. You don't have enough. Most of my men are former militia troopers. They never wanted to wear Matrite collars. Now . . . you try for some sort of stunt, like the one you're thinking, and you won't be able to hide what you did." Alucius projected a sense of his own command, and a feeling that the captain would be mustered out in disgrace. "Colonel Clyon will have your bars and your head. He needs every trooper he can get, and he'd really like some with knowledge about the Matrites."

"I can't make that sort of decision."

"We know that. We'll wait. You send a messenger to the colonel. We'll talk to him or Majer Dysar—no one else. We can also tell if someone's moving against us in force. That wouldn't be a good idea." Alucius used his Talent to convey the feeling of absolute strength. "You also send us some provisions, standard rations for a company for a week. You can leave them on the high road at the crest, a half vingt west of the camp. We'll leave a couple more of the broken torques. They're close to solid silver. You already have one."

"That will leave us short."

"Ask the colonel for more. He'll be happy to supply you for providing him with more troopers—and for handling a touchy situation with dispatch and caution. Remember, most of my company knows the Iron Valleys very well, and they all have families who wouldn't be too pleased if they weren't dealt with fairly. I'm sure you understand all that, captain." Alucius added a sense of authority to the words.

"You have the torques there tomorrow before noon, and we'll leave the provisions."

Alucius could sense the caution, but the resolve to provide the provisions—and the captain's concern that he was treading on dangerous ground.

"You're an honorable man, captain. Keep it that way, and we'll all do fine." Alucius guided Wildebeast back out of sight. He could feel the sweat pouring down his forehead, and down the back of his neck.

In some ways, battle was easier than negotiating, and that was even when he had tools for negotiating that most officers didn't.

126

The provisions arrived, left in haste by some very worried militia troopers, and Alucius and his company settled in to wait—with precautions. He had Egyl and Longyl sending scouts everywhere, and he spent much of his own time using his Talent to scan the lands to the east.

He also insisted on spending three glasses every morning, and two in late afternoon, on various training exercises. The first four glasses were spent with the green troopers, and last on unified company maneuvers. After six days, Alucius could see definite improvements.

At midday on the Tridi after they had met with the Eleventh Company captain, Longyl and Egyl interrupted his mounted sabre training efforts with the first two squads, riding up.

"Sir!"

"Halt! Take a break!" Alucius ordered, urging Wildebeast toward the two squad leaders.

"There's someone on the high road," Egyl said. "Not a

full company, but two squads, we'd judge, and they've got a banner, black with a gold starburst."

"That's the commandant's banner, I'd wager," added Longyl.

"We'd better have the company form up," Alucius said.

"How are you going to do this?" asked Longyl, concern in his voice.

"I'm going to have to go down and meet them. Same place as before. You'll be in charge, and you'll have all the squads ready on the hillside."

Again, Alucius used the white banner as a signal, but this time, if nervously, he rode halfway down the slope and waited, totally exposed.

A small contingent rode toward the stream, two senior officers in blacks, then the Eleventh Company captain, and one squad of militia. The captain and the squad halted thirty yards back from the stream.

The two senior officers rode forward, stopping short of the stream by about five yards. The silver-haired Colonel Clyon wore the formal black uniform of the militia, despite the hot sun of late summer. So did Majer Dysar, who appeared little different from the time more than two years before when Alucius had last seen him. The squad behind them looked and felt, to Alucius, very nervous and jumpy.

Alucius rode down to the western edge of the water. He wondered why both Dysar and Clyon were there—unless Clyon wanted Dysar to verify who Alucius was and didn't trust Dysar to handle the negotiations.

Dysar rode forward, almost to the stream edge, studying Alucius. "You look like the man you say you are."

"I'm Alucius, majer. Your wife and my mother have been friends for many years. Years ago, she and your daughter visited the stead."

"Captain Koryt"—Dysar gestured toward the captain who commanded the squad behind him—"said that you had insisted on some ridiculous settlement."

"No, sir. I made no demands, other than our wish to return home and to be treated fairly. I don't believe either is unreasonable for troopers who were captured in war, enslaved, and who have managed to escape."

"Just how did you manage this miraculous escape? None have ever done that before."

"The Matrial died, and when she did, the silver torques that could kill a man instantly no longer worked. We provided several of those as both payment and proof."

"You're a traitor!" snapped Dysar. "Anyone who wears the green is a traitor."

"We were supposed to die, rather than escape?" asked Alucius calmly.

"You took the enemy's colors."

Alucius looked at the man, trying to project calm, and realizing that persuasion wasn't about to work. So he had to play to the silent Clyon for a bit. "We've fought our way back across half of Madrien. We've brought you weapons, silver in the form of torques, and even two wagons. That doesn't count the information we can provide. For this, you're calling us traitors?"

"Anyone who was captured—who didn't die in the cause—" Dysar's voice rose in pitch and in apparent rage.

Yet Alucius could not feel that much anger, but a certain fear. Fear? Because Alucius might reveal his lack of tactical ability? Or because he disliked herders?

"Isn't it better that we survived and returned, majer?" Alucius's cold words cut through the tirade.

"You surrendered—"

"I *never* surrendered," Alucius replied, struggling to maintain a calm appearance. "I was wounded at Soulend and knocked unconscious. That was true of most prisoners who had collars put on them." Alucius could sense both a calculation and a certain amusement from the colonel, but the commandant still hadn't spoken.

"You owe—"

Alucius could sense, finally, that Dysar was unwilling to negotiate in any way. It was a gamble, but . . . he reached out with his Talent, hating to do it.

Dysar grasped at his chest. "What—" Then the majer slumped forward on his mount.

Alucius offered a surprised and gaping look, if but briefly.

"Hold!" snapped Clyon. "Attend the majer, Captain Koryt!"

Beyond the commands, underneath, Clyon did not seem surprised, and did not move in the slightest. Captain Koryt rode forward and caught the limp form before Dysar's body slipped from the saddle. "He's dead."He glared at Alucius. "What did you do?"

"I didn't touch him," Alucius said. "You saw that. I'm on one side of this stream. He's over there. How could I do *anything*." Alucius was gambling that what his grandsire had told him was correct, that herders never revealed their Talents except to other herders. If the gamble didn't pay off, then he could move the company northward through the Westerhills and see if he could get some of the herders to intervene. He hoped it wouldn't go that way, but he was ready . . . if he had to.

"You did *something*," Koryt insisted.

Alucius shook his head. "Me? I'm a simple herder, and I was a horse trooper. You know that, captain. I was captured by the Matrites at Soulend, when I was left for dead. Was I supposed to slit my throat when I recovered and found myself a captive? They'd even taken my belt knife."

Koryt was silent.

Alucius turned his glance to the still-silent colonel. "From what I've heard, colonel, it would appear that no one wants us in service. Should we turn over our equipment and wagons to you, sir, and then head home to our families? They, at least, would be glad to see us." As he studied Clyon, Alucius had the distinct feeling that he had *pleased* the colonel. That bothered him, and, in a way, it did not.

Colonel Clyon lifted his felt hat, and pushed back wavy silver hair. After readjusting the hat, he looked at Koryt. "Captain Koryt, I think that Captain Alucius and I can work out something. Take your men and Majer Dysar's body back to the encampment. I'd warned the majer about accompanying me, but he insisted."

"Sir?"

"You heard me. Go!" Clyon looked to Alucius. "I'm not about to yell out an agreement. Would you please ride over here?"

"Yes, sir. I'd be happy to."

"I thought you would. You look a lot like your grandsire, and he was always a reasonable man." Clyon waited.

Alucius guided Wildebeast through the shallows of the stream and reined up about two yards from the colonel.

"Your grandsire was most accomplished as a herder. Some even said he was a Talent-wielder," Clyon said evenly. "He always said he was just a herder. It looks like you take after him, young Alucius."

"I might, sir. I'm just a herder."

"So was he, and more than a few things occurred around him." Clyon smiled, almost sympathetically, as if dismissing the clear implication of his words. "I checked your records. Even if we count all the time . . . the Council raised the term of service to four years."

Alucius could sense that the colonel had something in mind, that the older man was scheming, but unlike Dysar, there was neither anger nor pettiness. "I hadn't heard of that. Then, I'd guess I wouldn't have."

"You've brought back a company or so . . ."

"Not quite, and some were Reillies, colonel."

"Most won't have any family or steads to go back to, not after what the Matrial's troops did." Clyon paused. "Did any of your men have anything to do with that?"

"Not that I know, sir. Most of the ones with me were in Hieron. I was in the south fighting the Southern Guard."

"So you know something about them as well?"

"Yes, sir."

"Better and better." Clyon paused. "I have a proposition for you."

"Yes, sir?"

"By the time this is all sorted out, I imagine you'll have

about a company, perhaps an undersized company, but a company. You owe time. I need another company. The militia needs more than that, but this I can work out, and we can add to your company over time. You and I both know that the Council would rather have you and your men in service and grateful than loose in the Iron Valleys."

Alucius waited.

"With your knowledge, and your actions, you've served the militia, even done me and the Iron Valleys a favor. Poor Dysar, I told him his heart would give out if he didn't calm down." Clyon smiled knowingly, and Alucius could tell that Clyon had a very good idea what had happened. "That sort of thing happens, at times, when people get herders upset. Dysar and the merchants of Dekhron never quite understood that."

Perhaps they didn't, but Alucius understood all too well what Clyon was saying, and the implicit bargain that was being struck. Alucius had done Clyon a favor, if desperately and inadvertently. At least, it was a private bargain that would keep Alucius's Talent mostly hidden because Clyon would lose almost as much as Alucius to reveal what he knew—or suspected.

"We'll promote you to captain, allow you to keep or choose your own squad leaders."

Alucius nodded. "You'll have to give furlough, and some back pay."

"A quarter pay for all time served in Madrien for those who were in the militia and have families and no militia obligation remaining. The rest stay in service for at least a year or for the length of their remaining militia obligation, but they also receive back pay. Two month's pay to those Reillies without militia service as a reward for their service to you, and half pay for time-served for all those who still owe time. You get half pay for that time—as a captain."

"Furlough?"

"How about a month?" Clyon smiled. "And you can promise another month sometime after six months."

Alucius considered. Clyon had come with his terms ready.

He hadn't even had to think about things. He'd already decided . . .

Alucius had never wanted to be an officer. He was probably still too young. He'd only wanted to come home and be a herder. But he also owed his life to the men who'd followed him, and the Council could make life more than a little difficult on his grandsire and his mother. If . . . if Wendra . . . he hoped that she would consider being married to him before he got out of the militia.

Alucius looked at Clyon, then smiled slowly. "I think I have a great deal still to learn, colonel . . ."

"And . . . captain . . . when we received word, I did take the liberty of sending a fast messenger to your family and your intended. Your grandsire sent a very persuasive message to me, and they would very much like to see you, the young woman especially."

Persuasive message. Alucius almost grinned. For once, he was more than happy to accept any aid his grandsire might have offered. Then he took a deep breath. "Yes, sir. If the men agree—or most of them do—I'll do it."

"I know men, captain. They'll do it. They wouldn't have followed you back here if they didn't believe in you, and they didn't want to live here. And we will honor those who have finished their commitment." Clyon smiled ruefully. "We have to. If we didn't . . . well . . . word would get out, and that wouldn't be good for the Council. I can assure them that it wouldn't be good. They need the herders now, as never before." He reached into his pocket. "Here are your captain's bars. You and your company have one last task before you go on furlough." He extended the silver insignia to Alucius.

"Sir?"

"After you pick up some proper militia tunics, you're going to escort me back to Sudon. There, you'll all be fitted—those who are staying—for uniforms and paid." He smiled. "And you'll debrief me and some senior captains on what is happening in Madrien."

"We can manage that, sir."

"I thought you could." Clyon nodded. "Your grandsire was one of the best ever. He and I expect the same of you."

Expectations—for now, he could deal with those, especially since it was very clear to Alucius, through his Talent, that the militia commandant intended to keep his word.

127

By **midmorning on Londi**, nearly a week later, Alucius was mounted on Wildebeast and riding eastward from Sudon to the high road that would take him north to Iron Stem and then home. It had only been late on Decdi, almost seven days after working out the agreement with Colonel Clyon, that Alucius had finally finished filling out all the forms, briefing the colonel and Majer Weslyn—the replacement for Majer Dysar—and writing all the reports that he had promised to the colonel. Because it was the end day of the week, he had to wait until Londi morning for the clerks and functionaries to come to work so that he could draw his back pay—and so that his troopers could do so as well, before they could all leave on furlough.

The Council hadn't even balked at creating the new company—Twenty-first Company. Not much, according to Colonel Clyon, and not when the colonel had pointed out that the weakening of Madrien meant that the Lord-Protector of Lanachrona could turn more troopers to the north against the Iron Valleys, especially if the southerners' on-going campaign to seize Southgate proved to be as successful as the early reports of recent events in Zalt suggested. Clyon had also suggested to the Council that unfair treatment of those who had been enslaved by the Matrial and had the courage to escape would create far too much unrest among the smaller merchants and crafters at a time when the Council would need support—and might need to raise tariffs. Beyond that, it certainly wouldn't have gone well with the militia, because almost everyone in service knew someone who'd been captured.

Clyon had told Alucius that Zalt had already fallen and that the seltyrs of Southgate were trying to work out a surrender that would leave their trading houses intact. Alucius hadn't been that surprised, but he'd only nodded. His thoughts were on the month ahead, and getting back to Wendra and to his mother and grandsire. He had few illusions that he would see his grandmother.

Still, as he rode through the warm late summer morning, a morning he once would have called hot, but not after nearly two years in Madrien, he was looking forward to seeing his family and Wendra. Wearing the uniform of a militia captain was strange indeed, and even stranger was the weight of coins in his wallet, between the Matrite silvers, and the golds and silvers of militia back pay. Yet . . . all those coins were less than the yield of a year's worth of nightsilk from the stead, far less.

There had been a letter waiting for Alucius at Sudon—a brief note from his mother, expressing gladness at his return, the restrained gladness that revealed more than it hid, and the forceful suggestion that, since Wendra was at the stead, he head directly home when he was free to do so.

He rode alone, since he had seen his troopers off first. That was but one indication of how so much had changed in two years. His eyes took in the fields of grain on each side of the road, the stalks still green, except in places where touches of gold had begun to appear. To the northeast loomed the Aerlal Plateau, lower against the horizon than it would be at the stead, but still imposing. And stark, compared to the wooded slopes of the Coast Range in Madrien or even the Westerhills. Yet he was a herder, and the plateau was part of home.

He watered Wildebeast at the public pump a vingt south of the center of Iron Stem, knowing full well that if he stopped for water at the square, he'd be delayed. Even after two years away, some would recognize him.

After watering his mount and stretching his legs, he remounted and headed north. His eyes took in the small houses—huts with crooked walls, roofs with irregular slate tiles cobbled together from older structures long since dismantled or destroyed . . . mean dwellings compared to most of those in Madrien. He could not help frowning as he made the comparison.

Before long, he was riding Wildebeast toward the south side of the square in Iron Stem. In the early afternoon sun, more than ten carts filled with produce and other goods were set out in two lines on the sun-warmed stones. The square was far busier in late summer than it had been in the winter of the last times he had ridden through the town—far busier, but the carts were carelessly painted, and the peddlers in clothes not much better than rags, and the produce smaller than he recalled, and often blemished.

One of the cart merchants glanced up, took in the uniform and the captain's insignia, and nodded. Alucius returned the nod and turned Wildebeast slightly to the right, in order to avoid an oncoming wagon. Alucius did not recognize either the man driving the wagon or the young woman beside him, except to note that both looked thin, and the horse pulling the wagon was close to being bony.

As he passed the front of Kyrial's cooperage, he could hear loud whispers, and the sound of feet on the small front porch. He could sense the curiosity . . . and something more. Someone had to have passed the word about him.

". . . the dark gray hair . . . has to be him . . ."

". . . Alucius . . . heading home . . ."

". . . first man to escape the Matrites . . ."

Alucius did not look to his left, but kept his eyes on the street that was also the high road northward. Even so, it seemed to him that the buildings around the square slanted slightly, in different directions. He did listen—carefully.

". . . takes after his grandsire, then . . ."

". . . say he brought back a whole company . . . made him a captain for that . . ."

". . . still a herder born . . . never know what they'll do . . . don't talk much . . ."

". . . Wendra . . . said he'd return . . ."

Alucius smiled. Wendra had faith. He hoped she liked the scarf—the only personal item he had brought.

The whispers behind him, he continued riding northward, past more small dwellings and shops, some with peeling shutters, others with crooked or no shutters, and all surrounded by mostly bare ground, saving an occasional apple tree or patches of weeds. There were no neat courtyards or well-tended enclosed gardens. There were no stone walkways or sidewalks.

In time, he reached the Pleasure Palace, small and sad-seeming, with its patchwork walls of indestructible blue-and-green and blue-and-yellow stones. Beyond it, to the north, was the spire of the tower, rising into the silver-green sky, its outline and its brilliant green stones as crisp as they must have been even before the Cataclysm, its interior as gutted and empty as always.

Alucius glanced toward the Pleasure Palace, where two horses were tied out front. For some reason, he recalled the girl who had gone to school with Wendra, whose mother had been one of the women there—and who probably still was. He'd never seen anything like the Pleasure Palace in Madrien either, but he'd seen an innocent man killed unjustly. Here, he reflected, innocent women were used unjustly. And from what he'd heard, that was true still in most of Corus.

He glanced to the tower, proud against the sky—proud and empty. Then he looked to the road ahead, stretching northward.

Before much longer, the enclosures of the dustcat works appeared on his right, long low buildings of weathered wood that looked as though they would collapse under a high wind, although they had not, not in years of winter winds out of the north and off the plateau. The dustcat works—another structure whose like he had not seen elsewhere, raising yet another question.

How could anything justify the torques—and the purple evilness behind them? Yet . . . when he saw the houses in Iron Stem, the Pleasure Palace, the dustcat works . . . saw them all for what they were for the first time . . . he could understand the impulses that had created the torques.

Even in the warm afternoon sun, he shivered, if slightly, before shifting his weight in the saddle. There was Wendra—and his family—they had to be as he had remembered them. Didn't they?

He could feel a rider approaching. He studied the eterna-stone pavement that seemed to stretch endlessly to the north, making out a dark figure moving swiftly southward toward him. The single militia rider—a messenger from the green sash slung over his black tunic—rode closer and closer. The trooper glanced toward him, apparently taking in the uniform and insignia, then slowed his mount.

"Good day, trooper," Alucius called.

"Sir . . ." The rider's eyes opened. "Sir? Weren't you with Third Company?"

"I was. That was several years ago. I've just been promoted to captain of Twenty-first Company."

"Congratulations, sir." The messenger paused. "Beggin' yer pardon, sir . . . weren't you wounded pretty bad at Soulend?"

"I was left for dead," Alucius replied. "I wasn't." He didn't recognize the man, but there were certainly those in Third Company he had not met.

"Thought it must have been something like that, sir." The messenger nodded. "Thank you, sir." He nodded yet again and urged his mount southward.

Alucius could sense the combination of fear and awe. What had so troubled the trooper? Troopers were wounded. Some died, and some survived. Alucius had been lucky, as some troopers were, yet the messenger had clearly recognized him and been more than a little surprised to see him. And frightened.

Was it just because his head wounds had looked so bad? That had to have been it. Even though he nodded to himself, he wondered.

It was nearing late afternoon when he turned off the north-south road to take the lane to the stead. After the messenger, he had seen no one on the road, no one at all, but that was as it always was. The quarasote lands were empty.

The stead lane was rutted, not any worse than he remembered it, and dusty, but not so dusty as the mountain logging roads near Zalt. Still, he must have raised enough dust, because as he neared the stead, he could make out the figures of Wendra and his mother, both standing at the foot of the steps before the stead house, and that of his grandsire on the porch, leaning on the railing.

He couldn't help but smile as he rode up to them.

All three of them were smiling as well, but his mother's face was lined and weathered, more so than he had recalled. Wendra's face was finer, more refined, and, without a word, in a long single glance, he could sense that she had been on the stead almost the entire time he had been gone. Her brown hair was shorter, but more lustrous, and the greenish gold eyes were deeper, more intent—and deep flashes of green—herder green—ran through her life thread and being. She was no longer a girl, but a woman, and one who had been waiting for him, believing in him.

"I'm back. It took longer."

For a long moment, no one spoke.

Then Alucius dismounted. He had to drop the reins as Wendra's arms went around him.

"You came back. No one does, but you did." Her words were smothered, and her face was damp.

Alucius didn't care as he held her, and as their lips met. The shock of their meeting was as intense as if both life webs had melded.

When they finally parted, Alucius turned and stepped toward his mother, giving her a long and gentle hug. "I didn't mean to worry you, but I did promise I'd come back."

"You did," she murmured. A smile appeared. "You'd best have time to get married."

"A month, and we will, if Wendra"—he looked to the golden-eyed woman—"will still have me."

"I will." She smiled softly. "How could it be otherwise?"

Royalt stood at the top of the steps and called out. "Well

. . . I see they recognized some value in you." His grandsire was still tall and straight, but far more gaunt than Alucius had recalled. "A captain yet. They didn't let you out?"

"No. Colonel Clyon gave me full credit for time served, but that still leaves almost two years."

"They let young Vardial out earlier." Royalt shook his head. "We can talk about that later. It's just good that you're home."

"I'm glad to be here. Let me get Wildebeast stabled . . ."

"I'll do it—" began Lucenda.

"I can do it," Alucius replied. "You can tell me everything I've missed."

"There's not that much . . . little changes on the stead . . ."

Alucius led Wildebeast away from the steps and back down to the stable, and inside, taking the third stall on the right, one clearly cleaned recently, and readied for him. He glanced from the clean stall to Wendra.

She flushed. "I wanted everything to be ready for you . . . once we heard."

"Grandma'am . . ." Alucius said slowly.

"She . . . held on . . . until about a month ago . . . None of us expected she would live that long," Lucenda said slowly. "Your grandfather couldn't explain it."

"That . . ." Alucius had trouble speaking for a moment. "That was when I started back from Zalt . . . but I didn't know . . ."

"She did," Lucenda said quietly.

Alucius swallowed.

"How did . . . don't the Matrites have silver collars?" Wendra ventured.

"They did." Alucius loosened the girth. "I'll tell you all about it when we go inside. Grandfather will want to hear it."

"He will," affirmed Lucenda.

"Lamb will be glad to see you," Wendra said after a silence.

"How is he?"

"He's getting old. He doesn't lead the flock anymore,"

Lucenda said. "We let him graze the nearer quarasote during the day."

Alucius understood the underlying message there as well. He racked the saddle and the saddle blanket, and then began to brush Wildebeast.

"He's gentle for a stallion," Lucenda offered.

"Only around me, or so they say."

Grooming Wildebeast and making sure of the stallion's feed and water seemed to take a glass, but it was less than half that when the three walked toward the house. Alucius carried the saddlebags with the new uniforms inside—and the screen scarf that he had carried a thousand vingts.

"It is good to be here." Alucius motioned for his mother to go up the steps to the porch first. "It's different. Nothing's changed, and yet everything has."

From the porch where he had waited, Royalt laughed, a sound of amusement and rue. "Could have told you that. Every trooper who comes home after a long time away feels the same way. It changes you."

Alucius could feel Wendra stiffen, and could sense her sudden concern. He leaned toward her ear and whispered, "It hasn't changed what's between us."

And it hadn't—that he also knew, knowing as well that, as his experiences had changed him, so had Wendra's work on the stead changed her.

Wendra did not reply, but Alucius could feel her relax, if not completely.

"You look older," Royalt observed.

"I am," Alucius replied. "Two years."

"Older than that." His grandfather offered a wistful smile. "Wish Veryl had been able to see you. She knew you were coming home."

Alucius nodded. He wasn't surprised, but he still felt the emptiness when he thought about his grandmother.

"There's a stew in there," Lucenda said, "and it won't be long before it's ready. I'd have had something grander—"

"Except you didn't know when I was coming," Alucius

said with a laugh, half forced. "A good stew would be wonderful."

"You can eat—you need to eat after that long ride—and
you can tell us everything."

"There's a lot to tell." Alucius wasn't about to recount it
all, not at the moment, and perhaps never, but, when they
were alone, he would tell his grandsire about the crystal, the
torques, and the Matrial. Royalt deserved that, and so did
Wendra.

"You can start," said Royalt.

"Yes, sir." Alucius grinned as he followed the others into
the house.

128

The dinner was outstanding, stew or not, but
the narration Alucius offered before, during, and after the
meal was a slight strain, because while he did tell them about
the Matrial's death and the failure of the torques, he did not
tell all the details, nor did he ever intend to, not for years,
and perhaps not ever. Without a word passing between them,
he also knew none of them needed the details about Dysar's
death.

His grandsire nodded several times, but did not offer a
single word or question about either aspect of his tale, and,
finally, Alucius and Wendra escaped the house—or, Alucius
reflected, were allowed to leave. For several long moments,
they stood on the porch, looking at the Aerial Plateau, looming large in the east, its crystal edge shimmering in the light
of both moons.

Alucius turned and looked at Wendra, wearing the green
scarf that somehow brought out her eyes, as he had known
it would.

"I'll always treasure it."

Alucius blinked.

"The scarf." She smiled.

So would he, if for slightly different reasons. He offered his arm. "I'd like to walk a bit."

They walked north, arm in arm, and then westward, away from the house. The slightest of breezes had begun to whisper out of the north, bringing with it the faint sweet scent of blooming quarasote, a harbinger of the coming harvest season.

"I'm glad you've been here." Hearing an old echo in his own words, Alucius stopped and studied Wendra, taking in her face, as he had once so many years before, seeing this time not a girl, but a woman.

"So am I."

"You belong here."

"With you . . . yes." Wendra paused. "Do you remember the last time we were here? There was only Selena, and a star where Asterta is now."

"You asked me to look, to see how beautiful it was," Alucius said. "You were worried that your father would call you."

"You *do* remember."

"It's more beautiful now." Alucius fell silent, wondering about what he needed to say, but finally spoke. "You don't mind getting married . . . with me still being in the militia?"

She laughed, softly, warmly, turning to him. "I'd mind much more not getting married now. Life goes on. It doesn't wait for the perfect moment. I'd feel more like I was helping you by being here."

Their lips touched.

As they held each other in the summer evening, Alucius could feel once more the dark webs of life entwining, not as a shock, but a flow that was meant to be, that would be, and would continue to grow stronger as the years passed.

A pale silver-green radiance flowed over them . . . a radiance that bore warmth of a sort.

They both fell away from each other, looking to the east where the soarer hovered, seemingly halfway between both moons, her delicate winged figure suspended between the evening sky and the bare ground, her eyes fixed upon the couple.

Green radiance . . . Alucius felt both warmed and chilled within. The silver-green radiance had surrounded him on three occasions, although this was the first time he had seen the soarer. The first had been just before he had been struck down at Soulend, the second when he had destroyed the purple crystal . . . and now . . . with Wendra.

They both watched the soarer.

"She's smiling . . ." murmured Wendra. "She is . . . as if you're the soarer's child."

Soarer's child? That was a nursery rhyme. Still, he could sense the warmth projected by the soarer, although he would not have called her expression a smile. "She wishes us well, I think."

"You can tell that?"

Alucius did not answer, instead watching the soarer, seeking an answer he knew he would not get. Instead, the radiance diminished, and then, suddenly, the soarer was gone.

Wendra turned to Alucius, inquiring, but not speaking.

"We're meant to be together," Alucius said with a smile. "The soarer means that nothing can tear our spirits apart."

The second time they kissed, there was only the light of the stars—and the two moons.

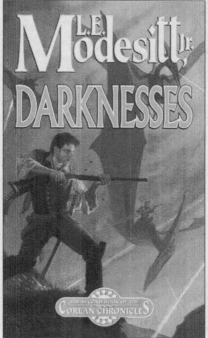

3

Alucius woke in the darkness, knowing that he had to rise. His winter's-end furlough was over, and he had to report back to the outpost at Emal. The ten days of the last week had flown by all too quickly, and now he had a three day ride ahead of him, and he had to leave a day earlier than his men and squad leaders would, so that he would be there as they reported.

"I wish you could stay longer," Wendra whispered, snuggling against him.

"So do I."

For a time, Wendra clung to him before he kissed her and said, "It's a long ride."

"I know."

Alucius eased out from under the heavy quilts and headed from what had been the guest bedroom across the back corridor to the washroom. The water coming from the hand pump in the washroom was like liquid ice, and shaving left his face chill. When he returned to the bedroom, Wendra had pulled on trousers and tunic and her heavy winter jacket. She sat on the edge of the bed, watching as he pulled on his nightsilk undergarments and then his captain's uniform.

Then she stood and embraced him again. They kissed for another long moment, before she turned slightly and pressed the black crystal of her ring against the crystal of his herder's wristband. For an instant, warmth and closeness enfolded them, and they clung to each other.

Wendra stepped back to let him finish dressing, but did not sit down, standing at the foot of the bed. Once he was dressed, he reached down and shouldered the saddlebags, then lifted the rifle from the high wall rack. Except for what he had on, and his personal toiletries, he'd packed the saddlebags the night before.

He wore the heavy cartridge belt over his militia winter parka. While he did not expect trouble, if he encountered it he'd need the cartridges in easy reach. The rifle was his— but met militia standards, which meant that it was designed for use against sanders and sandwolves, with the magazine that held but five cartridges, each thicker than a large man's thumb.

Wendra accompanied him out of the house, carrying the basket of travel fare. As they walked through the darkness toward the stable, a darkness that was more like early twilight to Alucius, she said quietly, "It's colder than yesterday. You'll be careful?"

"I'm always careful, dear one. Even in Madrien I was careful."

"I worry."

Alucius worried, too, although he had less reason to do so than he had when he'd first been conscripted years before in the middle of a war. Still . . . Corus was an unsettled place, and there were raiders and brigands, even if there were no battles. Yet.

After saddling Wildebeast, and slipping the food from the basket into the top of his saddle bags, he turned to Wendra and wrapped his arms around her. "Just another four seasons, and I'll be here all the time."

She did not speak, but lifted her lips to his.

After the embrace and kiss, Alucius pulled on the skull mask of nightsilk that shielded his entire head, with only eyeholes and slits for nose and mouth.

"You look dangerous in that," she said with a faint smile.

"I don't know about dangerous, but the nightsilk keeps my face from freezing. I'll have to take it off at sunrise, or someone will think I'm a brigand." He led Wildebeast out of the stall and then from the stable out into the chill air of a winter morning three glasses before sunrise.

In the west, just above the horizon, the green-tinged disc of Asterta was setting. The larger moon—Selena—had set a glass after sunset the night before. Alucius closed the stable door, and then mounted. "I'll walk you back to the house."

"I can—all right." She turned and began to walk back to the house, Alucius riding beside her.

Once Wendra stood on the porch, Alucius turned Wildebeast.

"You *will* be careful," Wendra said again, looking at her husband.

"I will," he promised. "You take care as well."

Wendra nodded, as if she dared not to speak.

After a long moment, of just looking through the darkness at her, he turned his mount toward the lane, heading southwest, swallowing as he did.

He understood her fears, her concerns.

So much had happened. Three years earlier, he had been conscripted into the Iron Valley Militia. He'd served in the militia as a scout, then had been captured at the battle of Soulend by the Matrites and forced by the Talent-torque welded around his neck to serve as a captive trooper in the Matrial's forces. He'd discovered his own Talent-abilities, and broken the power of the torques and returned to the Iron Valleys at the head of company of other captives—only to discover that the price of freedom was to become a militia captain over that company. Now, after a little more than a year of service since his return, in command of the Twenty-first horse company, he had just less than a year before he could return to the stead, and the life of a herder—and to Wendra.

As he rode past the outbuildings, he turned and looked back at the stead house. Wendra still stood there watching. He waved, not knowing whether she might see his gesture in the darkness, but he could not tell whether she did or not.

He had ridden less than a vingt from the stead buildings when he sensed the others. There were four men—none with Talent, for his Talent revealed that the being of each was blackness without the flashes of green that revealed herder Talent or the flashes of purple that revealed the only other kind of Talent in people that Alucius had come across.

He slowed Wildebeast into a walk, letting his Talent-senses reach out to locate those who waited. They were waiting in the low wash less than two hundred yards from where the stead lane met the old high road that ran from Eastice south through Soulend and then through Iron Stem to Dekhron. Two were on the north side, and two on the south, all of then less than twenty yards from the road—a clear ambush.

Alucius could also sense the grayish-violet of the sandwolves, doubtless waiting to see if there would be carrion left for them. Alucius smiled grimly behind the skull-mask. There would be carrion.

He continued to ride until he was less than two hundred yards from the ambush site. In the darkness, far enough away in the now-moonless night that none of the men would see him, he reined up, dismounted, and tied Wildebeast to one of the posts marking the stead lane, then took the rifle from its holster, holding it in his left hand.

Moving as silently as only could a man who had been both herder and scout, he slipped through the quarasote, using his night-vision and Talent sense to make his way to the wash on the north side of the lane.

He hoped he could use his Talent to stun the men, and then to sever their lifethreads, rather than using the rifle. But he had to get within yards to use Talent that way, and there was every chance that one of them might hear him. So he held the rifle ready as he eased toward the northern-most of the ambushers. When he reached the edge of the wash, only about a yard and a half deep, he slid down onto the lower ground, and began to follow the wash south.

He froze as he heard the faintest of sounds. Remaining silent, he listened.

". . . thought I heard something . . ."

". . . scrats probably . . ."

". . . not at night in winter."

". . . quiet . . . he'll be along . . ."

Alucius edged along the chest-high miniature bluff toward the men, rifle ready, still hoping not to use it, especially not at first.

A good half-glass passed before Alucius reached a gentle

curve in the edge of the wash, a position from where he could sense the nearness of the closest man. He paused. Then he reached out with his Talent-senses—and struck with full force at the man's yellow-brown lifethread—a thread invisible except through Talent-senses.

There was but the faintest gasp, and then a muted thump, and the reddish-tinged void that signified death washed over Alucius.

"Silyn. . . . you there? Silyn?"

Ignoring the whispered inquiry, Alucius kept moving, until he was less than ten yards from the second man, where he once more extended his Talent and struck, wincing as the death-void swept across him.

Then, for several moments, Alucius stood silently, shuddering, and feeling the perspiration gathering beneath the skullmask, despite the chill and the light night wind that swirled around him, with the iron-acrid scent that always accompanied any wind on the stead that came out of the northeast and off the Aerlal Plateau. Finally, he took a long and slow deep breath, and then crossed the ten yards of the wash to the western side, where he climbed out, and silently began to circle west and south toward the remaining two men.

The second pair were far closer together, less than three yards apart, and lying prone behind quarasote bushes on the edge of the far shallower section of the wash south of the depression where the stead lane dipped and ran through the infrequent watercourse.

Neither even turned as Alucius Talent-struck.

Alucius had to sit down, with his legs over the crumbling edge of the wash, breathing heavily and shuddering. He'd killed with his Talent before—but never more than one person at one time. He'd had no idea that the effort was so great—or the reaction so violent. But it explained why those with Talent didn't make that much of an impression on the world, especially since there were few who had great Talent. He doubted that he could have used his Talent against a fifth man—not if he wanted to remain conscious.

After a time, he stood, slowly, and walked back to the first pair of dead men, rifling through their wallets, and winter jackets to see if there happened to be any sign of anything that might say why they had tried to attack him. All he found that indicated their motivation was five golds in each belt wallet, in addition to some silvers and coppers. He took the golds, but left the lesser coins. Then he trudged back to the first pair, where he found nothing revealing, except five golds more in each wallet.

He took a deep breath and made his way through the darkness toward Wildebeast, his Talent-senses still extended. The sandwolves were closer, perhaps a vingt to the west, across the ancient eternastone high road. Only when he reached the stead road, and Wildebeast, did he concentrate on the image of carrion, of food for the sandwolf pack. Then, with a grim smile, he mounted.

He frowned. His Talent indicated someone was riding toward him—quickly. He relaxed slightly as he sensed the green-shot blackness that was his grandsire. Rather than ride on, he waited.

Within another quarter glass came a voice.

"Alucius?"

"I'm here. I'm all right."

"I can tell that now. Wasn't sure what had happened until I was headed out here. Was certain something had. Could feel you were worried. So did Wendra. We both caught that. Not like you. You just called the sandwolves," Royalt observed, reining up on the stead road. "I didn't know anyone could do that."

Behind the skullmask, Alucius grinned raggedly. "Someone told me not to tell anyone. Herders don't tell, remember?"

"You can do more than that."

Alucius ignored the statement. "There were four of them. I don't think the sandwolves will leave much. They're hungry." He eased Wildebeast toward his grandsire and the gray that the older man rode, then extended his hand. "They'd been paid in gold. Five golds each. Use it for the stead."

The twenty golds clunked into the older man's hand.

"I left the silvers and coppers in their wallets," Alucius said.

"What do you think about their mounts?" asked Royalt.

"They're tethered. Leave them where they are. I thought you and Kustyl could find them and the bodies—or what's left of them—early tomorrow. I was going to ride back to the stead and tell you, but you've saved me the trip. I'd guess that the four, whoever they were, were travelers who got lost in the dark and had the misfortune to run into hungry sand-wolves."

"That's what Kustyl and I will say. But I'll get the mounts now. Wouldn't want to lose them to the sandwolves. Waste of good horses." After a pause, Royalt asked, "Do you know who it could be?"

"If Dysar were still alive . . ." Alucius said slowly. "But I can't think of anyone else. You said Wendra felt it, too?"

"She wanted to come. I thought it was better she didn't."

Alucius nodded. "She has Talent. She might show more. You ought to take her out with you."

"I will. I'd thought about it."

Left unsaid was the understanding that the stead needed a herder, and, in Alucius's absence, should anything happen to Royalt, there would be no one else to herd the nightsheep—unless Wendra could. The last woman herder had been Royalt's mother, the last woman with Talent in Alucius's family. Alucius didn't know—or hadn't asked, he corrected himself silently—about any female herders in Wendra's family.

After another silence, Royalt said, "You'd better get going, before the sandwolves get here. Kustyl and Wendra and I . . . we'll take care of things."

"Thank you."

Once more, Alucius turned Wildebeast westward, leaving his grandsire behind once more.

In less than a fifth of a glass, he was traveling southward on the ancient high road. The gray eternastones, laid down at least a millennium before, remained unmarked by the passage of time or traffic. Within a day, any few scars that might mar the gray stone surface vanished. In the darkness the gray stone emitted a faint glow perceptible only to those with Talent, a line of illumination that ran straight as a rifle barrel from Soulend to Iron Stem.

As he rode, Alucius pondered the attempted attack. Why would anyone wish him harm? He was the most junior captain in the Iron Valley Militia. His death would not turn the stead over to anyone outside the family, not while his grandsire and mother and Wendra still lived. He had never been involved in trade. His only skill was that he was perhaps the best battlefield captain in the militia. He was certainly the most experienced, if not through his own desires.

Yet there was no war and, so far as he or Royalt knew, none in sight. From the brief words he had heard, the would-be killers had either been from the southern half of the Iron Valleys, from Deforya, or from Lanachrona. While the Lanachronans might wish a less effective militia in the Iron Valleys, Alucius couldn't see how his death would affect anything. He'd been a captive Matrite trooper when the militia had repulsed the Matrites—if with some earlier help from him and from the Lord-Protector of Lanachrona.

All Alucius could come up with was the idea that the ambush meant he was in a position to do something, or to stop something—or no one would have bothered with trying to kill a lowly captain. The question was whether he would recognize whatever it was before it was too late, and that might be difficult, because he hadn't the faintest idea of what he was looking for.

A glass passed before, in the darkness, he could sense the dustcat works, the long wooden sheds that confined the animals, kept and groomed for the dander that provided exquisite pleasure when inhaled—and which made gold and gems cheap by comparison. He'd only met Gortal a handful of times, and not in years. Even when he had been much younger, Alucius had found the man who confined the captured dustcats and who sold their dreamdust to the traders of Lanachrona cold, almost without spirit, for all of Gortal's manners and fine clothes.

The scutters who labored for Gortal would do almost anything to be around the big cats, just to inhale the vagrant dreamdust, and it was said that the women scutters made those who served at the Pleasure Palace seem virtuous. It still amazed Alucius that people would destroy themselves so—and that Gortal could accept the golds that came from such degradation.

Then, he reflected ruefully, golds affected everyone. The traders of Dekhron had pressured the Council to reduce the size of the militia in previous years, almost inviting the Matrial of Madrien to attack, all because they had not wished to pay the tariffs necessary to support a strong militia. In the end, they'd paid more by having to expand and equip the militia rapidly—and they'd been forced to borrow the golds—a debt it appeared they could not repay. And, once more, right after the war, they'd pressured the Council to reduce the size of the militia—and the tariffs that could have serviced that debt.

Were there those on the Council so much like Gortal that they would do anything for a gold? In the chill, Alucius snorted. From what he'd seen, there was little difference, except that Gortal was probably more honest.